HORSES
of
FIRE

HORSES

of

FIRE

A Novel of Troy

A. D. RHINE

DUTTON

DUTTON

An imprint of Penguin Random House LLC
penguinrandomhouse.com

DUTTON and the D colophon are registered trademarks of Penguin Random House LLC.

LIBRARY OF CONGRESS CATALOGING-IN-PUBLICATION DATA
Names: Rhine, A. D., author.
Title: Horses of fire: a novel of Troy / A. D. Rhine.
Description: [New York]: Dutton, 2023.
Identifiers: LCCN 2022055496 (print) | LCCN 2022055497 (ebook) |
ISBN 9780593473061 (paperback) | ISBN 9780593473078 (ebook)
Subjects: LCSH: Trojan War—Fiction. | LCGFT: Fiction. | Novels.
Classification: LCC PS3618.H556 H67 2023 (print) | LCC PS3618.H556 (ebook) |
DDC 813/.6—dc23/eng/20230320
LC record available at https://lccn.loc.gov/2022055496
LC ebook record available at https://lccn.loc.gov/2022055497

Title page art: Hawk line drawing © Singleline / Shutterstock
Interior art: Sculpture silhouettes © Olga S L / Shutterstock

Printed in the United States of America
1st Printing

BOOK DESIGN BY ALISON CNOCKAERT

To our mothers and grandmothers. The walls do not stand without you.

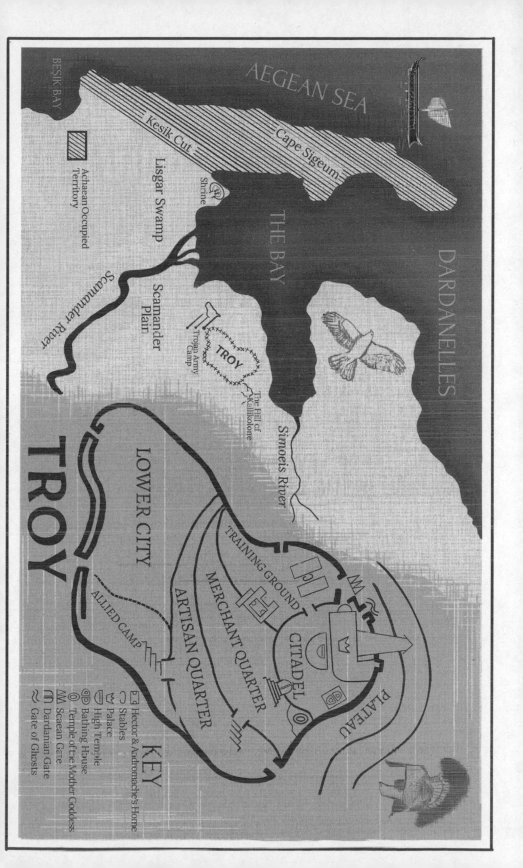

Here is the world. Beautiful and terrible things will happen. Don't be afraid.

FREDERICK BUECHNER

HORSES

of

FIRE

THE HAWK

Sing to me, cries the Hawk.
Fly for me and I will sing, answers the Voice,
strange shadow who rides his wings.
The Hawk dives down from the tower.
Tallest perch in a city bound for the sun.

Slow circles over the golden Citadel.
Sharp bank west over vast walls and vaster plains.
The Hawk glides over rows of black fish with tall white fins.
Beaches swarming with strange termites.
Men, says the Voice. *From across the sea.*
The Hawk knows men.
They burn and they cut and they kill.
The Hawk kills too, but not the way they do.
The Hawk kills to live.
Not to feel alive.

Sing to me, the Hawk asks again.
Come back, and I will sing, promises the Voice.
Song that has yet to be sung.
Of men? The Hawk cares nothing for their songs.
Not of men, says the Voice. *Of Shadows.*

The Hawk chases the light back to the walled city.
Under its wings, the wind changes.

BOOK

I

1

ANDROMACHE

THE BOY IS *lost.*

And so is his mother. I can tell with one glance.

With a warrior this young, there is only ever one reason for such a clean spear wound. A neat hole right between the shoulder blades. Slowly, I roll the stiff corpse back onto the stone slab until he lies face up, eyes unblinking. Across the room, I meet his mother's raw, wild gaze. Her hands fidget anxiously.

There is no hiding what I've seen. She knows that I know.

The primal wail that follows is like no sound I've heard, and yet I've listened to a million variations of the same tune. Every mother's cry of lament is her own. As unrepeatable as each new life she carries. Only this woman's groans speak of a secret.

A song of betrayal. Of cowardice. *Shame.*

I take a step back from the washing slab, letting the wet cloth in my hand hit the floor with a soppy splat.

"*Please,* Harsa Andromache. I beg you."

The mother throws herself at my feet, arms wrapped around my calves. She thrusts the rag back into my hand, closing my fingers before returning unceremoniously to her seat at the other end of the slab. There she presses her tearstained cheeks against the soldier's feet. The part of him farthest from the light that once filled her boy's eyes.

For that *is* what he is. A boy. Large for his age but younger than a soldier should be. I may not have sons, but I have washed enough of them to know what fifteen summers looks like. This child is at least a year shy of the minimum age for serving in Troy's army. Not that most captains care to check so long as he can carry his shield upright.

"He wanted to follow his father and brothers. For Prince Hector. He was . . . too strong . . . I, I couldn't stop him." The woman's explanation unravels into sobs. "I've given a husband and two sons for Troy already. Will you deprive me of my youngest even in the afterlife?"

My throat tightens. I open my hand. The flax-colored cloth is now pink in most places, a rusty red in others. No one in Troy, not even Hector, expects me to cover myself in blood that stains my nail beds brown. But that is exactly why I do it.

I want to get my hands dirty.

When I muster enough courage to look into the eyes of the desperate, childless widow again, I see that she is far from old. Despite her tears, the firm line of her mouth says she would do anything to guarantee her son's safe passage across the Great River.

My eyes land on the knife at the edge of the slab an instant before she lunges. I am fast, but she is faster. The mother brings the blade to her own quivering throat before I can exhale.

"If he is condemned to wander, then I will wander with him."

Her eyes blink fire. A thin, crimson drizzle travels to her collarbone.

"Have you heard me issue such a condemnation?" I ask calmly.

The mother's gaze flickers. Her grip on the knife handle loosens slightly even as her voice shakes. "My son was *not* a coward."

I nod. "No man who stands across the plain from Achilles can ever be called one."

And the boy who turns and runs from Achilles's spear? Surely the only name for him is *human*.

But the King's Council is not interested in shaping men. It is demigods they seek to mold. Names, after all, cannot be speared in the back. Names can live on, ringing glory throughout the ages. Which is why the punishment for fleeing the battlefield isn't so merciful as a clean death. It is eternal shame followed by a corpse left exposed. An unburned body that becomes a lost soul, doomed to wander the shadow lands. Even worse, there is nothing the warrior or anyone else can do to redeem his name. The last note of his song has been sung.

But only if you sentence the boy to this fate.

I look down at the blue, bloated face. The full cheeks of a child. With a swift stroke of my hand, I close the black holes of the boy's eyes.

"Eda, the stones."

The aging woman in charge of Troy's dead rushes toward me from her stool in the corner. She presses the smooth, flat stones made from smoky quartz into my hand. Compared to the boy's flesh, they are warm. As usual, Eda looks somewhat surprised to see me here.

She shouldn't be. If Hector is the type of commander who walks among his men, thanking even the lowest-born for his sacrifice, then I intend to be the kind of queen who reaches for a washcloth when the women of her city must bury sons who cannot yet grow beards.

If I live to be queen, that is. Or have a city left to rule.

I turn back to the mother. "It is time to let go."

With aching tenderness, the mother places the *atamanui* in her dead son's palm. A symbol of a life, carried into death. A fare to be paid at the Great River for passage across.

The *atamanui* the mother chose is a piece of jade carved into the shape of a small bird. The artistry is as impressive as the stone itself. It would have cost the woman much. By the looks of her ragged tunic, more than she could afford.

"It is beautiful," I tell her. Somehow, it is also confirmation that sending the boy to the pyre instead of the refuse heap is the right choice. "Fitting."

The woman's lips tremble as she closes her son's stiff fingers around the jade bird. "From birth, Antinous woke with the dawn. I would hear him singing in his sweet little voice. Just like a sparrow."

A sweet little sparrow.

Not the kind of soul there is room for on the plains of Troy. But perhaps there is a place for him in whatever lies beyond.

I place a smooth stone over each half-moon of lashes, then kiss the boy's forehead and whisper, "May your journey across the Great River be swift and your rest eternal."

The mother's lament crests.

"Not a word of this to anyone," I whisper to Eda as I refit my headscarf. When I move toward the door, I stop to rest a hand on the mother's shuddering shoulder.

There is nothing more that I can do. There never is.

Outside the Citadel bathing house, the scent of the jasmine bush spilling over the wall hits me before my blinking eyes adjust to the bright day. Its luscious perfume overwhelms the pungent aroma at my back. Still, in Troy, one cannot escape the stench of death for long.

It was not always this way. When I left my home of Thebe under Mount Placos and glimpsed Troy for the first time, the city felt even more like a bridegroom than the prince who was to be my husband. Its high outer walls shone like the stores of bronze that could be found in every household past her great gates. My mountain-girl eyes had never glimpsed such a blue-green sea, nor had they encountered such wealth. Troy seemed to contain the colors, smells, and sounds of the entire world.

The stone streets inside the Citadel are quieter these days. Troy's common men defend the walls while her women secure food stores in the Lower City. The royal Citadel—home to the palaces of King Priam and his many children—sits at the top of the plateau. Its High Temple to the countless gods Troy has imported from every land hovers over the city, a shadowy place where the incense always burns. I am told the shimmer cast by the pearly white stone of the palaces can be seen from far off the coast, but I have never set foot on a ship. Nor do I ever intend to.

Still, before the war, I often gazed upon Troy from the shoreline. The city's many rings unfold like an artichoke, that uninviting vegetable I've watched our cook Bodecca prepare often, seeing as it is Hector's favorite. Despite a hard exterior, Troy contains the most tender heart.

"*You are much the same,*" the old woman told me after I married the prince she'd nursed at her own breast. Somehow, I knew not to take offense.

The memory begins to thaw the chill in my chest, the one that settles in whenever I spend a morning at the bathing house.

It is a short walk to the home Hector and I share a few paces beyond the Citadel's walls, but the modest house feels a world away from the ruling center of Troy's Old Blood. That's precisely what Hector intended when he moved us there after our wedding feast. The house has direct access to the army's training grounds and stables, the place Hector spends every free moment, but it is far from the gossip that turns the lives of Hector's siblings into a whirlpool that rivals Charybdis's. My husband may be the heir of Troy, but he is a soldier first. And soldiers value action over idle talk.

My Hector.

The mere thought of him quickens my pace. Hector returned from the battlefield late last night, but he was up with the dawn as usual. Every morning he is home and before tending to his horses, Hector begins his day with a run around Troy's outermost walls.

"I have circled the city twice, but never three times," he sighs when I ask why he invokes this extra pain upon himself. *"Even if I'm never the fastest warrior, I intend to endure the longest."*

Given how long this war has lasted already, I pray to Tarhunt, god of storms, that Hector is right. Entering the courtyard that leads to our home, I pluck a ripe lemon from the tree that grows near the central fountain. Its crisp rind fills my nose, a welcomed change from the weary scent of lavender. The herb reminds me of dressing corpses, and I wish to inhale *life.*

The promise of submerging my body in a fragrant tub of citrus peel draws me toward the house. I intend to stay in the water until the blood beneath my nails turns it the color of the rose oil we have not imported since before the war.

There, I will do my best to forget the mother's moans. And my own betrayal of the Citadel's rules that somehow doesn't feel like a betrayal at all.

"A fresh robe, Harsa Andromache," Faria offers as I climb the stairs to my bedchamber. Her arms are heavy with the colorful garments she's brought in from drying in the sun. Our servants know better than to ask if I want their assistance when drawing a bath. All I ever want once I have fled the wails of grief is *silence.* A few minutes to whisper the name of the dead warrior whose wounds I have washed—my best attempt at a plea to the gods.

"Antinous. Antinous. Antinous," I whisper once I slip into the steaming tub.

For how long is such a soul remembered? A boy who does not have any sons of his own? Even if he had not fled in shame, his name would not last an entire generation. It will be blown away as quickly as the dust soars from his funeral pyre to the sea.

Still, it is a fate better than wandering somewhere in between. But he will be gone just the same.

I push away the thought, as we each must do a thousand times a day if we are to endure this world. This endless war. The water's warm caress nearly lulls me to sleep, but the moment I hear a horse's whinny and the crack of a whip, I open my eyes.

The breeze kisses my damp skin as I step onto our balcony, wrapped in a clean linen robe. Hector is in the horse ring below, helmet removed, his bronze face streaked with mud. From my perch, I watch his muscled arms glistening in the Anatolian sun.

Each evening that I wash his body before rubbing his sore muscles with olive oil, he tells me of the day's conflict. Of the strategies that worked against our enemies, and those that ended in more bloodshed. More dead sons.

Unlike most Trojan wives, I tell him what I think.

Unlike most Trojan husbands, he listens.

I only wish I could convince him to let me tell the rest of them.

My eyes follow Hector's lean body as it moves with the horse he is intent on breaking, an unruly colt. They never resist him for long. I should know.

"*You will be his partner, the iron rod that sharpens his sword,*" my father, King Eetion, assured me when Hector came to Thebe at the base of Mount Placos to pursue my hand. "*He is equal in dignity, even if you have your own spheres of influence. There is no other prince in all of Anatolia who can offer you that.*"

"*But why have the Amazons train me if you intend that I end up another coddled queen?*"

"*Coddling is neither in your future nor your nature.*" My father, who'd grown frail in a way I'd never thought possible, had pulled his chair close to mine until our knees touched. "*Andromache, your mother gave birth to seven sons— the pride of any king—before she placed you in my arms. It was then that I knew fear, for every father knows in his heart that losing his daughter to another is as inevitable as winter's return. I had Penthesilea instruct you not because I wished to send you off to war, but because the gods gave me a premonition.*"

"*Of what?*" I'd asked, crossing my arms like only a girl of seventeen can.

"*Of a war that will come to you.*"

Hector looks up from the colt and meets my gaze through a cloud of dust. His eyes smile even if his mouth does not. Ask the people of Troy and they will tell you their dutiful prince does not know *how* to smile, but I know better. My husband is weary from defending his city, but his eyes have always smiled for me. From the moment I asked him the question that forged our fates—a melding of tin and copper.

"Will you let me fight by your side if the time comes?"

"Women do not fight, Harsa," Hector had replied in his quiet, stalwart way as we walked through the orchards beyond my father's palace. *"They are what we fight for."*

"Fight for? Or fight over?"

A boyish smirk I have rarely seen since danced across his lips. Back then, the face of the Whore of Sparta was but a whispered rumor.

"And what of the Amazons? They fight. Father says they're fearsome warriors because *they are forced to go beyond their nature. You forget I was trained by Queen Penthesilea herself, just as all my brothers were."*

"I haven't forgotten."

He'd said it with such admiration, I'd felt the ground shift beneath my feet. The only way to remain upright was to raise my chin and press on.

"Not only did she teach us to wield a sword, she taught us how to strategize so that swords would rarely be needed. Perhaps that is the true difference between women warriors and men."

The smile that had been hiding at the back of Hector's eyes emerged in full display. *"You may know how to fight, Harsa, but not, I hear, how to ride. Tell me, what good is a bow if you can't stay on a stallion long enough to use it?"*

For that was surely the spark behind Hector's initial curiosity in courting me. The peoples of Anatolia were master chariot-drivers but not skilled in mounting the small horses themselves, a deftness that could be claimed by few. The prince of Troy had a rare ability to ride, and so did the Amazons. I imagine Hector had envisioned mounting the beasts side by side with his queen.

How I'd cursed my brothers for telling him of my awkwardness on horseback! If Hector's face hadn't broken into an unfettered grin, I would have sent his household on the long road back to Troy.

But he *had* smiled. In turn, I'd elbowed him in the ribs. He'd caught my arm with a boldness that startled me to laughter. We'd laughed until my back was pressed to the trunk of a fig tree and Hector's hungry lips were pressed to mine.

By the time we'd wandered back to my father's palace—Hector's waist belt torn and my hair tousled with leaves—I'd known he was the only man

I'd ever desire to laugh with. By the time his lips climbed to my ear and whispered, "*There's no one I'd rather fight beside, Harsa Andromache. But I would travel to the Underworld and back so you never have to,*" I knew I would be his queen.

Beyond my balcony, the high sun begins its slow descent, and Hector comes inside. He marches straight to the alabaster basin in the corner of the bedchamber, torso stripped bare, strands of thick hair pulled loose from the knot Trojan horsemen wear at the base of their neck.

"That colt is impossible." Hector scrubs his arms and chest with his usual ferocity—as if the dry earth caked to his golden skin is blood or bits of brain. Often, it is both.

"You will break him." I set a cup of wine on the table and give Hector a strip of linen to dry his hands, enough time for him to catch my wrist. In one quick movement, he pulls me to him, burying his stubbled face in the cavern of my collarbone. Wrapping my waist with hands accustomed to gripping a horse's mane, he moves toward our bed, piled high with silks that once came to Troy from lands across the sea. Until the day the Achaeans followed.

"Is it time yet?" Hector's voice is hoarse from breathing in dust.

I laugh. "How am I to regard the changing of Arma's moon when it has not made an appearance yet?" I wiggle from his grip and cross the room to close the door. I have no qualms with trying for a son before nightfall, even if the gods have scorned our previous offerings. Or should I say, they've scorned Queen Hecuba's offerings.

"Sometimes duty must come before pleasure." Hector grins. This time, I do not laugh. "What is it, Andromache?"

There are only two times he ever says my name like this—when he is on the edge of exasperation, or when I am beneath him.

I join Hector on the bed. "The war council meets tonight."

I strive to remain focused while his hand runs from my hair to the crease between my breasts. He reaches for the flash of rust that paints a streak from my forehead through otherwise black hair, tucking the gilded piece behind my ear. A kiss of flame, my father used to say.

"Yes. It does."

"I have a plan, Hector. It has been racing through my mind for weeks."

"You always have plans, my *alev*." My fire. "And I always consider them, do I not?"

"I know you value my counsel, but your father—"

"—is not in the habit of basing his war strategy on the advice of women who've never set foot on a battlefield."

Heat rushes to my cheeks as I sit up. "And whose fault is that?"

Hector rolls away, his eyes on the ceiling in the same position as the dead boy. "How often must we have this discussion? That may be how your father ruled Thebe, but it isn't how things are done in Troy. Even still, you will find no city on either side of the Aegean where Harsas have more freedom."

The grieving mother's face fills my thoughts. "Ah, I forget myself. In Troy you give women the liberty to start wars rather than end them."

A flash of anger grips Hector's mouth, but he's too weary to fight it with his usual patience. "I've asked him. You know I've asked him. I've told my father about your training and your gifts, but *he* is the king. What would you have me do when he continues to refuse?"

"Allow me to accompany you regardless. Your father and brothers would never dishonor Troy's future queen to her face."

Hector says nothing for a lengthy moment. This man who carries his power without pomp or presumption. This faithful guardian of Troy who tries so hard not to offend those he loves, and so he never pushes, never goes beyond duty's rigid boundaries.

He sighs. "You are as relentless as that colt."

I smile at the unspoken agreement between us, suspended on the winds that assault Troy's ramparts day and night.

"But if I bring you to the council, you must do something for me in return."

My eyes skate across the bed, bathed in an afternoon glow that wraps us with a false promise of peace. The illusion is nearly enough to make us forget that not far from here, more men will die by the hundreds—entire households shattered with each thrust of Achilles's spear, each blow of Ajax's sword.

"It's my mother." A sheepish look stifles any desire flaring in Hector's eyes. "Almost every day, she asks why you will not accompany her to visit the fertility goddesses." He pauses to search my face. "She doubts you truly wish to give Troy an heir."

My eyes fall to the tile design at our feet. A pomegranate. It has been years since our wedding, and still I remain childless. Outwardly, I act as if I want nothing more than to bear Troy the heir she demands, tracking my cycles and the phases of the moon, so that Hector can come home from the battlefield to share my bed when Arma is likely to smile upon us.

That isn't enough for Queen Hecuba. But if Aphrodite and Demeter ignore her daily clouds of incense, if they refuse the lavish offerings she makes on behalf of her most beloved son, what good would my halfhearted prayers to her foreign gods do to sway them? They are Greek, after all.

I meet Hector's gaze head-on. "What does your mother suggest?"

His answer is not at all what I expect. "Tarmack died yesterday."

"Your Master of Horses? I thought he was too old to go to battle."

"He is . . . He was. An illness took him suddenly." Hector clears his throat. "Nobody else in Troy has his skill. I must travel to Cyzicus to look for another master and to replace the stock we've lost to the Achaeans' fire arrows."

"How many?" I can read the worry in his eyes.

"Almost half of our horses and a third of our chariot fleet. I've never seen arrows dipped in fire before . . ." Hector trails off, rubbing the back of his neck. "It is brutally effective. Agamemnon isn't capable of such creativity."

"But Odysseus is." A burning spreads through my chest. After almost nine years camped on Sigeum Ridge, the Achaeans are finally branching out from their usual strategy of raiding smaller cities across the Troad, terrorizing the lands all around us since they cannot take the city of Troy itself. Now, when the Achaeans do take to the battlefield beyond the Scamander, they have started using fire arrows. It is clever and a tactic I would admire if it weren't wreaking havoc on our chariot force, the backbone of Troy's army. "Is there no way to defend against them?"

"We have tried soaking the wood of the chariots in water to keep them from burning, but we can't train the horses not to be afraid. One whiff of smoke and they run wild. The drivers can't control them." Hector's frown lines deepen into sorrow. "I am tired of leaving them lame on the plain for the Achaeans to butcher."

"There has to be a way," I murmur, occupied by this new problem. Just like a storm cloud of arrows, they keep coming, one setback after another.

"Cyrrian is working on the chariots, but we can't build horses out of wood. We must buy more." Hector takes me in his arms. "I hate to leave the men, but if the Achaeans see how badly they have damaged our force, it will make them bold."

I nod, glad to hear Hector will be leaving the battle for a time. Less than a week ago, Hector's and Achilles's swords finally clashed. It must have been the gods who spared him—that or the dozens of Trojan warriors who rushed in to protect their prince, many of them dying at Achilles's hand. Since then, there has been a strange lull in the fighting. We should be grateful for the sudden quiet in the Achaean camps, but it has left me more uneasy than anything. I am not alone. Sailing so close to the Great River has left Hector shaken in a way I've never witnessed. This journey to Cyzicus would give him a chance to rest, and rest would do him much good.

But I also know my husband, and there is more to this than he is letting on.

"What does this errand have to do with your mother?"

Hector hesitates. "There is a large temple to Demeter in Cyzicus. A cult has initiated a new fertility rite, rumored to be especially effective. Their festival begins in a few days, and Mother hopes you'll take part in the sacred Mysteries." Words pour from a mouth normally dammed shut. "She thought it might correct the offenses of the last rite, seeing how it was so many years ago and never finished."

Yes, never finished thanks to Helen of Sparta.

"I was there, Hector." Teeth grinding, I get up to pour myself a cup of wine.

"Please, Andromache."

When Hector looks up at me from the bed, there is no smile, not for a two days' hard ride. There is only grief seasoned with longing. The longing for warm flesh in a world strewn with corpses. For the scent of a new baby, unsoiled by the greed of men. For his name, his house, his memory, to last beyond days that grow shorter with each season. The longing to put an end to an uncertain future that has made the Citadel a whirlpool of speculation.

Shame floods me like the fields of the Scamander in spring.

My primary duty is to give Troy an heir that will cement Hector's position as the future king and prove he is a man capable of siring many sons. Just like the virile Priam, whose bastards fill the streets of Troy, carrying the recognizable spark that animates all of his children's chestnut eyes. More importantly, I am the only one who can give Hector the desire of his heart—a family—even if doing so will break my own into a thousand pieces. For there is a stark reality I can no longer deny, not even to myself.

Fulfilling my husband's great longing will increase my inevitable loss tenfold. Ours is not a world where men outlive their women. I have given Charon a thousand river stones to prove it.

My bare feet cross the tiles between us, still hot from the rosy sun that is starting to slide behind Troy's walls. I raise a hand to Hector's cheek. His eyes close like he wants to hide his war-battered body in the shallow space of my palm.

"I will join you in Cyzicus," I assure him, straightening my spine. "And I will also join you at the council."

"ARE YOU SURE about this?" Hector asks as he lifts me onto the ruddy mare.

"I'll be fine. We are only riding just past the walls." Pulling the hood of my cloak forward, I tighten my grip on the lead. The mare whinnies as her muscles go taut beneath my legs. I've no idea why horses fear me, but it has always been this way. With both feet planted on the ground, my archer's aim is true. But as soon as the Amazons placed me on the back of a horse, the unease that overcame us both made it hard for me to string a bow, let alone shoot one. An inconvenient weakness for the wife of a man who practically communes with the beasts.

"I will not have it said that you are the only half of this union who can ride." Even if the sight is atrocious.

"You would have made a fine warrior," Hector says softly.

When I reach for his hand, the horse stiffens beneath our palms. "I never wanted to fight unless I had to, Hector. But it seems I do require challenges that go beyond determining which color thread I ought to spin next."

"You're exaggerating." A smirk rises in the corner of Hector's mouth. "We both know you hardly give a thought to what you weave. It's why my men joke that I'm the most poorly dressed prince Troy has ever seen."

With a laugh, I slap his hand and the mare brays. "The next time you hear such slander, you can tell your men the reason they are still alive is because your wife prefers discussing battle tactics in bed."

Hector's smile fades as he climbs onto his horse. "But that doesn't mean my father will listen to what you have to say. It doesn't mean he'll even give you the floor. What he knows of women warriors has left him bitter."

I sigh. "After all this time, he still resents that an Amazon got the better of him in his youth."

"That is the rumor, though he will never confirm it."

I glance down at the bronze breastplate Queen Penthesilea gifted me when I was seventeen. It is too late to change it now.

At the click of Hector's teeth, his horse trots toward the Trojan camps that guard the Lower City's west walls, where King Priam gathers with his captains and council advisors once a moon to discuss the war. I squeeze my thighs and the mare takes off. Though I do my best to sit with some dignity, the horse's awkward gait makes it difficult. My insides quake from what I am about to do.

From what I am about to say.

Despite my doubts about the gods' interest in our paltry affairs, my heart calls on Athena, goddess of battle strategy and an Achaean deity I never thought I'd beseech, as I approach Priam's tent.

Hector turns to me as he lifts the hide flap, his face mirroring the turmoil I strain to hide. "This is your one chance, Andromache. There will not be another."

I nod and follow him into a murky space, a hot enclosure that smells of smoke and sweat and roasted animal flesh.

A place that reeks of men.

King Priam and his sons, his captains, along with members of the King's Council, sit at the tent's center, telling stories and jokes, as if this single day has not seen the demise of at least a dozen Trojan youths. I scan the faces, recognizing most of them. To my disappointment, none of the representatives from our allies—small armies sent to support Troy from both sides of the Black and Aegean Seas—are here. A slight to their captains that I cannot be alone in registering.

The chuckling stops when they see me. All the men rise to their feet. All except for King Priam.

"Harsa Andromache, to what do we owe this . . . honor?" Helenus's perplexed eyes shift to Hector. Of Hector's six siblings born of the queen's womb, Helenus and his eldest sister Creusa have been the kindest to me. Perhaps they see what the others do not—an uncertain spirit beneath a stern face and sharp tongue. Traits that Queen Hecuba has described on more than one occasion as "manly." Or so I've heard, since she'd never say such a thing to my face.

Hector shifts his weight and turns to the princes and commanders. "Most of you know that Harsa Andromache was trained in the arts of military strategy from an early age. Many of the orders I've given have come directly from our hours of shared deliberation."

"Then perhaps that is why we are losing," Paris mutters loud enough for all to hear.

My face remains impenetrable, a line of Trojan shields. I expected the most resistance from Paris—vain, self-centered Paris. So oblivious to the world beyond his own desires that even after all these years of war, he still does not acknowledge that *he* is the cause of our woes.

Hector shoots his brother a warning look. "She is touched by Athena. You will hear her counsel."

I cringe at the comparison, a reminder of my own disloyal plea. If even Hector is forgetting Hannahanna and Runtiya in favor of the armed owl goddess, then Queen Hecuba's mission to overhaul Troy's favored Luwian and Hittite deities is nearly complete, trading the immortals of one imperial power for another.

But battles in the sky are the least of my concerns.

Each day, the Achaeans grow bolder. Each day, our allies grow restless in their longing for home and our crop stores dwindle.

"What do we have to lose in hearing a fresh perspective?" Hector continues, an assurance we are still of one mind.

"Oh, merely our honor and self-respect," Paris murmurs. If Hector catches the slight, this time he lets it go to keep the peace.

The tent falls silent as I pull back my hood, the bronze of my breastplate gleaming in the firelight. Hector gives me a firm nod.

There will not be another. The wails of the war widow echo in my ears. My heart quickens and my palms go slick. If this is my chance to spare the women of Troy more nights of agony, then I must make it count.

"*Tread softly, Andromache,*" my father warned before I set off for Troy. "*Though their ways may be different from ours, the Trojans are your people now.*"

The expression of each face around this fire couldn't be in sharper contrast to the one that overtakes them when Helen enters a room. Though she has kept her troublesome face hidden behind a veil since the day it nearly got me killed, it isn't merely her legendary beauty that inflames their lust. It is her unabashed softness that reinforces their own sense of strength. One glance from Helen and they *feel* like men, even as they chase servant girls and roughhouse like they've barely begun to sprout chest hair.

If Helen is an affirming embrace that makes no demands, then I am a stone wall men slam into. One glance from me is a battle cry—not to feel like a man, but to *be* one.

I clear my throat and step into the center of the circle.

"Twenty-seven."

The men stare back at me skeptically. But expectantly.

"That is the number of villages Achilles and his Myrmidons have razed to the ground thus far," I explain, pulling back my shoulders. "The main problem with our current strategy against the Achaeans is we are fighting on the wrong front."

A few men chuckle. One laughs outright. It is only Priam and Harsar Antenor, the king's twin brother and right hand, who sit in a stony silence.

"And where would you have us fight?" asks Polydamas, Antenor's son and one of Hector's most trusted captains. "If not for Troy herself?"

I meet his gaze without blinking. "I would have you fight for our neighbors. For the defenseless people living in the coastal settlements in reach of the Achaean ships, some of whom have already fled to Troy's protective walls. These friends never asked for war, but it is they who suffer the most because of it—thanks to the constant raiding of their villages by Achilles and his thugs."

"But why would we stretch our own defenses thin for those who mean nothing to us?" Paris scoffs.

"Because it will stem the flow of hungry people seeking asylum behind our walls. Because it is the only way we defeat the Achaeans. Because *winning* matters more than glory." My words are sacrilege, confirmed when their scattered chuckles rise into a unified roar.

"Tell us, Harsa, when we ride out to rescue these women and their helpless babes, will we need to change the little ones' soiled rags as well?"

My fists clench. I should have known. They will not give up their chance for the immortal fame that is *kleos*. They will not risk their reputations for anything but a glorious death the bards might recount for generations to come. Not the unadorned death that comes from defending the most vulnerable in a hovel far from their own soft beds.

"Harsa Andromache, if I may," interrupts Deiphobus, Hector's most war-
hungry brother. Much like the ox he resembles, he chews the inside of his
scarred cheek, as if weighing my words on a scale. "We've been fighting for
years and Troy's walls still stand. Why should we divert the energy of our
army to the coast just to rescue a handful of farm girls from having to share
Achilles's bed?"

"Come now, I'm sure most of them enjoy it!" shouts a council member I
do not recognize. And now I do not care to.

My skin prickling with heat, I shrug off my riding cloak, just as my father
used to when he was about to give orders no one would like. "Tell me, how
do Agamemnon, Menelaus, and Achilles *feed* their armies? How do they keep
their soldiers from sailing home to their wives after all this time?"

Deiphobus stares like I've gone mad. "They do as foreign armies have
always done. They rape and they plunder."

"And what happens if we make that strategy impossible? What if we *arm*
those farmers, the very people who provide the Achaeans with fresh-ground
wheat and warm thighs? Better yet, what if we station small groups of soldiers
at each settlement, a trap set for when the Achaeans inevitably come to raid?"

"You are really suggesting we train our inferiors to fight for their own
worthless homesteads instead of calling on them to send men to Troy?"
Paris's lips twist into a smile. "On second thought, maybe that isn't such a
horrible idea. Why don't we send the foreign allies to the coastal settlements
in our stead? Their unruly captains have been a pain in our side since this
war began. How many Citadel liaisons had we run through before you were
stuck with the job, Helenus?"

"Seven." Helenus massages the bridge of his birdlike nose. "They're impossible. I spend half my days moderating the petty squabbles between
them. Last night, I was called to the Lower City because one of them tied
another to a post and shaved him bald. The only thing they seem to agree
on is their mutual dislike of one another."

"Then perhaps this is a stroke of brilliance after all," Paris says. "I'm sure
the women of the Lower City would be glad to have a few weeks' reprieve
from their foreign stench."

I gnaw my lip and turn to King Priam. "Troy's allies are here because we called upon the oldest ties we have. The Assuwa Federation that rose against the Hittites had been dead for generations before *you* resurrected it. These men left their homes to answer our call for aid. And now, even as the Hittite threat from the east grows yet again while the Achaeans are pounding on our doors from the west, they remain by our side. Still, we so flippantly dishonor them."

Paris shrugs. "You would paint them as noble only because you've never had the pleasure of their company." His words are arrows that do not miss. "You are sheltered from that unfortunate necessity. As well you should be, like all of Troy's Harsas who are spared the harsher realities of this war. Yet for some strange reason, shielded as you are, that is the same war you would now seek to counsel us on."

"Because I know what it is to be an outsider, even inside these walls," I say before I can stop myself. "Walls we hide behind while our neighbors suffer for a fight that isn't even theirs."

The men shift uncomfortably. Some look to Hector, uncertain but not hostile. Many more nod in agreement with Paris. So many that my heart goes from a smooth canter to a jerky trot. This fruitless debate is precisely why Hector and I have always lived along the Citadel's edge instead of firmly inside its walls. But as I take in the obvious rifts within the council, I almost regret keeping the distance that has guaranteed our independence. Perhaps I have miscalculated the depths of the divisions that exist within the Citadel. Divisions with Hector at their center.

I see them now. Feel the danger in the gooseflesh traveling down my arms. Paris's slow smile assures me these factions have been building for some time. As the son that King Priam made his Master of Trade, Paris was the gatekeeper of the Dardanelles before the war, collecting taxes from merchant ships that wished to pass through those narrow straits and in turn made Troy rich. But with sea trade reduced to a trickle, Paris has turned his attention to politics instead.

I hold his gaze. "The only reward on offer here is saving your city when we drive our enemies into the sea. Which is exactly what will happen if we cut off their food source." I pause when Paris begins loudly sharpening his blade, though for all his talk of my sheltered life, he's never gotten close enough to an enemy to use it. His smugness grates because now I see that it may well have been earned. While I have been worried about the actual war, he has been worried about his private schemes, securing his own support from Troy's elite.

"Careful, brother," I continue over the din of bronze meeting stone. "One might think you prefer reveling in this war over winning it. Or fighting it, even."

Paris is well loved by the decadent Citadel, after all. The common soldiers do not adore him as they do Hector, but they at least respect him because by some miracle, his company of archers have become the deadliest in Troy. Paris's raucous boasting in the Citadel's wine halls about possessing the favor of Artemis's arrow and Aphrodite's ardor is as legendary as the beauty of the Spartan woman who shares his bed.

But my latest castration is too much. All the captains glower at me and then at Hector, their eyes berating him for allowing his wife to speak so willfully. He flashes me a look that tells me I have crossed a line. The only man who isn't burning is Priam. The old king just sits there, expressionless, staring into the crackling flames.

"What do you think, Father?" Paris asks, still sneering at me.

Antenor leans over to whisper into the king's ear. Hector loves his father, but he knows Priam's twin has the sharper mind. Born minutes after the king, Antenor is just as gray haired. But with his tall, regal bearing, he looks a decade younger when seated beside the king's ever-stooping shoulders. A hunchback that would be even more pronounced if Priam did not have his brother to carry some of the weight.

Priam looks up from the fire as though stirred from a deep sleep. "It is an interesting approach. Far more innovative than any of the strategies the rest of you have proposed."

My heart races with hope. The hope of recognition.

"Unfortunately, every able-bodied male within a hundred miles is already conscripted into our army. Women and old men would never be able to stand up to Achilles's warriors, no matter how well-armed—"

"They would if *we* sent soldiers to reinforce their efforts!"

It doesn't take Hector's grimaced mouth to assure me that interrupting the king is another mistake. One I will pay for dearly.

The men erupt into argument and the animal skins of the tent flap in the wind. Whatever divisions already existed among Hector's kin, I have made them worse. My hands tremble with helplessness. It does not matter if I am right. The war inside Troy's walls is one of numbers. And we don't have them on our side.

"You've no idea what a mother will do to spare her children from death or slavery," I say to a room of men who are no longer listening.

"No. And neither do you." The voice that replies does not belong to Paris. Or Priam. It is as cold as a long-dead corpse, but as familiar as my own.

I turn and meet Hector's cutting gaze across the flames, his eyes glistening like obsidian. Not one of his brothers, not even the king, dares to speak as the wave of Hector's fury passes through the tent. Outside, my mare whinnies.

His words are a lash, flaying me open. Shining light on words we have never dared to speak out loud. Hector knows I will always do my duty, but that in my heart, there is something I want even more than a son with my husband's earth-laden eyes.

My freedom.

That's when I see it. The inner workings of our bedchamber from the perspective of the Citadel. As king, Priam is rumored to have produced over fifty sons between his queen and countless concubines. Sons that are a solid mark proving Priam is blessed by the gods. And thus fit to rule. As of yet, I have not given Troy's current heir a single child.

For an instant, the razor-sharp rage in Hector's gaze softens . . . but into what? Pity? Regret? I lick my dry lips, tasting the metallic tang of the truth he's been protecting me from. In this one thing, perhaps I have been sheltered.

My barrenness may not just cost Hector his joy. It may cost him his throne.

Even worse, Hector refuses to see what I suddenly can—that his beloved brothers are waiting in the wings for a chance to improve their own prospects.

"I need to water the horses."

Hector's hard shoulder hits mine as he brushes past. He slips out of the army tent and into the night. One that will never be dark enough to cloak the humiliation I've brought upon him.

That I've brought upon us both.

2

RHEA

LIVE, LITTLE MOUSE. You must live.

The four-wheeled cart hits a bump, jolting those of us inside. Animal hides hang over the rickety frame, steeping the interior in darkness. A low groan rises from the front. The only part of the crying woman I can see are her hands, twisted with age and hard work. Unlike my own, hers are bound. They also haven't stopped praying. I don't recognize the melodic language flowing past the old woman's lips, but desperation sounds the same in every tongue.

Horses whicker. The men outside call to each other. I concentrate on the flow of sounds. Guttural. Staccato. The language of the men who found me half-dead is no longer completely foreign. Since they threw me in here ten days ago, I've had nothing to do but listen. And regret.

I've told myself it doesn't matter. That any interest in this world is a betrayal of all the people I loved who are no longer in it. But my ears and my eyes have made a liar out of me. After all these days, they've been greedy for every sound. Every sight. By now, I've collected two hundred and eighty-four strange words and attached them to their meanings.

Horse.

Water.

Danger.

Death.

There were fifteen of us in this cart when the journey began. After two days without food, we are now down to ten.

I've noticed other things too. The reek of spices from the second wagon. The grunts of poor donkeys who struggle to pull the third, loaded down with tin. Ten horses and forty sheep, guarded by seventeen armed men. Valuable cargo. Expensive goods. Wherever we are going, it isn't a small village. If we ever get there at all.

Hunger claws at my insides. If the dizziness is any indication, I won't have to bear the pain for much longer. The thought fills me with a strange peace, but then my sister's voice is there, driving the peace away.

Live, Rhea. You must live. For all of us. For me.

Kallira's eyes burn through my memory. The approaching fire reflected in their depths, bringing out the golden threads of her irises. The soot on her cheeks and the way the flames painted her beauty with a starkness the sun had never dared.

Voices drifted toward us from outside the stable where I spent the sixteen years of my childhood. Our heads jerked toward the single door. We were squatting in a pile of hay in the back of an empty stall. It was where I had run when I first saw the men coming onto our land with their arrows nocked and spears drawn. That was right before I first heard the screams from inside the house where my mother and sisters were preparing the barley bread for the evening meal.

The scents of smoke and terror were thick in my nostrils. Death was everywhere, but it didn't look like the creatures from my papa's stories. No, death wore the faces of men, lean and haggard. Their eyes glinting with words for feelings I didn't yet know.

When they came, I was pulling up onions in the garden beside our house. I crouched down low, making myself small. My eyes trained on the stable. The only structure on our land that wasn't burning.

Scurry scurry, little mouse.

It was what my papa always called me. Said with warmth and affection as I sat before our hearth. My spot was by his side, directly next to the statue of the Mother goddess—the first thing he brought into this house he had built with his own two hands.

You see all, my little mouse, he would say. *But nobody sees you unless you want them to.*

It would have made me feel proud if not for the unfortunate fact that I didn't simply move like a mouse. I looked like one too. Ears too big. Wide teeth in a narrow face. The only thing I liked about myself were my eyes. The same color as the spring pastures that ran from the side of our house all the way to the mountains.

Mountains that had gone smudged, seen through the smoke of the world burning all around me.

The men came closer. The tips of their weapons smeared red. At the sight of those spears, I closed my eyes and forced my body to still the way I did whenever I worked with our horses. Just like Papa taught me. Hands steady. Breaths even. I focused on the stable and waited for the men to turn their backs.

Scurry scurry, little mouse.

They turned, and I flung myself toward the stable doors.

The familiar musk of horses and hay greeted me inside. A dozen of their heads stuck out over wooden rails. Even in the shadows, I knew them by their shapes and smells as easily as by their shining coats.

Our horses' fear danced through me. For them, I buried mine deep and approached the first stall.

My hands trembled as I pulled the latch free.

Run. My heart sang out in the language of whispers.

More doors and more latches. Animals streaked past me. One stall after another until there was one left.

Ishtar and Carris watched me come. Nostrils flared. Hooves stomped in defiance.

I threw open the door, but they did not move. My brave, brave girls. They wouldn't leave me. Not unless I made them go.

I pressed my head to the white star on Carris's forehead. A shudder ran through me as I took a step backward and smacked her hard across the rear. I did the same to Ishtar.

Pain. Confusion. Fear.

Tears ran down my cheeks as I watched my horses run through the doors, now flooding with smoke from the fire consuming our home.

A shrill scream pierced the night outside. With one last glance at the doors, I scrambled into a bed of hay.

More smoke. More screams. They seemed to go on forever. I lay there shaking. Finally, the screaming was done.

That was how Kallira found me.

A hand grasped mine through the straw, her other hand wrapping around my mouth to cut off my scream.

"Quiet, Rhea. They are just outside."

Kallira. Who looked just like our mother.

Kallira. Who made men stop and stare whenever she walked past.

Kallira. Who was the one Papa loved best even though he would never say so. I was his little mouse, but Kallira was his prize mare. Older by three summers, she wasn't kind like Zaria or talkative like Tannsa and Megari. Kallira was a puzzle I couldn't solve no matter how long I sat and watched. And oh, how I'd watched. It was what I'd done for as long as I could remember. I collected details the way a mouse collected straw, but Kallira . . . Kallira was different. No matter how much I watched, I could never really *see* her. She didn't let me. She was my sister. I loved her, and yet I didn't know her. I wasn't sure anybody did.

"What do they want?" I asked as the sounds of the men outside grew louder. But for the two of us, the stable remained empty.

Kallira looked into my eyes. *"We don't have time for questions you know the answers to."*

I nodded. Winter on the steppes had been harsh and the summer dry. Hunger was a wildfire burning through the Hittite Empire. There were rumors of raiding men in the north. Shipments of grain from Egypt to Hattusa. It had only gotten worse since Papa had left with his men to fight a foreign war in a distant city. My mother said to leave us alone was to invite evil. It had taken two summers, but evil had finally come.

Something crashed against the wall from the outside. I flinched back.

Kallira met my eyes. The horror in mine reflected back in hers. And then I watched that horror bleed out of her face to be replaced by something fierce.

"It is time to run, little mouse."

Run? I couldn't run. I shook my head, but Kallira grabbed my chin, forcing it still.

"You will run when I tell you to. And you will live."

Grief. Doubt. Fear. Kallira saw them all on my face. Her grip on me tightened until her hands were the only things I could feel.

"Live, Rhea. You must live. Promise me."

The fire in her eyes burned into me, cutting through my terror.

"I promise."

The last words I ever said to her.

Her perfect face cracked and all the love she never showed bled through. The truth of herself I never saw because she hid it for reasons I will never know.

I ran for two days. Until I couldn't run anymore. Until the pain in my body took over even the ache in my chest, and I fell down at the foot of an ancient yew tree.

That was where the caravan found me.

Another jolt from the cart. I bite back a moan and make the same wish I've been making ever since the wheels beneath me began turning.

I wish I could go *back*. This time, I wouldn't hide. This time, I would run toward the house instead of away. I would grip Kallira's hand the way she had gripped mine, and I would tell her that I would only go if she went with me.

I would never have made the promise that sent her running out of that stable.

But I had.

Live, little mouse. You must live.

Only, living was suddenly too hard.

The wheels hit a bump that tilts the wagon on its axis. It sends the girl next to me careening sideways. Her cheekbone collides with my shoulder. A hiss escapes her teeth. It's the first sound she's made in eight days. Since the first night the men came for her.

Three of them had pulled back the cloth covering us. The girl's eyes were wide. Her hair long and dirty. Even covered in rags, her soft curves stood out among the rest of us. For the first time in my life, I was grateful for a body that resembles a stack of sticks held together with string.

She fought. Like a wild animal she kicked and flailed, drawing blood before they dragged her out. There was a moment. Before they took her. When her eyes met mine and something passed between us. Something that I couldn't have explained if I tried, but that I felt in the place deep inside me where I hear the horses whisper.

When the men brought her back an hour later, she wasn't fighting anymore.

The men have come for her twice since. Even beaten and dirty, the girl is still pretty.

My sisters were pretty too.

The wagon pitches upward again. Up. Up. Up the cart climbs. Until it feels like we are poised on the very edge of the world, and one wrong step from the horses might send us hurtling over.

Voices outside. Not those of the men who hold us. These voices are calling from somewhere farther away. The sounds fracture toward us. I track the echoes in my head.

Wood groans as we shift course, the ground growing smooth under our wheels. The cover is thrown back from over the top of us. For a moment, I'm struck blind by the sun.

We have stopped at the entrance of a city. Beyond the fortified gates, flat-roofed, two-story houses sit in stacks of rings around an open ground alive with movement. Endless rows of carts overflowing with colorful wares and more people than I've ever seen at one time or in one place. Enclosures packed with livestock and horses. Hundreds of horses that must have been gathered from every corner of Anatolia.

Noise drifts toward us on the breeze. Men and women talking, hawking, bargaining in many languages.

This is no ordinary market.

I've heard of such places. Bustling centers where the trade routes north of the Black Sea connect with those stretching past the lands of the Hittites and the Assyrians in the east and the Egyptians in the south. During the dry seasons, Papa and his men would visit trading grounds like this one to sell our horses and barter for goods we could not produce ourselves. When they returned smelling of sweat and the spices of distant lands, I would soak up their tales and wish that someday I might see those lands for myself.

Two hills overlook the village from opposite sides. On the eastern summit lies a temple carved directly out of the stone it sits upon. Rock reliefs adorn the rough walls of the imposing sanctuary, from which the thousand gods of Hatti gaze down upon me. Their faces are mixed with the cult gods of western Anatolia. I recognize only Tarhunt, god of storms, and Tiwad, the Luwian sun god. These deities are joined by the ancient grandmother, Hannahanna, and the Hittite Kumarbi and Telepinu and many more I can't make out, but whose familiar forms give me the sense that I am being watched over.

The temple on the western hill is like nothing I've ever seen. Made of light-colored stone and many pillars, it seems to be fashioned more of air than rock. Bright banners dance in the wind from the temple's heights, as if welcoming all below to join in the celebration. I search its façade for some distinguishing characteristics—some clue as to exactly where I am, but the banners are just scraps of dyed cloth. The stones are just stones.

The wind blows with the sharp scent of salt and fish. I spin around and am greeted by the sight of long, narrow beaches pressed like golden hands around a jewel of the deepest blue. Waves send ripples through the water. It twinkles in the sun, stretching on so far, I might think it goes on forever.

In sixteen years, I've never once traveled beyond our pastures, but that doesn't mean I know nothing of the world. Long ago, Papa sailed across the Aegean. A boy with no family born in a land far to the north where horses ran wild across the plains, he worked as a rower on a trading ship. Every night, my sisters and I would listen while Papa told us of the paths he trod before he brought his first horses over the sea and settled on our farm in the heart of Anatolia.

The Hittites call the small number of settlers like us Phrygian, but they let us stay in their lands so long as we provide grain for Hattusa and horses for the king's chariots. Papa repaid this hospitality in kind, and no traveler or trader ever passed through our stables without an invitation to our table. As word of our magnificent horses spread, there were many, many traders. They came from the east and the west, north and south to our small farm at the foot of the mountains. As a little girl, I collected their tales, even those in languages I didn't know, and when Papa asked, I would recite them back to him word for word. I remember the moment I first realized this was not something everyone could do.

"*Your mind is like the wind, my little mouse,*" he told me once, his sun-dried face creased in lines of pride that bathed me in warmth. "*Always running. Collecting secrets and forgetting nothing.*"

I lived for those days when visitors came. My father asked them his questions, and the travelers gave him their tales. And while I cherished all the words the same, regardless of where they came from, Papa loved the tales of the Achaean gods best. It was where he found my name.

Rhea. A goddess born of the earth and sky.

I stare at a sea like the one my father crossed when he was even younger than I am.

Our cart traverses a ramp to the high gates of the port city. A man steps forward to intercept us. Plates of armor span his chest and a sword hangs heavy in the hilt at his belt. Like the sea twinkling in the distance, my mind screams *soldier*, even though I have never seen one.

The soldier waves our convoy onto the wide dirt street beyond the gates, where we are immediately swallowed up by the jostling crowd.

Words rise up out of the chaos all around me. Shouts of tradesmen and patrons. Sharpened by fear, my mind cuts familiar sounds from the air.

Horses.

Trade.

Water.

Slave.

A weight settles in the pit of my stomach. Past the goods and the enclosures filled with horses and cattle, another bustling trade is being conducted on a patch of bare earth. Bound men and women are brought to stand in lines at the center of the circle with strangers surrounding them on all sides. The spectators reach out to grasp them with rough hands, inspecting before goods exchange hands. Then the next group of captives is brought forward and the process begins all over again.

My heart starts a rhythmic pounding in my chest.

I'm not a slave. I am Rhea, daughter of Haskim, and our horses are the finest in Anatolia.

I run over all the words I've gathered, trying vainly to fit them together into a plea that makes sense. Even if I could, I'm not so naïve as to believe these men would listen. Where I come from doesn't matter to them any more than where I am going. Just so long as they get paid.

Whoever I was, I am nobody now.

The horses walk forward a few more paces before stopping in the long line leading to the slave market. A man approaches our cart. His bright, richly woven clothes set him apart. As does the small armed guard that hovers in his wake. A prosperous gut hangs over the golden belt wrapped around his middle, and the small leather bags at his sides jingle with the precious beads and gemstones used to make trades.

The rich man leans forward, his eyes halting on me for less than a breath before moving on to the girl beside me. His tongue darts out over his lips, revealing a mouth of brown teeth.

He says something in the language of my captors, which must be Palaic or Luwian, the tongue of trade in the Troad. Hands are clasped. The rich man turns away. When he does, five girls trail after him, their hands bound by rope and tethered to the golden belt around his waist.

The girl beside me tracks the rich man's movements. Her eyes run blankly over the bound women for a moment before something deep inside them flickers.

Her expression tears at me.

Shifting her weight, the girl brings her bound hands into her lap. That's when I see the rock hidden in her fist. Viciously sharp. She grips it so tightly, blood trickles from her palm down the crook of her arm.

The girl raises the rock to her wrist. As she does, the angle of the sun changes, bathing her face in orange fire. Suddenly, it is Kallira sitting beside me. Her face inches from mine as she forced a promise from my lips. And then it is my sister's words coming out of my mouth, as if she is the one speaking them.

"Live," I tell the Hittite girl whose name I don't know. "You must live."

She glances at me then, her suffering so stark it strips us both.

"They took my baby." Bound hands lift her tunic, revealing engorged breasts beaded with unspent milk. She is only a few summers older than I am, but the shadows in her eyes are ancient. "They ripped him from my arms."

My gaze lifts from her mottled skin. "Then live not for yourself, but for him."

She shakes her head. "They will force another child on me, and then they'll take it away. I can't bear it. I *won't*."

The rock shakes against her wrist, opening a shallow cut.

"Stop." My words are a whisper. "This isn't the way."

Slowly, the girl takes in my face as her hands move upward, running over her own features. The delicate bones. Smooth skin. Full lips.

"Perhaps there is another," she agrees.

Understanding twists my stomach. "No."

"Either you do it, or I will." A flicker of fear. A harsh swallow. "It will hurt less if you help me."

She waits. The path forward is clear now.

When I reach out, she places the rock in my hand. A shudder runs through me.

"You'll have to be silent," I say, unsure if I've won or lost.

The girl glances at the men who hold us. The naked hatred on her face steals my breath. "I won't make a sound."

The wagon moves one more place forward.

"Do you have a protector god?" I ask the girl to buy time, because though I agreed to do this, I don't want to. Don't even know if I can.

The girl stares into the distance. "It does not matter. They have forgotten me."

Something about her answer starts an echo of Kallira's final plea. Only, the words don't speak to the beat of my heart or the intake of breath in my lungs. No, they dance to the tune of my mother's singing, my sisters' laughter, and the rhythm of Papa's voice as we sat together around our hearth.

I am trying, Kallira. I swear to you. I blink back tears, and for the first time since I made my promise, I wonder.

Is living enough?

I open my eyes, but my sister isn't there. Instead, it is the girl grieving the son who was taken from her. A life that is no longer her own. We have lost everything, the two of us, and yet, we are still here.

We are still here.

I grip the rock so tightly, it bites into my palm. "Perhaps now is the time to make them remember."

The girl grits her teeth. The sound that escapes her throat is low. Savage.

I swallow once. And then I raise the rock to her face.

3

HELEN

FOR HER SAKE.

I flex my stiff hands so they can travel across the loom, weaving a web of many colors.

Crimson.

Indigo.

Black.

Olive.

Violet.

The tapestry's intertwining threads are the only prayer I have left. And so, my fingers move at a pace my mind cannot, in rhythm with the guttural intonations of the priestess I always wanted to be.

Why don't you hear me? What can I do to make amends?

The Unnamed One does not answer. It comes as no surprise.

Again, I open my hands. Two pale swans swim in my vision, blurred from my last cup of wine. The rest of my body may be weak, but my hands are more muscular than most. Weaver's hands. Though clumsy, the fingers are strong, and that alone makes them lovely to behold. Blood rushes to my head as my senses sharpen and the darkness along the edges recedes. A thin crimson stream travels from the bleeding tip of my finger down my arm, past the wrist I've imagined slicing into countless times. Yet I've never had the courage. Nor the permission. The Unnamed One forbids it.

I see the blood, but I can barely feel a twinge of care or pain. Wrapping the wound in a scrap of cloth, I turn back to the loom. Always, I return to the work. An outpouring of grief, a record of all the deaths my life is bound to.

The deaths they will say *I* caused.

They aren't entirely wrong. This land of bright cobalt sea and sky has faded to a mute gray after so many years at war. Sometimes, I feel like the fog from inside my head has grown, on a mission to spread out and consume everything that is good.

The cut in my finger throbs now, a reminder of what awaits. I reach for my wine cup again. Forgetting calls to me from beneath the surface. A few drops of poppy tincture, just enough to eliminate the sweet memories of her face for some moments of peace. One gulp and grief's bite loosens its fangs. Another sip and the stirring of rage is reduced to embers. The silver cup falls to the floor, jarring me awake for an instant before the lull of walking sleep takes over.

I reach for the tapestry threads, but I can no longer feel them. Feel much of anything.

Is this my altar now? Is the sacrifice of my guilt and my grief before the loom the only consolation I will receive from You?

All pleas to the Unnamed One are in vain. They cannot harness the silent deity's attention, just as they cannot stop the rivers of blood spilled in my name. A punishment for choices tied in a thousand knots that can never be undone.

For her sake.

As the dense fog swirls, I pray with my hands. The only part of me permitted to speak, but in pictures instead of words. With each loop of thread, I pray into being the struggles of the horse-breaking Trojans and the bronze-clad Achaeans. The one part of this story I am permitted to tell, though there are others who would tell it for me.

Crimson for Odysseus and his cunning.

Indigo for Hector and his loyalty.

Black for Achilles and his wrath.

Olive for Paris and his greed.

Violet for Agamemnon and his power-lust.

If they saw this tapestry now, it is possible they would each recognize their faces and their deeds. They would look, but they would not *see.* The moment I cannot fully escape, no matter how many sips I take from my cup. The thread beneath the threads. A color woven into all the others, so fine it can barely be perceived.

Gold.

Priceless treasure. Delicate yet forged in flame. Beautiful but deadly.

My vision blurs again as the poppy completes its work. The woven figure of a woman standing on the bow of a galley next to a handsome prince contorts and changes shape.

Not treasure taken, but a monster made. A Gorgon with a grotesque head of snakes. Devourer of men. As empty and lifeless as the stone her gaze makes.

For her sake. For her sake. For her sake.

My fingers reach out to touch the threads as if they were the soft curves of her face. Yet they are only threads. This tapestry my only witness to that which can never be revealed—for her sake.

The truth.

～ ✦ ～

I BLINK AND time slows, then speeds up all at once. When my eyes open again, the arrowheads are laid out across my workstation like the row of corpses they will soon create. I do not remember doing this, but I must have. Nobody else comes here. Nobody else is allowed. The work I do, I must do in secret.

Paris secured this private space for me, a small room attached to the gardens near the bathing house, a place that smells of jasmine. It is where the Citadel's women harvest herbs used to prepare the city's many dead.

I take an arrowhead and dip it into the shallow clay bowl, into the last remaining drops of poison, before returning to my mortar and pestle.

Wolf's bane is not an easy root to grind, but I do not mind the effort. The release. It's as if the beads of sweat forming beneath my veil carry crimes that are not so easily wiped clean.

You are made to heal. Never to harm.

The vow of all healers, all Paeanas of Sparta. A land I have not seen in years. A promise I have not been allowed to keep for nearly as long.

Warriors do not realize how much better it is to *see* the life you are snuffing out. With every batch of poison I make, I must imagine the hundred faceless spirits who will haunt my steps.

"How I love the little noises you make while you work."

I did not hear him come in behind me. Then again, I rarely do.

Pinpricks dance across my skin. I take a long swallow of wine before turning to face him. Slowly, the memories fade. Her pale, helpless face retreats into the fog, and I am able to speak.

"Paris. You are back from the battlefield early."

"Tomorrow I travel to Cyzicus with Hector to find a new Master of Horses. It seems the old one caught something fatal from an overworked whore." Paris nods at the drying arrowheads. "Good. The archers have nearly run out. Now that Odysseus has caught wind of our tactics and is returning the favor with fire, Troy cannot afford to hold back."

I take another drink. Paris speaks as if the entire Trojan army, not merely the archers he commands, will benefit from these poisoned arrowheads. A poison that makes the Achaeans fall to the ground in brief agony, never to rise again. It is the only reason Paris has remained in the army's good graces despite his unwillingness to fight in the front alongside Hector. If anyone knew the secret behind his archers' deadly success, the shame would be too much for him. So instead, I bear it for us both.

For her sake.

"This poison." Paris leans over my shoulder, his hand resting lightly on my hip. Curiosity takes over his fine features and stirs something in the mist around me. Something that almost feels like fear. "What happens if it is ingested?"

I reach for the wine, for the softening of ragged edges and a swirl of accusations. Paris pulls my hand back from the cup. "Tell me what it does."

I take a deep inhale. "Drinking wolf's bane is as deadly as a tainted arrow in the flesh. And nearly as immediate. The victim's muscles will tense into convulsions. They begin foaming at the mouth." I hear the words, though I cannot feel my lips speaking them.

Paris shakes his head. "Too violent." His lips press against my bare shoulder. I close my eyes. "Do any of your plants accomplish the same task but with more subtlety?" His next kiss presses to the top of my spine. As if he might seduce the answer from me. "I need one that makes it appear as if the person is dying of something natural. A sickness, perhaps."

"Why?" I cannot remember the last time I questioned Paris. Judging by his expression, neither can he. The almost boyish light in his gaze dims, exposing the long-standing grudge he hides from everyone but me.

Hector.

The thought escapes me as a soft gasp, though Paris doesn't seem to notice. My hands reach for the cup again, wanting, *needing* its dulling powers. This time, Paris permits it. As the bitter tincture slides down my throat, I tell myself I am mistaken. Paris has long coveted his brother's position, but he knows well the gravity of the consequences if our misdeeds were ever found out.

Paris pats my cheek. "Do not worry, wife. I have as many enemies as there are stars, yet I am still here." He kisses me again. "You do your part, and I will do mine."

4

ANDROMACHE

CYZICUS STINKS OF salt water and rotting fish. They are not smells I ever thought I would relish. I have forgotten what the sea looks like without the blight of Achaean ships. It has made me miss the sights and scents of the shore.

It's strange to enter such an open, bustling city. A city oblivious to a war that has consumed Troy's former glory like a ravenous fire. Much of the trade and goods that once flooded our markets have been redirected here. It seems our loss has been Cyzicus's gain.

Hector's watchful eyes never rest, darting around the throng brushing up against our party, his hand ready on his spear. It isn't customary for a prince of Troy to leave his post, but with a war as long as this one, it is sometimes unavoidable. The tasks that have brought us here are equally vital to Troy, each in its own way.

"Look there, Andromache. We're nearly to your retreat," Paris says from where he rides in a cart on the other side of Hector. He joins our small party under the guise of helping Hector, since Paris is a self-professed natural when it comes to haggling for horses. But I've no doubt that the chance to sample different vintages and different whores is the real reason Paris is here, eager as he is to play the prince again far from his city's war.

Paris smiles, knowing the best way to ignite my wrath. "Three days should be plenty to bond with your fellow females while you all hold hands and sing odes to the great goddess."

He seems to know more about this fertility rite than I do. Perhaps his harlot—who, for all her years in Troy, has never borne her Trojan prince a child either—provided him with the details. One might suspect the shared misfortune of barrenness would bring us together, but Helen has made it clear that she, a former queen, views herself as my rival. If she ever manages to give Paris a son, Hector's position as first in line becomes that much more precarious.

She may well get there first. The gods have seemingly granted her everything else.

My fast-approaching prison rises up before us. Demeter's temple sits on a small hill at the end of the long market street that has swallowed us. Its white, rounded stone is covered in colorful banners that flap in the breeze. The serenity of the sacred space could not be in sharper contrast to the older temple that guards the opposite end of the city. Carved from dark limestone that has kept its ragged edges, the rough sanctuary honors the less fashionable gods of the Hittites and Hurrians, along with local deities from across western Anatolia.

It appears that even here, our worlds are at war.

Only this battle has a clear victor. The Anatolian temple honoring the gods of my childhood sits empty and neglected, more like a ruin than an active place of worship. In contrast, the hillside dedicated to Demeter has that irresistible sheen of *the new*—a fresh take on ancient wisdom that makes the seeker feel uniquely enlightened. As if we are the first humans to come up with the notion that lighting an oil lamp is more productive than wandering in the dark.

I turn away from the older sanctuary, though I loathe accepting the undeniable conquest of the Achaean gods. Could our enemies have had the patient foresight to plan such a covert and gradual takeover? First, export a few goddesses with the jars of olive oil from Crete and jugs of wine from Thessaly, then move your army in once the coveted peoples do not know which gods should have their loyalty?

And here I am, one of those city women who will apparently pay for the privilege of bowing before the latest fashion while the ghost of Huwassanna stands at my back.

A hum of voices draws my attention to the living hillside. Dozens of servants rush up and down Demeter's temple steps like insects, busy making preparations for the three-day festival in honor of the goddess and her daughter, Persephone.

Three days spent in the Underworld.

Lips turned up in amusement, Hector studies my frown. His horse nuzzles my mare. She lurches forward, making me seize on the lead. After an awkward crossing yesterday that resulted in the beast throwing me into a river, Hector tried to talk me out of riding beside him today. But I refuse to sit with Paris in the cart. If Hector is the only Trojan Harsar to ride on horseback, I will be the only Harsa.

"Relax, Andromache. How bad can the rite be?"

"Likely much worse than you're imagining."

Hector casts me a teasing grin. "Aren't you at least curious? No one knows what takes place during the Mysteries but the honored women who participate in them."

"Trying to make the veiled affair seem exclusive does not make it more appealing."

"But the rite *is* exclusive. Men are forbidden to talk about it, let alone know what takes place."

"Then you'd better hush before some fat old priestess has you stripped naked and flogged in the streets for prying." Despite my tone, a smile lurks. Ever since our disastrous meeting with the council, Hector and I have hardly spoken about anything that matters. I've tried to keep our conversation light and full of banter, but it hasn't had much effect on him, which worries me. Hector's anger is usually a bolt of lightning, not an enduring blaze.

Thankfully, the look he gives me now flickers with amusement. A softening. "You know as well as I do that we only give the gods our most sumptuous virgins. What better way to torture men for their impiety?"

I bury my face in the mare's mane so I am not the first to break our stalemate with laughter. Then I sit up and meet Hector's gaze. What happened at the council may never be addressed directly, but according to Queen Hecuba, a lack of communication is the secret to a long and happy marriage.

We reach the base of the temple mound, and Hector helps me down from my horse, smoothing my veil before reaching for the single bronze curl beneath.

"What will you do with three days to yourself?" I ask, suddenly wishing I had one more night to share his tent and make the mending of our union official.

Hector pulls me close, his low voice tickling the flesh along my neck. "You mean besides purchasing enough horses to get Troy through the fighting season, all while counting down the hours until you return to me renewed?"

I pull back from his embrace.

"Andromache, that's not what I—"

Gesturing for my servants to follow, I break away before he can make excuses. Hector is a good man, but he is still the son of a Trojan king with more bastards than he has fingers to count them on. A king's might is bound to the fruit of his loins. Which means so is my worth as a wife.

The long years of our marriage are more than enough time for doubt to fester in the Citadel. Hector may be Priam's firstborn and the commander of the army, but he cannot remain the king's heir if he does not produce a son of his own, and Priam grows more feeble by the day.

"Why not take a concubine?" Hector's mother asks whenever I step out of the room, but not out of earshot. Hecuba wants me to hear. She wants me to know I am failing in my only duty to this city that has become my home. *"You have the love of the people, Hector. It matters not that those children would have none of your wife's blood, only that they carry* yours. *Andromache will understand."*

And I would. I would hate it, but I would understand. There is no one else who could rule Troy without breaking her. No one but Hector. Still, he refuses his mother in this one matter. We have always been the sun and the moon. We both know that to bring another star into our orbit would be the end of a union, stable as few have known. Even when we fight as fiercely as we love.

This rite, as much as I dread it, may be our last chance.

Without looking back, I stride toward the temple of Demeter. For the first time since we arrived in this town of merchants and fishermen who plunder land and sea, I am looking forward to paying homage to the goddess who makes the earth's crops flourish, and then wither unto death.

All for her unbearable grief over Persephone. The lost daughter she might have kept, not the son she surely wished for before she knew better.

Before she learned the harsh truth that boys never belong to their mothers—
they belong to the sword.

~⁓~

THE FIRST TWO days were not as horrible as what my imagination
had conjured. Opening ceremonies began with a procession around the
mount that ended with an ascent up the steep temple staircase, followed by
a visit to the bathhouse behind it. I have given many baths in my day, but I
have never enjoyed being on the receiving end of such intimacy. The ladies
around me, however, seemed overjoyed at the prospect of a little pampering.
Only the latest of many indications I did not belong to this strange world of
women.

At least not these women.

Queen Penthesilea's face must have visited me a thousand times, an ap-
parition rising in the bathhouse steam. From the age of nine when my father
first sent me to her through to my seventeenth summer, I'd trekked the
Scythian steppe, roaming the lands around the Black Sea with a tribe where
the women fought as bravely as their men. The Amazons never cared about
the things the daughters of kings were told to value from the moment they
recognized their reflection in a still pond—elaborate hairstyles adorned
with precious stones, the number of silk robes one could wear in a single
day, eyes lined with kohl and lips dyed with rouge.

Can you wield your sword with skill but know when to set it aside?

Is your mind sharp enough to sniff out an enemy and recognize a friend?

*Does your heart beat with a love so fierce, it gives refuge to the despairing and
defends the weak no matter the cost?*

These were my lessons in what made a woman beautiful.

After our long, communal soak, the temple servants rubbed our bodies
with clove-scented oil that burned and scraped away the dead skin with a
coarse wool glove. They then led us to a plunge pool where a toad of a
woman directed us to jump in one by one, our emergence from the cool
waters a symbol of our newfound purity.

We were each given an identical tunic of white linen. Once the servants
had pulled back our hair in simple plaits, they led us to a cluster of tents
beside the temple mound. There were nearly fifty of us, all women of

nobility from across Anatolia. Our offerings to the foreign goddesses were
not on behalf of our own fertility alone, as we would also bring back gifts to
bolster the fields of our homelands. Fields to the east, which rumor has it are
left barren by famine.

No wonder these women have turned their prayerful gazes west.

On the second day of the festival, a day of mourning, we fasted in soli-
darity with Demeter's grief. The entire day was spent praying in front of the
temple while sitting on beds of chasteberry leaves—an herb said to kill sex-
ual desire and return our souls to a virginal state.

It did not work.

My frustration over the way Hector and I parted, coupled with a lack of
food, manifested itself in dreams that left me in a cold sweat. Ours had always been a union of combatting desires. It wasn't unusual for those battles
to extend to the bedchamber, where almost any disagreement could be
smothered by our beating hearts and tangled limbs.

Not this time. Even in the heat of my dreams, though I longed for him,
Hector was as cool and distant as a stranger. His only purpose the son who
must carry on his memory and ensure his future place as king. For the first
time, I fear I am losing him.

I fear I may have lost him already.

When my eyes open to the next dawn, it isn't Hector's firm jawline I see
above me, but the round face of Faria, my personal servant, a girl as dimwit-
ted as she is dull.

"You must get up, Harsa. Or you'll be late for the final rite."

"Ah, yes." I yawn. "The supremely secret one."

As I sit up, the throbbing behind my eyes rushes to my temples. "I don't
see how starving makes a person any more pious."

Faria gives me a hesitant smile. "Not to worry, Harsa. It is the last day.
Prince Paris said there is to be a great feast in your honor."

"Paris is not a trustworthy source of anything." When the poor
girl flinches, I soften my tone. "I don't see why he has concerned himself
with—"

Of course. Paris does not want this rite to succeed. Not if it results in the
heir who would send him from second in line to third.

That thought alone is enough to rouse me from my bed. Feeling no more blessed by the gods, I make my way to the temple, where all desire for food flees as soon as I enter its hazy cavern.

What is that stench?

Based on their sour expressions, the other women seated around the central altar notice it too. But the temple is pristine, a dimly lit space clouded by incense that isn't strong enough to mask the rot of death.

My gut lurches as I join the circle, but my stomach has nothing to offer. A young temple priestess hands each woman in white a simple pitcher. We then spend the next half hour trying not to choke on the stench while the priestesses lead us in prayers to Kalligeneia, nymph nursemaid to Demeter and Persephone, honored as the giver of a beautiful birth.

"In order for there to be new life, we must first face death," the high priestess intones, inviting two of her sisters to aid her in pushing back a stone slab on the floor before the altar.

With the stone removed, the foul odor grows overwhelming. My desperate eyes search for a place where I can step aside discreetly, but such a sanctuary does not exist. It wouldn't matter if it did—there is no time. I heave the bile scorching my throat into the clay pitcher. The woman sitting next to me follows suit, as do several others around the circle.

We meet each other's humiliated gazes, all feeling as though we have done something disgraceful in the presence of deities. But the priestesses are hardly fazed. A young acolyte whose role I do not envy makes her way around the circle, exchanging the soiled pitchers for fresh ones. Another girl is right on her heels, handing each of us three roasted acorns dusted in sea salt. I choke them down greedily, hoping to settle my stomach. But this food of pigs and famine-time is a far cry from the feast Faria promised.

Next comes a middle-aged priestess who carries a tray lined with two-handled depas cups. "May the harvest prove abundant," she says with an unnerving smile as she hands me my portion of steaming liquid.

I breathe in its steam. Like overripe plums. Whatever herbal concoction these priestesses have brewed, it is strong. It smells better than the rest of this temple, but still too rich to drink on a nearly empty stomach without consequences.

Again, Paris's face flashes before me, though I cannot say why.

A few of the women make a toast to Demeter before throwing back the mysterious elixir. Their lips twitch, but no more than a child swallowing an unpleasant tincture. My reservations are surely ridiculous. There is no sinister shadow lurking here. There are only people doing what people do, in every land and by every tongue. Attempting to conjure order out of chaos and bend the wind to our will. Trying to control the outcome. By any means necessary.

A hand lands on my shoulder. I lift my chin and meet the bright, creaseless eyes of another young priestess, eyes that simultaneously hold the wisdom of all the ages. "Drink," she urges gently. "Drink and you will see the face of Love."

There is only one face that comes to mind when I raise the bitter herbs to my lips.

To Hector.

The drink is surprisingly smooth. The effects, immediate. My hands and feet begin to tingle. The rest of my body grows heavy. Although the stench still lingers, I notice it less. Everything slows, the circle of robed women blending together in a swirl of white. One by one, a chanting priestess leads each toward the hole in the floor. There must be a staircase, because they descend without effort, eventually returning in a new robe—this one dyed the deepest scarlet.

Beneath the thick veil of incense, I can barely make out what happens once the women exit the cavern. They bring their pitchers to the altar, dumping the contents onto the broad slab. Their offering to the goddesses. Only then the women do not return to the circle. I do not know where they go.

What if we are the sacrifice? This rite a way to dispose of broken women?

More and more questions build in a fearful swirl.

Out. I need to get out. I take a wild step, but a figure in white suddenly appears before me.

"Breathe deeply. The herbs make the mind run with dreads before they reveal what you need to see. Come, it is your turn." The same ageless priestess who gave me my cup takes my hand.

I follow, each step weighed down by what feels like copper ingots tied to my ankles. When we reach the top of the narrow staircase, I remember what I am being asked to enter.

A pit. One that harbors all the rot of the Underworld.

Again, my guide places her hand on my shoulder. The gentle touch rushes through me, lighting a fire of tingling warmth that heightens every sensation. Whatever these women gave us to drink, any wife would pay her weight in bronze to bring the tea home to her husband. Perhaps that is the true secret to this fertility rite's effectiveness.

"New life begins in death," the priestess says, urging me toward the staircase. "Do not be afraid."

I descend alone.

Inside the pit, it is so dark that I don't see her at first.

A voice from the darkness beckons, "Come closer, child."

A woman with a face more ancient than the three Moirai stands beside a large basin at the center of the chamber. She holds a small torch, the only light inside this shallow space. I take a step toward her but stop when my foot comes to rest on something soft. Another step and there is more of the same, but this time it—whatever *it* is—collapses under my foot. The only sensation I can compare it to is the time I joined my father's servants in stomping grapes.

But even the sourest wine does not smell this wretched.

In the dim firelight, the woman's strands of oily hair resemble snakes. With her leathery skin and toothless grin, she looks more like a beggar than a servant to the gods.

The crone speaks in a low voice lined with gravel. "To begin, you must gather your offering to the goddesses."

"And what, exactly, am I offering?"

The woman startles. "The remains of a thousand piglets, if you must know. Brought here to decay so they might one day feed fresh soil."

I gag but force the bile down. The only reason I am able to stand in this vile space at all is the drink that makes me feel like I'm hovering just above my body, and I am not willing to give the herbs up.

Holding my breath, I bend forward to scoop up the piglet corpses with my pitcher, unable to grasp how this horror might bring me closer to bearing a son.

"He will never come unless you welcome him," says the old woman.

I look upon her ugliness with new eyes. "What are you saying?"

"You know. But first you must admit these fears to yourself." She beckons me closer, flashing another toothless grin before raising a thin wooden pipe to her prunish lips. Inhaling its contents, the crone blows rings of smoke into my face.

An assault of questions rises with the sweet-smelling vapor.

What do I fear? That bearing a child means losing everything I am? That I sometimes love my freedom more than I love . . . Hector?

No.

We may have our difficulties as all couples do, but there is nothing in this brutal world I love more than Hector.

"Then why deny him the gift that will enable him to live on?" The old woman answers my unspoken questions, speaks as if I have any choice in this matter. "Why refuse him that which will cement his place and end the striving of those who seek to take it from him?"

"Because I do not want to lose *him,*" I blurt out.

The old woman smiles.

So that is the truth. The worry at the bottom of this well. The fear that each year of this war brings Hector one day closer to his death. Knowing he would leave behind not only me, but a son who would be a mirror image of my beloved, a perpetual reminder of my loss, feels like more than I can bear.

For what woman would wish to feed her own flesh to such a gluttonous war? I have walked Troy's ramparts for years, watching countless sons pass through her gates, never to return. The weeping in the bathing house drowned out only by the chorus that fills Troy's alleys as soon as the sun begins to set. That's when the mourning of women grows so violent, it sounds as if someone has set a pack of wolves loose in the streets.

All because of that Spartan who's brought us nothing but death and disgrace. Thousands of boyish smiles slashed, countless tender skulls caved in—all for a face most have never even seen.

Still, the body does not lie. I admit there is some dark, feminine part of me that longs to give Hector the son he desires, even as the sinewy muscle beneath my softening flesh screams *Not yet.*

For as soon as my belly grows, the small freedoms I have secured in Troy will wither on the vine. Even Hector, good man that he is, will value me more for the life I suckle at my breast than for the schemes of victory that race through my mind late into the night.

Surely the gods, whether Anatolian or Greek, have glimpsed the turmoil of my divided heart.

The gods.

This savage rite has only reinforced my distrust. There is surely some power, some mystery, behind the life that sustains us, but can that mystery really be so vain, so petty, so unbelievably cruel?

Releasing the breath I've held in too long, I set the pitcher of remains down at the foot of the washbasin. The room no longer spins, but my neck muscles throb.

"Now that you know what has been holding you captive, you can focus on the future," the old crone says, holding the torch over the basin. "Look closely."

The water beneath me is a sheet of obsidian. I barely recognize my own reflection. The gaunt woman staring back looks . . . afraid.

The crone waves a wand of incense, chanting in a language so ancient, I do not recognize one guttural word. The waters tremble and then . . . my face disappears.

Everything is dark. Lifeless. Hopeless.

Until it is not.

A light appears in the long tunnel that stretches before me. First, a rhythmic sound. A gallop. The most beautiful horse appears, though I do not usually think of horses as such. A boy sits high on the beast's back. He is young. Six or seven summers. The water ripples again. When the boy's face comes into focus, I hear myself gasp. A distant echo from the tunnel behind me.

A strong nose. Dark eyes that are both bright and brooding. Thick hair that curls at the ends where it falls loose and long.

Hector's son.

A tingling warmth travels up my legs and down my arms, pooling in the space beneath my heart. *Hector will have a son.*

Then perhaps this vision means Hector will live to grow old. That he will one day watch his eldest ride through the wheat fields surrounding Troy, its black soil rich with the ashy remains of a thousand Achaeans.

Perhaps we will live to see it. All of us.

A woman suddenly calls out to the boy, igniting a shiver that rattles my core. The voice isn't mine. It is younger. Strong, but gentle.

My heart lurches with a feeling I do not recognize.

When the boy looks up, his eyes alight with a love that scatters my dreams with one strong gust. A boy this young only looks at one woman like that.

And she isn't me.

Before I can make sense of this revelation, the water moves and the vision vanishes. I am back in the stinking pit, body and soul reunited in a way that can only feel like a disappointment.

My one consolation? Hector will have a son. Hector's blood will live on. But who is the woman who will make this possible?

"Is it certain?" I ask the crone. *Will I never be a mother?*

"The Mysteries bring clarity, never certainty," she replies.

Then there is a chance. A chance to alter what I have witnessed. A chance for that woman calling out to the boy with Hector's eyes to be me.

But only if I find the courage to *want* it.

The woman dips a pitcher into the basin and beckons to me once more. "Do you surrender to the fate that awaits you?"

"Yes." So long as this fate agrees with my will. I close my eyes, waiting for the cool water of another ceremonial cleansing.

The liquid poured over my shoulders is sticky. Warm. I have already grown accustomed to its pungent smell. The final act of this rite isn't, in fact, the donning of a fresh red robe.

It is a bath, and a promise, in blood.

5

RHEA

BLOOD. SO MUCH blood.

It runs down my forearms. Jumps off the cliffs of my elbows to splatter the cart floor.

The girl sucks in a breath, her skin breaking like an overripe fig. My hand falters.

A low hiss. Tears mix with the blood and dirt on the girl's cheeks, but there is nothing weak about her grip as it snags my retreating wrist.

I swallow an ocean of bile and lift the stone again.

The girl is true to her word. She doesn't make a sound. The buzz of the crowded market fades into the wind. It wraps around the two of us as I carry on about my task. When the rock becomes too slick to grip, I lean back to survey my handiwork.

Pretty girl. Not so pretty anymore.

Grief overwhelms me as the cart moves forward with a jolt.

The wheels roll a few times before coming to a stop next to a line of raised troughs covered in a thick swarm of flies. The stench coming off them is strong even over the reek of my own filth.

Dozens of hands shoot out of the cart toward the water. I catch the man across from me staring. He jerks his gaze away, but not before his terror has sunk its claws in deep. I glance down at my sullied tunic and bloody hands. Two thoughts crystallize in the chaos.

Our bodies are not our own anymore.

Somebody will be made to pay for this.

I drop the rock down the side of the cart and plunge my hands into the water, scrubbing furiously. It's no use.

Beside me, the girl leans out over the murky water, looking for some glimpse down the path she has chosen. I know the moment she sees, because her shoulders go rigid.

She turns toward me slowly, and the sickness I've been holding back rises up in a violent wave. Green bile splatters the dirt beside the muddy wheels.

I rest my face against the wooden floor of the cart and pray for the darkness to take me far away from this miserable place.

"Here." The voice is hoarse.

I turn my head.

The girl's expression is calm. Almost serene as she digs something out of the filthy folds of her cloak and presses it into my bloody palm.

I study the scrap of yellow fabric before wiping my mouth.

The girl's gaze clings to the swatch in my hands. "I wove that at my mother's loom," she says. "Wrapped him in it the day he was born. He was wearing it when they stole him from my arms, but not before I stole this first."

I pull the fabric back from my dirty lips. "I can't take this," I say, pressing it back to her.

She shakes her head. A fresh trickle of blood runs down her cheek. "Everyone who loved him is gone. I can't carry his memory alone." She closes my fingers tightly around the cloth. "Simursu. His name was Simursu. Beautiful boy with midnight eyes." Her voice breaks, and a part of me breaks with it.

It's been two years since Papa left our farm to answer the call of a prince I don't know, only to fall outside the walls of a city I've never seen. Now, everyone who loved Papa is gone, too. Except for me. His stories and his secrets are mine to carry. Just as I carry my mother's songs and my sisters' laughter. If I die now, all of them will die a second, more permanent death.

The thought settles heavy on my chest. "And you?" I ask. "What is your name?"

"Once I was called Lyria. Mother of Simursu. Daughter of Annaza and Hyme and wife of Zulliama." Every word is a rasp.

"A beautiful name." I cringe the moment the words leave my tongue.

She smiles. I'm not sure which of us it pains more. "I am not that girl anymore."

The men outside spring into action as the cart moves into the crowd at the end of this line. The girl who was once Lyria and I crouch down low, away from prying eyes and reaching hands. I press my shoulder into hers. She presses back.

"I am Rhea. Daughter of Haskim and Elliana. Sister to Tannsa, Megari, Zaria, and Kallira. What should I call you?" I study the girl to avoid looking at the men arguing, jostling, shoving one another.

Midnight eyes blaze. "Vengeance."

One final lurch sends Vengeance slumping against my shoulder.

The wagon stops. Even the old woman's prayers fall into silence.

Our captors bang on the edges of the cart, pulling us out one by one. They scream words my desperate mind clings to.

Move.

Down.

Now.

Eight of us exit the wagon. Two remain inside, bodies motionless on the floor. One of our captors turns them over before growling back to his men another word in my growing collection.

Dead.

They assemble us in a line and push us through the crowd. The stench of unwashed bodies mingles with the scent of animal dung and sea salt. I glance across the way to a table where a young girl is gutting fish from a basket. I lose sight of her as we are propelled into the circle at the center of the throng.

Men press in around us. Reaching out with their hands. Someone pinches my waist above my hip, hard. The pain is so sharp and sudden, it floods my eyes with tears.

I am blinking them out of existence when someone takes hold of my hand.

I glance back at Vengeance. Her grip on me tightens.

Our captors push back the mob with wooden prods. I steel myself for the haggling to start, but instead, a tear forms in the crowd. A man approaches us, his guards carving a clear path to the front. My pulse hammers at my throat. It's him. The rich man with the golden belt.

One of our captors, a short man with a long, black beard, moves forward eagerly. He bends at the waist and smiles as if he and the rich man are old friends before leading him to where Vengeance and I stand side by side.

The smiles quickly slide from their lips.

The rich man makes a choked sound when he sees Vengeance. A hot torrent of Luwian spews from his mouth. The words are flowing too quickly for me to catch them all, but his fury needs no translation.

Our captor with the black beard grips Vengeance by the arm. She doesn't move. She just dons the same blank expression she wore every time he and his men tore her out of the back of the cart. She gave them nothing then, and she will give them nothing now. Not even her fear.

I watch her shoulders straighten, her chin rise, and I pray to any gods who are listening that they might make me brave like Vengeance. Like Kallira. Like a hundred other girls who aren't me.

The rich man is yelling again. Black-beard gestures widely, protesting his innocence. They hurl insults at one another until the rich man throws up his hands. He waddles forward, the bottom of his robes dragging through the muck. His cheeks are red, dotted with perspiration, as if this ugly business has tested the very limits of his stamina. He grabs Vengeance by the chin, paying no mind to the cuts as he jerks it from side to side.

Vengeance bears his inspection without flinching. It strikes me that she is tall for a woman. She also doesn't hunch like the rest of us. Instead, she wields her height like a weapon. The only one she has. She towers over the rich man, and a flush creeps up his flabby neck as finally, they are speaking the same language.

All at once, the rich man's gaze falls on me. A sneer twists his lips as he takes in my tunic and my hands, both stained with evidence of the part I've played. Fury paints his cheeks. It's the only warning.

The blow sends Vengeance sprawling. Before I can move, she is already staggering back to her feet. She sways, and I reach out to steady her.

The rich man spits first at her feet. Then at mine.

Our captor makes soothing sounds behind him.

Girl.

Skinny.

Gold.

Slave.

Their words form a cyclone around my head, but I am not listening. Instead I am focused on Vengeance. The song of triumph in her eyes. One that echoes inside my chest as our captor presses a bag of goods back into the rich man's hands.

The rich man makes a dismissive gesture, and I almost smile as our captor ushers us toward the center of the waiting circle and whatever new horrors await us there. Vengeance moves first. I take a step to follow when a hand clamps around my arm.

A vicious tug yanks me backward. Before I can make a sound, a length of rope slips over my head. It tightens around my neck, cutting off my scream. Vengeance turns. Her eyes lock on something over my shoulder. The expression on her face sends my stomach into a free fall. She reaches for me with her bound hands, but the rope jerks before our fingers touch. The force spins me toward the rich man, who is watching me with a smile that is not a smile, but a vow.

He slips the end of the rope through his golden belt.

~ ❧ ~

FEAR. IT IS a taste as much as a feeling. Bitterness coats the back of my throat as the rich man, whom the guards call Bengor, walks through the market, dragging his purchases behind him on a leash.

The rope burns my skin. My thoughts are leaves chasing each other in circles. I can't catch them. Can't do anything but follow the man dragging me like one of my papa's stallions. Only no horse in our stables was ever treated like this.

Drip.

Drip.

Drip.

My eyes jerk to the sky. The clouds are a dark gray above my head. It hasn't rained on the central plateau in months. This coastal city can't be so far from the heart of Anatolia that it is much different here. Drought. Dead crops. Desperation the likes of which brought those men with spears and torches to our farm.

I don't know where I am or where I'm going, but I know this rain. It paints the pastures green. It makes my mother smile with thanks to the gods. It turns my father's irrigation trenches into fast-flowing streams and breathes life into dust. I tip my chin so that it might breathe life into me too.

The drops are gentle. Cool. I let them wash away some of the blood and the grit, and then I do the only thing I can. I open my eyes to the strange world around me.

My gaze focuses on the back of the girl directly ahead. There are six of us tethered to this rope. All female. All young. That is where my similarities with them end. From what I've glimpsed of the others, they are pretty with thick hair and lush curves. Just like Lyria before I helped remake her into Vengeance.

Live, Kallira told me, and I have. But in my heart I don't believe she would have made me swear those words if she had known where they would lead me.

My feet tangle, and I fall to my knees. Bengor turns. His fat lips compress in a tight line as he takes in my fair skin and dark hair tied in many braids.

"You are not Hittite born. Phrygian?" he asks in the language of my father's people.

It's a moment before I can gather enough saliva to form a word. "Yes."

He seems to consider. "You've come a long way to the Troad."

Hope shoots through me.

"My father was a horseman," I say through cracked lips. "Though we live on Hittite land, when King Priam sent out a call for aid, my father came west with horses and his sword. He died for Troy."

Bengor weighs my words like copper ingots before he tosses them back in my face. "Then he would be pleased to know his daughter will serve the brave soldiers who died at his side." A pensive sneer reveals rot no gold can fix. "Those jade eyes do not save you. The angles of your face are too sharp and you've the body of a hairless boy. No respectable Trojan soldier would pay for that. It'll be the docks for you. Sailors and Achaean scum. I hope you like the stink of fish."

He releases me roughly and starts walking again. The burning around my neck. Bengor. This whole city. Everything fades as I retreat deep within my own head. I've all but left this world behind when a familiar scent pulls me back against my will.

Earthy. Musky. It tickles my memory with hay and long hours mucking out the stables.

I wipe the tears from my eyes and there they are. As if I dreamed them into life.

More than one hundred sleek bodies are crammed in a single paddock to my right.

Horses.

Not just any horses.

These are from the Anatolian steppe. Beautiful, hearty animals like the ones my family raised and that by rights should be first on offer to the chariot forces of Hattusa. The fact that they are here instead means that, like me, they are stolen goods brought to one of the few places where they might be scattered to the winds before the Hittite king can stake his claim.

I trace their lithe forms, and my heart leaps with recognition. For a moment, I forget to breathe.

The black with the proud tilt to her head. The steady bay with white stockings. I watched them both foaled. Stood by my father's side as he weaned them and taught them to follow a lead. Not just familiar. *Home*.

Ishtar. Carris.

My heart sings to them. As if she can hear it, the black mare my mother named wickers in answer. Carris breaks against the tide of horseflesh, working toward me. My trembling hand is inches from Carris's soft muzzle when someone calls out Bengor's name.

The rope yanks me back. Carris whinnies as I am dragged toward a group of men gathered at a nearby enclosure. The space around them is clear but for guards and a few servants, who are dressed more finely even than Bengor.

My eyes race back to Carris, finding her immediately in the packed stall. Ishtar dances beside her, straining toward me. I want to run to them. I want to scream to anyone listening that they are mine and that we don't belong here. But this is a place where the unifying tongue is one of silver and gold, and the truth is that I have none.

Twenty more paces and the horses disappear in the crowd behind me. It is like watching our farm burn all over again. I am straining for any sight of them when a burst of heat licks across my skin.

As if pulled by an invisible rope, my head swings toward the paddock, where the men who summoned Bengor have gathered along the fence line. This enclosure is exactly like the others except in one regard. It is empty, but for a single horse.

Whatever breath I have left leaves my lungs in a rush.

I could ride almost before I could walk. Some of the greatest horses in Anatolia have come through our farm, and still. I've never seen a horse like this.

His coat is a rich copper that burns like fire. His mane and tail are black threaded with gold. The smoke to his flame.

He tosses his head as he charges from one end of his prison to the other at dizzying speeds. His movements are liquid. Every muscle coiled with unleashed power. A crowd has gathered to watch him in silent awe.

Beautiful. Wild. Bigger than any horse has a right to be. He runs at the fence where Bengor has ordered us to stand and skids to a halt directly in front of me.

Panic licks at the back of my neck. Anger. Restlessness. It is his and it is mine. One spilling over into the other.

I see you, Fire Horse. I hear you, I whisper back in the same language.

The fire horse leaps sideways, galloping for the far edge, where men jump down from the fence before he can do the honors for them. Mesmerized, I follow his movement until the sound of Hittite calls my attention back.

A squat man beside Bengor is boldly proclaiming himself to be the greatest of Phrygian horse breeders, though the wry expressions painted on the faces of his companions suggest they know full well what he is. A murderer. A thief.

"He's a savage beast," says another man, studying the "trader" with barely disguised contempt. The speaker has aquiline features and black curls that fan artfully as he lifts a cup of wine to his ruby mouth. His high voice and fine cheekbones do not match the hard glint in his eyes.

"True, Harsar. You have a keen eye. Which is why you must also agree that his beauty is matchless. Look at those legs. The shape of him! He is a chariot horse fit for a king!"

The pretty man's smile turns sharp. "That horse will never be broken. He is too proud. Horses like that should be disposed of before their distemper sullies the bloodlines."

"Quite right, Harsar Paris. Quite right. You are the epitome of wisdom. Kill the beast, and cut your losses, Fagos," Bengor snivels.

Paris. The Trojan prince they say stole the heart of the most beautiful woman in the world. He is as handsome as the stories say, but his beauty holds an edge. The kind that might cut if you allowed yourself to get too close.

"Perhaps another horse, then?" the thief turned trader offers quickly. "Something strong and noble, as befitting his master?"

"Or perhaps you're after a different type of ride," Bengor suggests, eliciting a chorus of laughs from the men.

"Not today," the man says.

Not a man. A prince.

"I am here at my brother's behest," the prince continues. "He is looking for horses and is not overly concerned with their origins so long as they can pull a chariot. Ours are dying faster than we can train them, and Hector can train them in a day. Our father would rather cut off his own nose than beg help from Hattusa, and so we are forced to acquaint ourselves with necessity." The words are as lovely as roses, but something in the way they are spoken gives them thorns.

What Prince Paris says next is lost to me. I have room in my head for only one name, and it echoes over and over.

Hector. Breaker of Horses. Bastion of Troy.

But that is not what my father called him.

When Papa came to Troy seeking his fortune as a young man, Hector, then just a boy, had been kind to him. The prince even bought some of our very first horses. Papa didn't have much to say of Troy's Old Blood, but when he spoke of Hector, he always did so with the blessings of the gods on his lips. I didn't understand his devotion, and I hated that it was the thing that took him from us.

"*I don't want you to go,*" I said the night before he was meant to leave with a caravan of men bound for distant Troy in answer to their call for aid against the Achaeans.

"*And I don't wish to leave you, but there are greater callings than those of our own hearts' desires, my little mouse.*"

"*Like glory?*" I asked, because that is what the stable boys spoke of. The thing that called them. But none of their reasons had ever called to *me*.

"*Glory is nothing.*" Papa batted the word away with a swish of his sundarkened hand. "*You can't hold glory. It does not light your way through the dark. Not like other things.*"

"*What things?*"

"Honor. Duty. Love." He listed each with a pat of his finger against my nose.

Not even three summers have passed, and already, the young girl in my memory feels like a stranger.

"You speak of the Trojan prince," I said.

He smiled down at me. *"Clever little mouse."*

"Who is he? How can you love him so?" I asked, but what I really meant was *How can you love him more than me?*

"He is a prince. The greatest of all warriors," my father said. *"But more than that, he is a leader of men. The rarest of all breeds."*

My brow furrowed as I went over the scraps of information I'd collected. *"They say Achilles is the fastest man alive. The fiercest. They say his aim is without fail. That he is the son of a goddess."*

"He may be all those things, but they do not make him great." My father leaned forward so that we might be eye to eye. *"To be a great warrior, one must first be a great man. Among men, Hector has no equal."*

The fireside evaporates along with my papa's face, and then I am back in this busy market, listening to the language of my people uttered by men who have done nothing but *take* from us.

"Will Harsar Hector come today?" the horse thief asks. "If so, I will save the best of my stock."

Prince Paris shrugs, as if the subject bores him. "It all depends on his shrew of a wife."

The other men do not laugh. But neither do they speak in defense of Prince Hector. Or the woman he is married to.

An uncomfortable silence descends, and then everything changes in an instant.

A nearby cart falls sideways, sending pottery raining to the ground. The sound lashes through the crowded marketplace.

The fire horse rears up on his hind legs. I somehow feel his heart take off in my chest a moment before his legs move to follow. He is fire unleashed as he tears across the enclosure and sails over the fence.

People rush to clear the way, but the fire horse doesn't move to avoid them. If anything, he chases them down. I watch a man's leg crack under the hammer of his hooves.

The fire horse dances around another cart, sending a wave of persimmons tumbling. He turns and gallops, straight for us.

The girls beside me scream. Bengor scrambles for the stone partition, but he can't pull his bulk over the structure even to save his own life. Prince Paris's guards stand in front of us, a line of spears before their prince as the horse charges in our direction. He will trample them. He *wants* to. They stole him, and caged him, and now he hungers to make them pay. I know it just as I know these men will snuff out his fire for no other reason than that they couldn't control it.

No! The scream rings through my head even as the distance between us evaporates.

I grab the rope around my neck and yank it hard to give myself room. Shouts echo around me. Blades slide out of sheaths as I push past the line of armed men and run toward the charging horse just like my father taught me.

Show them respect, but no fear, and they will feel you even when their passion is high and their eyes cannot see you.

If the horse feels me, he gives no sign.

He closes the distance between us. The rope cuts into my neck.

A yell tears from my throat as I throw up my hands. The stallion slides, pulling up his stride. He dances in front of me, and though this can only end one way, I can't help but be struck again by his beauty.

The lead rope dangles from his neck. With no thought, I reach for it. The moment my fingers close, the horse rears. His front legs come crashing down.

The rope around my neck gives a vicious jerk.

My back hits the ground a few steps from his hooves. I curl into a ball, the lead still clutched in my hand, and I do the only thing I can. I speak low and quiet in the language of the whispers. Above me, the fire horse goes still.

Men move. A rope sails out of nowhere, looping around the animal's neck. More join it. Someone pries the lead from my clenched fists. It takes a total of ten men to muscle the fire horse back into the enclosure, where he rages and paces like the beast they have named him.

All of this happens in a hazy blur before my eyes. When my vision finally clears, it is focused on the strong hand suspended in the air above me.

I look up into a face that is sun-bronzed and striking. Heavy brows set above eyes the brown of the richest earth. His square jaw is clean-shaven, and his hair is long and tied back in a low knot. This man is large, and he is wearing the armor of a soldier, complete with a sword at his side.

He says something to me, but after a word from Bengor, he switches to Hittite.

"That was very brave," says the soldier. "And very stupid."

Before today, those are two words that have never once been used to describe me. Too winded to speak, I simply stare.

"The horse," he calls to the men holding the stallion. "I will pay whatever price you're asking for him. So long as it is fair." The way the men respond with reverent nods leaves no doubt that this man's will shall be done.

"As you say, Harsar Hector."

Hector.

"You know horses?" he asks me, again in Hittite.

Unlike my trembling legs, my neck is still capable of obeying my commands. I nod.

"How did you know that horse would not run you over?"

I look from the fire horse back to the prince and find no reason to lie. "I didn't."

"And yet you placed yourself in his path." It is both a statement and a question.

"Your men would have killed him."

"He was a danger." There is a lie buried under the truth of his words. For reasons I can't explain, it feels like a test. And though I don't know exactly what is at stake, I want to pass. If only because my papa loved this man.

"He is frightened. And angry." Like me, he has every right to be. "You cannot catch the fire in your hand and not expect to feel the burn." It was one of my father's favorite sayings, and it has the prince narrowing his eyes as if it is one he has heard before. I rush to fill the heavy silence. "He will calm down with time. It . . . it would have been a shame to lose such a valuable animal."

"It would have been," Prince Hector agrees. "I take this all to mean you can tell good stock from a twenty-year-old plow horse with worms?"

I nod again, and he openly takes my measure, but not in the way so many others have done today. The way Prince Hector looks at me makes me want to stand up and be counted.

"What of those?" He jerks his thumb to the enclosure where the other horses are kept. "Which of those would you choose if you had your pick?"

Carris's whicker rises up from the paddock, filling me with longing so sharp it is hard to speak past it. "The black and the bay with the white stockings. They are the best this market has to offer."

"How do you know if you have not examined them?" the prince asks. Another test.

"Because I helped to raise them." I offer the words with a pride I didn't know I had left. It runs wild under my skin like the fire horse ran wild through the market. Speed and strength and power with nowhere to go.

This time when his eyes narrow, the expression is searching. "There is something . . . Have we met before?"

"No."

Prince Hector's silence suggests he does not fully believe me. And yet it is the truth.

"My father raised horses," I add when it is clear that he is still waiting. "He was a Phrygian breeder."

Hector spares Bengor a blank look. "Where is your father now?"

"Gone."

The brown of his eyes seems to soften, or maybe I am imagining it. "I knew a man from Phrygia once. He was the best horseman I ever knew." He helps me to my feet, but before I can so much as thank him, Prince Hector addresses Bengor again. "I'll take the girl too." There is no give in his tone now.

For the first time, the fat Trojan seems genuinely flustered. "This girl? But . . . but she is nothing. If you are looking for companionship, I have others that would . . ."

"I am not looking, and I do not want any others," Prince Hector says with an edge of distaste, but maybe not for me. "Give my man your price, and he will meet it." It is not a request, but a command. And that is exactly how it is received.

"Certainly, Harsar Hector." Bengor bows his head low as he unhooks the end of the rope from his belt and places it in the prince's hands.

A muscle tics in his jaw as Prince Hector removes the rope from around my neck. Coarse fibers have embedded themselves into the burns on my skin. I wince, and the prince hesitates.

"Steady now," he says in a low voice not unlike the one Papa used on our horses. I draw a breath, and the rope pulls free with brutal efficiency.

I bite through my tongue in an effort to hold back a cry.

The prince drops the bloody rope to the ground and turns toward the other paddocks, where Ishtar and Carris wait.

People stop and stare. A storm of whispers passes the prince's name back and forth across the marketplace, and a path clears in front of him as if by magic.

I am still watching the prince of Troy walk away when he turns to look over his shoulder. He doesn't say a word. He merely jerks his head and continues on his way, leaving me no choice but to follow.

6

ANDROMACHE

THE SIGHT OF Hector's broad shoulders at the end of the crowded market street makes my breath catch and my heart flutter.

Then I see the girl.

The flame of a new sensation flares. Has he beat me to it? Perhaps there's no need to tell Hector of the plan that came to me in the depths of that stinking chamber. Most men would view three days in a foreign city, far from the war as well as their wives, as a chance to unwind in a brothel with an oenochoe of strong wine.

Faithfulness has never been a requirement of a Trojan marriage.

Faithfulness is simply who Hector is.

I can't make out the details of the girl's face, but she is bone thin where I am lean, petite where I am towering. She isn't bound, but there's little doubt she's a slave. My insides twist. Perhaps I have pushed him too far. Even if this is a way for him to have a son, would it be enough to save my place beside him? He would never cast me aside entirely—Hector is too noble for that. But he is also the kind of man who can only hold one person in the secret chambers of his heart at a time.

And I was the one who opened the door by refusing to yield in the smallest ways. Before me, that recess beneath his chest was occupied by Paris. In recent years, it has been my home alone. Paris has never forgiven me for that, and if this girl ever took my place, I surely wouldn't let her escape my scorn either.

I walk down the hill of the market street, ignoring a hundred offers shouted from stalls, waiting for my husband to notice me. A thorough scrubbing followed the gore of the final fertility rite, so in spite of minimal food and little sleep, I feel surprisingly refreshed. A renewed woman, indeed.

Finally, Hector lifts his gaze. His eyes spark, and he raises a hand in greeting. The robe the priestesses gave us for our journey home is made of crimson silk, dyed with hematite this time. It has always been a color that makes me stand out in a crowd. At least it did. Grasping merchants pitch their wares, but not a man in the marketplace lingers on me for more than a passing glance.

I stop in my tracks. My mother warned me this day would come. *"Especially if you keep romping around with your brothers, barefaced in the sun."*

My eyes have only just glimpsed my thirtieth summer, and already I am a withered weed among lilies.

"I've missed you," Hector whispers when he reaches me. But not even his warm embrace can soften the startling realization that I am no longer young. That from this day forward, any girl who captures his attention, let alone his affection, is likely a girl I am almost old enough to have birthed. If I were capable.

Fortunately, the creature in front of me couldn't rile the ardor of a sailor stuck at sea. *Poor child.*

It isn't that she's ugly. Her look is simply . . . strange. With those feline eyes the color of grass at the end of the harvest. No one has ever claimed I am a conventional beauty either, but I've known when men look at me and wonder, *What would it be like to bed a woman whose arms are cut from stone?*

Only this plain child has an innocence that promises no such novelties. Her narrow hips and grinding-slab chest do not promise much fruitfulness either.

All the words I want to say to Hector get caught in my throat. I can't let this girl, who watches my every gesture like she's committing it to memory, see my great need for him.

"You've been busy, husband," I say, finally noticing the massive horse the girl leads. Bigger by far than any other I have seen, and yet with the graceful lines of a creature made for speed.

"Yes," Hector replies. "I managed to secure fifty, but I tell you, Andromache, this one is worth them all."

The stallion is handsome, I'll give him that, and red as an open fire, but I have too many questions to linger. "And the slave girl?"

Hector glances at her the way he looks at all of our servants, at all of his soldiers for that matter, no matter how lowborn. It is another trait that sets him apart from his family. Priam may have outlawed slavery within Troy's walls, but his ban was purely pragmatic. For a city built on a desirable strip of land between two waterways and two gluttonous empires, a fiercely independent spirit is everything. Priam knew that inhabitants who were free to take up arms to defend their home would fight with a fervor no slave could muster when that city was inevitably attacked.

But not everyone in Priam's household sees the prudence of elevating their inferiors, and it makes them spiteful. One need only look at the way Troy's ruling class treats the foreign allies who fight with us, allowing even their captains to live in conditions unworthy of their rank. Paris once boasted of how he enjoys striding through their Lower City camp dressed in his finest imports from across the sea—*"to remind them that they need us to protect the trade of the Dardanelle straits far more than we need them."* Hector's mouth had sagged when his brother spoke such callous words. He wears a similar expression now as he watches me watching the girl.

"She comes with the horse," he says, turning toward our camp.

———※———

RAIN DRUMS ON our tent pitched in the grasslands outside Cyzicus. In the darkness nearby, the horses Hector purchased refuse to stifle their neighs. I cannot sleep regardless. Not when I am trying to figure out the best way to tell Hector the decision I came to in that temple's bowels.

Almost as soon as we returned from the market, Hector disappeared with the horse that shone like polished copper. And with the girl.

He hasn't returned. Not even after the rain started.

It is nearly the end of the first watch of the night when the hide flap to my tent flutters. My servingwomen depart as Hector's forceful presence fills the space. I rise from my fur-lined pallet and reach for the bedside pitcher. "Wine, husband?"

I wonder if he can hear the tremor in my voice. If I've learned anything from this war, it's that the thicker the walls we build, the more eager we are to fall back on formalities and familiar rituals.

"No more wine."

I'm not surprised. There are few things Hector hates more than feeling out of control. But when I see his pained longing, I realize too much wine isn't the problem.

"Some tea, then," I say softly, calling for Faria to fetch hot water from the fire outside. Along with the bag of blessed remains I am to spread across the scorched fields of Troy, Demeter's priestesses gave each of us a leather pouch of the herbs we'd taken before the pit.

"Drink this tea at the same time every night, and the herbs will plow the fields of your womb. If the gods still refuse to give you a child, at least you can make the effort as enjoyable as possible," my young priestess had whispered with a sly smile.

I pour the hot water over cups for Hector and myself. For a few moments, we sit in silence, studying the floating leaves as though reading our fates. Two lines that seem to be diverging as quickly and violently as they came together.

"Do you feel . . . different?" he asks finally.

"I don't know." More sips and more silence. Now is not the ideal time to bring up the thought that nags me, but then again, time has eaten up most of our ideals.

"Why didn't you tell me about the divisions in the Citadel?" I ask softly.

Hector sighs. "What would be the point? There is nothing to be done."

"That may not be the case. How long have these wounds been left to fester?" Because the divisions I saw in the war council were deep. It would have taken some time for things to grow so dire. And Hector never told me.

"My father has been feeble for some time, but over the last year of the war . . ." Hector swallows a mouthful of tea. "He won't be around much longer, and there are those who believe Troy is vulnerable so long as her succession is in doubt."

He does not need to say more. If the city is seen as weak, the independence we have fought so hard to keep will be swallowed up by the Achaeans in the west or the Hittites in the east.

Strange that what takes three generations to build can be lost in the space of one.

The face of the boy I glimpsed before my bath of blood flashes across the wall of our tent, dancing with the shadows.

Clarity, not certainty.

The Fates may weave our webs, but we are still the spiders who must walk them. We are the ones who must hunt and strike.

"Hector," I begin carefully. "If things are as bad as you say, your father may soon name a new heir. He will be *forced* to. There are those in the Citadel hungry for a more pliable replacement, lest the Hittites try to plant a puppet of their own once Priam is gone. They have done it before." I bring the tea to my lips, each sip more bitter than the last. "Your brothers have many strengths, but they cannot rule Troy. Not if we want the city to survive this war."

"You think I don't know that?" Hector's stony look softens. "It is why we are here."

"Then I hope our prayers are finally answered." I pause. One sip becomes two. "If not . . . there are other ways you might sire a son."

Hector swirls his cup, staring into its murky core.

"Have you considered taking a concubine?" I ask. Another long pause of drumming rain follows. "It is not as if it isn't expected . . ."

His eyes meet mine, and I *know*.

He hasn't taken a lover because she would be the final stone in the wall that's been slowly creeping up between us, one layer at a time. Many wives endure the status of second-best by looking the other way or focusing on the children they already have to satisfy their longing for devotion.

We both know it would never be that way for me. For *us*. I am willing to do our duty if necessary. But then duty will be the only chain that binds us.

"It wouldn't matter," Hector says, picking up where the silent exchange of our eyes left off. "A bastard could never inherit the throne when Priam has plenty of legitimate sons ready and willing to rule."

"Yes, but not to *lead*," I insist. Does Hector not see that having a child with a concubine has less to do with siring the heir and more to do with proving he is capable?

"You are the only son of Troy who has ever been chosen as the commander of the army by her people and heir by her king," I continue. "*You* are the one who fought against the Egyptian pharaoh as a mere youth and won Hittite respect by your sword. The ability to produce sons of your own is the

only tile missing from the most glorious mosaic the independent cities of
Anatolia have ever witnessed."

If my flattery has any effect, Hector shows no sign of it. Then there is
only one tactic left to me, but I take no pleasure in the words I must say next.

"Even your child by a concubine could be named heir if few of Priam's
sons are alive by the time this war is over. And if that boy was the son of
Hector, then *he* is who the people will want." I let my bold claim sink in. "You
know the people's will has weight. It can make any son of yours the king."

And I could help the boy rule. Teach him what it means to lead as well as fight.

It matters not if the boy is mine, so long as he is Hector's. At least that is
what I will keep telling myself until my heart submits to my mind.

Still, this new ambition leaves behind a sickly-sweet aftertaste. Perhaps
the promise of influence is always sweet. It is the actual taking of it that
turns the flavor rank.

My words do not appear to move Hector. But the tea is a different story.
He shifts uncomfortably in his seat, and he is not the only one. The tingles
traveling up my legs have set my blood on fire.

"No, Andromache. No."

I halt the coming storm by resting my hand on his arm. Hairs stand on
end. The light touch feels like the most sensual of caresses. "Think of it,
Hector. Troy grows weaker by the day and so does your position. Imagine
how this sign of hope might bolster the men."

Hector pulls me to him with such intensity, my body shudders. "But he
would not be *ours*."

My mouth trembles, then hardens. "No. But he would be Troy's."

Something inside Hector shifts. Either that, or the tea has done its work.
I wait for his advance, my pulse echoing each hoofbeat of the coming charge.

Instead, his kiss is long and slow, flavored with the swallowed tears for
the child we may never share. When he pulls back, his eyes travel along my
body as he slides the brooch from the shoulder of my gown. It hits the floor
with a *thud*. Robes follow.

"I will consider your counsel, wife. Just as I always do." Hector slides a
hand up my bare hip, lighting a fire the entire way. "But not before I see for
myself what the gods have to say about our most recent offering."

7

RHEA

A HORSE WHINNIES somewhere in the distance.

I scramble to my knees and push back the hide flap covering our wagon. The girl beside me leans away from the bright light, muttering in angry Luwian. I ignore Faria's scowl and scan the caravan for any sign of Carris or Ishtar. There's nothing but an endless procession of soldiers and carts moving southwest under the sweltering sun.

I haven't seen the horses since we started on this journey two days ago, but I am sure I can feel them. Overwhelmed by the strange sights and smells. Lost in a world that's become impossibly vast. Longing for the green pastures and silver mountains of home as desperately as I do.

I close my eyes and send my thoughts out on the wind.

Don't be scared. I'm here. I'm right here, and I won't leave you.

The covering yanks out of my fingers with a sharp *snap*. Faria glares at me. Chastened, I hug my knees and study the other occupants of this cart. At Prince Hector's command, his servants bathed, fed, and dressed me. They saw me cared for with efficiency and thoroughness, but they also haven't spoken to me. Not a single word in three days. They do their jobs, and they watch. Someone is always watching.

Low laughter echoes from the other side of the wagon. I look up to find two stable boys staring at me. The first, one or two summers younger than I am, flushes and looks away. The second brazenly meets my gaze before pushing out his ears and sucking his lips around his front two teeth. It's only when Faria laughs unkindly that I realize he's making fun of the way I look.

Heat scorches my face. The older boy smirks, his dark, satisfied eyes accusing me of crimes I can't fathom.

It's been like this since I left that slave market with Prince Hector. A cold wind follows me wherever I go. Chills me with the sight of pursed mouths and angry glares. I don't understand it. What could I have done to make these people hate me?

A high-pitched nicker cuts through the music of the caravan. I bolt upright.

Ishtar.

She's terrified. *Calling* to me. I want to jump out of this cart and find her. Instead, I avoid twelve sets of probing eyes and make myself small.

The mood inside the wagon lightens as the sun lowers in the sky. Servants chatter. Men call to each over the grinding wheels. Theirs is a growing eagerness to match the restlessness of the horses. The animals' anticipation dances across my skin. It's reached a fever pitch when the wagon comes to a sudden stop.

This time, nobody complains when I pull back a section of the hide cover.

A great river cuts through the land in front of us, a froth of white through a brown, barren plain. Directly ahead, a group of soldiers wrangle the horses across a ford.

The chatter of the servants cuts off abruptly when I lean over the side of the wagon, straining for a better view. My pulse stutters when I see Carris at the front of the herd. She rears back from the soldier attempting to drag her through the rushing water.

The sound of a whip cracks through me. When the soldier jerks her lead, I feel the burn around my own neck.

Easy, girl. It'll be all right.

Ever the steady sister, Ishtar moves to Carris's side, gently nipping her forelock. Together, they ford the river and climb onto the broad expanse of plain.

The two stable boys fold back the covering, and the landscape is laid bare before us. To our right, a thick ribbon of dark blue shines between the mainland and the peninsula that runs beside it. The rocky bank smooths out into a long line of white beaches that end in a glittering bay. A cape juts out into the sapphire sea, sheltering the west side of the cove.

I take in the jeweled water, every bend and curve of the coast. Bits and pieces of Papa's stories weave together, forming a tapestry that aligns so perfectly with the land before me, it draws a gasp from my lips. For the first time since I left my stables, I know exactly where I am.

Papa told me once that the Hellespont is the sacred gateway between east and west guarded by the pearl of Anatolia. None other than . . .

My gaze jerks south.

It sits like a crown upon the sheer plateau, towering over the plains and the opposite bay. Walls slightly slanted, and so high, they must have been pressed by the hands of the gods. Painted buildings shine like ripe fruit in a bowl of the brightest gold. The sun winks off the tips of palisades and gates more befitting giants than men. Behind those gates, the city is a mountain of cut stones stacked in layers that climb into the sky. Every higher ring is smaller and more colorful than the one that came before until they reach the pinnacle. A palace of white where a single tower pierces the sky. Its needle roof is a spear of bronze reflecting the fire of the setting sun.

Troy. The place where my father died fighting a war that wasn't his.

My vision blurs. The memory of Papa's sun-weathered face dances in front of me, so real it causes a pang in my chest. The worst part is wondering what became of him. If they burned him as is the custom in Troy, or if his body was interred in the earth so that he might return to the Mother, whom he loved. I don't know if he suffered, or if he suffers still. A spirit weighted down by the anchor of his bones.

I'm coming, Papa. If you are trapped here, then I'll be trapped too.

As we draw closer to the city, I see fields that should be dotted with waving crops but are largely devoid of life. The earth is scorched in places, as if the farms that once stood there have been burned. On the ridge beyond the bay, a flock of strange birds covers what little I can see of the beaches.

No, not birds. Ships. Hundreds of them.

A shiver skates across my arms as our convoy travels south. Arrow shafts stick out of mud blocks set high on stone foundations. Broken chariot wheels clutter the muddy bottom of the trenches that lie just beyond them. We approach a gate crowned by a wooden palisade and guarded by dozens of soldiers.

The armed escort leading our caravan parts, and Prince Hector rides through on the back of a black stallion. For a moment, I can do nothing but watch him and the horse move together as one. I've never seen another person ride a horse's back the way that I do.

The way my father always told it, he left me in the pastures one day and returned to find me sitting on a horse as if I was always meant to be there.

The prince of Troy is a large man, but his horse is big to match. Other than the fire horse, the black stallion is the only animal here with enough size and strength to carry an armored man. The soldiers watch them pass with reverence.

Hooves pound the dust as Harsa Andromache joins her husband. The horse she rides stoops in discomfort. It's hard to decide which of them is less at ease. Watching the Harsa cling to the poor animal's mane, I can't help but admire her. She is a match for her husband in determination, if not skill. Half a dozen soldiers follow in their wake, pulling something behind them.

The fire horse's body glistens. Ribbons of foam fly from his neck as the soldiers drag him up a ramp and through the gates guarded by a tower on one side. Every step is a battle. The stallion's spirit calls to me. The fire inside him burning brighter than his coat. I wish I had a fraction of his courage, but even if I did, I've no home to escape to. No family waiting for me. All I have left in the world are Ishtar and Carris, and they've already slipped through the gates up ahead.

We pass through those gates, adorned with six stone pillars crowned by horses' heads, and the sights and sounds of Troy roll over me. In every direction, streets run together in a twisted maze of two-story houses of painted stone and mudbrick. Ornate tapestries cover the windows and bright linens hang to dry in the sun.

The scent of roasting hazelnuts and foreign spices dances through the air. The wind sings with trade in dozens of languages. Strange and familiar words run together. So many that my mind struggles to capture them all.

The crowd clears for us to pass. Near the southern wall, the sturdy two-story homes give way to hastily constructed huts, the spaces between them cramped with livestock and valuables—a makeshift camp of some kind, mostly made up of tired women and the barefooted children they watch over. All of them stop and make a sign of blessing as Prince Hector and his Harsa ride by. Love for him shines in their lean, hungry faces.

Our wagons turn north, following the upward grade. Whispers on the wind call my attention back to the shadows where the south and east walls meet. A cascade of neighs rises from a stable constructed with rubble and dirty straw. The horses inside are taller than any others I've seen with the exception of the fire horse. They look better cared for than the group of redheaded men who stand guard around them, and the song they sing is one that boldly claims that they, like me, are strangers here.

The crude stable sits in a forest of shanties that make the wooden huts of Troy's asylum seekers seem opulent by comparison. Worn sails flap in the wind from warped planks to provide meager shelter from the elements. Grizzled men wearing hard weapons and even harder expressions stare at the back of the royal procession. Like the thousand gods of Hatti, their faces represent the many peoples of Anatolia and beyond. And none of them are pleased.

Our wagon turns up a narrow street, and the unsightly camps disappear behind us. They are replaced by winehouses and outdoor ovens. Courtyards and multistory homes grouped around fountains spilling water through stone as if by magic.

From the inside, the divisions within Troy are clearly drawn. High walls of stone partition the city into crescents. From the crowded Lower City, we pass through an inner gate and onto paved streets lined by artisans and craftsmen. The people here are better fed than those below, their bodies cured hard as leather by the work of their hands. The next gate leads higher still, into a world of wide lanes, stone domiciles, and leisurely faces that represent a wealth I had not known to exist. And even still, it is not Priam's palace.

We approach the fortified gates that lead into the Citadel.

Men call out in raised voices as our caravan splits into two. The royal wagons continue up into the Citadel while the soldiers and their supply carts take a sharp turn left, taking the horses with them.

I grip the edge of the cart. Ishtar and Carris dance sideways, straining toward me. Breath blasts in my ears as I study the distance to the cobbled street. The heart of Troy is a fortress. If I'm swallowed by those innermost gates, I may never find my way out.

My gaze sweeps the cart. For once, nobody is watching. Slowly, I release a breath. My leg is halfway over the edge when our wagon follows the supplies and horses away from the Citadel.

A tremor of relief runs through me as I draw my leg back into the cart and sink down. Directly ahead, a stately home stands at the end of the street that hugs the outer Citadel wall. Vast grounds stretch out behind it. Enclosures and extensive training yards where the clash of steel echoes from the green. The small flame of hope inside me stokes to a blaze when I catch sight of an impressive stable through the neighboring alleyway.

An army of servants greets us when we come to a stop in front of the well-tended home of sunbaked mudbrick.

"Nekku! The horses!"

At once, the older stable boy scrambles out of the cart to do as he is told. He barks over his shoulder, "Come on, Larion. Move your skinny hide."

The younger boy, Larion, starts to obey. At the last moment, he squares his shoulders and turns to offer me his hand. Hesitantly, I let him help me down into the street.

I am breaking toward the alleyway where the horses are being funneled toward the stables when a hand locks around my wrist.

"Bodecca will want to see you."

Faria's nose wrinkles with distaste. At my blank stare, Harsa Andromache's servant gestures impatiently toward a set of stairs built into the side of the house. My gaze drifts down the alley toward the stables, but I do as I'm bid. The two stable boys from the road pass me on the way. Larion regards me with something like pity, but Nekku takes one look at those stairs and smirks.

～◦§◦～

PRINCE HECTOR'S KITCHEN is a kingdom unto itself. Servants scurry, hearth fires roar, and pots bubble under a heavy cloud of spices. My eyes are immediately drawn to the woman who forms the quiet center of this storm.

The woman called Bodecca is almost as small as I am. She is also old in that indefinable way mountains are old—well past the measure of seasons. Despite all this, the others dance around her, scrambling at the slightest wave of her gnarled, sun-spotted hand.

She watches me approach with eyes blue as ice and equally cold.

"So this is what all the fuss is about." Whatever the exact Luwian phrasing, Bodecca makes it clear that she is less than impressed.

My mind scrambles over her words. Cataloging the hills and valleys of sound and assigning meaning. Every day, I understand more of the Trojans' speech, which is not so different from Palaic or even Hittite, but this woman's accent is strange. Yet, at the same time, achingly familiar. She wasn't born here any more than I was.

I take a stab in the dark. "My name is Rhea," I offer in Greek that is only as strong as my father's was, which is to say, it is not overly strong. "I come from the Hittite steppes."

The eerie lightness of Bodecca's eyes is especially unnerving when they're pointed right at me. "And yet you speak Greek."

"My father taught me."

"But who taught him?"

"He was born in the lands far north of Attica," I explain in a rush. "He learned when he sailed across the Aegean as a young man."

Bodecca's hard mouth becomes even harder. "Trouble," she decides at last. "That's what you are."

Prince Hector ducks his head through the doorway. The servants scatter before him like mice. All except Bodecca.

Her brows are storm clouds gathered over flashing eyes. "You don't belong here," she tells the prince of Troy. "Off with you before you cause mayhem in my kitchen."

He leans against the wall. "The girl. I came to see that she was well taken care of." Prince Hector speaks Greek with the same accent as the white-haired woman. It makes me wonder if perhaps she was the one who taught him.

"Has harm ever come to any person under my care?" Bodecca asks crossly.

"Never." The corner of the prince's mouth twitches. "They would not dare."

"Then why this journey to my domain? You've never before troubled yourself to check on the well-being of a servant."

"I've never had a servant of my household receive such a poor welcome."

The shock on the old woman's face must mirror my own. I'm not sure what catches me more off guard: the fact that I haven't been imagining the others' coldness toward me, or that the prince of Troy would trouble himself to notice.

Bodecca's scowl deepens as she looks me over. "Skinny little thing with arms like sticks. She'll make a terrible kitchen maid."

Kitchen maid?

The smile in Prince Hector's eyes travels briefly to his lips. "I have faith you are both up to the challenge." His expression grows somber. "Bodecca will watch out for you," he tells me in Hittite.

Why? Why would the prince save me in that slave market only to bury me here in the kitchen? As much as I want to ask, I know it is not my place. Especially not with Bodecca's eyes burning a hole through my skin.

The prince of Troy searches my face. A deep line cuts across his brow, leaving me to wonder what he is hoping to find.

Bodecca clears her throat, and the prince nods before taking his leave. Bodecca watches him go, her expression filled with love she would not let him see. When she turns back to me, all that warmth is gone.

"I raised that boy from a babe. Queen Hecuba gave him life, but the milk in my breasts gave him strength." Her nostrils flare. "You've been here less than a day, and already there's talk among the men that you and that red beast have put a spell on him. Why else would he have claimed you?" Bodecca steps in close enough for me to smell the herbs on her breath. "I don't hold with gossip, but I swear to every last one of the gods, if you bring trouble to Prince Hector's door, I will kill you myself and spare Harsa Andromache the trouble."

She glares at me for a moment longer before turning on her crooked legs. "You'll sleep with the kitchen girls. At the end of every moon, you'll be paid for your work in grain."

I stumble. "Paid?"

"Not only skinny, but ignorant too." Bodecca places her hands on her ample hips. "There are no slaves in Troy. That is another story, but as far as it concerns you, every man, woman, and child within the city walls is entitled to their freedom. So long as they don't forfeit that freedom by breaking Troy's laws.

"Harsa Andromache insists all servants bathe once a week," Bodecca continues. "You will be silent and you will be clean. Prince Hector does not look kindly on the practice of flogging, but give me a reason, and I can make things painful for you all the same."

With that, she leaves me in a small room off the kitchen. It's clean and neat, with a row of cots and a deep sink with water that seems to spring directly from the stone through clay pipes. My father once told me that in Troy there were many such wonders, but they do not seem wondrous to me now. Only strange. And frightening. I pick the bed closest to the narrow window overlooking the courtyard. If I crane my neck, I can just make out the top of the stables. I stare at those stables until the last trace of light bleeds out of the sky.

⁓

"GIRL!"

I wipe my hands on a rag and cross the kitchen to where Bodecca waits by the scarred table. My stomach sinks when I see the brown mass in her hand.

"By what foul magic did you manage to transform flatbread into *this*?"

My first full day in Troy has proven Bodecca right about one thing.

I am a terrible kitchen maid.

"I'm sorry."

The other girls don't laugh. They value their lives too much for that. Instead, they bite back smiles and go about their work. Prince Hector's visit did nothing to endear me to them. If anything, it's made things worse. For the first time in my life, I curse the skill that helps me learn more Luwian every day. It'd be easier to ignore the constant whispers if I didn't understand them.

Faria takes a bowl of olives from the table with a smirk. I want to ask her *why?* If I were truly a witch with the power to bespell the prince of Troy, why would I still be here in this dungeon? Scrubbing pots and ruining meals under the icy eyes of a tyrant when I could be out in the stables with my horses instead?

I force myself to raise my chin. "I've never baked bread before."

"Never baked . . ." Bodecca's words trail off. "Tell me, girl. What is it you Phrygians eat? Because I've held rocks that are softer than this." She tosses the bread to the floor, where it lands with a *thunk*.

"At home, I worked with our horses. If you let me go to the stables, I could make myself useful. I could—"

A flour-coated palm slaps the table. "Those stables belong to the army. Women are not allowed. Most especially *you*."

"But—"

"Not another word. Go fetch some lemons from the tree outside. Before I think of some less pleasant task to occupy you."

Movement behind Bodecca draws my gaze to the interior door, where Harsa Andromache's tall form stands motionless, her dark eyes cast in my direction. Is she listening in? Before I can dwell on why she'd bother, the Harsa turns and disappears down the hall.

Outside in the courtyard, the scent of lemons greets me along with the familiar aroma of horses. I glance back at the kitchen. Fewer than a hundred steps separate me from the stables. It wouldn't take long. A minute or two to slip inside and—

Hoofbeats echo in the alleyway. I duck behind a fountain shaped like a bull just as two stable boys cut through the courtyard. A pair of stallions trail behind them on lead ropes.

Blood stains both animals. Deep indents of chariot harnesses crease their coats. One of the stallions is gray with white stockings. The other is the great black beast Prince Hector rode the day we entered Troy.

They come closer, and my hand presses flat over my mouth. An arrow is lodged deep in the gray's shoulder, but it's the flesh around the wound that makes my insides clench.

The skin is blistered. The hair blackened and burned as if the arrow itself had been doused in flame. It's the worst kind of wound. The kind that doesn't kill cleanly but that leaves a horse forever lame.

The black stallion isn't visibly injured, but there's a stiffness to his gait. The animals' pain winds through me, causing my breath to come hard and fast.

"Useless creature." The older stable boy yanks the gray's lead. "A little flame and he lost his wits." Nekku glances around the empty courtyard before he takes his whip and lashes the injured gray across the nose.

A cry lodges in my throat.

The younger stable boy, Larion, steps forward. "Don't."

"Why? This one's as good as dead anyway." Nekku isn't much taller than Larion, but he weighs easily twice as much.

"It isn't his fault. Any horse would've run when struck with one of the Achaeans' fire arrows. He's a brave one. I wouldn't count him out yet."

"A brave one? He's a horse. A dumb animal. You sound like one of the bloody Thracians," Nekku sneers. "Though I suppose those redheaded bastards are hardly better than the beasts they like to ride. You'd think with a Trojan father, you'd have more sense."

Larion reaches for the maimed animal's lead. "Prince Hector wouldn't like it."

The whip strikes the boy across the mouth. With an ugly smile, Nekku jerks the gray and leaves Larion moaning on the ground at the foot of the black stallion.

I wait for Nekku to pass out of sight before I ease out from behind the fountain.

Larion scrambles to his feet. He uses his sleeve to wipe the blood and the tears running down his face, wincing when it touches the beginnings of an ugly welt.

Without a word, I pull off the cloth covering my braided hair and dip it in the basket of water by the courtyard well, offering it to him the way he offered me his hand yesterday. Larion hesitates only briefly before he accepts. While he cleans himself up, I step toward the black horse.

The animal stills under my hands. Singing to him in the language of the whispers, I run my fingers down his foreleg until I reach the chestnut above his hooves. The stallion graciously lifts his leg.

"What are you doing?" Larion watches me with open interest.

I lean back, and the boy's eyes widen when he spots the splinter wedged into the animal's hoof. I meet Larion's gaze to make sure he understands what is needed. He nods at me, and I nod back. When he starts for the stables again, gently pulling the stallion behind him, a smile creases his swollen mouth. My own smile dies as soon as he and the stallion disappear out of sight.

I lie awake that night, unable to banish the memory of the gray. The blood on his coat and the arrow buried deep in his muscle. The blackened skin and the way his terror had clung to him like the scent of charred flesh. What kind of monsters are these Achaeans? Who could do something like that to an innocent animal?

I've seen horses injured before. I've even seen them burned, but never like that. Never *on purpose*. They are too valuable.

By the time the moon has risen and the soft chatter of the other girls has faded to deep breathing, my heart is running at a full gallop. I throw off my blanket and slip quietly into the kitchen, past the dying hearth fire and out into the night.

The autumn air stirs anxiously outside. It nips at my cheeks as I scurry through the courtyard and into the training grounds, quiet except for the howling wind. In the moonlight, I can make out an armory, three enclosures, a chariot yard, and two stables. Drawn by the whispers, I move toward the smaller of the two structures.

Ishtar and Carris call out a greeting when I enter the dimly lit building. I follow their voices to a stall at the end of the row. Their heads bump into my shoulders. Laughing, I wrap my arms around their necks. "I missed you too," I whisper, breathing them in.

We sit together in the straw, drawing comfort from each other's nearness until a loud *thud* brings me back to my feet.

It comes again, this time accompanied by the splintering of wood. One calming touch to my friends, and I ease out of the stall.

A horse nickers nearby. Its distress cuts through to my bones.

Slowly, I approach the opposite stall. It is easily large enough to fit five horses but is currently occupied by only one.

The fire horse is every bit as big and beautiful as I remember. He spins in dizzying circles, pausing to hammer the walls with his hooves. Winded from his efforts, he stops in front of me.

His mane is a nest of tangles, his coat covered in a layer of grime that does nothing to dull his fire. I'm wondering how Prince Hector could've allowed him to reach this state when I notice the handful of brushes in the straw at his feet.

"Are you making a nuisance of yourself?"

The fire horse snorts and tosses his head, and I can't help the laugh that bubbles up my throat. "You are not alone." Wistfully, I rest my arms on top of the stall door. "It seems they don't know what to make of either of us."

Hoofbeats sound in the training yard, making my blood run cold.

I glance back at Ishtar and Carris's stall, but there's no time to hide.

The fire horse's nostrils flare at my intrusion. He stamps his feet but, after a terrifying moment, magnanimously decides not to trample me. Offering silent thanks, I peer through a crack in the door.

No stable boy greets Prince Hector when he enters. No soldiers flank his sides. Instead, he sees to his horse alone, his broad silhouette cut out of the moonlight.

His loneliness calls to me.

The prince leads his horse deeper into the stable. Only after tending his mount does he lay his weapons down beside a trough. He washes the blood from his hands and face, every one of his movements singing of an oft-repeated ritual. Next, he turns to his armor. It's a task that Bodecca or Andromache would surely take on, but watching Prince Hector in the dark, I know he'd have no one else do it. His heart whispers to me like one of the horses. It says this blood was shed by his hands, and his hands will be the ones to clean it.

When the bathing is done, Prince Hector straightens, his eyes fixed on something too far away to see. I don't know what he's thinking. If he's praying to his gods or if he senses the quiet comfort the horses offer him. But somehow, I know that here and now the prince of Troy is not living or fighting or pretending for anyone else. In this one moment, he exists for himself alone. For reasons I can't explain, the thought makes me glad.

The prince turns toward the fire horse's stall. "You can come out now," he says in Hittite. On trembling legs, I stand.

The prince watches my approach with dark, inscrutable eyes. "I . . . I'm sorry," I stammer. "I didn't mean to intrude. I was here before you came. I should've announced myself."

He tilts his head. "It's the middle of the night. What are you doing here?"

Sensing my fear, Ishtar and Carris stir. Their anxious cries drift through the stables.

The prince's gaze travels from Ishtar and Carris to the fire horse watching us from the shadows. "I see. Well, you picked a curious place to hide. This is the third stall he's been housed in."

As if sensing that he has become the topic of conversation, the fire horse rams his head into the boards holding him.

"What became of the others?"

"Splinters." Prince Hector's tone betrays more admiration than anger.

"He is beautiful," I say, though my heart senses that his true beauty lies not in his coat but in his spirit.

"That he is."

"Have they tried to bring him into the ring?" Unbidden, my mind conjures an image of Nekku and his whip.

Hector approaches the horse cautiously. "My new Master of Horses claims he's angrier than Kupapa's attack hound. So far, my men haven't even managed to groom him." He picks up a discarded brush. "You are the first person he has allowed to come so close."

"He's frightened." I chew my lip before deciding to speak further. "Some of the men are heavy-handed."

Prince Hector doesn't deny it. "I wish him to know he has nothing to fear. No one here will touch him against his will."

"You won't force him into the harness?" I must do a poor job of hiding my surprise, because the prince smiles. It feels like the full strength of the mountain sun on my face.

"His spirit is indomitable."

It's a truth any good horseman would've known from the very first moment.

"Why did you buy him if you knew he could not be broken?"

Hector looks at me sideways, and for the first time, I realize that a servant doesn't ask her master questions. A servant shouldn't speak to her master at all unless commanded, but Prince Hector doesn't look at me as if I am a servant. He doesn't even look at me as if I'm a trespasser in a stable where I do not belong. And therein lies the danger, for it causes me to forget myself.

He leans over the door to the stallion's enclosure. The fire horse voices his protest. "It seems I have a weakness for stubborn creatures." A small smile creases the prince's face. Unlike the other, this one is not meant for me. "Some things cannot be changed without being broken, and I like this one the way he is. Wild, but whole."

"His heart is fire," I say with an admiring glance at the pacing animal. "When he runs, his coat catches the flame."

"*Atesh*." Prince Hector offers the word for fire. "So he is. And now that you have given my beast a name, it is only right that I should have yours."

"Rhea."

At the sound of my name, Ishtar and Carris dance in place. Hector runs his hands down their necks. "I worked with these two on the journey back to Troy." He looks at me. "You said they were your horses. Did you train them?"

My cheeks flush with pride. "My papa said the trick was in bending the will without breaking the spirit."

Hector gives Carris a final pat. "Your papa taught you well."

Hope whispers through me like wind. Ishtar and Carris toss their heads, urging me on. "He was the best horseman in Anatolia." My heart drums in my chest, because if I am going to do this it must be *now*. "Haskim." The name lodges in my throat. "Haskim the Phrygian."

Hector's eyes widen. Every doubt I have been harboring leaves me in a rush of breath.

"You have your father's look," the prince says after a moment. "I knew you were familiar the first time I saw you, but I couldn't place how." It's as if a wall has fallen between us. "Your father was a good man. I had never met anyone who understood horses as he did. He trained the stallions I took with me to fight the Egyptians. It was my first battle." Hector leans one shoulder against the fire horse's stall. "I was so scared I could scarcely hold the reins. In the end it was those horses who steered me, not the other way around." A ghost of a smile haunts his face. "I tried to make him my Master of Horses even back then. He turned me down. Said his girls were waiting for him. I never expected to see him again."

I close my eyes. "When he heard Troy's call for help, he couldn't ignore it. He said he owed Troy a debt and would fight for her to repay it. When he didn't return . . ." I force myself to behold the man for whom my father left us, and I find that I can no longer blame him. "All I have left now are Ishtar and Carris." And the things my father taught me. If only I might be allowed to use them.

Hector sits with me in my loss before he speaks. "Your father was more than a gifted horseman. He was a friend to me."

I lick my lips and ask the one thing I have wondered since I first saw the walls of this city. "Do you . . . do you know where he lies?"

Prince Hector's eyes soften. "It is our way to burn the dead, but I saw Haskim buried outside the walls of Troy because he once told me that was the custom of your people. It is by the sea. Too close to the Achaean camp, but when the plains are safe again, I'll show you the spot. It is marked with a stone in the shape of a horse's head. I thought it fitting."

My knees weaken. It is what he would have wanted, and I have the prince of Troy to thank for it. Drawing a breath, I muster my courage. "I would ask you for one favor in his memory."

The prince straightens. "Name your favor, Rhea, daughter of Haskim. If it is within my power, I will grant it."

My nails dig into my palms. "Let me work here. In the stables." I push on before he can object. "I've heard the stable boys. You're in desperate need of chariot horses. It is the reason you came to Cyzicus. Now you have the horses but not enough capable men to train them. I can help."

Hector's eyes are the only part of him that yields. "There are many ways to serve. None more important than another. Troy is a city of the world, but it is also a place of tradition. There are places outsiders are not permitted to walk."

"But why?" I ask. "Troy has always been a city made of people from many lands."

"Yes, but it is also a city made of many rings," Hector replies. "And the Old Blood are not willing to let those not born in Troy into her innermost. Not even allies. For even our friends harbor old resentments."

My mind recalls the haphazard stables surrounded by squalid huts as Hector continues. "Women are cherished here. You will find no city that honors our common Mother more. But they do not fight. And they do not work with animals."

The fire horse churns furiously in his stall. The song inside him charges through my blood.

"I don't wish to be cherished. I wish to belong."

The words ring out between us. Mortified, I drop my gaze to the ground.

"I wish it were that simple. Troy could benefit from your skill. The Achaeans know our chariot force is superior and so they have found a way to disable it."

"The fire arrows?" When Hector raises a brow, I swallow. "I saw the gray stallion. What will happen to him?"

"The same thing that has happened to all the others. He will die, or he will live. Either way, he will never again bear a harness."

"They aim the arrows at the chariots, not the horses," I guess.

Hector nods. "We could put out the flames easily enough, but there is never enough time. The horses' fear makes them difficult to control. They run into each other or the Achaeans' trenches, injuring themselves and decimating our chariots."

I look back at Ishtar and Carris. My heart aches at the thought of them broken.

"To control the horses, you have to control their fear," I say. "I can help you." I can help *them*.

"Even if you could, I'm not convinced Haskim would want this for you." The prince studies me closely. "These stables are a hard place made up of hard men. The best among them have their wounds. It makes them strangers sometimes, even to themselves. It is why our traditions are so important. They help us hold on to who we are meant to be, especially when we are most in danger of forgetting. Your presence here could upset that careful balance."

"I'd wait until dark when the rest of Troy was sleeping. I'd muck out stables from dusk until dawn." Anything. Anything so long as I might be near my horses.

A shadow crosses Prince Hector's face. "Could you bite your tongue when you wished to speak? Could you take orders from those who, based on merit, should be taking orders from you?" His gaze turns probing. "Could you train these horses only to send them out to die? Because they will, Rhea, daughter of Haskim. Even if you trained them perfectly, they will die."

Grief crashes through me when I look at Ishtar and Carris. I would do anything to spare them the fate of the gray stallion, but that isn't within my power. They'll be sent to this war whether I work in the stables or not. The only thing I can do now is be here for them. And train them. Train them to *survive*.

I square my shoulders and meet the prince's gaze. "I am good at becoming invisible."

Prince Hector studies me in the dim light before he reaches down and picks a brush off the ground. "In these stables, invisible is the last thing you would be." He places the brush in my hand and leaves me in the darkened stall, wondering what he means.

8

HELEN

ONE GUST OF wind and the doors to my weaving hall burst open. Paris marches into the room, reeking of sour wine and horse sweat. His younger brother, Helenus, follows on his heels. The sudden smells of an entire world beyond these walls stirs me from the fog.

"Imagine my shock that you're exactly where I left you." Paris trails a filthy finger across the tapestry scene I've been working on halfheartedly. It depicts his brother Deiphobus killing four of Achilles's best men in a single day—a moment of glory that has been the talk of Troy the entire time he has been gone.

A familiar resentment fills Paris's eyes. Except for the opening scene with the galley ship that brought me here, he is nowhere on my tapestry. That is because he has not committed a single feat worth remembering.

My gaze sweeps the tapestry until I find it. Prince Paris's ship, sailing a sea darker than the wine swirling in my cup. Among the spiraling waves woven by indigo thread, I stand on deck beside him, the noose around my neck invisible to all but me.

My eyes travel along other scenes. I do not know where these violent images come from, for I have never set foot on a battlefield. They might well descend from the realm of Muses, though I prefer to imagine they are gifts from a bird who soars high above the plains, sending me whatever it sees.

Or maybe this is the only way the Unnamed One speaks to me now. Not even in whispers, but through images. Through silence.

I am sorry. What else can I do to prove it?

Helenus gives me a slight bow as he walks by my loom. It appears the two men aren't merely passing through my weaving hall on their way to Paris's rooms.

No, Paris is here to play.

"Will you take wine?" I ask, even though he always takes wine. As I stand, my eyes search the weaving hall for servants who are suddenly scarce. I lean against the loom until my spinning head slows.

Paris smirks. "Not from your pitcher."

I nod. One of the more unfortunate things about my second husband is he is occasionally smarter than he looks. "I'll call for Aethra to bring a fresh cup," I say quietly.

"Good. It seems I've given you a household of servants just so they can gossip in the halls." He looks at me with what might almost pass for concern. "You shouldn't be alone, wife. Everyone knows too much time in her head makes a woman lose her mind."

Helenus chuckles because he knows his brother expects it. I alone catch his uneasiness at Paris's reminder of the mad sister who kept Helenus company in Hecuba's womb. The sister who is locked away, though her family would like the world to believe she's praying in Athena's temple day and night. Poor Cassandra.

Of all of Paris's brothers, Helenus remains mostly a mystery to me. I force my heavy eyes to take in the details of his face. He is an ill-looking man, a baby bird with fragile bones and thin wisps of hair that have gone silver much too soon. It is said Helenus also has the gift of Sight, taught to him by Cassandra. Both were sickly children; Helenus of body and Cassandra of mind.

I would try to heal them, if only they'd let me. Yet Troy's priests prefer burnt offerings over hands that mend. The only work I am allowed to do in this city is that which brings suffering, not that which takes it away.

I reach for my cup before remembering that I left it on the other side of the room.

"The sickness in the Lower City has worsened since you've been gone," Helenus tells his brother. "A number of families are holed up in their hovels. Laocoon believes it is a sign we are losing the gods' favor."

At the mention of the illness that has begun to decimate Troy's poor, a fluttering sensation stirs beneath my breast. Something long dormant. I hold out my hands in front of me, drenching them in sunlight.

Strong, but so pale. *So useless.*

I jerk them back into the shadow of my loom. To hope is folly. He would never allow it.

Paris shrugs, unmoved. "Or perhaps the illness was brought to Troy by the allied filth. And to think they've been pestering us to allow them entrance to the higher rings."

"They say that with the influx of asylum seekers fleeing Achilles's spear, their living conditions are too cramped." Helenus's expression turns harried. "A day does not pass when one of their captains isn't sending some message of complaint."

"They're almost as vulgar as the Achaeans," Paris says. "With their habit of sleeping so near animals that defecate in every shallow hole, it's a miracle we haven't had sickness earlier." He pauses in a way that makes me go cold, despite the humming in my blood. "On the other hand, who is to say my mother's priests aren't right? This *could* be a sign."

"But of what?" Helenus asks, though he is the one supposedly able to read them.

"That we should no longer pretend the factions taking over the Citadel aren't becoming problematic. Uncertainty about the succession is weakening our ability to wage this war effectively. What if this sickness is a sign Hector must finally do his duty by casting off the yoke of his Amazon?" Paris gives a careless shrug that is anything but. "That, or he must finally forfeit the throne to one who knows his duty better."

"I can help with the sickness." I hear the words, and suddenly find myself between the two men with no memory of how I got to the other side of the weaving hall.

"Helen in the Lower City?" Paris scoffs.

My belly burns at his instant dismissal. Paris has never taken my gifts seriously, not unless he is using them for his own ends. I glance around for my cup. It is too far away if I am to keep Paris's attention, so I continue.

"Please. Let me use my healer's knowledge to aid the people of Troy."

Paris casts his brother a weighted look that causes Helenus to rise from his chair uncomfortably. "Father and Mother are expecting me. Thank you for the wine, Helen."

Once Helenus is gone, Paris stalks toward me. When we are face-to-face, he wraps his hand around the bones of my wrist. "Have you done what I asked of you before I left for Cyzicus?"

I search the misty corridors of my mind for any words at all. I don't know why I haven't worked harder to find the plant he demanded. Maybe because I have no idea how he intends to use it. Creating a weapon for battle is one thing, yet the throbbing beneath my breast tells me Paris intends to use this new poison *within* Troy's walls.

"I've searched the bathhouse gardens for an herb that causes vomiting and fever, but all the ones that do have a strong aftertaste—"

"No. We can't have that." Paris's hand tightens. "But such a plant exists? One that causes the symptoms of sickness only without detection? Don't bother—your eyes tell the truth even if your lips refuse." He leans in until his breath tickles my ear. "You know what I can do if I discover you are being difficult on purpose."

I squeeze my eyes shut. It is the one thing even my cup cannot help me to forget. "There are other plants. Yet none of them grow within the walls, and they can be dangerous to harvest."

"Ah." Paris smiles to himself, as if pleased this conversation is flowing two ways for once. "So this is where the bargaining commences."

I look toward the sloped climb of the Hill of Kallikolone beyond the balcony. I want to be of service, I want to make amends, yet it is more than that. Something is rising. Clarity. A sensation I haven't felt since the night I glimpsed pure terror in my child's eyes and vowed to avenge all that had been taken from us, one way or another.

"There is an abundance of healing plants on the hillside slope just beyond the east gate. If I can harvest some to help the Lower City, I might also use the opportunity to search for the . . . the plant you require."

Forgive me.

Paris smiles as though genuinely pleased. "You sometimes surprise me. That is good for you, and more importantly, it is good for her."

His words dry all the moisture in my mouth. I break free from his grip and rush to my cup. To the banishment of memories. When my hand grazes the edge, he is right beside me, already pushing the rim down before the seasoned wine can reach my lips.

"No, Helen."

I startle at his gentle use of my name.

"We have both been trapped in our heads for too long." His fingers play with the soft edges of my veil before pulling it away. And then he looks. *Takes.* Takes as he looks. As if both acts were one and the same.

"Soon it will be time for us to claim what is ours." As quickly as it came, the softness is gone. Paris downs the rest of my tainted wine. "If you are going to set foot outside this palace, you must have your wits about you."

He struts from the room without looking back.

Not long after Paris is gone, there is a knock. I stumble toward the door on heavy legs, but when I pull it open and see the face on the other side, the fog lifts and I am quickly sober.

"Hector. Come in." I take a step back and gesture to the small couch Paris likes to lounge on whenever he comes here seeking solace.

Hector hesitates, and in the brief space, I see it. How strange a request to come in and sit must seem to this man of action.

Or is that fear? Does the prince of Troy fear *me*?

"I'll only be a moment." Hector clutches his helmet awkwardly, like a green soldier half his age. Another pause and his eyes find mine. In their earthy depths, I read nothing but concern. "You do not look well, Helen."

My hand reaches up to find my cheek bare.

My veil.

It has become such an extension of myself that most of the time, I hardly feel its gossamer prison. I might even be grateful for its shield, if only the element of mystery lessened the stares cast my way instead of heightening them.

"I'm sorry . . . he took . . . I hadn't realized."

Hector's expression does not alter. Of all the men I've ever stood before, barefaced and eye to eye, he may be the only one to remain constant. Unflinching. It isn't that he's cold or unfeeling. It's more that he feels no urge to possess what he sees.

Hector's eyes skate over the couch behind me, and still, the levee behind them does not break. Maybe that is why I have always felt secure in his presence. Every sparse moment I am with him, I am an actor, not a pawn. Hector only ever responds; he does not initiate. For a fleeting instant, it makes me feel as Andromache must whenever she walks into a room. Knowing without a doubt that anything she says or does will have a consequence. What a wonderful, terrible power.

Hector glances over my shoulder into the cavernous hall again, emptied of servants. "You are lonely." The words are as uncomfortable for him to say as they are for me to hear.

"As are you."

At that, something in Hector's gaze sparks. It is his secret. One he has not confessed even to his wife. Not because he lacks Andromache's companionship or the camaraderie of his men, but because of the many burdens he alone must bear.

Burdens that keep his gates barred and his walls reinforced, lest some silent enemy sneak through the smallest crack and burn everything he loves to the ground.

It is a loneliness I know better than he will ever realize.

"I am looking for my brother," Hector says.

Somehow, I sense he has been looking for him for a very long time. Long after Paris returned from the mountain shepherds who raised him. Whatever tenuous bond still existed between the brothers when I first arrived in Troy, the severing of it is nearly complete now.

"He isn't here."

Disappointment. It is there before he can hide it. And something more painful still.

They were close once. Paris told me the story of how it all changed. A tale of two brothers with a stolen jug of golden apple liquor, playing in the boughs of the ancient oak beyond the Scaean gate. A high branch. A dare to blow Aphrodite a kiss. And a fall that left Paris with a limp in one leg that he has become a master at concealing with the help of the finest garments.

"It is not your fault," I say softly.

"What isn't?"

"His injury. And all that was wounded after."

Hector's shoulders sag. A reminder that the opposite of love is not hate; it is indifference. The thing Hector pretends to feel in order to hide his pain, but that he cannot feign now.

"The fall did not damage anything that could not be mended." Those parts of Paris were already broken by a childhood spent in squalor at the foot of Mount Ida, a baby abandoned on the slopes. Stolen from the city for reasons unknown, by people who have never been found.

All those years I lived in a shepherd's hut with a floor covered in goat shit.

Always knowing I did not belong. That I was meant for greater things but never knowing why. They were so close, and yet they did not find me. Because they did not look. None of them looked.

By the time the missing prince was discovered, the clay that was Paris had been molded and fired. "You cannot accept responsibility for the choices of others," I tell Hector.

He drops his gaze. "The day Paris came home, I was elated to meet this long-lost brother. But no matter how much praise and affection Father heaped on him, he always remained unsure. Resentful, even. I vowed I'd never give Paris reason to doubt my loyalty." Hector closes his eyes and shakes his head. "The way he looked at the bottom of that tree. I couldn't bear waiting to see if he would live through the night. So like a coward, I left for Thebe to meet King Eetion's daughter. Paris and I didn't see each other again until I returned with Andromache." He rubs his hands over his face.

I nod as if Hector pouring out his past griefs is the most normal thing in the world. In a sense it is, given that grief is an endless spring. It eventually bubbles over, but it always fills back up again. Especially when words are left unspoken and wounds are not mended properly.

After Andromache added to their wedge, things were never the same between the two brothers once so inseparable, Troy's people called them the black stallions harnessed to Priam's chariot.

But that is not why Paris loathes you.

"The people who were meant to love him best have failed him," Hector says, swallowing hard. "That is why I'm glad he has you. Why I have not berated him for what happened in Sparta . . . as others have."

I want to tell him that he would have been right to, but the words won't escape.

"Gods only know why we love who we love," Hector continues. "Even when they seem to be doing everything in their power to make it impossible." As if suddenly aware of the moment's expanding intimacy, Hector clears his throat. "Paris is meant to participate with our allies in an archery training in the Lower City, but he has yet to show."

"Maybe it slipped his mind."

We both know nothing slips Paris's mind, even if his curls are the most well-oiled in Troy.

"It would mean much to our allies if he would take more of an interest," Hector continues. "Show his face more often. As their prince."

As if that prince listens to me.

"He left not ten minutes ago. You might try Helenus's rooms."

Hector starts to turn, then stops. "They are thick these days. Those two."

I can't tell if that is envy in his voice, or merely regret.

"Take care of yourself, Helen," Hector says. He pauses again midpivot and taps his helmet three times. I can tell he wants to offer some other courtesy. To assure me he will send Andromache to check in on me from time to time, as she often does with his captains' wives.

Instead, the words that leave his sun-chapped lips are ones I do not expect.

"This will not last forever."

⁂

MY BACK ACHES as I bend over a clump of sage wilting in the sun. Two of my servingwomen search the overgrown vegetation alongside me, though what they are looking for is anyone's guess.

"If you go beyond the walls, you must take Aethra and Clymene. I will station my personal guards nearby. It is for your safety," Paris said. *"We can't risk another misstep like the one at Andromache's ceremony . . ."*

An occasion my sister-in-law has never let me forget, despite the years that have passed. It is the reason I always wear a full veil when most Trojan matrons only cover their hair outside their homes—to guarantee such an incident doesn't occur ever again.

If only it weren't so difficult to breathe through the fabric on this oppressively warm day. Or maybe the heat is coming from inside me. A scant few hours away from my cup and every muscle screams to the throbbing beat behind my eyes. It is a sharp, precise pain. Like walking on bits of glass or stepping into a bright light upon waking. And yet, a part of me savors the stab of it even as I curse the sun.

I breathe in honeysuckle on the tail of the wind that rustles my robes. The fabric tickles like a caress. Another sign the mist that weighs down my thoughts is slowly dissipating.

The relentless warmth of the sun.

The trembling ache in my hands.

The gentle kiss of the wind.

If I close my eyes, I can almost hear the Unnamed One calling to me through each of these things. In Sparta, where our walls are humbler and our cities are made solely of mudbrick, the still, small voice was more audible than it has ever been in Troy. Yet the whisper echoing in that inner chamber we all know but do not know how to name seemed to grow loudest whenever I chased the color green.

My eyes rise to Kallikolone, and the pulsing beneath my breast grows stronger still. The forest at the base of its slope is a wilderness of medicinal treasures. Linden flowers, shallow trees, and the tenacious dandelion, used to reduce swelling.

So many plants, so much life. All old friends. Wild, growing things, born from the womb of damp soil. Many with the power to save, some with the power to kill.

All gifts from the Unnamed One.

I used to know them on sight. The memories return with each scent riding on the wind. Mint. Licorice. Fennel. The herbs we've encountered near the olive groves beyond Troy's east gate are common enough, and many can be brewed into teas or mixed into salves that will bring comfort to the sick in the Lower City.

Poisoning without detection, however, is another matter.

You must remember.

Aethra looks at me sideways, and I realize I am standing utterly still, like a hunted stag who's heard a crunched leaf.

An old ache stirs. More than any pain, this makes me long for my tincture. Unwelcome memories dance along the edges of my mind.

Remember.

I push the stirring aside and refocus on my task, yet my thoughts refuse to go where I direct them. There are only more questions as the comforting fog recedes.

Whom does Paris intend to harm? Hector?

Is he tired of waiting for Achilles to do his dirty work for him?

The unknowns carry on in an endless stream, and with them the vague shape of something else that *wants* to be known. It lurks deep in the shadows. A possibility. Yet strain for it as I might, it remains just out of reach. My mind is still befuddled by the lingering fog.

"What are these?" Beside me, Clymene reaches for a cluster of mushrooms. A deceptively beautiful trail of fungus with rich golden tops.

I slap her hand aside, surprising us both. "Achlys's Fingernails. Merely touching them can have . . . ill effects."

Clymene scowls but stays her reach. "Mother brews me a tea of the very same for moon blood pains."

"Listen to the Harsa." Aethra approaches her daughter with a protectiveness I've never noticed. "I've only ever purchased dried ones from the merchant's stalls. I've never harvested them in the wild myself."

"And harvesting is where the danger lies. Achlys's Fingernails are nearly identical to Apollo's Wreath, used in teas that benefit the female organs. That is what the merchant gave you. Otherwise you would not be here."

Clymene scrunches her nose like she has smelled something foul. "How can you tell the difference?"

My lips turn up slightly. "The gods."

The two servingwomen stare at me with doubtful expressions. They come from an old Trojan family that has long served the king and his many children, and Paris trusts them implicitly. Yet they have never trusted me.

"Apollo's Wreath is one of the few mushrooms that grows well in the sun, so its glistening tops can be found on hilltops or in meadows." I point to the shaded mushrooms at our feet. "Achlys's Fingernails are like the goddess of eternal night herself. They grow only in the shadows."

"They look the same," Aethra says with a shrug. "I'm sure we aren't the first to almost make such a mistake."

"Sadly, we won't be the last."

I search through the fog for a list of the fungus's effects. In Sparta, if the young acolytes I mentored accidentally collected the lethal mushrooms with uncovered hands, it led to raised blisters, as if they'd been badly burned.

A gust of wind has me gulping in fresh air. I look down at the soft round caps.

What would happen, I wonder, if they were crushed into a fine powder and added to a drink? Another moment of wringing hands and the dormant knowledge suddenly seizes my throat. As the truth always does.

Consuming Achlys's Fingernails would lead to violent emptying of the bowels, muscle cramps, delirium, convulsions. And eventually, a long, slow, agonizing death.

All symptoms that resemble other illnesses, including the one assaulting the Lower City.

I stare at my pale hands, knowing not all blemishes are visible. Yet some are.

Blisters.

An opportunity.

If I can find the courage to take it.

I turn back to the servingwomen. Aethra and Clymene inhale sharply when I remove my veil and wrap it around my hands for protection. "On second thought, this is exactly what we are looking for."

9

RHEA

A WEEK AFTER Prince Hector discovered me in the stables, I've all but given up hope when he ducks into the kitchen. The plate in my hand clatters to the floor.

Bodecca shoots me an irritated look. "Two visits in one moon. Have I reached the banks of the Great River, and nobody's seen fit to tell me?"

"I am confident you will outlive us all, Bodecca," Hector answers smoothly. "I am here for Rhea."

Bodecca's gaze turns withering. "*Rhea*, is it?"

"You may employ her in the evenings, but during the day she will work in the stables."

It takes every bit of control I have not to let the rampant joy inside me spill out onto my face.

"The stables," Bodecca repeats with absolutely no inflection. "Either my ears are failing me, or your reason you."

Silence descends. The other servants wisely take the opportunity to flee. Hector watches them go with a flicker of amusement.

"You heard me right. We're short of horses and time. The girl helped raise some of the new stock. Her presence will make them more agreeable."

Bodecca crosses the kitchen. It's hard to imagine Achilles himself could be more fearsome. "Women do not work in the stables. It is unheard of."

"It is necessary." For the first time, weariness creeps through Hector's guarded voice. "Last winter was hard. With another on the horizon, we can't let the Achaeans know how badly they've diminished our chariot force. We lose more horses every day to their fire arrows. The army needs horses, Bodecca."

She sighs. "Why does it have to be the girl?"

Because I can do it better.

Hector looks at my face as if he can read my thoughts and is waiting for me to voice them. During the pause that follows, I bite my tongue, sensing he needs to know I can.

After a long moment Hector nods. "Rhea knows these Phrygian horses better than any of my men. We are no longer in a position where we can afford to let the tools we have sit idle."

"There'll be talk. Not in the household, but in the stables." Bodecca regards me evenly. "There is already talk where the girl is concerned."

Broad shoulders shrug. "Then people need more worthwhile endeavors to occupy their time."

"Don't dismiss the weight of their words," Bodecca warns. "There's precious little to do these days but mourn and gossip. The love of a people is a fickle thing. Your position as commander could be stripped as easily as it was given." Her gaze brings a flood of heat to my cheeks. "Do this now, and the men will wonder."

"The men will do as they are commanded."

"And Andromache?" Bodecca's tone speaks of grudging affection and respect.

Prince Hector's jaw softens. "You forget Harsa Andromache was born with a bow in her hand. She knows women are sometimes needed in the world of men."

Bodecca harrumphs. "The world of men would collapse if women weren't there to hold it up. And you know very well that I forget nothing."

"Neither do I, old woman." Prince Hector places a quick kiss on her cheek.

Bodecca makes a sound of protest, but she doesn't push him away. Neither does she throttle him when he grabs a strip of cured meat before moving toward the door.

"Finish breaking your fast," Hector instructs me. "One of the stable boys will be waiting outside." With that he leaves the kitchen as abruptly as he entered it.

I grab a piece of bread and stuff it in my mouth.

A cup slams down in front of me.

"Don't look so pleased with yourself, girl." Ominously slow, Bodecca lowers herself into the opposite chair. In all my hours in this kitchen, I've never once seen the woman sit.

"Heed my words if the prince won't," she says. "The men won't want you in their domain. The stables fall under the protection of Tarhunt and Pirwa, lord of the horse. Neither is particularly welcoming of women. You are drawing attention to yourself, girl. A dangerous habit."

The bread sticks in my throat. "I only wish to help." And to be with my horses—the last link tethering me to everything I've lost.

Bodecca sighs. "I suppose what's done is done. The prince has asked for you, and there's no way to refuse him."

Eager to escape the old woman's dire predictions, I stand and make for the door.

"Wait."

When I turn, Bodecca is bent over, rummaging through a chest in the corner of the kitchen. She straightens and tosses something at me. The tunic has seen better days, but it is clean and roughly my size.

"You won't ruin those new robes on my watch. If you're going to play the part of a stable rat, you might as well dress like one." She crosses her arms over her ample chest. "If we're lucky, the men will mistake you for a boy. Better yet, the prince will take one look at you and come to his senses." A deep trench cuts across her brow. "I pray to Hannahanna he does. For both your sakes."

※

LARION PUSHES HIMSELF off the wall when I step out into the courtyard. The welt on his jaw has turned a painful shade of purple, but he smiles when he sees me.

"I'm supposed to bring you to the stables." He starts walking, leaving me to jog to keep up. "I told Prince Hector what you did for Lightfoot. Maybe that's why he's asked for you." Larion speaks in rapid Luwian though he knows I'm a Phrygian born in Hittite lands. Either he's lonely, or somehow he senses that I can understand him. Since that day weeks ago when that caravan found me, my collection of words has expanded by leaps and bounds.

Larion flashes me a grin made up of crooked teeth. "Zikari turned the color of a pomegranate when Hector told him. That's the new Master of Horses," the boy explains. "His temper is as short as he is, and he walks around looking like he's sucked a lemon." He screws up his face for emphasis.

The men in the training yard lower their swords as we approach. I fasten my eyes to the ground and follow Larion toward the larger of two stables. Bodecca's prayers that I go unnoticed must have fallen on deaf ears. Conversations trail off as every soldier and stable hand stops to stare at me. The boy clears his throat and takes a small step away from me. It is hard to blame him.

He points toward the doors. My stomach takes a sharp tumble, but I suck in a lungful of air and enter the stables. Stalls containing Troy's famous horses stretch out in front of me in two neat rows. Directly in their center waits Prince Hector.

The prince of Troy frowns when he sees me. "What's wrong?" he asks in Hittite.

I wipe my damp palms on my tunic. "The men don't want me here."

Hector considers what I've said. "Most are curious. Some will resent you. Act as if you are meant to be here, and they will have no choice but to accept or ignore you. Either way, they will leave you alone. If they don't, you will tell me."

It's an impossible command. Despite Troy's strange laws, a servant is still a servant and a soldier a soldier. We are not the same, and they still have authority over me, no matter Prince Hector's or King Priam's lofty decrees.

Hector is on the verge of speaking again when someone enters the stable behind us.

The man is broad-shouldered and lanky. One hand is cupped behind his neck so that all I can see as he walks is a headful of black hair. In the dim light, I can just make out the slash of high cheekbones and the elegant line of a nose. For a moment, I think it's Prince Paris. Then the man looks up, and all my thoughts scatter.

Until now, I did not realize a man could be beautiful, but this one is. If he and Paris were standing side by side, no one would give the Trojan prince a second glance.

"Cyrrian." Hector switches seamlessly back into Luwian. "I expected you an hour ago."

"My apologies." The young man grimaces. "There seems to be a very small man with a hammer trying to split my skull from the inside."

Hector frowns. "You need sleep after a day of fighting. Not wine and women."

Cyrrian smiles with half his mouth. "All soldiers need wine and women. Why else would they fight?" He walks over to the water trough and dunks his head inside. When he tosses it back, beads of moisture fly from the ends of his curls. He yanks them back and ties them into a knot at the back of his head like the one Prince Hector wears. "We can't all be so noble as you."

Hector watches the young man with an expression that is equal parts exasperation and affection. "Don't be late again. Andromache will be displeased if I'm forced to flog you."

Cyrrian grins. A flash of brilliant white in his deeply bronzed face. "Andromache is not someone I would ever wish to displease." He tucks his errant hair behind his ears. "I doubt you've missed me too much." His eyes touch upon me for the first time, and it becomes a little harder to breathe. Not just because of their intensity, but because of their color. Cerulean. Like the Aegean.

"Rhea will be helping Zikari train the horses," Hector says. "I'm counting on you to ensure the men keep their distance."

Though he doesn't say a word, it's clear Cyrrian thinks Hector is concerning himself over nothing.

"Cyrrian is my driver and the most skilled charioteer in Troy. When he can be bothered to show up on time. If you need anything when I'm not here, find him."

"At your disposal." Cyrrian is looking right at me, but I have the strangest sense that he doesn't see me at all. His eyes sail past me toward the entrance, and that half smile blossoms into a devastating grin. "This should be interesting."

A man strides through the stable doors. Troy's new Master of Horses looks exactly as Larion described. Short of stature with an uncommonly sour face.

Zikari wastes no time on pleasantries. "Forgive my boldness, Harsar, but this is unacceptable. It is well known that women frighten large animals."

I bite my tongue hard.

"I think we can both agree that there are exceptions to every rule." Hector's voice is calm, and yet a vein of authority runs through it. One the Master of Horses apparently fails to note.

"When you hired me in Cyzicus, you assured me these stables would be mine to run."

"And so they are," Hector replies evenly. "But we have fifty new horses to train, and no more men to spare. I am merely offering you extra help."

"Pirwa will not be pleased. Her presence will distract the men," Zikari announces.

Cyrrian coughs into his hand.

Hector sends his driver a quelling glare. "All I ask is that you see for yourself what she can do before you make a final decision."

Zikari finally deigns to acknowledge me. "I take it you know the back end of a horse from the front?"

The prince speaks before I can. "Luwian is not Rhea's native tongue."

The Master of Horses casts his eyes skyward before he spins on his heels. After a reassuring nod from Hector, I follow Zikari out of the stable and toward the corral packed with twenty Phrygian horses. They mill anxiously around the pyre of wood stacked high.

Zikari unlatches the door before leaning against it, barring my way. His expression turns beseeching as he jerks his chin back toward the house. As if to remind me that it isn't too late to go running back to the kitchens where I belong.

I look over my shoulder. There is a warning mixed with the warmth in Prince Hector's eyes. He has given me this opportunity, but he won't override his new Master of Horses or undermine his authority. If Zikari takes a firm stand against me, this will be my first and last trip to these stables.

Unbidden, my hand moves under the sleeve of my tunic to the strip of cloth tied around my forearm. My fingers touch the piece of the blanket that Vengeance gave me and then I square my shoulders the way I saw Harsa Andromache do the day we came to Troy. The Master of Horses shakes his head and ushers me into the paddock as if he fully expects to carry me back out again in pieces.

A ripple of awareness runs through the herd as I call out to them in the language of the whispers.

Ears prick. Muscles twitch. Hooves tap the dirt.

Zikari frowns. With a sideways glance at me, he unfurls a massive whip. The crack of the leather sings through the training grounds, sending the horses into flight. Their panic screams through my blood, drowning out Zikari's bellow as I step into the center of the storm.

Living thunder. Screaming wind. Dust and hot sun. And then the world falls away until a thousand memories eddy with the grit all around. My sisters' laughter. Papa's weathered hands on mine, guiding me through the motions. For a moment, I can almost feel him walking at my side as I place myself into the path of the charging horses just the way he taught me.

My hands move in slow circles. I raise my palm, and as one, the horses change direction.

Dimly, I hear Zikari crack his whip again. The horses pick up speed, circling us in a cloud of muscle and heat.

The scowl falls from Zikari's face, replaced by beads of sweat. For minutes that feel like moments, he drives the horses as I direct their course. Again and again until the horses are dancing to the music between us. My heart leaps as I watch them run. That joy quickly dies when I notice the danger. Dozens of men have gathered at the edges of the paddock to watch us. Larion flashes me a grin of crooked teeth. A few feet away, Nekku glares with undisguised hatred.

Bodecca's words of warning parade through my head.

The Master of Horses scowls at me, and any remnant of joy dissipates like smoke. It isn't enough. I might make the horses dance in circles, but what good are useless tricks to men who must take these horses and drive them onto a plain raining with flaming arrows?

"Rhea."

The prince of Troy stands at the edge of the fence, but now, there is something in his hand. A bow.

Hector nocks back an arrow tipped with glistening black. Though he scowls all the while, Cyrrian touches the end with a small torch. It burns hot and bright.

Prince Hector lets the arrow fly. It sails over the fence and strikes the pile of wood in the center of the corral. Wood, I suddenly realize, that has been drenched in oil.

The pyre bursts into flame.

Heat and fear.

Thick, bitter smoke fills the corral. The horses rear up. Their cries fill the yard as they crash into each other in an effort to escape the flames.

To my left, Zikari dodges a horse and dives headfirst over a rail. I start after him when I catch sight of the prince of Troy. He is watching me. Waiting. My gaze locks with his, and I stop at the edge of the enclosure.

The horses' fear washes over me in a wave. Gritting my teeth, I turn around to face it.

The horses churn in circles. If they were connected by harnesses, they would've destroyed each other and their chariots by now. It's a natural instinct—one that is wreaking havoc. Their fear makes them uncontrollable. But to beat the fear out of them would cripple them as surely as any broken bone. No. I can't steal their fear when it is fear that keeps them and their drivers alive. What I need instead is their trust.

I step into the corral.

Easy. The fire can't chase you. I won't let it.

A few of the horses trot over, drawn by my promise of protection. I run my hands over their bodies, sealing the pact with touch, as horses do.

A few minutes pass and, slowly, the horses grow used to the stench of smoke. A few minutes more, and they have stopped their pointless running.

"You see. The fire cannot chase you," I whisper to the bay beside me while I walk in a slow circle around the flaming wood. One by one, the horses follow.

When I dare a glance at Prince Hector, he is surrounded by slack-jawed soldiers. They watch as if they aren't sure if they are meant to cheer me on or curse me. Perhaps the god Pirwa is not clear on the subject.

"What do you think, Zikari?" Hector asks smoothly. Cyrrian stands at his side. The young charioteer isn't smiling anymore.

The men await Zikari's answer, and I wait with them. My heart races in my chest as every one of my hopes and wishes hangs suspended in the silence.

The Master of Horses takes his time folding up his whip. At last, he turns to the prince of Troy with a shrug. "I might find some use for the girl."

<hr>

ON THE WAY back to the house, my heart is brimming in a way it hasn't since before I fled our farm. It's why I don't see the figure lying in wait in the courtyard until it is too late to avert my course.

"You were in the stables."

It is not a question, but I answer anyway.

"Yes, Harsa Andromache. I'm helping with the horses."

Her head tilts to the side. "Your Luwian is coming along rapidly."

I drop my chin, unsure if this pleases her. Not knowing why it should matter to me, only that it does. I've never seen another woman command a room merely by entering it. Not even Kallira had that power. Harsa Andromache speaks without a flicker of doubt that her words will be heard. By men. Women. Servants. Members of the Old Blood. Hector's wife walks among them all as if she fears nothing and no one. I've watched her from the shadows and wondered what that must be like.

"What of my husband?"

The Harsa's words carry a dangerous edge. I lick my lips and walk it carefully. "He is with the fire horse."

"The fire horse?"

"Atesh. The stallion," I explain quickly.

Dark eyes skewer me where I stand. "My husband hasn't bothered naming the horses since the second year of the war. By now we would have gone through every pantheon twice."

I nod, but she isn't looking at me anymore, but past me. Toward the stable and the training ground ringing with the clash of bronze. A playground for brutality where Hector and his soldiers train for a war that may never end. And yet, for the briefest moment, something flickers over the Harsa's face. An expression that soothes the bite of her words and speaks to something deep inside me.

Longing.

But what is it that a Harsa of Troy could long for?

I drop my gaze, but it's too late. Andromache's expression has turned to stone.

I saw something I was not meant to see, and we both know it.

THE HAWK

When they come, the Hawk is waiting.
Feathers preening in the sun.
Passing through the gates below.
Horse of fire.
Little Mouse hiding in plain sight.
Death.
It enters on their heels.

No, sings the Voice. *It is already here.*
Yes, the Hawk has tasted it.
Mixed with bits of flesh and gristle.
Invaders.
Not the army on the beaches, another.
Crawling low over the ground.

And so it begins, says the Voice.
They have all come.
Just as the Voice said they would.

The Horse fights.
The Mouse scurries.
The Weaver weaves.
The Spindle turns on the loom.
And the Hawk makes lazy circles.
Lonely bird that sees too far
high above a city built of bones.

BOOK
II

10

ANDROMACHE

THE ACCUSATORY SLASH of crimson stings in a way my other
failures have not. It is the first moon cycle, the first rejection from Demeter,
since our journey to Cyzicus. Only there is a finality to it. A sense that I have
done all that I can to be a normal woman.

I wash the undergarment in a basin, waiting for a release from this destiny. An unfettering from the well-worn path of a wife and mother. A road I
never even wanted to walk until it was the only route left open to me.

The release does not come. Nor does any relief. There isn't even gratitude
for the promise of again living on my own terms. There is only failure. And
the whispers in the streets about things that shouldn't be but are, and things
that aren't as they should be. The spark behind a gnawing fear.

Change is coming faster than the first frost. For all of us.

Out on the balcony, I shake the damp undergarment so it can dry in the
morning sun. But the late-autumn rays cannot dispel the coldness from my
bones. A hawk cries out from the clouds.

My eyes follow the red bird on its flight toward the Scamander and the
Achaean camp on Cape Sigeum beyond. Smoke rises above the shoreline as
it always has, but the billows seem thicker as of late. What are they burning?
A harvest offering to their gods?

A growing desperation, theirs and ours, confronts me from every angle.
The fatigue we all feel from fighting this war. Priam's health is failing. Hector and I remain childless. And now the Citadel is scheming against us. Only

what good is an heir if there is no city left to rule? This obsession with securing the succession is a vain distraction from the real threats to Troy.

Again, I breathe in ash, unable to shake the hunch that this sudden silence from the Achaeans is an ill omen. Their behavior may seem mysterious, but human nature acts in accordance with certain rules. There is *a reason* the Achaeans are staying away, refocusing their efforts on raiding settlements along the coast. I just have to figure out what it is.

My chest burns, only for what I can't say. For the child who would save both my husband's affections and his place as Priam's heir? Or for the chance to finally prove myself, if not in armor then at least with my mind?

Why not both? the wind whispers back.

I grit my teeth. *Because I am a mortal woman, not a goddess.*

And yet the longing to do and be everything will not subside. I slip back inside the bedchamber, where Hector sleeps naked on our pallet. He lies flat on his stomach, face buried, his stone-chiseled body beckoning me back to bed.

What would be the point? There was a time we used to enjoy exploring every surface of each other like an uncharted land. These days, Hector makes love like he does everything else—with purpose, with honor, but from a safe distance that guards his heart. There is a shadow between us. It makes me wonder . . .

My mind has always seen hidden connections and natural consequences where others cite magic and the will of the gods. Still, I cannot deny the spell the stable girl has cast.

It isn't that I fear Hector longs for her. It's that I long to be for him what this girl has become.

Useful.

"Husband," I say softly. Not a muscle stirs.

Then, at the blare of a distant war horn, Hector shoots out of bed like a taut arrow, reaching for the armor never far from his side. He has at least agreed to keep his sword and spear by the door instead of right by the bed. We have enough battles there of our own.

"How long have I slept?" His eyes dart around in a frenzy. "Is the sun high?"

"No run around Troy's walls today." I wrap him a paltry breakfast of day-old bread and figs in a cloth. "You needed rest. You've slept in the mud with the men long enough."

Hector's worries chase him even into the land of dreams. There is good reason for that.

The harvest has been poor, so our food stores are dwindling and there are fewer men than ever to farm. And yet our population continues to grow, as more and more asylum seekers from the Troad's razed villages flee to our gates. That they can make it across the plains at all is merely another indication the Achaeans are uniquely preoccupied. Priam may soon regret his benevolence toward our homeless neighbors. Friends we would not have to provide refuge to in such great numbers if we'd only sent out men to defend them weeks ago. But we didn't, and now there are the rumors of sickness. So far it seems to be isolated to certain wards of the Lower City, near the asylum camp, but I can tell Hector is worried. If the illness hits our soldiers . . .

Before his return late last night, I'd not seen Hector in days. When he isn't in the stables with *her*, he's sleeping with his men in the army camp in front of the west walls of the Lower City, awaiting word from the scouts he sent to the beaches in an effort to understand the sudden quiet on the part of the Achaeans. So far, not a single scout has returned.

"That is Aeneas's horn." Hector secures a belted kilt of wool dyed in thick black and red stripes around his waist before fitting his breastplate over his tunic.

It is obvious he hates himself for this small luxury he's taken. For the privilege of sleeping in a bed beside his wife when his men are denied the same. I hand him his gleaming helmet. As I have a thousand times. Only now, my farewell includes a request I've only had the audacity to utter once before.

"Let me come with you."

"Andromache."

"Not now. But soon." When his frown lines do not disappear, I clear my throat and stand firm. "I can no longer sit here doing nothing. *Being* nothing."

The shadow that overtakes Hector is as familiar as the phases of the moon. I can tell he understands what I am trying to say. "You mean . . . ?"

My eyes fall.

When I raise my chin again, I have no doubt this is the only time in our shared life that I have seen Hector of Troy defeated. He says nothing. But he knows.

A desperate sound rattles in my throat. I grasp Hector's armguard. "Let me fight! Permit me to be of some benefit to Troy."

Hector grips my chin gently, his eyes drinking in mine. "You are of irreplaceable benefit to *me*. Let that be enough."

I shake my head. "They will change the succession. They won't want to wait."

"I have not given up hope."

The little boy with Hector's chestnut eyes flashes before me.

"You must hear me, Hector. I completed the rite of Demeter and it did not work. They will find a way to use this failure against you. And now, with this illness . . . if it takes hold, the people will grow frantic. The Citadel will look for any scapegoat, and they will lay the blame at our door."

Hector's silence scares me, but I press on regardless.

"You have not helped matters by making yourself an easy target."

After all, there is not a person in Troy who has not heard that Prince Hector has given a girl free rein in his army's stables.

"You may be right," he says finally. A surprisingly measured response that is scarier still. "Some speak of a prophecy that says Achilles is destined to die in Troy, but not before he earns his eternal glory."

Achilles? "What does he have to do with thi—"

Hector throws his shield to the floor. The frustration he keeps buried to spare the morale of his men boils over without warning. "So which is it? Who sees the truth? Does Achilles fall in this war? Or do I?"

A possibility too bitter to linger on.

"I don't know," I say as calmly as I can manage. "But you need the support of the Citadel all the same. Which means you need a son." I clench my fists around an illusion of composure.

"Hard as it may be for you to believe, there are many other pressing matters that require my attention."

"What could be more pressing than solidifying your throne?"

He shakes his head. "Forget I mentioned it."

At the look on my face, Hector sighs. "Helenus is at his wits' end trying to manage the allies. Paris thinks the role of royal liaison beneath him.

Deiphobus has all the diplomatic finesse of a hammer, and Polydorus is too young. I have run out of brothers to entrust the task. I would ask Aeneas, but his sense of decorum isn't . . . well-suited to such men."

"Are our allies really so difficult to deal with?"

"On their own, no. But together? They are growing more restless by the day." Hector shakes his head. "At this moment, one of the captains is loudly requesting an audience with the council. Sarpedon refuses to take the field again unless he is heard."

"Sarpedon? The Lycian?"

"He is a cutthroat and a pirate. Before the war, he and his brethren made a nuisance of themselves to our ships trading down the coastline toward Mytilene. But as far as our Assuwa allies go, he is as loyal as they come. To refuse him outright would be a mistake, but it seems the council would rather chew off their own hands than bow to the demands of an outsider."

"He sounds like someone I would like at my table."

"Leave it alone, Andromache."

"But don't you see? Customs based only on long-standing grudges are precisely what *you* could change if you were king. Until you are established without question as Priam's heir, there will be nothing but instability and machinations among the Old Blood. And in times of trouble, they will cling even more to what is familiar and safe, no matter how harmful those ways have become."

"*I am* the Old Blood," Hector says. "But I am not the king, Andromache. I'm a soldier, and I will carry out whatever my father commands. If you're so eager to take to the battlefield, you must first learn what it means to obey orders."

"Fine. Then give me a mission that matters." My jaw tightens further when his doesn't soften. "Tell me, as a Harsa of Troy, where am *I* permitted to give any orders of my own? I don't even have authority over the servants in my own kitchen—"

Hector strides away in exasperation. The bright plume of his helmet swishes behind him like a stallion's tail. When he reaches the doorway, he clenches his spear before glancing back. "You want to be of service? Then think less of the old men on the council and more of your own people. Dozens in the Lower City are falling ill. Mostly elderly who were already weakened, but I have heard of a few children also." His eyes flit between me and the door, the only sign of the battle waging within him. "More are needed to nurse the sick, but the Lower City women are consumed with replenishing the army's food stores, and there are few in the Citadel eager to expose themselves. If you could organize a—"

"I'll do it. I'll go."

And just like that, all the many reasons I love Hector come rushing back. Queen Hecuba might make a Lower City appearance from time to time to put on a good show, but I know the sole reason Hector has asked me to take this risk is because he is genuinely concerned for those in his charge.

"Have the women you organize separate the sick, but do not linger with them. This illness is spreading, but it does not appear to be serious." Eyes glistening, Hector crosses the room. He stops just short of an embrace, stroking my cheek instead. "Be careful."

Something sinks inside me as I recall the Achaeans' sudden quiet; remember the stench of smoke billowing from the camps. But I do not want Hector to see my hesitation. I do not want him to see anything except my resolve.

"We will do what we can to break their fevers," I say. "When the situation is under control, we will come back."

Come back.

How many times has my heart screamed these words to him?

"Do this well and I may be able to convince the council to let you do more." A fleeting smile plus one more stroke of the cheek and Hector is gone.

Once his footsteps fade, I cover my head and slip from our house, eager to go unrecognized. Our servants would insist on an escort if they knew where I was headed, seeing that it's the last place I am expected to show my face.

The day is early yet. There's a good chance she's still mucking the stalls. I haven't seen much of the mousy girl up close since we returned from Cyzicus, but Hector has spoken of her. Or he *used* to. His enthusiasm over his recent rescues waned once he sensed that my disinterest was in fact poorly disguised hostility.

I don't know why I let the girl bother me so.

Or perhaps I do. From my balcony, I've witnessed the two of them dancing in the ring with the horses. Hector's eyes shine with something worse than desire. They shine with respect.

The same admiration I saw when he arrived at my father's palace and watched me sparring with Podes, my closest brother, a sword in my hands instead of a spindle. It's the look I long to see again on the day we face Troy's enemies the way we were always meant to—as a united, terrifying force.

But first I must convince a handful of Citadel women to leave their looms to face an unknown danger in the service of Troy. These women of higher status have at least been trained in the basic arts of herbal remedies, and we need their skill. It would also bolster the people of Troy to see some of the Old Blood walk among them. With the growing numbers in the Lower City limiting the available resources, the lines separating the many levels of Troy have become more deeply drawn than ever.

Besides, if I am to kick the nest of hornets that is the Citadel, I will need someone with me I can rely on. Bodecca has too many years behind her to risk, and Faria grows faint at the sight of blood. It occurs to me suddenly that while the customs of Troy mean I am constantly surrounded by women, I do not have many friends. But perhaps it is not a friend I need . . .

Hector's horse girl is clearly clever. Her quick mastery of Luwian proves that if nothing else. More importantly, she has enough fear in those strange eyes to act with sense.

Fear is what keeps people alive.

If I'm being honest, there's another reason I seek to bring the girl beneath the wing of my cloak. Those who fear me are beyond my influence. But those who love me? They are as loyal to Hector's Harsa as they are to him, if not more so. I have let myself be threatened by the girl's usefulness to Hector, and it has blinded me to all the ways she might be useful to me.

Useful in one way in particular, though the thought had not occurred to me until now . . .

The girl doesn't even notice when I enter the stalls. I rarely come here, but I know the musky place from the stench that clings to Hector's clothes. Crouched in front of a mare and her foal, she grooms the baby horse like she has no other care in the world. The girl is even younger than I remember. Or at least she seems younger with her dirt-streaked cheeks and the thin tunic that underscores her shapelessness. When the mare brays at my intrusion, the girl grabs the horse's nose, whispering in a tongue I cannot decipher.

Hay crunches beneath my foot. The girl startles, the brush slipping from her hand as she turns. "Harsa. I, I did not see you there."

Her Luwian is perfect. Not a trace of an accent. That skill alone is worth the trouble of welcoming her into my household. Fortunately, I know the one foreign word that will get her attention.

"You are an *assussanni.*" The term lingers like the stable smell.

After a long pause, the girl says, "I've not heard that name since I left home."

"My mentor learned how to ride from an *assussanni* along the banks of the Black Sea," I explain. "They say the Hittite woman could talk to a horse in its own tongue."

The girl's eyes fall to her feet. "I can do no such thing."

"You can. I've seen it. So has my husband." I notice how the girl's eyes flash at my mention of Hector. "It's a gift from the gods, not to be scorned. Though of course . . . not everyone feels that way."

The girl's pale green gaze glows. "What do you mean?"

I cut to the question on the lips of every Trojan with two working eyes. "Do you have my husband under a spell?"

"I don't understand."

"Soldiers are a superstitious lot. What else but sorcery could explain why Prince Hector has allowed a young woman to work in his stables? You practice horse-magic. Or have you not heard the rumors yourself?"

"I've told you. I know of no such magic."

The girl was hesitant to contradict me, and yet she *does.* Perhaps I have indeed come to the right place. Her hunger for approval is plain, but I suspect there may be more to her. We shall soon see.

"I speak to the horses as I have been taught," she says.

I soften the thin line of my lips. "It doesn't matter what is true if you give up control over what is spoken. If these horses can hear you, then you have a power no man for a thousand miles can lay claim to. Still, they will do whatever they can to reap that power's rewards. And one day, when your gifts no longer serve them, they will blame you for their troubles."

I let my words sink into the silence before I spring the trap. "My husband says you are almost done training the last of his new stock. That there is to be a demonstration for the king and his council in three days' time to signify the completion of Troy's new chariot force."

"That's right." It is a whisper.

I resist the urge to smile and take a step closer. "Troy's supply of horses is limited, and as a result, so is your usefulness. How much longer will they stand for your presence once you have given them what they desire? Do you really think they will thank you for what you have done once they no longer need you?"

"Why are you saying this?" The girl's disbelief tells me her whole life story. She is the youngest child, as am I. But whereas I had seven brothers who shoved me in the dirt, she must have had sisters who carried her on their hips longer than they should have. That isn't to say the girl is weak. No, her center is as hard as the gemstone cut of her jade eyes. Still, she has never been alone in the world before.

She doesn't yet know that women like us are *always* alone.

"My husband is a good man. He feels responsible for bringing you here, and he would be aggrieved if something happened to you . . ." I drum my fingers along the stall's railing. "I will give you my protection by taking you on as one of my personal servants. No one would dare accuse you of sorcery if they knew I trusted you enough to bring you into my household."

The girl studies me warily. "That is kind, but how will I—?"

"Do you doubt what I've told you? If you wish to remain in the stables, we must ensure you are not driven out by idle tongues. You may continue your work with the horses, but you will also attend to me and sleep with my personal servants instead of . . . where do you currently reside?"

"The kitchen."

"Good. You know your way around it, then." My mind rushes forward, adjusting my plans. "We will need supplies. Linens for poultices. Basins for water." I turn to face her. "What is your name, child?"

"Rhea."

"A Greek name." Why am I not surprised? "Do you speak that crude tongue as well?"

"A bit."

This pleases me, though I can't yet say why. "I will keep watch over you, Rhea, *assussanni* of the steppes." I pause to watch how my promise of protection settles over the girl's shoulders like a warm shawl. "But in return, I need your assistance."

The fear that conquers Rhea's calm demeanor doesn't escape my notice.

"I have eyes and ears all over this city, and they tell me the fighting men grow weary."

"How could they not?" Rhea replies. "I can barely keep the horses fed. Surely the soldiers grow hungry as well."

"Yes, well, unlike horses, men need more than fresh straw and a good rubdown. They need to believe they are fighting for something. Dying for something."

"They fight for Troy. For Prince Hector."

"And yet some begin to doubt his judgment. Some even doubt he is fit to lead."

"What?" Her eyes ignite at the blasphemy. "How is that possible?"

Is she playing a game, or is the girl truly that naïve? "It does not matter how. There will *be* no Troy without Hector."

And his son.

Shame stifles any further words bubbling in my throat.

"But who would spread such lies?" Rhea's hands tighten into tiny balls.

Oh, I have an idea. After all, where has the rot in Priam's line always festered?

Still, Hector's position as commander and heir won't matter if the council keeps hamstringing him and we lose this war. In that case, my barrenness may yet be a blessing. For it will take every warrior in Troy to hold off our enemies.

Every warrior, including me.

The girl studies my face, as if she can see the yarn of plots twisting around the spindle of my mind. "What must I do?"

The girl's blind loyalty is almost endearing. "If the Achaeans ever decide to see sense and launch an actual advance, a full-scale siege, then our current strategy of chariot skirmishes on an open plain will do us little good. Troy's horses remain the only weapon we possess that the Achaeans lack." I nod toward the beast stomping his hooves. "Wouldn't you agree?"

Rhea casts the horse a fearful glance, giving the white stripe between its eyes a stroke of reassurance.

"They are warhorses, child. You cannot save them. Surely you realize that?"

Her lip trembles as she nods.

"Few among our allies know how to fight from a horse, but the day may come when that is the only advantage we have left. Hector has the gift, as do the Thracians from the north. The Amazons know the secret to shooting a bow on horseback, but they haven't yet responded to our call for aid. Still . . ." I look away as the mare brays, almost in protest to what I am about to ask. "Not even the Amazons could teach me how to ride well. The horses always seemed . . . afraid."

The look on the girl's face tells me she has no trouble believing it. My voice shakes as I strive to hide that I am a Harsa of Troy about to ask a servant for assistance in an area where she clearly has the superior skill. When Rhea meets my gaze again, I can tell she understands. And she does not judge.

"After we tend to the Lower City, I want you to find me a suitable mount." As reassurance, I give her the gift of a rare smile. "Help us . . . reach an understanding. Teach me how to ride into battle without dishonoring my husband, and I will guarantee your gift with the horses does not become your curse."

11

HELEN

THE WARNING TREMORS travel from my hands all the way up my arms. I turn and find Paris in the doorway of my bedchamber.

"What are you doing here?" I lower my ivory comb. There are only so many answers he can give. None of them are promising.

"Your opportunity has presented itself." Paris's eyes drink in the rare sight of my face. "Andromache is calling on the women of the Citadel to join her at the old sea trader's inn to care for the sick of the Lower City. Hector must realize how close he is to losing favor and has finally decided to give a care to his image." He shakes his head. "That or Andromache browbeat him into putting her in charge of something other than his cock."

Hands tremble. Hope stirs. "And you . . . want me to go?"

"You asked to tend the sick." Paris saunters across the room to plant a kiss on top of my head. "I always hold up my end of a bargain."

His smile transforms into the snarl I hate to remember but would do well not to forget.

"If you cooperate, you'll see her again. But make me appear a fool, and I will gut you like a sacrificial offering to be placed at Menelaus's feet."

My mind races as Paris runs his hands down my arms. Why would he suddenly want me to venture into the Lower City when he was set against it before? Out of habit, I search for the pitcher that has been banished from my bedchamber. For several days already, I've survived without it, but it would take the crushed seeds of an entire poppy field to endure Paris's touch.

"It has been a long time . . ." His lowered voice feels like a forked tongue flicking at the back of my neck. "The Citadel grows uncertain about Troy's future. About who is best fit to lead her after this war is over. It would not hurt to strengthen our alliance in all the ways that count."

He should know by now that this route has never been open to him. Paris has surely tried with a hundred palace servants and Citadel concubines, and not one of them has ever brought forward a child for him to claim. Which Paris would gladly do to assure Priam he'd inherited more than the king's jawline. The people talk about their two childless princes, though of course the blame is cast on me. Just as it is put on Andromache.

Yet at the middle of my life's fourth decade, at least he now thinks me too old to help him in his cause. Most of the time.

"I am not well." I shrink away from his hands, the stench of suffocating myrrh. When we first came to Troy, it didn't take but a few months for Paris to stop visiting my bed.

Any lively girl is preferable to a corpse.

"You are never well." He shrugs, but his sigh is laced with something else. Actual disappointment?

"My moon cycle . . . it is . . ."

"Say no more." Paris drops his hands and turns for the door. "But soon." He nods at the strip of sheer fabric lying across my bed. "Don't forget your veil."

Another growl from the past rises at the back of my mind. Oceans and years between then and now.

"It is best to keep one's greatest weapon hidden until the moment it is needed most."

What Paris fails to realize is it will take more than a covered face for Andromache to tolerate my presence, let alone hear my advice when it comes to caring for the Lower City sick. Yet she must. I've no doubt Andromache would inflict wounds when necessary, but she has no idea how to heal them.

My hands tingle again. Not with a craving for oblivion, but with the promise of doing what they were made to do.

Only how am I to heal when Andromache despises me so? One look at my "harlot eyes," and she will send me back to the Citadel before I can convince her otherwise.

For Andromache's memory is long, and I am certain she hasn't forgiven me for the last time I stole the thunder Zeus meant for her. The memory floods through the cracks left by the loss of my cup.

Queen Hecuba held the ceremony not long after I arrived in Troy, an official acknowledgment of Andromache as the future queen and mother of the next heir. I'd worn a silk head covering, as is the Trojan custom when in public gatherings. Each of Hecuba's daughters had pulled back her headscarf when she approached the altar, revealing the full glory of her face and hair before giving Andromache the blessing of a sisterly kiss on the cheek. I stepped forward when my turn came.

Never had I shown my face before Troy's people. They'd only glimpsed me at a distance from my seat high on the ramparts. The murmurs that rippled over the temple's stones as I turned to face the crowd will never leave my dreams.

Awe and horror sound much the same.

They look similar, too. Yet Andromache's wrath was quickly replaced by terror when the throng rushed the altar—to get a closer look? To pluck a strand of my hair as a keepsake? Whatever their reasons, the mob pushed against the row of armed guards with such force, the ceremony was cut short and the royal family forced to flee.

The prayers for Hector and his future son were never finished. Andromache surely blames me for this as much as she blames me for the war.

If only she knew . . .

An idea rushes with the blood to my head. I race to the wooden chest brought with me from Sparta. At the bottom lies the ceremonial blue garment reserved for ritual mourning—an even darker midnight shade than the Egyptian blue pottery Troy once imported by the boatloads. It's an unflattering robe donned by the city's many widows, a dowdy dress I would wear every single day if Paris would allow it.

After pulling the shapeless garment over my head, I turn back to the chest and plunge my hands through soft robes until they graze cool metal at the bottom. The gilded face of my father stares back at me, the only piece of dowry treasure I managed to hide from Paris before he took the rest for himself. Not even I know where he has hidden it within Troy's walls, or if there will be any gold left by the time this war is done.

The Spartan Death Mask is exquisite. My father's goldsmith captured every wrinkle of King Tyndareus's face, even the short bristly hairs of the mustache that tickled my cheeks when I was a girl. As with many others, the Achaean custom of widows donning a funerary mask to honor their fallen men is one that has made its way to Troy. Among the showy sorts within the Citadel at least, who fawn over any fashion from across the sea.

I stare into the hammered silver plate on the wall where my reflection ripples. How many years has it been since I smiled? The gesture widens as Helen of Sparta disappears behind a golden wall. In her place stands a matronly widow who draws no eyes and incites no lust. A woman capable of determining her fate instead of the path thrust upon her.

A woman with a king's face.

~ ⁓ ~

"OVER THERE. PUT him down over there."

The inside of the mask fills with sweat as my breathing quickens. Andromache stands at the center of what must have been the Fair Winds' main hall, back when Troy actually hosted sailors while they waited for the currents through the Dardanelles to change in their favor. Now it is a large room with a cold hearth, empty but for the sick who are slowly filling it.

Andromache gives orders with the authority of a general, but so far hers is a scant force. Creusa, Priam and Hecuba's eldest daughter and the wife of Hector's cousin, Aeneas, lifts an elderly man under his armpits. An even smaller girl with strange green eyes carries his legs. Yet, just barely.

Creusa's grip starts to slip as she lowers the man to the pallet. I rush forward to assist before they drop him on the hard ground.

"Thank you," Creusa says, bloodshot eyes widening as they take in the striking Death Mask.

I nod, afraid to speak. Of all the women in Troy, Creusa is the most likely to recognize my voice. For while most Trojan Harsas have not bothered to hide their hatred, Creusa has followed her parents' lead and behaved as if my marriage to her brother is nothing but legitimate. Her tolerance is genuine, for Creusa's heart lacks all guile.

"He is heavier than he looks." Creusa gives a gentle nod to the old man with skin as thin as papyrus. Her slight shoulders rise and fall rapidly. For as long as I have known Creusa, her poor lungs have ailed her, especially during the spring and the harvest. Sadly, the affliction has passed on to her only son. I open my mouth to tell her to sit and rest, but close it for fear of raising her suspicions.

"Have you come from the Citadel?" asks a metallic voice behind me.

I turn to Andromache, bowing my head in reverence to her station. "Yes," I say in a tone much lower than what feels natural. "I am called Theana."

The name of the Spartan midwife who taught me materializes out of nowhere. I pray Andromache will not ask questions I do not have answers to.

"One Harsa of Priam's line, my own servant, and a war widow," Andromache mutters under her breath, arms crossed. "This is what the Citadel sends when I request aid on behalf of her city's most vulnerable."

"I am trained as a healer," I offer weakly, gesturing to the leather satchel on my hip that carries an array of herbs.

"Well, I am trained as a warrior. Not a nurse." Andromache sighs, a slight softening in her eyes revealing her relief. "Forgive me. I am grateful you have come. You've sacrificed much for Troy already."

A pang of guilt jabs me in the ribs. In a way, I *have* done much for Troy. If causing the deaths of my own countrymen is any consolation for the war she blames me for in full.

Images of poisoned wounds foaming in the sun launch an assault no mask can block. A scratch at the back of my throat has me reaching for the small vial of poppy tincture buried in my healer's satchel.

A cry stills my hand. For a moment, I forget where I am. Tears prick my eyes as they seek the source. A baby lying on a pallet next to a woman too far gone to care for her child.

My gaze locks on the infant seeking her mother, and I drop the vial back into darkness. "I have missed being of use."

Something sparks in Andromache's gaze. "That I can understand. Troy's walls are meant to protect. But when does that protection become imprisonment?"

"It is much the same with illness." I look down at the old man writhing on his pallet.

Andromache's heavy brows narrow. "How so?"

The uncertainty on her face does not become her, but it makes me bolder. For all of Andromache's confidence, she truly has no idea what she's doing. She intended to transform this inn into an infirmary because it would be easier to care for the sick all in one place. She has no idea this decision might be the Lower City's salvation.

"If this fever is like others . . ." I trail off as I walk among the three rows of a dozen pallets. About half are filled and both men and women make up the sick. The men are all elderly, the only males spared from the fighting. When I return to the man Creusa and the servant girl first carried in, he is sweating profusely yet shaking as if submerged in icy waters.

"I have never seen anything like it," Creusa whispers. "This sickness seems to burn them from the inside out. Yarri spare us . . . I fear it may prove catching."

I fear worse. Much worse.

The fever. Tremors. A dry cough. My heart pounds as the old man lifts his gnarled hand, clamping it around my wrist. A bluish-green hue stains his fingertips like dye.

All my saliva dries up. I have seen dead fingers like this only once before. The walls of the inn seem to collapse around me.

"Do you recognize this sickness?" I hear Andromache ask, though she now sounds worlds and lifetimes away.

When the room stops spinning, I crouch beside the pallet and lift the man's tunic above his waist. Creusa and the girl gasp at the sudden indecency. My trembling hands travel up the man's leg to his groin.

Swollen nodes. A red, pinprick rash. My eyes fly around the room, taking it in as if for the first time. In total, there are enough beds for about forty people.

We will need many more.

"This is no seasonal fever." I meet Andromache's steely gaze. "It is plague."

Her hard face blanches as she charges over the claim. "Impossible. Troy is a walled city. We haven't allowed visitors past her gates in months. Except . . ."

I can tell Andromache is thinking of the recent flood of asylum seekers from the coast. Of her journey to Cyzicus. Though of course, I cannot reveal I know anything about it. So how to make her understand the gravity of our situation without betraying who I am?

Give her the truth.

Yet just enough so as not to condemn myself with one turn of the loom. "I was not born in Troy. When I was a girl, my city experienced a bout of this very plague. Many people died." I point to the rash along the man's swollen upper thigh. "These are signs. Wait and see if you wish—I predict they will start to appear in the others." I work to keep my voice low despite the panic I feel rising.

"But where did it come from?" Andromache asks, missing the point. It's as if the source of this contagion matters more to her than the remedy. "Hector says no one in the army has fallen ill beyond the walls. So how could such a deadly illness suddenly appear from within?"

"Ill spirits have a way of riding the wind," Creusa offers halfheartedly as she sways on her feet.

"No. There is more to it than that." Looking entirely like an Amazon, Andromache gnaws her lip and turns to me. "It must not touch the army. What do we do to prevent it?"

For a moment, I am left stunned by the word *we*. "To begin, we wash often, preferably with strong wine. We must make sure all the sick are brought here. No exceptions. And we burn any corpses as quickly as we can." I glance at the paltry beds again, certain we will run out before dawn.

Three women and a servant girl. Is this really all the aid we have?

"This one is burning up," says Andromache's servant. The sick child drenched in sweat at the servant girl's feet looks to be about nine or ten years old.

The dam inside finally breaks open, sweeping me away in the flood. Hermione's heart-shaped face flashes before me, the promise of the Unnamed One echoing in my ears.

She will be the light of your days.

And she was. For nine glorious years, Hermione belonged to me, and I to her. Alone in our halls, I watched my daughter crawl, then walk, then run, happy to call the small world of the women's quarters our home.

"But that sun has set," I whisper behind the mask.

My work as a healer? Forgotten.

The only child of my flesh and bone? Gone.

Yet what of this child here?

Slowly, I back away from the women looking to me for answers. What right do I have to give them? If only they knew all that I have done . . . My shifting feet freeze when a breeze from an open window tickles the back of my neck.

Paeanas are meant to heal, not harm.

I hold out my hands. They've hardly stopped trembling since I arrived, but now they are as steady as they have ever been.

"We should push back the drapes," I hear myself order. "Let in as much fresh air as possible. And someone fetch us water. We must cool her down."

The new strength of my foreign tone turns the golden mask into a gong.

Creusa wobbles as she brings over a basin for the girl and pushes the damp hair off her brow. "I can always tell in one glance when my Ascanius has a fever."

I nod at her mother's wisdom. "It's the glassy look in their eyes."

"Go, Rhea." Andromache's command cuts through our reminiscing like a lash. "The sickness is worse than I thought. Hector needs you for the chariot demonstration, and you cannot help him if you fall ill."

I study the young servant girl. Rhea. It is a name I have heard Paris mention in passing, his expression one of smug satisfaction. Though I never bothered to question why.

The girl is thin as a weed and plain as one too. And yet hers is a face that like the rarest of flowers might one day bloom into something uncommon. A distinctive look as lovely as her disposition. The girl's desire to please is as obvious as the turmoil it creates within her.

Rhea glances over her shoulder. "If the widow is right and this is plague, you'll need more help than this. The horses will be fine without me for a day or two." She directs her stance and her words to Andromache alone. "With your permission, I'd like to stay."

Piercing eyes take her in from every angle. If I didn't know better, I would almost say they were pleased. "I suppose you have the right to make your own choice," Andromache clips.

"And she's right about needing the help," I add. "Many more will likely fall ill."

"Then they'll surely say it's the curse of the gods," barks a new voice. I turn toward the older woman who has burst into our make-do sick hall.

"Bodecca." Andromache uses the same flat tone one might use to describe the weather. "That makes our force five."

"I have sent for my maid, Isola," Creusa offers weakly. "That will give us one more pair of hands."

Andromache clenches her own around the cloth she's using to cool the old man. It is obvious to all that Hector's wife would be much more comfortable gripping a spear while fresh blood drenched her robes.

"Tell me what needs doing." Bodecca is already rolling up her sleeves.

Andromache scans the room. She stops on me, eyes pleading in a way I never expected. "What do you say, Theana?"

This time, my answer comes quickly. "We have to keep everyone here. This sickness cannot reach the army or the Citadel. Fortunately, it mainly spreads through fluids."

"Fortunately?"

"Yes," I say. "There are some illnesses that seem to spread through the very air, but this is not one of them. If we keep clean, we may yet keep it contained."

Andromache studies me for a long moment, then nods. "We'll travel door to door and tell all we meet to send any with the sickness here. Perhaps we'll rouse a few more nursemaids while we're at it. Bodecca, you're in charge of the sick until we return. Rhea, assist her in any way you can."

Andromache sighs as she studies her paltry force. "Leave the rest to us."

～ ❧ ～

THE FIST THAT smashes against the door sends an echo down the otherwise silent alleyway tucked in close to the western wall.

"Do you think they will help us?" I ask Andromache as she lowers her arm and waits.

"The people here love Hector," she says simply, though I can tell by her dull tone that they have not always extended her the same warmth. "They will answer his Harsa."

It is her overconfidence that betrays the doubt she harbors.

Yet if anyone will help us battle this sickness, it's the mothers who fear that Death might come for their dozing children next. Andromache pounds her fist against the door once more.

Somewhere inside, a baby cries. Finally, a haggard woman glares at us through a crack in the doorway. While the toddler on her hip runs his sticky hands through her hair, the mother blinks as if to assure herself she isn't dreaming. She goes pale at the sight of my mask, and paler still when her eyes take in the towering Amazon beside me.

"Harssi?"

"We need your help," Andromache demands. "You've heard a deadly illness has come to Troy?"

The way the woman grips the baby closer while peering into the empty street behind us is answer enough.

"We can stop its spread," I tell the mother gently.

"But to do that, we will need steady hands and strong stomachs," Andromache cuts in. "Can you spare anyone who might help us tend the sick?"

The woman stares at us blankly. "I am a widow. My children. I . . . I can't just leave them."

"What was he called?" Andromache asks without ceremony. "Your husband."

"Hamza."

"A lion." Andromache offers the words like a prayer that might pass her lips. "My friend here has also lost her husband. She shares your grief."

Not for the first time, I'm grateful that I wear my father's stern face. It hides the tear sliding down my cheek. Not only for the weight this mother must bear alone, but for the wishful thought that I might actually grieve either of my husbands.

This poor woman and I share nothing. Though I am not sure which state is worse.

Andromache's face twists when a girl emerges from the dark hovel to stand beside her mother. The two women in the doorway barely look a decade apart in age, but the tone the adolescent uses with the slightly older woman marks her as a daughter. The girl holds a baby that has a scar marring its upper lip. Judging by the thinness of all three, along with the hungry wails behind them, this household contains more children than there are means to nourish them.

I meet Andromache's gaze and know we are thinking the same thing. Here we both are. Harssi with no mouths to feed but our own.

Yet the only visible emotion this sight ignites in Andromache is anger. "If you wish for your children to survive this sickness, you will leave them with your eldest and join me to do what must be done."

"And why would she do that?"

My gaze lands on the girl clutching the harelipped baby. Her tin-colored eyes challenge Andromache directly. She lifts her chin like it is the only thing holding up their roof.

"What did you say?" Andromache replies, more intrigued now than angry.

"Lannaka, quiet now," the mother hisses, attempting to pull her daughter back into the shadows.

Lannaka will not be silenced.

"My father was killed fighting the Achaeans two years ago, and this is the first time anyone from the Citadel has ever knocked on our door. Why should my mother help you nurse the sick when all that is likely to do is leave us orphaned?"

Andromache grits her teeth. It is unclear if she is frustrated with others or with herself. "You are right. More should be done to honor those who have sacrificed their lives for Troy. But tell me, do you still have a roof over your head?"

"Thanks to Hippothous and his men." Lannaka shrugs carelessly. "They replaced the leaking thatch just last week."

Andromache raises an eyebrow. "Hippothous? The Pelasgian captain?"

"That's right," the girl continues with brazen eyes. "Sad, isn't it? When Troy's allies care more for her lowly inhabitants than the city's own king." She shifts the baby on her hip with a possession that makes me wonder if the allied captain left more here than a new roof.

Lannaka said her father was killed in battle two years ago, yet the child sleeping in her arms has barely been on this earth for more than two months.

A detail Andromache does not miss.

"Come back inside, Mama," the younger woman says with a gentleness she does not extend to us. "When the Lower City finally falls, will you answer our calls for help as you would have us answer yours?" With a smile that descends into a sneer, Lannaka adds, "I didn't think so."

She uses her bony hip to close the door.

"Wait." Andromache thrusts her arm into the doorway's crack. "Our army is doing everything they can to defend your homes. What is it that you want?"

Lannaka glances down at the sleeping babe before her eyes flash back to us. "A say in what becomes of us."

For the first time, I see Andromache speechless.

"We will do whatever we can," I offer. "You have our word."

"My father warned me not to heed empty promises that come from full mouths. If only he'd taken his own advice."

The door shuts. Andromache stares at it for a long moment before she strides down the cramped street toward the south wall, almost as if she could outrun the accusations at her back. Accusations that ring more and more true, the farther south we go. Andromache marches up to a two-story building attached to a large, pleasant courtyard. It is nicer than the dilapidated homes around it. A business of some kind. The sound of female laughter trickles down from a terrace above.

Again, Andromache raises her fist to the wood. The whispers that rise in response are immediately quieted by another. Still female, but harsh. Authoritative.

No one answers right away, but Andromache does not move. Finally, an older woman with droopy, kohl-lined eyes throws open the door with a bark. "What is it? My girls are sleeping."

"It's midday," Andromache says.

The woman's painted smile is without mirth. "Some of us must take our rest when and where we can, Harsa."

Unimpressed, Andromache delivers the rest of her summons.

The only reply the made-up woman gives is the sound of another slamming door.

Andromache's teeth grind in the silence. It is the only betrayal of her frustration as we knock on the next door and the next, where the welcomes we receive are much the same.

And so, we return to the Fair Winds as we departed, just the pair of us. Somehow, that in itself softens the failure, though I can tell Andromache is simmering at her own impotence.

The dimly lit rooms we return to, however, are much changed.

An unfamiliar figure labors at Creusa's side. A nervous girl who looks much younger than her years if she is indeed the maid Creusa sent for.

"Word spreads quickly in this part of the city," Bodecca says over deep groans and a child's high-pitched cry. "The sick keep arriving."

I count pallets. Twelve more have filled in our absence. Soon we will run out of floor space. "It is good that they are coming."

"Has more help arrived from the Citadel?" Andromache asks, though the answer is obvious. Her jaw hardens. "Perhaps the request will be better received from softer lips. Creusa!" she calls across the room.

Slowly, Creusa turns from the woman she was nursing.

At the sight of her ashen face, my insides go cold.

The cup in her hands slips from her fingers, staining the front of her robes. The sound of shattering pottery cuts through the Fair Winds.

"Isola, help!" Creusa reaches for her maid before crumpling to the floor in a heap of silk.

Rhea and Andromache run to Creusa and place her on a pallet. I conduct my assessment quickly, though my heart knows what my hands will find even before they reveal the rash in Creusa's swollen armpits.

"She has it," I say. What I do not tell them is that the signs were there before this. I just failed to read them.

As much as I wish to stay at Creusa's side, there is no time to linger. I leave her maid, Isola, to look after her and continue attending to the others.

More sick arrive. Bodecca and Rhea move between the pallets as quickly as they can, delivering herbal compresses and sips of water from a wooden ladle.

There are too many.

There were even before Creusa fell ill. Hours pass. How many I cannot tell. In the dim light of the inn, they all bleed together.

"Theana!"

I shake myself from a stupor and join Andromache at Creusa's side.

Clumps of wet hair stick to her feverish face. The linens twist around her thrashing legs as the woman's spine arcs with a strength she does not possess in normal life. With a grunt, Andromache grabs the princess's legs while I throw my arms over her chest.

"Will you not remove your mask even now?" Andromache says breathlessly once the thrashing stops. "There's no need for the ceremony of the Citadel here."

"Yet the shield that ceremony provides is strong," I say with similar force.

Andromache's lips twitch. "Who taught you the healing arts?"

"I was trained by my mother and she by hers," I lie. My head throbs with craving to the point of blindness, another sign of my betrayal. My weakness. What would the Paeanas who taught me think if they could see me now?

"It must be satisfying . . . to learn from other women. To be a woman judged by merit alone."

"It must be," I agree.

Andromache snorts indelicately. A smile creeps in behind my mask. It flees when Andromache speaks again.

"We can't do this alone."

I shake my head. "No. We can't."

Andromache places a firm hand on my shoulder, only to pull back when the doors of the Fair Winds part.

In walks the matron with kohl-lined eyes and ample curves. The number of golden bangles lining her arms, as well as the eight young and heavily painted girls who trail her, tell me the source of her income at once.

"Where do you want us?" The woman's gravelly voice is obviously more accustomed to giving orders than asking questions.

At first, Bodecca studies the woman like a rival. Then she hands her a smock. "Put this on and follow me."

Andromache's shudder of relief is perceptible to none but me. But then Creusa seizes up again, pulling me back to the sharp scent of urine and the sickly sweetness of death.

One of the new arrivals rushes over to help. A small girl whose cutting black gaze needs no kohl to stand out. We hold Creusa's legs while Andromache grips her ears so she does not hit her head. The convulsion passes, yet the moan that leaves Creusa's throat has me shoving a basin beneath her chin. Blood and green bile hit the clay bottom with a slosh.

"I'll get rid of that," says the girl with hematite hair and eyes that dart around like daggers.

She takes hold of the basin like she's seen worse.

"What is your name?" I ask.

"Salama."

"Thank you for coming," I say softly. "That was brave."

Salama shrugs. "Bravery has little to do with it. A plague is bad for business. Especially if it touches the army."

"Are we too late to help?"

The question comes from the inn's entrance. Again, Lannaka stands in a doorway beside her mother, but this time her arms are childless.

"You aren't too late." I approach the mother and daughter who look more like sisters. "What changed your mind?"

The widow gives me a small smile as her daughter moves to assist Rhea. "My Lannaka has always been our protector, even before Hamza left us. Whereas I tend to be the one who tries to mend what is already broken."

"That is the way of many mothers," I say with a knowing nod.

The woman stands a little straighter than she did in her hovel's shadows. Despite the agony around us, it's as if she's come home to a part of herself, unfettered from the endless needs of her children.

Though needs there are plenty still.

"I am called Theana."

The name gets stuck on the roof of my mouth. The woman offers her own with more ease despite more syllables.

"Paskuwatti."

"How many children do you have, Paskuwatti?"

"Call me Watti. Five in this world and three who have crossed the Great River."

"And would you do anything to keep the others from joining them?"

Watti shakes her head. "Not anything. Death is not always the worst fate."

Tears choke any words that might escape my mask. I know with the certainty of my entire being that what this woman has said is true.

"There is always a way out," I say finally. "For those with enough hope to see it."

"The only hope I have for my children is that they will not taste the bitterness of needless suffering."

"I pray to the gods it may be so." Seeing that Andromache needs fresh rags, I leave Watti with her fragile hope and hurry back to Andromache's side.

"Shhh. Rest now." Andromache pulls Creusa's head into her lap, pushing back filthy strands of hair with a surprising tenderness that stirs an unknown longing inside me.

And then Andromache sings. Sings in a voice that is low and rich as honey. The enchanting sound rolls through the hall in a language I've never heard. Every person lying on every pallet falls still. Even Rhea, who hasn't stopped moving since Bodecca took over and started giving her tasks.

Andromache's voice rises and falls. Soaring high and diving down low, where it resonates with a dull ache. When the last note is sung, Andromache studies my mask as if she can peer past its gilded sheen. "Is it really so difficult to imagine?"

I make my reply extra hoarse. "Imagine what?"

The usual sternness vanishes from her features. "That I might be capable of giving tenderness as well as orders."

"No," Rhea answers, settling down beside us. "It isn't."

Andromache's expression softens further as she comes out of the spell cast by her own song. She removes a brown pouch from her robes and beckons Rhea. "It's late. Please ask Bodecca to heat the water for my evening tea."

I gesture to the bag once Rhea and Salama have both disappeared. "May I?"

Andromache hesitates.

"Herbal remedies are an interest of mine," I explain.

"It is nothing special."

"Yet you drink it nightly?"

"A treatment for inflammation of the bowels."

That sounds like a lie, but Andromache relents regardless. I open the bag and push around the leaves. Red raspberry leaf. Stinging nettle. Fenugreek. Dried pieces of some kind of fungus, though I'm not certain which variety. Yet even through my thick mask, the mixture smells foul. Not earthy, but stale. Stripped of potency.

What's more, none of these are the right herbs for any bowel problem that ails her. If anything, some might make matters worse. And I can tell by the hawklike way Andromache watches me that she knows it.

I hand her the bag back, gather a damp rag, and wipe the crust from Creusa's lips. Moments creak along, a cacophony of ragged breathing. Around us, our growing force of women continues the grunt work of caregiving that is so easy to undervalue, though it has surely saved as many cities as the soldiers who guard their gates.

"Of all Priam's children, people overlook Creusa," Andromache says finally, smoothing the blanket over the ill woman. "Even more than Cassandra, who is mad, they view Creusa's kindness as weakness. Once I was no better. She alone was warm to me when I first arrived in Troy. Not because she wanted something, but because she knew what I needed. Not that I have ever . . ." Andromache swallows hard. "Kindness is its own type of courage, I think."

They are the most words Andromache has ever spoken to me, yet I know she'd never utter them if she knew her true audience.

Andromache checks Creusa's fever before sliding down to the floor in exhaustion. She stands again with a start when Hector and Aeneas stride into the sick hall. "You shouldn't be here, Hector."

The prince gives a reverent nod to my Death Mask, as if I am the very king it depicts. Aeneas walks right by me, dropping down to his ill wife.

"Do not touch her," I advise when he reaches for Creusa's hand.

Finally, he scans my ceremonial garb. No scoffer of traditions or the elders who uphold them, Aeneas heeds my warning.

Hector gives a light touch to Andromache's arm. "We have much to discuss."

"Come, Theana." Andromache nods for me to follow them into the adjoining kitchen.

I follow slowly. This inclusion in her circle almost makes me forget the stench at our back, if only for a moment. Inside the kitchen, Bodecca and Rhea dip strips of linen into a vat of boiling water with long wooden sticks.

"What happened to Creusa? I asked you to be cautious," Hector says to Andromache when we're out of earshot of his sister.

"Spoken like a man who has never nursed anyone," Bodecca grumbles.

"You asked me to organize the women of the Citadel." Andromache gestures toward me without taking her eyes off Hector. "This is who has come. Your sister was brave to be among them."

Andromache gives me an urgent nod. With her, it is always the truth.

"A plague has visited Troy."

My thick pronouncement seems to float in the center of the room.

"This sickness will spread like a fire in drought if we do not keep it here." I pray the men hear the desperation in my voice.

"But is that even possible?" Much like his cousin, Hector keeps his thoughts tightly guarded. If he has tasted fear in this place, he does not show it.

"Will she survive?" Aeneas runs a hand through his hair. "Our son. Ascanius. The boy is frightened at how long his mother has been away."

Andromache looks to me again.

"It's hard to say," I answer both men at once. "If Harsa Creusa makes it through the night . . ."

Aeneas's unflinching eyes fall. He cares about the mother of his child, that is plain. Yet his concern for Creusa is not the same bloom of love that binds Hector to Andromache.

"Creusa will rally." Andromache leaves no room for failure. "But we must prevent a panic. Especially until after tomorrow's chariot demonstration. If they discover a plague has besieged the Lower City, the army will despair. Despairing men make poor warriors."

"People will die," Hector says softly. "They deserve to know."

"People are dying everywhere," Andromache returns. Not cruelly. Honestly. "You invite death every time you leave our door. The risks you take are always to defend Troy. Her walls and her people. If those people riot and those walls are breached by this plague and it spreads . . . Death will have come for us all."

"Even so, we must alert my father," the prince continues. "Call the King's Council to meet—"

"This enemy cares nothing for horses and chariots!" Andromache's fierce eyes sweep over Bodecca and Rhea before landing on me. "I would have you leave this battle to *us*."

The strange warmth beneath my breast at her gaze has me resenting the words I must speak all the more.

"Prince Hector is right," I say. "The plague may not be contained by nursemaids alone. We will need to enforce a curfew and secure a larger infirmary for the sick. It will take an organized effort at all levels of the city. The people, and the king, must know."

"The people will do what we deem best." Andromache looks slightly betrayed that I have spoken out against her. Yet some of what I've said must make sense because she relents without a fight. "Call for a dinner with the King's Council, then. See if the Citadel cares to send more than one widow the next time we call on them for aid."

My eyes lock on Hector. A warning reverberates through me.

Hector does not dine at the palace often. Surely Paris has been waiting for such an opportunity . . .

"You should hold the dinner in your own household," I say suddenly. "Not at the palace."

Three sets of eyes turn to stare at my golden mask.

"And why is that?" Andromache raises a thick brow.

My throat tightens. If I accuse Paris openly, he will know I am the one who betrayed him. Worst of all, he might finally make good on his threats against *her*.

The scream I've drowned for a decade rises up like one of Poseidon's storms. Beneath my robes, my hands grasp for the vial, craving the numbness it offers, but it is empty. Not a drop of the poppy's magic remains. I poured it out on the lips of a dying woman with the most beautiful eyes to lessen her pain.

Beauty and pain. Two horses pulling a single chariot.

I shake away the fog and look up. There is only one way they will listen to me without also turning my husband into my enemy. Yet the move is not without its own risks.

"The Citadel has always been too insulated from this war and the widespread suffering it has caused," I begin. "And yet King Priam loves his people. Far more than the council that seeks to take advantage of his slowing mind. The king must learn about this plague in a venue where he can hear his people's tormented cries with his own ears."

Hector's chestnut eyes are searching. "How do you know my father?"

I take a deep inhale. "Because I have loved him like a daughter. And he has loved me in turn."

Slowly, I pull the Death Mask away from my face.

Aeneas's mouth falls open. Bodecca grunts and Rhea drops a wet cloth to the floor. Hector and Andromache simply stare.

Andromache goes crimson as she unravels my deception. She gnaws her lip, but she does not speak. Maybe because she knows what I have said about Priam is true, and it is yet another reason for her hatred. Priam never blamed me for this war, one he believed was the will of the gods. We became companions almost as soon as I arrived in Troy. For all the many hours the royal family sat on the ramparts watching the early battles play out—Paris, Helenus, and Polydorus jesting like spectators at festival games—Priam could tell I truly listened to what he had to say. Invisibility may be a death blow to a king, but it is the very reason I welcome old age.

"*Liar,*" Andromache spits at my feet. "I might have known Paris would send you here to spy."

"I came of my own free will." There are few things Andromache loathes more than a timid tongue, and right now mine feels like it's coated in sand. "You know what I've said is true. Priam will not hear your warnings in the lavish safety of the Citadel. Your home is the threshold between two worlds. Warn the king *there.* Create a plan of action on your own ground. For unless this entire city comes together, there is no circle that will be spared."

Her fists tighten, but I can tell Andromache has heard me. And she knows I'm right. "You are not welcome here. You will never be welcome here. Leave."

"I may not be welcomed, but I am needed. This is a mistake, Andromache."

"I said get out." She rushes toward me with each syllable. *"Get out!"*

I hold up both hands, as if the wave of her wrath could ever be slowed. Then, my own regret overflowing, I flee to where the shadows grow long.

12

RHEA

AN EXPECTANT SILENCE runs wild with the wind through the training grounds. Men are packed shoulder to shoulder along the wooden rails. On a temporary platform, Priam sits in a hulking chair, little more than a shrunken shadow of the brother who stands at his side.

Horses dance in their harnesses. Behind them, drivers clutch leather reins. Sixteen teams of newly appointed chariots face two pyres stacked high with wood. Along the perimeter, a line of archers stands ready with oil-tipped arrows.

I pull myself up onto the wooden rail and look over the grounds, legs shaking from the long run up through Troy's inner gates. Zikari's eyes find mine. Every line of his face threatens murder. I should've been here long ago to help harness the horses and go over everything with the drivers one last time. I study my hands, scrubbed raw with vinegar at Bodecca's orders. Zikari is no more interested in my excuses than I am in making them. Besides, there is no time.

Whinnies sound. The hard knot in the center of my chest loosens slightly when I spot Ishtar and Carris bound to a gleaming chariot. My gaze sweeps Troy's Old Blood next. Every member of the King's Council is well dressed and better fed than anyone else in the city. After two days in the rank darkness of the Fair Winds, the sight of their perfumed skin and pressed hair is as jarring as the low-hanging sun. Servants drift among them offering wine and food from bronze plates covered in stable flies. My eyes snag on a fat man in a tunic as he dips his fingers into a bowl of oil.

The Old Blood occupy their raised seats like untouchable gods; their greatest concern is for the chariots that have been made vulnerable to Odysseus's fire. They either don't know or don't care that another fire has sparked right under their noses.

Helen of Sparta was right about one thing.

These people have no idea what is coming for them.

A hushed awe settles over the small arena. Zikari bows low before the king. Early-evening sunlight glistens off the Master of Horses' brow. He looks to me one last time, and the eyes of Troy's people follow. Bodecca's warning plays through my head as I shrink back from their curious stares. Around the ring, the archers lift their bows. Hooves tap the dust.

The horses sense it too. All the eyes on them. The weight of this moment.

I search the crowd for Prince Hector, but I don't find his face. Last night, I overheard him telling Andromache that the Achaeans had finally roused themselves. Another attack was expected, and it must have come, detaining him at the army camp on the western plain.

Unable to stall any longer, Zikari throws back his shoulders. Around us, dozens of archers set fire to their arrows. Even the king's stooped back grows a little straighter.

Smoke winds through the air. Ishtar's and Carris's fear is a sharp tang in my nose. My hands itch to comfort them. To talk to them. But I hold myself back. I can't do this for them. Just like I can't be there when they finally leave the safety of the ring for the battlefield. It is the driver who'll have to care for them then. Just as it is Troy's drivers who must rise to the challenge now.

As one, the second man in every chariot leans forward. Firm leads and soft words wash over the ring even as a wave of calm bathes the horses. Zikari looks at me to gauge the horses' readiness. I nod. He turns back toward the king and gives the signal.

Arrows fly. A shower of flame. Horses squeal as the pyres erupt. If they balk now, half of Troy's chariot fleet will be destroyed while her Old Blood look on.

Wood crackles and flames hiss. The horses' fear flares up with the heat, but the drivers are there, overriding it not with force, but soothing it with assurances the way I taught them.

Not a horse steps out of line.

The pounding in my heart subsides as the chariots break into synchronized motion. The drivers urge their animals around the pyres. A hush runs across the platform. From somewhere to the side, Larion whoops out loud.

My eyes find Ishtar and Carris at the front of the line. Pride mixes with sorrow. They are warhorses now.

The rest of the demonstration doesn't last long. Zikari accepts the cheers and raucous stomping with the same sour face he usually wears. The crowd clears quickly as the drivers set the horses free.

"Good girl." I run my hand over Ishtar's soft muzzle and press my face into the latch of her warm throat. After days holding the clammy skin of the dying, it feels like coming home. "You made me proud today."

A hard nudge to the ribs. I look over my shoulder to find Carris watching me with the horse's equivalent of a scowl. It fills me with tenderness. "I've missed you too. And there's no need for jealousy." I press my forehead flat to her white star. "You are much too lovely for that."

Larion jumps up onto the enclosure and dangles his long legs over the edge. He flashes the gap between his front teeth. There's a dark bruise around his eye that wasn't there two days ago. I don't ask him where it came from. By now I have plenty of bruises of my own. Nekku haunts my footsteps, taking every opportunity to shove me into a wall or trip me when Zikari isn't looking.

"We gave 'em a show, didn't we?" Larion grins. "Did you see Zikari smile?" The boy shivers even as he sticks out his thin chest. "It's enough to give a man nightmares."

I want to smile back, but my memories from the Fair Winds won't allow it. Despite our best efforts, the number of sick has doubled. Already the plague has spread into the Merchant Quarter. If it reaches the stable—or worse, the army . . .

One of the drivers in the ring makes a sound halfway between a cough and a groan. A gob of phlegm hits the earth at his feet. I stare at it long after he has walked away.

"The drivers did well." I offer Ishtar and Carris one last rub.

"We both know it wasn't the drivers." Larion's legs stop swinging. He glances over his shoulder before leaning in close. "How do you do it, Rhea? Is it magic?"

"It isn't." I stroke Ishtar's neck, trying to shake the chill that is rapidly setting in despite the glare of the sun. "Horses are like people. They just want to be seen." Only, with people, it isn't the words they speak, but all the meanings veiled behind them.

Carris ruffles my hair with her muzzle, offering comfort. I run my hands down her neck and lean into her warmth.

"Hector will want these two beauties for one of his captains. Maybe even Polydamas. He lost his horses a few weeks ago."

Captain Polydamas is quick to argue and to laugh, but his hands are also heavy on the reins, and according to the stable boys, he's lost more than one team of horses already. "We haven't picked the driver yet," I say quickly.

At least they hadn't before I abandoned the stables for the Fair Winds.

"It won't be long now," Larion says.

My grip on the lead tightens. If it comes to it, I'll beg Hector to spare Ishtar and Carris. Given the success of the demonstration, he might even agree. Unless the plague spreads and the army grows desperate. Or unless he finds out about my riding lessons with Harsa Andromache first.

The song the Harsa sang to Creusa reverberates in my memory along with the secret it revealed. A softness hidden under all the strength. A deep caring shown not through her words but through her actions. I was proud that she chose me to help her at the Fair Winds, just like I was secretly pleased when she asked me to teach her how to ride. For reasons I can't explain, I *want* her to value me the same way she does Bodecca. But how can it be that helping his own wife still feels like a betrayal of Prince Hector?

Zikari joins us at the edge of the enclosure. "That wasn't the utter disaster I feared it would be. No thanks to you."

I gnaw the inside of my cheek and strive for an even tone. "Any word on when the new teams will be sent to the plain?"

Zikari scowls. "The council called the captains back behind the gates. The army is making camp in the Lower City as we speak."

"What?" I step back from the rail. "What happened to make them call the army back?"

Andromache would have told Hector this is the worst thing they can do with a plague festering near the west wall, but would either of them have the power to stop it?

Zikari's scowl deepens. "Our illustrious council is not in the habit of discussing their battle strategies with me."

"They are overly cautious. Cowards who would rather hide behind walls than ride out to defend them," Andromache said to her husband last night when he'd come with Aeneas to check on Creusa.

I stood outside the door, frozen by the venom in her voice and the weariness in his.

"Why have the Achaeans fallen silent, Hector? You've seen the smoke."

When he didn't say more, she'd pressed.

"They have it, Hector. It explains their fires. The eerie quiet. If the Achaeans are suffering from this plague even worse than we are, now is the time to drive them into the sea."

"The order to hang back has come from my father and my king. Whether or not I agree, I am bound by blood and duty to honor it."

The *crack* of wood draws me back to the present and sends my gaze hurtling across the training grounds. In the small ring next to ours, the fire horse dances, his back legs unleashing fury upon the innocent fence. Behind him, Prince Hector drops over the rail. His armor lies discarded on the ground behind him. His bare chest and face are speckled with blood—a sure sign that Aeneas's scouts were right about the Achaeans' rousing. Hector must have come here straight from the battlefield. The darkness in his eyes as he raises them to Atesh makes me wonder if part of him is still there.

I glance back toward the courtyard, where the shadows are lengthening. Bodecca and Harsa Andromache will be needing me back at the Fair Winds, but my eyes return to Hector stalking to the center of the ring. The sun setting behind him highlights every cut and ridge of his sweat-slicked skin.

Atesh tosses his head. An open challenge. Prince Hector doesn't back down, but neither does he rise to it. It's the way he works not just with the horses, but also with the men. Guiding them with a firm will, a steady hand, and endless patience. Frustrated, the fire horse makes a mad dash along the walls of his cage, sending men toppling backward to clear his path. Their armor still dusty from the plain, the soldiers gather to watch their commander face off against the wild stallion. They hoot and holler as Hector stalks Atesh until he is pinned to the opposite fence. Hector raises his hand, and silence falls over the training grounds.

The fire horse's body goes still. The prince and the horse regard each other in pregnant silence. I catch my breath when Prince Hector takes a single step forward. Atesh bows his head. Hector raises his other hand and slowly closes the distance between them.

I feel the tension coiling in Atesh's muscles a second before he springs. The horse leaps to the side, bucking wildly.

Hector, prince of Troy, hits the dirt flat on his back.

"I suppose I asked for that." Hector climbs to his feet. His eyes find mine across the paddock. The shadows under them have grown darker since yesterday. "You should have named him Ares, Rhea. It would have suited him better."

Atesh's tail swishes back and forth as he prances.

"He likes you," I tell the prince as I lead Carris and Ishtar to the partition separating us.

"Then I pity anyone on his bad side." Hector joins me at the wooden fence line. I open my mouth to ask him if he has been to see Andromache when a voice speaks up behind me.

"I'll take them, Rhea."

Larion sneaks a glance at Prince Hector before he busies himself inspecting the ground. I place the leads in his hands, and Larion turns, tugging my horses behind him. The bruise under his eye is almost black in the fading light.

"Larion, wait," I call.

Even with Nekku lurking between the stalls, these stables will be safer for him than going home to his mother in the Lower City. "Can you stay in the stables tonight? I . . . need your help with . . . something."

Larion frowns, but another glance at Hector, and he nods. I release a breath.

"Larion?" Hector says. "Kazuwa's son?"

It is quite possibly the first time I have ever seen Larion speechless.

"Your father was a fine soldier." Hector's expression grows solemn. "You favor him."

Larion ducks his head, but not before I catch the flush. When he leads the horses away, he seems to stand a hand taller than before.

Hector watches the boy go for a moment before he catches me staring at him. "What is it?"

"Nothing." Only that Larion is more likely to forget his marriage feast or the birth of his first child than the day the prince of Troy paid him such a compliment.

Hector frowns at the boy's retreating back. "I send men to their deaths every day, Rhea. It doesn't seem too much to ask for me to remember their names."

I fear I'm starting to look at Prince Hector with the same glazed expression of awe that Larion does.

Before he came to look for Andromache at the Fair Winds, it'd been days since I'd last seen the prince. No matter how early I climb from bed, he is already gone on his daily run around Troy's walls. When the dawn breaks over the battlefield, he's on the sun god Tiwad's tail. When darkness falls over the city gates, Prince Hector is there, ushering the last fighter through ahead of him. And his people love him for it with the kind of devotion that can't be bought by gold or the oldest blood.

What would Troy even be without him?

On the nights Hector stays outside Troy's walls, Bodecca sits by the hearth, her milky eyes staring at the flames as her hands—hands that are never still—lie clenched in her lap. Every evening finds her in the same place, sitting and waiting and thinking her own secret thoughts until the sound of Prince Hector's horses, Lightfoot and Golden, comes clomping past the kitchen and toward the stables. Only then does she retire to her bed.

On the opposite side of the house, Andromache keeps her own vigil. Under the gaze of the servants, her expression and her posture are armor without weakness. But on those long dark nights when I lie awake in my new bed next to Faria, I hear footsteps pace the floor of her rooms as if they are a cage.

After watching Andromache care for the sick with little food and less rest, I'm more convinced than ever that a fire smolders beneath her skin of ice. I felt it the day I watched her ride into Troy at the prince's side. Fierceness and longing. Grief and helplessness. The kind that she would never show, but that for better or worse, the horse beneath her could *feel*.

Horses have a way of seeing past the armor we wear. Perhaps that is the real reason she doesn't like to be around them.

Making a sound deep in her throat, Ishtar leans over the fence to rest her head on the prince's shoulder. Hesitantly at first, his hand comes around her neck to claim what she offers.

When Hector's shoulders rise and fall, they seem to carry the weight of the world.

Ishtar makes the sound again. Less subtle, Carris joins the cause, nudging me in the back. I shoot her a look before I clear my throat. "Is everything . . . all right, Harsar?"

I don't really expect him to answer, but he does. "They came across the plain at dawn. The horses held steady despite their arrows. We had them on the run. Even Diomedes and that giant Ajax had broken the line and fled when my father called us back." The wooden fence groans under the prince's weight. "I can't win a war I'm not allowed to fight. And with this plague, I am starting to think none of it matters. I told my father we should bring the army and the allies into the Citadel. Away from the sickness."

"And?" I lean forward.

The look of frustration on his face is answer enough. "Certain members of the council would rather keep the common soldier where he belongs."

I rack my brain for some comfort to offer him. "Things will change now that the council has seen what our chariot forces can do." If those forces aren't wiped out by sickness because the Citadel refuses to see the truth right in front of their faces.

"I fear it will take more than one demonstration. Fortunately, more is what my wife excels at." He sighs. "Thank you. Not just for what you've done for our horses." He studies me from his great height. "Andromache says she has taken you into her personal service."

I duck my chin before he sees the guilt I can't hide. "Harsa Andromache is kind to have taken an interest in me."

At this, the corners of Hector's eyes crinkle. "My Harsa is many admirable things, but kind is not one of them." His gaze moves to the horse running wild in the corral. "I worry sometimes that her spirit is lost on this city. She was not built to sit on her hands."

I can't imagine it is easy for Andromache to spend week after week waiting. For the sickness to pass. For the war to progress. For a son that might never come. Based on the whispers in the stables, all of Troy is waiting with her. Expecting. Demanding. The sympathy in Hector's voice makes it painfully obvious he has no idea his wife has moved on to other, more dangerous plans.

Guilt churns in my stomach. "She wishes to be of use."

Hector's smile is soft. "Not just clever with horses, but with people too."

I tuck a strand of hair behind my ear and watch Atesh. "It's not so clever to see what is."

"You'd be surprised, Rhea, how many people miss the things that are right in front of them." Hector turns to face me fully. "Harsa Andromache has asked for you back at the house."

I push myself off the fence. "But . . . I'm needed at the Fair Winds. I want to help."

"And you will." Hector gives my shoulder a fortifying pat. "Your escort is right that way."

I turn in the direction Hector points.

Cyrrian stands in the chariot yard. A group of men are gathered around him, laughing, carrying on as if just a ten-minute run away, people aren't dying.

His smile grows hard when I meet his gaze. A flush accompanies the unpleasant memory of our first meeting. The way he made me feel small without a single word. I've seen the young charioteer many times since. He seems to live here when he isn't fighting the Achaeans or, according to stable gossip, spending his nights in the Lower City.

"Andromache wants you both at the house," Prince Hector tells us after waving the young man over.

"Are we in trouble?" Cyrrian wields his half smile like the lethal weapon it is.

"I suppose that depends on how you feel about granting a small favor to the one reputable Harsa in Troy who still welcomes you at her table," Hector says.

Cyrrian groans. "Please tell me you aren't asking what I think you're asking."

"I ask nothing." Hector retrieves his armor. "If you wish to tell my wife no, it will be from your own lips."

Cyrrian grimaces before gesturing for me to proceed him toward the house. On the way we pass a long line of soldiers headed to the stables. The wind blows around them, kicking up storms of dust. I cover my face, all the while fighting a growing sense of doom.

"Do you know what this is about?" I ask.

Cyrrian pushes his unruly hair out of his eyes. "No doubt Andromache is planning on enlisting my help to provide entertainment at her little gathering tomorrow. It is said that my voice can make maidens weep."

I ignore that infuriating smile as it makes another appearance. "The dinner for the council? You'll be there?"

The familiar tang of lemons wafts over us when we enter the courtyard behind the house.

"Yes. All the important Old Bloods are set to attend except for our queen, who prefers the incense-steeped halls of the palace to the stench in the lower rings." Darkness stirs in those Aegean eyes. "I don't know why Andromache bothers. They have never accepted her, and they will never stoop so low as to heed her counsel."

"But they have to. If they don't, the Achaeans will be the least of their problems."

Cyrrian frowns down at me. "You mean the sickness?"

"You really don't know?"

"Know what?" His long, rangy body pushes into my space.

I refuse to cower. "It isn't merely a sickness. It is plague. Andromache needs help from the Citadel to contain it."

He takes in my ill-fitting clothes and raw hands, and I can almost hear the whirling blade of the sharp mind he takes pains to hide. "They'll come, but she will be hard-pressed to make them listen. Especially Paris." Cyrrian's gaze skewers me in place. "If Hector has a weakness, it's that he occasionally gives people more credit than they deserve."

This time, I don't have to guess at his meaning. "You don't like me."

"Don't take it personally. I don't much care for anyone."

"Except for Prince Hector and Harsa Andromache."

"Except for them." He leans down so that I can smell the honey and cloves on his breath. "Which is why I won't stand for anyone putting them in danger."

He looks at me as if every ill tiding that has befallen Troy is my fault, and it makes my blood run hot. "I would never do anything to endanger them."

"You really don't know?" Cyrrian throws my own words from a moment ago back in my face.

"What do you—"

"You already have."

He steps inside, leaving me standing there alone to wonder what he could mean.

Inside, the kitchen smells like a market and feels like a pyre. Everywhere I look, preparations are under way. Faria smiles prettily at Cyrrian from beside the hearth. I suppress a stab of irritation when he returns the favor.

The last time I saw Bodecca, she was calmly spooning water into a dying man's mouth. Now her skin is scrubbed raw and every one of her white hairs is standing on end. "The Harsa has sent word to the Citadel. The Old Bloods will be descending on us tomorrow night."

I join Bodecca at the hearth, where she is stirring a pot of simmering lentils. "She and Prince Hector will make them see reason," I say.

Bodecca smashes the lid on the pot with more force than necessary. "Reason and politics mix like shellfish and chicken livers. What if Troy's finest decide it would be better for them to simply bar themselves in the Citadel until the plague passes?"

"Would they do that?" I gape at her.

"They've done it before." Cyrrian speaks up behind us.

"And they will do it again if we don't make this good." Bodecca shoves the spoon into my hand.

"You ladies obviously have much to do. Far be it from me to get in your way." Cyrrian bows smoothly.

"Wait!" The word comes too late. He has already disappeared through the door.

Coward.

At a loss, I stare at the spoon in my hand. "I'm useless in the kitchen."

Bodecca casts me a sideways glance. "If there is a point to this speech, you'd best get to it."

I no longer live in terror that she will send me back to the nearest slave market for displeasing her. Everybody displeases Bodecca.

"Would I not be of more help at the Fair Winds?"

Pale eyes narrow on me. "Do they have rock vipers where you come from, girl?"

I nod.

"Then you know how they hunt? Passive until it suits them. Then mean as any creatures fashioned by the hands of the gods. The Old Blood are like that. Vipers hiding in plain sight. Waiting for the opportunity to strike. When it comes, they'd devour their own young sooner than see it pass by."

"Prince Hector isn't like that. Neither is the Harsa." Andromache would never hide from an enemy. If she were to strike, it would be the same way she bargained. Charging forward so that others were forced to succumb to the sheer strength of her will.

Bodecca grunts. It is as close to a sign of approval as she's ever given me. "Which is why you are needed here. Those of us under this roof are loyal to the prince and his Harsa. We might hear, but we do not discuss. We may see, but we immediately forget. Do you understand me, girl?"

Always *girl*. Never Rhea, and yet, I find I don't mind.

"I understand."

"At the dinner we will all have roles to play."

Helen of Sparta's face flashes through my mind. So lovely it wrenched something deep inside. "What about Harsa Helen?"

Bodecca's sudden stillness makes me want to swallow my own tongue. "What about her?"

"Will she be attending the dinner?" Though Helen was staring right at me in the Fair Winds when she revealed her face, I can't recall one solid feature. The thing I remember is the compassion in her gaze and the way that kindness seemed to radiate from somewhere deep inside. It's easier to picture her bent over the sick and dying. It wasn't the mask that drew my notice, but the way she moved. Shoulders hunched and hands shaking. But once Andromache pressed a washcloth into her hands, Helen's movements had become graceful. It left me with the feeling that comes over me whenever I see my horses run.

Bodecca harrumphs. "Helen of Sparta is as helpful as a house made of feathers. I don't know what role she would play in such matters."

"But she helped us already," I insist, risking Bodecca's wrath. "If not for Helen, we would not have known what we were dealing with until it was too late."

"Then she must have had her own reasons," Bodecca says. "Reasons that have nothing to do with *you*."

Her tone warns me to let it go, but I can't. Helen of Sparta is a puzzle, and I've never been able to leave those alone. I can't help but feel that Helen's beauty, like Kallira's, hides a deeper truth. I didn't see the truth of my sister until it was too late, and it makes me wonder: Does anyone truly see Helen?

"Is it because Andromache dislikes Paris?"

Bodecca's gaze turns sharp. "Careful, girl. You see much, and one day those eyes of yours might land you neck-deep in boiling water." She drops the bedding she was mercilessly beating. "The Citadel might be fooled by Paris's smiling face, but I was there from the first when Paris returned in his youth, and I saw how it was. Prince Hector loved his lost brother, and maybe in his own way, Paris returned that feeling as best he could. But it is not the same. You just have to look at the queen to see it. All love is not the same. For selfish love only lasts as long as the skies are clear. It does not hold in foul weather."

"Paris may be all that you say he is, but it's still possible that Andromache is wrong about Helen." The words rise up like a wave. "She seemed so intent on helping . . ."

A sharp *bang* cuts through the kitchen as Bodecca slams down her broom. "Harsa Andromache is worth a dozen Hecubas and a hundred Helen of Spartas. She would fight to the death to defend Hector from his enemies," Bodecca offers with a grudging respect that was not given, but earned. "She is the iron in his spine. She is *ours*, and I won't have anyone question her in this house."

Her knotted hand wrenches the stirring spoon from my grip.

"The prince might not have known what he was doing when he bought you in that slave market, but he knew full well the risks when he allowed you to work in the stables. Now, Harsa Andromache must bear not only the whispers of what happens in her bedchambers, but also the idle gossip of those who claim you're an *assussanni* witch who's placed her husband under the same spell as Troy's horses. Why else would a son of Priam allow a girl into the army's stables, flouting the gods? It would be less worrisome if they thought he was bedding you," she says, making my cheeks flame. "As it stands, they merely accuse you of controlling his mind and compromising his judgment. And so, it is a far more dangerous game we are playing. Remember this, girl. Image in Troy is as valuable as gold, and you have tarnished theirs."

You really don't know?

You already have.

My stomach sinks. Is it true? Could I have unintentionally tarnished the

Harsa's and Prince Hector's reputations all because I begged a favor in my father's name that Hector could not refuse?

One look at Bodecca's face, and I have my answer.

"What can I do?"

"Tomorrow, the vipers come to dine. Andromache is focused on protecting the people and Prince Hector on safeguarding his army. They are both too busy to spare much thought to the dangers to themselves. It'll be up to us to make sure no harm comes to them." Her eyes narrow. "Don't think it's escaped my notice or the Harsa's how words seem to stick in that head of yours. You will use those skills here. Keep your eyes open. Use that memory for the benefit of this house, understood?"

I nod.

"Go," Bodecca orders. "Take off those rags and do something with that hair. You'll be serving wine tomorrow at the king's table."

The king's table.

I blink. "Is that . . . wise?"

Bodecca arches a brow. "Andromache does everything for a reason." At my obvious terror, Bodecca's expression softens. "Come, girl. Let us see if you can charm the snakes as easily as you do the horses."

13

HELEN

THE WEIGHT OF the small pouches, one in each hand, is far heavier than the contents.

One carries life, the other death.

One is safety, and the other proof.

Paris will not be delayed any longer. Tonight, he demanded the poison, and so I walk the twisted path to his rooms, every step increasing the load that threatens to break me. If I give him the pouch containing lethal mushrooms my pestle crushed into a fine powder, there's a risk someone may die—*Hector*, if the signs are to be believed. But if I give him the other, I'll have missed my chance to expose the treacherous side of Paris only I seem to see.

My fingers tighten around the harmless herbs. If Hector drinks these instead of Achlys's Fingernails, he will be spared. Until the next time Paris is so emboldened.

And there will be a next time.

My skin itches beneath my robes. If I'm seated beside King Priam like usual, I should be able to stop Hector from drinking the poison in time. It is enough that Paris places it in his cup and in so doing condemns himself. Yet the mere possibility of bringing harm to one of the few Trojan men who has shown me any regard makes my gut seize as if I'd ingested the toxin myself.

It is a risk.

Yet like the others I've taken, it will be worth it if it paints Paris's hands in red blisters that reveal who he truly is.

For her sake.

I pick up my pace, each *pat, pat, pat* of sandaled feet a war drum. There will be no coming back from this. If things go wrong, Paris will know I am the one who deceived him.

The primal fear overtakes me in the echo of her girlish cry. A sound so disbelieving. Shock that our tranquil world could be disturbed with such cruelty. Then came another voice, crystalline like the Mad Honey that Paris gave me in those early days to calm my grief, the vision-producing nectar of the rhododendron a rare gift from marauders who roamed the Dardanelles to the Sea of Marmara.

"I've hired men all over the Aegean who would think nothing of killing a child. Perhaps they'd use an arrow made by your own skillful hands."

The back of my throat burns. There is no decision, then. There never has been. I must give Paris the poison that will betray its handler. Then I must wait until the moment Hector raises the cup to his lips.

As I pass through another courtyard, I lift my eyes to the square of night sky and ask for courage. Courage to act, but even more, to speak.

Because only when Paris's attempts at fratricide are undeniable will they invoke the Law of Bound Blood. Only then will Paris be forced to glimpse the beauty of his own reflection in the glint of an executioner's sword. This long-standing law is why Paris has cultivated his own faction within the Citadel, men who speak in low tones on the other side of my walls. Having Hector killed outright has never been an option. If it were, Paris would have taken it years ago, for there are plenty among the Old Blood who'd prefer the more pliable prince to the unmovable boulder that is Hector.

All my thoughts dissipate as soon as I walk into a cloud of myrrh. Paris hasn't summoned me to his bedchamber in almost three years. I managed to deflect his renewed advances a few nights ago, but his lust for power—over me and everyone else—will not be put off for long. I pray he only wants the poison before tonight's dinner and nothing else.

"Helen. Wife. Good of you to come."

Wife. The untruth of that word makes the corners of my mouth tighten. From where he sits, receiving a close shave from a scantily robed Clymene, Paris speaks as if I have any choice but to obey his every command.

The rows of bronze oil lamps cast shadows along the tapestry-covered walls. Paris waves an impatient hand. Clymene lowers her blade and secures the knot of curls at the nape of Paris's neck, her hands slick with oil. The source of the sappy, overpowering stench.

Dozens of Luwian shoes with upturned toes cover the floor. Fine-woven kilts and colorful garments imported from every corner of the Mediterranean lounge about the bedchamber like rags, though the gold-etched tunic Paris decided on for tonight is far from tawdry. Like everyone in the Citadel, his congenial existence has not altered much since the war began, and it won't so long as Troy's walls stand. His covert alliances with the raiding Sea Peoples have seen to that. As a result, nothing will move Paris from that plush pillow at his back. Not the plague ravaging the Lower City. Not the nine years of fighting that have killed hundreds of his own people.

Not my dowry of gold. Nor my body of ice. Nor my tears of salt.

My eyes sprint across the unmade bed as a scene from the last time flashes before me, a dagger of lightning across a dark sky. Paris's smug cruelty. The sour smell of his breath behind his false compliments—a boasting not intended to bolster my confidence, but his own at having claimed me.

A wave of nausea surges.

Clymene leaves us, but not without giving me a jealous glance on her way out. She has shared Paris's favor and his bed of late. I would thank her if I could.

"Do you have it?" Paris nods at the hands I hold stiffly at my sides.

Another flash of memory fills the space of my hesitation.

"*Why do you weep?*" Hector had come up beside me on the ramparts before he and the army marched out to meet the invading Achaean ships for the first time. "*If it is for your people, take comfort in knowing this war will be brief. No attacking army has ever made it beyond our beaches.*"

I'd gestured to a plain that, by nightfall, would be stained with both Achaean and Trojan blood. Yet if I'd opened my veins and offered my own, which side would it be on behalf of?

"*Hear me now, Helen, and we will never speak of it again.*" With little formality, Hector had lowered my outstretched arm. The rich soil of his eyes generous enough for any plant to put down roots. "*Men find many reasons to wage war. Beauty is not one of them.*"

Once, I thought I knew what Hector meant. Not anymore.

With a long exhale, I lift my right hand to Paris.

"Must you do it at the king's dinner? It seems so very . . . public."

Paris studies me closely. He has not shared the details of his plan and seems somewhat taken aback that I've put the pieces together on my own. Yet his lips quiver with the desire to spread his sin around, and I have always been a blank wall for his splattered mud. "Hector and Andromache think they are too good to dine at the palace. An entire rainy season might come and go before we have another opportunity. By then, the plague will have passed. It must happen tonight."

"Two pinches dissolved in wine." I gesture to the pouch, willing my hand to remain steady. He must not see my fear. "Measure it with your fingers so you do not add too much."

Paris dismisses my warning with another wave. "I understand."

"This is important, Paris. If you overpour, the effects of the poison will come on too strong and won't resemble sickness. You must be precise."

"A little goes far." Paris nods. "Will it mix the same in all liquids?"

My brows narrow. Hector's household is far from conventional, but I cannot imagine the men would drink anything but wine.

"It will dissolve. But remember, a pinch or two is plenty." *And you must use your hands.* I mimic the motion to reinforce what is left unspoken.

"Pity you won't be there to observe." Paris tosses the leather pouch up in the air, over and over.

Every muscle tenses. Fear, I suddenly recall, has a taste. "What do you mean?"

"You aren't invited. Andromache made that most clear. Not that her mannish ways are ever anything but direct."

Andromache's contorting face as she banished me from the Fair Winds is still fresh. A deep imprint to accompany the more distant memory of her enraged voice the day I pulled back my veil.

"Whore. Your presence has stripped us of everything."

I recall the same voice when we tended to the sick, only it is gentler. Trusting.

"What do you say, Theana?"

There isn't a woman in Troy who has hated me more, yet by some twist of fate, *she* is the woman whose acceptance I crave most.

"It matters little." Paris pulls me back to his perfumed room. "Since Hector refuses to assert control over his wife, the damage is already done. His standing as commander of the army and Troy's heir hangs by a thread. Soon the Old Blood will see the Gorgon who really holds the reins to Hector's chariot."

Why is he telling me this?

It strikes me suddenly that I am the closest thing Paris has to a confidant. He has his admirers, yes, but no true friends. Plenty of toys, yet no lovers. At least none who love him for himself. In that way, we are similar. Two fired-clay faces others long to possess. A flicker of sympathy sparks in my breast.

It is promptly extinguished.

"I can always tell when you're frowning by the arch of your left brow." Paris peels a North African orange with a knife, the rind coming off in one long piece. "It isn't becoming. For one who is otherwise exquisite."

My throat feels parched. I have not stared into the blank darkness of my cup in days. Not since before the plague. I had thought too much rested on my clearheadedness, but now I see that I have been useless to contain both the plague and my husband alike.

Paris puts down his fruit but not the knife. He approaches slowly, laying the cool, flat side of the blade against my throat.

The smile on his face is identical to the one he wore that night. For the first time in all the nights since, the desire to kill Paris with my own hands, by poison or otherwise, stirs.

"When I return, I expect you to be bathed and awake." Paris slides the knife down the front of my robe until the fabric tears. I do not move. I do not breathe.

"The people and the gods," Paris murmurs, as if to himself. "He always said that whoever rules Troy must hold those two routes through her golden gates."

He?

"And you, Helen, are the treasure that will pay my fare."

Before I can ask questions, Paris rips away my veil and presses his lips to mine. The shock of his assault makes me gasp. I shove his myrrh stench back, but Paris's eyes just laugh, mocking me. Exactly as they did that night. Back when my hands brought only life, not death. Back when I could still remember who I was.

Who you are.

"Good. I prefer it when you have a little fight in you." Paris's tongue dances across his lips. "For when has frailty ever borne fruit?"

Tossing his peeled orange into the air, he strides from the room. My body shakes as his footsteps fade, the terror growing stronger even as the echo softens. Paris will visit my bed tonight, and I have no more tincture to make it bearable.

More questions swirl as I search his chamber for something, anything, to dull the rising panic, even if it is simply enough wine to drown the entire Achaean fleet.

Yet there is no way to soften this blow. Paris will poison Hector at the king's dinner, and I will not be there to stop him. Then he will return to use my body in celebration of his triumph.

I close my eyes and wait for the tears to flow, but they don't come. Instead, my eyes snap back open in defiance.

Paris's plan is straightforward enough. Remove Hector from the succession. Sire his own royal son by me or any woman within reach so that Paris might be named heir in his brother's place.

When has frailty ever borne fruit?

And when has unbridled force? I pace the room, in search of something, though I don't yet know what. The nagging sensation is relentless, digging a painful trench behind my eyes.

Minutes pass. Maybe hours.

"The reins to Hector's chariot . . ." I repeat Paris's words as the wind flutters the balcony drapes. But if Hector is not the driver, who else has the ability to secure the succession?

I look down at the pouch of mint and fennel still hidden in my left hand.

Will it mix the same in all liquids?

The shades of all the babes I never bore seem to lurch within me, a united effort to spare one of their own. I should have seen what Paris was planning much, much sooner.

After all, he has done it before.

Paris is too much of a coward to strike his target directly. Instead, he goes through the person they love most. He lies and he manipulates. He makes you lose yourself.

What other choice do you have?

The whisper of some of the first words Paris spoke to me force my feet out onto the balcony. Tears prick my eyes as they search the fiery horizon for a distraction, something that will pull me back from the one memory I've fought so hard to drown. Even when it meant numbing myself to all that remains good in the world.

It is too late.

One long exhale, and she is everywhere. In the golden hour that ushers in twilight, her favorite time of day. In the bag of dried peppermint clutched in my hand, which I drank daily for morning sickness during those months when her irreplaceable life caused me no shortage of torment.

It all resurfaces on the Ilium plain before me—in colors just as vivid, a detailed scene from my tapestry whirling through clouds of dust.

He was *handsome. There was no denying it . . .*

Yet I'd hardly noticed his presence in the palace, even if my serving-women were giddier than usual as they discussed the charismatic prince who'd arrived on a diplomatic mission from Troy. Menelaus left me to my work as a Paeana among Sparta's women and never talked with me about politics or commerce, so I was never forced to feign interest in his greedy schemes. For how could trading treasure ever hope to compare to the cloudy blue of a newborn's gaze?

Iron. Bronze. Gold. It is not the metal but the power it represents that drives men to nearly anything. And it seemed my dowry treasure contained enough power to lay claim to the entire Aegean.

Only the blade Paris pressed to the flesh of my daughter's throat that night did not shimmer. Against his crisp, finely woven tunic it looked dull, almost rusted, the kind of weapon a second-rate assassin used in a brothel back alley.

"What is this?" I demanded when I entered my bedchamber and found a strange man curled around my only child like a snake.

Hermione's eyes widened at the sight of me, her little lungs rising and falling beneath her sheer nightdress. Paris held her in the moonlit doorway of the balcony.

"How did you get in?" The words flew out of my mouth on their own wild wings.

"I have eyes in every corner of the Aegean," he said. Not the last time I heard those words, though I'd felt his eyes upon me from the moment Menelaus

received him as our guest. *"The only thing that concerns you here and now is the choice that you must make."*

"Please," I begged, prepared to drop my gown and go with him if what he wanted was to know if all the rumors were true.

He smirked. *"If only it were that simple."*

If only I had known it wasn't my body or even my gold that he desired, but the chaos that the taking of both would unleash.

"I have a ship ready to depart to Troy. You will board it."

"Why would I do that?"

"Because your dowry treasure is loaded already, and despite your famed face, you are worthless without it." He smiled with vicious satisfaction. *"If you don't come willingly, I can take your daughter for my queen instead."*

"She's a child." My panic swelled as tears poured down Hermione's pale cheeks.

"Lower your voice," Paris hissed, clamping a hand over her mouth. *"If guards come knocking, you'll find you no longer have anything to barter."*

"She isn't even old enough to give you sons."

"She would not be the first child bride. Nor will she be the last."

Who knew this better than me, my father's bidding prize before I'd begun to bleed?

"I'll go."

"Perhaps you have more sense than your reputation suggests." Paris loosened his grip on Hermione. *"But if either of you screams, I can just as easily slit one of your throats while throwing the other from this balcony."*

"I'll go quietly." The entire room grew dark except for the moonbeam dancing across Hermione's face. *"Now release my daughter."*

When he did, she flew straight into my arms. I'll never forget the sweet honey of her hair as she sobbed against my chest, old enough to know she was about to lose her mother forever, yet young enough to still need her desperately.

"It will be all right," I whispered, knowing full well that the only thing right in the world was about to be ripped from us both.

"Be quick about it," Paris ordered as I tucked Hermione into my bed, humming the lullaby that always put her to sleep when she was a babe.

"Listen carefully, my sweet girl. You mustn't cry out until we are gone, otherwise he might hurt me. Can you be brave?"

Hermione nodded, lip quivering. I wiped her tears with my veil and gave her forehead one final kiss. Then I met the dark eyes of a man whose elegant manner and polished speech left his admirers more than willing to be deceived.

And I knew.

He was no prince. He was one of those men who wanted nothing more than to set the world on fire and watch it burn.

Mouth turned up in self-satisfaction, Paris pressed a finger to his lips before leading me to the balcony.

At the sound of Hermione sobbing, every muscle tensed. *"Why bring her into this? You could have easily dragged me to your ship without involving her."*

When Paris's lips stretched into a full smile, I knew that while I had little love for Menelaus, I would anxiously await the day my Spartan husband shoved his spear through this Trojan's neck. If there was one thing Menelaus cared about, it was honor, and there was no greater dishonor than taking another man's woman. Menelaus would not rest until he saw Troy's princeling dead at his feet.

"Why?" Paris sneered. *"Because no matter how the child recounts these events, there is one detail she'll never be able to deny—her mother left this palace willingly and of her own accord."*

"That doesn't matter," I spat, my grief igniting an untapped rage.

"Ah, but it does. There is nothing remotely interesting or even memorable about a man who abducts another man's wife." He paused, as if the source of this notion came from someplace deeper than his own vanity. *"No, I much prefer that when our love story is recounted, the poets will sing of how Paris, prince of Troy, seduced the most beautiful woman in the world."*

Revulsion traveled the entire length of me. *"I will never love you."*

Paris's glistening gaze betrayed the months he'd spent preparing for this moment. *"Fortunately, Queen Helen, I am not in the business of love. I am in the business of war."*

14

RHEA

THE WINE JUG trembles in my hands as I bend over King Priam's gaunt shoulder. Harsar Antenor lifts his brother's cup and takes a discreet sip. It is the same thing he has done with every morsel of food that has passed the old king's lips.

Harsar Antenor waves me away, and I resume my place near the wall, where I can watch the small army of Troy's Old Blood that has invaded Hector and Andromache's hall.

Twenty-nine men. Five women. Five of Priam's legitimate children. Ten high-ranking members of the King's Council. Seven army captains and five priests.

Seventeen. The number of cups I have filled this evening.

Four hundred sixty-two. The new words heard and stowed away in my memory.

Forty-three. The number of times I have already wished to be somewhere, anywhere else.

A loud laugh draws my gaze across the table. Unlike his absent wife, Paris is on full display. He talks even more than he drinks, and he drinks heavily.

His younger brother, Prince Helenus, is seated across from him. A man with a weak chin and pallid complexion that gives the appearance of sickliness. At the far end of the table, Helenus's twin, Harsa Cassandra, sits hunched in her chair, a curtain of dark hair obscuring her features. Bent over the piece of bread in her twisted fingers, the princess resembles an exotic bird. Beautiful despite her strangeness. It's her eyes. The color of amber, they seem to stare not across the room but through it.

Paris raises his two-handled cup, and I rush to refill it. The cloying scent of oranges and myrrh hovers in the air when he speaks. "Let us dispense with the pleasantries. Tell us, brother, to what do we owe the honor of this invitation to your charming home?"

Andromache's eyes flick to me. I nod and quietly take my place against the wall directly behind Paris. From here I am able to see what nobody else can. Though the cup lifts again and again to Paris's mouth, the wine never touches his lips.

Prince Hector clears his throat. "The purpose of this meeting is twofold. First, we would ask the council and the king to move Troy's armies back to our camp outside the walls. Both to press our advantage and to protect our own forces from the sickness that has taken root in the Lower City."

Antenor speaks from his seat beside the king. "What is the latest word from our scouts on the plain?"

"Of the four men we sent toward the Achaean camps, only one returned with his head. Regrettably, not with his tongue." Harsar Aeneas's gray eyes are ringed with shadows from the late nights at his wife's bedside.

"We can't get close enough to the camp to see what is happening inside," Captain Polydamas says from the other end of the table.

"I don't trust it." Harsar Antenor leans back in his chair. "Like their arrows dipped in fire, this quiet is not natural." His lips twist in distaste. "The council feels that to risk an offensive would play right into this latest trap. Better to keep the army behind the shelter of our walls until we divine the meaning of this."

Andromache's nostrils flare, but one look from her husband, and she grits her teeth.

"There is always the possibility of trickery," Aeneas concedes. Tall with sharp, solemn features, Harsar Aeneas is seated in the honored spot at Prince Hector's right side. Both at this table and in the stables, he is Hector's second-in-command, and yet, I notice a distance between the two men that becomes loud in the heavy silences.

"You would distrust milk from the teat of your own mother, Aeneas," Paris says, dismissing his cousin. "However, caution in this case does seem advisable." He runs his finger around the rim of his cup, now miraculously half-empty.

Paris's eyes glint as they drift across the table to Andromache. "After all, there is more to strength than beating one's naked chest like a brute."

"How very true." Andromache's smile is the opposite of friendly. "Knowledge and wisdom count for much. Which brings us to the second reason for this dinner." She focuses her next words on the king and his brother. "Hector and I have ascertained the cause of the Achaeans' weakness and their pyres. I have spent the last few days viewing the truth with my own eyes in the Lower City. This is no trick. It is plague. The Achaeans have it, and now, so do we."

Murmurs sweep the table as the Old Bloods take in this announcement. The only one who does not seem bothered is Paris. He waves his hands in an exaggerated movement that is meant to appear sloppy. I track the cup closely. When it moves below the level of the table, Paris quickly tips the contents to the floor at his feet.

"Impossible," says one of the wives of the council members at the far end of the table.

"You would not think so, Salsani, if you had bothered to answer my call for aid in the Lower City," Andromache says.

"My wife has been caring for the sick," Hector explains.

"Not alone. Helen was there as well," Paris cuts in. "She has a heart for those less fortunate. As do most women who possess the maternal instinct."

I look up and down the table and wonder if the rest of them can see the dagger he has hurled right at Andromache.

"Helen was renowned as a healer among the Spartans," Paris continues. "She did not seem overly concerned about the illness. Perhaps if she had been extended an invitation to this affair, she might have given her opinion herself."

Andromache meets my eyes. We both recognize Paris's brazen lie.

Aeneas's somber voice cuts through the room. "It isn't only the inhabitants of the Lower City who are suffering. Creusa went to care for the sick and now stands with one foot in the Underworld." His glare skewers the far end of the table, where the council members sit with their wives.

"The plague is here, and it will be the end of us if we do not find a way to stop it."

"How certain can you be that it is a plague?" Paris sits up straight, all pretense of drunkenness forgotten as he fixes his attention on Aeneas.

Aeneas meets his gaze. "You are more than welcome to visit your sister and form your own opinions."

Paris leans back, for another moment forgetting to play the drunken fool. Calculation gleams as he glances briefly down the table to the priest, Laocoon, a man whose fine robes speak more of wealth than servitude to any gods. "Plague would be a serious matter indeed." The hand not holding the wine cup taps a rapid tune against the table. "We have not had it within our walls since the Hittite puppet king died. Do our servants of the gods have anything to say on the subject?"

There is a shift in the air. A trap being set. I can't see it, but I can feel it.

"Helenus brought us word of an ill omen yesterday," the priest, Laocoon, intones somberly. "He saw a raven circling the Citadel, a harbinger of death."

Andromache's gaze is sharp. "Is that so?"

"Most disturbing news. Rest assured, my brothers and I have consulted the gods," Laocoon continues.

A terrible noise erupts in the hall. Like the creak of old wood or the howl of a dying animal. The wine jug jerks in my hand when I realize where it is coming from.

Harsa Cassandra.

"The gods . . ." Her voice is a wheeze belonging to a woman ten times her age. "Are not in the habit of revealing their plans to men who make a mockery of them by performing cheap tricks." She stares at her twin through a dark scraggle of hair. "Once, you saw the Truth. But only when Cassandra took pity on you and led you to it by the hand. And then you left her to rot." Cassandra sucks in her lips, smiling without teeth.

Helenus's face turns a sickly shade of yellow.

A cold draft blows through the room, making the oil lamps gutter. "No." The old woman wearing Cassandra's face laughs without humor. "Your birds and your fish bones can't help us now, Helenus. Death is already among us. He sailed over the walls while we were looking the other way." Bloodshot eyes pass over the table to linger on me, sending a chill up my spine.

"Cassandra, please." Priam's voice ends on a quaver.

"Cassandra is not here." The way her lips cover her teeth like gums distorts her words. "Do not speak to me in that tone, for I am older even than you, deaf king. Do you think I don't recognize death's shadow when I see it?"

"Your dinner conversation is illuminating as ever, little sister. It's a wonder Mother and Father keep you all to themselves." In the flickering lamplight, Paris's beauty is razor sharp. "We must remain focused on the issue at hand. If Helenus and our trusted priests are right and this truly is plague, it can only have one cause."

"What do you mean?" The rare emotion on Aeneas's face is one that I too share.

Unease.

"There is only one thing that could move the gods to such wrath." Aware of his audience, Laocoon pauses. "As long as the succession remains in doubt, we are weakened from the inside. Apollo and Yarri are not pleased. Regrettably, it is why the council and I have recommended that the king choose a new heir at the Festival of the Divine Twins. If the matter is not resolved by then, of course."

A death blow of silence falls over the room.

My eyes fly to Andromache. Her bronze face has gone stark white. There is no fight in her. No fire. Only shock. It is perhaps the first time I have witnessed her caught off guard.

"You have agreed to this, Father?" Hector's expression is made of stone, but even so, I can hear the pain grinding between each word.

King Priam does not meet his son's eyes. "I am considering it."

Fury paints Andromache's face as she glares at the priest. "You would come into my home and lay the blame for this sickness at our door?"

"Of course not," Paris scoffs. "It is not your fault that you are . . . struggling to perform your marital duty."

"You of all people would speak to me of duty?"

"Andromache," Hector warns.

A sharp intake of breath. When her dark gaze refocuses on Paris, the fire inside it has cooled. "What you are saying makes no sense."

Paris tilts his ebony head. "Do you doubt the word of our esteemed high priests? Or is it the will of the gods that you question?"

Danger screams at me from that place where I hear the horses whisper.

"I do not question the will of the gods. Merely your interpretation of it. If the gods meant to punish *us,* why make the Achaeans suffer too?"

Paris spreads his hands wide. "Tell us, what proof do you have that the Achaeans had the plague first? Whatever it is, we are eager to hear it."

"The smoking pyres—"

"Are common enough in war," Paris cuts in. "You are grasping at straws when Laocoon and Helenus have their ear to the pulse of Olympus. We must trust in their superior wisdom."

In the silence that follows I can almost hear Andromache's jaw clench.

"It seems Helenus has been divining much lately from the splattering of pigeon droppings," she says.

From my vantage point behind the table, I alone glimpse the gentle hand Hector places on his wife's leg. I will her to heed the warning, but she does no such thing.

"What a shame the gods weren't so eager to reveal their will before you brought Helen of Sparta into our city and the Achaean blight to our gates."

The table falls as silent as it did at Harsa Cassandra's outburst.

Paris's smile is barbed. "I so enjoy our banter, Andromache. Few women are gifted with such wit. In the spirit of fun, I remind you that it could be considered bad sport to evoke the name of a Harsa you did not see fit to invite to your table."

Andromache's nostrils flare. "A bedmate does not a Harsa of Troy make."

"None would know this better than you." Paris nods gravely. "Surely you must miss your clan of warrior women who roam their primitive hillsides in the nude? Tell me, do all Amazons share your contempt of the gods, or is it merely their humble servants that you revile?"

"Enough," Hector says just loud enough to be heard over the wave of nervous laughter sweeping the room. "Regardless of the cause, we must take the necessary step to protect the army from the plague in the Lower City by moving it back outside the walls. Aeneas and I are of one mind about this."

"I have seen this illness up close." Aeneas's deep timbre casts a spell through the hall. "I would risk the Achaeans' tricks before I risked the spread of this blight."

"It is a risk we must take," Hector says, meeting the old king's eye directly in a way that no one else has bothered to do. "The other matters I leave in your hands, but when it comes to Troy's army, I am still commander, chosen by the people to take care of her sons. To do that I must remove our troops from the Lower City where the plague may soon run rampant."

"We need to find another liaison, then." Helenus chimes in quickly while on the subject. "The allies no longer show me the proper respect. Captain Sarpedon has all but refused to fight until he gains his audience with the council. I can't risk sickness or be tied up with such matters when I'm supposed to be divining the will of the gods."

"The selection of a future liaison is a question for another hour." Antenor places a hand on the king's shoulder. The brothers seem to have a discussion without words. "As far as the plague is concerned, you may move the army as you see fit."

"For now the army will camp back outside the walls," King Priam echoes. An afterthought rather than a command.

Andromache's shoulders relax.

Her relief is short-lived.

"On the matter of the succession. We cannot risk losing Apollo's favor." The corners of Antenor's mouth turn down, making him look almost as weary as his twin. "The Festival of the Divine Twins is fast approaching. Our course must be clear by then. As difficult as it may be to let go of our traditions, sometimes change is the only means of preservation."

They will strip Hector of his birthright.

The startled faces around the table confirm it. Along with the smile in Paris's eyes that no cup could hide. Andromache's cheeks go as red as her robe. This time, Hector's hand on her knee is not gentle. Neither is hers as she physically removes his grip. There is a spear at the end of her tongue, and I am suddenly certain that if she launches it, this night will end in blood.

My feet move on their own, bringing me to Prince Paris's side. Slowly, I pour wine into Paris's already full cup, blocking their view of each other.

Pain stabs my arm. Sudden and sharp. The wine jug wobbles in my hands and red liquid sloshes over the rim.

Horror dawns as my eyes move from the welt on my arm—two deep indents in the shape of crescents—to the stain on Harsar Aeneas's tunic.

"This wine is weak, and your servants are clumsy." Paris pays me a dismissive glance. His expression quickly changes to one of calculation when it lingers on my face. "This girl. She is familiar."

I take a hasty step backward. Paris's fingers around my wrist cut short my retreat.

He turns to Hector. "She is the slave you bought when you found the devil himself on four legs. The one they say has the touch of the *assussanni*."

"This is Rhea." Hector leaves it at that.

"*Rhea*, is it?" Paris's scrutiny chafes. "The servant you have given free access to the army's horses? First a woman addressing the King's Council. Now girls in the stables. What next, Hector? Nursemaids on the battlefield? Perhaps we can send Helen."

"This *girl* is the only reason we still have a chariot fleet," Andromache says, surprising no one more than me.

One of Paris's dark brows makes a break for his hairline. "They say she has accomplished in weeks what we haven't managed in a year. I can't help but wonder how such a miracle was possible." He leans toward me. "Is it true then what they say? Can you put animals under your spell? If animals, why not people?" I see the danger in Prince Paris's eyes before his words ring through the hall. "Given the bastion of unruly women Troy has become, it seems the gods have countless reasons to be displeased with us."

The eyes of the Old Bloods weigh heavy on me. Assessing. Judging.

A song of danger sings inside me. There are other forces at work here. Faceless shadows I can't count. Whispered words I can't commit to memory. But I can feel them. And I refuse to stand by silently and let them make me part of their plots.

"I am a horse trainer. My methods come not from magic, but from the lessons my father taught me." Going on instinct, I direct my next words to the head of the table, where Harsar Antenor and King Priam sit. "He came with his sword and his horses to fight for Troy, where he died. Now I honor his memory by serving the city he fought to save."

The beautiful lyre music that has been humming in the background falls silent. I lift my gaze to where Cyrrian is seated in a corner and meet his eyes. Startling this time not because of their color, but because of the flash of respect they radiate. The fire is out as quickly as a flaming arrow shot into sand.

The king and his brother say nothing. No one does. For one agonizing moment, I am certain I've made a terrible mistake.

"Go see to the next course, Rhea," Andromache says at last.

A dismissal. Ducking my chin, I flee the hall as quickly as I can without running.

The sweet air of the courtyard greets me outside.

"Are you all right?"

I turn to find Cyrrian watching me from the kitchen doorway.

"Paris does not take kindly to anyone getting in his way," Cyrrian says. "You have marked yourself as his enemy. It's not a particularly enviable title to hold."

A cold wind runs over me as I rub the bruise on my arm. "You were right. About my presence endangering Hector and Andromache. I didn't see it before, but I do now."

Cyrrian sighs. "You are far from their biggest concern. If Paris and the priests have their way, Hector and Andromache will need all the friends they can get. Lowly as we may be."

"I don't understand. Hector and Andromache put Troy first in everything and are good at everything they do."

"You are operating under the illusion that goodness is rewarded and competence is what makes people love you."

My belly burns. With anger at his presumption or because he might be right? "How can Hector and Andromache live like that?"

"Because they have no other choice. We adapt or we die." Cyrrian shrugs. "There are exceptions, of course. Andromache would rather bend the world around her than change. Aeneas will one day snap those iron bands he places around himself and use them to bludgeon everything in his path. And Hector. Hector is too busy accepting the responsibilities for those around him to have a thought for himself."

"You know them well."

"I should. They're my family."

A cold spreads through my insides. If what he says is true, then I have overstepped my position immensely. "Forgive me, Harsar. I didn't realize you were of the house of Troy."

"It was Cyrrian before, and it's Cyrrian now." He shrugs as if it was nothing when we both know it is everything. "I'm an illegitimate cousin to Priam's sons like half the inhabitants of Troy's innermost ring. But I don't much care for the palace or her rules." That smile again. "Not when they have never cared for me."

My mind rushes to fill in the gaps between his words.

A bastard. It explains his closeness to Prince Hector, but also the distance he keeps from the Old Blood. The distrust must be mutual. Cyrrian has always seemed more comfortable in the company of men who laugh and joke as if he were one of them. And yet when he leaves the stables after a long day of fighting to go wherever it is that he goes, he always does so alone.

It seems I've noticed the young charioteer more than I care to admit.

He studies my face for a moment before nodding toward the kitchen. "Have Bodecca take a look at your arm." Before turning toward the stables, he adds a parting thought. "And, Rhea? With that lot, the greater danger lurks in the words they don't say."

I wait for his outline to fade into the darkness before I walk back into the kitchen.

"All of Troy knows him as Cyrrian of the Two Shadows."

I swivel toward the source of the voice. A girl sitting on a chair by the hearth, her arms wrapped tightly around her knees.

Princess Cassandra.

"Excuse me, Harsa?"

"If you watch closely, you can see her ghost haunting his footsteps. He shows the world the face it can love, but the truth is in his eyes." The hunch is gone, as is the papery rasp of the Crone's voice. Her tone is now a rich alto, drenched in melody. Her eyes are no longer unfocused. Instead, they are clear as tourmaline.

"Are you lost, Harsa?" The way the others treated her at dinner gave the distinct impression that she is not often left alone.

"Lost?" Entire worlds reflect back to me from the golden waters of her irises. "I am always lost, little mouse. Sometimes lost is the safest place to be."

"What . . . what did you call me?"

"Is that not what you are? Scurrying about? Seeing everything and forgetting nothing?" The princess cocks her head. "The time is soon coming, little mouse, when you must set loose the lioness within you. His life depends on it."

"Whose life?" My weight shifts. I don't know if I should go to her or run hard the other way.

"There you are." At the sound of Hector's voice, Cassandra's face transforms again. The sadness and intensity melt away, replaced by a joy that is every bit as unsettling.

"Hector! Hector! Hector!" She launches herself into his arms and wraps her legs around his waist. It's the behavior of someone much younger, and it is almost obscene considering that Hector is a man, her brother, and this young woman is not a child.

He sets her down, smoothing out her gown. "We'd better get you back before Father sends his minions searching."

"I'll go," she answers in a high, whiny voice. "But promise you will take me riding first. Promise me, Hector. *Promise. Promise. Promise!*"

After everything that has happened tonight, Hector still finds a smile. "As soon as I can."

With a flounce of her robes she leaves the kitchen.

Hector watches her go with an expression that causes an ache in my throat. It says he doesn't just have a fondness for unbreakable things, but for broken ones as well.

"Princess Cassandra is kept under strict watch for her own safety. I would appreciate it if you wouldn't tell anyone you had found her down here."

Not a command. A request.

"I won't say a word."

His shoulders relax. "She isn't simple. Despite how she acts or what people say. Sometimes, I believe she is the most perceptive of all of us."

Andromache enters the kitchen in a whirl of red silk. "That did not go as I had hoped."

"At least we got them to agree to move the army," Hector says wearily.

"Of course they agreed," Andromache growls. "It was a concession that cost them nothing. They care as much about the common soldier as they do the Lower City."

"Andromache." Hector casts a glance in my direction.

"Do you really think there is a word spoken in this house that does not reach that one's ears?" Andromache's nostrils flare. "You brought the girl into this when you took her into your stables. A place where she could not be missed. Now she has drawn the attention of our enemies. Ignorance will not protect her, Hector."

The prince of Troy bows his head. My chest tightens at the sight. I want to take his sadness from him. I want to beg him not to regret his choice to trust me, because *I* don't. Instead, I say nothing.

"They granted our request because it is the succession that they are obsessed with," Andromache continues. "And now with the support of the priests, Priam will have no choice but to change it."

"Then let them."

Andromache flinches as if slapped. "You cannot mean that."

"Can't I?" In the space of Hector's shallow breathing, I catch a glimpse of a different man. A soldier who fights for his city and for the thrill of being alive, but never for position or power. Blinking rapidly, Hector releases a sigh, and that simpler man vanishes. He walks toward the door before looking over his shoulder. "I can only wage one war at a time, Andromache." Then he leaves us alone in a kitchen that suddenly feels too small.

Painful silence. I am opening my mouth to break it when a rasp echoes through the room.

Princess Cassandra fills the doorway Hector just left. Bony hands grip the frame as she leans forward, black hair obscuring her features.

Raised voices echo in the hall. Cassandra's head snaps toward them. Her expression is like none I've seen before, and tonight, I've seen several of the Harsa's faces.

"You should not be here," Andromache scolds. "It was no easy task for Hector to convince Hecuba to let you come—"

"A storm is brewing." Cassandra stumbles into the kitchen. Her gaze finds mine, and this time, it is filled not with madness but with genuine *fear*.

"Calm yourself, Cassandra," Andromache warns. "If you carry on like this there will be no more visits. You know how protective your parents can be."

"Protective . . ." The girl's features ripple with a despair so profound, it causes my breath to hitch. "Listen to me. You must *listen*. Not just to the words but to the whispers behind them." The flame of her yellow gaze finds mine again. "Troy will rot from the inside with the same sickness that is taking the Achaeans. You must find its source. By the west wall. Your proof and your salvation."

"Cassandra, if you've seen something, the king—"

"The king is deaf by choice," Cassandra hisses. "There is no help from him. You know this, know it . . ." Her body is racked by a fit of coughs. Suddenly, she is several inches shorter. Back bent over twisted hands. A hundred years she hasn't lived echo in Cassandra's voice. "Take the mouse. If you fail to find the truth, Troy will burn with fever before it ever burns with flame." She hobbles back to the door before glancing over her shoulder. "And, Andromache . . . bring your sword."

"Harsa Cassandra is unwell," Andromache says in the echoing absence. "As long as I've known her, she has been not one, but five different people trapped in a single body. Always with Hector it is the Child. With me, there are others." The corners of her mouth sag. "They say the faces came with the visions. Helenus was gifted with divination. And to Cassandra the gods bestowed madness."

"She seemed frightened," I say. "Would it not be better to tell the—"

"No!" Andromache turns on me swiftly. "The king and queen guard her carefully in her tower. The young woman's life is already a torment. We will not risk what little freedom she has for the sake of these delusions. Is that understood?"

"Yes, Harsa."

Andromache's skirts rustle, the beads on the ends of her robes making soft music as she walks toward me. "I meant what I said to my husband. You are part of this now, whether or not we want you to be. As you seem to be collecting this family's secrets, I suggest you do yourself a kindness. Guard them well."

She searches the kitchen for something, eyes landing on a small brown pouch sitting on Bodecca's workspace. A pot bubbles on the fire beside it. Andromache leans over the liquid, breathing in its earthy steam. Even from where I stand, the smell of boiled dirt is overpowering. She coughs. "You would think I would become used to the stench, but it seems to be getting worse, while its former pleasures are weakening."

She stares into the pot with a frown. "I forgot to ask Bodecca to prepare the tea, but it seems she has taken matters into her own hands." A strong smell wafts toward me again and my stomach pitches.

Shadows move in the corner of my vision. The sound of low laughter from the courtyard beyond the kitchen door. I am moving toward it when Andromache speaks.

"Come, Rhea. Troy's Old Blood do not like to be kept waiting."

The atmosphere in the hall is still tense when we return. Andromache regains her seat but does not touch her plate.

As soon as she sits, Paris raises his cup. "I propose a toast to our hostess. To the end of this war, and gods willing, a new heir. Perhaps that is what we should drink to." Paris smiles. "The will of the gods."

"I couldn't agree more," Andromache says. "Rhea, will you pour my tea?"

Something unsettling whispers over me. Despite Andromache's clear command, my feet won't move.

"There is no need." Paris hands her a cup of steaming liquid. It is only then that I notice the raised red marks on his hands. "To the gods and their infinite justice."

Andromache studies Paris carefully. Steeling herself, she lifts the cup to her lips.

15

HELEN

I WATCH FROM my balcony as a lone bird makes circles across the darkening horizon. Every minute that passes feels like a lifetime while I wait for the arrival of dark. I try to keep busy at the loom, but my shaking fingers can't grasp the threads.

What can I do?

The only answers I receive are my own tangled memories and knotted thoughts.

When the sun is submerged in the sea, I put on my veil. The royal family will have reached Hector's house, and the wine will be flowing. Since the poison won't take an immediate effect, I cannot imagine Paris will wait long to make his move.

I consider taking to the streets before it is completely dark, yet memories of Andromache's fertility rite force me to sit with the uncertainty a while longer. I cannot risk being seen.

When the last traces of daylight are gone, I move through the palace halls, across the courtyards, and toward the Dardanian gate. Five soldiers stand guard, their gazes fixed on external threats. I pray they'll pay no mind to a lone woman going the other way.

I've never left the Citadel on my own. At least not as myself, unmasked. My veil isn't enough to suppress my identity, merely the acute reactions to it. Heart pounding, a river of sweat cascades down my neck, yet I walk toward the gate as if I have every right to be there. The guards glance my way, but none make a move to stop me. I *am* a Harsa of Troy, no matter what Andromache claims.

Eyes fixed, I maintain my course until my feet round the corner. Only then do I press my back against the wall and remind myself to breathe.

For a few inhales, I wait for the trembling in my hands to cease. It is a new sensation, caused not by poppies but by my own liquid fear. Slow, deep breaths lessen its flow. I follow the Citadel's outer wall all the way to the west side of the city, where the training grounds lie. It's easy enough to spot Hector's house, though I have never been inside. The sturdy structure is modest and close to the horses and the army. Just like its master.

A handful of armed men stand in a ring outside the front door. The black stallions on their shields identify them as the king's personal guard. If I recognize them, they will surely recognize me. At the very least, someone will summon Paris, who'll have little difficulty determining why I am here.

If I am not too late already.

Two soldiers walk by with a small cart covered in animal hides. They take a narrow alleyway to the left of the house. I slip in behind them. The alley spills out into a courtyard that separates the house from the training grounds. The smell of lemons and verbena follows me, along with the bubbling of a fountain spring. I'm moving toward the side door that must lead into the kitchen when I notice a pair of shadows lurking on the threshold. Despite the darkness, I recognize them easily enough.

Aethra and Clymene.

I draw myself back behind the stone fountain. If my servingwomen are here, it can only be because Paris ordered them to come. I've long suspected they were more his servants than mine. Yet there is no other way in.

I step out of the shadows and meet two matching sets of almond eyes.

"Harsa Helen." Clymene looks as if I've caught her with my husband. Again. "What are you doing here?" Her confidence takes me by surprise, for it is new. As new as the growing roundness of her breasts and her ever-rosy cheeks.

I study her face anew. Pretty. Young. Certainly guilty of something. "I've come to join Paris as his Harsa."

"But you were not invited," the younger woman points out.

The mother pulls her daughter in close, wisely choosing to bow her head in deference to my status. "We only mean that you would not wish to cause a scene. Prince Paris wouldn't be pleased."

"Yes, he wouldn't like it at all," says Clymene, confirmation that she knows enough of his plans to make her dangerous. I'm sure Paris pontificates from his pillow often enough.

My shoulders pull back. "I'll see for myself. Andromache may have changed her mind."

"Your nerves are frayed, Harsa," says Clymene, her tone firmer than before. "Go home to your tonic."

The words sting, but not because of the thinly veiled insult. These two women, daughters of a family that has served the Old Blood for generations, clearly view themselves as my wet nurses. They expect me to back down, to return to my old ways of coping.

"You are surely right," I say timidly, drawing near. "Yet allow me to rest a moment and catch my breath."

Thinking me oblivious to the smirk that passes between them, mother and daughter part to create room for me on the stoop. As soon as there's a gap, I dart past them, slamming the kitchen door and securing the iron lock.

Pounding commences. At the hearth, Bodecca barks, "What's this?"

I don't stop long enough to answer. I sprint through the kitchen, chasing the river of raised voices, straight into the hall.

One sweep of the room reveals a dozen reactions. The disapproving glare of Apollo's priest at my interruption. The frown crease between Hector's thick brows. The shock twisting Paris's mouth. The eerie smile on Cassandra's lips.

I ignore them all and focus on the other person at the table's head. Andromache. The cup in her hand on its way to her lips.

"NO!" I am halfway across the room before the guttural cry has left my mouth.

No one sees the flash of my white arm until it is too late.

The cup soars over the table, landing in the center of the hall. Its contents seep into the dirt floor and vanish. There is no bubbling or foam. The poison is just gone, and with it, all proof.

Unless . . .

I look up, searching for Paris's hands. Willing the mark of his deceit. What I find instead is the hard ground as Andromache pushes me away from her. The room goes black. Then red as my ears ring. All the faces at the table blur together as everything around me swirls.

"I thought I made myself clear." Andromache's voice shakes with fury above me. "You are not welcome here."

The spinning stops. A single hand, strong yet gentle, wraps around my waist, pulling me back to my feet. Hector's presence at my side is a wall of solid warmth. "Deep breaths, Helen." The command is both tender and impossible to deny.

The ground becomes solid once more. I look up at Hector, but his gaze is focused on where his wife stands watching us like two strangers.

Hector's grip stays firm on my waist. Though he does not say a word, his actions on my behalf are the worst kind of rebuke. One that Troy's Old Blood was here to witness.

I part my lips to speak, but a hand clamps over my mouth, drawing me away from Hector. The stench of decaying flesh overtakes the warm smell of hay.

I struggle to break free, until I feel a needlelike blade at the base of my spine. "Forgive my wife. Even after all this time, she finds the customs of Troy strange."

"Customs such as common decency?" says Andromache flatly, though her chest still rises and falls.

"You forget she was once a queen." I can hear the ragged edge of Paris's rage, even as he defends me. Insulting his wife is a pleasure that belongs to him alone. "It's difficult for such a woman to be upstaged."

"And so she endeavors to steal my honor every chance she gets."

I try to speak, try to tell them about the poison, but the festering hand over my mouth tightens. We are nearly to the door.

"I don't have to tell *you* about the vanity of the Achaeans, sister. You can take the girl out of Sparta . . ." Paris trails off.

"Just get her out of my sight," Andromache demands, seething.

King Priam shifts forward as if he too would come to my aid if only his body would allow it. "Andromache, this is not behavior fitting of a Harsa of Troy."

"Forgive me, my king. But this is my husband's table." Andromache's wrath simmers as she glares first at me, then at Hector. "And I'd like the woman who has brought death to our gates for too many years to leave it."

The last thing I see before Paris drags me out the door is Cassandra. She looks at me and raises a pair of red hands, dripping with wine, though wine is not what it looks like.

A shudder passes through me.

She smiles. Gleefully.

Like she has a secret.

Paris hustles me through the kitchen. Rhea looks up from her crouched position by the hearth. I try to scream again. Bodecca's pale eyes scrape over me as if they would peel the skin from my bones.

Outside, Paris releases my mouth. He grabs a fistful of hair, his needle sword pressing deeper until it almost breaks skin. When we're a few steps from the house, he releases a long, low laugh. "Well. I suppose I should have seen that coming. Bitch that you are."

I raise a hand to my tingling lips. The residue of poison left behind on Paris's fingers is stronger than I imagined. If Andromache had taken even one sip . . .

Paris studies the eyes above my veil as if he's seeing them for the first time. "You really are a strange creature. Our entire army would die happily at the tip of Achilles's spear if my brother commanded it, yet you are the one person in Troy who prefers his harpy. Even if she loathes you most of all." The needle's pressure lessens as his shoulders round. "Andromache does not deserve your loyalty. I am the only one who cares for you."

My body stiffens at this strangest of lies, one he wholeheartedly believes. "She could be with child," I say simply.

Paris shakes his head. "Silly of me to forget your great weakness." His hot breath hisses in my ear. "Unfortunately, *wife*, killing any child she might carry was the entire point."

Like a flailing animal dragged to the altar, I throw my weight against the courtyard wall. The urge to run is overwhelming, but Paris is far from done.

"And then I'm forced to watch my brickheaded brother put his paws all over you. As if he had a right to touch what was *mine*."

"Helping a woman off the floor was once considered a courtesy." The excuse feels feeble as it leaves my lips.

"You are truly an idiot if you believe that," Paris snaps. "He meant to show every Trojan who matters that he can care for my wife better than I can." Paris drags me down an abandoned street toward the Citadel. I can see his twisted mind whirling tighter with every step. "Fortunately, Hector showed his underbelly tonight. He'd have us believe otherwise, but my brother is only a man. Susceptible to the same weaknesses as any other."

The sudden hitch in Paris's stride has me stumbling.

Pressing me against a high wall, he grips both of my hands with a feigned tenderness that masks the violence building beneath the serene surface. "Calm yourself. We don't want to make a scene and incite more rumors, do we?"

"I will scream. I will tell them everything."

Paris laughs. "Tell who? The woman who just threw you to the ground in front of guests in her own home? There isn't a soul in Troy who will believe anything you say."

"Then why drag me from them as if they might?"

He snickers in the dark, his hands twin serpents strangling my wrists. "Your tender heart nearly cost me the throne, but I know you could not help yourself." Paris pauses as if to catch his breath, though in the moonlight, I see the sharp glint that overtakes his eyes. "In fact, I will give you an opportunity to make things right."

"What do you mean?" I ask, more carefully this time.

"Hermione." Paris's slow smile spreads like poison. "I've received word she's getting married."

The buried wound breaks open at the mere sound of her name, the agony as fresh as the day Paris tore her from my arms.

Hermione . . .

The thing no one tells you about birthing children is you lose them gradually. Over and over, from the moment they first nestle into the crook of your arm. The ever-present pain of the loss is a part of the joy.

"Married? To whom?"

"The gods appear to have a sense of humor. She will wed Neoptolemus. Son of the infamous Achilles."

The ground beneath my feet rises like a wave. My daughter is to marry the offspring of the world's most proficient killer, a swift-footed monster who'd never show mercy should he take this city. Why would I assume his boy is any kinder?

"How can you know this?"

Paris shakes his head. "How many times must I say it before you'll believe that I have hired eyes everywhere?"

Eyes that share faces with mouths he has fed well in exchange for information. With my gold.

Something inside me sinks. I may be guilty of mixing poison that has sent a hundred men to the Underworld, but that is not my most tragic folly. My greatest weakness is my hope.

Hope that I might protect her. Hope that I might see her again.

And Paris knew it all along. Now, he will use that hope against me.

I take a step back, regretting that I did not tell someone, anyone, about Paris sooner. All the secrets kept for her sake, the evil deeds done to keep her safe, the words choked down so I might one day hold her again. They have all been for nothing.

If Hermione is sent from Sparta, we will never meet again. Not in this life.

I fall to my knees.

"She will be married in Phthia, the land ruled by Achilles's father." Paris stands over my crumpled form like there's no position he prefers more. He crouches down, lifts my trembling chin, and peers into my eyes with such benevolence, it almost looks sincere in the fickle moonlight. "How would you like to attend the wedding, my love?"

All the air leaves my lungs.

"Your presence must go unannounced, of course." He releases my face with a harsh shove. "But thankfully, the Sea Peoples who now dominate the Aegean in the convenient absence of your countrymen are old friends. They would provide us with a safe passage, though the ship I sent you on would be guarded heavily—don't think for a moment this is an opportunity to escape. Regardless, no matter how this war ends, you'd have a chance to see your child one last time. It's what I always promised for your silence, is it not?" Paris turns to me with a look of grandiosity that he alone is delusional enough to believe. "I am nothing if not a man who keeps his word."

I rise to my feet, wiping streams of salt from my cheeks. I am not the same woman who stepped onto that ship in Sparta. I may not know who *I* am, but I know him. And this is what Paris does. He figures out what people want and he uses it against them. It was enough to purchase my silence for nine long years.

"Why would you go through the trouble?" I ask, stalling him. For such a generous act makes no sense unless there's something in it for him.

Paris sighs. "I have been shortsighted. Too focused on safeguarding this city from our external enemies instead of those within Troy who are leading her to ruin."

We both know this could not be further from the truth. Yet I continue staring blankly ahead.

"This is something I must correct," Paris continues. "I meant what I said. I will let you see Hermione before you lose her to the house of Achilles."

The bait cast, I wait for the sharp stab of the hook. "But . . ."

"*But* you must first do what your face has always promised and your body has never delivered." Each degree of Paris's smile is a blade dragged across my skin. "Seduce my brother. Take Hector into your bed and make it so he never wants to leave."

Horror and relief flood me at once. "Why?"

In the breath that passes, I find I already know the answer, for I caught a glimpse of it in those two skewers the priest Laocoon calls eyes.

Because the time Hector and Andromache have left is nearly up.

"His shrew-wife needs to learn a lesson. Besides, my poor brother deserves to know what it's like to lie with a real woman who not only looks the part but is its paragon."

I clench my fists. "Andromache does not deserve this."

Paris rolls his eyes. "She is a heartless hag who scorns your help each time you offer it. And don't think I haven't noticed the way you look at Hector." His words carry a dangerous timbre.

"What you saw is my respect."

Paris snorts. "With women, the distance from respect to desire is hardly a step."

How a man like him would gain such an insight is beyond me. But then a deeper understanding dawns.

The slight twitch of his lips. The torment behind his razor-sharp glare. Paris is desperate. He started this war because of his deal with the Sea

Peoples, bands of masked pirates in gray ships who've been wreaking havoc from Mycenae and Crete all the way to the Nile Delta. If the marauders provided him with the only safe trading route to Troy, keeping the Citadel rich in exotic goods, Paris would draw the entire Achaean navy to his shores to fight an unwinnable war. Of course, Paris also hoped Hector would die on the battlefield, clearing his path to the throne. But since that ambition never materialized, he has now attempted a more duplicitous attack against Andromache.

Only I ruined it, and as long as there is a possibility that Andromache and Hector might yet have a son, Paris's position remains tenuous. All his plots to bring down Hector without violating the Law of Bound Blood have failed, but he has this final move to play.

I am still the one thing he possesses that his brother does not.

A wife he can control, a woman whose beauty can be sharpened into a weapon. I am the final brick Paris would wedge between Hector and Andromache.

"If you refuse, I could just as easily have an assassin target your daughter with one of your carefully crafted arrows," Paris adds. "Wouldn't that be a wedding to remember?"

The breath snags in my lungs.

He could be bluffing. Harming Hermione gains him nothing, and Paris surely knows it would mean losing his hold on me.

Without wanting to, I imagine Hermione's face as it must look now. A young woman at the peak of loveliness, her whole life ahead of her. My eyes squeeze out the vision, but I manage to hold back my tears. Does she still hum those little songs in her sleep? Does her laugh still carry enough life force to shake a cornerstone? Does Achilles's son realize how the gods have blessed him?

Paris waits for my consent. My complicity. *Again.* I am as powerless to stop him now as I was then. Stripped of choices and allies. Abandoned even by the god I devoted myself to in a life I'd hardly recognize now.

My hands vibrate. For the first time since they tended the sick at the Fair Winds, I long for one thing and one thing only.

Grasping for something, anything, to keep me planted *here*, I send up the question, though I do not expect an answer.

What must I do?

My own heartbeat is an echo rattling around my skull. All I know for certain is this:

I am no match for Paris on my own.

His captivity is more crippling than my tincture ever was. It is time to put the cup down once and for all, so I might pick up something else.

I need help.

16

ANDROMACHE

"OFF WITH YOU. See to your husband before he leaves to attend his army." Bodecca adds a platter to the tray before lifting the tower of clay bowls like a woman half her age. "How will the servants react if they see their mistress clearing the table of her own dinner party?"

"Perhaps they'll think it right that I clean up my messes," I mutter, eyes on the dark patch of dirt in the middle of the hall.

Some stains are not so easily scrubbed out.

Whatever the consequences of the words said here tonight, the tightness in my chest promises they cannot be undone. It isn't even that Laocoon and his supporters blame me. Or that Paris blames me.

It's that I worry they might be right.

I have fought too hard to keep a firm grip on myself. It's a secret I am only starting to admit to myself and would never dare say aloud.

So, is my barrenness a curse? A punishment for having too strong a will?

Will Hector now suffer because of me?

The image of him holding Helen with such care grates. I shiver in spite of the heat.

"A good splash of vinegar should remove the spot," Bodecca observes, joining me. "Past resentments, however, are another matter."

I look down at the stout woman and meet the arched wisp of an eyebrow.

"She insulted me in my own home." Though what Helen of Sparta hoped to accomplish is a mystery to rival that of the gods. Why invite the punishment? Unless she *wanted* Hector to come to her aid. "You would defend her to my face?"

Bodecca's nostrils flare. "Hardly. It is you who concerns me." Her mouth turns down at the corners. "Don't let your hatred prevent you from seeing the dangers at your back."

Hector has said the same often enough. It's the soldier blinded by rage who fails to see the spear flying over his shoulder.

My memory circles back to the disastrous dinner. If I'm being honest, I glimpsed no malice in Helen's eyes when she struck the cup away. No desire to humiliate me, yet again, in front of the King's Council.

I glimpsed only fear.

It skitters up my spine now. I retrieve the pummeled cup and set it on Bodecca's tray, mind churning over all that happened here tonight. Paris's drunken insults. The blame of Apollo's priests. Cassandra's vague riddles and empty ramblings.

By the west wall. Your proof and your salvation.

Why mention that wall specifically? The place where our most external defenses, those encompassing even the Lower City, meet the internal walls separating Troy's rings is by far our weakest. It's a truth not widely known, but Hector has admitted that he worries the Achaeans might one day discover this vulnerability.

Perhaps they have already.

Your proof . . .

What could Cassandra have meant? Proof that I am right about the sickness? Paris's smug face at the dinner works its way into my mind. He fought so hard against any word I uttered. If there was ever any doubt he is behind the rumors on the collective tongue of Troy, I am certain of it now. Paris and his spineless brother Helenus are surely the ones stoking the divisions on the council. After all, it is Paris who has the most to gain if the succession is changed.

There are days I believe our task would be simpler if we adopted the merciless strategy employed in the lands surrounding Mount Placos and in the Hittite realm. Whenever an Anatolian king wished to guarantee his position, he eliminated all siblings who might attempt to take his throne.

It's a custom as old as the gods, and the reason King Priam's predecessors instituted the Law of Bound Blood. That law alone has made Troy's succession much more stable than her rivals and the city richer too, but has it made her stronger?

Troy will burn with fever before it ever burns with flame.

Alone in the kitchen, Cassandra spoke with a force I've rarely seen. An ancient wisdom had filled her eyes, and for the briefest flash, she revealed herself as the woman she might actually be, buried beneath neglect and the five faces who help her endure this world. A Harsa of Troy, perceptive and powerful. But as with any gift, when the Sight isn't granted room to stretch its wings, it becomes a blade turned inward. A decay that rots from the inside out.

I shake my head at all Cassandra might have been. Priam and Hecuba have poisoned their own daughter's mind by locking her away.

But do *I* see the face that is true?

When it comes to his sister, Hector tries to. He and Aeneas made for the Lower City as soon as everyone left the dinner. By now, they're moving Troy's army back outside the walls—the night's sole victory. It's no easy task to move that many men and all of the things that accompany them. But when they do, the western wall will sit unguarded. Briefly.

My chin lifts to the moon, willing it to rise faster. Hector has enough worries without adding his sister's ramblings. Still, in the unlikely event that Cassandra's warning is warranted, I may need help to deal with whatever I find there.

But who is left that I might count on?

Take the mouse.

A tray of pottery crashes to the floor. Bodecca's round backside is gone, replaced by Rhea's slight form. It's a good thing she also sits low to the ground—despite her clumsiness, not a single bowl stacked on the tray has broken.

"You did well tonight."

Rhea raises her eyes, then lowers them quickly. "Harsa?"

"What you said to Paris about it not being horse magic, but the lessons your father taught you. That was smart." I hold the girl's gaze. This time, she holds mine back. "Paris meant to trap you with your own pride, but you would not let him." I glance at the small blade I always wear on my left hip, a gift from King Eetion on my wedding day. "I also learned much from my father. He respected the gods of his ancestors, but he never claimed to fully understand their mysterious ways. Instead of hurling stones of certainty at innocents whenever trouble visited our gates, he first looked for a simpler cause behind our woes."

"Is this about Harsa Cassandra? The things she said?" There is fear in Rhea's eyes, but unless I am mistaken, it isn't merely for herself.

"Yes." I wonder if Cassandra can see us now from that faraway place where her third eye resides. "Our horseback riding will have to wait. I think perhaps it's time for a different lesson." I pause in the long corridor beyond the dining hall, where several weapons hang on the wall, waiting for Rhea to follow.

"What kind of lesson?" asks the girl.

I choose my weapons as carefully as I choose my words. "I will not lie to you, Rhea. When you first came here, I resented you. Perhaps I even envied you."

Surprise paints her features. It lasts a breath before she notices the object in my hand. A knife. One I've worn on my right hip since Queen Penthesilea gifted it in my twelfth year soon after my moon blood appeared. The blade resembles a leaf. One side straight. The other elegantly curved to a deadly point.

Rhea looks like she's wondering if I'm about to reward her or slit her throat. The desire to laugh rises up. Knowing that would terrify the girl completely, I keep my expression calm. "It occurs to me that it's within my power to atone for my past mistakes by rewarding your loyalty."

"Reward?" Her hands shake. But as when she faced off against Paris, she holds her ground.

This time, I cannot help the small smile that cuts across my face. "I'm prepared to spare your horses from taking part in this war."

"Ishtar and Carris?" She offers their names as one would speak of loved ones.

"If that's what they are called." I shrug. "I will have Hector keep them far from the plain."

"You would do this for me?" The tremble in the girl's hands works its way into her voice. "Why?"

Brave and clever. This night may well require both.

"Contrary to what you may have heard, I am not unfeeling. I honor loyalty above all things, and I give mine where it's earned." I hold her gaze. "You heard Cassandra's warning. What we're about to undertake could be a fool's errand, or it might hold hidden danger. Either way, it must be attended to with no one the wiser. Can I trust you?"

Rhea needs no deliberation. "Yes."

"Then your horses are safe." I let this linger before I tell her what she will not want to hear. "Your work in the stables has aided Troy greatly, but after tonight's spectacle, it will be safer for all of us if you were to keep your distance for a while."

"I understand."

I nod, pleased. Young as she is, the girl seems to recognize the danger closing in around us. She must also realize there's a price to pay for my favor. "My husband and I have many enemies. Now that you belong to our family, our enemies will become yours."

Pink rises in Rhea's cheeks.

Her contentment at being claimed stirs an old longing, but I stomp down the ache and lead her into the courtyard. At the small fountain in the center of the lemon trees, I turn to face Rhea in the moonlight.

My feet slide until they are shoulder width apart. "It will take Hector and Aeneas some time to move their men out of the Lower City. We cannot move until the streets are clear, which makes this as good a moment as we are likely to get." I lift my chin. "Come closer."

Having committed to her path, the girl walks without hesitation.

I place Queen Penthesilea's knife in her hand and close her fingers around it. "This blade is sharp not just at the tip but on one side as well. Weapons for women must be versatile. For so too are the threats facing us." I adjust her grip. "You are strong for your size. This will come as a surprise to any foe, but it will gain you only a brief advantage. Fight only as a last resort. And if you ever pull this blade, be prepared to use it."

"I don't know how—"

"Like this." I cover her hand with mine and guide her body through a series of simple motions.

One. Two. *Dodge.* Three. Four. *Thrust.*

Again and again until sweat beads on her brow.

"I can teach you the basic forms," I say, taking a step backward, "but it will be up to you to practice until they become second nature. One day your life may depend on it."

Rhea squares her shoulders and goes through the movements again.

One. Two. *Dodge.* Three. Four. *Thrust.*

Her recall of the movements is perfect, but her form is another matter. "Speak the steps out loud. It will help." It certainly can't hurt.

The weapon wobbles in her fist as she swings the blade first left, then right. "One. Two. *Dodge*—" She makes a clumsy movement and nearly takes out her own eye in the process.

Perhaps I've finally found something at which Hector's protégé does not excel.

"You hold that knife as if you're afraid it will rear up and bite you."

"You sit on a horse as if you are afraid of the very same thing."

Her quick response startles a laugh out of me. The sound is a sharp bark in the night. Rhea smiles, and it does something remarkable to her face. It transforms it from something strange into something strangely . . . beautiful. I see a flash of the woman this girl might become, if she's given the chance.

"We are both a bit right." I grin and wave her forward, taking the blade from her hand. "I'll give you a strap and sheath so you can keep this under your robes. Never be without it. I've carried not one, but two blades for most of my life. I still practice with them every morning while Hector races the wind around Troy's walls."

I toss the knife in my hand and catch it neatly out of the air, offering it to her again.

The awe on her face reflects back to me the memory of another girl. Another life.

"Where did you learn to do this?" she asks quietly.

I close my eyes against the desires it feels like a betrayal to long for still. The feeling of being honored for my strength. Respected for my mind and its strategies. Revered for reasons that have nothing to do with being a vessel for others to fill—and then blamed when the waters do not rise.

"I was reared by warrior queens."

"I am not a warrior." Rhea lowers her gaze.

I grab her chin. "That was the first lesson the Amazons taught me." My grip is not gentle, but then neither is the world. "Every woman is a warrior. By the very nature of her birth."

Rhea nods. I follow her eyes to Arma's moon. Its height in the sky says we have waited long enough. The army should be out of the city by now, so this is our chance. Though what that chance is or what we may find at the western wall remains as opaque as the night.

We slip through the alley that connects our courtyard to the streets of the Merchant Quarter. The internal gates leading down from one circle of Troy to the next are staggered, and so we must first move east in order to go west. Unlike those below it, the lanes in Troy's second innermost ring are wide and paved with stone. Stately homes rise over the streets, mudbrick layered over rock foundations, with muraled alleyways hinting at secret courtyards where veiled women lounge. The wealth in this part of the city comes not from old bloodlines but from trade and calloused hands grasping for the heart of Troy.

I hasten my steps, giving the Dardanian gate a wide berth. The chances are slim that anyone will be leaving the Citadel at this hour. Even so, I cannot risk being seen. Signaling Rhea to stay close, I cut southeast through the gently sloping streets and make for the smaller gate connecting Troy's Merchant Quarter to that of her many craftsmen. The acrid smoke of forges and the sharp tang of curing leather greet us on the other side. Paved stones give way to packed earth lined with workshops run by the artisans who live above them. The numbers here have swollen with the influx of farmers and fishermen seeking refuge from the Achaeans—a fact most obvious where the leaking clay pipes running along the streets suggest that Troy's drainage system is struggling to keep pace with the demand.

It takes us another ten minutes to reach the gate leading into the Lower City. Unlike the others, this gate is guarded by men whose primary task is to keep the lowliest in Troy from straying where they are not wanted. The changes wrought by war are somehow even starker in the dark. Hastily built houses lurk in shadowed alleyways. Brittle choruses of drunken laughter are pierced by the soft cries of children behind slipshod walls. There are too many people and not enough room. The rancid smell is overwhelming. More unsettling than sewage. It is the smell of desperation.

Few things are as dangerous.

My eyes search the alleyways for hidden threats as I grab Rhea's arm and move toward Troy's western wall. It is the section that lies closest to the Scamander plain, and so it is the most easily reached from the Achaean camps on the beaches of Sigeum Ridge. Thanks to Cassandra, it is also the target for our search.

Stepping into the shadows, I remove my father's dagger with my right hand and tighten my grip on one of Hector's spears with the other. Rhea doesn't speak as we make our way through the sleeping streets. Farther away from the bustling taverns, they are eerily silent out of fear of the sickness.

"What are we looking for?" Her voice sounds disembodied in the dark.

"I don't know." I grip the hilt of my blade, feeling half-ridiculous and half-glad to be doing *something.* "Let's hope we recognize it when it comes out to meet us."

We approach the west wall of Cassandra's ramblings, where a foul smell reaches us on the wind. A single oil streetlamp hangs high from a pole. The solitary bit of light in all this dense black tar.

The stench grows stronger with every step. I look down at the waste trough running along the inside of the wall.

"There's nothing here but shit." I drop my blade, defeated in spite of myself. I don't know why I expected otherwise.

"Where does that leave us?" Rhea asks.

The conversation at tonight's dinner echoes in my head. Cutting compliments and thinly veiled threats. My jaw clenches. "In a dangerous position."

I start to walk away from the wall, but Rhea does not run to keep up. Instead, she lingers.

"It isn't safe here, Rhea."

"That smell . . ." Her words trail off into the sound of faintly dripping water.

"It's the city's waste." I spare the trough a quick glance. "That entails all manner of things."

"No." She shakes her head. "I've come this way before. It was not this bad then."

I watch the girl's eyes, zipping around as she takes in everything, moving like a creature used to scuttling around, unseen.

I hold myself still and resist the urge to question.

She walks back toward the trench. I follow, and together we peer over the edge. Together, we recoil.

The trough is filled with dead, bloated rats, submerged in a murky bath that burns my nostrils. I fight the urge to gag. Rhea scans the trench, the furrow in her brow deepening.

Noise echoes from an alleyway to our right. I swivel toward it, spear raised. When no threat emerges, I lift my gaze to the rising moon.

We need to get back to the house before Hector does. "It's past time to go, Rhea."

"But there are so many." The words are almost a whisper.

I do not bother to turn around. "Troy would hardly qualify as a city if there weren't rats."

"Yes, but why are they all *here*?" Rhea's voice gains strength, making me pause.

I turn, frowning down at a collection of rat bodies toward the back of the trench. That mass, I realize, is moving.

I didn't notice right away because the vermin swarm beneath a molding blanket. The stained material undulates with the steady movements of the creatures it hides. I notice a glint of metal just beneath the edge of the woven fabric.

Gripping my spear, I lean forward and catch the edge of the blanket with the tip. One quick jerk is sufficient.

Rhea makes a choked sound before she heaves up her dinner on the stones. I barely manage to choke down my own as I stare at the source of the foulest smell.

A body.

Half rotted and nibbled away, but not so much that the armor does not reveal it for what it is.

An Achaean. An enemy.

Inside Troy's walls.

My eyes focus on the red rash at the man's neck, and all my rage from tonight's dinner forges together in a single lightning bolt. I heave Hector's spear at the warrior's bloated, one-eyed face. When it lands, rats scatter in every direction.

Your proof and your salvation.

Cassandra may be mad, but at least one of the faces crouching inside her wishes to save the city that's made her such a laughingstock. This corpse proves it.

More importantly, it is proof that *I was right.*

"The s-sickness . . ." Rhea stutters, putting the pieces together. "It isn't a punishment from the gods. It is coming from *here.*"

"Yes," I say. "And that is no accident." I rip my spear free and use it to drag out the helmet also hiding under the blanket.

One made of leather and boar's tusks with an Ithacan crest.

Rhea's chin jerks toward the wall. Though weakest in this portion of the city, it is still difficult to climb. But if multiple men hoisted a single body over . . .

Only how did they even get close enough to try? We have lookout soldiers positioned on every rampart.

Understanding is a wave that crashes over Rhea's face. "What kind of monster would do this?"

I eye the dead warrior's helmet again. "Not a monster. A man. One who is as tired of this war as we are. And clever enough to find his own ways to end it."

"Odysseus," she says.

The mere utterance of his name sends a shudder through me. Of all the Achaean kings, I fear Odysseus most. Even more so than the swift-footed Myrmidon who hunts Hector's steps.

"His cunning is his greatest weapon. One that makes his men fight differently than the rest."

"How so?"

"Their approach is more . . . intentional."

Our gazes drift back to the bloated body in the trench.

"You have to tell the council. Show them where the blame for this truly lies."

Oh, I intend to. "In good time, Rhea." Before we turn our attention to the rot inside the Citadel, we must first banish this sickness from the Lower City.

I glance around the alley, eyes locking on an overturned cart used for hauling waste and rotting vegetables to this trench.

"Help me flip the cart over. We'll need to haul the body to the west gate so the guards can burn him outside it. But first . . ."

Rhea follows my gaze, which chases the rats as they scurry up and down the street.

"They are four-legged soldiers of the war god Yarri, carrying this corpse's plague-ridden flesh everywhere." Clutching my spear, I nod at Queen Penthesilea's blade, still on Rhea's hip. "Do you think you can use it?"

The girl's eyes grow as large as the moon as they take in the sheer number of rats. And what I intend to do about them. "I . . . I don't know."

I remove the blade from its sheath and shove the handle into her small hands. "Tonight, you learn."

17

HELEN

WHO CAN I trust?

I consider my options. Helenus. Deiphobus. Aeneas. Polydamas.

So many threads woven into one family, where each envisions a Troy in their own image. Yet there is really only one choice.

A young woman all of Troy fears. A woman they have painted as insane.

I have no reason to doubt them. Cassandra was the first of Paris's siblings to welcome me to Troy. Only instead of greeting her brother's new wife with a warm embrace, she'd attacked me like a Fury from the pit, tearing at my jeweled headdress and shredding my robes with her fingernails.

"Blood! Can't you see it?" she screamed, dark curls circling her face like Medusa's snakes. *"Soon her lily-white hands will be stained with the blood of a thousand Trojans!"*

And she was right. Yet for once there was no malice in the face that so intently held mine before Paris dragged me from Andromache's table. There was only curiosity.

Will you see the truth behind their lies, Helen? Before it is too late?

My skin prickles as I leave Priam's complex of palaces and step into the courtyard of Cassandra's tower, a place avoided by all. I've heard Paris's servants speak of another young woman who threw herself from its balcony a generation ago. Some claim to see her shadow walking the ramparts. A dead girl whose screams can be heard in the wind that batters Troy's walls.

At the end of the circular staircase that carries me up the tower, a man stands outside a single door. He leans against the stone wall, eyes closed.

The guard is old, nearly as old as Priam. Certainly well past serving in the king's guard. Yet his broad, barrel chest assures me he was once a soldier, as do the faded threads of battle scars disappearing into his scraggly white beard. Something tells me the deepest are hidden, for there's a sadness about this stranger, and it is bottomless.

"I am here to see Princess Cassandra."

The guard's eyes snap open.

"I didn't mean to startle you." I nod toward Cassandra's door. "May I enter?"

The man hesitates but doesn't say a word. I watch the debate taking place behind his eyes. I am a member of King Priam's household . . . yet I am also a Spartan. An enemy.

"What is your name?" I demand, imagining how Andromache would speak in this situation.

The man jerks his head toward an alcove around the corner from Cassandra's door. Beneath the torch glow that bathes the wall, I follow him to an elaborate chalk sketch. One only the guard who sits here day and night would have the time to make. It is a drawing of a city as large and detailed as my tapestry.

An image of Troy at peace. A kingdom I hardly recognize.

This Troy features women weaving in their halls or walking through the city's concentric spheres, their children running in between them. More men than I've ever seen inside the city line its ramparts, protecting their people from everyday threats, not from thousands of enemy soldiers. Even more men, accompanied by young boys, hold scythes in the abundant farmlands beyond Troy's gates. Along the path leading to the Hill of Kallikolone, lovers walk arm in arm beneath pleasant summer skies.

I turn to the guard, recognizing an artist's most cherished memories. There is love in this rendering, but there is also grief. The grief of one who knew intimately this great city as it once was.

The city it may never be again.

"I admire your work." I pause, throat tickling with thirst as the words of my old mentor Theana rise in my mind.

If we do not create, the only option left is to consume.

And I have had my fill of consumption, though it has left me no more satisfied.

"Only this woman at the loom . . ." I lift my arms to paint a picture in the air. "She would hold her spindle like this. Not like this."

The old man colors, but he smiles. An almost painful expression.

"I do not mean the princess harm," I assure him. "We have much in common, she and I. We are both prisoners of this palace."

By the sorrowful stoop of his shoulders, I suspect he is a prisoner too. One of us. The powerless who walk among so much power. He turns from his drawing, removing a ring of keys from his cloak. Enough to unlock every door in the city. The old man lifts a stick of Hittite iron and meets my gaze.

I wait in silence as this Master of Keys turns the iron bar over in his gnarled hands. When I hear the loud click of the lock, my thoughts rush ahead.

I am about to cross a threshold. One I can never back out of. A door I cannot shut.

"Thank you," I tell the old man before moving into the entrance's shadows.

She sits by the hearth in a rickety chair, staring at the door like she's been expecting someone, though not even the king or queen visits her here.

"Helen of Sparta," says Cassandra, as if introducing me to an audience that leans against the wall behind her.

This is how it has always been. We do not cross paths often, but despite her isolation, I've never sensed that Cassandra is lonely. That she even perceives of herself as *being* alone.

I know what that is like. At least I did before the Unnamed One abandoned me.

"He is with you still." Cassandra's eyes peer into mine with a rare lucidity. I know she wears many faces, but this one is a stranger to me. "Sometimes, in order to be heard, we must first be silent. And sometimes that silence must last for a very long time."

Bolts of lightning travel up my spine. "How do you know—"

"I know more about my brother than any person living!" Her expression alters as her lips curve over her teeth, producing a toothless grin. "And I tell you, the time of silence is coming to an end. Hector's song is about to be sung."

I release the breath burning in my chest. The roar between my ears fades to a light pulse.

"That's why you are here, isn't it?"

I hold my tongue. She is testing me, but for once, I am not the one with something to prove. "Do you know what they are saying about him?"

With a chilling giggle, Cassandra brushes a greasy curl away from her eyes. "You mean, do I know the rumors your treacherous husband and my fool of a twin spread for their own gain?" She nods eagerly. "Not only that, I know the role they'd have you play."

Bitter cold floods my veins. Cassandra rocks back and forth, shoulders slumping forward more each time, until she resembles a frail old woman long neglected by her children. "They're right about one thing, the twin and Apollo's foolish priests. The name of Troy will fade to dust unless Hector has his heir—it was Cassandra who taught Helenus to read the signs, after all."

"Then why do you call them foolish?"

"Because Hector's destiny is not fixed!" Cassandra shoots up straight in her chair. "Fate is never so straightforward. Even Achilles had a choice."

I frown. "Achilles?"

Cassandra shakes her head impatiently. "Two paths were set before the son of Peleus: a long, peaceful life surrounded by many sons, or the bright flame of glory that barely lasts the night, yet whose smoke lingers for all the ages."

"Yes, I've heard it said." No one needs to be told the fate Achilles chose. "And Hector? Must he also choose between life and glory?"

And will the warmth of my bed give him one or the other?

Cassandra's breathing grows shallow. Her voice drifts further into the centuries. "His choice is not so simple . . ."

I wait.

When she looks up from the fire, the Crone is gone. A fresh innocence takes over Cassandra's gaze. This time, she speaks in the high-pitched voice of a little girl.

"Please, pretty lady. My brother must have a child." Another giggle drips like ice down my spine. "And only you know the soil where his line might grow." A slow smile spreads an instant before it twists. "The question is, will it grow in the shadows, or in the light?"

In the space of her rapid breaths, Cassandra's eyes age several lifetimes.

"The time to choose is nearly here. For the winds are blowing."

IT IS NOT a long walk from the base of Cassandra's tower to the twisting hallways of the Citadel's central palace. My mind is so focused on unraveling Cassandra's web that I do not hear the other voices until I've walked right into their midst.

"Helen. What are you doing awake at this hour?"

Paris's voice slices through me. A warning that I have strayed somewhere I am not wanted, and yet he smiles for all the world as if he's delighted to see me.

"Sit. Have some wine." Paris's fingers press into my forearm as he pulls me toward the central fire of the palace hall where King Priam and his sons have gathered.

I rack my mind for some excuse for my presence so late. If he knew where I had gone . . .

"I could not sleep. Walking clears my head."

"Which must be full of many complicated matters from the days spent weaving with your servants." Paris forces me into a chair with an easy grace.

I scan the hall. Andromache is the only other woman here. Her glare makes it no secret she prefers it that way. We have not been in the same room since I struck the poisoned cup from her hands and she struck me. I'd hoped the days since would have thawed her somewhat, but the air between us is crystalline cold.

All the princes are accounted for. Hector, Paris, Helenus, Deiphobus, even young Polydorus. As is their trusted cousin, Polydamas, along with his father, Antenor, and King Priam himself. Only Aeneas and his father, Anchises, are missing. The omission of the Dardanian branch of Priam's line cannot be accidental. Much like Hector's dinner to discuss the plague, this is no casual family gathering. Whatever its purpose, there will be no witnesses here who are not bound by either marriage or blood.

"More late-night wanderings, Helen?" Andromache's voice yanks me out of my head. "I'd have thought you'd have worked that out of your system by now."

"You should be grateful my wife loses sleep over this city's fate. As a Spartan and a healer, Helen is the only person here who can speak to the issue you have raised." Paris says these words with a pride that is alien to my ears.

"Do not sing her unearned praises to me."

"This is the Citadel, sister. You have no power to exclude because of your own petty jealousies." The heated gaze Paris levels my way almost seems protective. More than anything else, it puts me ill at ease.

"What is this about?" I ask them. All of them.

"Nothing that concerns you," snaps Hector's Harsa.

"Everything about this war concerns me."

Andromache grunts. "Truer words were never spoken."

"Ladies, let us work our way back to the point," Paris interjects. "Andromache insists the plague was a deliberate attack by the Achaeans. She and Hector would have us believe that Agamemnon can command sickness over high walls."

All the princes except for Hector smirk. Hector's troops may be the ones whose deaths earn them glory, but Paris's archers stationed along the ramparts are Troy's last defense and most elite force. Bolstered by my arrowheads, of course. Other warriors make jokes about their shielded position at the back of the fray, but everyone knows shooting arrows over and over takes an endurance that is mental as well as physical. An archer must be strong, fit, and sharp—thus, Paris's men are the best fed in Troy.

And yet, Andromache believes they can still be deceived.

"How?" I ask.

Andromache gives the room an account of the body found by the west wall. That she chose to save the revelation for this moment tells me it is part of some weightier strategy. As she speaks, my mind races over the many faces of the Achaean kings I have seen lounging in my first husband's hall. There is only one capable of such brutal efficiency.

"It is Odysseus." Andromache hisses the name like a curse.

"Impossible," Deiphobus says. "Odysseus could not approach the city unmarked by our archers."

The younger princes of the Citadel believe the walls of Troy make them invincible. For that is the only world they have ever known.

"'Impossible' is a dangerous word in wartime, Deiphobus," says Andromache. "You forget that not so long ago, the house of Troy was held hostage from within by a false king from Hattusa. Our walls can be either our greatest asset or our most profound weakness, depending upon the angle from which our enemies choose to attack us."

"With all due respect, Harsa," Polydamas begins with an apologetic glance at Hector. "Most of the warriors in this room have faced Odysseus across the battlefield. He is a man. Not a god. Only gods have the power to walk invisible."

"Then how do you explain the body of a plague-riddled Achaean lying in our sewage trench?" Andromache snaps.

"What leads you to believe the man is Achaean?" Unlike Deiphobus, Antenor does not dismiss her outright.

Andromache addresses him gratefully. "You are right, Harsar, we can be more specific than that. He was Ithacan. The corpse was unknown to my husband and was wearing Ithacan armor."

"Many wear the bronze taken from our slain enemies," Paris says, "especially those who cannot afford armor of their own. And even Hector cannot claim familiarity with every farmer who fights for Troy."

"The body was an Achaean," Andromache insists, but the hard line of her jaw makes it clear it is her own intuition driving her to this conclusion. Just like it was my own gut instinct that drove me to intervene on Andromache's behalf and at my own expense.

Yet those gathered here will never trust our intuition. Not over the infallibility of their walls.

They would also ignore the many tales I have heard, filtered through Paris's seafaring spies, given that they are mere stories and not treaties stamped with a royal seal. How Odysseus went to great lengths to avoid taking part in this war, going so far as to feign madness. That is, until his own son was placed before his plow and he gave up the ruse to save the infant's life. And yet, I alone know the *man* behind these myths, and he is as smart and cunning as they all fear. He is also much more.

As Andromache's lips continue moving, a memory sparks. One of Odysseus's many visits to Sparta, back when Hermione was only a few months old. I'd excused myself from dinner to nurse her. None of the men seated at Menelaus's table would normally notice my departure, but when I passed by Odysseus's seat, he'd stopped me for the chance to coo at the rosy child in my arms.

"*You feed the babe at your own breast,*" Odysseus observed, eyes crinkling in a smile of approval. Or maybe surprise. "*My Penelope was the same. They say a mother's milk is second only to the ichor of the gods.*"

My insides clench. Strange how that moment has remained with me after all these years.

It is because you know Odysseus is capable.

True, he may not be the monster Andromache describes. The Odysseus I knew was a decent man. A doting father and husband. And yet I know the horrors he would enact in order to return to those he loves.

Am I not living proof? A witch who made Paris his poison, killing hundreds, though I convinced myself I had no other choice.

And after everything, I am no closer to Hermione now than I was when I first arrived in Troy. Not unless I do Paris's bidding once again . . .

My gaze falls to Hector. He looks at his brother in a way that suggests he does not see Paris as his most dangerous rival, though he should.

"Helen. What can you tell us of the Achaean kings, my love?" The falseness of Paris's endearment should be obvious, yet the room appears not to notice or care. "Are these men as devoid of honor and good sense as Andromache claims?"

The pinpricks along my arm assure me this is a trial to see if I will side with him. To determine if I am trustworthy and can be given the chance to do what he wants. I must somehow answer in a way that pleases him. My eyes slide toward Andromache's stern face.

Yet how do I answer without widening the chasm even further?

"Agamemnon is not clever enough for such a strategy," I offer halfheartedly, giving Paris some of what he desires. "Menelaus is even less so."

"And what of Odysseus?" Andromache says, though she does not wait for my response. "*He* is the cause of our woes. I care nothing of the others."

"Odysseus is a pig farmer whose bloodline is as murky as the Scamander." Paris pounces. "The Ithacans aren't even trusted by the other Achaeans."

"What would you bet on that, Paris?" Andromache snaps. "The comfortable life you haven't risked for Troy even once?"

Antenor interjects before their personal enmity takes over this unwieldy chariot. "The plague is contained to the Lower City, where it is burning itself out. How it came to be is not our main concern, and there are others more pressing."

I can see the fury rising in Andromache as she steps forward to press her point, but Hector rests a hand on her arm and she pulls back. They will never believe that Odysseus made it all the way to Troy's walls unseen. Not without something undeniable.

"Then why are we here, uncle?" Paris asks, clearly eager to move on.

Antenor lifts his regal chin. "We have received word from Achaean heralds that Menelaus has challenged Paris to a duel. The Achaean forces were worn thin by this sickness, and they wish to determine the conflict's outcome man-on-man. The winner of the fight wins the war. And Helen, of course."

Andromache laughs maniacally. "This is absurd. For countless reasons, the first of which is Paris cannot fight."

"I agree," Hector adds, casting his brother an apologetic glance. "Not because Paris isn't capable, but because I am the leader of the army. If the city's fate rests upon it, this duty should fall to me."

Andromache is not laughing now.

"Menelaus will never agree to that!" Deiphobus's thick neck throbs. "He wants to fight the man who stole his woman. He will accept no substitutes."

"We have all seen Menelaus in action," Hector replies in a measured tone. "He is far from their best warrior. But he is also far from their worst."

The subtle insult thickens in the silence. Every person in this room knows that Paris's fighting talents are to be found among the dregs. The limp he is adept at masking becomes undeniable when he runs. If he takes even one step off his chariot, he will never be able to outpace Menelaus. And Menelaus is not fast.

I dare to look his way. Paris inches farther to the edge of the circle, staring at his tight-lipped father all the while. Willing King Priam to speak, to save him from this humiliation. Not only from the fatal reckoning of a duel that would undoubtedly be Paris's end, but from the shame of refusing to volunteer for it in the first place.

"Then it's settled," Polydamas declares. "A prince of Troy must participate in this conquest, and Hector already represents the people as Troy's commander and, to date, her heir."

A troubled look passes over King Priam's face when Polydamas reiterates with admiration, "Hector must fight in Paris's place."

"No!"

The cry I am not permitted to utter flies from Andromache's lips. All the men stare while I exhale relief. Andromache will change their minds. She *must*, for I know Menelaus. He fights with fervor, but he lacks endurance from long years of idle living, whereas I have witnessed Hector's morning runs around Troy. If Hector takes to the field, he is more likely to win. If Hector fights, he saves Troy, and this horrible war will end.

The stone beneath my breast sinks as a new realization dawns.

If Hector fights, all of Paris's plots will be thwarted. If Hector fights, I will never see my girl again.

And if Paris fights—and loses—I may only glimpse Hermione as I walk to whatever grisly death Menelaus has planned for me.

Paris shoots a warning glare my way before he finally speaks. "It's true, brother, that you are better suited to fight man-on-man," he concedes, casting Polydamas an equally sharp glance. "After all, you practice the maneuvers daily, whereas my duties draw me elsewhere . . ."

While Paris makes his excuses, I imagine Hermione in the temple of Hera on her wedding day. I envision my hands securing the Egyptian headdress from my own dowry over her golden hair.

What would I give to be there? What sort of Gorgon am I willing to become?

"Do not speak of *duties*." Andromache rises to her full height, black eyes burning. "Unless you mean whoring by night while you hide behind your archers by day?"

It is all I can do to keep my torn heart from screaming, *Please. Let Paris fight!*

Let him lose and while Paris's blood is congealing on the ground beneath him, let King Priam give me back to Menelaus. At least he might have enough pity to let me hold our daughter one last time before he slits my throat.

"The Achaeans will never back down, Hector. Even if you win the duel, do you really think they will simply pack up and leave? No, this is another ploy. An effort to cut down Troy's commander and the army's morale with it; that way they can use the hidden route they have to the city and take it when we are weak with grief." Andromache paces the room like the general she might have been. She only stops to send Paris another biting glare. "I will not sit by while your brother has you fight his battles for him once again. I was right about Odysseus and the plague, and I am right about *this*."

Hector chews on his cheek along with his wife's words. Everything she has said is true. I know it even if I cannot say it, and so does every man in this room.

Paris breaks the silence with a snort. "Remarkable."

Andromache narrows her brows. "What is?"

"Your elaborate efforts to deny that you have earned the gods' disfavor. To avoid that unfortunate reality, you would instead turn Odysseus into some kind of monstrous creature from a child's tale."

"Then let's give the tale its proper end . . ." Andromache clenches her fists as she stalks toward Paris, but again, Hector rests a firm hand on her arm. She composes herself before looking to the other men inside the circle. "Use the gift of reason the gods have granted you. If Paris *truly* cared about ending this war, he would have given Helen back to Menelaus long ago. Any fool can see he's tired of her."

If only she knew that the pleasures he takes from me are not of the flesh. Paris has plenty of women for that. It is having a plaything he can control that inflames his power-lust.

"Don't any of you see? The Achaeans are growing desperate after so many years and the ravages of the plague." Andromache meets my gaze head-on before shifting back to Paris. "The question is, if Paris no longer loves his adulteress queen—if he ever really did—then why does he keep her here when the solution is simple? What possible other purpose could it serve to drag out this war until every man in Troy is slain on the battlefield? Every man but *him*?"

What she is insinuating is lost on no one, least of all Paris. And yet the accusation she heaps on him is secondary to the triumph painted on his cheeks. That's when I see it. The embarrassed hesitation of the other men at this sight of a fully enraged woman. A woman who does not wait for permission to speak. And rightly so, for she is quite possibly the only person here who can match Odysseus in wit . . . and ruthlessness.

Paris does not miss the opportunity before him. Nor will he waste it.

"The source of Troy's troubles is straightforward enough," he begins slowly, a picture of self-control. "Her future queen, presently at least, refuses to give up *one shred* of her selfish willfulness. Perhaps that is why she has failed to grant my brother the son he, and this entire city, so desperately needs."

Andromache blanches.

"Enough." Hector grits his teeth. "I have had enough of your constant battles and childish bickering. I am commander of Troy's army. I will fight Menelaus."

No! I barely swallow the cry.

"I agree with Hector," Antenor chimes in, striding between Paris and Polydamas to place a hand on each of their shoulders. "I am sorry, Paris. You are a worthy warrior, but Hector has the best chance of victory. And it will be a victory for all of Troy."

"That may well be true, but I'm afraid it isn't possible."

All eyes drift to the shaky voice that slices through the air, reminding everyone that he is still here. King Priam lifts his head, glassy eyes passing between his firstborn and his twin, the two men he trusts most in all the world. It is a rare thing for him to contradict them both. "This is Paris's fight. There will be no other way to assuage Menelaus's pride."

"But, Father—" both Hector and Paris protest.

"I've made my decision," Priam says, doing what I could not. "I am not dead yet."

Something flutters beneath my breast. Hope that Paris will be slain? Or relief that the choices I may yet have to make have been pushed a bit further down the road?

I search Paris's face for the fear that is surely lurking there. Yet the only reaction I find hides in the grimaced corners of his mouth. And it is *pain*. Raw, genuine hurt. The unbearable wound of a man who can no longer deny a truth he's suspected all along.

If Priam must offer up one of his sons to save this city, it will be the one he respects the least. The one he needs the least. The one he loves the least.

Wrapped in his own silent rage, Hector storms from the hall. Had the command come from anyone else, Hector would fight it to the bitter end. Yet never against his king. He is too good a soldier. And a son.

That Andromache watered the seed of this outcome makes it even worse. She starts to follow him, but when she reaches the door, she stops, wringing her hands. Knowing, I suspect, that despite her best efforts to protect him, the prince she loves so fiercely might not listen to her counsel as openly as he once did.

Unable to stop myself, I take a step toward her, aware of Paris's eyes at my back. My hand reaches for her shoulder, then drops to my side. "When he is done being angry, he will come to you. Doesn't he always?"

Even now. Even after all the scorn she has heaped on me. Even when I may be forced to hurt her in ways she will never see coming, I can't help but hope Andromache will hear the words I cannot speak out loud. That she will accept my help and give me hers.

That she will see the truth of our common enemy.

"You are an Achaean," Andromache says simply. "Your advice means nothing. Go tend to your pitiful husband. And leave me to mine."

18

RHEA

"RHEA, YOU NEED to come with me." Larion stands in the kitchen doorway, red-cheeked and panting.

Across the kitchen, Bodecca whacks her spoon against the table. "You don't give orders here, boy. Now get off with you before—"

"No."

Every servant in the room turns to stone.

Bodecca spears Larion with a glare that has him swallowing whatever is left of his tongue. "I . . . I only mean . . . That is . . ."

"Out with it, boy. We would all like to find our pallets before the sun rises."

Larion pales beneath his bruises, and I start forward. "The horses . . ."

"Ishtar and Carris are well," he says. "It's Prince Hector. He is in the stable, and he's asked for you."

"Well, why didn't you say so?" Despite Bodecca's bluster, the lines deepen around her mouth.

When Andromache returned from the palace, we assumed Hector wouldn't be far behind, but it's been hours and he hasn't come home. That in itself wouldn't be cause for alarm, but we both saw Andromache's face before she retired to her rooms. She hasn't left them since.

Bodecca gives me a curt nod, and I leave the kitchen without a backward glance.

Larion's longer legs eat up the ground, forcing me to run to keep up. The hour is late and the training yards are completely dark.

Atesh snorts his greeting when I enter the stable lit by flickering oil lamps. Smiling, I move toward him, halting when I notice Prince Hector in the shadows. His knuckles are scraped raw, as if he's been brawling with mudbrick. I step closer, and the smell of sour wine stings my nostrils. But none of these things concern me as much as the way he half leans against the wall.

In all my months in Troy, I've never seen Prince Hector stand anything but straight.

"Leave us." His command is a whip lashing through the silence.

With a worried glance at me, Larion backs out of the doors.

"I used to know every horse in these stables," Prince Hector says after a seemingly endless pause. "Now I am all but a stranger to them. I don't even give them names."

I don't say anything. He does not expect me to.

"Those nights when I came here alone. You sat with me in the shadows."

My heart beats faster. Since Hector never spoke, I assumed he didn't realize I was there. Now I fear that I have intruded on his most private moments.

"Why?" Hector shifts into the lamplight, and I notice the wineskin in his hand.

Because you risked the opinion of men you value to help me.

Because you saw my worth and helped me to see it too.

Because my father once told me that to be a great warrior, one must first be a great man, and among men, you have no equal.

"Because . . ." With great effort, I coax the words out of my throat. "I thought it might help to have someone sit with you. Even in silence."

Prince Hector nods. "You helped me when I did not ask. I need that help again, Rhea, only this time I am asking for it."

"I am proud to serve you. Just as my father was."

Hector moves out of the shadows. "My brother is to fight tomorrow. A duel with Menelaus for the fate of Troy. Menelaus was given the choice of field, and Paris his pick of weapons. Menelaus chose the Ilium plain. Paris chose the chariot."

I've seen Prince Paris drive on the training grounds. His estimation of his own skill with the reins is as inflated as everything else about him.

"How can I help?"

"Choose his horses and choose them well. If they aren't his usual animals he will hardly notice." A complex history Hector never betrays is laid bare upon his face. "Paris's left leg was injured when he was younger. It makes him half the soldier he might have been. On the ground, there is no way he can best Menelaus. I would fight this battle for him, but it is out of my hands. He must win, Rhea."

They are the words not of a prince but of a brother.

The weight of his trust settles over my shoulders like a mantle. "I will choose well."

Hector nods. "Menelaus is a better fighter, but he has all the grace of an ox. On a chariot driven by the right horses, Paris might stand a chance." Hector looks deep into my eyes, and I hear the words he does not say.

Paris's chariot is his best hope of leaving the plain alive. His only hope.

Footsteps echo behind us. Cyrrian's face is covered in a sheen of sweat, his black hair escaping the low bun to form a messy tumble around his ears. "I just left the house. Andromache said . . ." He trails off when he notices me.

At the mention of his wife's name, Hector's hands turn into fists. The fresh wounds on his knuckles reopen, releasing a trickle of blood.

Cyrrian's gaze dips to the wounds. "So it's true, then. Our fates rest in Paris's uncalloused hands. Andromache—"

Hector turns and stalks deeper into the stable, where Atesh dances in his stall. Cyrrian looks at me with a question that is also an accusation. He jerks his head. A dismissal.

When I don't immediately flee, the young soldier spears me with a look of pure resentment. I lift my chin to meet his glare. If Hector wishes me gone, he can say so. Until then, I stay.

Cyrrian's nostrils flare, but he merely follows his friend toward Atesh's stall. "Aeneas told me what happened. You can't fault Andromache for wanting to protect you."

"It is not her job to protect me." The wineskin flies from Hector's grip to *smack* against the stable wall. "It is her job to obey!"

Even the fire horse goes still.

Bodecca told me once that Hector's name means "holder," and that is what he is. Solid. Like the earth, he roots everything to him so that it might grow, but he is still a *man*. Something Troy seems to forget but that I never will again.

Hector's rage is a crackle in the air. I want to hide. I want to cower before it, but there is nowhere to go.

"I am trying to hold this city together. But I can't do it if she doesn't trust me to do it my way."

Cyrrian takes a step closer than any other man would dare. "I remember the day you brought Andromache home. How she strode through the Scaean gate at your side like the Achaeans' goddess Artemis. Proud even though she must've been afraid. She had her reasons then and she has them now. She's done everything that was asked of her, and still, the Citadel does not fully accept her."

As they have never accepted Cyrrian, a voice inside me whispers.

The shadows highlight the perfect lines of Cyrrian's face. "Everything she's done since that day is to protect this city, and you."

Hector runs his calloused fingers along Atesh's stall door. "She seeks to protect Troy, but she wants to pick and choose the parts worth saving." He looks at me as if the words are as much for my benefit as Cyrrian's. "The sanctimonious men on the council who do nothing but talk. The pampered Old Bloods in the palace. Our customs, and our omens, and the infighting of the Citadel. They are as much a part of Troy as the women who mourn for it. The whole can't survive without all of its parts."

An image flickers before my eyes. Andromache wielding her weapon in the shadow of the wall. The bodies of a hundred rats at her feet and the moonlight shining off the bloody ends of her hair. Nobody else was there that night. Nobody else saw what I saw.

Her utter desperation to save a city that would never truly know her.

"Perhaps Andromache merely sees the ways Troy needs to change in order to survive," I say.

Surprise registers briefly before Cyrrian nods. "Our traditions won't endure if our people don't live to pass them on."

Prince Hector regards his friend. "Your mother sought to change things too. I'm afraid this will end much the same for us if we don't proceed with caution."

"Andromache is learning," Cyrrian offers with unexpected tenderness. "Give her time."

"If only I believed that was something we had." Hector sighs. "Thousands of Trojan men would lay down their lives at my command, and yet I can't make a single stubborn woman hold her tongue if the fate of Troy depends on it."

"But that is why you love her," I say quietly.

Cyrrian's gaze bores into the side of my face, but by the time I look up, he is focused on Hector again. "If you expected anything else, then you do not know the woman you married," he says. "She follows no laws but those of honor as she sees it. You can't simply pick and choose the parts of her worth loving."

Cyrrian's admiration for Andromache is betrayed in the vibration of his voice. There's affection there. Maybe even love. It makes me wonder about his own mother. The woman Hector spoke of.

"I know." Hector's shoulders slump. "And I don't blame her. I should have stepped in before she could goad Paris to his death."

"Paris does not deserve your loyalty or your protection. You think he has not been prodding those priests to spew their lies? That he doesn't know Andromache was right about the plague's source, but would rather innocent people die than admit it? You shouldn't—" Cyrrian glances sideways at me.

"Say what you must," Hector says wearily. "I trust Rhea as I trust Bodecca. As I trust you."

A fierceness fills me at his words. It is pride and it is pleasure. It is faith I thought I'd lost. I meet Cyrrian's gaze.

The charioteer looks away in exasperation. "This is Paris's mess. You can't clean it up for him like you always do. He treats you with indifference and your wife with contempt, and you are the only one who still refuses to see his treachery."

"I know what he is," Hector says. "He is my brother."

"Yes." Cyrrian dares a step closer. "He's your younger brother. Which means you stand between him and the one thing he covets. Don't let your love for him expose you."

"I am not ignorant to his nature, but I also know it isn't something he can deny any more than I can deny mine." Hector grips his friend's shoulder. "There is good in him. Just as there is good in every man I have ever fought beside. I've seen brave men cower and weak men made brave by a single moment." Hector's eyes look past Cyrrian, right at me. "Paris's moment is coming."

His hand falls away from Cyrrian's shoulder as he moves toward the stable door.

Cyrrian speaks up behind him. "Might I suggest you extend your wife the same generosity. She can't help who she is. Our time on this side of the Great River is short, Hector, and she loves you well."

Hector studies his friend for a long moment. "Andromache may do what she does out of love for me, but everything I do is for love of Troy." He reaches out and grips my shoulder the same way he gripped Cyrrian's. "Paris must win tomorrow. For Troy." He looks between the two of us. "I trust you both to see it done."

When Hector exits the stable, his back is straight once more.

～◦～

I'M SORRY. MY heart begs forgiveness.

I'm so sorry. But Hector told me to pick the best, and that is what you are.

The shadow of Troy's outermost wall shields me from the sun as I run my palm along the taut skin of Ishtar's neck. "You must be brave." My other hand rubs Carris's soft mouth. "And you must be sure."

Carris whickers. Ishtar stomps her hoof. As much as I have tried, I can't hide my fear. Not from them.

Soon, someone will come to collect my horses so that they can be harnessed to Paris's chariot. To the surprise of no one, he has requested that Hector and the army proceed him out onto the field. A perfectly choreographed entrance onto a plain where thousands of men have died, but where Paris has never once set foot unguarded.

Today that changes. Today, Paris will face Menelaus, son of Atreus, and when he does, it will be with my father's horses under his hands.

"Be brave and be fast. Be sure and be wise." Carris dances in place. Ishtar moves in close, steadying her sister. Papa always said that one was air and the other earth. There is no other pair in Troy more in step. No other pair I would trust to see Paris through this day alive.

But at what cost?

I reach out with both hands and bring their heads to mine. "But most of all, come back to me."

I run my fingers through their coarse manes. "And if it isn't too much trouble, could you bring the Trojan prince back with you? Preferably in one pretty piece?"

"Though nobody would complain if he was slightly maimed," a voice speaks up behind me.

I spin to find Cyrrian watching me from the shadow of the wall. There is a cloth in his hand and oil streaked across his exposed forearms. He's been working on Paris's chariot, doing whatever he can to give the prince a chance of saving himself, and indirectly, all of us.

"Do you think he can win?"

Cyrrian's smile is sharp as the spokes on the chariot's wheels. "In an honest contest? Never. Luckily for Troy, I've never known Paris to fight fair."

The bruise on my arm throbs. I remember the way Paris had covered his wife's mouth in an iron grip and a blistered hand. The rest of them looking on as if there was nothing the matter.

I tighten my hold on the leads, already dreading the moment I'll be asked to let go. "Is the chariot ready?"

"As ready as I could make it. Not that it matters. He won't be the one driving it."

The breath leaves my lungs in a rush. "Prince Hector—"

"Is an unparalleled fighter and horseman, but somewhat awkward with the reins. Though maybe don't mention that to him." Cyrrian flips the hair out of his eyes with a carelessness that belies the tension in his neck. "I'll do what I can to keep the bane of Troy alive." He walks up to the horses and pats Carris's neck. "Who do we have here?"

I swallow the growing lump in my throat. "Carris and Ishtar."

Cyrrian runs his hands beneath the harnesses. A frown creases his brow. Assessing eyes travel over the horses before returning to mine with a coldness that wasn't there a moment ago. "No."

The word is a slap. "Hector said I could choose—"

"Hector's trust in you was obviously misplaced. Run back to the stables, horse girl, and pick two others before all of Troy suffers for your mistake."

A spark kindles in my stomach. "Perhaps you should worry about the chariot, soldier. And leave me to worry about the horses."

"I wish I could, but the fate of Troy hangs on this charade, and these two are mares. Even worse, they're so green I can practically smell it. If they've ever seen battle, I'll retire my whip."

The spark inside me erupts into a blaze.

He would have me choose from Paris's preening stallions. Or from Hector's strong and sturdy stock. But Ishtar and Carris are the best Troy has to offer even if Cyrrian can't see it. Not only because they are strong and true, but because they are mine. They were raised in my family's stables. My love for them is interwoven with my memories of home and all the faces I will never see again. It is that love that makes me brave now when I have never been brave before. It will make them brave too.

"I would match these horses against any in Hector's stables save one, and he will not be harnessed." I will my spine into an arrow. "Hector told me to choose, and I have."

"Any gelding would be stronger, and a stallion better still." Cyrrian answers my challenge with one of his own.

"Stallions are temperamental, loud, and easily distracted. Their endurance is inferior and they are less adept at handling pain, whereas mares are built for it. These two learned to run side by side. They are as steady as any team that has ever pulled a chariot, and we both know that Paris requires balance more than strength if he is to stay off the ground."

Which he must, if Troy is to survive.

Lightning flashes in those cerulean eyes. "Says a stable hand who belongs in the kitchens."

"Says the woman who helped to raise them." The words fly out of my mouth before I can call them back.

A ripple of confusion passes over his features.

Pride wells up from somewhere deep inside. "Ishtar and Carris were bred and foaled on my father's farm. Before . . . Before I came here." When I was still Rhea of Phrygia. "As I said, they will serve you well."

"So these are the horses Andromache demanded be spared," Cyrrian says carefully. "If you fought so hard to save them, why endanger them now?"

"Because I owe Hector my life." I bite my lip, surprised that there is more. "And because Troy is my home now too. Paris must not be unseated, and there are no other horses I would trust to ensure that does not happen."

Cyrrian considers me for a long moment. "No harm will come to them. I swear it."

The sudden ferocity of his promise loosens my tense muscles. "Be sparing with the whip, and gentle on the reins. Carris is the bolder of the two, but Ishtar keeps her sister steady. Don't be afraid to give them their heads, and when you need speed, I promise you, they will fly."

"I appreciate your instruction on the finer points of driving." Cyrrian's smile is unlike any of the others he has given me. Rueful and surprising. Real.

He runs a large hand down Ishtar's side. She nuzzles into his shoulder, drawing a deep chuckle from him.

I narrow my eyes at her. *Traitor.*

"Ishtar," he says, offering her his palm. She all but revels in it.

I can't help but smile.

"The Achaeans call her Aphrodite." Cyrrian quirks a brow at me. "They do say Paris is beloved of the goddess. Though he'll be furious when he sees these two at the front of his chariot instead of his usual beasts. For that alone, it might be worth it."

A soldier calls out to Cyrrian, and the smile slips. "Time to see what's to become of us."

My throat goes tight. One more time, I press my nose into Ishtar's and Carris's necks. Their scent fills my nostrils, sending memories of my mother and sisters swirling through my head.

Be strong. Be brave. If all else fails, come back to me.

With surprising gentleness, Cyrrian takes the leads from my hands and walks the horses toward the group of soldiers gathered around a gleaming chariot. As I watch, his normal rolling gait gives way to a steady tread that is a perfect imitation of Prince Hector's. Just before he reaches the chariot, Cyrrian turns. "Andromache is watching the duel from the forward battlements. Your presence was requested. Go by the west gate where it meets the Citadel walls. Take the stairs directly up to Priam's private battlement." Aegean eyes lock with mine. "If you run, you can still make it."

I should thank him, or wish him luck, or say *something*, but none of the words I know feel right for the moment. So instead, I turn my back on Cyrrian and run. With little effort, I find the steps he spoke of built into the shadow of the wall. The sheer extent of them only becomes clear once you start to climb. I climb until my legs feel like water, and the breath saws through my lungs.

Sweat sizzles on my brow when I exit the stairs and spill out on the narrow ledge of the battlement facing the western plain from above the Scaean gate. The sight below pulls me up short.

Two armies face each other on the field below me. A line of men that stretches as far as I can see. The killing field of Ilium is a plain of utter stillness. Thousands of Trojans and their Anatolian allies, divided in disciplined companies, stand mere yards across from the Achaean horde, a host of warriors standing shoulder to shoulder and oceans deep.

So many men. So many lives and loves connected to them. Mothers and wives. Daughters and sons. I can feel their spirits in the silence, screaming their grief into the wind. And on the narrow strip of land between these armies, the two men who brought all of their fates crashing together.

Paris, son of Priam. And Menelaus, son of Atreus.

The spot directly between them is stained with blood, the bodies of three ewes all that is left of the oaths spoken. Now there are only these two men, facing each other in full armor, the harsh light reflecting off the winking tips of their spears. Both of them are mounted on the backs of sleek chariots. Menelaus's driver is a tall, thin man whose face is covered in a helmet. In the barest of leather armor, his dark head completely bare, Cyrrian has no such protection. He has forgone a shield to keep the chariot light, more maneuverable.

My fingers dig into the stone. Menelaus has the look of a man who has seen too many battles. His armor is covered with nicks that are visible even at distance. There are no unsightly dents in Paris's armor. No stains that will never come clean. He is a picture of youth poured in a cast of bronze, a plume of white horsehair sticking proudly out of his helmet to fan around his shoulders in the wind.

For the first time since Hector called me into the stables yesterday, I am really and truly afraid.

If Paris loses this fight, all of Troy will burn as Harsa Cassandra said. I'll be a slave again, only this time, there will be no Ishtar and Carris to keep me company. No Hector to rescue me and grant me free rein in his stables. No Andromache to sing aching songs that remind me of home. There will be no Bodecca to leave out honey-roasted nuts under the guise of forgetfulness, and no Larion to make me laugh with his shy jokes.

My eyes drift across the battlements. In the harsh Anatolian sun, King Priam is as gnarled as the wooden chair he sits upon.

The king's brother, Harsar Antenor, stands at his side, his expression grim. On the other side of the king is Queen Hecuba, her hair pulled back in a severe coiffure that exaggerates the deep hollows of her face. Eyes as black as Paris's look coldly upon the scene below. One of her hands clutches the godstone around her neck, while the other rests firmly on Harsa Cassandra's shoulder. Based on the princess's grimace, it is a touch meant to restrain more than to comfort. On either side of them, the princes and princesses of Troy have amassed in force. Harssi Helenus, Deiphobus, and Polydorus. Harsa Andromache, a wasted-looking but alive Creusa, and more I don't recognize. And standing apart from the rest at a distance, a shroud of flowing silk. Helen of Sparta.

The look in Helen's eyes is impossible to decipher. I can't decide if it holds whole worlds of emotion, or none at all. I wonder if she hides more than a beautiful face behind her veil.

Andromache summons me over just as voices raise from the Ilium plain. A rush of murmurs. A gasp.

Down below, Paris descends his chariot.

Cries of confusion run along the ramparts. They are quickly picked up by the men down below as Paris makes his intentions clear. Cyrrian grabs his arm, but Paris shakes him off and stalks across the earth, horsehair plume fanning out behind him.

Hector takes a single step forward. Though I cannot see his face, the horses echo his anxiety. Paris has signaled to all that the duel will occur on the ground. A choice that, once made, cannot be unmade.

"Fool," Andromache hisses between bloodless lips. "He will be the death of us all."

Menelaus climbs down from his chariot in a nearly synchronized movement, except that his driver does not attempt to stop him. Why would he? Even I can see that on level ground, Paris stands no chance. So why does Paris do it? Is it arrogance? Some trick up his sleeve?

Carefully, Paris holds his spear in front of him, tip pointing toward the sky.

"What delusion is this?" Andromache seethes.

"One man's delusion is another man's talisman." Helen's voice is utterly removed. "He thinks himself safe."

"Hubris," Andromache snaps. "That's what comes of relying on signs to make your choices for you."

Helen's eyes spark behind her veil but remain fixed on Paris's gleaming spear tip. As if the weapon itself is the talisman she spoke of; one that holds her captive.

A cry flies high on the wind. At first, I think it's the call of a bird, but then the sound fractures into a series of jagged notes. High-pitched and shrill. Harsa Cassandra throws back her head and lifts her hands to the sky, her childish giggles spilling over the wall in a waterfall of sound.

Fidgeting in the ranks below.

Menelaus answers with a roar that assaults the ramparts. Paris must hear his own death in it, because he suddenly appears less than eager to be standing in front of this hardened warrior in his finery. He manages to raise a single, gleaming spear, issuing the challenge for all to see. Menelaus grabs the sword at his hip and advances, clearly unwilling to do this at a distance. Caught off guard by this breach in protocol, Paris stumbles backward. He turns his back on Menelaus and makes a hasty, limping run across many yards behind the safety of the Trojan front line. Every person present watches his coward's retreat in grim silence.

A man moves through the Trojan line. Hector grabs Paris by the arm. Whatever he says can't be heard from the battlements, but when he is done, Paris has collected himself.

The Achaean ranks grow rowdy at Paris's retreat, and the neat companies of Trojan men and their allies rise up in answer. It is all fury and violence. Spears flash and swords bang against shields in a deafening song that rings in my bones. Hector moves forward with his brother until they are closer to the Achaean front line than to their own men. Hector's hands are empty. It would be so easy for the Achaeans to kill him, and all of Troy's hopes, but none of them makes a move. Instead, every man both Achaean and Trojan falls silent when Hector speaks.

His words are lost on the wind, but when he raises his arm, all the ranks of Troy fall to their knees like felled wheat. Hector turns his back on the enemy and makes the lonely walk back to his men. And then it is just Paris and Menelaus again. As it was always meant to be.

With a cry that is high and shrill, Paris launches his spear. It hits Menelaus's shield and bounces uselessly to the ground. For a moment, both warriors stand frozen, but then Menelaus takes his turn. His aim is true, striking Paris's shield and puncturing it clean through.

Helen falls forward against the parapet. Her hands claw at the stone. I look into her gemstone eyes, expecting to see the same fear I feel reflected there, but there is only hope. So bright and burning it rivals the sun for its splendor.

A wave of murmurs brings my attention back to the plain, where Menelaus is holding something. His sword. The blade has shattered in his hand, cleaving down to the hilt. I didn't see it happen. Didn't even know a sword could break like that.

Cassandra laughs. Deadly sharp and serrated, it is not the laugh of a woman at all. But the cry of a Fury.

With a shout, Menelaus tosses his sword to the ground and lunges at Paris with his bare hands. Another cry from Paris. This one more of a yelp. It echoes across the field as Menelaus grabs Paris by the pompous plume of his helmet and begins to drag him toward the Achaean line. Paris reaches desperately for his spear, still lying in the dirt.

All of Troy takes a single breath. Helen seems to be the only one who is frozen.

This battle is over. It was over before it ever really began.

Hector moves forward, but Cyrrian jumps down from his chariot and intercepts him halfway to the Achaean line. Then Aeneas is there, their dark heads pressing close. Hector's shoulders drop as he watches Menelaus drag Paris to a death that will bring Troy nothing but ruin.

"No." Andromache's word is a plea. One that echoes in my own heart.

Menelaus is almost at the Achaean line when the chin strap of Paris's helmet snaps, and he falls free. The Trojan prince scurries on his hands and knees, scrambling through the dirt back to his broken spear. As if that might be enough to save him.

Cyrrian once called him a varmint, and in this moment, crawling through the muck and the blood in his golden armor, that is exactly what I see.

What everyone sees.

Menelaus watches him with a naked disdain that is palpable despite the helmet hiding his face. When he starts advancing again, his steps are unhurried.

"It is over." Andromache's pronouncement is hollow.

"Leave the prophecy to those who can see beyond the tips of their spears," Cassandra says, coming up behind us. Her back is hunched and her voice whispery and frail. "Troy will endure so long as Paris lives," the Crone rasps.

"He can't win this fight," Andromache says.

"It is not winning but survival that counts. Paris learned to survive on the foothills of Ida where his own mother forgot him. There is still one way he might yet leave this plain alive." The Crone wearing Cassandra's face looks at me with eyes that are ancient and searching. "They say he is favored by Aphrodite. I wonder. Will the goddess ride to his rescue? Or will she let him die, and all of us with him?"

The Crone's words ring through my head as I look across the battlements, down into the patch of barren earth to the empty chariot drawn by Paris's horses. *My* horses.

Ishtar. Aphrodite.

She is there with him after all.

A few feet away, Menelaus stalks Paris, who is twenty paces back from the Trojan line. Menelaus lifts his weapon over his shoulder.

My heart cries out first, and then the word follows.

"Ishtar!"

I do not recognize the power of my own voice as it rings across the battlefield.

Down below, Ishtar dances in her harness.

"Rhea." Andromache whispers my name, though I don't know if it's an encouragement or a warning.

"Ishtar!" I scream again until my throat aches. "Carris. Come!"

Come, my heart cries. *Please, please, come back to me.*

And they do. Two streaks of black and bay, Ishtar and Carris burst into motion. Though Cyrrian pulls hard on the reins, they do not stop. Instead, they move with a burst of speed that throws the charioteer against the wooden frame as they gallop in a tight circle, turning back toward Troy. As they do, they pass right by Paris, who uses the last of his strength to throw himself into the chariot. And then my horses do what they were born to do.

They run.

As one, they burst through the Scaean gate and into Troy, leaving two stunned armies in their wake.

And when they go, they take the disgraced prince of Troy with them.

19

HELEN

ON THE TAPESTRY before me, Menelaus and Paris face each other with weapons drawn. A broken sword hangs in Menelaus's hand. Paris clutches his poisoned spear, a detail I'm unable to portray, for reasons artistic as well as practical. The anger on Menelaus's face is plain as Aphrodite wraps her arms around her lover in an embrace strong enough to block a thousand blows. It is the version of events least likely to upset Paris. In this retelling, he did not flee out of cowardice, or because of his limp, or as a result of his poorly aimed spear that so easily snapped under Menelaus's heel, but because the goddess of desire desired *him* above all.

Yet the truth is there in plain sight for anyone who wishes to read between the threads. Only the tapestry does not show the hundreds of men who will now bleed in Paris's place. There would not be room for them all.

It seems there is no escaping the choices that chase us.

My fingers are securing the last thread of Aphrodite's fiery hair when Paris bursts into the weaving hall. Aethra and Clymene scatter like flustered pigeons.

Paris has grown thinner overnight, the circles beneath his eyes dark blue from little sleep. If there is one thing that could ruffle the feathers of this peacock, it is the thought of the entire city laughing behind his back.

With some men, humiliation makes them cower and hide. With Paris, it makes him cruel.

To delay the inevitable, I gesture to a plate on a side table loaded with fruit. "Have some refreshments, husband. You need to regain your strength."

"Don't you mother me." The way he growls his command is all the confirmation I need. Paris is here to pick a battle with someone he might actually have a chance of beating.

My heart races as he walks along the tapestry, studying the scenes before grabbing a cluster of grapes from the platter. He stops in front of my latest addition. "I think I understand now. Why you do . . . *this*." He waves his hand as if banishing a bad smell. "The stories we tell ourselves are all we really have in the end."

And there it is. A flicker of a man. Fragile. Uncertain.

Paris takes a leisurely seat, resting his filthy boots on the table that holds my yarn and spindle. He looks thoughtful, and on his careless face the expression is utterly menacing. A few more grapes and he releases a slow breath. "It must be tonight."

The tickle at the base of my spine spreads in every direction. "Do you think that is wise? Surely Hector is displeased with the outcome—"

"Which is why you must make him forget!" Paris stands violently, knocking over my side table. He seizes my chin and rips the veil away. Foaming spittle lands on my cheek. "You know all about *forgetting*, don't you?"

I almost pity him. He is ashamed of himself, and so he would shame me. I look ahead as a silent stream flows down my cheeks to the faint scars of his blistered fingers.

At the sight of my tears, his grip softens. "This is the only move we have left to make. That cheating brute you once called a husband has cost Troy much. But at least the duel confirmed that I have been looking inside Troy's walls for solutions when perhaps I should be focused on our resources outside . . ." He releases me with a rough shove. "No matter what I do, it all depends on that bitch remaining barren. Which means it all depends on my brother licking his wounds in another's bed."

My tightly coiled thoughts unravel. The chaos rages for a moment before I am met with an eerie stillness, a deeper knowing.

My chin jerks toward Paris. "I will go to him tonight. Alone. But you must keep Clymene and Aethra here."

Paris raises an eyebrow. "It wouldn't do for you to prance around Troy after sunset all by yourself."

"I'll be heavily veiled. The walk from the Citadel gates to Hector's stables is short. Isn't that where he likes to end his days?" Or so his servant Rhea mentioned. "It will surprise Hector to see me there alone. Men enjoy surprises, don't they?"

A muscle tics in Paris's cheek. "You must bring him back here. I will have your servingwomen prepare your bedchamber and make it known that I will be spending the night in the Lower City. My personal guards will stand outside your door."

I nod as blood rushes to my head. "Tonight, then."

"Steady, my love." Paris raises a hand to my face. "This task will not be a pleasant one. For either of us." His hand hangs there in the air, trembling as mine has so many times before. What is it lurking under his words? Hesitation or genuine regret? Either way, his hand falls and he steps away.

"Tonight my brother may bed you, but never forget . . ." Paris presses his mouth firmly against my neck, a kiss meant to leave a mark. "You are mine."

~ 2 ~

AS THE MOON rises, I walk the length of my tapestry one more time, studying the details of this endless war. The faces of all the lost lives who have been laid at my feet.

In the center of every scene that matters stands Hector, breaker of horses. Hector, prince of Troy.

Paris is deceiving himself if he thinks there will ever be a city worth preserving without his brother to lead it, not even if Paris somehow produced a dozen sons with his countless concubines.

Hector of the gleaming helmet and the cobalt thread practically leaps off the tapestry, one hand gripping a short sword while the other rests on his horse's back. His is a likeness I took extra care with, each woven stitch a whisper of the truth I have long kept hidden. A truth I would not willingly tell another soul.

A truth I've not told even You.

It isn't love, of that I am certain. Any capacity I had to love a man died when I became the prize a hundred princes fought over.

No, what overcomes me whenever I glance Hector's way is longing. A longing to *be* loved. Not desired, but cherished—as Hector treasures Andromache.

It is hard to understand what moves him to such devotion. For while Andromache is strong and sure of herself in a way that makes both men and women tremble, she does not seem easy to love.

But I would be. I *would* be.

And then would Hector, who grows more burdened by the day, finally know a moment of happiness? I am certain I would—once I embraced the slight frame of my Hermione as reward for my betrayal.

Betrayal of them? Or of myself?

My eyes land on a snag. There is always a snag.

It starts in the flaming hair of the fire horse Hector adores but never rides. I used three colors to capture the shimmering movement of the mane, and the gold strand woven beneath the others has come loose. I finger the thread loop and it becomes looser still.

With little hesitation, I pull.

The fire horse is gone in a breath. All ten tips tingling, more fingers fly. Hector and the bronze of his armor vanish next. Instead of working methodically to create an entire world of thread, I move across the tapestry in a fury, pulling one strand of my guilt that leads to another, then another, the pile spooling at my feet as I traverse the length of this gluttonous war.

Gone is Agamemnon.

Gone is Deiphobus.

Gone is Odysseus.

Gone is Ajax.

Gone is Diomedes.

Gone is Aeneas.

Gone is Achilles.

Gone is Sarpedon.

Gone is Menelaus.

Gone is Paris.

By the end, all that remains is a single, grotesque figure standing on a galley bow.

Helen of Sparta.

Helen of Troy?

Helen of the Unnamed One.

My lungs burn as I gasp for air, staring at the mountains of color strewn across my weaving hall. Is this what it is like for the Three Fates? The intoxication that comes from destruction with one snip of a thread?

Beauty is much harder to build.

My breathing stills as the drapes over my balcony doorway flutter, causing snakes of thread to slither across the floor. I follow a knotted ball onto the balcony, raising my eyes to Kallikolone.

I glance back over my shoulder at the tangled intestines of my tapestry. All this time, I have stood there, weaving threads but saying nothing. Hoping, *praying*, my fate would change. Staying silent for a child who is no longer mine to keep, if she ever truly belonged to me in the first place. And the Unnamed One has responded in kind.

For a step to be directed, it must first be taken. For what is most real is more than we can see.

More realizations rise like the dawn. Slowly, then with a stallion's breakneck speed.

The time for standing motionless on this threshold is done. I have woven silent prayers into a thousand threads, but they have only risen up to strangle me. In order to be spoken to, I must also speak.

All this time, I thought I received no guidance from the Unnamed One because I boarded that ship with Paris, exchanging the life of my sweet girl for the blood of a thousand Trojan boys. Even now, I would make the same trade.

Yet what if the only punishment I've inherited is for all the decisions I've refused to make? The sides I've not wanted to take? All the possible good left undone?

Even Achilles had a choice.

The faint echo sings to my heart in the voice of a little girl, speaking from the mouth of a broken woman.

Soil. Light. Shadows.

My unsullied hands dig into the earth that nourishes the potted herbs on my balcony. For the first time since I entered these city walls, I know what I must do.

⁓ ❧ ⁓

THE SHADOWS ARE growing long when I set off for the stables. The fringe of my finest gown drags down the stone walkway behind me. Its neckline is low and fitted, and the snug belt of gold makes it difficult to catch my breath. Paris approved of the choice. The material woven tightly in taupe and plum stripes is new—brought here from Egypt by the Sea Peoples that Paris has his hired sailors meet in the Aegean. Bands of gold cover my bare wrists, and the loose waves that fall past my waist are held back by a jeweled headband. A touch of kohl liner and a few dabs of oil of iris perfume, and I feel as if I'm ready for yet another marriage ceremony.

It is hard to believe it has come to this.

When I pass through Hector's courtyard, the outlines of two figures enter the stables ahead of me. One is tall and broad shouldered, the other low to the ground. Despite the difference in height, they walk in step with one another. The girl's musical voice drifts to me on the wind, followed by the low sound of Hector's laughter. I keep my distance, following both into the musty den where horses snort and stomp their hooves. The figures separate, the man going into a stall on the left while the shadow enters a stall on the right. For a moment, I linger there between the two. Waiting. Breathing.

I take a step forward. The darkness of the stable greets me, illuminated by a single oil lamp. Horses poke their heads out of stalls as I move forward. With every step, I weave my pattern. I pull the final thread through to set the scene.

One more breath, and I step out from the shadows.

The girl looks up at me, startled, her hand gripping the hoof of a dappled mare.

"Harsa Helen." Rhea sets the horse's foot back on the ground. She stands and adjusts her dirt-smeared tunic. "What . . . what are you doing here?" Her eyes dart toward the stall doors. It is possible she might flee to the main house. Or to Hector. After all, this is not the first time I barged into her home uninvited.

"I need your help, Rhea." I keep my voice low.

"*My* help?" She straightens.

"You were at the Fair Winds when we fought the plague. And you were there at the dinner with the king. I know you saw things," I say, praying my instincts about the girl are right.

Her face closes down. "I saw you attack Harsa Andromache."

"That may be how it appeared, but that is not the truth you saw." I take another step closer.

She frowns but does not retreat. "What do you mean?"

"Prince Paris. Did anything about his behavior that night strike you as unusual?"

Something sparks in the depths of Rhea's eyes that tells me I was right. The girl is a watcher. Like me, she sees things without being seen, though in an entirely different way.

The sound of footsteps outside has me pressing my back to the stall's wall. The horse Rhea is caring for stretches out her large head to chew on my gown. "There isn't time to explain now. Yet I need you to believe that what I will ask of you is in the service of Hector and his cause." I take another deep breath. And then I wait.

Rhea fidgets with an uncertainty I know like an old friend. "Why me?"

It is a fair question. "Because I saw the way you cared for Troy's sick. Your attention to detail. Your loyalty to Hector *and* Andromache." I pull my veil down and hold the girl's gaze. "She trusts you, and that is no easy accomplishment."

And yet her trust is what I need.

The girl hesitates again. "You promise your only intention is to help Prince Hector?"

"I do," I say, though Rhea still looks unsure. How to make her understand? "I have a daughter. Hermione." My voice trembles. It has been years since I've spoken her name to a sympathetic soul. "She would be about your age by now."

Rhea's mouth softens. She sees.

"You must miss her desperately."

"And I would do anything to protect her. Just as Andromache would do anything to protect those she loves."

I can see her nimble mind making the connection. "Is that why you would help the Harsa? Even though . . ." Rhea breaks my gaze and turns to brush down her horse.

"Even though she loathes me?" I smile gently. "It is easy to hate what you do not know. What you fail to understand. Yet if you help me, Rhea, that may change."

Rhea takes several breaths as she runs the bristles over the glossy coat in front of her. A horse that is plainer than the others but obviously one she loves well. The animal seems to study me before it tosses its head and nips the girl on the shoulder. Rhea raises her strange eyes. "What do you need me to do?"

A sudden warmth for this small, shy girl glows within me. I pray my Hermione is as quietly brave. She will need to be for the life ahead of her in the house of Achilles's son.

"Is there someone in the stables you trust? Someone you might ask to deliver a horse to the east gate?"

"Larion," Rhea says without hesitation. "He would do anything for Hector."

How many of them are there? I wonder. How many boys still breathe and girls continue to walk this city's streets with wrists unbound, all because of one man?

I reach out to rest a hand on Rhea's arm. "Tonight, we must summon all our courage if we are to defend Troy's prince. Just as he has defended us."

With one last stroke of the horse's mane, Rhea turns to me and nods.

"We must make our way to the east gate," I continue. "I have a friend who will see us through it. That is where your friend is to meet us with a mount."

"I will tell him."

Rhea returns from doing so as silently as she departs. We leave the warmth of the stables for the coolness of shadowy streets. Rhea doesn't speak as we walk back to the Citadel, passing through the sleeping halls and gardens of Priam's palaces. Her eyes are too busy drinking in every sight.

"What are we doing here?" she asks when we reach the lonely courtyard of Cassandra's tower. A fearful edge has crept into her voice.

"Do not worry. We will not disturb her at such an hour." For tonight it isn't the prophetess but her protector we seek.

The old man rests in the position I always find him in when I come to Cassandra's chambers. My initial visit moved me to such pity that I've returned to sit and spin thread with her three times since. There have been no more wild claims, no more opaque prophecies. Just the empty chattering of a sick, sick girl whose mind is filled with even more accusatory voices than mine.

My heart breaks for her loneliness, if only because I know it well.

The Master of Keys has been a balm to us both, his protective presence providing what none of the servants in my lavish prison can. He never speaks, and I am starting to wonder if his tongue was cut out for some crime committed years ago. Despite his silence, I am sure the man understands the city, its history, and its inhabitants better than most. The more I've studied his elaborate rendering, the more I've noticed details King Priam himself isn't likely to know.

If anyone can help us move through Troy's gates with ease, it is the Master of Keys. Though it will cost him greatly if we are caught. As it will cost all of us.

With Rhea and the old man on my heels, I approach his chalk sketch of Troy. He has added more to it since the last time I was here, just as I am always adding layers to my tapestry. Or was.

Unlike the faded images of Troy's former glory, these fresh markings show the city in the present. Or at least, they show the people in charge of her fate. All along the ramparts stand King Priam's children. Down on the Ilium plain is a crude drawing of Paris and Hector facing the Achaean army. Yet where my tapestry aimed to soften the blow of Paris's defeat, the Master of Keys has chosen to highlight the pinnacle of Paris's disgrace, as Prince Hector drags his shamed brother through the dirt and back to the battlefield.

The bold depiction stokes my confidence. Whoever the Master of Keys is, he is no friend of Paris. I point to his sketch of the Hill of Kallikolone, rising up to the east of Troy.

"I have an old friend. A god who is not worshipped in temples but *here*. A place of rich soil where Hector's line might grow," I explain in a hushed voice, repeating Cassandra's strange words. "Yet that soil must be nourished, and I believe I've figured out what it needs."

Rhea and the Master of Keys stare at me blankly, so I point to Cassandra's locked door. "She has confirmed it."

The old man studies me. Warily.

It isn't enough. The quiet moments we've shared over a twirling spindle and a piece of chalk. The silent understanding that sits between us as we seek to provide company to a madwoman rejected by all who are meant to love her.

Without warning, the Master of Keys turns, raising a thick arm for us to follow. He leads us through a maze of tunnels and alleyways only he must know how to maneuver. When we reach the east gate, our guide motions for Rhea and me to wait. He passes through the small side entrance that leads

to the top of the watchtower. What will he say to the guards, I wonder, if the
man can even speak? What sort of influence does this phantom actually
hold?

Not for the first time, I begin to think this plan is folly. My doubts only
increase when I see the animal meant to carry it forward.

The horse Larion has left tied to a post near the gate is not what I expected. Mainly because it is not a horse at all. I glance at Rhea, her head
covered by her cloak, making her seem even more childlike despite her old
soul. She strokes the pony's nose with affection. "Astra is better suited to our
task than any warhorse."

The stocky pony looks as though the short walk from the stables was
enough to wear her down. Maybe her chestnut coat was glossy once, but
now her fur is matted and dull.

"Don't worry, Harsa. Astra is stronger than she looks." Rhea gives me a
gentle smile. "And she is less likely to attract unwanted attention."

"I am sure you are right. It is just—" Heat rises to my cheeks. This old
pony and I are more alike than I care to admit. Once my legs were strong
from walking the vineyards around my father's palace. Even when I was
Menelaus's queen, I chased Hermione through my gardens almost daily. Yet
here, Paris has denied me even the privilege of pulling weeds. Since I've been
in Troy, I have hardly moved except to reach for my wine. Other women may
say they envy my lithe build and narrow waist, but all I feel these days is
weak.

"Thank you." I stroke the sturdy pony's forelock. "I don't think I'd have
the strength to make this trek without your help."

The servant girl glows like I've handed her a sunbeam from Apollo's
crown. There is a low creak as the gates part. The Master of Keys reappears,
looking rather pleased with himself.

Rhea helps me onto the pony and leads us through the exit. From my
perch, I turn to say good-bye to the old man, but I can tell by his stalwart
face and steady, soldierlike gait that he intends to accompany us farther.

Before long, the humming of cicadas fills my ears in between the clip of
Astra's hooves, two songs I have not heard in ages. They set loose a vibration
within me until everything feels like a single heartbeat.

"How long has it been since you've known a night without oil lamps?" I
ask Rhea as we move deeper into the darkness, away from walls that have

been more cage than sanctuary. The wind whistles through the silver of the surrounding olive trees, and I sense a stirring I have not felt since I came to Troy.

An entire world unseen. The Unnamed One calling me home.

"It's been some months since I've been able to see the night sky so clearly," Rhea admits, turning her face to the heavens. "My father taught me to read the stars. But I have never been on the sea."

I do not ask her to explain, but I can tell she wishes to continue. As if my simple question has opened a wineskin long sealed.

"Before his voyages, my father always asked the Mother for safe passage."

"The Mother?" I say as we move north. "You mean the Phrygian goddess Cybele?"

"She has many names."

I nod. "The things that are most real often do."

When we fall silent, I again hear the soft patter of the Unnamed One playing in a thousand places. In Astra's labored breathing. In the star-kissed sky that gave the pony her name. In every muddled thought and tenacious hope that has brought me to this untamed place.

From my perch, I survey the pulsating wildness of this hillside. The purple outline of Kallikolone rises up in front of us. The road we must follow to reach its summit does not look as steep as I expected, but it is far longer. Only this one way up and one way down.

The Master of Keys sits on a large boulder beside the start of the incline, wheezing in a way that betrays his age. His curt nod says this is where he'll wait for us to complete whatever female magic we came here to conjure.

Rhea searches my eyes for a sign that I am ready. When I give it, she tugs on the lead and the pony begins to climb. Astra is an easy ride—slow and steady, as consistent as the day is long.

For the next half hour, I am free. Free to wander the dark. Free to listen to the wind. I hear nothing clearly distilled enough to be called a *voice*, but I can feel the Unnamed One's presence ripening in all that lives and grows around us. Things that are born and must die but that are also reborn. A million earthly monuments revealing as much care and intention as my tapestry once did.

I glance at Rhea and remember what it felt like. To be young. To have limitless possibilities and few disappointments. To so easily trust in people and in the goodness of the world.

"I can see you have a willing heart, a heart that longs to serve," I say finally, breaking through the blanket of silence. "I was once the same."

When Rhea looks at me, I realize my mistake. This girl has seen her share of grief and heartbreak. Yet her face still harbors an innocence I can't help but envy.

"I was a healer among my people," I continue, my own amphora tipped over. "That was the work the Unnamed One called me to."

Rhea raises a brow. "A god from your homeland?"

I gesture to Kallikolone. "As a girl, I first heard the whispers on a rocky hillside much like this one, the wind dancing with my uncovered hair. It was the first time I'd escaped the women's quarters and found myself entirely *alone.*" Alone, except for that infinite echo we each feel inside us but find difficult to identify. "When I asked what the deity was called, the answer I received was strange. *The Name behind all others.*"

So let me tell you your name instead.

Helen.

Healer.

Beloved.

The memory is still so vivid, I can taste the wild honeysuckle I'd plucked from that verdant hillside.

"Where is this god's temple?" Rhea asks.

"There isn't one. When I asked the Unnamed One where I could serve as a priestess, I was told to *seek the east wind, which blows where it pleases.*"

Only this trackless path did not end in the holy life of an unmarried Paeana as I'd hoped, but to a contest among suitors. A war between the beds of Menelaus, king of Sparta, and Paris, prince of Troy.

"I can no longer hear the Voice," I admit. "Not since I've been in Troy."

Rhea looks especially thoughtful. "I wonder if you cannot hear it because the Citadel is too . . . full. Because the clamoring within its walls has grown too loud."

As it has within my own mind.

"I also hear things," she continues. "They are clearest when I am alone and the moment is . . . plain. Simple. In the stables with my horses. In the stillness of Andromache and Hector's household after everyone else is asleep."

I marvel at the wisdom in one so young. "Then that is your home. A place where you may be alone but are still seen. A place where you are fully known and yet fully loved. When you have that, nothing else can frighten you."

A new expression takes over the girl's strange features. "I suppose it is like that now, even if it was not always," she says at last. "But where is your home, Harsa Helen?"

My gaze travels up the hillside. "I used to know."

Rhea gives me a small nod that says what words cannot.

Now that we are out in the open, I see how truly homeless I have been. What if the Unnamed One was there all along, speaking in whispers instead of shouts? The vibration behind all my soul's stirrings?

Astra stops at a clearing near the top of the crag. The summit. A ring of fiery pink surrounds us as the sun begins to crest. Yet it is not so tranquil over the sea to the west. There, black clouds gather, swirling with Poseidon's wrath.

At the sight of this looming darkness, Rhea kneels down to release a handful of grass to the wind. "The storm is moving this way. We must hurry."

"Do you know how to build a fire?" I ask, suddenly aware that I do not.

"For an offering?" Rhea removes a piece of flint from beneath her cloak and smiles. "I was raised on a farm. By a most pious man."

While the girl gathers twigs and bits of dry brush, I search for the plant that is our primary purpose here. As the sky lightens, a flash of gold winks from Kallikolone's black soil.

There. A small ring of Apollo's Wreath. Right on the clearing's threshold, where the light meets the dark.

"What is that?" Rhea asks at my back.

"A mushroom that will make Andromache's tea more potent," I explain. "I smelled her herbs at the Fair Winds. The mixture was rancid, yet it has taken me some time to figure out what ingredient might be missing."

What I don't tell her is we have Paris's poisoning attempt to thank for that.

"Is that the reason we have come here?" Rhea glances back to the small fire she has built.

"It is one of the reasons." I remove my sandals and step toward the flames, relishing the feel of sacred earth between my toes.

Dawn is about to break. A hawk circles the dusky sky. When the bird releases a shrill cry, my eyes fly back to Rhea. In a flash, everything changes. As if the wind scatters a cloud of ash that's been hanging over my gaze all this time.

Rhea now sits high on a stallion instead of standing beside her pony. Her face looks older and harder, yet the spark in her eyes speaks of a love as untamed as the horse of fire she mounts. In her arms rests a bundle swaddled in reams of colorful cloth.

I blink and the vision is gone.

"Are you all right, Harsa?" Rhea asks, once again a disheveled girl holding a feed bag.

My knees sink to the ground. "This child. Who . . ."

I find I already know. I would know him just as I'd know the flash of his father's helmet. As I would know the bold swish of his mother's stride amid countless shadows.

It isn't your sacrifice that will save him, Helen. It is your love.

The wind whips the veil around my face, the Voice stronger than it has ever been.

My eyes drift to the few pale stars still hanging in the sky. How little of this vastness can we glimpse from here? The sight of the flickering heavens only deepens the ache that gnaws at me. Watching stars on a summer night was one of Hermione's favorite pastimes.

I have no idea what makes her smile now.

You promise to keep her close?

The wind caresses my cheek.

I will hold her as I hold the stars. As I hold you. I will take your mother's love and multiply it tenfold.

I let the cool gale run over me, needles along my skin. Opening my satchel, I inhale the musky aroma of the damp earth before me. Another deep breath of black smoke.

Again, the hawk circles.

If I openly disobey Paris by helping Andromache and throwing myself on her mercy, there is no going back. Hermione will marry the son of Achilles, and I won't be there to see it.

She will be gone.

A rush of blood blasts through my ears as I dig my fingers into the soil around a cluster of Apollo's Wreath. Once I free several mushrooms from their beds, I place them in the satchel and draw even closer to the flames. With dirt-streaked hands, I lift my veil and let it dance on the breeze. It is the same veil I used to wipe Hermione's tears the night Paris ripped her from me as if from my womb.

Pale arm trembling, my fingers hold out the veil to the fire's greedy tongues.

I raise the leather satchel in one hand. The other lets go.

A single strand catches, and then all the finely woven fibers are consumed. The only things in this world that survive fire are the things unseen.

"Give Andromache her son."

I close my eyes and turn my face upward. Up toward flecks of ash the wind blows to destinations unknown.

20

RHEA

THE SKY RUMBLES above us. The sound has grown louder ever since we left the clearing at the top of Kallikolone. The day should be getting lighter, but instead, the world grows darker around us.

The air smells sweet with an edge of sharpness. Maybe it's the sea. The beaches are too far away to glimpse, but there's a distant crash, like the sound of waves throwing themselves upon the beaches, making the Achaean ships groan. Or perhaps those are the ghosts of the dead I hear.

A shiver runs up my spine as Astra tosses her head, eyes wide and panicked.

We are halfway down the side of Kallikolone when it starts to rain. Cold, stinging drops that slice as they fall. Wind lashes over the hill, making it hard to see. Astra's panic dances through my veins. I try to calm her, but it's impossible to hear anything over the building storm. We are near the bottom of the hill when it becomes unsafe to ride. I stop the pony and reach up for Helen. Her hands lock with mine. Gracefully, she slides down from Astra's back.

"Stay low to the ground," I yell over the wind. The rain pelts our shoulders and backs with painful force.

Helen nods. She's been silent since she completed her ritual. As wrong as it had felt watching the woman pray, I couldn't look away, and what I saw left me certain of one thing.

Helen of Sparta is not who she pretends to be.

Entire worlds lie buried under the topography of her face. I caught flashes of them in the firelight as she bent in supplication, Andromache's name a whisper on the wind.

That was when the storm came.

I hope this wasn't a terrible mistake. My heart tells me Helen wishes Hector and Andromache no harm, but I don't know how to make that fit with what I know of Prince Paris. He is small and cruel, and, as all of Troy learned yesterday, a coward. What kind of woman would leave her husband and daughter to run away with a man like that?

Perhaps a woman who had no other choice.

The thought strikes me as a bolt of bright light slashes the sky. Astra dances on her feet, the whites of her eyes glaring in the dark. I look across the open plains toward the sea as a dozen of Tarhunt's bolts fall from the churning clouds at once. For several heartbeats, the world in front of us is laid bare with stark clarity.

The killing fields of Ilium. The distant beaches strewn with Achaean vessels and endless camps of men. And beyond their monstrous ships, a wall of churning black stretching out as far as the horizon.

In sixteen years at the foot of the mountains, I've weathered many storms, but I've never seen a storm like this.

"We must hurry, Harsa." I grab Astra's lead and jerk her hard, cutting a path straight down the slope.

Helen's longer legs keep pace with mine, though it is a struggle for her in an elaborate gown better suited to Priam's gilded halls than this mountain trail. In front of us, the path back to Troy materializes in the unnatural dark, marked by the boulder where we left the man Helen introduced as the Master of Keys. The old man is gone now. He must have wisely sought shelter.

We head down the narrow walkway that leads toward Troy's easternmost walls and the same gate through which I first entered the city all those weeks ago. We're nearing the turn to that gate when a hand reaches out of the darkness.

The cry that leaves my lips is stolen by the wind.

The Master of Keys' bearded face presses close to mine. He takes Astra's lead from my hand and drops it, slapping her hard on the rear so that she takes off at a trot. With another cry, I move after her. The old man pulls me and Helen into the rough bushes that lie alongside the path, jerking us down into a crouch.

"What is it?" Helen finds her words at last.

The Master of Keys' beard is wet and dripping, his eyes gleaming in the flashes of light that are almost right on top of us. They are fixed on something up ahead.

Shadows move in the darkness to our left. They creep across the shrubbery that lies at the foot of Kallikolone, between the bridge and shrubs at the edge of the trench.

Men. A dozen of them. They're not wearing armor, but I can tell who they are by the weapons strapped to their sides and the stealthy way they move.

Achaeans.

How did they come so close without raising an alarm?

I glance up at the walls, but any archers who might be there have long since taken cover from the storm. The small party of Achaean soldiers splits into two groups. One moves to the left of the bridge toward the southern wall of the Lower City. The other moves right, toward the plateau and the Citadel that sits at its highest point. They disappear into the bushes that run along the trench's edge. The same bushes we are using for cover.

My pulse pounds in my ears as I survey the open space that leads to the swaying bridge and the gate beyond. The Achaeans are somewhere out there, between us and the entrance to Troy. We can't get past them unseen, but we also can't remain out here in the open. Not with those black clouds closing in. Beside me, Helen bows her head like she is praying all over again.

The Master of Keys drops to his knees and crawls through the bushes at the edge of the path. He jerks his chin for us to follow.

The ground is wet and squelching under my hands. The old soldier is just a few feet ahead of me, but several times, I lose sight of him through the near-solid sheets of rain. Behind us, Helen struggles to keep pace.

Several minutes pass before I realize we are following a trail. It's overgrown, but below the grass and weeds, the stones have been worn smooth. Troy's northeast bastion towers over us like a specter. To the left, the trench ends in a sheer wall of earth.

We've reached the base of the bastion. A more effective barrier to invaders than any men could build. From here, it's impossible to reach the city walls, never mind any gate that could let us in.

The ground under my hands drops away without warning. I tumble forward, directly into a pair of arms. With surprising strength, the Master of

Keys brings me down onto a narrow ledge under an overhang of crag. Just beyond the tips of my sandals, the ground falls away.

The plateau.

I press my back against the vertical slab of earth. Beside me, the Master of Keys hands Helen down until she is standing at my side. The ledge under our feet is carved into the face of the plateau and barely wide enough to walk on. With no other choice, we follow our silent guide's lead as he walks along the treacherous path.

Wind and rain whip into our faces, turning the sharp blade of the ledge slippery under our feet. With every step we travel toward the center of the plateau, the drop below us steepens. Behind me, Helen stumbles. I reach out and grab a fistful of her gown. We keep moving.

After a few painstaking minutes, the ledge widens. Ahead of me, the Master of Keys drops to his hands and knees and crawls again, this time through a tunnel of earth that leads into a narrow, sideways opening cut into the face of the plateau. He slips through the darkened slit.

The inside smells of earth and rain. Flickers of light from the guard station on the wall high above us puncture the narrow grotto from various places in the ceiling, providing just enough contrast to make out the barest of outlines. The Master of Keys melts into the darkness ahead. I stifle a gasp when his hand takes mine, leading me to a place where the plateau wall seems to come together in a solid mass.

Something sparks. A small flame in the old man's hand. It illuminates the darkness, revealing what I could not see before.

Helen's ruined robes, hanging in tatters. The bloody cuts on his face and my arms. And the slight gap in the wall to my left. A hole. One that is barely wide enough for a child.

"What is this place?" Helen's voice echoes in the silent grotto.

The man takes our hands and runs them along a rough seam of wall.

I let out a breath of wonder. "This is where the plateau meets the man-made walls of Troy." The old man nods. "And this hole, it leads into the city?" Another nod.

Helen frowns down at the opening. "Only a child could hope to pass through. Or someone nearly as small." This time, the old man doesn't bother to nod. He merely looks over Helen's shoulder. Helen's gaze follows, and I take a step backward.

"There is no need for desperate measures. We can rest here until the storm passes and then—"

Helen's whisper is cut off by an echo from the front of the grotto.

Voices. The harsh cadence of Greek.

A visible tremor moves through Helen. The Master of Keys douses the small flame in his hands, sending us crashing into darkness. As one, we huddle behind the waist-high boulder obscuring the small opening behind us. Four figures carrying torches step into the open space directly ahead.

Our hiding place lies just beyond the reach of their lights. If they move any deeper, they'll see us, and the hidden entrance to Troy that lies at our back.

The Master of Keys reaches for the weapon at his belt. Gone is the lonely, silent man who led us through Troy's gates. I can see the moment he abandons the thought of fighting his way through these men. There are four of them, young and strong, and he is only one, well past his prime. His hand falls from his weapon, and we are left to sit in silence.

The Achaeans study the walls around us, speaking to each other in voices low and urgent. One of them steps forward, raising his torch high. He is shorter than the others and wide across the chest with an impressive amount of hair. His eyes are sharp as they pass over the wall directly above our heads, searching.

Helen makes a sound beside me. A word passes her lips in a breath of air too soft for anyone to catch but me.

"Odysseus."

There is no fear in her voice. Instead, there is something even more powerful.

Longing.

Helen leans forward before she remembers herself. Her gaze turns sideways, running over me and the Master of Keys. Hope flows from her eyes, leaving them utterly empty. But hope for what? For whom?

It's in this moment that I see the thing I only glimpsed on the battlements during Paris's duel with Menelaus. The one that flickered in the shadows of her face on the hilltop while she made her offering. A truth hidden by the startling beauty of her features and the spell they cast over anyone who beholds them.

Helen wants to go home. A desire she can fulfill now with a single word.

In her face, I watch two sides at war, a battle between loves and loyalties, and a faith that takes my breath away as it shines from the light of her eyes.

I read the truth of her choice a moment before she slumps against the wall.

Helen of Sparta is gone.

Now there is only Helen of Troy.

The Achaeans retreat to the opening that spills onto the plateau, but the shadow of their light lingers. They are staying for now, seeking shelter. If they got this close to the walls once, they will surely come back. Next time, we might not be so lucky.

Helen rests her head against the rock, chest rising and falling rapidly with each breath.

"Are you all right, Harsa?" I ask, because I know without a doubt that had she revealed herself to those friends of her past, the Master of Keys and I would already be dead.

"I had to let her go. I had to so Hector might have his child." Her voice is low and trembling.

"Let who go?"

The fierce love in Helen's eyes when she turns to me is answer enough. I've seen eyes like that before. Once in a cart in a slave market in Cyzicus. Every day of my life before those men burned my home to the ground.

This is a mother's love. Those are a mother's eyes.

She clasps my hand in hers. "They are searching for a way past the wall. Andromache was right, for all the good it's done her. I have not seen the fires from their pyres burning for days, but even if the plague has passed, the Achaeans will be weary of losing men. If they can't win by duels or force, they will attempt victory by trickery. That is Odysseus's way." Her grip on mine becomes painful. "We need help. We need Hector."

My gaze shifts to the wall and the dark hole it hides.

Fear clenches my throat in a fist of iron.

"Look at me," Helen says in a voice that gives me no option. "If you didn't care for Hector and Andromache, you wouldn't have risked so much to aid them tonight. Now you must risk once more. Hector must be told that Odysseus is sniffing around his walls so he can send soldiers to guard the plateau and get us to safety. You must go. Go if you wish to live."

Live, Rhea. You must live.

"I'll go." My voice sounds small even to my ears.

Helen presses my hands in hers. "To Hector and Andromache. Nobody else."

I face the wall. It will be completely dark inside the narrow tunnel. I could get stuck. Or the weight of the city could come crashing down on my back.

Panic rises up inside me, but I push it down.

If these Achaeans discover Helen, they'll as likely kill her as kidnap her back to Sparta. If they find a way in, that will be the end of Troy. The end of Hector and Andromache. Of Bodecca and Creusa and Larion and Cyrrian. My stables will burn again, and this time, Carris and Ishtar with them.

My hand moves to my forearm, and my fingers find the scrap of child's blanket tied around it.

The fabric fills my hands even as helpless rage fills my heart. It is Vengeance's and it is mine. Because she could do nothing to protect the child she loved. Just as I could do nothing to protect my mother and my sisters when those men came to our farm with spears in their hands and blood in their eyes. I watched it happen then.

I meet Helen's eyes one more time, and I let her see my choice just as she showed me hers.

Then I thrust my head into the dark. And I crawl.

<hr />

"WHERE HAVE YOU been?" Andromache stands alone by the hearth. The kitchen should be bustling at this time of morning, but there is only the blazing fire and the coldness of Andromache's gaze resting solidly upon me.

The moment the warmth touches me, my legs give out. Andromache is at my side in an instant.

She lowers me into a chair. Concern takes the place of anger as she bends her tall frame into a crouch before me. "You're bleeding. What happened?"

"A band of Achaeans." I moisten my cracked lips. "Helen says they're excavating our walls for weaknesses."

At the mention of Helen's name, Andromache's eyes go as black as the storm clouds above Troy. "How do you know this?"

I wish that there were any other answer to this question than the one I am forced to give.

"Because I was there. We saw them."

Surprise flashes across her face for the briefest of moments. "You witnessed them crossing the plain?" The sheer intensity of her focus is unnerving.

"No. They . . . they were already at the city walls under cover of the storm when we sighted them."

She stands. "I will get Hector. And you. You will not move or speak a word until I return." With that, she leaves me alone with the fire and my worries, which seem to have multiplied over the last several hours.

My legs ache. My skin is scraped raw from the inside of the passage. My throat clamps shut at the memory of that darkness. The weight of the stone all around me. I close my eyes, but when I open them again, the room is no longer empty. Hector is kneeling in front of me where Andromache was just a moment ago.

"Tell me what happened."

When I've finished explaining about the plateau, Odysseus, and the secret entrance, Hector places his warm hand on my shoulder. After a few whispered words to Andromache, he opens the door and braces himself before marching out into the storm that's raging even more fiercely than it was before. My body tenses as I wait for Andromache to attack me with questions. What she does instead is much worse. She settles down into a chair opposite mine and sits as still as an effigy of the Hittite sun goddess Arinna, her dark gaze fixed on the flames.

An hour passes, maybe more. I'm exhausted, though not foolish enough to fall asleep. It is a long time before she speaks.

"I don't know what you were doing with that woman beyond Troy's walls in the dead of night, but whatever your reasons"—she takes a steadying breath—"you may have saved this city." Another endless pause. "Be that as it may, I have taken you into my personal service and my confidence. Tonight, you have rewarded my trust with betrayal."

Her words are a blade slipped between my ribs. It's exactly what I feared. A fall from Andromache's favor. And what's worse is that I deserve her wrath. I did betray her trust, and my motives don't matter as much as my actions. Not when my actions are the only thing that she can *see*.

The smell of the stables. Lying in the hay at night with Ishtar and Carris. My morning chores with Larion. The long evenings in Andromache's rooms listening to the rise and fall of her voice. Hector's quiet kindness and Bodecca's fussing. The peace and happiness I've found when I didn't think I'd ever know peace or happiness again. I can feel them slipping through my fingers because of a decision I can never take back.

"I understand, Harsa."

I can almost hear the sharp blade of Andromache's mind whirl in the echoing silence.

"There is only one way you can restore my confidence in you."

"Anything." The word spills from my lips with no thought whatsoever.

Andromache places her hands in her lap, the picture of composure, but after all these months, I read the distress in the small lines around her mouth. "When Hector returns, I will ask something of you. I need you to agree even if it frightens you. Can you do that, Rhea? Can you do what must be done no matter what it requires?"

Before I can respond, Hector enters the kitchen with a blast of wind and rain.

Andromache stands at once. "The Achaeans?"

Hector moves toward the hearth and warms his hands. "They scattered when we passed through the Scaean gate. Whatever path they used to reach our walls, they weren't so foolish as to reveal it as they fled."

Andromache gnaws her lip. "Odysseus?"

"Is a hard figure to miss." He shakes his head. "But he was not among the ones we saw."

"Then he is still lying in wait outside our walls. The men you saw were meant to misdirect us. He'd have us believe the storm is what allowed them to come so close." She paces the length of the hearth. "He will leave the city on the same path by which he approached it."

"Wherever he hides, we won't take him by surprise," Hector says. "Not if he is watching our gates."

I wait for Andromache to argue. Hector must expect it too, because her easy nod of acceptance draws a frown from him. "Paris's trophy?" Andromache wastes no time changing the subject.

"She is a little worse for wear, but mostly unharmed," says a figure stepping in behind Hector.

Helen's elegant robes are covered in mud. The dark kohl smudges under her eyes give her the look of the dead. Her hair has fallen from its coiffure to form a tangled mane around her head, but for all that, her beauty still hits with all the force of the storm we just fled.

"What is she doing in our home?" Andromache sets her feet the way she did the night she placed a blade in my hand and taught me how to use it.

"She had nowhere else to go." Hector rubs a palm over his face. "I said she could stay here so that we might make some excuse to Paris for her absence last night."

"And what concern is it of ours if Paris cannot keep track of his prize?"

Hector looks at her with equal parts plea and command. "Because if my wife turned up cold and bleeding at my brother's door, I hope he'd see her cared for. Because we haven't fallen so far as to have forgotten who we are, Andromache."

The silence that stretches is heavy with hidden meanings.

Helen clears her throat. "Thank you, Rhea. I owe you a debt that I hope someday to repay."

"The only thing we would welcome at this moment is an explanation," Andromache snaps. "Rhea could have died in that wall because of you."

"I'm sorry for it. Yet Rhea's courage tonight has spared Troy much suffering."

"She was disobedient." The hardness in Andromache's tone makes me flinch. "And as a member of my household, she is none of your concern. Which begs the question why she was with you to begin with."

Helen draws herself up, and for a moment, I glimpse the woman from the grotto. The one who gave up the future she wanted so that two innocent people would not pay the price for it. "That is something we must discuss." Her eyes dart to Hector.

"No more of your games. This is my home. If you wish to speak you will do so now and on my terms."

"You are angry, and not without cause." Helen presses the leather satchel to her chest. "But there are things I must say to you in private. I have my reasons. You must believe me."

It is the wrong thing to say.

"I do not have to do anything." Andromache strides forward, and Helen takes a step back. "We have Achaeans sniffing around our walls and wayward servants to question. Now is not the time for whatever petty schemes of Paris have brought you here."

"This has nothing to do with him." A brief flicker of anger passes over Helen's face, but she collects herself. "You were right. Odysseus is the greatest danger facing Troy. I know him. His cunning is matched only by his determination. He will not stop until this city is rubble and his ship is bound for Ithaca."

"How unfortunate you could not offer your support when it actually mattered," Andromache says coldly.

Helen swallows. "I was not free to speak then, but I wish to atone for that now. I can help if you let me."

"I want none of your help."

The act of drawing her shoulders back seems to take all of Helen's courage. "Be that as it may, you will have it. I'll give you all a moment, but what I have to say can't wait longer than that." Helen toys with the bag still clutched in her hands. Her eyes rove over Hector with something akin to regret before they return to Andromache. "I hope someday you realize what you have." She walks to the door leading to the hall and pauses on the threshold. "I hope someday you stop punishing people for the actions they take for love of you, Andromache."

Helen walks out of the kitchens for the guest rooms. An oppressive stillness lingers in her wake.

"We are missing something," Andromache says at last. "If she knows Odysseus so well, how do we know Helen didn't leave the city precisely to help him through our walls? She was in the Lower City when it was struck by the plague. Perhaps she played a hand in that too."

"She didn't. She wouldn't." I speak from weariness and from the fear that has dulled my sense. "She was only trying to help."

"Help how?" Andromache demands.

I start to tell her about Apollo's Wreath but stop myself. Andromache will never believe Helen would so blatantly undermine Paris's chance to take the throne. No, she is far more likely to suspect Helen of attempting to poison her. "She could've turned herself over to Odysseus tonight, but she didn't," I say instead.

"Then she must truly love Paris. Which is all the more reason to doubt her motives."

"No!"

The word from my lips is a bolt of lightning slashing through the room.

The rigid line of Andromache's shoulders lets me know the thunder will soon follow. I want to duck my head and hide from her anger, but I don't. Andromache needs to hear the truth, even if it costs me whatever is left of her trust. "She doesn't love him. If anything, I think she is afraid of him. She didn't leave the walls of Troy tonight for him or for the Achaeans."

"Then why did she go?" Andromache asks yet again.

Yet again, some deeper instinct cautions me against revealing the full truth. "She was . . . praying. Not for herself, but I think . . . for Troy." I shiver and meet the full force of Andromache's gaze. "There's more to Helen than she would have anyone believe."

Hector sinks into a chair by the fire. "If Odysseus has found a way to approach our defenses unseen, Helen's reasons for leaving the city aren't our most pressing concern."

Andromache straightens. "After tonight, there will be no way for the Citadel to deny the threat he poses."

Hector tips his head back. "It isn't that simple. They will use the storm to explain this away just as they did the body. Subterfuge isn't how the Achaeans fight. It will be hard for the council to concede that so much power could be given to one man."

"Because Paris has them convinced this is all some diversionary tactic on my part!" Andromache stalks to the hearth. The flames set her white robe glowing orange at the edges.

Hector sighs. "I believe you, Andromache. But unlike bronze, people's minds cannot be bent with fire and force."

"You should not have to win over every weak-chinned man who sits on your father's council! As commander, it is your right to decide how to deploy Troy's sons. They owe you their allegiance." Her voice goes quiet. "But if they continue to withhold it, we will be forced to protect our city by other means."

"What means are those?" Water drips from his hair down into his eyes. Hector does not wipe it away.

"The only ones left at our disposal." Andromache turns and looks directly at me.

The room shifts. I hold fast to the chair with my broken hands.

Hector looks between us, brow furrowed.

"Odysseus's men will be watching for any troops that leave our gates," Andromache says calmly. "We will never catch him that way. If we wish to discover how he is advancing on our walls unseen, we must approach him from an angle he is not expecting."

Every ounce of emotion bleeds out of Hector's features when her meaning finally dawns on him. For a moment, he looks like a stranger, and that frightens me almost as much as what Andromache is proposing.

He leans toward me, as if he could protect me from the words that haven't yet been said. "You would send Rhea through the tunnel and back out into the storm?"

The declaration is a wind blasting through the room, sucking out all breathable air. Suddenly, I am trapped in that tunnel again. Surrounded by darkness. Unsure of how I'll ever get out.

"She has safely made the passage through the wall once already. Wherever Odysseus is hiding, he will not expect a scout from the plateau. All she has to do is watch and wait for him to make his move back across the plain. If we discover *how* he is reaching the city walls, it will be proof the council cannot deny."

"The council?" Hector's tone is as limp as the hands that fall to his sides. He studies his wife as if he has never seen her before. "Look at her, Andromache. She is hurt and terrified. So exhausted she can hardly stand."

It would seem unspeakably cruel if I didn't know Andromache. And she is never cruel. At least, not without reason.

"She is stronger than you give her credit for and cleverer than most of the men who sit on your father's council. More importantly, her safety depends on the integrity of our walls every bit as much as ours does."

Her eyes land on me, and for the first time, I glimpse the desperation in them. *Do this for him,* they beg. *Do this for Troy, and I will forget what happened tonight. Do this for* me, *and I will see that you never go a day without family again.*

I don't want to let her down. More than anything, I want to justify her faith in me, but I'm terrified of the darkness under the wall. Even if I weren't, taking Andromache's side now feels like a betrayal of the man who saved my life in every way that matters.

The muscles in my body tense in response to his silent anguish. His nostrils are flared, his chest rising and falling too rapidly. Heedless of the danger, Andromache barrels on, oblivious to everything but her own plans.

"This may be the only opportunity we get to stop him."

"Andromache—"

"No, Hector! I will not sit idly by while he brings down our walls around us. It is the succession all over again! We both know what needs to be done." She steels herself, and then she hits him where she knows it will do the most damage. "The difference between us is that I am willing to make the sacrifices required. No matter what they cost us."

And you are not . . . The words hang in the air unspoken.

Hector draws a ragged breath and rises to his feet. His hands clench and unclench at his sides. And then the painful silence breaks with all the fury of the storm.

Roaring, Hector picks up the chair and flings it against the wall.

Andromache flinches. A deep pain flashes across her face, but she hides it away before he turns.

"Enough, Andromache. *Enough!*" He stalks toward her. "This is not about the succession or Odysseus. This is about you and the way Troy's customs chafe at your pride. And so to take it back, you'd have this child risk her life to do what you cannot? A girl who is in our charge? One you *know* would do anything to gain your respect and who holds no true power to say no to your reckless demands?"

Andromache's temper rises to match his. "That is what you have always failed to understand. True power lies in the choosing, husband. You live in a world of choices laid out before you like garments. They are not easy, but they are yours. What choices am I given? What choices do girls like Rhea have?" She raises her chin. "Every day, I watch you ride out of our gates and face death with a spear in your hands. I have no weapons here, Hector. All I have is a body that will not do what I need it to and the wits in my head. I will wield them both to defend what is mine. As you wield yours. Without remorse. It is the only power I have left. Do not strip me of it, Hector. And do not strip Rhea of this one opportunity to decide her own fate."

"Hector." The voice comes from the doorway. We all turn to find Harsar Aeneas standing there in his armor, soaked through with rain.

He frowns at the scene. "The rain has stopped, but the Semiosis and the Scamander have already risen dangerously high. We need to check the levees before they break."

Hector doesn't lift his gaze from Andromache. "Leave us, Aeneas."

The tic in his jaw is the only indication that the Dardanian prince resents being ordered around like a common soldier. "The rain will not hold off for long. We have to—"

"I said, leave!" Hector bellows.

"I'll wait outside." Aeneas's eyes are large when he ducks out of the doorway.

"I have always trusted your counsel, Andromache," Hector says when his cousin has left. "Out of love for your strength and your spirit, I've looked the other way when you acted in a way that would have shamed another man. Because for all that you push me, I have the strength to push back. This is not the same. You will trample Rhea in your rush to slip your lead, and I don't believe you are prepared for the consequences. If the worst happens, I'm not sure either of us could forgive you."

"I am not asking for your forgiveness. I am asking you to put aside your own stubborn sense of duty and let her decide what risks are worth taking."

All the strength seems to go out of Hector at once.

They both turn to me. These two people I have come to respect. To love, even. They wait for me to make the choice between them. And I find I can't do it. I can't choose.

So I do the thing I did the first night my world burned around me.

I run.

21

ANDROMACHE

THE STORM RESTS for a few breaths before it returns with the ire of Tarhunt.

It batters the brick floor of the terrace outside, causing the tapestry in the doorway to flap without ceasing. But that isn't the sound that wakes me.

I lift my aching head from the bed and move toward the chamber door.

"Andromache? I must speak with you."

Helen.

My apathy intensifies with each of her knocks. I turn back to the bed, intending to nurse my throbbing head. A punishment following Hector's outburst and Rhea's flight. As well as all the bitter thoughts I have spent the morning ruminating on.

It's as if all these years of fighting have turned my very being into an arena of war. One where I am a battler not just of men but of everyone. Including myself—if I even know who that is anymore.

It must be close to midday. Hours since Hector left with Aeneas to deal with the flooding of the system of levees that surrounds the city. The lack of light makes it difficult to tell. When I step to the doorway of my balcony, all I see is a bluish-green wall. The dark clouds that swirled above the sea at dawn have regathered over the Ilium plain, blotting out the sun.

"Why aren't they back yet?"

My voice is lost in the wail of the east wind. If Rhea were here, she would give me an answer. Come up with a sensible reason for their delayed return.

But Rhea is not here. Neither is Hector.

And it is all my doing.

Pressing my ear to the bedchamber door, I listen for footsteps. Hearing none, I open the door and make my way down the narrow staircase, pausing when I land on the creakiest step. There is a distinct lack of commotion coming from the kitchen.

One face and one face only greets me when I enter it. The one I least wish to see.

"Andromache." Helen's hands fly under her robes. She stands before Bodecca's workstation, a long table lined with clay pots of spices, jugs of oil, and a mortar and pestle. I push past Paris's harlot without speaking and grab the bag that contains my tea.

Why do I bother?

When I glance up, Helen is watching me. Her gemlike eyes flit between my hands and a hardened face that has more battle lines than hers ever will.

"I hope now is a better time to talk. Surely you have questions."

"The only question I have is why you are still here—"

Before I can finish, my vision blurs. The shock of a pain so intense, I can't help but grip my head in one hand while the other holds the table. A streak of light from Tarhunt flashes outside the window. Another similar bolt strikes me behind the temples.

"Are you all right?"

Nothing is right. Helenus and Laocoon have their signs for the imminent arrival of blood, and I have my own. Headaches are the most prominent.

"There is water on the fire," Helen notes, taking a seat across from me as I ease into a chair. "Do you always have headaches like this before your moon cycle?"

I snap open my eyes.

"It is not an uncommon ailment," she continues. Helen nods at the bag on the table between us. "Does the tea help?"

Another surge of pain overcomes me. "Sometimes . . . I don't know."

"The trick," Helen says, rising to approach the fire, "is to pour the water over the leaves as soon as it reaches a rolling boil. Allowing the water to bubble for too long makes the tea go flat, and its potency is weakened."

As am I. All the bloom of youth gone.

With a firm shake of the head, I sit up straight, newly aware. Helen of

Sparta is in my kitchen. She is bringing a ladle of hot water toward me. Helen holds my gaze, keeping her movements slow. Steady. As she lowers the ladle, I add a few pinches of dried tea to my cup. She pours the water over and I inhale its soothing steam, almost forgetting who she is.

As much as I do not want to admit it, Helen may be right. The tea smells different. Fresh. Almost sweet.

It tastes even better.

The Spartan's eyes remain locked on my face as I take a few small sips.

"Bodecca always leaves pots boiling for days on end," I murmur. "I will have to tell her to change her ways."

"From what I've seen of the woman, I can't imagine that is an easy task." Helen smiles hesitantly, and I find myself wanting to rail against the simple yet infuriating gesture.

But I cannot find the strength to abhor her now. Not when my own shortcomings have never been so pronounced, causing two people I care about to flee into a storm rather than face me.

The regret and self-loathing swirl into a cyclone.

"It does no good to dwell on what cannot be changed."

Helen's voice again breaks through the chaotic rumbling. Normally, I'd have a curt reply ready, but the way she speaks—it's almost as if she understands.

The soothing tingle from the tea spreads out from my belly. I have not felt its warming effects, not like this, since Cyzicus. After a few more sips, my thoughts begin to clear. Not enough for me to be so foolish as to think Rhea was right about Helen, but enough for me to wonder if perhaps she was not entirely wrong.

"I know you have no reason to listen, but you must hear me, Andromache," Helen begins. "There are things you *don't* know. Things I must—"

The kitchen door bangs behind me. I assume it's the storm, but the way Helen's face blanches has me whirling around in my seat.

Drenched to the bone, Paris looks even more like the scrawny, spoiled boy he is.

I rise from my chair. "In my household, visitors use the front door."

Paris stares right past me, his viper's tongue oddly silent. "You. Cover yourself. We're leaving."

Helen does not move from her chair, but I hear the sharp intake of breath. Her hands resting on the table start to tremble. She reaches for my gaze with the look of a frightened animal. And then she does something stranger still.

She stretches her hands wide, fingers splayed across the wood. Her eyes close. It's as if she has laid down all weapons and surrendered. But to what?

Helen's lips move in a silent plea. She does not flinch or cease her voiceless murmurings as Paris storms into my kitchen.

"Stop this idiocy," he growls, grabbing one of Helen's arms and yanking her out of the chair. Still, her lips continue moving. With what, a prayer? When his wife does not snap out of her trance, Paris strikes her across the face.

The loud *smack* brings me a step closer. "Paris, this is uncalled for!"

Helen is no friend of mine, but I will not suffer abuse under my roof. I move toward Paris but stop when I hear more footsteps. In the doorway behind me stand three soldiers from Paris's personal guard, along with two servingwomen, heads covered by the hoods of their long cloaks.

Paris pulls Helen toward his armed entourage. "Concern yourself with matters of your own household, Andromache. As you have so often told me."

"Hector will hear that you stormed into his house ready with weapons."

"Let him," Paris replies. "Hearing complaints and doing nothing about them is about all my brother is good for."

It isn't until they are outside beneath the rain that Helen returns from the otherworldly realm she has fled to.

"Andromache! Andromache, please!"

Doubt gnaws at my insides as the courtyard flashes with Tarhunt's light. *She could've turned herself over to Odysseus tonight, but she didn't.*

And that was her choice. She chose Paris, miserable wretch that he is. I stand in the doorway, watching them go. My thoughts swirling like the sky above.

Thunder booms. The very walls of Troy seem to shake.

Whatever strife exists between Paris and his prize, it is none of my business. I have my own pressing concerns.

Namely, the storm is worsening, and Hector has not returned with his men.

It isn't like him. What if Odysseus and his men laid an ambush? At least Achilles fights in the open, whereas Odysseus has proven himself most dangerous when moving in darkness.

Outside, that darkness gathers.

I pace before the hearth as more clouds roll over the plain. We've seen countless rainy seasons over the years of fighting, and always Hector pulled the army closer to the walls as soon as the weather turned the battlefield into a bog. There was no need to lose chariot wheels or break our horses' legs in the mud. No need to expose our infantry to Tarhunt's angry bolts when the rains would not last forever.

Rounding up supplies and checking the levees shouldn't take this long.

I pour another cup of tea. For the entire first year of this war, I could hardly sleep during the long nights Hector spent with his men in the camp beyond the Lower City walls. To keep my mind off the spears flying past Hector's head, I pressed into the work of running this household. I prepared the bodies of Troy's dead, and I worked my loom day and night.

Now, I sit and drink herbs.

And I wait. Hoping against hope, though I have no reason to.

I set down my cup, drained to the dregs, with every intention of returning to bed. But when I reach the staircase, something makes me pause. On the wall hangs my wedding present from Hector. The large copper disk he commissioned from a skilled craftsman. Painted a deep violet-blue, it is inlaid with the golden symbols of the royal seal we share as indication of our authority. And our unity.

A stallion's head and a tongue of flame.

My fingers trace the flame that has become as much a part of me as my name. One that burns bright but is also capable of consuming everything in its path. I know I speak without tact and push others too hard along the path I have in mind. But I also know the many shades of Hector's anger. The resentment I saw in his eyes before Aeneas dragged him back to the battlefield was new.

And what of Rhea? She may never forgive me for seeking to use her free will like a tool to achieve my own ends.

Once I reach my rooms upstairs, I can hear the horses outside in their stables, whinnying in terror as they stomp their hooves at the storm.

They want to run. To move.

So do I.

Rushing to the bed, I search for the riding tunic hidden beneath it. Apprehension tightens around my waist with each cinch of the leather belt that keeps the wool tunic in place. What will Hector do when he sees his wife charging down the plain, looking as though she was born to ride?

It is a moment I have planned for weeks. Practicing my riding with Rhea whenever the men are away. Learning to trust the horse as she does—which, it turns out, is the first step to the horse trusting me in return. Still, this is not how I intended my grand entrance to go.

But it is my chance to make things right. Even if it is the only time I set foot among Hector's ranks, *I must go to him* instead of demanding that he always return to me. Whatever it takes, I must put an end to Hector's rage.

For he has said it himself. It is anger that sends men to the pyre too soon.

As I'm strapping on my boots, the door to my chamber opens. Aeneas's face is the first I see, his mouth set in a thin grimace. A helmetless Cyrrian is with him, covered in mud from head to foot. Between the two men hangs a limp figure whose features are hidden by his horsehair helmet. Not that I need to see his face to know him.

"What happened?" I am by Hector's side before the words can escape.

"It is nothing," Hector groans, lifting his head like it is dead weight.

I unclip the chin strap and let his helmet drop to the floor, releasing him from the one piece of armor that can transform him from a gentle husband into a fearsome warrior. "Nothing, Hector? In all these years, you've never been carried to our doorstep by your friends."

My insides clench at how much worse it might have been. Aeneas and Cyrrian could be bringing Hector's body back to me on a burial cart.

And it would be my fault.

"In all these years, you've never made me so willing to meet my death." Despite the agony twisting his face, the corner of Hector's mouth lifts slightly. "And that is saying something."

The clip of my laugh is trailed by a sob.

He is still here. He is still mine.

Aeneas and Cyrrian hold him up awkwardly as I throw my arms around Hector's neck. When I pull back, our gazes lock. My hands search his battered body. "Where are the wounds?"

"Nothing to stitch," Cyrrian explains. "It's my doing. We hit a boulder in the darkness, and he was thrown from the chariot."

"This storm has the beasts spooked," Aeneas says as they sit Hector down on the bed.

"As they should be," Hector grunts. The look on his face reminds me of a fear he once admitted, back when our sheets harbored shared secrets as well as passion. Ever since he was a boy, Hector has hated the clash of thunder. It seems that even as a child, Troy's most dutiful son couldn't bear this wrathful sign that the king of the gods might be displeased with him.

"Forgive my men." Hector rests against the pillows. "They fuss like mother hens over a few bruised ribs."

"Or broken ones," Aeneas counters. "You could hardly breathe when we got to you."

"Even one busted rib makes hurling a spear feel more like throwing Agamemnon's fattest whore." Cyrrian turns his striking eyes to mine. "He'll be fine, but he needs to rest."

I point to the sheet of rain hung along our veranda. "Then we should thank the gods for providing a respite for us all." For if the rainy season has truly come early, we will soon have more rest than we can stand. Looking to Aeneas, I add, "Get home to Creusa so she can tend to those scrapes."

"And me?" Cyrrian asks with a wry grin.

"You can head off to the bed of whoever is fortunate enough to have your favor this week." Smiling, I nod toward Hector. "I will take care of him."

Our friends depart, leaving nothing between me and Hector but unsavory memories and the hammering of rain. His glassy eyes follow me across the room as I clean up the mud the men tracked in.

"I will draw you a bath. Do you think you can stand?"

"If you pour me a cup of our strongest wine while the water heats."

Then his pain must be intense, no matter how he tries to deny it. I head to the bathing room to light the fire that will warm the water.

When I return, Hector grabs my wrist as I reach for the wine jug on the bedside table. His eyes shine with regret as he opens his mouth to speak.

"There is no need. I should never have accused you of being afraid to do what must be done." I grip the jug in both hands. "You spend your days outside our walls breaking horses. I am only sorry you must do the same when you return home."

But I am not sorry about what I asked, because the strategy itself was right.

His grip travels up my arm. The look on his face tells me Hector understands the evasive nature of my apologies.

When he releases my wrist, I bring the wine to his parched lips. His eyes won't leave mine as he drinks in large gulps, welcoming the warmth that dulls his pain. The tingling heat incited by his gaze is merely intensified by the herbs still steeping in my belly. I look away.

My voice cracks. "The water should be ready."

It isn't, not yet, but as I pace in front of the fire in the connected chamber, I feel more naked than ever. What would I have done if Hector's injuries were worse and the harsh words we exchanged were the last we'd ever spoken?

Finally, I pour hot water into the deep clay basin. As I stare at my reflection on its surface, the truth becomes as plain as the simple braid hanging over my left breast.

No matter how much armor I don, I would never survive the loss of him. Hector's death, whenever that is, will be my own. And today, the fire of my will and my wrath could have ended us both.

But we have been granted another chance. One that should not be wasted.

I add a cup of coarse salt to the basin, along with a handful of dried rosemary to soothe Hector's aches. A calming aroma rises with the steam, even as another barrage of thunder shakes the walls of the only home we've ever known.

Back in the bedchamber, I'm surprised to see Hector sitting upright on the edge of our bed. He has managed to remove the remainder of his muddy clothes. His stare holds all the intensity of an archer who knows his target.

"Is it ready?"

I nod. The gruff edge of his voice makes any words catch in my throat.

Slowly, one hand gripping his ribs, Hector rises to his feet. As he walks toward me, the full glory of him—this man I have seen naked a thousand times—has me lowering my eyes.

He pauses to lift my chin until it is level with his. Perhaps for the first time, I feel what an uncommon thing it is to see eye to eye with a man. A prince who, by birthright, is meant to rule me. Even though my equally regal bearing has always made me bold, the tears at the backs of Hector's eyes make me feel more like a blushing bride than any command he has ever issued.

His calloused hands cradle my face. Hector's kiss wraps me in a tenderness both foreign and familiar. Without speaking, he releases my chin and walks away. My gaze trails the battle scars along his back until he steps into the tub, slipping beneath the surface. I release the breath that burns through my chest.

Outside, the sky is now so dark it might as well be night. I light a few oil lamps and bring them into the bathing chamber. The hot steam has curled the hair around Hector's ears. The rest is released from the knot at the back of his head and floats loosely in the water.

I hope someday you realize what you have. I hope someday you stop punishing people for the actions they take for love of you, Andromache.

My tunic hits the floor before I know what I am doing.

As I lower myself into the water by his feet, Hector's eyes snap open like a soldier who's been ambushed. But instead of reaching for his shield, he reaches for me, pulling my body through the water until my breasts rest against his chest. The moan that escapes his mouth is surely one of pain, but any sounds I make in return are fueled only by longing.

A desire for the walls we've built with our words to come crashing down.

A need for Hector to look at me as he once did—not as a threat to his honor, but as the fulfillment of it.

Most of all, my hunger is for *him*. For a night that is for us alone, not for Troy or our duties to its king and council.

Hector draws me even closer. Needy mouth trailing my collarbone, he slides his hands up and down my back until they grasp my hips, sending a fire through me. He winces as I pull myself out of the water and lean back, skin glistening in the faint light of the oil lamp.

"Will it hurt too badly?" I whisper, heart racing. "I can be gentle."

Hector grabs a handful of my hair and guides my mouth back to his. Water sloshes over the edge of the tub as I throw my legs around him, thighs strong from the nights spent gripping a horse in a similar fashion.

When our bodies come together, there is no storm except for the one raging beneath the water. There is no more war. No more Odysseus. No more Citadel. There is only Hector and Andromache, and nothing about us has ever been gentle. Our union builds with the thunder until the heavens open and we are left trembling in the aftermath.

"I love you, my *alev*," Hector breathes, my rapid pulse keeping time with his.

"And I you."

All the other things I long to say now taste saltless on my tongue. So I return his declaration with another kiss that reignites the dance from the beginning.

We can dance all night if we must.

THE HAWK

Hot bolts of death flash.
Heat and burning feathers.
Fly. The Hawk must fly.
See. The Hawk must see.
Rivers rising.
Naked fields and rusting swords.

The Hawk climbs on the wind.
To a stable, where a Mouse
cowers at the feet of a Horse.
To a Spindle dancing with a blunted edge,
sowing seeds of life in fields of death.
To a palace where a King cries.
Where a Weaver waters her loom
with the blood of choices made.

And all of this is as it should be.

The Hawk glides along city walls.
Around men who act like gods
and gods who behave like men.
The Hawk sees all this and more.
But the Shadow on its wings sees farther still.

Across ages and folds.
Of histories written in the blood of men.
Of stories told with the ending wrong.
Songs missing the final refrain.

One hero will fall
Another will rise.
A great deception.
An even greater sacrifice.

The Hawk carries it all as it soars.
Higher, higher, higher still.
To the very edge of destruction.
It does not fear.
The Hawk tucks its battered wings.
It dives.
Into the eye of the storm.

BOOK III

22

HELEN

HOW MUCH DO I love you?

Her giggle finds me in the dark. Sunshine on bare skin.

More than all the stars in the sky.

More than all the leaves on the trees.

More than all the grains of sand on all the beaches of the world.

Her soft caress. Little fingers running down my cheek. The scent of her skin. Yeasty, like fresh baked bread. I breathe it in. Hungrily.

Cold.

Metal.

Wrong.

One eye blinks, forcing me through the haze.

Blood.

Coating my tongue. Drizzling down my chin. Pulsing behind my eyes.

Where am I?

Why can't I move?

A moan erupts, yet only a gurgle escapes. Cold hands tighten along my collarbone as more metal forces my teeth apart. As more slick blood slides down my throat.

No. Not blood. *Wine.*

Spreading its diluted poison. Unfurling its dense fog.

I gag. *Please . . . someone . . .*

Then gulp. *No. Don't.*

Then drink. Eagerly.

He will kill you if you refuse.

All the blunt edges return, and the pulsing pain recedes.

"Good girl. Back where you belong."

Everything warms at his hot hiss in my ear. I give in to it. Fully.

"How much do I love you?"

I am too far away to answer, yet I know this.

The route to love is overly steep. There is only one path left open to me now.

Oblivion.

23

ANDROMACHE

AS SOON AS I hear a break in the rooftop thrumming, I set down my spindle. Rhea looks so bored she might be half asleep, even on her feet. I've tried teaching her how to weave over these long weeks of rain, but I'm secretly delighted to see that the girl isn't any better with wool fibers than I am.

"Come. I've had enough of threads," I say with a sigh. "Let us break our fast."

Rhea steps away from the loom. "I'll put on the water for your tea."

I grimace. Between Rhea's and Bodecca's frequent reminders, I've hardly drunk anything else. Though I don't know why I still bother. Now that Paris is rumored to have sired a child with one of his concubines, the king will feel renewed pressure to change the succession. Then we can all stop with this pointless charade. My one consolation is that Hector seems to be at peace with this unjust fate. Perhaps I can be as well. Our bond has been stronger since the night of the first storm. It is the one thing we have that they are powerless to take away. But will it be enough?

I abandon the woven abomination I was working on, ready to move more than just my hands. "After breakfast, we can have a riding lesson while the rain holds and the men are off at the camp outside the west wall."

The girl's expression brightens. Rhea hasn't spoken much since the night I asked her to go beyond the walls alone. Not that she was ever one to speak without cause. Thankfully, her silence carries neither resentment nor fear.

"Sometimes I hold too tightly to the things I wish to protect. The things that

most matter to me," I said to her when I found her huddled in the stable, sleeping among the horses. The morning after she ran from my tireless will.

Rhea nodded. *"Prince Hector is worth holding on to."*

"As are you."

I had not realized how much I meant the words until they escaped my lips.

"Though I can be as stubborn as your fire horse, I am learning that we must let go of things we would cling to in order not to lose them entirely. I cannot lose Hector. And it seems I've grown fond of you as well." I'd held out my hand. *"Come back home, Rhea. Come back, and I will never again put you in a position to choose between us."*

"I am your loyal servant," Rhea replied without hesitation.

"No. Not merely as a servant."

"Then as what?" she'd asked, confused.

"As a companion." But that wasn't quite right either. *"A friend."*

There is no friendly sun to greet us as we cross the courtyard now, but at least the rains have stopped for a time. We need no omen to tell us they will soon return. These daily downpours have assaulted the plain for weeks, stalling the war and driving the trapped citizens of Troy to the brink of madness.

I pity them. The mothers with cooped-up children, especially. And I understand their sorrow. There's something new about this particular oppression, a dampness that has settled in like a bad cough, turning one's own household into a prison.

Still, my house may be the only refuge I have left in this world.

"It is enough." That word again. Hector has said it often since the rains began. Usually on stormy nights after making love, while we talked quietly among the shadows. Much like we used to in the early days before the war. *"It has always been enough."*

But can it be enough for me? Could I sit by, doing nothing and saying nothing, while an exceptionally virile dolt like Deiphobus or—gods forbid—Paris brought this city and her people to ruin from Priam's throne?

I stare down at my hard middle, the taut muscles nearly as defined as Hector's from all my recent riding with Rhea. Perhaps it is better this way.

"The plains." Rhea calls me back from a future I could never control. "They're more like a lake."

"They might as well be." I gaze across the glasslike surface of the stagnant water and long stretch of plain that separates Troy from the Achaean camp. It isn't all that deep. Still, the way the mud would suck down a man decked in bronze, he'd end up looking more like a flailing pig than a warrior. Multiply that man by thousands and this war would become a swamp of laughable chaos, all chance at a hero's afterlife lost in the mire.

Of all the things that might tempt Agamemnon and Menelaus to turn toward home, I can't fathom why *this* isn't it. Not when famed warriors like Achilles and Ajax the Great have undoubtedly grown restless in their sopping huts.

To say nothing of Odysseus. The boggy plain has surely made it more difficult for him to sneak up on the city by his hidden route, but I worry what seeds of cunning and deceit this extra time will allow to germinate.

"Their poor women," Rhea whispers.

My stomach recoils. Though I try not to dwell on it, many of the slave women Rhea speaks of once spent their days weaving in fine seaside houses just like us, dressed in silks from the east and gold from across the Aegean. That is, until their husbands and sons were slaughtered, and their daughters dragged off in stiff ropes. All because no one came to help them when Achilles's black ships appeared in their harbors.

Because *we* did not help them.

On our way into the stables, Rhea and I pass a pile of armor lying in the muddy training yard. The shields of the fallen should be gifted to their sons or widows, but with supplies becoming scarcer by the day, we can no longer afford to cling to formalities. With all trade by sea cut off by the Achaean horde and the routes by land flooded, tin is nearly impossible to procure. Our forges have fallen silent. More importantly, what few crops we boasted have been washed away. By some miracle, there are people within the Citadel, Paris's household especially, who never seem to go without. But as it stands, our cattle and our walls are the only things keeping the army alive. And thus, keeping Troy alive.

How much worse will it be for the rest of Anatolia if Odysseus finds a way to break Troy's back without ever stepping foot past her walls? If Hector and I are stripped of all power to stop him, it is not a question of if, but a matter of when.

Rhea makes a quick stop at the largest stall on the right. The one where

Hector keeps the horses that survived Odysseus's fire arrows. Scarred, miserable-looking creatures.

Rhea brings them treats from her satchel, taking time to shower each animal with her attention, though she must know my patience for such things is short. Despite her smile for the horses, the girl looks tired. A weariness known most keenly by women. The kind of fatigue I myself have felt more deeply as the Festival of the Divine Twins draws closer and the King's Council prepares to give its ruling on Priam's succession.

"He won't stop, will he?" Rhea asks, her voice echoing in the quiet. As if sensing her distress, a white beast mottled by burns rests its head upon her shoulder.

I watch the maimed animal return the comfort Rhea offers, and I wonder what it would be like to give and receive so freely. "Who do you mean?"

"The Citadel can't defend against their most dangerous threat because they refuse to see it."

A clever mouse, indeed.

But whether cleverness is, for women, a gift or a curse remains to be seen.

"To some, the truth is only as valuable as the voice that speaks it." A gust of wind brings on a strong waft of manure that makes my insides lurch. I should have taken bread with my tea, but my appetite has been less ravenous lately, thanks to so many immobile days spent indoors.

I follow Rhea to a stall that houses a large gelding with a dappled gray coat. Like sea-foam in a storm. The beast no longer bristles at the sight of me. We appear to have reached an understanding.

The horse greets Rhea by bending its head low. Gently, she runs her hand down its crown.

"Would you do the same as Odysseus?" she asks quietly. "If it was the only way to end this war?"

It is the question I have asked myself time and again. If only in the safety of silence.

"When you fight your enemies with identical tactics, soon their evil becomes your own." My father's words seem to echo through the stall.

I recall Helen's calm demeanor before Paris so forcefully dragged her from my kitchen. Her hands splayed across the table, silent lips summoning some mysterious source. I rest my hand on Rhea's shoulder. "Still, there are other forms of resistance."

A wet cough has me glancing across the aisle, where a young stable hand feeds the mares. The boy has pools as deep as Hector's for eyes, making it easy to imagine my husband here in the stables at his age. The one place he could stroke a stallion's coat under a mantle of silence just like any other boy.

"Good morning, Harsa." The boy gives me a deferential nod and Rhea a shy smile. "Rhea."

"Good morning, Larion," Rhea returns.

The boy called Larion lowers his feed bag. "If you're looking for Prince Hector, he isn't here."

All the better. "Do you know how long he will be gone?" I ask.

"The prince rode out with Cyrrian and Harsar Aeneas to check the levees above the olive grove."

The scent of turning oats joins the musk of animal dung. Another queasy wave hits me, but I push it down. The land around the olive groves has flooded multiple times since the night Hector was injured weeks ago. Aeneas fortified the levee once, but it is full to bursting again, and the rains show no signs of stopping. "We need to prepare Kasirga for riding." Rhea nods to the gray horse.

"Riding?" The boy starts to open his mouth, but a poorly concealed pinch from Rhea and he bites his tongue. Clearly my reputation with horses has spread far and wide.

"You have no reason to fear, Larion. Rhea has taught me well."

The boy glances at her and sighs, as if resigning himself to this folly. "Kasirga is calm and should be easy to control. Unlike the whirlwind he is named for."

As a vote of confidence, it leaves much to be desired.

While Larion helps Rhea prepare the horse, I sit down on an overturned trough. Cold sweat spreads across my skin. My head swirls as I search for a pitcher in case I lose what little tea I managed to drink.

"Are you all right, Harsa?" Larion asks.

"I'll be fine." I force myself to stand. "I just need some fresh air."

Out in the ring, the horse doesn't flinch when I mount him. My grip on Kasirga's lead tightens. The beast takes a lurching step forward, and the training yard is consumed by a black ring at the edge of my vision. A roar fills my ears as the ring moves inward. Soon I can't distinguish the horse's breathing from my own.

"Andromache?" Rhea never addresses me by name.

A violent wave of nausea has me grasping the horse's mane. I throw my body forward, expelling everything inside me. Memories of the Lower City's sick launch their assault as I lift my head.

"You are ill." Rhea's watchful eyes run up and down my body.

"The wave of plague subsided almost as soon as the rains began." I wipe my mouth. "There hasn't been a death in weeks, if that's what concerns you."

"Andromache." My name again. A whisper this time. "Helen said . . ." My hard expression has Rhea swallowing the words on her tongue. "How long has it been since your last moon cycle?"

"I . . ." My grip on the horse tightens. In the wake of the council's mounting threats, I've lost track. It hasn't helped that the ceaseless rains have kept the moon hidden behind a veil of clouds. "It might be late. I suppose."

Rhea nods, eyes shining. "Bodecca put me in charge of washing your bedding and undergarments. It's been some time since . . . I hadn't thought . . ."

The urge to be sick overtakes me again, but I keep the lump at the back of my throat. I can barely entertain what Rhea is suggesting. The burden of hope is too heavy. "I know little of these matters, but I do know animals." Rhea bites her lip. "There have been other signs . . ."

The roaring returns. I shake my head to silence it. "It isn't possible. Not after all this time."

"It may not be likely . . ." Rhea shifts on her feet, then raises her chin. "But I stand before you. The daughter of a Phrygian horse breeder who now serves Troy's future king and queen. Nothing is impossible."

My thoughts race over the past few weeks. Hector has visited my bed more often since our reconciliation. Resigned to barrenness, I thought little of it. Still, to appease Queen Hecuba and curb the pestering of Rhea and Bodecca, I have been drinking the tea blessed by Demeter morning and night.

"Do not speak a word of this. To anyone." I shoot a warning glare to the stable boy. He sits awkwardly along the ring's railing, suddenly consumed by the task of tying endless knots into a lead rope.

Larion lifts his shy eyes in agreement before returning to his task.

"You won't tell Hector?" Rhea asks.

I set my jaw. It grieves me to keep a secret from him when the rift between us is much improved. But that rekindled closeness is even more of an incentive not to break his heart by giving him a dream I cannot yet guarantee. "Not until I am certain beyond a doubt."

"There may be ways to be sure," Rhea says. "I once heard my mother speak of them."

"What ways?"

"I don't know, exactly. But Helen would," Rhea offers quickly. "They say she was even more sought out by Sparta's women than she was desired by their men."

I study the girl closely. Since that night in the grotto, Rhea has become taken with Helen. For reasons beyond the obvious, it bothers me.

"Nobody has seen Helen for weeks. Not even at the temple sacrifices meant to quell the rains." I shrug. "Paris must be keeping her on a short lead for venturing beyond the walls."

A consequence she ought to have anticipated.

Andromache, please! I must speak with you.

A pinch gathers at the base of my spine, but whether it is guilt or simply unease, I leave it for later. One day soon, when these current storms have passed, I will get to the bottom of that nymph-eyed Spartan and demand answers to my questions.

"Helen is no friend of ours," I tell Rhea sharply.

She gnaws on her lip. "But the tea."

"Has what to do with Helen?"

"Nothing," the girl answers quickly, wisely dropping the subject. "Only if it has done its work, you must keep drinking it."

I feel a rush of tenderness at the caring reflected back to me from Rhea's eyes. "I will. Though I would warn you that hope is a double-edged blade."

Rhea's gaze sparks. "Bodecca will know what to do. She—"

"Has had enough disappointments in her long life. We will not subject her to another until time has taken our side. Is that understood?"

After a slight pause, the girl nods.

I roll my aching shoulders. "Come, Rhea. Our riding lesson is finished for today."

When we are returning the horse to his stall, a cry goes up from the walls. Hector enters the stables looking weary. That he does not immediately question why I am here suggests something is wrong. "What is it, Hector?"

"Chariots are riding toward the walls," Hector clips, glancing around the stalls. "Have you seen my helmet?"

"Hector!" Cyrrian comes racing down the aisle. "A small band of Achaeans approach the Scaean gate."

I exhale slowly, willing that the news these heralds bring is somehow good. "Perhaps the rains have finally made Agamemnon eager to discuss terms of peace."

Hector studies me sideways. "Since when does my wife look for light among the shadows?"

"I'll walk with you," I say by way of an answer, picking up Hector's horsehair helmet from where it's fallen behind a pile of straw.

He places it on his head, a prince of Troy once more.

And her heir? A restless, hopeful hand grazes my belly.

Once we reach the gate, we climb the ramparts to watch as the emissaries approach. Only a well-placed arrow could do us damage from this height, and still my hands seek to cover my core, struck by this new vulnerability. The sense that there are hidden threats everywhere I turn.

A strong gale nearly blows my headscarf over the walls. It carries on its back a shrill scream.

"He is here among us!"

My skin prickles as I search the Citadel's many layers for the source of the cry. There is only one place from which this shriek could sail such a distance.

Cassandra stands on her tower balcony, hair twisting in the wind as it rises and falls.

"Water the seed." This time, she does not scream these words. And yet they somehow carry. As if they are meant for my ears alone. "Be his soil."

A violent shiver travels through me as another shrill cry cuts through the air, this one nearly loud enough to shake Troy's foundation stones.

The Fury.

"Three times! Three times his webs will wrap around the city walls!"

The Fury spits each word like a curse, leaving no doubt that the one she speaks of now is not the one she foretold a moment ago.

Dread scrapes at me with sharp fingernails. Like everything else, Cassandra's cries are light and shadow both.

Be his soil.

I cling to the small hope Rhea threw to me as if it's a rope tossed over a ledge.

Shouting soldiers bring my attention back to the emissaries. The Trojan guards are gesturing wildly to where a small group of Achaeans is expected. There are six warriors outside the gate, but the only man I recognize among them isn't a man at all.

Her threadbare robe hangs off her body in long strips. Her wrists are bound by the ropes of a slave, though there is no need for them. The woman is clearly on the verge of collapse, but she still walks toward the walls of Troy as if they hold all the water in the world. My stomach heaves again.

I know the woman approaching the Scaean gate.

She is my mother.

24

RHEA

"ON THE BED." Andromache's voice is tight.

Hector places the bundle of rags down onto the clean blankets in their private quarters.

The woman doesn't move or speak. Other than some low moaning, she doesn't even stir. Not since Hector carried her all the way from the ancient oak tree near the Scaean gate.

I help Andromache arrange the limp body on the bed. Every bit of visible skin is coated in grime. The stink coming off her is one of stale urine and blood gone bad.

Faria and I work together to push up the woman's robes. For a moment, nobody speaks.

The old woman's legs are covered in scratches with dark welts at the knees. Her hands are cracked and bleeding. She's been made to do the type of back-bending work that breaks more than just the body.

Andromache's normally golden skin drains of color. She looks as pale as she did right before she almost fell from Kasirga's back. Only this time, I know the cause isn't the child that may be growing inside her but the broken woman on the bed.

I wait for Andromache to say something. To take control of this situation like she always does, but it's as if she is paralyzed. Andromache who has washed hundreds of bodies for the pyre. Andromache who battled the plague and killed rats and tended injuries much worse than this. Her grief twists inside my chest as I grab the pot of honey salve she uses to clean Hector's battle wounds and gently place it in her hands.

"Her wounds need cleaning," she says hollowly.

Nodding, I walk across the room to fetch the stirrup jar full of water. Faria retrieves a handful of clean linens. She dips the rags in the water as I pull the ruined robes even higher, releasing another wave of stench.

Faria wrinkles her nose.

"I'll do it." I take the wet rag from Faria's hands and move the cloth up and down the woman's legs while Andromache applies the salve, wrapping her thin bones with the strips of bandage cloth. A deep gash runs horizontally over the woman's hip bone. The source of the smell.

Hector places a large hand on Andromache's shoulder.

"It will be fine," Andromache says in a voice that is nothing like hers. "Go make sure our enemies do not linger around our walls. If you are needed here, I will send Rhea."

With a nod, he turns to leave, but at the last moment, he grabs his wife gently around the waist with one arm and presses a hard kiss to her temple.

Andromache washes the blood from her hands in the basin. Only I can see the way they tremble. "Faria, tell Bodecca to mix a healing draught."

Faria all but runs from the room.

"Who is she?" I ask when Faria is gone.

"She is my mother."

My hands still. I lift my gaze to find Andromache standing with her own hands stretched over her stomach as if to protect what's inside from this sight it can't even see.

I drop my gaze to the shriveled figure on the bed. A woman I've heard Andromache speak of with equal parts affection and exasperation. Ariasti. Wife of Eetion, king of Thebe under Mount Placos. A queen.

Mother.

As hard as I try, I can find no resemblance between them. No trace of the vibrant woman with the gentle heart Andromache has described to me. Whatever strength and beauty there was, the Achaeans have stripped it away.

"What happened to her?" I press the last of the bandages to the gash that didn't have to be a death sentence if only it had been properly cared for. Ariasti of Thebe received no care.

"The Achaeans have sacked Thebe. I had hoped my father's walls would hold and that my brothers . . ." Words catch and hands fist. "It is what I always feared. They have raided the coasts and now they are moving inland. Safety is an illusion so long as these men live and breathe."

"But why would they do this?" It's cruelty for cruelty's sake. "Why bring her all this way? They didn't even ask for a ransom."

Andromache moves to the head of the bed. "They didn't do this for gold. They did this to break us. They want Hector to know that they have slaughtered his wife's family. That we can't protect our loyal allies, and we won't be able to protect ourselves."

"I'm sorry." My heart aches for this woman. For Andromache. For my own mother and sisters, who met their end at the hands of ruthless men like the ones who did this.

The woman on the bed stirs. Her eyelids flutter as a whisper passes her lips.

"Podes."

A single word. A world of anguish.

I look up to find Andromache's cheeks wet with tears. I've been a member of this household for months filled with moments of joy, but also with suffering. And through it all, I have never once seen Andromache cry.

"He was my closest brother," she whispers.

Her sadness fills the room along with the labored sounds of her mother's breathing.

I am moving forward with a cup of water when the woman speaks again. Another whisper. Weaker than the first.

"Chryseis."

I look up at Andromache, afraid to see this latest grief in her eyes, but there is only confusion.

"Who is she?" I ask when it is clear Ariasti of Thebe will speak no more.

"The daughter of a priest of Apollo in Thebe." The furrow between Andromache's brows deepens.

"What does it mean?" I ask quietly.

"I don't know, Rhea." Andromache brushes back the filthy hair from her mother's cheek.

Helplessly, I wet a rag and place it on the woman's cracked lips. I remember even gentler hands as they tended the sick and dug into the soil on the

Hill of Kallikolone. "I know you don't care for Helen, but she is the best healer in Troy. Perhaps she could—"

"No."

My mouth snaps shut. Since that hilltop dawn, my mind has run back to Helen over and over. I've spent endless nights wondering if I made a mistake in trusting her. At least a dozen times I've started to tell Andromache about what Helen did to help her, only to swallow down the words and pour another cup of tea. If Andromache knew who was responsible for her possible miracle, she would not thank me. Instead, she would stop taking the tea altogether.

Andromache places an animal hide over her mother's legs, restoring some of the dignity that was stolen from her. "My mother has seen her home razed. Her husband and seven sons slaughtered. She will not open her eyes to this barren world again."

"But the world isn't barren." My eyes lock onto Andromache's.

"Don't," she warns. "It is bad luck to speak of new life in a room full of death." Her shoulders set in an unyielding line. "My mother's world was burned to ash and can never be reborn. This is the fate of all women in fallen cities. We watch our sons and brothers butchered. Our husbands and fathers die in a vain effort to protect us. And then we alone are left to pay the price of their failures."

Memories stir like the breeze. "I've seen it," I say softly.

Andromache pauses in her grieving. "You told me once you had sisters."

My throat swells. "Four of them."

Andromache sits with me in my pain, as I sit with her in hers. Though she is completely still, it's as if I can feel vast lands shifting inside her.

"If the walls of Troy are breached, they will take us. If I have a child, they will rip him from my arms and force me into the bed of my enemy, their hands still red with my husband's blood. As bad as it will be for me, it will be ten times worse for the common women." Her gaze is a pointed spear. "Women like you, Rhea."

My hands move to the cloth tied around my wrist. I've relied on the blanket talisman less and less as I've woven myself into the fabric of this household. This city. As I have finally found my place. A place that will burn just like my farm if what Andromache says is true.

I grip the bit of blanket now as I watch Andromache ease herself onto the bed, taking her mother's head into her lap. Cradling the older woman as that woman must have once done to the infant daughter in her arms. All the sons who came before. Bodies lying dead and charred in the rubble of a once-great city.

Andromache sings. Her voice moves through the room like wind, carrying melodies of innocence and girlhood. Of gratitude, regrets, and farewell.

The songs fade into silence. The soundless tears she sheds are ones I have cried. They are the same tears that have been stored by every woman in Troy from the first moment the black-hulled Achaean ships appeared on the horizon.

Ariasti of Thebe doesn't wake. Together, Andromache and I stand watch over her final hours. Every minute that passes, her breaths grow shallower; the pauses between them longer. Until the breaths cease to come at all.

Andromache bows her head. She kisses a limp hand that must have once caressed a sleeping child at her breast, and she presses it to her own belly, so that for at least this moment, two generations of flesh can cradle the hope of a third, not yet born.

"I'll call Bodecca." I rise to give Andromache room to grieve.

"No." Andromache's eyes are alight when they meet mine over the body of her mother. There's something fevered in her gaze. A determination that stretches the boundaries of reason.

It scares me.

"Let me draw you a bath," I offer quickly. I know what grief and her delicate condition demand. And it isn't whatever idea has possession of Andromache now. "You are overwrought. You need to rest." I move to help her off the pallet.

She grabs my arm and holds me fast. "What I need is to stop waiting for my fate and the fates of those I love to be decided for me. What I need," she says through gritted teeth, "is to act."

Our faces are inches apart. This close, I can see the beginnings of faint lines around eyes that struck fear in me when I first came to this city. Eyes I now wish to light when they are cast my way. It's what I've come to want more than anything.

Whispered words from the past echo in my head from the last time Andromache made a request of me. They mix with those from the night she found me in the stables and called herself my friend.

"Show me where you entered the wall that night the storm broke," she says.

A thousand questions fly through my mind on the heels of a thousand doubts, but one look at the still, broken body of Andromache's mother, and I swallow them all.

I will do whatever she asks. I will go wherever she leads, no matter where it takes us.

We don veils to hide our faces and leave the house by the courtyard out back. Following the rampart that separates the Merchant Quarter from the Citadel, we make our way east past the Dardanian gate and cross into the less crowded section of Troy's second ring. Over our heads, Priam's palace looms with its sprawling temple and jutting tower. I guide Andromache as far east as the road allows, to the juncture where the Citadel wall meets the exterior defenses of the towering northeast bastion. There in the shadows stands a small stone building. Older than all the rest.

We enter a single room with a vaulted ceiling. Its ancient walls were forged long ago to honor the goddess carved into the stone stele above the offering table. A goddess I recognize even in her earliest, crudest form.

The Mother.

The door is so low, Andromache must bend to duck inside. The cramped interior of the temple is kept neat and clean. Offerings from the city's inhabitants are laid out upon the hearth before the statue of the Mother goddess. The one my father loved. I walk past the jars of prayers to a shelf carved in the stone, deep enough that the back of it is obscured in darkness.

I know what that darkness hides.

"There." I kneel beside the shelf and climb halfway in, using my body to show Andromache how the shadows trick the eye.

Andromache drops to her knees beside me and peers inside the opening. "Where does it lead?"

"Straight through the earth, down a twisted path of worn stone to a small break in the wall where it touches the plateau. There's a grotto in the sheer face. It's invisible to the eye, but once you leave its shelter behind, you are fully exposed to the plain."

Andromache probes it with her hands. "It's too narrow for a man or even a grown woman."

"What are you thinking?" I ask the question, though in my heart, I already know.

"I am thinking that I can no longer rely on Troy's walls to protect what is mine. If there are indeed any gods who have heard my prayers, then this is their test to see if I am worthy." Her chest rises and falls. "If I sit and wait, my fate will be that of my mother. Hector's fate and the fate of our unborn child will be that of my father and brothers. These are not outcomes that can be changed. Only delayed." Her jaw clenches. "Unless we take them into our own hands. Starting tonight."

A chill settles in me that has nothing to do with the musty temple at our back and everything to do with my memories of Hector's wrath the night the storm came to Troy. "Andromache, what about—"

"No." Her voice is a blade hacking off my words. "I am done asking permission to protect the ones I love. If the plague taught me anything, it is that there are other women in this city who feel the same. Not all battles are won or lost by the tip of a spear." Her gaze drifts toward the Mother and the secret she keeps. "This is the way out. A chance for us to give those women a choice if all others are stripped away."

"You would send Troy's children through the wall if the city falls."

It is a cunning plan. Just as importantly, it is not a complete disregard of Hector's wishes. Relief is a heady rush that is painfully short-lived.

"If worst comes to worst," she says slowly. "But more than that, I intend to prevent the need from ever arising."

Clarity dawns with a sense of bone-deep dread. If I'm right, the game that she would play now is far more dangerous than the one she suggested all those months ago. "You mean to send people past the wall. Just as Odysseus is sending his men to steal around us in the dark."

"Aeneas's scouts are little more than foot soldiers, marching in a straight line toward our enemies' camp without the benefit of numbers. What I have in mind is a new type of battle," Andromache offers coldly. Methodically. "More than all the others, it is one that we must win. And I will win it, Rhea." She reaches out to run her hands over the face of the goddess. A carving just like the one that marked the hearth of our farm.

"The plague was just the beginning," Andromache says, yanking me out of the past and back to this cold, stone room in a city surrounded by death. "Odysseus won't stop his efforts. *Three times.* That is what Cassandra screamed."

That was not all she screamed. I was there and I heard it too.

Water the seed. Be his soil.

But soil does not move. It does not plan and plot. It abides, waiting for the sun to send its rays. And that is not something Andromache can easily do.

"All of Troy may think her mad, but we alone know better," Andromache says. "Cassandra's words were a warning. As they were about the west wall."

"You really think Odysseus can find a way past Troy's walls?" Andromache's fear is stark, and it knocks me off-balance because until this moment, I would have sworn that she feared no one.

"Agamemnon is a brute with more power than imagination. Menelaus a witless follower. Diomedes is a hotheaded idiot, and Nestor is wise but old. Ajax the Great is as gifted a killer as the gods ever made, Idomeneus the Cretan death with a spear, and Ajax the lesser is only lesser because of the giant who shares his name."

"And Achilles?"

"Achilles." Andromache's catalog of Achaean kings trails off into silence. She opens her mouth but seems to swallow whatever words she wished to say. Instead, she shrugs. "You know what is said of Achilles. He is the fastest man living. And yet none of them pose the threat to Troy that the farmer king from Ithaca does. Odysseus is clever enough to realize Troy's walls can only be breached by two means. Outright siege, which will be costly and long, or . . . by his wits."

"Three times." I repeat Cassandra's warning.

Her nod is grim. "While the rain pours and the men sit idle on their shields, Odysseus will exploit our weaknesses. We can't let him."

I draw my shoulders back. "What do you need me to do?"

Andromache's face softens. "I won't ask you to risk yourself again. There must be other girls in Troy small enough to fit through that hole. A few of those who are smart enough to see why it is necessary. They will be well paid in gold for their service. But when we find them, only you can show them how to descend to the plain from the exit at the plateau. Will you do this for me, Rhea?"

My eyes drift to the hole. Air too thick to breathe. The clawing fear at the back of my throat. It is all waiting for me right there in the yawning darkness.

"Rhea."

I yank my gaze back to Andromache. I want to say yes. I want to do this so that she will look at me with the pride and affection of the mother and sisters I lost, but I can't make myself say the word. "What then?"

"The Achaeans are camped above Lisgar Swamp and near Kesik Tepe. It is a good defensive position. The only access and exit point is at Kesik Cut, which is easily protected from attack. But that also means it is easily watched.

"Odysseus will have to pass through the cut on his nightly missions. If we can track the movements of his men, we can discover how he is approaching the city unseen. Perhaps we can even anticipate where his next attack on the walls will come from."

"You know Hector will never agree to this," I say, because one of us must.

"Which is why we will not tell him."

I squeeze my eyes shut. It is the very thing I was most afraid of.

"Hector is a good man." Regret flashes across Andromache's features so briefly it might be a trick of the shadows. "He would do anything to protect those most dear to him. To protect us." Her expression hardens with resolve. "But that sense of duty occasionally narrows his vision, and that love would become a prison if we let it. If Troy falls, Hector will not be here to save us. He will be gone, Rhea, and it will be up to us to save ourselves. I would tell a thousand lies to keep that from happening. I would pay any price."

Seeing the anguish I cannot hide, she sighs.

"I am not asking you to choose between us. I am asking you to help me defend him as he has always sought to defend us. He fights for us every day, every moment. None know this better than we do. This is our chance to fight for him."

Unbidden, my fingers trace the small scar at the base of my throat where a rope once bit into the skin. My hands drop to my sides.

"I'll do it," I say. "I'll show them the way."

Andromache's smile is small, but even so, it makes me feel as if I had swallowed the sun. "I promise we will not keep it from him forever. We will tell Hector as soon as we know that it is possible to reach the Achaean camps by way of the Mother's pass." She runs her hand across the face of the goddess one last time. "May she give us strength and courage to face whatever comes."

"Who will you send?" The thing she would ask is not easily done.

Andromache frowns. "I wish I could send the war widow Watti's daughter. Lannaka. She had the spirit for such a task."

Yes, but not the diminutive size required. Trenches break across Andromache's forehead as she reconsiders. "There was the girl who helped us during the plague. Creusa's maid."

"Isola." I remember her. She remained by Creusa's side, and when the sickness came for her too, she never cried out. Never complained. In a rare act of fairness, the gods rewarded her bravery with life.

Andromache's lips lift at one corner. "Have you ever forgotten a single thing you've seen or heard, Rhea?"

"My memory is a curse as much as it is a blessing." Unbidden, Kallira's face rises in my mind. The way it had looked the last time I saw her. Quickly, I push the image aside.

"The gods are strange in their gifts. We don't always see the meanings behind them until the moments when they count." Andromache's hands drift down to her stomach again, and a fierce light shines out of her eyes. "No more waiting, Rhea. No more trusting in others to protect the things that matter."

"What do you need me to do?"

"Go to Creusa's rooms. Tell her I sent you for the girl. Meet me back at the house at sundown."

She takes a breath as if to steady herself. It gives me a bad feeling.

"Where are you going?" I ask.

"To the Lower City." Andromache places her hand on my shoulder much like Hector did not so long ago. "Before the day is done, we will complete our small army. One the Achaeans will never see coming."

25

ANDROMACHE

THE MERCHANT-LINED STREETS of the Lower City once fanned out in a maze of colors—bright textiles, fruit stands, piles of spices from distant lands. Those colors are muted now. Not only by the brown wash of a muddy street but by a grief that gnaws at me. A grief not only for my mother but for all that once was. This part of the city has always felt the most alive to me. At dawn and dusk, the streets ring with the bells of sheep and cattle heading in or out to the grazing fields. Women used to chat while doing laundry at the city's many springs and fountains, their children laughing as they kicked balls made from bundles of rags. At mealtimes, the clatter of pottery could be heard from simple homes made of mudbrick and wood, the aroma of fresh bread rising up from every outdoor clay oven.

Now the only sound I hear is the song of a lonely lute.

Large puddles line the road—cumbersome obstacles that have made Troy's citizens less patient with each other. Every person I pass either scowls as he splashes through mud or shouts something nasty to his neighbor.

Is this the divided people we are fighting for?

Is this ugliness truly Troy?

All my plans suddenly feel foolish. Hector has given every drop of his sweat for this city. Why risk ourselves when that same city is willing to strip him of his birthright all because of the direction a few bird feathers sailed on the wind? I stop in the middle of the street, arms wrapping around my own middle.

We could run away. We don't have to end up like Thebe. Like my mother.

Something hard collides with my back, sending me staggering. A man bent under a load of textiles pushes past without a word of apology. I am in the process of hurling a curse after him when a stabbing pain lances my lower abdomen. It has me crouching on my heels in the middle of the street. Breathless, I wait for the familiar feeling of dampness. The bright red smear of my shame.

"Forgive them. They grow weary of the weather." I turn to the voice and see a merchant in his run-down stall—a display of figs and dates covered by a tattered awning that barely shades the fruit. "Come. Rest a moment. Out of the rain."

The merchant's skin is nearly as black as the obsidian bracelet around my wrist. I force myself to straighten. "By now, you'd think we would all be accustomed to the damp."

"You are from the Citadel, no?" He smiles warmly. "Surely the gods make it rain less up there than they do down here."

I pull my cloak around my shoulders, feeling exposed. The way I have felt since the moment Rhea told me her suspicions about my condition. Street brawls and petty thefts have become nightly crimes in the Lower City thanks to the pent-up frustration that comes with sitting on our hands. Still, this new fear makes me feel like a stranger in my own skin.

The ripe scent of the merchant's fruit assails me. Clenching my jaw, I lean forward and fight back the sudden swell of nausea.

All at once, a fresh wave of grief hits with a ferocity that stings my eyes.

Sickness is common enough among expecting women, but this pain dull and then sharp, then dull again . . . it doesn't feel right. The fear it ignites can only be compared to the overwhelming dread of those first few times Hector rode out to fight.

Back then, at least, I had the company of Troy's women, every one of them standing on the ramparts, side by side, watching their husbands, their fathers, and their sons set off to taunt Lelwani, the Hittite goddess of death. Still, this loss—if that is, in fact, what is happening—*this* grief would be mine alone to bear. Rhea's companionship has given me great solace, but of such matters she knows little.

And still you refuse to seek out the woman who might help you.

I bite the inside of my cheek. The day I show up at Helen of Sparta's door begging for her aid is the day this city burns.

"You must eat something, Harsa."

I crack my eyes open to find two hands extended. One offering dates. The other figs.

"Thank you. But food is the last thing I want."

"Strange how the things we want are often not the things we need."

Something in the man's firm yet kind voice compels me to comply. I study his humble offerings again.

"A few dates, then," I say, overcome by the sudden desire for something sweet. I hold out my bracelet to the merchant. A vast overpayment, but one well deserved.

Cardamom eyes spark, but the man shakes his head. "I cannot accept payment from my future queen." His gaze falls to my slim waistline. "Nor my future prince."

"How did—"

"My wife is also ill, and she is also expecting. Our fifth. She is hopeful this one will be a little girl who can join her at the loom. Seeing that she is only eating figs these days, she may finally get her wish." The merchant chuckles, his ebony face glowing with pride. "A boy craves dates and a girl figs, you see. At least that was what the grandmothers in my homeland claimed."

Smiling again, the man wraps a few dates in a cloth and hands them to me. "Thank the Divine Twins that the festival is nearly upon us. The people will be glad to hear the succession has been set in stone."

Another twinge around my middle and my craving vanishes. "There has been talk of the succession in the Lower City?"

"I doubt there is any water poured out in the Citadel that does not eventually make its way to our cisterns. If you'll forgive me."

"No, I appreciate your candor. Thank you . . ."

"Ekon." The man bows slightly. "Merchant and former fruit farmer from the kingdom of Aethiopia, as well as father to many young Trojans."

I smile for the first time in days. "Thank you, Ekon. I will not forget this kindness."

"Harsa Andromache," he calls out as I turn to depart.

"Yes?" I look back, my mouth full of sticky dates.

Ekon's warm eyes are heavier now. "My eldest. Zaidan. He will be fifteen soon."

My heart sinks with understanding. For the first time, I feel the sting of a parent's worst fear. "We will watch for him."

The man nods, knowing this is the most I can promise, and the best he can hope for.

It is a cruel irony of Troy's more generous laws. The ones that allowed the city to flourish as a center of commerce, bringing in people from as far as Thrace in the north, Egypt and Canaan in the south, and Assyria in the east. Our foreign merchants are not required to fight in our army so that some trade might continue. Any children born within the city gates, however, belong to Troy.

My baby, should he take his first breath, would belong to Troy too.

Pushing my private worries aside, I refocus on why I've come here. A search for Troy's daughters rather than her sons. Turning away from the fruit stall, I face down streets I have not visited since the night I held a spear and hunted plague. Everything looks different in the light.

"A question." I hesitate, not knowing a more dignified way to phrase it. "Where is . . . the brothel?"

Ekon grins, nodding down the road in front of me. "Just follow the spears."

I grasp the merchant's meaning once I round the next corner. Dozens of spears and shields line the outer wall of a two-story limestone structure with a well-maintained courtyard near the south wall. It is by far the best kept of the dwellings in this area. I recognize it by the arched trellis over the doorway, decorated with a dozen veils.

"Gods above. Every soldier in Troy is here," I mutter.

"Not every soldier," says a heavily accented voice behind me. A wiry warrior with a careless smirk nods toward a larger courtyard, not far from the brothel entrance. Over the low wall float grunts and raucous laughter.

His accent is of Lycia. And if I know anything about Lycian men, it is that there is only one woman they fear even more than their wives.

"I imagine your mother would approve of your restraint, soldier."

His smile widening, the warrior looks me up and down. "My mother does not approve of land soldiering at all, but since the woman has given me her name, I do my best to honor her where and when I can."

I smile in turn. Lycians are known to take the names of their mothers instead of their fathers. They are also known for their plundering, seafaring ways.

"And that name is?"

"So direct." He tsks and gives me a mocking bow. "Sarpedon of Lycia."

Something clenches inside me. "The captain who refuses to take the field unless he has an audience with the council?"

"I see my reputation extends beyond this mud pit." Sarpedon's teeth are a flash of white in his handsome face as he moves in closer than is good for him. "Hurry along, Harsa." He leans forward, his pine-resin breath tickling the side of my neck. "What will the women of the Citadel think if they see you conspiring with one such as me?"

At my snort, confusion flashes across his face. "They will find precious little odd about it, I imagine. Tell me, Captain, were you successful in your demands?"

"Sadly, no. It seems you Trojans have all manner of rules to keep people in the places your Old Blood appoint as proper. Which is why I, Sarpedon of Lycia . . ."

I resist the urge to roll my eyes as the inebriated boasting commences.

". . . son of the princess Laodamia and grandson of Bellerophon, slayer of the Chimera and a hero to rival Perseus, am standing *here* instead of lounging on one of your plush pillows in the Citadel."

I spare the miserable alley a glance. Two men stagger past, holding each other for support. A few feet away, a lone child plays with a wooden toy on the filthy ground near a wall a soldier is currently pissing on. "If it is any consolation, Captain, the company here is far better."

Sarpedon barks out a laugh before rubbing his face. "Undoubtedly. But the accommodations leave something to be desired. Now if you'll excuse me, Harsa, I must return to my drunk cousin and his companions." The slight slur at the end of Sarpedon's speech assures me he isn't joining these friends for their first jug of wine.

When the Lycian enters through the brothel's courtyard, I follow him the same way but stop at the side door. The last time I knocked on the main entrance, these women weren't so eager to answer my call. But this side door is unbarred.

Once inside, I follow the spiced perfume down a long corridor to a small room. It's quieter than I imagined it would be, given the number of spears outside. Though I suspect that as with the circles around the Citadel, this entry chamber is merely one layer among many.

"How can I assist you?"

Slowly, I turn toward the familiar voice lined with gravel and remove the hood of my cloak. The mistress of the house greets me with the hard, figlike face of one who has known years of grinding poverty—even if her gold-bangled wrists speak to her rise above it.

"You." She infuses the word with decades of long-suffering.

"Madam Morgestia. I'm glad to see the plague didn't hamper business."

"What do you require now, Harsa? Another mess you need my girls to clean up?"

I don't bother with pleasantries. "As it happens, I am looking for a girl. Or more accurately, the house of Priam is."

At the mention of a possible transaction, her demeanor shifts. "Of course, Harsa. Of course." The woman's eyes glisten as they take in my many rings. "We have the most beautiful girls in all of Troy."

"I don't doubt it. But I do not seek a beautiful girl. I want one who is plain, smart, and small. *Very* small. Preferably one who speaks Greek and isn't afraid of her own shadow."

Madam Morgestia harrumphs as if I have requested a daughter of the gods. "Such a girl! In all my years, I can't recall having ever met a creature like the one you describe."

I remove one of the gem-studded bangles from my arm. "Perhaps this will stir your memory."

"In fact," the old lady reconsiders, snatching the bracelet, "one of our youngest might be what you are looking for. *You*," she barks at a languid woman who lounges on a nearby sofa. "Go fetch Salama."

The name strikes me as familiar, though I don't know why.

The proprietress gives me a slick grin that reveals two teeth of gold. "The girl's mother was once in high demand. Regrettably, the poor woman died when Salama was young. Her father, a hired soldier from Egypt, was already slain. Salama has been raised by the women of this house, but I must be frank—she does not have much experience. For you see, as you requested, she is plain." The old woman shakes her head again, as if counting the years of lost income. "Nothing like her mother, whose beauty was second only to Harsa Helen herself."

My mouth sags. "Plain is best. I doubt I need to tell an experienced pro-prietress like yourself of the tragic consequences that come from vanity."

"Right so, Harsa. There will be none of that from Salama. She mainly assists with cleaning and laundry. But she is hardworking and obedient."

It is obvious this old swindler is trying to get rid of a girl who does not bring in bronze. Still, I nod and reach into the pouch at my belt, filled with precious gemstones and pearl beads.

"Ah, and here she is." The woman's eyes move from my pile of treasure to the girl who passes through the purple curtain.

Salama is indeed small, but her high breasts indicate it's been a few years since she started to bleed. Her sly gaze and slender limbs remind me of a cat. Though not a beauty by any means, if this girl looks nothing like her mother, it is because she takes after her father with her strong, straight nose and those striking Egyptian eyes. They cut like a razor and require no kohl to stand out.

"The gods have blessed you, child," the proprietress declares. "Today you will return with this Harsa to the household of King Priam."

"The household of Prince Hector, actually."

Both women stare with mouths reaching for the floor. Not long ago, I might have stood in this very spot and made the request they are imag-ining, if not for the small heart now beating beneath my own. At least I pray it is.

In the end, Madam Morgestia drives a hard bargain. I return to the alley with far fewer gemstones than anticipated. By now the sun is gone, and it wouldn't be wise to wander these sordid streets after dark.

"This way."

"Not until you tell me why."

I turn slowly. "It seems your mistress's characterization of your obedi-ence was somewhat overstated."

The girl shrugs. "She's been trying to get rid of me for years. It's not my fault you fell for it."

"I see."

"Well, I don't. My question stands."

"Is it not enough that your father died serving Troy and I require that service now?"

She takes a few steps forward. "My father served no one but himself." The flash of hatred masks a deeper sorrow. It intrigues me. That's when I realize where I've seen Salama's scowl before. She was one of the girls Madam Morgestia brought to assist at the Fair Winds.

"Be that as it may," I continue, "he sacrificed everything on behalf of my husband. For that alone your father deserves respect."

Salama freezes in the street. "Then I would ask you something as well, Harsa." She speaks my title with an edge of contempt. As much as I am testing her, she is testing me in turn.

"Go on."

"My mother spoke of knowing Hector's bride before they both came to Troy." Narrow shoulders pull back. "Her name was Melanippe."

"Melanippe?" The word falls from my mouth like a stone. Our earliest memories always create the widest ripples. "Sister to the Amazon queen, Penthesilea?"

The girl nods.

My chest tightens as I recall my mentor's face. The woman who taught me how to wield a dagger and string a bow. Her younger sister was just as fiercely beautiful, but she never fought with the same passion as Penthesilea. Melanippe battled like she had no other choice. Perhaps that is why she abandoned the nomadic life of the Amazons and came to Troy.

"The Achaeans have taken everything from me. My father was cut down by Achilles." Salama nods at the brothel behind us. "Since my mother was all I had left, she was not willing to put her own life at risk as a hired soldier. She came to Madam's instead. Ironic, isn't it?"

For a girl to lose her mother to a silent disease in a brothel bed rather than a resounding blow on the battlefield? No. Sadly, it sounds just like the twisted humor of the gods.

All because Melanippe gave up her freedom. All because she gave up her spear and her bow.

I look down at my middle and wonder if I am making the same choice.

"You were her sister-in-arms. Did you not know she was here?" Salama's voice shakes with rage as she finally asks her question.

"No." To my own shame. "How would I? Men do not always speak openly of who they lie with."

Salama's sneer holds dark secrets. "My experience suggests otherwise."

She is angry. So she should be. The blood of Amazonian queens and the might of Egypt runs through this girl's veins, and still she spends her days hanging sheets to dry in the most miserable corner of Troy.

I close my eyes and imagine Melanippe arriving to the city in her youth. Falling in love with a handsome soldier. Giving birth to a healthy baby. Doing all the things a woman is supposed to do . . . and where did that leave her? Who was there to help her feed that child when her husband was cut down?

If only I had known, I could have . . .

What? What could I have done?

If I lose Hector and am carrying his child, Melanippe's tragic fate may be my own.

My eyes fall back to her razor-tongued daughter.

Salama's resilience will be a great asset to what awaits us. If only I can find a way to channel her indomitable resolve without it breaking both of us.

"Come with me," I assure her, "and you will find yourself on a very different road."

The girl studies me, and much like Rhea's horses, she searches for something she can trust. When she takes another step forward, I know she will follow wherever I lead.

But only ever by her own choice.

When we pass by the wine hall next door, the sounds coming from its walled courtyard aren't merely lewd talk. There is the *smack* of flesh. The angry curses of a man who believes himself cheated.

Roasted meat a day too old hits my nostrils, making my stomach churn. "Stay close," I tell Salama. I know the beginnings of a brawl when I hear one.

Holding my arm in front of me like a shield, I intend to quickly pass by the gate in the courtyard wall. But a collective roar has me halting in my tracks.

At least sixty men sit at long, wooden tables positioned around a large open fire in the center of the courtyard. By the potent smell in the air, their clay cups must be filled with ozüg—a dreadful cocktail of poor wine, strong ale, and a liquor made from pine resin and honey.

Before I can question the impulse, I step through the gate. The men do not even notice. They are too busy watching two armor-clad soldiers standing on either end of the table closest to us, shouting obscenities even as they draw their swords.

One of the men is Sarpedon. Another Lycian, shorter, stockier, and surely the cousin he mentioned, sits by Sarpedon's feet, attempting to talk him down. His opponent is a warrior I don't recognize, but the way he wears his flaming red hair in a high knot at the top of his head tells me he is a Thracian, while the emblem on his breast assures me he too is one of our allied captains.

"Until now, Troy's allies have always kept to different winehouses." Salama speaks up beside me. "They only mix when visiting . . ." She nods back to the brothel. "Though then they have other things on their minds."

The group of men in front of me is very much mixed. "What has changed?"

"There were two other winehouses serving soldiers nearby, but the first was owned by a man taken by the plague. The second lies in the bottom section of the Lower City and is currently underwater." Salama shrugs. "Boredom will drive men to drink even with those they dislike."

A platter crashes against a wall. A young man's head follows it as he is shoved hard from behind. Another warrior goes sailing into a table, upending clay bowls and spilling an oil lamp onto the floor.

For a moment, the captains seem distracted by the fire hazard, but any illusion of peace vanishes when the two leaders face off against each other again.

Wild cheers rise. Insults are flung in their own many languages, whereas others are shouted in the Luwian that binds Troy's allies together, even if the knot is tenuous.

I watch as the rope begins to fray down the middle.

Reaching for the blade beneath my cloak, I take a step toward the gate. Then pause. Once these captains resort to blows, this entire courtyard will erupt into violence. I can't risk getting caught in the fray. Not now.

All because she gave up her spear and her bow.

But I also can't risk doing nothing.

Unbidden, Helen's face takes the place of Penthesilea's warning. The way that face can silence a room. The power it holds, much as I resent it.

My face holds no such charms, but Helen and I do have other things in common.

"Hold my cloak, please." I hand it to Salama without taking my eyes off the two men. The gown I've kept covered as Trojan custom demands is one of my best, its rich silk the golden-green of pressed olive flesh. The jewel-studded belt at my waist only accentuates my hips and breasts, both fuller as of late. Half of my hair is worn up in pin curls while the rest flows in loose waves in the late Minoan style, recently back in fashion. The bracelets lining my arms jingle as I walk toward a table of warriors, the group parting to make room as I step onto the bench between them.

Weapons for women must be versatile. For so too are the threats facing us.

And the threat building in this courtyard is not one that can be subdued by a knife.

The men's weighty gazes stick to my curves as I climb to higher ground. A wave of nausea overtakes me as I step onto the table opposite Sarpedon and the Thracian, but it passes quickly, feeling more like a promise than a hindrance.

I have never felt more like a woman than I do in this moment.

And I am glad of it. Perhaps for the first time.

All shouting ceases. Not a cup moves as the eyes of every man fall upon me. There is a total, tranquil hush.

My hands fall restlessly to my sides.

"Tell me," I ask calmly. "What is the source of this foolishness?"

Sarpedon's gaze holds a faint flicker of the libertine I met in the alleyway earlier. "Naturally, Harsa, it concerns women. What else can cause a war that lasts so long?"

I raise an eyebrow. "You expect me to find wife-blaming a valid excuse for such behavior from Troy's finest?"

"My jest was about the whore who gave him birth, not his wife," says the Thracian with a grin for his men. He turns back to Sarpedon. "Though no one is stopping you from jumping on your ships and sailing home to your mothers. Gods know how much you Lycians love them."

The warriors in the crowd behind the Thracian captain release laughter tainted with resentment.

Sarpedon's smile could cut stone. "I won't deny it, Akamas. Just like I can't deny that any one of our mothers would sooner fight on two feet than from the safety of a horse's ass."

The cords on the Thracian captain's neck stand out like iron bands. He opens his mouth, but I speak before he can.

"And *this* is the matter our allies are willing to slit each other's throats over?" I cast a desultory glance around the courtyard. "You speak of moth-ers, but I fear yours would die of shame if they could see what I see now."

Sarpedon looks at me as if we are the only two people in the courtyard. "And what is it that you see, Harsa?"

I cross my arms over my chest. "Boys. Hurling cheap insults like they would stones."

So, like boys is how I treat them.

"Find your beds." I study the men around me. "Perhaps in the morning you will remember why King Priam summoned you to our shores."

"Then perhaps in the morning you can remind him of how guests should be treated when resting within a king's walls," Akamas returns, his glare unflinching. That he is clearly referencing his rival Sarpedon's request for an audience with the council speaks volumes.

I take in the captains' threadbare tunics. Our allies have been living on stale bread and unspiced meat for too long. Strangers who washed up on a foreign shore would be given better hospitality. These men we regard as friends stare back at me, daring me to deny it.

I nod. "I will speak to Prince Hector and see that your provisions are improved."

"Tell him to trade in his pale brother for a liaison who doesn't balk at his own shadow while you're at it," suggests a wizened warrior with obsidian skin and a full head of thick white hair.

Sarpedon's eyes dance languorously up my gown. "I have long said that Troy has more riches than just gold. Yet I can't help but wonder why the wife of Prince Hector would care that we are vexed by fleas and forced to shit in cracked pots."

"Because I too was once an outsider in Troy." In many ways, I still am. "I understand what it is like to long for home, which is why I give you my word that if you leave this courtyard in peace, I will take your grievances to my husband and see that they are heard."

When the men don't immediately agree, I alter my angle of attack. "I may not be your preferred advocate, but I am currently the only member of the royal family who is taking an interest. There will be no better bargain than this. I suggest you take it."

"Forgive us, Harsa." Akamas's shoulders bow slightly. "If you will do as you have promised, I will make sure my men return to their camp and cause no more trouble."

"You have my thanks," I say.

The men begin clearing the winehouse. A sinking feeling overtakes me as I watch them go. These warriors are dry tinder waiting for a flame. Only the soldiers' shock at seeing me, Hector's Harsa, rising up before them kept it from igniting today.

The other Lycians leave, but Sarpedon lingers. When he passes me, he leans in close enough for his lips to graze my ear. "No man could have done what you just did." His smooth voice is sober now. "We will never bring shame to the house of Hector again."

"I will hold you to that, Captain," I say, unable to resist the parting gift of a smile.

Then I turn back to Salama. The girl waits near the courtyard exit with my cloak, her mouth agape. "That was . . . unexpected."

"It was, indeed." Before I can say more, a firm hand grabs hold of my wrist. I recognize the placement of the finger calluses long before the cloaked figure, who is seated alone at a rear table, lifts his hooded head.

"Hector."

"Not here," he says, pulling me through the gate and back into the alleyway.

"What is this about?" I hiss.

"I should ask you the same thing." His intense eyes flit from me to Salama on my heels.

"She has nothing to do with this," I insist.

"You still have not explained what you are doing in the Lower City."

"And you have not explained why you did not reproach your captains for brawling yourself."

Hector sighs. "It is not my place. The allies are under Helenus's charge, and I can't be seen to overstep. But sometimes, I observe these idle men from the shadows. It's only then that I'm able to see the grievances they are too proud to tell me to my face."

I nod. "To start, the stewed goat is shit."

"Yes, I heard." Hector's lips quirk, but too quickly the hard line returns. "Helenus's efforts to appease them have left much to be desired."

"These men came here to fight," I say, feeling every ounce of their frustration. "Instead, they sit languishing in winehouses, far from their families and their homelands. These aren't Trojan troops trained to heed your every command. They are commanders in their own right, and they won't be content to hide behind our walls forever."

"I know that. But I would not pave a different path if it means breaking with the ways and the alliances that have gotten us this far."

"Nor would I ask you to trade in one set of problems for another," I agree. "But you can't expect these men to follow our traditions if we do not give a care to understanding their own."

"Perhaps." Hector turns back to Salama, who stares at him like he is a god. "What is going on here, Andromache?"

My eyes fall. In all our years of marriage, I have never lied to Hector. Even when he was most likely to resent me for my honesty. Now, I seem to be withholding the full truth left and right.

"Bodecca isn't getting any younger. I didn't want to trouble you, but we needed another kitchen maid to ease her load."

Hector nods and his eyes glaze over. "I see."

The reality that he sees nothing—that my misdirection works—floods me with guilt. I change the subject.

"Your strength is in the army that stands at your back, Hector. But we do not have enough men. We *need* these allied captains, and their enthusiasm is waning. It's no longer enough to merely defend. Odysseus will find a way to breach these walls unless we employ equally cunning tactics that can stop him."

Three times.

Hector says nothing, but I can tell he's considering my words. It gives me hope that one day he may be open to receiving my small army of spies, so long as we are able to prove what can be done. What must be done. His large hand reaches for one of my loose tendrils. It's a hairstyle I've not worn since we were first married.

Hector's hand digs through the curls until it clasps the back of my neck. His grip softens, as do his eyes. "What happened in Thebe will not happen here, my *alev*. Not while I breathe."

My hope starts to slip as I reach for his neck in turn, gently pulling his forehead to mine, until I can hear his exhale as clearly as I hear the east wind.

That is what I fear most, Hector. That your breath will stop.

But I cannot say the words.

The rising flood of all that is left unspoken between us may soon breach the levees, no matter how well we fortify them.

26

RHEA

"WILL YOU BE all right here with Bodecca for a few moments?" I ask.

Isola sits straight-backed in a wooden chair by the kitchen hearth. She looks as old as my sixteen summers, but the unsure way she carries herself makes her seem much younger. In the hour we've been waiting for Andromache's return, she hasn't said a word. If I didn't see the occasional rise and fall of her slim shoulders, I might think she'd ceased to breathe.

Slowly, Isola lifts her chin. She's as small as I am, but where I now have some softness to my figure thanks to Bodecca's forced feedings, she is all harsh angles.

"I am just going to step outside," I tell her.

Isola merely ducks her head so that a curtain of hair hangs over her face. The long strands are stick-straight in the strangest shade of brown mixed with copper. It clashes oddly with her olive skin, marked with red bumps that have been picked at repeatedly.

It's hard to reconcile this timid girl with the one who cared for her mistress before suffering the plague herself with such courage, and it makes me wonder if Andromache and I are making a mistake to ask so much of her.

I leave Isola in the kitchen under Bodecca's guard and slip into the courtyard. The rain is falling again in a miserable drizzle that sinks into my bones.

It's been hours since Andromache left me at the temple, that strange fire burning in her eyes. What could be taking her so long?

I've heard talk in the stables. Of the asylum camps overflowing into the lower rings. Livestock shortages and bands of desperate men who hunt for easy marks in the Lower City when the sun goes down. Add in several thousand idle, foreign soldiers and a flood, and I imagine the situation is rapidly nearing a breaking point.

A familiar silhouette cuts toward the house.

"Andromache!" I barely stop myself from throwing my arms around her.

"Careful, Rhea." Her lips twitch. "One might think you doubt my ability to fend for myself."

"It's getting dark." I glance over her shoulder to see we have an audience. One of Madam Morgestia's girls. From the Four Winds.

"So it is." Andromache observes the darkening sky. "Isola?"

"In the kitchen. Creusa said she could stay as long as necessary. So long as Isola herself agreed."

"I'd expect nothing less of Creusa." The tone that might sound sharp to anyone else rings with clear affection to my ears. "It seems there is no reason to delay. Take Salama into the kitchen. Wait a few moments and then join me in my chambers."

She leaves us in the looming dark.

"This way." I gesture toward the kitchen, but the sharp-chinned girl doesn't budge.

"I'm not for sale." Color rides high on her cheekbones.

"I . . . I'm sorry?"

"I earn my keep by cleaning sheets, not warming them. If the first family of Troy wishes for a plaything, they can find one somewhere else."

"You . . . No. That's not why . . . Andromache would never . . ."

The girl offers me a mocking glance. "It's not unheard of for couples married many years to seek a bit of sport. Especially ones desperate for a child." Her eyes go hard as obsidian. "You can't imagine the things desperate women will do."

Kallira's face flashes through my mind. "You know nothing about what I can imagine and even less about the reasons you've been brought here. And if you don't hold your tongue and follow me into the kitchens, you can walk right back to your brothel without ever finding out."

We face each other in the rain. After a long moment, the girl pushes past me into the warmth of the house. Letting out a long breath, I follow.

Isola is still sitting exactly where I left her. Salama studies and dismisses the other girl in the span of an instant. She lifts a knife from the table, spears a piece of salted meat Bodecca has left to cure, and eats it directly off the blade.

Fearfully, I glance across the kitchen to where Bodecca is stacking platters with her back to us.

"Follow me." I hurry them out of the room.

We find Andromache in her personal chambers. Ariasti of Thebe's body has been removed for preparation, but I can still feel the woman's presence haunting the room. A reminder of what is at stake.

At Andromache's signal, we take our places against the wall.

"This must seem strange to you," Andromache says. "I promise, if you decide to stay, things will become stranger still."

"Why don't you tell me what this is, and then I'll tell you if I'm interested." From the way she holds herself, one might think Salama was royalty, but her plain clothes and red-calloused hands tell a different story.

"Do either of you speak Greek? Anything other than Luwian?" Andromache asks.

"My mother and father came to Troy with Harsar Aeneas from Dardania." Isola's voice is barely audible. "I also speak Thracian."

Andromache nods, pleased. "And what of you?"

Salama shrugs. "My father was Egyptian. I have Greek too. I can understand and converse roughly in a half dozen more languages."

Andromache's dark brow arches. "How did you come to be so learned?"

"Growing up in a brothel is an education all its own." Salama's smile is a sharp slash across her face. "Our visitors hail from every kingdom east to west. Men pay more when they are made to feel at home, and they all speak with one tongue when it comes down to it."

Isola's cheeks turn a deep shade of red to match my own.

"How do you feel about confined spaces?" Andromache asks.

Salama offers another shrug. "They don't bother me so long as I'm not bound. I refuse to be tied for any reason."

"If the city falls, that may lie outside of your control," Andromache points out.

"I'll slit my own wrists before I surrender to the Achaeans." Salama's voice is Hittite iron. "But I'd rather force them to do that work on my behalf while I take as many of them with me to the Underworld as I can."

Andromache and I share a look.

Daring. Burning with hatred for the Achaeans. Alarmingly low levels of self-preservation.

Salama may be just what we are looking for.

If only Andromache can get her to do as she is told.

"What about the dark?" I ask, because I've never known blackness like the one under the wall. The memory alone has my breaths going shallow.

"What about it?" Salama snaps.

"Does it frighten you?" I say through gritted teeth.

"I am not a child."

"What about you, Isola?" I ask the girl who has barely spoken.

"The dark does not frighten me." The way she says it, with a slight emphasis on the word *dark*, makes it seem as if it is one of the few things that doesn't.

I nod at Andromache, who accepts my judgment without another word. "I have something to ask of you," she says. "Do not agree if there is any doubt in your heart that you are prepared to fulfill the terms." Her face sets in hard lines. "This is a matter of the utmost secrecy. If word gets out, I will know exactly who to punish. Is that understood?"

"Tell us what you want from us," Salama says. And so, Andromache begins to speak.

When she is done, silence lingers.

"You wish for us to spy on the Achaeans on their own ground?" Salama asks, this time without a trace of belligerence.

"No. You will watch the Kesik Cut to see who crosses and report back to us where they go. Obviously, the mission is not without risk. You will be rewarded accordingly."

"I'll do it," Salama says quickly. "But I have a condition of my own."

"Speak it," Andromache says.

"When we beat the Achaeans, I want to be there on the beaches when they set fire to all the ships with the men inside. I want to hear their screams."

Andromache glances at me sideways. "I'm . . . sure that can be arranged."

"And if we're seen?" Isola whispers.

Andromache opens her cloak to reveal two more daggers like the one she gave me—the one I still carry beneath my tunic.

"You should be safe from the regular army during the rains, but there may be scouts on the plain. Or scavengers. Once you leave these walls, the only protection you can count on is that of the gods and your own quick thinking."

Salama snatches the dagger from Andromache and begins passing it between her hands with an ease that suggests she's no stranger to a blade.

Isola, on the other hand, cradles the dagger as if it might catch flame.

"You don't have to do this," I tell the girl, feeling a wash of sympathy for her. "We can find someone else."

Isola meets my eyes for the first time. "One of my brothers died on the Scamander plain in a raid last year. The other two are members of Harsar Aeneas's company. My brothers are the only family I have. If this will help them, I'll do it."

"It is settled then. You will both answer to Rhea," Andromache says.

It's a struggle to keep my face impassive.

"Her?" Salama asks scornfully. "Why?"

I can't help but wonder the same thing.

"Because I trust her," Andromache says simply. "You lack her judgment, her tact, and have yet to earn my trust."

Every one of my doubts melts away under the warmth of Andromache's gaze.

"I'll show you how to wield the dagger so that you won't hurt yourself," I say. "If I can learn it, so can you. And then, I'll lead you through the wall and show you how we are to access the plain."

Andromache points to some wine and bread on a side table. We leave them to eat while we watch them from across the room. Salama sticks a piece of bread in her mouth and starts tossing her dagger up and down. Isola ignores the food and stands with her back pressed against the wall as if she is in danger of fainting.

"How long until we go through the wall?" I ask quietly.

"Odysseus won't wait, and neither can we."

I nod. The longer we put this off, the greater the chance that Hector will notice something amiss. And though Andromache has her reasons, I fear the growing list of secrets between them will only lead to grief.

Quietly, I reach for a cup of cold tea left on the table and place it in Andromache's hands.

She grimaces, but for once, Andromache does not protest as she raises it to her lips. It is almost enough to assuage the prick of guilt.

I watch Salama slice a piece of fruit as if it were an Achaean throat. Pulp flies across the floor. Whatever the source of her hatred, it makes her more than a little frightening.

"I almost pity the Achaeans," I say under my breath.

Andromache laughs and grips my shoulder. "Perhaps they are finally about to get what they deserve."

THE SERVANTS' QUARTERS are stifling with the heat of a dozen bodies. I've been lying here for hours wedged between Salama and Isola, but sleep refuses to come.

It's been weeks since the night of the storm when I traveled under the wall. The rain hasn't stopped. There's a chance the passage will be flooded with groundwater. If that's the case, then Andromache's plan will never work. Maybe it would be better for all of us if that were so.

I ease myself off the bed. Throwing on my cloak, I slip from the room, past the kitchen, and out into the night. For once, I don't head back through the courtyard to the stables. Instead, I make my way through the empty streets of the Merchant Quarter, between rows of impressive houses lit by the occasional oil lamp and the Dardanian gate that leads to the Citadel. Other than the guards who stand watch, there is no one about at this hour. The people in Troy's second ring may be wealthy, but theirs is a wealth that is earned, not given. In order to maintain it, they must still rise early like those in the lower rings. Meanwhile, light shines out from the many door-ways and balconies of Priam's palace high above, leaving me to wonder if the men and women who live there ever sleep. After a few more twists and turns, that light is blocked out by the towering northeast bastion. There, in the darkest corner of Troy's second ring, the ancient temple sits.

Inside, embers burn low in the hearth, casting a soft glow over the face of the Mother goddess. Someone must've come here recently to make an offering. I glance around, but the temple is empty.

My breaths turn ragged as I bend before the shelf of stone. If I'm being truthful, it wasn't the threat of flooding that brought me here. It was the dark. I'm not sure I can face it again. Even for Andromache. And I can't bear the thought of shaming myself in front of her.

I suppose there's only one way to find out.

Bracing myself on my hands and knees, I crawl into the narrow opening. My frame takes up most of the available space, and at once, the blackness of the tunnel swallows me. Every muscle in my body goes rigid. I close my eyes and think of Andromache. Of Hector and Carris and Ishtar in the stables.

I've forced myself forward another inch when a hand wraps around my ankle.

Stone scrapes skin as I am yanked out of the narrow passage and back out into the dim light of the temple. I hit the floor with a hard body on top of mine. My scream is cut off by the blade pressed to my throat.

I look up into eyes as blue as the Aegean. It takes me a moment to put those eyes together with the features of the man they belong to.

"Cyrrian?" My heart stutters. "What are you doing here?"

"Rhea." The blade drops, but his weight still pins me to the stone. "I was just wondering the same thing about you."

I wiggle to free myself, but his arms form a bronze cage around my shoulders. "I asked you first."

Cyrrian's jaw clenches. "I come here to pray. These were my father's gods. Now, you."

I rack my mind for some way to answer that doesn't betray Andromache's trust or secure me swift passage across the Great River. "My comings and goings are none of your concern."

"Troy's security is my concern." Cyrrian's breath tickles my cheek. "As such, so are any and all people who sneak through her walls."

"Perhaps I'm on Troy's business," I say, channeling some of Salama's insolence. It seems to work well enough for her.

"What do you mean?"

"Nothing." I instantly regret my words. "Let me go. I'm here for Andromache. If you don't believe me, let's go together and ask her."

A dark brow arches. "There's an idea. Perhaps I'll drag you through the streets and demand answers. Civilized though we think we are, the people of Troy do love a good stoning."

"You can't do that!"

"Why? If nothing's amiss, what does it matter?" The heat of him sets the front of my body on fire. He leans down so that our faces are inches apart. Suddenly, I can't breathe.

"Let me up," I gasp. "Please."

Within seconds, his fingers span my rib cage, lifting me to my feet. He doesn't give me a second to catch my breath. "Tell me what you're doing here. I am out of patience."

The silence hangs suspended between us. There's no give in his expression. His blade remains ready in his hand, assuring me he'll do exactly as he threatens. Unless I tell him what he wants to know.

My shoulders droop. "There's a passage here out of the north walls of Troy. We plan to use it to sneak onto the plain at night and keep watch on the Achaean camps."

Cyrrian's expression turns immutable. "You aren't serious."

Annoyance flares through me. "Why force me to tell you the truth if you only refuse to believe it?"

"This is Andromache's doing. She'll send you out to do what she can't." Cyrrian takes a step backward. "Hector will put a stop to it. I might end up with one of Andromache's knives in my back, but at least nobody innocent will have to die."

He starts to walk away, so I say the only thing that I know will stop him. "Andromache is with child."

Cyrrian turns. The dying fire throws shadows across his impossibly handsome face. "What?"

"Nobody knows. Not even Hector. She found out moments before she learned of Thebe's fate and it is making her"—I search for the right word—"*determined* in a way I haven't seen before. If you betray her plans to Hector, you'll only set her on an even more reckless course." I draw a steadying breath. "At least this way, neither she nor Hector's child will be in any direct danger."

"I would trust Andromache with my life, but this is madness." The charioteer rakes his hands through his dark curls, sending them flying. "Her grief is no excuse for putting innocents at risk." He nods to himself. "Hector will make her see reason."

"Have you met anyone who could make Andromache do anything?"

His lips twitch. A blink and then it's gone.

I take advantage of his silence. "You underestimate what lengths she would go to protect Hector and their child from threats the Citadel refuses to acknowledge."

"I'm not saying there isn't value in what she is proposing. But if someone needs to go beyond the wall, let it be a man who knows how to defend himself."

It is my turn to snort. "They've tried that. Odysseus has men watching the gates. Any scouts Hector and Aeneas have sent out are spotted before they ever reach the plain." My back straightens. "The tunnel to the plateau is the only way to leave the city unseen, and it is too narrow for a man to pass through."

"Then we find another way."

"There *is* no other way." Anger rises up from a dozen secret places inside me. "Why is it so hard to accept that a girl could do this? That she'd take the risk to defend her city and her people? Why must we always wait for misery to find us when we could act to prevent it instead?"

"Your people?" Cyrrian asks sharply. "I didn't realize you were of Troy."

My face heats at the dig. "I wasn't born here, but neither was my father, and he died on the Scamander plain at Prince Hector's side. When he was gone, our farm was burned and my family slaughtered by men just like the Achaeans."

The coldness melts from his face. "I'm sorry. But if your father were alive, he'd want you to stay behind the walls and let the men whose job it is to protect you do their duty."

His words break something inside me. Anger and pride fly through my blood on a flood of images I've tried desperately to forget. The terror of horses. The smell of thick smoke. Muffled groans and high-pitched cries. Rhythmic knocking and animal grunts. Ugly sounds that reached down into the depths of fear within me.

Screams.

They rise up in my mind, only now, I can't deny where they are coming from. I know it with the part of me that hears the horses whisper. They are my mother's cries. My sisters'. They scream and scream and scream, calling out for help that does not come.

And then Kallira is there, kneeling in front of me. Forcing a promise from my lips in a burning stable before she burst out of the doors. For the rest of my life, I will never forget the way she stood. Proud and graceful in the dying sun as she waited for the men outside to spot her. They called to each other, eager for the game. She waited for them to come close, and then she picked up her robes and broke from the gardens beyond the stable. Clearing the way so that I could run from the only home I'd ever known. So that I could *live*.

Pain, guilt, and desperate love war inside me as I face Cyrrian in the shadows of the lonely temple. "No man protected me from the monsters who came to our farm. It was my sister. She gave her life for mine." The ache in my throat makes it difficult to speak. "I lost everything once, Cyrrian. I can't lose it again. No matter what happens."

The words are truths that feel like lies. When it comes down to it, Isola and Salama are the ones taking all the risk. And why?

Because Andromache didn't ask it of me this time?

Because I want to believe she cares too much to put me in real danger?

My heart knows the answer in the flush of shame that travels up my neck.

Because I am afraid.

"This is madness," Cyrrian says again.

"If you think you can stop her by telling Hector, you don't know Andromache." I repeat the very words that Cyrrian spoke to Hector in the stables all those weeks ago. "She follows no laws but those of honor as she sees it. You can't simply pick and choose the parts of her worth loving."

Cyrrian's face grows pensive. "You have an uncanny memory."

"It occasionally proves useful in showing people their blatant hypocrisy."

Cyrrian's eyes flash as he presses me farther back against the stone. "I can't decide if you are incredibly brave. Or incredibly stupid."

"I find you every bit as confusing."

"How so?" It's a challenge.

This time, I speak knowing exactly how reckless it is. "You smile at everyone, but you have no real friends other than Aeneas and Hector. You pretend to be the disinterested wastrel others paint you as, but when nobody is looking, you do what needs to be done. These are not the actions of a man who shows his true face to the world. They are the actions of someone with something to hide."

He studies me closely. "You see much even though you speak little."

"I've been told this is one of my most endearing qualities."

This time, there is no mistaking the quirk of his lips. "No doubt there are many." He rubs his hand over his face. "Persuasive as your arguments are, I'm forced to disappoint you. I will not lie to Hector. Not even for Andromache."

Sympathy wells inside me. I know better than he realizes how loving them both is occasionally like being torn in two.

"Please." I hear the desperation in my own voice. "Before you decide, approach her yourself. Do the one thing the rest of Troy refuses to do."

"And what is that?" Cyrrian asks.

"Listen." The word tastes like defeat even as I utter it. He will not be moved by anything I say. Only Andromache might wield that power, and he will not let her try. "Listen to her, before it is too late."

Cyrrian flinches. I watch in confusion as he fights to master his emotions. For a moment, the temple of the Mother goddess is filled with ghosts, though I'm not sure if they are his or mine.

"Cyrrian, what is—"

"Don't," he warns. Whatever I said to upset him, he will guard his hurt as closely as all the other things he hides.

A muscle jumps in his jaw as he turns to study the Mother's pass. The curls he tries so hard to tame into a low knot like the one Hector wears riot around his face.

"What path will Andromache have you take to the cut? That's where she'd have you wait? For Odysseus and his men?" he asks without looking at me.

"How did you—?"

His eyes pierce me. "As you so generously pointed out, I'm not as stupid as I look. It's the most pragmatic place to watch the Achaeans' movements and discover their secrets, and Andromache is nothing if not pragmatic." Cyrrian frowns. "How do you plan on getting there undetected?"

"I . . . I had thought to figure that out as we went."

The warrior in front of me looks less than impressed. "The marsh will be impassible. Flooded with bogs and insects. You can't take the plain or the higher ground without risk of exposure."

"How can you be sure?" I ask him.

"I grew up in this city, and I spent a great deal of time beyond its walls. There is only one way you might hope to get to the cut undetected from the plateau, which is the only place we don't bother with archers because it is impossible to scale."

Without knowledge of the Mother's pass.

He does not say it. There is no need.

"Tell me."

"I'm not agreeing to anything. If nothing else, this little misadventure proves how ill-conceived this plan was from the start. At the very least, you should have had someone guard the temple at your back. Thank the Mother for staying my hand before I slit your throat tonight."

As much as it irks me to admit it, he's right. "I hadn't thought of that."

Cyrrian's laugh cuts through the damp. "I'd say you haven't thought of a lot of things."

"Help us or don't." I am tired of his criticisms.

His eyes scan my face for a long moment before he asks, "Are you as good at memorizing pictures as you are other people's words?"

"I can memorize anything."

"That remains to be seen. What time has Andromache set for this calamity?"

"End of the second night watch. Tomorrow."

He nods. "I will meet you both here. I'll agree to hear her out, but that is all. That is all, Rhea."

He leaves the temple as silently as he entered, a solitary figure slipping down a dark and empty street, holding on to his own secrets as tightly as he does those of others. As I watch, his broad shoulders seem to bend under the weight of the black sky, and it leaves me wondering who has won tonight. And who has lost.

ANDROMACHE

"DO YOU THINK the trenches will be enough?" I stare down from the ramparts into what has become a passageway of mud stretching around the southwest corner of the Lower City. These trenches are meant to stop a full-scale chariot attack, but filled with standing water, they will soon become a haven for hatching mosquitoes and the ill spirits that feed on them.

"I can add more archers to the walls, especially during the third watch when Odysseus is most likely to be on the prowl. Even if he avoids crossing the trenches here, more eyes mean more chances to see which direction he is coming from." Hector flexes his arms against the wall of sunbaked mud-brick, weighing the few options we have at our disposal. "Why the stern face, my *alev*? Providing the people of the Lower City with greater protection was your idea."

"I know." The despair on the faces of the Lower City's women during the plague has never fully left me, so knowing Odysseus would press in on our weaknesses *here* has filled me with fire. What right do we have to ask these people to fight for us if we do not stand for them? Unsurprisingly, not everyone agrees.

I can already hear Paris's complaints before the council about having to send more of his archers down to the Lower City. Why would Hector stretch the defenses of the Citadel thin?

Instead, Paris would risk these homes and businesses so long as the Citadel stands. Never mind that we would not last a week without a granary or wells in the lower rings of Troy. Without the struggling forges that still manage to keep Paris's archers well supplied with arrowheads.

Pull back. Dig in deeper. Hide behind the walls.

That has always been the Old Bloods' way.

And it may yet be their downfall. The Citadel is at the center of Troy, but the Lower City is her pulsing heart.

I watch a woman in the street below us, a large water jug on one hip and a baby on the other. She turns back to call out to the small child straggling behind her, and I catch a flash of her profile. Young and familiar.

As if sensing me there, Lannaka meets my gaze. Her eyes are ringed with shadows and the hollows of her cheeks are even more pronounced than before.

She starts to turn away, but at the last moment she offers me a curt nod.

Not all omens are bird signs.

The boy runs to catch up to his older sister, wielding a large stick like a spear. When he wags it at her baby, Lannaka snatches up the stick, breaks it over her thigh, and tosses the two halves aside. She hands the crying boy a crust of bread and beckons him onward.

I watch them go.

"Andromache?"

Hector's voice calls me back to myself.

"The walls here are too short," I tell him. "Especially by the fig tree where the earthquake during King Laomedon's reign did much damage. It will never hold if the Achaeans grow smart enough to launch an assault from there."

"Then thank Zeus they'll first have to make it over these mosquito-ridden moats," Hector says.

I frown at yet another encroachment of Queen Hecuba's western deities. "Zeus...Tarhunt...Taru...Teshub. Why do we give so many names to the same catastrophe?"

Hector sighs. "Regardless of the god responsible, if these two defenses fail, we will have to sound the horns and bring the people to the shelter below the Citadel."

I can hear the pressure of the council building beneath Hector's words. "And if Odysseus's cleverness guarantees we fail to perceive the attack before it's too late?"

Because if the plague-corpse was only the first, then there are two more coming.

A shiver skitters up my back, followed by a sharp cramp that leaves me dizzy. I swallow the rush of saliva in my mouth. Though every day that passes with no sign of blood increases my hope, I'm not ready to invite Hector onto this narrow ledge. Not until I am certain it will hold.

Hector sighs again. "You know we don't have enough men to launch a full-scale building project at the west wall. If the allies abandon us, soon we may have even fewer."

My eyes meet his. I came out here to distract myself from the dangers I have asked Rhea and the others to walk into willingly, but the peril seems to be piling up.

"The situation has not improved?" I have already begun to keep my promise to the allied captains. The servingwomen of my own household have been weaving new bedding and tunics for the men.

Hector places a hand over the one I am resting on the wall, aware of what I'm really asking. "Under the best of circumstances, the memory of a hired soldier is short. And the song of his homeland is sung by a siren who never shuts up."

"These are far from the best of circumstances."

Hector nods. "There is that."

I gnaw on my lower lip. Without plenty of men to guard the walls and fight on the plain, the future of Troy's girls and boys will be equally grim.

"We can't lose the support of our friends, Hector." Especially not when that support seems to have lent itself to those in the lowest rings of the city everyone else has forgotten.

"Many fear to leave their homelands undefended for much longer. I can hardly blame them. The Achaeans aren't the only common threat we face. The famine and unrest in the Hittite Empire is beginning to spread. It has kept the eyes at Hattusa focused inward, but that will not last if they sense an easy conquest." Hector sighs. "I've already offered the captains every incentive I can think of to stay, and my father's promises of more treasure are growing stale. The only thing they want is the thing I have no power to provide." He sighs again. "They came here to drive Agamemnon into the sea, and the longer it takes, the less faith they have it will ever happen."

They are not alone.

I recall the courtyard of disgruntled men I happened upon in the Lower City. "Then we must remind them of what is at stake. We must do what the King's Council has failed to: show our allies they are indispensable. Not just the captains, but the lowest-born foot soldier and everyone in between."

Again, I look down on Lannaka and the children before they disappear into a vine-covered courtyard. The girl is too young to be tethered by such a frayed rope, trapped by sickness and rains and high walls for half her life. There are few things as tragic as being denied a childhood.

Perhaps we may yet give her a taste.

"The Festival of the Divine Twins," I say as a vision of the Lower City dressed in vibrant colors spreads out before me. "Instead of limiting the festivities to the Citadel like we have since the war began, we should invite everyone. The citizens of the Lower City, as well as the asylum seekers. And, as our guests of honor, Troy's foreign allies."

"I like the notion, but I'm not sure my father or his advisors will approve of the added expense." Hector frowns, and I can hear all the thoughts he doesn't say. The change in succession will be hard enough to bear with the Citadel as witness. To include the whole city . . .

The desire to reassure him rises up with nausea, but I hold strong against both.

Patience. My greatest weakness. One I must master if I am to give Hector an even greater victory over all who seek our downfall.

"Prior to the war, the festival *was* open to everyone. So you see? We are not breaking with Troy's traditions. We are merely reinstating ones she has forgone in the name of expediency."

Hector chuckles and shakes his head. "And this is why my father wants you nowhere near his council. Your arguments, like our walls, have few visible cracks."

Unlike my resolve when I think of all that I am trying to make invisible. The things I am keeping from him. To drown the inner accusations, I force a smile. "A real festival, Hector. We will ask the Divine Twins to bring back the sun with their solar steeds. There will be music and fresh food. And games, of course. As many competitions as our allies have homelands. It will be a great reprieve for those who have suffered during these dreary days."

The people of the Lower City will know they are not forgotten. And if the gods grant me this child, it will prove to Paris and all his supporters that I have won.

An image of Rhea and the girls shivering in the wind of the plateau attempts to steal my joy, but I force it away.

"The festival will surely boost morale," Hector says. "But I'm not certain it will be enough to convince the captains to stay, and they are the ones who hold sway over their men. They are still refusing to deal with Helenus."

"You really don't think Aeneas could step in as liaison?"

"My cousin can't mask his disdain of their unconventional ways, and for their part, the captains won't take orders from . . ." Hector stands up straight. "You. If anyone can keep them from killing each other, it is you, Andromache."

I know every inch of the man who stares at me with his usual intensity, but these words cannot be coming from my husband. "What are you asking?"

"Serve as my liaison to the allied captains. Keep them happy. Well, happy enough not to leave."

"How can you imagine they'd liaise with a woman when my predecessors have failed?" I ask in disbelief.

"You are always telling me how the queens of eastern Anatolia and Egypt rule beside their kings. I saw it with my own eyes in the winehouse. They will listen to you."

I study Hector, reading between the words he says for the truth he won't speak. "You mean, you are confident they won't spear a Harsa of Troy between the eyes like they might any of your other brothers."

He doesn't even try to deny it.

"I am no administrator." The thought alone is enough to make me shudder. "I am also no orator."

"They have heard a hundred old men pontificate on the glory to be gained in battle." Hector pulls my arms so we are standing face-to-face. "These men were not born in Troy. My father and his advisors struggle to understand their ways, so they keep them apart. Most of our allies are children of the east. Appeal to them in a language they will understand."

"The Citadel will not like it."

"Is there a more compelling reason to say yes?" Hector's smile is full of faith. It makes my heart swell and my stomach sink.

"By the end of this war," Hector continues, "every man, woman, and child in Troy will know that their future king and queen intend to rule this city with a single heart and mind. Let us show them our united front."

And, if the gods are just, the son who is born of it.

Hector kisses me softly on the cheek. "We are one, Andromache. Even as we each set our own offerings on the altar."

My hands turn to ice. There is nothing that makes a marriage bed go cold quite like deception, however noble the reasons. I reach for my face, still warm from Hector's touch, which felt more fraternal than anything. Stripped of all desire to keep me for himself.

"What's wrong? I thought this is what you wanted."

"It is." And the brutal irony is he gave it to me right after I took it for myself. In secret.

For years, I've urged Hector to let me play a greater role. But the way I am most needed now rubs against the grain of my former vision. Armor-clad, seated on a stallion reared by Hector's own hand. Riding into battle beside him, both of us smeared in our enemy's blood.

"You spoke to them as a woman, Andromache. As a queen. A warrior queen."

The lump in my throat thickens. "That is what I was trained to be."

"Then be one. Now is your chance."

"You truly think you can convince the council?"

"The council will be happy to wash their hands of the allies once and for all. Besides, the king is the only one who can order me. But I get to approve the liaisons who advise my men because I alone command them . . ." He gives me a playful squeeze. "Just as I command my wife."

Swallowing the bitterness at the back of my throat, I grin and shove him gently in the chest. "You'd like to think it."

Hector catches my hand, pulling me in for a long kiss.

In this, I obey.

When he pulls back, he asks, "So. What will be your first act as royal liaison to Troy's allied captains?"

"I will get to know them." I chew on the inside of my cheek. "And I must offer them something. Not just better provisions, but perhaps a better place to train."

"There are few suitable places in the Lower City."

"So we bring them to the stables and the upper training yards. They are your domain, Hector. You decide who is welcome there."

Concern flies across his face. It is no small thing for him to bring outsiders into Troy's upper rings, but I know it is also the only way to make this work.

At last, Hector nods. "You can use the smaller yard. I'll have Cyrrian move the chariots elsewhere." He rubs the back of his neck. "The council will have to make an exception. It is the least that they owe me."

Again, my secret burns. How I wish I could tell him there will hopefully be no more need to worry about the council.

I *will* carry this child, I will subdue the allies, and I will silence Paris.

I will give this man I love everything he needs to rule, and then we will display our full power at the festival.

"What else are you thinking, my *alev*?"

Hector knows me too well. But there are also things he does not know.

"I must use a woman's oldest attack," I reply vaguely. The wry wisdom of Sarpedon and his beloved mother rings in my ears as I squeeze Hector's hands. "I will remind our captains that a man's courage is often born in his gut before it takes root in his heart."

***

AENEAS OF DARDANIA is cut from the same noble cloth as Hector. It makes him a natural leader, but whereas Hector is known to laugh on occasion, I have never seen Aeneas's lips even twitch in that direction.

His steel-gray eyes dart around the amphoras set to cooling in the deep earth, the rows of jars filled with oil and flour. They stop to rest on the dead chickens hanging by their feet above Bodecca's workspace. "You . . . asked to see me?"

The discomfort that radiates from Aeneas's rigid body at this unexpected entrance into a woman's domain is palpable. It takes all my strength to stifle a smirk.

"Hector and I need your assistance."

"Of course." Aeneas's eyes ignite like struck flint. "As the gods command."

I have never met a man more devoted to the gods and their unbending ways. Aeneas may wear a soldier's armor like he was born in a cast of bronze, but it is hard to imagine his clean, patrician hands—with their trimmed fingernails and golden rings—spilling blood. But of course, they have. As often as the rest.

Aeneas is not an easy man to get to know, but I sense he is solemn because he is his own harshest critic. Still, no matter the walls of honor he hides behind, he is a man of great dignity and Hector's dearest friend. The soldier whose judgment he trusts more than any other.

He is also the warrior most admired by the army after Hector himself, with battlefield moves so graceful, some whisper that he must be the son of a goddess.

"We require the aid of the Dardanians," I tell him. Aeneas's love for his ancestral house is a close second to his devotion to the gods. He and his father, Anchises, first cousin to King Priam, came to Troy from Dardania when our troubles first began. Neither has seen their home city or countrymen since.

Aeneas nods. "The Dardanians are always willing to send gifts to their brothers in Troy."

"Yes, well, I'm afraid the supplies we require will be harder to transport than weapons. That is why you will have to go to Dardania yourself."

Curiosity and a dash of homesickness soften Aeneas's face, but I also glimpse something else. Concern? We have all endured enough of this war to know that any expedition could take longer than we anticipate, especially with masked Sea Peoples lying in wait along the coasts.

Only we do not have any time to waste.

"What do you need?" Aeneas asks.

"Spices!" Bodecca bursts into the kitchen with the ferocity of Hera herself. "If you're wanting me to prepare a dozen different dishes for this festival banquet, I shall require a great deal more than cloves of garlic as old and shriveled as—"

"Thank you, Bodecca," I interject. "That's precisely why I've asked for Harsar Aeneas." I turn to Hector's cousin, who backs away slowly toward the exit. "The arid lands to the east have been struck by famine, so we must look north. During the Festival of the Divine Twins, I am to hold a feast in honor of our allies. Not to mention we'll need additional provisions to feed the people of the Lower City."

Aeneas arches an eyebrow. "They are invited?"

"They are. Paris claims all our former trading partners to the west continue to refuse us, but the major trade route is still open in Dardania, so reaching out to your kin is the only way we'll be able to access the supplies we need. To anchor Hector's position in the eyes of the Citadel, this festival must secure the support of both the allies and the people."

"Let me make sure I understand. You are asking me to leave the army"— Aeneas's voice falls flat—"to make a kitchen run?"

"A kitchen run, he says." Bodecca's pale eyes alight. "This will be no slop meal like they serve in the common soldiers' camp. There will be fresh fish from Adresteia, soft cheeses from Larisa, lamb stew from Thrace, and—"

"Speaking of Thrace," I interrupt. "That is actually the more pressing reason for this expedition. And perhaps one more akin to your talents, Aeneas." I lower my voice. "We need more allies. It isn't enough to convince the ones we have to stay and fight. We will require more men if we are to advance to the next phase of this war."

"Next *phase*, Harsa?"

"Yes. Eventually, these rains will end. Just as the plague did." Not that Odysseus has let either stop him from scheming. "When they do, we must be ready." I stand a little taller. "Hector has made me a liaison to the allied captains."

The firm line of Aeneas's mouth parts, then closes again. He is too prudent to say anything against me, for that would be to criticize the judgment of Hector himself. "Why Thrace?" he asks instead.

I nod. "They are the most disciplined foot soldiers between here and the Black Sea. Plus, their leaders are trained horsemen like us. With the exception of a few of their best, the Achaeans can barely drive a chariot. We must use this specialty to our advantage in ways we haven't fully exploited. Imagine if we had an entire cavalry of warriors riding down the Ilium plain." It is why I have also sent a messenger to Queen Penthesilea, requesting that she rouse her Amazons and bring them to Troy's aid. "The sight will be one the Achaeans have never seen, and it will send them running straight into the sea."

My eyes move to the opening door. They're late. It seems the other captains I asked to attend this meeting track time according to their own customs.

Akamas's ginger topknot appears in the kitchen doorway as he ducks down to enter. Sarpedon is right behind him. That the two rival captains arrived at the same time without strangling each other feels like a sign that the gods may have sanctioned my plan. Still, it will take an even greater intervention for them to survive the command I am about to issue.

"You asked for me, Harsa?" Sarpedon casts me a wide, suggestive grin that makes Aeneas bristle. "There is no one at whose beck and call I'd rather be."

I fold my hands in front of me. "You may not think so when you hear my request."

"Name it."

"We need men and supplies. I am sending the three of you on a mission to obtain both. A journey to Dardania and then Thrace will take too long by land. The fastest route is by sea up the Dardanelles. While the Trojans have many strengths, sailing is not one of them. Lycians, on the other hand . . ."

Sarpedon's hazel eyes spark like he can already smell the seawater. "My men and I arrived here by galley. We hid the ship in a small cove to the north of the city. It would serve your purposes well, Harsa. And it would be my honor to man it."

"That is what I hoped you'd say." I smile at the Lycian captain, and it takes no effort to make it genuine. Sarpedon may be a scoundrel, but his magnetism would have made me pine for his attention when I was a virgin who didn't know any better. "The voyage is not without risks, of course. With the Aegean emptied of Achaeans and most of Troy's trade routes abandoned, the Sea Peoples have claimed the Dardanelles as their own."

Sarpedon's face lights up. "I've grown weary of land. If this journey involves paying those barbarians back for the last time they sacked Lycia, all the better." He casts a skeptical glance to his left. "I do have one concern. They say the Thracians mount their horses to make up for what is lacking between their legs."

I speak up before Akamas can retaliate. "My husband mounts his horse. And as of recently, so do I. What exactly are you suggesting, Captain?"

The Lycian grins. "Forgive me, Harsa, but the sea is a far more demanding mistress than the beasts these Thracians like to ride."

The spaces between the many freckles of Akamas's face run together in a solid blush. "Just sail the damn ship and leave the work of fighting to actual men."

"When do we leave?" Aeneas says in a pale effort to trim the flame at the quick.

My eyes pass from the fiery Thracian to the mocking Lycian to the austere Dardanian. "As soon as possible. But there is one more thing I must ask of you."

I take in the three warriors in front of me. Their mutual animosity is thick as smoke and shared by every one of our allies. If I am to unite them and keep them in Troy, I must know them. *See* them. And then I must give them someone to despise even more than they despise each other.

"Which of your men hold the most sway with the allies?"

Sarpedon perks up. "Glaucus is my second-in-command. I'll leave him in charge in my absence. He is a man Hector can trust."

"I am sure he is, but it is not Hector he'll be answering to."

The Lycian grins as he gathers my meaning. "Then you'll want to enlist Nhorcys the Strong, who leads the Phrygians. Also, Pyraechmes, who is captain of the Paeonians. Their bows are second to none, except perhaps Pandarus and his hunters from the foothills of Mount Ida."

"That is not a guess but a fact," clips Aeneas.

Sarpedon crosses his arms over his chest and leans against the wall. "Then there is Hippothous, who leads the Pelasgian tribes of spearmen. They are deadly but undisciplined. And Hippothous himself is an insufferable ass."

"On that we can agree." Akamas leans back, mirroring Sarpedon's stance. "The list is a fair one, though I have my own recommendations. Peirous is my choice. He is old as the hills but equally wise. Though why do you ask?"

"My husband has asked me to oversee his allied captains."

Akamas frowns. "Peirous will answer any question you have, but I warn you, Harsa. This endeavor is doomed to fail."

The look Sarpedon flashes him is full of derision. He returns his attention to me. "If you focus on courting Glaucus, Nhorcys, and Pyraechmes, you stand the best chance of keeping the allies in one place long enough to win them over before they start to kill one another."

"Are things really so dire?" I ask.

Akamas rubs the back of his neck. "Maybe I should stay behind and help facilitate."

I appreciate his willingness, but our brief acquaintance has left me with the impression that Akamas has all the ambassadorial finesse of a well-used club. "Leave it to me. Your armies will survive your absence."

"And how will we pay the Dardanians for the supplies?" Aeneas knows as well as I do that Priam's once-great wealth has been spread thin.

I remove the string of lapis lazuli hanging around my neck. "This should cover a great deal of the cost."

Aeneas's flint eyes widen as he accepts the cobalt-blue necklace. "But it was a wedding gift from Hector."

And I can still remember how patiently he and Creusa stood beside us during that endless ceremony, back when we were all so young.

"Like you, Aeneas, I understand that it is the gods' way to demand much of us." My chest tightens. "In truth, I fear even greater sacrifices than this will be required if we hope to defend those we love."

28

RHEA

MY FOOTSTEPS ECHO on the walkway. The temple of the Mother goddess takes shape out of the two joining walls in front of me.

It's a few minutes shy of the second watch. Andromache and the girls will be here soon. I made an excuse to come early to offer a prayer to the Mother, but when I enter the temple, there is already someone in it.

Cyrrian turns from the wall of offerings. His face is proof that the gods are not overly concerned with fairness when they hand out their gifts. If they were, Achilles of Phthia would have been born small and weak as any man, and Cyrrian of the Two Shadows would've come into the world with a face as plain as mine.

"It's impolite to stare."

A flush creeps up my neck. "It's impolite to lurk in dark corners and scare young women half to death."

"It's hardly lurking when you're expected."

I place my bundle on the ground beside a cloak of dark brown that should help me better blend in on the plateau.

Cyrrian's frown suggests my efforts leave something to be desired.

"You said you'd tell me the best way to the Achaean camps," I say before he can vocalize whatever thoughts are in his pretty head.

"I decided showing you will be more effective." Cyrrian's tone is entirely too ironic.

I don't trust it.

"We've established that the passage is too narrow for a man, and Achaean scouts are watching all the gates. You'll never make it onto the plain without drawing attention."

"That's not what I meant," Cyrrian says flatly. Stone walls glowing from the fire behind him, Cyrrian crouches next to what looks like a pile of ashes on the floor. I kneel down beside him and realize that it *is* a pile of ashes. One that's been smoothed out evenly and etched with a series of markings drawn with a sharp stick.

I follow the lines. "This is a rendering of Troy and the plain." My eyes fly to Cyrrian where he squats across from me.

"What do you see?"

I tear my gaze from his and focus back on the floor. "The Citadel is here." My mind analyzes every bend and curve. "Here are the Scaean and Dardanian gates. And the Lower City. To the southwest is the Scamander plain and Cape Sigeum." I chew my lip and follow the crude line of the bay. "Which means that the Achaean camp would be here on Sigeum Ridge. Right above the cut."

I look up. The hostility in Cyrrian's expression has given way to something entirely new. "It seems your tongue isn't your sharpest weapon after all."

His words fill me with pleasure, followed by a quick burst of annoyance at myself, because *why*? Why should I care what he thinks?

I study the ash pile to hide my flush. "Nobody has ever accused me of being sharp-tongued."

"Then they must not know you well."

"Or perhaps it's you who brings out that side of me?"

A spark lights his eyes for a moment before his face sobers. "This secret passage of yours. Where does it lead?"

I point to a spot on the plateau face that lies between the northeast bastion and the Citadel tower.

"The plateau there is almost sheer, which is why we do not bother to guard it."

"Mostly," I agree, and then I tell him about the hidden grotto.

Cyrrian follows the movements of my finger. "The flood channels and the levee have run over, drenching most of the plain."

"So which route does that leave?" I ask.

"Hypothetically speaking?" Cyrrian studies his drawing with an intensity he normally never shows outwardly. "The Achaean camp is built onto the ridge to the west of the Lisgar Swamp. It's miserable territory, utterly impossible to attack with an army. But if you are merely trying to observe . . ." His finger takes a curved path. "By cutting north across the plain to the bay, and then following the coast west to where the Scamander meets the sea, you should be safe from the Achaean lookouts on Cape Sigeum and the ones looking south over the Trojan plain. They'll be blind there."

Yes, but there is a reason for that. And as I watch him scratch another line into the ash, I realize that is entirely the point.

Cyrrian isn't trying to help me. He is showing me all the reasons this plan is doomed to fail.

"The Scamander." I grit my teeth and play dumb. If he is willing to share information, far be it from me to stop him. "How do we cross it without a ford?"

"Where the river opens up into the bay, there are two small clumps of land like islands. They are a bridge. There's a small dock in the marshy grasses with the fishing boats Hector and I used before the war. The grasses are high. The currents, unpleasant. It's unlikely any of the Achaeans would've come across them."

Marshes? Boats?

"And from there?" I ask weakly.

"From there you would have to move past the marshes, up the swell that sits before the swamp."

My stomach twists. This is no simple walk across the plains. The smug expression on Cyrrian's face confirms it.

"Do you see now?" he asks. "This is a truly terrible idea."

"Do you happen to have a better one?"

"If they catch you, the kindest fate you could hope for is a quick death. The Achaeans aren't known for their honor toward our women."

His words are meant kindly, but I can't help the spark they kindle inside me. "Achaeans aren't the only men capable of cruelty. You don't have to explain the risks to me." I stand. "We know what is at stake."

His brows draw together. "We?"

Voices echo behind us. Three figures enter by way of the narrow archway.

The first must bend to get into the small stone room. Behind Andromache, Isola and Salama look like children trailing after their mother's skirts.

"Cyrrian." Andromache smiles as he stands. "Rhea told me you'd agreed to join us. Allow me to introduce Troy's newest scouts. What we lack in size and numbers, we make up for with wit and good looks."

"I reserve judgment on the intelligence of anyone who's agreed to participate in this folly."

"I didn't expect to see you here, Cyrrian of the Two Shadows," Salama says with a wry smile.

"Salama." His grin matches hers, and I briefly wonder what it would be like to have him smile at me like that. "Has Madam Morgestia finally found a way to be rid of you?"

Salama shrugs. "Let's just say I've taken my talents somewhere they'll be better appreciated."

"It appears introductions won't be necessary," Andromache says dryly. "Your taste for the Lower City and its wares is clearly not exaggerated, Cyrrian."

A hint of color rises in his cheeks. "The upper rings are too cramped for my liking."

"Since this war began, this city is too cramped for everyone's liking." Andromache comes to stand beside him.

Cyrrian studies what is quite possibly the least threatening force ever conscripted.

"I came here tonight because I value your friendship, Andromache. And because I know if Hector learns what you'd attempt, it will hurt you both. So please." The word trips awkwardly from his tongue. "Leave this alone."

"I'm afraid that's not possible," she says.

"Then you will force my hand."

Andromache takes a step forward, undeterred. "You will keep my secret, Cyrrian." A gust of air moves through the temple, making the oil lamps flicker. "As I have always kept yours."

Cyrrian's normally bronze skin goes ashen.

"Andromache." Her name is a plea. The desperate way he utters it makes me want to comfort him. Instead, I fist my hands in my robes.

"We have both told our share of half-truths to protect Hector. All these years, I've granted you yours. Now you will grant me mine."

The apple bobs at the base of his throat. For a moment, he looks achingly young.

Whatever secret Andromache would use against him, it is one that she does not betray now. Instead, she places her hand on his cheek. "You are one of the few who I trust to defend Hector. You know this is worth the risk. You would not have come here tonight if you weren't already prepared to help us."

He jerks his face away from her hand. But he does not deny it.

I rush to fill the gaping silence. "Cyrrian has shown me the way to the Achaean camps."

Andromache nods. "Let us move quickly, then. The journey there and back will take several hours. That doesn't leave much time before sunrise to see if it can be done. Cyrrian, you will guard the temple while the girls are out."

His jaw clenches. "It seems you've left me little choice in the matter."

Andromache's smile is sad. "Some of our choices were made long ago, my friend."

She turns her back on us and crosses the room to the Mother's pass. It is only when she kneels before it that I finally realize.

This is really happening. We have a path forward, a grudging guard at our backs, and the dark on our side.

With trembling hands, I give each of the girls a cloak.

Her face solemn, Andromache presses her palm flat to the face of the Mother goddess carved into the wall. "Protect your children." She places the same hand on Salama's forehead. Then Isola's. She moves to stand in front of me, her height as towering as it has ever been. "Protect Troy." One of her palms presses to my forehead, but the other rests on her softening middle where only I can see it. "And come back home to her quickly," she whispers for my ears alone.

I let her touch and her words warm me, and then I do the thing I've been dreading. I move toward the hidden entrance carved into the offering shelf.

Crushing darkness comes at once.

So thick I can't breathe.

So heavy I can't . . .

Move.

I force myself into a crawl. Stone grinds against my hands and knees. The cloak offers some protection, but it still feels like washing my body with a handful of rocks.

Down, down, down the passage goes to a narrow bend. My shoulders catch on the edges, and for a moment, I'm overwhelmed by the cold, the dark. But then I hear them.

The low whisper of someone praying. A sharp swear in a foreign tongue. The sounds steady me until I'm calm enough to wrench my shoulder free. Up ahead, a break in the darkness.

The end of the tunnel comes unexpectedly, spilling out into the grotto and the hidden ridge of the plateau. Isola and Salama emerge one after the other. I motion for silence. Quietly, I lead the way across the narrow ledge beneath the towering Citadel walls until we hit the flat, soggy earth of the plain.

Collapsing against the sheer face of the plateau, I stop to gather my breath. Both my companions look a little worse for wear. Isola is winded and scratched but not visibly shaken. Salama, on the other hand, is trembling in a way that makes me wonder if she wasn't entirely honest about her easy friendship with the dark.

"Which way from here?" Isola's words are nearly whipped away by the wind. It drives rain into our faces and has us cowering against the plateau for what little shelter it provides.

"And the boats? What if we can't find the dock?" Salama asks, some of the color returning to her cheeks.

I huddle in my cloak. "Then turn around and come back. Take no unnecessary risks."

Salama looks up at the sky, where rain is pelting us sideways. "Tell me about the marsh again. How exactly do we get there?"

I search her face and then Isola's, stark white. My eyes move over the grass and mud of the plain, back to the safety of the Citadel walls, where Cyrrian waits.

I remember the route just as Cyrrian drew it. Only, it didn't occur to me until now that remembering it means nothing. Not unless I can somehow show them. And there's only one way to do that.

I pull my cloak tighter around myself, and I step onto the plain.

"Come," I say. "I'll walk with you a little farther."

"THERE ARE SO many." Salama's whisper echoes in my ear. Her body is a blaze of heat on my right side while Isola's is a shivering presence to my left.

We are pressed flat to the ground on a small hill that gazes westward over the Kesik Cut, overlooking the Lisgar Swamp, and beyond its tall grasses, the Achaean camps.

The wind whips over the bay, driving sea air into our faces. Sharp gusts set the smoke from the fires across the swamp billowing over us. In between the clouds, death peeks at us wearing a thousand barbaric faces that glow orange and yellow in the light of a hundred fires.

The Achaeans are close. Much closer than I imagined when I studied Cyrrian's crude drawing. The drawing didn't capture the brutal line of spears thrust into the ground. The sharp beaks of the great, black-hulled ships lunging out of the sea and up onto the beaches. It didn't sound like drunken singing and wet stones grinding and the roar of the sea, whose clean scent can't mask the sharp tang of burning flesh from pyres and human excrement.

It's been an hour since we crept up the shoreline. The boats were waiting right where Cyrrian told us they would be. One of them had a hole in it, but we were able to navigate the second across the tiny islands of marsh toward the opposite bank of the Scamander at the mouth of the bay. From there, we climbed up the hill Cyrrian described to a flat spot with a perfect view of the cut. A victory that fell flat the moment we glimpsed the stark reality staring at us from across a narrow field of stinking swampland.

Though it's late, warriors are awake. Thousands of them. They swarm the camps, and yet it isn't the men that concern me so much as their ships. They lie side by side in a row of arrows pointed straight at the heart of Troy. Their organized lines stretch all the way up the side of Sigeum Ridge and toward the Beşik Bay, where I lose sight of them in the darkness.

There are too many to count. Too many for the sons of Troy to fight and win if ever our walls are breached.

The sheer breadth and scale of the camp is startling to behold. The part that is on even footing with our hill is mostly flat and boasts huts built of mud and wood. These are no haphazard shelters. They are large and well-made structures fashioned with an eye for durability, organized in sections around carefully constructed settlements that can only be the camps of the individual Achaean kings, each an independent organism with its own grounds for horses, livestock, and housing.

It is not a camp made for men who plan on setting sail for home anytime soon.

Despite the hour, large fires blaze, around which warriors sing and laugh under the drizzle that hasn't let up in weeks. They wear their wet hair loose around their shoulders, their faces hidden by beards in many colors. In their hordes, they seem more like beasts than men. And yet men they are. Drinking. Laughing. Sleeping. Maybe even dreaming of the distant lands they left behind.

A storm of Greek words drifts toward us on the wind.

"Look at them. Feasting on our cattle. Drinking our wine. Sticking their sorry excuses for pricks into our women," Salama spits into the sand. "I'd set their tents on fire if I didn't think the rain would put them out."

"Your job is to watch the cut. Just watch." I gnaw my lip. "But if we can get some sense of their true numbers and the layout of their encampments, it might be of use."

The only other way to reach the camps besides the heavily guarded Kesik Cut is the marsh and the swamp where we are currently hidden. Any army attempting to attack from this angle wouldn't get very far.

"We've been here since the end of the second watch, and we haven't seen anyone cross the cut yet," Salama says. "How long do we have to wait here?" It's becoming quite clear that patience isn't one of Salama's strengths. Neither is silence. Unfortunately for us, both are fairly integral to the work of a spy.

"As long as it takes." My mind flies over the scene in front of me, making rapid recalculations, adjusting our plans. "It makes no sense to take this risk unless we can watch all the movements in and out of the camps. One of you will stay for a full day, then the other will come to relieve her. We'll keep a supply of food and water hidden with the boats. Whoever is watching can sleep for a few hours during the day. Just so long as you are awake during the three night watches when Odysseus and his men are most likely to move. When they do, we need to know exactly which direction they are headed."

"That is not what we agreed to," Salama says.

I stare right back at her. "It's what is required."

She raises a dark brow. "If this is so important to you, why don't you do it?"

I bite my lip and look away, because I have no answer. Andromache wishes to protect me, and I'm grateful for that. But part of me can't help feeling that I am hiding behind her. Just like I always do.

The thing that holds me back now is the same thing that always has.

Endless screams. The scent of burning hay.

A sound reaches us on the wind.

Isola stiffens. The voices are too loud to be coming from the fires across the swamp. No, these voices are coming from somewhere much closer.

Salama lets out a sharp breath as two men take shape out of the darkness in front of us. They work their way across the swamp, shadows that seem to be walking on the water. It isn't until they get closer that I see the wooden lattice that has been built over a small section of the swamp. It's anchored by poles set deep into the earth and hidden among the grasses. One of the men kneels down and lifts something out of the water by one of these poles. A net gleaming with silver fish.

More poles jump out at me in the shadows of the swamp now that I know what to look for. They are spaced out every ten paces in a line that leads right toward our small hill.

Salama looks at me. I shake my head.

The men work their way toward us. The shorter of the two bends down to retrieve the last net as Salama shifts slightly in the grass beside me.

A squawk cuts through the air as a flock of birds erupt from the marsh-land to our left. They take to the air in a storm of feathers, drawing a sharp squeak from Salama.

Both men drop their nets and pull short swords from the war belts around their waists. My heart thunders in my ears as I watch them come. Close enough to see the glow of distant firelight reflected in their eyes. Sal-ama reaches for the dagger in her tunic, but I place my hand over hers.

Salama jerks her hand free.

I shake my head again, but she is adamant.

"They know someone is here." Her expression is furious. Not at me, I realize. But at *herself.* "Better to let them catch one than all." Salama doesn't wait for me to answer. She merely rolls sideways down the edge of the hill. Once at the bottom she straightens, brushes off her robes, and walks toward the Achaean soldiers with a shamelessness to match that of their golden goddess Aphrodite.

"Countless greetings to you," she calls out in truly atrocious Greek.

The men pause when they see Salama emerging from the tall grasses, but they don't drop their weapons. Salama walks toward them across the narrow lattice without hesitation. It is, perhaps, this confidence that saves her.

"What're you doing out here, girl?" The soldier is a small man with a strange bend in one arm that speaks of a poorly set break.

"Combing the swamp for herbs," Salama replies easily. "For the bathhouse. So that the Trojans can't smell your armies on the wind miles before you arrive to attack."

The taller man jerks her chin toward him. "There's nothin' wrong with the way we smell."

"Perhaps the problem is my nose. It's large, you see, and therefore, sensitive."

The man lets her go. "It's unwise to speak that way to a warrior."

Salama smiles, and I can't help but wonder if she is actually mad. It isn't until she reaches down to pick up one of the nets of fish and steps toward the camps that I realize she is drawing them away from us.

"I am not your property. Lay a hand on me, and you'll answer for it."

"Then who owns you?" the shorter man challenges.

Salama's face shines in the dim light of the moon as it makes a rare break from behind the clouds. "I work in the bathhouse. I'm here to gather flowers for the scrubs the Ithacans favor." She cocks her hip. "The men of Ithaca have refined grooming habits. For Achaeans."

The shorter man steps toward her, his shoulders taut as a bow. "They sent you out here alone?"

Salama glares at them, but it's clear that this is one question for which she has no answer. The following silence feels like judgment. One that is not in our favor. Salama's hand moves to the hidden dagger under her robes. It's almost there when a soft, smooth voice drifts from the marshland to my right.

"She isn't alone." Isola steps out from behind the tall grass under our hill. She walks forward, her shoulders bent over the load in her arms. "We came here looking for feverfew," Isola says in Greek that is more refined than Salama's. "For the bathhouses and the healing tents."

"Feverfew?" the shorter soldier asks.

"It blooms here in damp soil." Isola holds up the armful of white flowers. "The petals are easily spotted at night." They are the most words I have heard the girl speak, and she delivers them now without hesitation.

"Come, then." The taller soldier jerks his chin back toward the camp. "They'll be expecting you back for the morning washes."

Salama scowls at him as she walks across the lattice and up the swell of earth toward the roaring fires of the Achaean camps. The men trail after her, disappearing into the high grasses that lead up to the flat land above. Isola glances over her shoulder only once. Terror is painted stark white across her face but her eyes are steady as they find mine across the distance. A silent scream rides on the wind. It echoes inside me long after Isola ducks into the high grasses that lead into the heart of the Achaean camp.

29

HELEN

TIME.

It isn't what we think.

Time is not one day passing into the next, an apple's skin unfurled by Kronos's cruel scythe before the old man eats your core.

No, Time is spun. Expanding in its significance. Always reaching.

It is a cheeky young Kairos with winged feet, sailing on the wind.

The season of perfect ripening. The opportune moment. The space between the breath taken and the breath exhaled.

A fixed threshold where fates are changed.

For the Moirai's thread is given to us, but our choices are what weave it into a fabric.

And my Kairos moment is coming.

Paris strokes my hair again, over and over. Like he is a child with too many emotions, and I am the cat who brings him comfort.

I stare beyond my balcony toward the sea, hands motionless. Eyes unable to blink, alive only inside my head. Trapped, but also not.

Whether Paris has forced more poppy wine on me is anyone's guess, yet I am firmly in Kronos's clutches, and he will not loosen his grip. A day is just a day. An hourglass where the sand never moves. By now, a hundred might have passed and I would not know it.

Or maybe none have passed at all.

A door opens and soft footsteps patter up behind us. Clymene glides in front of me to refill our cups, pausing to run a hand through her lover's curls.

If the girl's expanding middle is any indication, it seems Time has moved on after all.

I keep my blank gaze fixed to the endless horizon. They laugh softly beside me, murmuring sweet nothings, and all the while he keeps stroking my hair.

Clymene cradles her belly proudly. Paris smiles and says something about a festival.

A succession changed.

A chance that he must take.

His hand runs down my head and cheek again, slick fingers caressing my neck, causing my gag reflex to reignite. The taste of bile and smell of myrrh will smother me. Yet a statue I must remain. Only why does he keep me on this altar at all? He has the child he needs to show that his seed is not entirely useless.

Seeds. Scattered by a warm gale. They must move over mountains and valleys in order to take root in fresh soil.

Time. Is it standing still or moving fast?

Either way, I must move too. If I am to live, I must take a chance of my own.

The opportune moment is coming, and when it does, I must grab it by the forelocks.

My friend Kairos is flying toward me on the wind.

30

RHEA

TIME CEASES TO have meaning as I watch the Achaean soldiers escort Salama and Isola to a large structure in the middle of the four separate settlements on this side of the camp. Judging by the wafts of steam escaping through the open archways, it's some sort of bathhouse. My hands strangle the marsh grass as I wait for soldiers to come pouring out of huts to deal with the spies in their midst. Instead, the only movement comes from the steady stream of men passing through and a handful of women carrying large jugs of dirty water, which they pitch into a narrow ditch.

The sky lightens, hammering the island of Tenedos in gold. I have to move. Make my way back to the wall, or I'll lose what little chance I have left. If Salama's and Isola's true identities are discovered, they'll be questioned. The Achaeans will rip our secrets from their throats, and when they do, those secrets will lead them right here to this hill. I know it, and still, I lie in the grass as the sun rises behind the clouds over the Achaean camp, the harsh light of day revealing to me what the dark had hidden.

Puddles of mud and horse pellets crawling with flies despite the steady rain.

The low buzzing of thousands of men, swarming the ridge like bees do a hive.

They spill out of the huts and tents. Many enter the bathhouse. Others cut across the ridge, down to the beaches and the sea, where they bathe and fish and sharpen their blades with whetstones. There are fields for training, from which rise the clang of weapons. A stable of horses and two chariot yards. In every direction, men and a handful of women are working, building, farming, fishing. Going about the business of living as if their purpose here is nothing out of the ordinary. As if they are just like any other men.

Moments bleed into one another. One hour becomes two. Then ten. I don't know if I sleep. I only know that one hundred sixty-seven warriors have come and gone through the bathhouse since dawn.

Two hundred fifty-six basins of water have been drained into that ditch.

Another seventy-five have been fetched from a nearby stream and heated over a raging fire built into the pit by the bathhouse doors.

Thirty-two women have emerged from inside the steaming bathhouse to perform various tasks.

None of them have been the ones I am waiting for.

The sun begins to set again behind the endless clouds until the last trace of its light has slipped into the sea. Hundreds of fires light up Sigeum Ridge, casting the camp in a golden glow punctuated by shadows.

I have to go back. Before those men with the nets return. But every time I try, something holds me fast.

If I walk away now, Isola and Salama are lost, and Hector will hold Andromache responsible when he finds out what's become of them. My failure will become a wedge between husband and wife just as Cyrrian warned. Worse, Hector will never fully understand why we were willing to go behind his back. He feels the threat that Odysseus poses, but he wasn't there that night in the shadow of the wall. He wasn't there when Cassandra warned us of the plague, lifesaving truth swirling with madness. *Three times,* she said, and Andromache believed her.

I believe her too.

The rains will stop, and Odysseus will come again. We must be ready to stop him. Or every bow and spear in Troy will not be enough to defend against the vast army squatting on these beaches.

My mind spins in circles. The camp is fortified heavily at the Kesik Cut, but this area is mostly unguarded.

I study the open ground of Sigeum Ridge. There are plenty of women mixed in with the men. If I can get inside the bathhouse, maybe Salama,

Isola, and I could slip out of this camp the same way we slipped in. With nobody the wiser.

Or I could walk in there and draw attention to them, dooming us all.

It's a risk. But maybe it's one whose benefits outweigh the costs.

If I leave right now, I'll never know. And I'll always wonder.

I stare across the swamp toward the camp and count the steps over the latticework, through the grasses, and across the open camp to the bathhouse. As much as the thought of that walk fills me with terror, it's easier to imagine than crawling back under the walls to deliver the news to Andromache that her plan was doomed to fail before it ever really started.

I close my eyes.

A burning barn. Horses running in terror. The fields of our farm watered with blood. Kallira's face, which morphs into Salama's. Then Isola's—the way she looked before she turned her back on me and walked into the Achaean camp. Saving my life. As it was once saved by my sister.

But nobody was there to save Kallira then. And nobody is here to save Isola and Salama now.

Nobody except for me.

And then I'm moving. Down the hill to the wooden walkway across the black swamp. With the first watch of night so recently fallen, I have to concentrate on every step so that I don't end up neck-deep in the brackish water. Pole by pole, I cross the swamp to the tall grasses on the other side.

I crawl up the slope through the grasses. Wetness stains my knees. My mind sharpens its focus on the strange world in front of me. The rest of the ridge is crowded with men and structures, but the land directly ahead is empty but for a half-dozen ramshackle wooden huts.

The wind changes direction, and I am hit by a stench that makes my eyes water.

Those huts are the latrines for the Achaean army.

Gagging, I stumble out from the grasses toward Cape Sigeum. On my way, I pass a group of standing stones surrounded by a crumbling rock wall that must have been built by ancient hands. Papa spoke of other sites like this scattered across Anatolia. Open-air shrines built by people who have long since been forgotten. Their names may have been lost to time, but their ancient monuments still stand, and that thought gives me strange comfort as I creep past the rock formation into shadows behind the crude latrines. I go no farther.

You see all, my little mouse, but nobody sees you unless you want them to.

Hands hanging awkwardly at my sides, I step out onto open ground and start toward the bathhouse.

The walkways between huts are cramped with men, and I'm quickly swallowed up by the crowd. Most pass me without a second glance. All of them carry weapons. Spears. Axes. Swords. Other tools of death and destruction I don't even recognize. They tower over me like an army of giants with strange, bearded faces.

I keep my eyes trained on the ground until I've reached the open doors of the bathhouse. The smell of water and oil hangs thick with steam. With a shuddering breath, I duck inside.

The bathhouse floor has been laid with flat stones that are kept fastidiously clean. Even now, seven women are washing on their hands and knees. My gaze drifts over their bent backs as I make my way to a table stacked with tunics. In the center of the floor lie two giant pools expertly constructed to allow a dozen men to bathe at once. The first of the baths appears to be filled with cold water. The other is the source of the steam. A group of women with clay jugs are busy swapping out the water to keep it fresh.

Both pools are full of naked men.

I tear my eyes away from the bare bodies and stare deeper into the bathhouse. There are a few smaller, individual baths, presumably for more high-ranking soldiers. Between them, a dozen women lay out tunics for washing. Others hover around a circle of pillows where a handful of men are having their beards groomed.

A group of soldiers walk past me. I straighten the tunics on the table to give myself something to do. They exit without a word, and I step out from behind the table and toward the women in the back, the only place Salama and Isola could be hiding.

Nobody speaks to me. Nobody even looks my way. I'm halfway to my destination when there's a loud sloshing sound from my right. A figure lunges out of the hot bathing pool to land directly in front of me.

Beads of water run down well-muscled thighs to puddle on the stone floor. Drawing a sharp breath, I force my gaze up six feet of naked warrior.

His tan body glistens with water and oil. His manhood is proudly displayed above cut hip bones and below a torso covered with more scars than hair. Forcing my chin all the way up, I take in a striking face of sharp angles. Long, dark lashes framing a pair of gray eyes.

The tunics in my hand hit the floor.

The warrior reaches down to gather the textiles. Slowly, methodically, he uses one of them to wipe his face, moving lower over other parts of him.

When he is finished, the warrior places the stack back into my hands. With a slight dip of his head, he steps around me. The men in the pools on either side of us call after him in raucous Greek. At once, I remember how to breathe.

"Lissia," the warrior summons over his shoulder.

"Here, Patroclus." A girl breaks out of the crowd of women. Carrying a fresh robe and tunic, she moves forward gracefully. She draws even with me and her step falters. We regard each other in the steam-laden room.

The girl is beautiful. With long dark hair and eyes like a cat's. The warrior Patroclus calls to her again, and she moves forward with one final glance over her shoulder at me.

This was a mistake. These people have had years to get to know one another. Someone is bound to realize what and *who* doesn't belong.

Too far down this path to take a different route now, I make for the group of women laying out tunics in the back. I've gone three steps when a hand closes around my wrist. I look up into a face I would know anywhere.

After all, it is a face that I made.

"Vengeance." Her name leaves me in a rush of breath.

Shaking her head, she grips my wrist and pulls me through a back door. She doesn't look at me. She doesn't let go. Terrified of making a scene, I let her drag me all the way to the small stream that runs behind the bathhouse. Only then do I jerk free.

Vengeance spins toward me, her face stark white under the jagged red scars across her cheeks. Scars I put there with my own hands what feels like lifetimes ago.

"Vengeance. What are you doing here? How d—"

"It is Ven now. As for how I came to be here, the Achaeans sacked Cyzicus a few weeks after we were brought to that market. The gods have cursed me," she says simply. "The Achaeans haunt my footsteps. I was carted back here in their ships along with the rest of the plunder. It's the story shared by every woman in this camp. Except, I think, for you."

My heart thuds against my ribs. "What makes you say that?"

"The men built this camp, but the women make it run. I help assign jobs to the new girls when they arrive. With the exception of the most beautiful captives the Achaean kings bestow on one another as individual prizes. Are you such a prize, Rhea?"

We both know I'm not.

My mind flies over my options. I could lie, but instinct tells me Ven would never believe it. Those same instincts are screaming that in order to survive here, I'll need help, and Ven is as close to an ally as I'm likely to find. Her hatred for the Achaeans is as obvious as the scars on her face.

"I've come here from Troy," I tell her. "On an errand for her future queen, but I didn't come alone. I need your help. I'm looking for . . ."

"Two girls. Neither bigger than a child. One who can barely stand to face her own shadow and another with more mettle than common sense?"

My knees go weak. "Where are they?"

Ven motions for me to follow. With no choice, I trace her steps through a maze of huts until finally we reach a wooden structure that sits near the beach. The inside is crammed with rows of pallets set around looms where women are hard at work.

An older woman moves forward to greet us. She is wearing colorful robes and a cloak of authority. The sharp pinch Ven delivers to my arm warns me she is not someone we wish to cross.

The woman looks me over. "Who's this?" she asks sharply.

"This is Rhea," Ven says. "Another new arrival brought in from Thebe under Mount Placos. Machaon has placed her under my care."

The woman's nostrils flare. "I was promised the next group of girls."

"And you'll get them, Calis. Just not this one."

The woman, Calis, bares a line of small, widely spaced teeth. "I could complain."

"You could make a nuisance of yourself," Ven agrees. "It's what my predecessor did. Though I'd point out this is how I came to command the bathhouse in her place."

Calis's mouth goes flat. "Fine. So long as I take the next batch whenever they come in. The looms won't work themselves."

And then we are pushing our way past the unpleasant woman and into a narrow hallway that ends in a single door.

"This is where we stay," Ven says. "Those of us not chosen to warm the soldiers' beds. Though even the plainest of us can't avoid that fate forever."

I have no time to process her warning before we enter the room, occupied by two familiar figures.

Isola jumps up at the sight of us, but Salama hangs back, staring at me sullenly from her pallet. "Please tell me you didn't do anything stupid."

I should've known better than to expect thanks.

"Rhea!" Isola wraps her arms around me so gently I barely feel them. "They found you too?"

I return the girl's embrace. "No. I came back for you. I . . . I thought to help you find a way out."

"That is no longer possible," Ven says behind me. "These two have already been seen laboring in the bathhouse. I've covered for their sudden appearance, but if they disappear now there'll be trouble. Specifically, for me."

"Why would you do that?" I don't know if this is bravery or some hidden form of self-interest, and I need to understand Ven's motivations if only so that I can use them.

"I wasn't sure yet who they belonged to," Ven says. "The Achaean kings spend more time posturing against each other than they do plotting against the walls of Troy. It's unwise to be caught in their personal vendettas."

Her statement sits like a boulder in the pit of my stomach. I've risked so much for nothing. Salama and Isola are stuck here, and all I've managed to do is trap myself with them.

I look at Isola, expecting to see regret. Or fear. Instead, I'm met with determination.

She clasps my hand. "The men. The ones in the bathhouse. They *talk*, Rhea."

"What do you mean?" I've never seen the girl so animated.

"She means they're too busy comparing the size of their cocks to care much who's listening." Salama stands. "The things we learned today would set King Priam's head spinning. The Achaeans' food stores are dwindling. Their spirits are flagging after the plague and so much rain. The wind has been too strong for raiding, but that's changed this week. They're planning raids along the coast."

My breath comes fast as I realize what this means. "If Andromache knew where and when they're planning to raid, she could send warnings to the cities being targeted. Maybe even bolster their defenses." She could spare other cities the fate of her own. Just as she's always hoped.

Isola's wan face shines. "We could save them, Rhea."

Salama's mouth curls up at one side. "More importantly, we could hurt the Achaeans."

"You want to stay here," I realize. "You want to work in the bathhouse and watch."

"It's why we are here, isn't it?" Salama asks. "Only now, we can do more than just observe their comings and goings. Now we can actively gather the information needed to send these monsters sailing back home to their hovels across the sea."

"But we can't do it alone," Isola says quietly.

Me. They need me.

To come and go between Troy and the Achaean camps.

To hold what they gather in my head and deliver it to the people who might be able to use it.

It's exactly what Andromache was hoping for, but on a level that none of us dared to imagine. And all that's required of me are the two things that have always come as naturally as breathing.

Remembering what I see and hear, while at the same time remaining completely forgettable.

"Where did you enter the camp?" Ven asks, breaking into my spinning thoughts.

"By the latrines."

She considers. "There is an ancient shrine there. Did you see it?"

I nod.

"It's said that a healing plant grows inside. If you're caught, tell them that I sent you there to collect it."

"If the plant is so sought after, why hasn't it been gathered already?" Salama asks.

"Nobody goes near those stones. It's said they are cursed by the forgotten gods they were meant to honor." Ven's smile stretches the scars on her face in all the wrong ways. "They won't check to see if you speak the truth. And if they drag you back here, I'll confirm your story. But keep to yourself and nobody should question you."

"You'll really help us?" I ask. Though the girls and I are risking much, we're doing it out of necessity. The same isn't true of Ven. She's found a place here. Perhaps it's one she hates, but it also comes with a certain degree of security and power from what I've seen.

Ven runs a calloused finger over her cheek. "The information you give the Trojans will help them win this war?"

"Yes," I say.

So long as I'm not caught.

So long as Isola and Salama aren't discovered.

So long as a million other things don't go wrong.

"Then I'll help you," Ven says. "I'll see every Achaean on this beach hung over a fire like a goat."

"If the gods are just, they will be." Salama joins us, her lips peeled back over her teeth. "But not before we scour their skin with our nails and fill the bathing tubs with their blood."

31

ANDROMACHE

THE NOONDAY SUN infiltrates the darkness of my chamber, but I am still sitting on my undisturbed bed, dressed in yesterday's gown.

Hector left hours ago to make his run around the walls. I spent the first and second watches of the night lying beside him, trapped in my own agony. Wanting to tell him the truth but also wanting to hold on to hope.

So with heavy feet, I made my way to the temple of the Mother goddess by the fading light of the moon. Cyrrian was sitting by the secret pass exactly as I left him. We spent the last moments before dawn huddled in the cold temple, each gagged by our own helplessness.

"*She may be stuck on the plain,*" Cyrrian said as he rose to his feet. "*I'm going to look for her.*"

"*If the girls were forced into hiding, searching now would only draw attention to them.*" I shook my head. "*We must wait. It is all we can do.*"

The accusatory look Cyrrian sent my way burned. But it was surely a mere campfire compared to the pyre Hector's wrath will ignite once he finds out what I have done.

All the planning. All the hope of bolstering the allies and changing the course of this war. Gone like a scattering of leaves across the earth.

And I cannot find the strength to care about any of it.

Is Rhea dead? In pain? Is she calling out for help? The questions peck at me like carrion birds. I cannot outrun them. I cannot fight the rising tide that makes me itch to hold a weapon and paint myself in my enemies' blood.

Rage.

At Paris and the council for their schemes and stubborn ignorance.

At Odysseus and the Achaeans for threatening one more person who is precious to me.

But most of all, at myself. For believing that in order to protect the future, I had no choice but to risk the present.

My throat is parched. My skin burns to *move.* And then I'm slipping downstairs to the silent kitchen for a drink when a sudden voice speaks at my back.

"Rhea didn't come home last night."

Bodecca sits in her chair by the hearth. I know without asking that she has been there for all the long watches of the night.

"No." I release a breath. "She didn't."

"But you know where she is."

Though it's not a question, I can't bring myself to lie. "Please, Bodecca. Some truths are safer left in the dark."

Pale eyes glow in the low light. "Is the child you carry one such truth?"

The air around me grows too thick to breathe.

A snort. "Did you think that because I'm old, I must also be a fool?"

"How long have you known?"

"Long enough. It isn't as if I haven't carried babes of my own." A strange mixture of joy and hurt paints her profile. "Every day I hoped you would tell me, but then it occurred to me I might be waiting until the child was born."

My shoulders slump. "I didn't mean to lie to you."

"And what about Hector?" She leans back in her chair. "No. Of course he doesn't know. He never would've been able to hide it."

"Try to understand," I say, desperate to undo all the damage I've done. Though that may not be possible. Not once Hector learns that Rhea could be lost. "I have good reasons for keeping this from him."

"Everyone has a reason for everything they do." Bodecca sighs, her body going rigid as she lifts herself up from the chair. It hits me suddenly how old she has become. "But I understand, child. Better than you think. You see some people so plainly, and yet others you don't see at all."

"What do you mean?"

"Hector became my son the day Queen Hecuba placed him on my breast. And the day he brought you home to Troy, you became my daughter. I would hold you just as close. If only you would let me."

She leaves me alone in the kitchen with the heat of the fire and the weight of all my failures.

I'm not able to sit with either for long.

Not when I must still complete the task Hector gave me. The one he actually sanctioned.

My cloak settles across my shoulders as I cinch the material around my thickening waist and step outside. A light drizzle is falling. The shouts of a bored army drift toward me from the training grounds. I scan the area between the stables and find that the chariot yard has been cleared as Hector promised. At least one thing has gone according to plan.

For the second time in as many days, I make the long march down to the Lower City. Only now, I pass the brothels and wine halls without a second glance, my focus ahead until I have descended deeper into Troy's rings than I have ever gone before. To the very shadow of the south wall. A place from which even the lowliest of the city's inhabitants steer clear. For reasons that become self-evident at once.

The odor of five hundred unwashed soldiers stabs my nostrils.

Crudely constructed huts stretch out along the wall. A chaotic heap of molding wood, weaponry, and half-naked men, all in desperate need of a good scrubbing.

Lifting my skirts, I step over a brown puddle and in between two rows of ramshackle huts. Men struggle to rise as I pass. Many are still asleep despite the hour. The rest are unsteady on their feet, no doubt courtesy of the empty wine jugs that litter the ground.

At a second glance, I see that the huts are clearly partitioned. To my left, the Thracians are camped around their mounts, horses from the Balkans that, like their riders, are both taller and leaner than any found in our stables. Across a muddy walkway, the Lycians have strung their huts with flags from their ships, the once-bright colors now as dull as everything else in this wretched place.

I turn on my heels and recognize Pandarus's men, hunters from the foothills of Mount Ida. Then there are the Phrygians with their pointed hats, the Pelasgian tribes with their lengthy spears, the Paeonians of the longbow, even the burly men of Apaesus, Adresteia, and Mount Tereia with the large bronze gong they carry with them into battle. The differences between them are as impossible to ignore as the rain. In fact, from the muddy stretch of earth where I stand, the stench may be the only thing binding Troy's allies together.

It is the most pitiful excuse for an army that I have ever seen. But it is my problem now, and I am here to claim it.

Once Aeneas and his crew left to request more men from the Thracians in the north, I dispatched messengers bearing clay tablets with my seal to Queen Penthesilea in the east and King Memnon of Aethiopia in the south. It is in all our interests to maintain independence from both the Achaean invaders and the encroaching empire of the Hittites, but that does not mean these allies will answer my call with reinforcements. When Rhea and the girls vanished, so did our chance of uncovering Odysseus's path to our walls. The king of Ithaca will make his move, and when he does, this miserable lot before me now may be our only chance of stopping him. At least, until more help comes.

I survey the line of spears that divide the Pelasgians' territory from that of the others and tear one of those spears free. It sails from my hand like a hawk diving for prey. The bronze tip hits the Adresteians' gong with a clatter that has every conscious man in the vicinity scrambling for his shield.

"I have come for Captains Peirous, Pandarus, Hippothous, Glaucus, Pyraechmes, and Nhorcys the Strong." My voice echoes back to me from the wall. "Do any among you know where I might find them?"

For a moment, there is nothing but the sound of the steadily falling rain.

"I am Hippothous." A man steps forward from the Pelasgians' huts. He is muscular and uncommonly handsome—something the slow smile that stretches his face suggests he knows full well. "And I appreciate a woman who can handle a spear. Though I prefer she keep it in her hands."

The men behind him laugh.

"Are you lost, Harsa?" asks another warrior whose arms and legs resemble tree trunks. Under his pointed hat, the man's hair is braided in the Phrygian style.

The same way Rhea . . .

I force away her face. So young, so trusting.

"Not lost, Nhorcys the Strong. I am exactly where I mean to be." My guess is rewarded by a nod from the barrel-chested warrior.

"Then you've finally tired of pompous Old Bloods and Trojan boys."

Hippothous takes a basket of water and empties it over his head. His hands move languorously down his glistening torso.

This is the man Watti claimed fixed her roof? The likely father of Lannaka's child? That he cared enough for a babe he fathered on a poor Trojan girl to look after them both led me to hope he might be a reliable accomplice despite his reputation. But there is no promise of peace in his glare. No, his eyes do not leave my face as he stumbles sideways and sets his bare legs wide across a stinking trench.

He relieves himself into the ditch.

Insufferable. That is one word for him. Sarpedon and Akamas did try to warn me.

"Who the real men among you are is yet to be determined." I call out my list of names again. This time, more warriors come forward. I recognize Pandarus, Aeneas's cousin. Also Glaucus, Sarpedon's second-in-command from the brawl in the winehouse. The captains and their men look on with naked suspicion. My gaze travels over the filthy barracks, and I decide they have good reason.

"I am Peirous," says the wizened warrior Akamas left in charge of his Thracians. The snow white of his thick hair stands in stark contrast to his rich black skin. His rounded accent also suggests an origin closer to our allies in Aethiopia than those in Thrace. There will be a story there, though now is not the time to ask.

"What can we do for Andromache of Thebe, wife of Prince Hector?" Peirous asks.

My name is a fire catching through the crowd.

"It is what I can do for you that is the better question," I say. "It has come to my attention that you lack adequate space in which to train."

"No need to trouble yourself on our account, Harsa." Hippothous finally locates his elusive tunic and tosses it over his wet head. "The Citadel has made it clear how dearly she values her loyal allies." He throws his arms out wide to encompass the squalid camp. "What more could we ask for from the Old Bloods who like to claim that men of all lands are welcome in Troy?"

"Some ideals require several generations to take root," I reply evenly. "But who among you doubts that Prince Hector is good soil?"

Not a man speaks.

I spare the filthy huts a parting glance. "I will see what can be done about your accommodations." Then I turn on my heels and call over my shoulder. "Anyone who desires to take his destiny into his own hands, feel free to follow."

Without looking back, I retrace my path through the winding streets. More than any excuses about principles Troy has failed to live up to, I am counting on their curiosity to do the convincing for me.

Footsteps echo in my wake. I risk a glance over my shoulder. Roughly a hundred men have taken me up on my offer. They form a ragged line as we pass through Troy's Lower City to the gates that lead to the Artisan Quarter.

"Harsa, what game is this? Troy's blacksmiths have no more weapons to give us," Peirous says when we stop before the gates. The Thracian company forms a wall of freckled muscle at their commander's back. Interest glistens on their sunburned faces, but also distrust.

"No game. I promised you an adequate space to train, and this is where we must go to find it."

"Maybe you don't realize . . ." Nhorcys the Strong shifts uncomfortably. "But we are not permitted—"

"Oh, she knows," Hippothous snaps. "Tell me, is this how a bored Harsa of Troy would entertain herself during the rains? By seeing us shamed?"

I meet the Pelasgian's furious gaze. "The only shame here belongs to Troy." His anger bolsters mine as I greet the guard who walks forward to meet us. "Open these gates."

The guard's brow furrows as he takes in the long line of men behind me. "Our orders—"

"Come from the prince of Troy. And I am his better half. Your future queen. Now kindly do as I command and step aside."

The gates part. The men behind me go strangely silent as, one by one, they pass through them.

The walk to the stables is long and steep. On our way, we pass through one more gate, this one leading to the Merchant Quarter, where the welcome we receive is much the same. I lean into the grade. A few of the younger warriors draw even with me. Awe fills their faces as they stare at the fine homes. Well-dressed Trojans line the streets at the sight of our ragged procession. The wealthy traders wrinkle their noses. Women pull their children close and take discreet steps backward. My face burns. People looked at me much the same when Hector first brought me here from Thebe.

Like I was wild in spite of my fineries. Dangerous.

The men following me have been here for years without ever entering this part of the city. Instead, they have been left to rot in huts that aren't fit for dogs.

If nothing else, that is about to change. In this, I will not fail Hector.

At last, we pass through the alley and into the courtyard behind our home. Bodecca is waiting for me beside the lemon trees. Every trace of hurt is gone from her face, which sets with determination as she surveys the long line of unkempt men at my back.

"I can't do this without you, Bodecca."

It is less an apology than it is an appeal. Barely a breath passes before Bodecca accepts with a nod. I whisper a few words into her ear. She raises an eyebrow before rolling up her sleeves and bustling back into the kitchen to prepare. Deep affection spreads through me as I watch her go.

"This way, men." I cut a brisk path to the training grounds, now full of Trojan soldiers with nothing to do but wait for the rain to end. They lower their weapons, surprise painting their bronzed, beardless faces. Next to Troy's sons, my allies look like they have spent the past several weeks rolling in mud. Which, of course, they have. It fills me with outrage all over again, because this never should have been allowed to happen.

I turn to face the ring of men who have entered the smallest of the training grounds. There is a pile of equipment and practice weapons laid in a heap. Hector or Cyrrian must have left them for us. It is second-rate, but it is better than nothing—which is exactly what these men are used to.

"I am Andromache, daughter of an Anatolian king and disciple of the Amazons. I have been named royal liaison between Troy's allies and the Citadel."

The men murmur. Some of them laugh outright. They think it is a jest, but they will soon realize how deathly serious I am.

"As if that bird-fondling prince wasn't bad enough." Hippothous steps forward. "You are wasting your breath, Harsa. Most of these men are only waiting for this rain to stop so they can return to homes they never should have left behind."

His self-exclusion does not escape me. There are several among our allies who have already seen their homes fall to the Achaean raids. The Pelasgians relocated their people to the nearby Hellespont after being driven from Crete. If their cities have been sacked, Hippothous may have seen his world burn twice already. Anguish peeks at me through the visible cracks of his anger. It tells me that everyone he loved was taken from him while he languished here behind our walls.

Because he was not there to defend them when it mattered.

Because we asked him for help, and he answered.

The depth of his fury sends another stab of fear through me. Of all my plans, this one cannot falter. Troy will not stand without her allies any more than she'd endure without her walls.

"You would leave now? Just when things are about to get interesting?"

"I would leave before fat old men who want for nothing make a further mockery of us. That is why they sent *you*, no?" Hippothous's knuckles glow white around his spear.

"I wonder, Hippothous, if you've ever met an Amazon." That earns a few chastened glances. But not nearly enough.

Glaucus steps forward. "Forgive us, Harsa. It isn't your intentions we doubt. It is the Citadel. Placing a woman as our liaison seems yet another way for the Old Bloods to demonstrate how little they respect us."

"That is exactly how it was meant, Glaucus," I say. "Because the Old Bloods do not see what *I* see. Warriors who have left their homes to meet the rising powers of both east and west, powers that threaten to erase a thousand years of history. This history may have placed us on different sides at times, but at least it was *ours*." My gaze lands on Hippothous and once again, I think of the little girl with a roof over her head. "The Citadel thinks that because they did not inherit a culture, but instead invented one made of a thousand others, they are better than us. They would label our tribes backward and our traditions ignorant. They do not see the generosity with which you have treated the people of Troy whom they themselves have forgotten." I step forward. "Which will make it that much more satisfying when we use their shortsighted arrogance against them."

My words are met with immediate dissent.

Nhorcys the Strong's voice rises above the rest. "It is a pleasant thought,

Harsa. But in order to win this war, we must first be allowed to fight it. All you Trojans seem to know how to do is hide behind ramparts."

I can't disagree. Not when I have said the same thing time and again.

"Do not forget. I was not born in Troy, and I am not beholden to all her ways. If you do as I bid, I promise we will show those windbags on the council how real warriors fight."

And if I fail?

Self-doubt slams into me as soon as the thought arises. I envision Rhea's face before she entered the passage. Afraid but determined.

But mostly afraid.

My teeth grind. *This is the only way.*

Soon I must tell Hector about the girls who have not yet returned, but I will not fail him in this. I told Hector I would keep our allies from running home, and I am prepared to do it. By whatever means necessary.

A few heads nod at my critique of the Citadel, but most remain stony. After years in Troy, these men have had their fill of rousing speeches. I must give them something different. Something real.

I step closer to the line of captains. "That is my aim, at least. But first, I must determine if actual change is within your scope of power. Or perhaps you are as undisciplined as the council claims." I step up close to Hippothous. "Here is your chance, warrior. Cease with the empty boasting and show me what you can do."

The captains shrug at one another before calling to their men, who begin to arrange themselves into a sloppy line.

"I am not interested in your poor imitation of my husband's phalanx," I snap. "This is not your custom, and it is not my custom either. If you want the Citadel to look at you differently, you must *be* different. You must show them something new."

"What do you mean, *new*?" Peirous scratches his white head.

I survey the men in front of me. Pieces of a broken pot I am slowly figuring out how to put back together.

"I mean to play to your strengths. But to do that, I must first know what those strengths are." Hand pressed to my lower back, I sit down on an overturned crate, suddenly reminded of the small secret I carry.

None of the men move.

"Is no one up to the challenge?"

At last, Peirous signals to a few of his men, who hop over a nearby fence to an enclosure with a handful of horses. With fluid movements, Peirous and his men vault onto their bare backs.

The group of Phrygians breaks into rancorous laughter at the sight, but none more so than Nhorcys the Strong. In truth, it *is* comical. Unlike the Thracians' northern stock, our animals are much too small. The long-legged Thracians' feet nearly brush the ground. Not that this stops them.

Using nothing but their knees, the Thracians guide the horses into a gallop straight for the fence. Slingshots materialize in their hands. The horses sail across the wooden rails as stones rain down over our heads. Peirous is the last man over. His stone swipes the conical hat directly from the head of Nhorcys the Strong, who is no longer laughing.

Nhorcys knocks the dirt from his hat before handing it over to one of his men. He signals for his Phrygians to join him at a tethering post. They gather around their leader as Nhorcys bends down low to wrap his massive arms around the wooden beam. With a deep groan, he rips the post from the earth and sends it careening to the dirt at my feet.

I nod in appreciation at this show of strength, and Nhorcys bows before pushing his hat back down onto his braided head.

The next several minutes pass exactly as one might expect. Each group of allies takes their turn to outdo the others. Sarpedon's Lycians strip off their borrowed armor and pair off, sparring with the grace and speed of men who know how to defend themselves within the close quarters of a ship. The dust has barely settled from their exhibition when Hippothous saunters out in front of the crowd. One of his warriors tosses him a wineskin, which he proceeds to drink down to the dregs. A bit unsteady on his feet, he squints and lifts his spear, which he somehow manages to heave half a field's length. Unfortunately, it misses the post that was his target by nearly the same distance. Hippothous offers me a bow before staggering back to his men.

One by one, the allies take their turn. The men from Adresteia and Mount Tereia climb the side of the stables with nothing but their hands. Pandarus and his hunters from Mount Ida square off against Pyraechmes and his Paeonian archers in a contest of precision that has no clear winner. All the while, I watch, taking careful note and thanking the Mother goddess for men, who are nothing if not predictable.

Once every group has given an account of themselves, I rise. "You could do worse, I suppose. You could fight like Achaeans."

This produces another ripple of laughter.

Hippothous cuts it short by thrusting his spear into the ground so hard the tip shatters. I recognize the weakness in the act at once. He is young and his pride has been taken from him. He does not yet realize that unlike armor, no enemy can ever strip you of your worth unless you let them.

"What about you, Harsa?" he asks from where he rests at the foot of the fence, nodding at the bow he is handing me. "We've all made a fair account of ourselves. Shouldn't you do the same?"

I rotate my neck, relieving the stiff muscles. For a moment, I'm sorely tempted to borrow one of Pandarus's arrows and shave the scruff from Hippothous's chin, but my gaze passes over the wretched, beaten men around me, and I know that taking this arrogant warrior's bait to save face is not what the others need.

"Look around you," I say. "For the past hour, you have been training together without trying to kill each other. *That* is my strength. I can organize you. I can help you show the Citadel you are more than the undisciplined riffraff they claim you to be." I stand tall, fully aware that the success or failure of this experiment will come down to my next words. "Listen to me. Trust me. And most importantly, do what I tell you to do, and we will make more than a few members of the King's Council eat their words."

The captains look at each other. Their silence lasts so long I think my efforts have been in vain, but then Peirous speaks. "What assurances can you give us that you will keep up your end of the bargain?"

I nod. "The Festival of the Divine Twins. I am planning games. Contests of strength." I force a smile. "A chance to show off the skills you have just shown me, all while rubbing a few famous Trojan faces in the mud. Perhaps even my husband's."

More muffled laughter fills the training ground. Less hesitant this time.

"I invite you all to a festival banquet in your honor. Give me these next few weeks, and if you still remain unconvinced that things might change for the better, I will not hold you back from leaving Troy for good."

One by one the allied captains, with the exception of Hippothous, nod. I suppress a stab of victory, knowing it may take more time to bring him around.

"So." Old Peirous crosses his hands over his chest and looks about him with uncertainty. "Where would you like to start?"

I look over my shoulder at Bodecca, who stands in front of her own troops. A squad of servingwomen who bear all manner of oils and tubs of steaming water. A dull pain radiates through my chest. It is strange not to see Rhea among them.

Wherever she is, Rhea is fighting her own battle now. Fully prepared for hers, Bodecca steps to the front of the line with a bristle in her hand and a frown on her face.

"We start as all mortals must." I toss Hippothous a drum of soap made of beef fat and ashes. "Don't forget to wash behind your ears."

32

RHEA

I RETRACE MY route through the settlements and cut north up Cape Sigeum. My form melts into the shadows behind the stinking latrines. I've just reached the circular shrine of the old gods when I notice that one part of the surrounding wall is taller than it was just a few hours ago. Much, much taller.

A man crouches on the rock wall, watching me. The moon breaks out of the clouds above, emblazoning the golden strands of his shoulder-length hair. He leaps directly into my path.

This . . . this is not a man.

It is a giant.

"What are you doing out here?" the giant asks.

"I . . . I am . . . gathering herbs. For the infirmary." Ven's lie tumbles clumsily off my tongue.

The giant's expression is unreadable in the dark, but I can *feel* his frown as he studies the empty basket in my arms.

I take a step backward. An admission of guilt no matter what land you hail from.

The giant runs a hand over the back of his neck as he watches me. The gesture is unsure. So at odds with his size. The thought strikes me that I'm not the only one lurking out here in the shadows.

"I could take you back to Machaon." The giant's words are a river of honey flowing over rocks. "See what he has to say about it."

"You could," I whisper. If the giant brings me to the infirmary I will be found out, and then a quick death would be the greatest kindness I could hope for. Knowing the Achaeans, it isn't one I'm likely to get.

"Or," the giant says slowly, "you could give me your help, and in exchange, I could forget I ever saw you."

Wariness fills me along with a tendril of hope. "What kind of help?"

"A small task." The giant gestures behind him with one massive hand. "Inside the old shrine."

"The one they say is cursed?"

The giant's lips twitch though I can't be certain. "I'm not one for fanciful tales."

"Are you sure you are an Achaean, then?" I bite my tongue, but it's too late to call back the words.

This time, there's no mistaking the white flash of teeth. "As you've likely noticed, there are prying eyes all over this camp. My business requires privacy, and I'm not overly picky about where I find it."

This announcement sends me backward so quickly, I nearly trip over my own feet.

The shadows across the giant's face seem to darken. "It's not what you are thinking."

"Then what sort of help do you need?" My mind is running, desperate for any way out of this that doesn't require me to follow this giant into that cursed circle of stones.

"Your hands," he says. "They are smaller than mine."

I merely stare. Yes, my hands are smaller. I strongly suspect my entire body weighs less than one of his giant arms.

"Come with me and keep quiet, and I promise to return the favor." His eyes drift past the latrines, toward the campfires. "I can't imagine a little thing like you is up to anything too sinister. I suppose we all need a bit of freedom every now and then."

"All right," I say, because I really don't have a choice. Though you wouldn't know it from the wide, grateful grin that breaks across the giant's face.

The crumbling wall that encircles the open-air shrine is not half as high as the handful of stones that loom inside. Even so, it is twice as tall as I am. I watch in awe as the giant vaults to the top in one graceful bound. "Well, come on, then."

I study the barrier in front of me at a loss. The place where the entrance once stood has caved in on itself, blocking any access.

"Right." The ground seems to quiver when the giant lands, but perhaps it is my legs that are unsteady. "I'll have to lift you."

He waits for me to nod. A choice I regret as soon as he closes the distance between us. The top of my head barely reaches his sternum. When he bends down low, the ends of his golden hair tickle my cheek. And then his hands circle my middle.

A gasp leaves my lips, and he pauses, once again betraying a hint of uncertainty. The giant could easily span my waist with a single hand. Instead, he grips me carefully with two. The world shifts as the giant lifts me up onto the wall, several feet above his head.

I cling to the top and look down. The walls enclosing the shrine are sloped at an angle, allowing me to slide down to the other side. Four towering stones form the heart of the ancient structure. They rise out of the earth like fingers of a hand reaching for the starless sky. The giant has built a fire at their center. The flickering flames throw warmth and light over the circular walls holding us.

I approach one of the standing stones the people who built this place guarded so carefully. It is covered in elaborate carvings, many of their pictures too faded to make out.

The air shifts behind me. I turn to find the giant watching me from the other side of the fire. In the flickering light, I get my first good look at his face.

He is younger than I thought. His long hair is the color of a wheat field in the sun. A beard in the same shade is trimmed close to his square jaw, setting off eyes the color of green agate. There are several nicks where scars shine through, and the bridge of his nose is slightly crooked where it's been broken. Likely, more than once. The overall effect makes him more rugged than handsome, and yet there's something arresting about him. Something in his gaze that feels almost boyish despite his size and the handful of summers that lie between us.

It is . . . unsettling.

The giant returns my stare with the quiet patience of someone who is used to being gaped at. Before tonight, Hector was the largest man I'd ever seen, but this warrior is easily two hands taller and so wide across the shoulders, it's difficult to take him in all at once. The dramatic triangle of his torso tapers to a slim waist that ends in muscular legs that look capable of bearing the weight of the sky, if necessary.

Not a giant at all. More like a god.

The god's lips twitch, and suddenly, I remember who he is. An Achaean like the ones who came here to sack Troy. Who slaughtered Andromache's family. A killer. An *enemy*.

"What is it you need?" I ask briskly. A full day has already passed since I left Troy. Andromache will be sick with worry. And then there are the raids. I can't warn Andromache of the Achaeans' plans if I don't make it back before the sun rises.

The god doesn't speak. Neither does he approach me. Instead, he folds his massive body into a sitting position by the fire and lifts the sleeve of his tunic, revealing an arm carved out of stone and painted with gold. White pus oozes from a wound on the inside of his biceps. A bit of thread dangles free along with a bone needle covered in blood.

Not a god after all.

"Like I said, I need your hands. Mine have made a mess of things."

Yes, I can see that.

I take a few steps forward to inspect the wound. Most of it is covered by a cloth bandage. "I'm not skilled in the arts of healing. Would one of the men in the infirmary not be better?"

"More than likely."

"So why not seek help there?" It's unwise to question him, but it's equally unwise to make a butchery of his arm.

The giant shifts his weight. "Because the infirmary is full of ailing men with nothing better to do than run their tongues." He pulls back the bandage, revealing the wound.

I let out a gasp.

The cuts are deep. Obviously done by a very sharp blade to have made such precise lines. Precise lines that have been arranged carefully to create some sort of . . . symbol.

I lift my eyes to the giant's. A flush paints the hard panes of his face.

"I need it to heal exactly the way it has been cut," he says as if that explains anything. "I thought your fingers might be better suited to the job than mine."

A memory flies before me as I study the wound. Flies buzzing around my head and the hot drip of blood down my wrist as I pressed a rock to a young woman's face.

I swallow. "I've no talent with a needle."

"I'm sure you're just being modest." The giant stretches out one very long leg and crosses it over the other.

"I'm not." My mother had the patience of a priestess, and even she stopped trying to teach me. "There's a chance I'll do more harm than good."

The giant studies me from under tawny lashes. "You'd have me believe I've enlisted the help of the only female in all of Anatolia who doesn't know the sharp end of a needle?"

"I'm sure there are others." Unbidden, my mind conjures Andromache's face. What did she do when I didn't return last night? Is she sitting up at this very moment, unable to sleep, wondering where I am?

I have to get out of here. I have to return to Troy and tell Andromache everything I've learned, but in order to do that, first I must do this.

"I can sew for you, but it won't be pretty."

The giant tips his face to the sky as if asking his gods for deliverance. "I'll take my chances."

Cautiously, I step around the fire. The giant watches me work up the courage to approach him with what I might believe was amusement if giants or gods were capable of such emotions.

I kneel beside him. Between the warmth of the fire and the heat coming off his skin, I'm soon sweating. My fingers tremble around the needle. Letting out a deep breath, I hold it the way my mother taught me, and I start to sew.

Within moments, my palms are slippery with blood. The lines of the wound are intricate; the work demanding of my full focus. Long minutes pass before I notice the warrior watching me.

"You weren't lying." The giant assesses my handiwork. "You aren't very good at this."

My heart beats frantically in my chest. "I'm afraid . . . the scars will be bad."

"Then they'll be at home with all the others." The giant shrugs and goes back to watching me.

"What does it mean?" I ask to keep the focus away from all the questions he might ask.

"It's my mark." The giant's words are a low rumble from deep inside his chest.

I use the old bandage to wipe his arm. Anything so I don't have to look at him. "Your mark?"

"My father's mark, which makes it mine as long as I'm here fighting in his place. All the kings have them. We scratch them onto stones and draw lots when there's a task we all wish to do. Or not do, as is mostly the case these days." He runs his hand along a messy row of stitches. "I sometimes struggle with . . . remembering. It's the lines," he says with a naked vulnerability that causes my brow to furrow. "They move. When I'm looking at them. It . . . it's hard to pin them down. It has been this way since I was a boy."

I nod, even though I don't understand. Not in the slightest.

The giant who I've just learned is also the son of a king relaxes when I don't mock him. As if I'm in any position to do such a thing.

"Agamemnon is fond of saying I never make the same mark twice." He rubs a massive hand over his face. "It might not bother me if it wasn't also true."

"So you cut the mark into your skin? To help you remember?"

"I thought I could copy it if I had to. But for that to work the stitches have to heal clean."

It's a brutal but potentially effective solution. Sadly, I doubt the wound will heal as he wishes it to. My eyes fly over the mark. The one that I couldn't forget now even if I tried.

I bite my lip. The giant asked for my help, and my instincts tell me that there's a greater chance of him keeping his end of the bargain if I do the same with mine. "I . . . I think there's another way you might remember it. Even without the scar."

"How?" This close, I see the flecks of gold in his irises that match the threads of his hair.

"Look," I say before I lose my courage. Or regain my common sense. "Your mark is more than a series of lines. It's a picture." I run my finger above the swollen flesh. "Three mountains side by side and over them a bird in full flight. You see the mountains? And the bird?"

He looks at his arm as if he's never seen it before. "I see them."

I nod. "So when you're asked to make your mark again, don't think of the lines at all. Think of the mountains and the bird flying above them, and draw it just the way you see it in your head."

His eyes rise to mine.

"What's your name?"

"Rhea." I see no reason to lie.

"Rhea?" A grin lights up his face and reveals a dimple in one cheek. "That's a good name. A Greek name."

"My father bred horses, but before that he traveled on ships." The words echo through the hollow of my chest. "Your gods brought him and his horses safely across the sea, and he was deeply grateful."

That dimple flashes again. "Your father sounds like a wise man."

"He was," I whisper. "The very best."

The giant's expression sobers as he gazes into the fire. "Many good men have died in this war."

They are words that I've heard again and again. From Hector. From Andromache. From my papa when he was still alive. My vision flashes with red as I stare at this Achaean warrior, because *why*. If this is the truth that everyone can see, *why* must we simply sit back and let it happen?

"Would you tell me that is the nature of war?" I hear the challenge in my voice, but it's too late now to stop it.

"I've been fighting for a long time," the giant says quietly. "Since I was old enough to hold a spear. But I can't say I understand it any better than you do." A long moment passes before he looks at me again. "You must be tired, and I'm sure that they are expecting you back at the infirmary."

We both stand. The sudden awkwardness that passes between us makes me think I wasn't the only one tonight who said more than they meant to.

"Here." The giant steps in close so that his heat washes over me. "I'll lift you over."

He wraps his hands around my waist. His fingers only just skim my ribs. It's a careful touch, but still, I can't help the breath that escapes me. And then I am flying through the air to the top of the shrine wall.

"I'll walk you back to the infirmary," he says when we are settled on the other side.

"That won't be necessary."

"It's late. It'll be safer for you this way." He heads toward the latrines without waiting for me to agree. And why would he? As decently as he has treated me so far, there's no changing the fact that this young man is a warrior. The son of a king. And as far as he knows, I am a slave.

The giant starts north up Cape Sigeum in what I can only assume is the direction of the infirmary. After all, I have never been there.

My mind frantically searches for some excuse to get away from him when a loud voice bellows up ahead.

"Ajax!" the voice calls out, drawing a low oath from the giant.

The name stops me cold. I have heard it whispered often in Hector's stables. Usually before a long list of other names. Those of the many good Trojan men he has killed.

A tall warrior slides out of the shadows directly in front of us. He is slightly younger than the giant. Maybe two summers older than I am. For all his youth, he carries himself with an arrogance usually reserved for gods.

The warrior's lips bend in a mocking arc when he reaches us. "I thought that was you skulking in the shadows."

"Diomedes," says the giant. Ajax. I study him with new eyes. All the softness has fled his face, making him suddenly every bit as terrifying as he always should have been. "What brings you to this part of the camp?" he asks.

"The same thing that brings every Achaean at least three times a day. Even mighty Agamemnon isn't above taking a shit." Diomedes spots me over Ajax's shoulder. "I'd ask you the same if the answer wasn't obvious. Though I'd have a care you don't break the girl, if that's what she is." He looks me over critically, pausing on my meager bust. "Or maybe you have more in common with your cousin than all that pretty hair."

"Concern yourself with your own affairs," Ajax says shortly.

The sham of a smile drops from Diomedes's face. "As it happens, I was looking for you. Nestor has asked for an audience."

"What've I done to cross the old man now?" Ajax asks with obvious affection he does not offer the younger warrior.

"I believe he plans to send you up to deal with your temperamental cousin. I swear, Achilles has more moods than my sisters on their blood."

Achilles.

The name is thunder pealing through me.

I look up at the man I helped. Achilles's cousin. Only now, Ajax looks nothing like the uncertain giant who asked for my help in the stones.

"Careful." It is a growl.

Diomedes doesn't hear it. Or perhaps he's the sort of man who enjoys picking at scabs best left alone. "Why? Are we men or little girls?"

"I think you have to sprout at least one chin hair before you can call yourself a man, Diomedes."

The warrior's lips twist in a sneer. "Achilles has had long enough to stew in his own juices. Another man might think he'd lost his courage."

Ajax takes a step forward. "Achilles's courage is not in question. He is favored by the gods. He is also family. If you speak ill of him, you'll answer to me."

"And yet I can't help but wonder how he will reward you for your loyalty," Diomedes says. "By sitting back and watching you die at Hector's hands?"

"If I were you, I'd concern myself less with Achilles's honor and more about your own. Your spear arm is getting soft from underuse."

"Say what you will," Diomedes snaps. "When Agamemnon calls the men to fight, I'll be among them. Meanwhile, Achilles will be shedding bitter tears over Briseis."

"Agamemnon never should've taken her from him," Ajax growls. "It was wrong of him to replace Chryseis with Achilles's prize, and every man here knows it."

"And yet, every man here will also fight when he is called. Every man but one." Diomedes's nostrils flare. "Go to Nestor. Undertake his peace mission. Let us all hope that Achilles sees reason, or it won't be his great deeds the bards will remember."

Diomedes stalks off. I dare a glance at Ajax, and the ferocity on his face draws a rush of air from my lips. He seems to come back to himself. "It appears I'm needed elsewhere."

He walks away, making my legs wobble with relief. At the last moment, Ajax turns.

"Thank you, Rhea. Perhaps we'll see each other again."

I barely hear him. I'm too busy replaying the conversation between him and Diomedes. Something about Agamemnon and Achilles and an argument over two girls. One named Briseis. The other Chryseis.

Another name I've heard before.

⌒ ॰ ⌒

IT'S ALMOST LIGHT when I drag myself through the opening and fall onto the hard stone floor of the temple. For a moment, I just lie there in the incense-steeped air.

I don't expect to find anybody waiting for me. After we didn't come back last night, they would've given us up for dead. And we would have been. If it weren't for Salama's quick thinking. For Isola's quiet courage.

For Ven's help.

Andromache. I have to tell Andromache.

I've dragged myself up onto my hands and knees when the shadows to my left break toward me. An arm wraps around my waist, hoisting me roughly to my feet.

"Rhea? Where have you *been*?"

At the sound of the familiar voice, my legs give out.

Cyrrian scoops me up under the knees. He looks as if he hasn't slept since I left him last. Bloodshot eyes sweep my face. "What is it? Are you hurt?"

I shake my head, but worry still clouds his features. He tucks me into his chest and carries me over to a stone slab, where he sits me down before kneeling between my legs.

I try to form words, but my tongue can't catch up with my thoughts. The temple wavers in and out. How long has it been since I've eaten? Since I've slept? Hours and seconds slip through my hands as the light slips from my eyes.

Hands close around my arms.

"Stay with me, Rhea. Where are the others?"

My parched lips manage to form a single word. "Gone."

"They're dead?" Cyrrian's face goes slack, but the only thought I seem to be able to hold is that his eyes are almost impossibly blue in the flickering firelight.

My sense flies back into my head from wherever it's been hovering. "No. They were captured. But they're safe." I grip his arms with the last of my strength as the night washes over me. All the things I saw. All the things I heard.

"Andromache. I have to find Andromache." I try to rise, but Cyrrian holds me fast. "Please," I beg. "I have to tell her!"

"Tell her what?" His voice is low and soothing. Utterly unlike him. "Is it about Odysseus?"

"No," I say as the dark closes in on me, unwilling to be ignored. "It's about Achilles."

33

ANDROMACHE

MY EYES SNAP open, launching me from sleep like a stone from a sling.

Sleepless nights. Another outcome of carrying a child I hadn't anticipated. But at least this new discomfort seems a good sign, one that lessens
some of my worries about the pains that still strike me without warning.

Rolling toward Hector's side of the bed, I find it just as it has been as of
late. Empty.

Good. The more nights Hector sleeps with the army on the plain beyond
the western wall, the less likely he is to wonder about my slowly changing
shape.

And changing it is, though I can't yet tell if my constant body aches indicate a risk to my condition, or if they're merely the result of training with
Troy's allies. Knowing my chance for sleep is gone regardless, I throw on a
wool robe, grab an oil lamp, and start to leave the room for my nightly ritual
of pacing the halls. A small figure on my bedside table stops me. It draws my
gaze with an almost otherworldly pull.

The figurine is carved from rough stone. Though crude, the ancient
workmanship is tender and loving. Much like the goddess herself.

Hannahanna has long been revered, but unlike the Achaean gods and
goddesses with their dramatic bickering and licentious affairs, the quiet
grandmother of Anatolia is often overlooked. As is typically the case with
women past their prime in both beauty and childbearing.

Like all mothers, parts of her story are a whisper that will die buried in
the hearts of her children.

There is only one person other than Rhea who knows the whisper growing inside me. A woman who is far from quiet but whose service rarely receives the recognition it deserves. And it is just like her to place Hannahanna within my reach when I need her most.

The token of Bodecca's silent forgiveness nearly breaks me. She has been a mother to me where I have failed to be one to others.

"Oh, Rhea."

Dropping to my knees, my body rocks back and forth over the floor. Is this really what it is like? To bear life, to be vulnerable to love, only to be cracked open by everything it costs? Hannahanna's vacant gaze offers a fleeing comfort. But can it do any good to beg clay for help when the goddess has never sacrificed a son or daughter of her own?

Not knowing is the worst punishment of all. At least the mother of the sparrow boy whose secret I kept had the consolation of tending to his body. What if the Achaeans refused Rhea a pyre and threw her body into a swamp, barring her from peace? Or she could be chained to the bed of an enemy, where she'll be broken in ways worse than death.

No matter her end, the blame is mine. I asked three girls, barely older than children, to do something I could not do myself.

Sitting back, I hug my middle, wanting to hold the babe inside, but also wanting him—or her—to remain safe in the warm darkness for as long as possible. My fingers fumble with the bronze incense burner beside the bed.

Please, Mother. Keep them in your care.

Will she even hear my prayer when I have so failed to do my part? When even on my most pious days, my heart was filled with doubts? Once, I told Hector I didn't see the point in pleading with deities that did what they wanted anyway. He'd given me a look that landed like a blow.

"All men worship something, Andromache. If it isn't something higher, then our base human impulses are all that is left."

And the impulse to protect ourselves by protecting those we love? That is nothing if not human.

"I must tell him," I say to the rising incense smoke.

No matter how it breaks me open. No matter what it costs me. Our union will not survive this deception if Hector discovers it another way.

It may not survive it regardless.

On my way to the stables, the position of the waning moon tells me we are nearing the end of the third watch, but it is still an hour or two before sunrise. The time Hector likes to rise to care for the horses before his morning run. When all is quiet as the earth awaits the arrival of the rose-fingered dawn.

Inside the stalls, the oil lamp's shadows dance across Hector's face, reminding me of the younger man I strolled with in my father's vineyards. A man with fewer worries and endless possibilities before him.

He sits amid the stalls on an overturned crate, strands of hair loosened from their knot, his broad chest rising and falling slowly, as if horse sweat and manure are the most soothing scents in the world.

A horse flaps its lips. It is the red beast. Hector's fire horse. He stomps his hooves at my intrusion, making no secret of his displeasure. Hector's eyes snap to mine, but the sharp blade in his hand does not shift.

"I wondered how many nights would pass before you came looking for me here."

I open my mouth, but the words I must say get caught in my throat at this sight of Hector in his element. At the sight of his earthy beauty. I take a step forward, aiming to see what he's carving out of the oak log that sits upright between his knees. He follows my gaze and gives me a tired smile. "I did not want to upset you."

As I approach Hector's bare shoulder, what he's been working on these long nights takes shape. The log has been sliced in half, the side facing him hollowed out by the tool in his hand, creating a shallow bed.

"It will rock eventually. I'll smooth out the roughness, of course. Carve a few designs around the headboard. A horse head most likely."

Tears spring to my eyes. I fight them back.

Hector's face falls flat. "I'm sorry, Andromache. I never meant for you to see it . . . not unless . . ."

When he lifts his chin, Hector's own eyes are glassy. "It's how I handle the hope. Along with the grief." His hands move through the air as if holding a saw. "The back and forth of it all. Month after month."

I nod but still cannot speak.

"I do not blame you, my *alev.* I never have. If anything, I blame my—"

"It isn't that."

"Then what is it?"

How do I even begin to explain that until this moment, the life inside me had been a halfhearted wish? A wish I didn't even think I wanted until it happened. But now, it takes no effort to envision the boy lying in this cradle, looking up at us with dark eyes and his father's head of curls, as black and silky as a stallion's coat.

"If we ever have a child, I wanted to give him a gift," Hector continues. "Something made by my hand that wasn't a shield or a spear. Something he could pass on to his own sons. Or daughters."

The way Hector's eyes run to Rhea's lead rope hanging on the wall assures me he knows the kind of daughter he'd wish to have.

What I must tell him will break him. Not open, but in half. Dividing and then conquering as all betrayals do.

He looks back at me, a novel desperation filling his eyes. A fear he cannot make sense of, this warrior who has faced Achilles once and lived to speak of it. Hector holds up his scarred hands. Used for killing, not lulling a baby to sleep.

"Don't you see? You aren't the only one who has had doubts about their lukewarm prayers. If we are ever granted a son, war is all he will inherit from me. So long as Troy exists, she will be the envy of all kingdoms on both sides of the Aegean. It will never end. Not for him, nor his son, nor his . . ."

"That is the fate of any king who has ever ruled a prosperous city," I assure him. As if a long lineage of suffering makes it any better.

Hector shakes his head. "It isn't what I want for him. I want him to raise the best horses in Anatolia and watch his children grow in peace. But that will never happen. The only inheritance I can leave any son of mine is a bloodstained battlefield. Even if this fight ends, there will be another, and another, and another."

"Stop this, Hector."

Now. I must tell him now. But how?

He points to the half-carved cradle as I fumble for the right words. "That is why my son must have something else," he continues. "Something . . . simple. Not gilded in gold nor forged of bronze, but something that will remind him of me when I—"

"Please. Don't."

Uttering the mere possibility of his death feels like a curse. One I might somehow have the power to break by speaking the truth.

The stable doors blow open behind us. A cloaked figure enters, bringing news of the returning rain with him. He holds something small and wet in his arms. At first, I think one of the stable hands has helped with the birth of a foal, but then I see the cloak I lent her. Its wool the earthen color of the Ilium plain.

"Rhea!"

Cyrrian throws back his hood as he sets the girl down on a bed of clean hay. "I found her inside the temple."

"Is she hurt?" Hector asks, his voice unsteady and confused.

"No, just exhausted, I think. And in need of water."

Hector always keeps a jug of watered-down wine in the stables for the soldiers, so I pour a small cup and press it to the girl's chapped lips. Her eyes flutter at the strong smell. She releases a moan.

"You must drink, Rhea." At the sound of my voice, her lips part and she obeys. "We need to get her out of these soaked rags."

"What is this about, Andromache?" Hector's voice is as cold as the wind blowing through the stalls.

"First, I must get her warm."

Hector and Cyrrian turn away while I strip Rhea naked with shaking hands, wrapping her in the robe I threw over my sleeping tunic.

She looks up at me and I can't help but smile at the sight of her. Alive. "What a little mouse you are," I say softly.

Something drains the newly revived color from Rhea's cheeks.

"Achilles." The word is hoarse.

"Take more wine."

Two small sips and there's no stopping her.

"Achilles no longer fights. He refuses to . . ."

Rhea then tells us a tale. A tale of Agamemnon, Achilles, and two women, one of them the captured daughter of a priest of Apollo. There is plague and death and kings fighting among themselves. And at the end of it all, Achilles and his Myrmidons stew in their huts, feasting on stolen meat while playing their lyres. It is the most words I've ever heard Rhea speak at once, and the effort leaves her drained.

"I knew Chryseis when she was young," I say, recalling the little milkweed. Then I remember her name on my dying mother's lips. Is that what the poor woman was trying to tell me? That Achilles refuses to fight because a king lost a girl and took his instead?

"Our mothers were close friends in Thebe. Never would I have imagined that Chryseis would be the one to open the doors to victory." I give Rhea's cheek a light stroke. "It seems young girls have already left their fingerprints all over this war."

"They have them," Rhea says in a small voice. "Our girls."

"What do you mean?" Hector demands.

When neither of us answers quickly, Hector looks to Cyrrian. The truth he sees on his friend's face has his own bronze skin bleeding of color.

"Tell me you didn't, Andromache." It is as close to a plea as I have ever heard him utter.

"I did," I say. "And I would do it again."

Especially now that I know it worked. The Achaeans' greatest weapon has abandoned the war, and we are the only ones who know about it.

I turn back to Rhea. "Did you hear anything regarding Odysseus?"

Rhea shakes her head. "Not yet."

Her final word does not escape my attention. And not only mine.

"You really think you are going back?" Cyrrian snaps.

Rhea sits a little taller. "Isola and Salama are still trapped in the camp. What good does that do anyone if I don't deliver the information they gather?"

Cyrrian shrugs. "Little good, if it gets you killed."

I don't know how to name the faint flicker, but on Cyrrian's normally carefree face, it looks a little like pain. Like the longing in his voice on the nights when he and I have taken too much wine and sung sad Hittite songs on my balcony, a sober Hector looking on in amusement.

Hector is not amused now.

"The risk is too great," Hector says in a voice that tells me we will have words when we are back in our own house. For the first time in our marriage, I tremble at the thought. How to make him see why I kept this from him? How to show him what it was all for?

"Hector, I—"

"Later, Andromache." His glare burns like red-hot iron in a blacksmith's forge.

I open my mouth to defend myself, to say anything that will erase this look that says he does not know me any longer, but someone speaks before I can.

"Prince Hector, you told me once that Troy was a place of tradition, where outsiders are not permitted to walk," Rhea says. "But then you let me walk into the stables where you knew I was not welcome. Because you saw my talent and my need." She meets my husband's gaze without flinching, and suddenly, she is not the same meek girl who came to us. "You recognized something in me worth trusting. You cannot fault Andromache for doing the same."

"This is not the same," Hector says. "We are speaking not of Trojan stables but of the Achaean camps."

"True," Rhea says. "They are a place no Trojan soldier can hope to walk unseen. But we have walked, and we have seen." She draws a deep breath. "I once told you that my greatest wish was to be useful. You saw my gifts and then you granted me my wish. Andromache sees them too. Same with the others. She gave us the choice, but we are the ones who made it. Even now, I do not regret it. Please don't ask me to. If you are going to be angry, be angry at me."

Hector's face falls as every one of his shields lowers. Rhea looks to me, a plea on her face. The same plea my heart has issued time and time again. To be allowed to risk everything for those who have risked for us. To stand up and be counted.

With a small nod, I turn to my husband. "How will we defeat the Achaeans unless we figure out what Odysseus is up to? You've said it yourself, Hector. We must keep the walls from being breached until our reinforcements arrive." And until I turn the allies into the force they were always meant to be. A feat that is fragile and uncertain.

As is everything, it seems.

"Andromache." My name again, but this time, it does not burn or cut. I know he is still angry. More than that, he is hurt by my deception. But below both emotions, there is something every bit as powerful. Resignation. Hector knows why I acted as I did, and the part of him that is Troy's commander is perhaps a little relieved that I was the one who made the choice so he did not have to.

I place a hand on Hector's stiff shoulder. "When the plains dry out and the fighting resumes, we will take all the information we have gathered and launch a full-scale attack while their greatest fighter is down. We will send the Achaeans back to their festering excuses for kingdoms once and for all."

Cyrrian takes a step forward. "Do you have any idea what would happen to these girls if they were found out?"

"I do. But what would *you* do, Cyrrian? If you had this chance to give Troy such an enormous gift?" I look at Hector. The same question burning in my eyes.

They know.

"Can you survive their blood on your hands?" Hector asks me. "Rhea's blood?"

I think of the allies and the progress they have made already. All because someone was willing to place in them a scrap of the faith they deserved. "I believe in letting people determine their own destinies." My eyes find the wooden cradle. A reminder that this is about more than Rhea. It is about more than any one of us. "If we can use these weeks of waiting for the rains to end to strengthen the allies and gather details about what exactly the Achaeans are plotting, imagine how we might use both to our advantage. Imagine all of the city's many children who might be spared."

Hector considers these words carefully. "My father and the King's Council will mutiny if they find out we knowingly sent women into the enemy camps."

"Which is why we won't tell them," I offer.

"This will be a difficult thing to conceal, Andromache. How will we explain the information we come by?"

If only he knew how proficient I've become at hiding good news. My gaze drops, but the moment has passed.

"The plague was a difficult thing to contain," I remind him. "But we managed then, and we will manage again in the same way. By choosing our people well. We cannot afford any mistakes. If certain members of the council learn of this plan, it gives them one more spear to hurl at your head."

Just as they would use any complications with my precarious state against me if they caught wind of them.

Hector sighs. "How would such a thing even work?"

My heart races at his question. It is as good as an agreement. "We would have to be careful of how we pass on any information we collect. The safety of all three girls depends on knowledge of their circumstances never leaving this stable." My eyes find Cyrrian's. As much as I adore him, there's a reason his name is known throughout the streets of the Lower City. And it isn't for his discretion.

"I won't breathe a word." His expression is serious in a way I did not think him capable.

"I've already made contact with several Achaeans who will not find my presence in the camps unusual," Rhea adds. "The rest won't even notice my face."

Then she underestimates the power of a good heart. It is rarer and more desirable in war than tin. Even if they pay no attention to the modest way Rhea walks, such a heart can sing to men who are least expecting it.

"We cannot succeed in this without your support," I tell my husband. Rhea meets my gaze and holds her breath.

"Please," Rhea says on her next exhale. "Trust us to walk where only we can." She pulls back her narrow shoulders. "No more watching. No more hiding. Never again."

I don't know what her words mean, but the way Cyrrian shakes his head suggests there is something there. In the end, I don't have to know. They are the fuel to this new fire within her, and fire I can work with.

"I'll give you until the festival." Hector consents, repeating the same conditions the allies gave me without even knowing it. "If my father decides to change the succession and name another of my brothers as his heir, any thin blanket of authority I have to consent to such things will no longer protect us." His shoulders slump. "It is all I can offer you."

The festival. So much weight on this one day . . .

"Prove to me that it can be done," he says. "If you uncover anything of use, we will see what good comes of it."

Rhea and I share the glimmer of a smile. What my husband does not realize is that proving has become our native tongue.

34

RHEA

THE STENCH OF latrines drifts toward me on the wind, impossible to miss even in the dark. It has been less than a day since I ran through this swamp, my legs heavy with the burden of news I carried back to Troy. A handful of hours have passed since then and yet . . . everything feels different now.

Hector's and Andromache's trust is a buoy as much as it is a weight. It makes me both eager to repay their faith and terrified to fail.

The ancient stones rise toward the shrouded moon up ahead, filling me with the strangest sense that I am passing out of one world into another. And in so doing, I am somehow becoming someone else.

The night air is cool on my face as I dissolve into the shadows. A swaying Achaean leans on a wooden hut in front of me.

The soldier finishes his business. I stand still for one moment longer, and then I press my basket to my chest and step out of the dark and into the glowing light of the camp.

Warm air infused with scented oils washes over me when I pass through the arched doors of the bathhouse. This time, I walk directly between the two pools of soaking men toward the back, where Ven's voluptuous frame stands in the middle of a ring of women, all of them scrubbing out robes.

The raised scars on her face pucker at the sight of me. "This is Rhea," she announces for the benefit of the women nearby. "She'll be helping in the bathhouse. She'll also occasionally act as a messenger. If she tells you to do something, treat the command as if it has come from me or Calis."

The other women study me with open curiosity. I glance at Ven, wondering why she would draw attention to me when recognition is the last thing I want.

"Come on," she tells me sharply. "The rest of you, less wagging of tongues and more wringing of cloth."

Ven crosses to the hearth. A long line of clean tunics have been laid out to dry by the heat of the fire. She kneels to check the garments.

"Was that wise?" I ask under my breath.

"You will be coming and going. People are going to notice. The best way to avoid detection is to act as if you have nothing to hide." She snaps up two robes from the floor and hands me a third. "I'm not overly concerned about the women . . . most of them wouldn't reveal you even if they knew your purpose here. Many would even seek to aid you. But not all."

My mind conjures up the face of the dour woman who confronted us in the sleeping quarters. Calis. I nod to let Ven know I understand. "Will you tell more?" Ven is risking her life to help us. I'll be forced to trust her judgment just as she'll be forced to trust mine.

"There are a few with not merely the desire but also the skills to help. I'll wait a few days before I approach them." She folds a garment with brisk, efficient movements.

She means to wait to see if we are discovered before she risks anyone else. It's a sound strategy, and it makes me think that the Mother was guarding my steps when she placed them in Ven's path.

"I assume there have been no incidents since last night." I help Ven collect the last of the garments.

"You chose the girls well. They are plain enough to draw less notice than some." Her dark eyes drift over to the beautiful girl I noticed the last time I came here. She moves between the two pools, filling cups of wine while the men watch her with hooded gazes. She smiles and pours. Laughs at their crude jokes. But there is an edge to her laugh. A brittleness to her smile that makes me wonder what she really feels. For the first time since I can remember, I am happy for the sparse curves and strange features the Mother gave me.

"Lissia," Ven says, following my gaze. "She is Diomedes's prize."

"Then why does she labor in the bathhouse?"

"The Achaean kings are overly concerned with the way they look through other men's eyes, and Diomedes more so than most. He likes his trophy on full display. Tempting other men with what they can never have. The Achaeans are territorial about their women and cutthroat about what passes for honor among their kind. Otherwise, none of us would be here. Or have you forgotten?"

"You speak of Menelaus." I picture the large Achaean with the fiery red mane and the madman's roar I saw from the city walls. But even more vividly, I recall the expression on Helen's face that night in the grotto when she could have turned herself over to Odysseus. Acceptance and determination as she clutched that leather satchel to her breast and chose her side.

I haven't seen Helen since that night. What has become of her is anyone's guess. And though I still can't prove it, my heart says Helen is responsible for Andromache's happiness in ways she will never know.

Not unless I tell her.

At first, I didn't speak because I knew Andromache would've stopped drinking the tea at once. That fear has since passed, but still, a dozen other distractions have risen up to take its place. The allies. Our efforts in the camp. Since the night on the Hill of Kallikolone, one sunrise bleeds into another, and there is never a good time . . .

The excuse rings false even to my own ears. The truth is that my motivations for keeping silent are selfish. Because by revealing to Andromache all that Helen did to help her, I will also be revealing my own betrayal of omission.

I felt the crippling loss of Andromache's favor once. I don't think I could bear it again.

Which is why I have to prove to both of us that I am worthy of the trust she and Hector have placed in me.

Ven spits into the flames. "This war has little to do with Menelaus and even less to do with love. Menelaus would hardly dare to breathe without a direct order from his brother. He is a weak soldier and a weaker man. He has neither love nor honor powerful enough to have called down a fury as great as this endless bloodshed. We are here because of Agamemnon's need."

"Need?" I ask.

"All is not well in the west," Ven says. "You only need to listen to these men to know it. Talk of hotter summers and rising seas. The same unrest that has taken root in the Hittite lands is sweeping through the great cities of Achaea. Their people grow hungry. The great palaces require gold and goods to keep them running, and Agamemnon has come here to find it. Troy is filled with treasures from the Nile to Babylon. It is the gatekeeper between all major trade routes by land and sea, and whoever holds it grows fat. Agamemnon wants that access for himself. He will never return to a land on fire with empty hands. He cannot afford to."

I store all these pieces of information away for a time when I might pull them back out and study them again from different angles. For now, I focus on the task at hand.

"There will be a festival in Troy in a quarter cycle of the moon." I fold the tunic in my hand. "We have until then to demonstrate to the prince of Troy that this can be done."

Ven studies me closely. "That doesn't give us very much time."

She's right. It doesn't.

"The men here talk some, but this bathhouse is worse than any pharaoh's harem," Ven says. "It will take time to discern mere rumor from fact."

"Then we must work quickly," I say.

Ven's expression clearly says what she thinks about that.

"Where are Salama and Isola?" I ask to avoid dwelling on difficulties I hadn't anticipated.

"I moved Isola to the stream out back to wash garments with the other women. She will fit in better in a place where fewer words and more action are required. Separated, she and the foul-mouthed one might draw less attention."

Again, a good strategy. Not only because it decreases the likelihood that we'll be found out, but also because women working over washing tend to gossip.

"Girl, another jug of wine!" calls a heavily muscled warrior lounging in the nearby tub. Pottery cracks as he sends the empty jug spinning across the floor. It comes to rest at Ven's foot. Before she can so much as pick it up, Lissia has pressed a fresh cup into the warrior's hand. Whatever he says to her sends the men around her into uproarious laughter.

"Tell me this can work." I let Ven see some of my desperation, just as once, she showed me hers.

"I can't." Then she shrugs. "But I suppose there are worse ways to pass the time."

I search the bathhouse for the one face I am missing.

"Where is Salama?"

"See for yourself." Ven nods toward the circle of floor cushions where three Achaean soldiers are being groomed. Behind the man in the center, a girl is running a sharp blade down the length of his neck.

She looks up, and everything inside me goes still.

I stare, transfixed as the blade in Salama's hand runs up and down. Up and down. With each stroke, it pauses ever so briefly over the soldier's throbbing pulse.

Salama's grin slices across her thin face.

I swallow. "Are you sure about this?"

Eight days until the festival. Eight days of running back and forth between the camps.

Eight days for something to go very, very wrong.

Ven snaps another garment off the warming stones. "She hasn't killed anyone. Yet."

THE HAWK

Feathers glide across naked stars.
Black silk drenched in moonlight,
dancing across the Hawk's wings.

Do you see them? asks the Voice. *Do you see?*
The Weaver's skin a tapestry of bruises
bloody threads wrapped 'round her fingers.
The Spindle dancing on the loom
imperceptive to the hand that moves it.
A Horse of fire pacing in his stall.
The wind calling his name.
In the shadows of a waking army, the Mouse,
hunting a Spider in the dark.

Stirring on the plain below,
quiet movement in the gloom.
The Hawk circles and waits
for the moment it knows must come.
The Hawk dives, wings wide open.
Flash of white underbelly exposed.
Ancient question rings in silent
pause that comes before the kill.
Hunter or prey?

BOOK
IV

35

HELEN

GET OUT. GET out. Get out.

The cadence becomes the beat of my heart as my cracked fingers cling to the stone ledge.

One step, two step, three step, four. Kairos will catch you if you fall.

Child rhymes swirl. Stars shine above. The abyss below waits.

My moment has come, but there will be no mischievous son of Zeus flying in to save me.

There is only the ripe wind, blowing a warning from the Unnamed One.

I inch out farther onto the ledge. How many moments of opportunity will I have before he comes back? How many breaths?

Two more steps. Toward the sea and the sky and the wind. Toward freedom.

The emptiness howls again, tempting me to its numbing escape. Yet my toes cling to the outcropping of stone. A bird screams overhead.

Get out.

"Where are you going, my love?"

Time slows, like Kronos has caught my ankles with his scythe. I think I know what I will see when I turn my head, but this rage is new.

"Was one betrayal not enough?"

Get out.

The wind pulls at my gown. Pulls me away from him. Face pressed to the wall of the narrow ledge beyond the balcony, my arms and legs splay into a perfect X.

Reaching. Always reaching.

Not far enough.

A clammy hand clasps my wrist.

Not fast enough either.

One push. That's all it would take to send me flying backward. I can tell he is considering it. His bloodshot eyes have never looked so crazed. So tired of the cavern of emptiness that consumes him, issuing its haunting cry night after night.

They do not love you. None of them do.

Your own family left you to die. An innocent baby.

You will never be Hector. You will never be anything.

"Damn you!" Paris yanks me back onto the balcony by a fistful of hair. "You will not abandon me."

Something sinister widens his pupils. Something even worse than rage.

A twisted thing that looks a little like love but is really just a balm for self-hate.

"They are done for. Clymene carries my child, and the festival is upon us. We are close. He says all I have to do now is wait."

He?

Paris strokes my hair and then my cheek with icy fingers. "And you will wait with me."

My skull burns as he pulls me back into the room. I do not cry out, for who is there to hear me? Hands shaking, he pulls the stopper from the closest wine jug and presses it to my lips.

"Drink!" he screams.

I know this dance. I have memorized all the steps.

So I take a willing sip. To fight is futile.

Or is it?

Lips curling, I meet his hollowed gaze. So terrified. So broken. A pathetic little creature screaming for attention from an indifferent wilderness.

"Good girl."

I spit.

My craving gushes down my chin, much like the blood he has spilled.

Get out. Get out. Get out. Get out. Get out.

His face twists. He grabs me by the arms and hurls me across the room. Pain rips through my leg, through me, and it is total.

The dark ring closes in, and the world goes as black as his eyes.

36

RHEA

THE INFIRMARY IS a building of wood and mudbrick located farther up Cape Sigeum at the very heart of the Achaean camp. On our way, Ven and I pass a dozen more settlements like the ones near the bathhouse and the cut.

"Are you sure Machaon won't question me?" I stare past Ven toward the infirmary, the only building on the cape as heavily frequented as the bathhouse. Or so I am told.

"He did not complain when I sent Isola to him yesterday."

"And we've had no word from her since?" I ask.

"None. Which is why I am now sending you."

I force my arms to release their death grip on my basket. It has been nearly a quarter moon since I started working the second night watch at the bathhouse. Seven days of catching a few hours' rest behind Troy's walls before spending long nights scrubbing floors and fetching tunics for naked men with nothing better to do than complain and boast. I have heard many things. Some of which would make even Madam Morgestia blush. And yet none of it has proven remotely useful.

Each night, I've returned to Troy by way of the Mother's pass only to tell Andromache and Cyrrian that there is no news of Odysseus. Each night, Andromache has said a prayer of thanks to the Mother for my safe return. She would never betray her disappointment, and for his part, Hector has kept his distance. Though he is busy with his men, in my heart I know he is avoiding me. It's almost as if he fears the sight of me will somehow change his mind about what he has agreed to let us do.

Soon, it will not matter.

Any information we gather in the camps is only useful if there is some-one for us to bring it to. If Paris is named Priam's new heir, he will waste no time relieving Andromache of her liaison duties. And as for Hector . . . well, as Bodecca once said, the love of a people is a fickle thing.

With the festival two days away, it is time to take greater risks.

"Odysseus does not visit the bathhouse." Ven watches a group of men howl with laughter around a fire nearby, her expression bitter. "But I've heard he makes frequent night visits to the infirmary." She lowers her voice. "There are whispers in the weaving tent of discord among the kings."

I think of how the camp is organized, each contingent in their own set-tlement. That the Achaean kings seem to prefer the company of their own men reinforces Ven's suggestion that these invaders are not as unified as they appear from the walls of Troy. It makes me think that whoever ar-ranged the camp this way did so for a reason.

"Men won't speak as freely in the bathhouse. Too many ears," Ven con-tinues. "Machaon is known for his judgment if not for his bedside manner. They say he is decent for an Achaean. If there's something to learn, he'll have heard it."

With a heavy nod, I grab my basket and make my way inside.

I steel myself for the stench of death and sickness, but instead, I'm greeted by the sharp tang of lemons and drying herbs. The left side of the infirmary is dominated by rows of beds for ailing men. At the center of the room lies a hearth hung with pots for boiling water, the steam escaping through the round hole cut into the roof above. To the right is a scarred workstation covered with mortars and pestles, clay cups overflowing with seeds and powders under hanging bushels of plants.

The place is tidy and mostly empty, likely thanks to the idle weeks of rain. The two men who are currently lying in the beds seem to be more af-flicted with boredom than pain.

The only other person in the room is bent over the younger of the two men, changing the bandages around his head. Isola's eyes widen on me. I hold up my basket, and she quickly finishes cleaning the wound above the soldier's brow. Together, we move to the empty tables and begin to lay out the herbs for hanging.

"Are you all right here?" I ask Isola quietly.

She nods. "Machaon is a dedicated healer. It's only been a day, and already I've learned much from him."

"About healing and potions?"

"Among other things." She glances at her patients where they are preoccupied with some game. "Since yesterday, three kings have come to sit with Machaon. I brought them wine and may have lingered over the pouring." She offers me a small smile. "There's an unspoken worry among the kings. The men are growing impatient with the lack of action. They're planning a raid on Assos in three days. It will involve thirty ships and two Achaean kings."

I tie off another bundle of glasswort, a salt marsh plant the women in the bathhouse also use to make soap. "Which ones?"

"The Cretan Idomeneus and Diomedes."

"What of Odysseus?" I cut a fresh piece of twine.

Isola shakes her head. "I've heard the soldiers speak of him, but I've yet to see him."

"What do the men say?"

"That he's more like a fox than a man. That his mouth will say one thing while his hands do another. Ithaca is more isolated than many of the other kingdoms. Because of this, Odysseus's men are more like family than crew. He values their lives above all. In turn, they follow him implicitly."

Isola hangs a bushel above our heads without pausing in her speech. She acts as if the words will turn to smoke if she doesn't push them out fast enough. "Odysseus cares nothing for the esteem of the other kings, and therefore isn't easily drawn into their conflicts. They call him in when they need a dispute settled, but they don't fully trust him."

I nod, processing this. "Anything else?"

"Yes." Isola glances across the mostly vacant infirmary. "The plague ravaged the Achaeans. Even more so than we thought. They lost five hundred men and depleted their supplies. The raids are necessary not just for morale but also to replenish their stores of food. As it stands, they'll run out of meat in a matter of weeks."

My pulse speeds under my skin. Trouble for the Achaeans means opportunity for Troy. And for us.

"Thank you, Isola. You've done well."

Pink colors her cheeks. "It's not so hard to listen."

"For some, it's the hardest thing of all." I start to ask her about the other women in the camps when a voice drifts across the infirmary.

"You there."

A warrior emerges from behind a heavy drape that must lead to a private living quarters. He is well past middle years with the barest patches of white at the base of his skull. Though he is smaller than most Achaeans, his wiry frame and quick steps speak of good health.

I take a hesitant step forward. "I'm Rhea. I'll be back and forth to help you as needed."

"As you can see, I've little need of extra hands at the moment. But I'm expecting guests shortly. You may serve wine in my rooms while Isola deals with our patients." He shoots the two men a scathing look. "Most afflictions can be handled with the proper care, but as of yet, there's no effective cure for stupidity."

"None of your disapproving looks, Machaon," says the one with the bandaged hand. "It isn't my fault that Amphorous is a cheat."

"And so you decided to break your hand on his face?" Machaon shakes his head in disgust. "Any six-year-old girl in Thessaly could throw a better punch." The healer turns to me wearing an aggrieved expression. "Athenians."

I'm searching for a way to respond when two more men enter the infirmary.

Though the first of the new arrivals is tall, the rounded slope of his shoulders makes him feel utterly unassuming. Or maybe that is a natural consequence of the company he keeps. The second man is shorter even than Machaon, with a barrel chest and a mane of unruly brown curls that falls in a tangle down his back. His ungroomed beard isn't the only thing that sets him apart. It's something about the way that he moves. One of his stocky legs is slightly more bowed than the other, creating a prowl rather than a stride. A gait I would know anywhere.

The king of Ithaca approaches Machaon with a rueful smile playing on his lips. One of his hands holds a wineskin. The other is wrapped in a bloodstained bandage.

"Odysseus." Machaon sighs. "I've seen more of you during these weeks of wet peace than I did through years of war."

"I've become clumsy in my old age." Odysseus's deep voice rumbles.

Machaon jerks his head toward the hearth before turning to me. "Fetch cloth and a bowl of water."

With trembling hands, I grab the required items and quickly bring them to where Machaon is unwinding the stained cloth from Odysseus's hand while the third man looks on.

Machaon raises a white brow at what he finds. "This wound is deep."

"It appears that I've become *very* clumsy."

"He would've wrapped it in a rag and been done with it," the taller man says, scratching a nose that juts prominently from his narrow face. "But I thought it best to have it looked after."

"You thought right, Polites," Machaon says. "Does someone want to tell me how this happened?" He douses the wound with a clear solution that smells of sour wine. Based on Odysseus's pained expression, I'm not far off the mark.

"My hands slipped while I was sharpening my blade."

"Your blade must be very dirty, Odysseus. It must also be shaped strangely like a rock."

Odysseus offers a shrug. Cunning and charm in equal measure. I file away every detail to impart to Andromache later.

Machaon studies him from below heavy brows before he moves to his table of wares. The moment his back is turned, the king of Ithaca looks directly at me. And winks.

I'm still staring slack-jawed when Machaon returns with a bitter-smelling poultice. "There's dung in that wound. We'll need to fight the fever before it sets in. I'll prepare a draught and have one of my girls deliver it to you."

"When?" Polites asks, concern for his friend obvious in the thin press of his lips.

"Tonight."

"Can you be more precise?" Odysseus asks airily.

"Why? What are you doing crawling around in the muck when the sun is low?" Machaon tugs sharply on the bandage. "On second thought, I'd rather not know."

I study Odysseus covertly, eager for every word. So far, I've learned nothing about how he and his men have managed to approach Troy's walls unseen. But my gut is screaming that this is exactly what he's doing in the darkest watches of the night. The thing that surprises me is that Machaon, one of the most trusted of all the Achaeans, does not.

What can that mean?

"My men and I are farmers by trade," Odysseus says, throwing his good arm around Polites's shoulders. "We are merely returning to our roots. There's some good land beyond the cut. It seemed a shame not to make the most of it."

"Keep your secrets." Machaon shakes his head at both men. "I'll send the salve within the hour if that pleases you."

Odysseus pulls the sleeve of his tunic down past the bandage. "Thank you, old friend. You are a credit to us."

"Thank me by staying out of my infirmary." He directs his next words to Polites. "I grow weary of his face."

Grinning, Odysseus prepares to take his leave when two more men enter. I know they are important not just by the fine clothes they wear, but also because of the way the wounded soldiers nearby sit up in their pallets. Polites moves to stand at Odysseus's right shoulder. Even Machaon comes to attention.

Odysseus inclines his head. "Nestor. Agamemnon. I pray you are both in good health."

Nestor, a man of advanced years with long white hair and a withered frame, nods politely. Beside him, Agamemnon extends no such courtesy.

I recognize the Achaean king from the battle between Paris and Menelaus. Up close, he is even more imposing than he seemed from the ramparts of Troy. And while he is physically the biggest man in the room, it's his air of self-importance that takes up most of the space. "We've not seen much of you lately, Odysseus." Agamemnon does not spare Polites so much as a glance of acknowledgment.

The king of Ithaca shrugs. "My men and I have been busy with our crops and our livestock."

"So it would seem," Agamemnon drawls.

"It is an admirable use of time." Nestor adopts a conciliatory tone. "Nothing good is born of boredom."

"You have the gift of wisdom, Nestor," Odysseus offers with a respect that is lacking in his treatment of Agamemnon—something the king of the Achaeans doesn't fail to notice.

"You would do well not to forget your responsibilities, Odysseus," Agamemnon says. "It won't serve for you to miss another assembly between the kings. One might think you prefer the company of pigs to people."

"I suppose it depends on the people." Odysseus smiles broadly.

"Once a farmer, always a farmer." Nestor slaps Odysseus on the back with what seems like forced cheerfulness. They share a silent look that ends with Odysseus bowing his head and backing away.

"We bid you both good evening. If the gods are willing, we will soon reap the rewards of a rich harvest." Odysseus inclines his head once more before ducking out into the dark with Polites on his heels. A weighty silence falls in their absence.

"Would you join me for a cup of wine?" Machaon extends the invitation to the two remaining kings, though I catch the wistful look he sends his worktable. He waits for them to disappear through the drapery to his private chambers before he speaks.

"Rhea, was it?"

I nod.

"Fetch wine from the side table and attend us."

Detecting the hint of urgency, I quickly mix a bowl of strong wine the way that Bodecca taught me. My eyes meet Isola's for a moment before I duck between the drapes.

The two kings and Machaon sit around a plush rug in a plain but serviceable living chamber. Keeping my gaze low, I place three cups in front of them.

"He's up to something," Agamemnon says as I serve him. "It's more than farming a few miserable plots of land beyond the cut. They say he sleeps all day. At night his movements can't be tracked. What farmer works by the light of the moon? Twice last week alone my heralds found him gone. Of course, his men cover for him. They're almost as bad as the Myrmidons."

"It may be wise to leave him be," Nestor suggests.

"Why?" Agamemnon drains half of his cup in one swallow and lifts it for me. "He is part of my army. It undermines my standing if I can't control the men I lead."

"Odysseus is one of the greatest weapons we have at our disposal," Nestor reasons. "If he wasn't, you wouldn't have gone through such extremes to make sure he sailed with us. Whatever plans he's hatching can only be to your benefit."

"I don't know what drives him. I can't trust a man whose wants I can't determine." Agamemnon takes another slow draw on his wine. "Why was he here, Machaon?"

"He cut his hand while sharpening his blade."

Machaon does not express the doubts he voiced to Odysseus. The omission seems significant somehow.

"Farming." Agamemnon spits.

The healer glances down at the gob of wine-tinged phlegm on his beautiful carpet, the only luxury in this otherwise stark room. Machaon's expression remains perfectly neutral.

"I should like to know where he creeps to," Agamemnon says, confirming what I had already suspected.

Whatever Odysseus's plans to take Troy, he alone is master of them.

"I shouldn't think he'll be creeping anywhere at the moment," Machaon says. "I told him I'd send a healing salve within an hour. Polites will ensure it is administered properly. He is the only one whose counsel Odysseus heeds."

Agamemnon's gaze runs to me for the first time. "Send it with the girl. They may be less careful around her than they would be with my heralds." His next words are for me alone. "Insist on delivering it into Odysseus's hands." He doesn't bother inquiring as to my name. "I want to know if he's in his settlement or off somewhere making me look a fool."

Machaon frowns as he moves to a side table lined with a wide variety of wicked-looking instruments, some made of ivory. Others of obsidian. He uses a wooden spoon to ladle a thick paste from a pot into a small clay jar. It smells strongly of honey and herbs. "Tell Odysseus to apply it twice daily. Run along, then." He hands it to me.

My gaze passes over the three men, each one looking at me to fulfill this task for his own private reasons. None of which I can guess. Without another word, I turn on my heels.

I'm halfway through the camp, nearing the cut, before I remember to breathe.

Odysseus's settlement is easy enough to identify. As I approach, I'm struck by the sounds and smells of livestock. Specifically, pigs.

A low stone wall surrounds the cluster of buildings belonging to the Ithacans. It's the only settlement other than Agamemnon's that is so clearly partitioned. With brisk steps, I present myself to the soldiers at the exterior gate. As soon as I speak Machaon's name, they usher me toward a large house. The hall inside is modest but comfortable. Filled with men who seem perfectly at home with one another around the central fire. They look at me curiously as I pass with the jar clutched in my hand.

An older warrior offers to take it, but I refuse, repeating Machaon's order.

"King Odysseus is occupied at the moment." The old man scowls.

"I'll wait."

"Suit yourself." He leads me past the open hearth into a hallway, where I am instructed to stand against the wall. Muttering under his breath, the old warrior leaves me to my own devices.

The rise and fall of conversation drifts toward me through a curtain hung several paces to my right. I look both ways before approaching.

"Agamemnon suspects something," a high voice says on the other side of the curtain.

"It would hardly be possible for our great king to be as stupid as he pretends," comes a deeper voice. Odysseus's. "We have done the necessary work and waited patiently for our moment. Now Athena has seen fit to reward our patience with an opportunity."

"How so?" asks the high voice.

"The Trojans have been grazing their herds at night on the east side of the city so as not to attract our notice," Odysseus's friend, Polites, answers. "We've heard the beasts lumbering through the east gates on our previous trips to their walls. Five hundred head with nothing but a handful of boys to attend them."

"Their archers are trained to watch the plains. They don't know we are right under their noses. It has given them a false sense of security," Odysseus says.

"A cattle raid . . . at night?" The third man laughs. "It's utterly without pageantry. Agamemnon would hate it."

"Which is exactly why it will work, Silinus." I can hear the smile in Odysseus's voice. "Agamemnon is too concerned with his own glory to see beyond the allure of gold. And so to appease his pride, we've rotted here for years. Well, men, I am done rotting. The Trojans depend on these cattle for survival. For all the strength of her walls, Troy's people cannot survive on a diet of stone." His tone gains an urgency that draws me closer to the curtain. "Their crops have flooded, same as ours. If we can take Troy's last food source, we can simultaneously starve them out and feed ourselves. All the treasures in Priam's palace won't be enough to save them. The old man will throw open the gates himself and welcome us inside. And we'll be waiting to oblige him."

My palms go slick with sweat around the jar in my hands.

"When do we move?" Polites asks.

"Tomorrow night," Odysseus replies. "Take some of our men. A handful will do. Tell the guards at the cut that we need more timber for our garden enclosure."

"And you?" A trace of caution permeates Polites's voice.

I lean closer to the curtain.

"Silinus and I will take the rest of the men and finish what we started. The moon will be full and the rains have held off for days. The plains should be dry enough. We are closer to victory than ever before, brothers. If Athena is good, we will set sail for home by the next high tide. It is what we have been waiting for. There is no one else I trust to do this, Polites."

"Then there is only one small matter left to attend," Polites says at last.

"It is already taken care of. It required greater skill than any of us could claim, so I have enlisted the help of Ajax the Great."

The jar almost slips from my grip. Ajax? What would Odysseus want with him? If Ven is to be believed, the Ithacans like to work alone.

"It seems you have thought of everything," Polites sighs.

"Don't I always?"

The silence from the other side of the door tells me their plans are set. Before I can pull myself back, footsteps sound from inside. I barely have enough time to jump out of the way before someone strides through the curtain.

Polites stops short at the sight of me. "What're you doing here?" he asks.

"Machaon sent me. I'm to deliver this salve to Odysseus."

"Leave it with me."

"But Machaon—"

"Knows that Odysseus and I were raised as brothers in the same cradle," Polites says not unkindly. "He won't fault you for leaving it in my care."

Having already gotten more than I came for, I press the salve into Polites's hands and walk as quickly as I can out of Odysseus's settlement without running. As soon as I am clear of the gates, I bend low, grabbing my knees.

The enormity of everything I've learned crushes the air from my lungs. I have to get back to Troy. Before it is too late. If I don't warn Andromache, Odysseus will strike a crippling blow on the eve of her festival, and the already dire situation in Troy will only become more—

"Rhea? What are you doing here?"

I turn around to find a mountain at my back.

"Are you all right?" Ajax leans forward, his green eyes searching my face with what looks like concern. But how could that be? He is an Achaean warrior. A killer.

"I was bringing something to King Odysseus."

"So late?"

He seems to take my silence as an invitation to speak. "I came to the bathhouse looking for you days ago. And the infirmary. When that yielded no result, I tried the women's quarters."

My blood runs cold. "You were looking for me . . . Why?"

"I wanted to thank you. For your help. And I wanted . . ." His hands fidget at his sides. "I wanted to give you something. But I was starting to think I had dreamed you."

His words barely register as my gaze runs west, where the darkness beckons. Lighter than it was even an hour ago. It won't be long now before the third watch of night ends and with it my chances of getting back to Troy.

"I . . . I don't live with the other women."

He frowns. "Then where do you live?"

I search for some way to explain my absence in the women's quarters and my presence here so late at night. Some story that won't implicate Ven.

Or Machaon.

Or Agamemnon.

Or myself, for that matter.

Ajax is watching me with patient expectancy, so I say the first words that come into my head. "I live here. With Odysseus."

"You belong to Odysseus?" Ajax's expression seems to fall. "I thought you worked in the bathhouse."

Ven's words play in my head. The ones she spoke about Achaean men and their codes of honor. If Ajax thinks I belong to Odysseus, he'll have no reason to seek me out again. In fact, doing so might be considered a slight to Odysseus's honor. And that's not something that a man would risk. Especially not for me.

"He allows me to work there and the infirmary when there's little else to do."

Ajax's gaze cuts across to Odysseus's settlement. "I see." He takes a step backward. "I'm sorry if I startled you. I'll let you get back."

The words have barely crossed his lips when I turn back to the infirmary where Agamemnon and the others are waiting. As soon as I'm done with them I can retrace my path across the plains. If the Mother goddess is on my side, I might even make it back to the walls in time.

I have barely taken three steps when Ajax calls out my name again.

I turn.

"What time does Odysseus retire for the night?" he asks after a pause long enough to make me aware of my thudding pulse.

"Usually around the end of the second watch?" It comes out like a question even though I don't mean it to.

A strange sort of battle takes over his features. He gazes over Odysseus's settlement, and his jaw sets in a rigid line. "Meet me then. Tomorrow. At the tomb of the old gods."

"I don't think . . ."

"I have something for you." He says it quickly. As if to prevent either one of us from taking the time to ponder all the reasons this should never happen. "It won't take long."

My heart does a running jump into my throat.

"A few minutes. And then if you wish, I won't bother you again," he adds when I still refuse to speak.

Every part of me wants to refuse. Tomorrow night, Odysseus moves against Troy, making the plain more dangerous than ever. But if Ajax decides to ask about me in the camps again, my web of lies will come quickly undone. If I meet him tomorrow, he'll have no cause to doubt me or feel slighted. With some prompting, he may even reveal whatever secret part he is playing in Odysseus's plans. I can find out whatever he knows, and then I'll never have to think about him again.

"As you say."

Ajax smiles down at me from his great height. The expression softens the hard panes of his face, making him seem even younger than I initially thought. "Until tomorrow, Rhea."

37

ANDROMACHE

"DO IT AGAIN." I shift my weight in the chair Nhorcys the Strong carried outside for me. Above my head, the early-morning sun beats against the sail Glaucus and his Lycians strung up to provide some shade. It seems Queen Hecuba's daily offerings to the Dioscuri have paid off, as the Divine Twins have stopped the rains and turned the weather in time for the festival in their honor.

Which means our enemies will soon be stirring.

In the training yard opposite my perch, two dozen mounted Thracians circle a chariot while Pelasgian spearmen and Paeonian archers provide them with cover. The allies expressed their desire to train, and I have been more than happy to oblige them.

We have been drilling from dawn until dusk, working their bodies so their idle minds don't wander back to the homes they came from. By tomorrow's festival, they will be ready to present the fruits of their efforts while the Trojan army sat on its hands. And so will I.

Or that, at least, is how I envision it. But the spectacle before me tells of a different fate. It's the first time the allies have actually sparred with weapons, and as with most things, it has proven more difficult in practice than in theory.

Everywhere I look, men and weapons fly haphazardly. Compared to the neat lines of Hector's rank-and-file Trojan foot soldiers, it is nothing short of unmitigated chaos. With arrows and spears replacing the falling rain, it leaves the men little room for error in their maneuvers.

Hippothous hops the fence and lands in front of me. Since our first meeting, I have never once glimpsed the Pelasgian without a scowl on his face and a wineskin in his hand. His tunic, however, comes and goes.

"We've been running this exercise for hours," he slurs.

"And we will keep running it," I tell him. "Until you can do it stone-cold sober."

He bends over me so that our eyes are perfectly level. "Running seems to be a favorite pastime here in Troy." A bead of sweat travels down his nose to splatter my arm. "My men are tired of sprinting in circles. If we do not get to fight, all the rest is pointless."

I am well aware these men would rather keep drinking away their sorrows, but Hippothous is the only one who has the nerve to say so to my face. Repeatedly. His discontent is catching. It can be heard in the piercing clang of bronze spears on ox-hide shields. The frustrated thud of arrows striking their targets. These men crave more than drills, and I am beginning to doubt that even the festival games will appease them.

"If you and your Pelasgians aren't up to the task, don't let us keep you. The Achaeans aren't exactly trembling at your shirtless backs." I consider standing, but instead, I lean back farther in my chair. "Now if you don't mind, the rest of us have work to do."

My dismissal is not all for show. We are running out of time. At the festival, my allied captains must stand out in every competition and show the Citadel their worth. The more unusual their feats of strength, the better.

I just pray these games followed by my feast in their honor are enough to keep them in Troy until more allies arrive from Thrace. And from farther north along the Black Sea, if my messenger can even locate where Penthesilea is currently wandering.

Hippothous stalks back to his men. As he does, he passes Glaucus heading toward me and smacks his wineskin into the Thracian's chest. Glaucus starts, but Hippothous is already using both hands to pick up his spear and rejoin the drill.

Still holding the wineskin, Glaucus takes up a position beside my chair. "Are you sure this will make a difference?" He watches one of his men dodge a Paeonian arrow just in time.

"We will let the king himself decide once he witnesses our warriors outshining every Trojan in tomorrow's competition."

A gust of wind brings the scent of roasting meat from the courtyard. My stomach churns. "A moment, Captain." Turning sideways, I dry-heave into the basket already filled with the remains of this morning's breakfast.

The greasy aroma in the air may make the men drool with anticipation, but I can't seem to banish the effects of the nauseating smoke. How I wish someone had told me these early days of pregnancy would be my war. Worth the fight at every turn, though I'd have preferred to know the nature of the adversary lurking around my gates. For the past week, I've survived on nothing but bread, and I can't help but long for a sympathetic word, a kindness only Rhea or Bodecca might give. But Bodecca is busy preparing food for several hundred, and Rhea returned to the Achaean camps to do the job I tasked her with. Alone. While I sit here under a sail trying to hold down liquids as several dozen men grapple in the dirt on my behalf. Though at the moment, I think more than a few of them would take a swing at me, given the chance.

Another wave of nausea strikes, and I bend over my basket.

For the first time, I am beginning to understand the appeal of the sisterhood that mothers speak of, similar to the warrior bonds formed on the open plain. Only a woman's battle isn't against other mortals but the silent suffering and monotony that comes with sustaining a new life.

I was never close to my own mother. Achilles took her from me right when I needed her most. Bodecca, at least, knows what to do if not what to say. She fries my bread lightly in oil, but she hasn't exactly been a source of female encouragement. Once, when I was trying not to retch, she simply handed me a cloth and said, "I would tell you this will get better soon. But I would be lying."

Glaucus offers me the wineskin. Nodding my thanks, I swill the liquid around my mouth before spitting it back out again.

"Water with lemon. That's what you need."

I stare up at Nhorcys the Strong through strands of sweaty hair. The stocky Phrygian rubs down the muscles of one of his massive legs with a handful of oil that he also uses to smooth the ends of his intricate braids.

Could he possibly see what the others do not?

"I have six sisters," he says, as if that explains everything. Perhaps it does.

But it doesn't assure me Nhorcys will keep my secret if he indeed suspects it.

"It is the cattle fat. I am sick of smelling it." I force down a sip of sour wine.

"Of course, Harsa," Nhorcys says with a telling bow of his head.

I nod, satisfied with his discretion. "Have them do the drill again."

The chaos unfolds anew when a shadow catches my eye. Rhea bursts into the yard. She is red-faced, wet, and shivering.

I jump up from my seat, all sickness forgotten. As bad as I feel, Rhea looks a hundred times worse.

Memories of the night I prayed and waited for her in the temple of the Mother swirl. All the guilt and fear come rushing back to me like the tide.

"What's wrong? Are you hurt?" If she is, I will never forgive myself for letting her go. Again. "Rhea, I—"

My words drop off when she falls shivering into my arms.

"Here." I try to wrap a blanket around her, but Rhea's fingers dig into my skin. She leans forward and with great effort manages to speak through chattering teeth. Once she starts, she cannot stop.

All other thoughts cease.

"You are sure?" I ask.

"I'm sure." Her bluish mouth trembles. "I heard it from Odysseus's own lips."

I tighten the blanket around her shoulders. "Go. Get a warm bath and some sleep."

She nods. "I'm expected in the camps again soon. But Odysseus will attack the herds. Tonight." Her hands wrap around mine. "This is our chance. Your chance."

Her meaning is as clear as the summer runoff from Mount Ida. This attack could expose Odysseus's secret route to the walls, or, even better, lead to the capture of Odysseus himself. Either way, we would make the Ithacan's gamble an opportunity to show Hector that the risks of Rhea's small army have been worth it. As my gaze passes over Troy's allies, it occurs to me that *this* army may also have a part to play.

Rhea makes for the courtyard behind our house, her steps slow. Another wayward gust of wind. With a groan, I purge the wine I dared to take.

A dirty cloth appears before my face. I grab it from Glaucus and wipe my mouth. He stares at me with the same dull eyes of the slaughtered heifers Bodecca's kitchen maids are grilling over an outdoor flame. It seems these herds, Troy's greatest source of security, have become the target painted on her back.

Fortunately for us, when it comes to strategy, the farmer king of Ithaca and I like to plow the same fallow fields.

That Odysseus will act alone tonight without the knowledge of the other Achaean kings comes as no surprise. The arrogant Agamemnon would never sanction such an underhanded move. For him, *kleos* is everything, and Odysseus's plan is as inglorious as they come.

Whereas if we catch the Achaeans on their way to raid our cattle, the glory is ours.

A smile spreads. What would King Priam do if my allied captains marched into the festival arena carrying the heads of Ithacans on the tips of their spears?

"Have you seen Prince Hector's brother?" I ask Glaucus, another idea sparking. Since we began our training, Polydorus and his two hounds have been constantly underfoot. For their part, the allies seem to have taken the young prince on as their own sort of pet.

"I believe Hippothous is teaching him how to throw a spear."

I stifle a groan at the thought of what other things he is learning from the ill-tempered Pelasgian. "The boy has many better role models to choose from."

"The prince is more than a boy. He is an eager pupil to anyone who will treat him like the man he will soon become. The man Troy needs him to become."

"Are all Lycians so insolent?" I ask with a smile.

Glaucus returns the grin. "Need I remind you that Sarpedon is my cousin?"

"Your point is well taken. Go find Polydorus, and I will see what I can do to put your counsel to good use."

Once Glaucus has left to fetch the prince, I stifle another rise of bile and shout, "Pandarus!"

The captain puts down his bow and jogs over. "Yes, Harsa."

I rise to my feet. "I have a job for your men."

Glaucus returns with Polydorus. "You wished to speak with me, sister?"

"Yes, and this concerns your men too, Glaucus."

Hector's youngest brother bounds toward me like the child he still is, no matter what Glaucus claims. At fourteen, he is even younger than the sparrow boy who haunts my dreams.

In Polydorus's hands rests a Pelasgian spear, and a pointed Phrygian hat sits jauntily on his head. An ache for my own brothers, whose laughter and horseplay once filled my father's hall, wells up in my chest. This war did not spare them. It may not spare Polydorus either.

But I want my own child to inherit a different world.

"Hector has asked you to oversee the herds, has he not?"

Polydorus shrugs. "Father won't put me in charge of anything else. So I get the dull task of telling the drivers where to graze cows."

I nod. Hector and Paris may be the king's hope and joy, but Priam's youngest son is his slowly beating heart. And has been protected as such. Every year the boy ages serves as a stark reminder of how much time we have all lost.

"Tonight, Polydorus, that task will be far from dull. Tell the cattle drivers they have the evening off."

When I explain the rest of my plan, Glaucus's cheek twitches more than once. "How certain are you about this information, Harsa?"

"I never speak unless I am certain. But do not ask me about my sources. Lives depend on your discretion. I also needn't explain that the King's Council would not approve of these methods if they discovered them."

Glaucus frowns. "Can't say I am overly concerned with the council's feelings."

"I don't like it," Pandarus says. "What manner of men fight like cowards under the cover of night?"

I don't expect Pandarus to understand. His blood runs with as much nobility as the high-born Aeneas. But as boys, they spent their summers on the cool slopes of Mount Ida, learning the ancient ways of warfare. Methods passed down since before the settlement at Troy even had a name.

"If I am not mistaken, most of the mountain men you lead were once farmers and shepherds who know what it is to be hunted by a lurking predator they cannot see . . ." I retrieve a torch stick from the sand and thrust it toward Pandarus's chest.

"Trust me when I tell you, they will know their way around the night."

38

RHEA

MY DOUBTS ARE a building scream as I stare down the darkness ahead. With the light all but faded from the sky outside the temple doors, it is nearly time.

"Don't meet him."

I frown at Cyrrian from my seat on the lip of the offering shelf.

We are alone in the temple of the Mother. I didn't tell Andromache about my meeting with Ajax. Just like I didn't tell her the truth about Helen. With Odysseus setting his sights on Troy's cattle tonight, she already carries the weight of the city on her shoulders. All the same, if something should happen . . .

I won't leave Andromache to worry what's become of me ever again.

Cyrrian listened as I recounted almost everything. I couldn't bring myself to share what Ajax told me about his mark. It has no bearing on our plans, and still, I berated myself for protecting the Achaean by keeping his secret. Judging by the savage glower on Cyrrian's face, I'd already shared too much.

Cyrrian's demand echoes loudly in the otherwise silent temple.

"I don't have a choice. If he goes looking for me again and doesn't find me, he'll suspect something is wrong."

"Then don't go back," Cyrrian offers with a carelessness that sets my teeth on edge.

"I can't stop now. Tonight, we have the upper hand, but if a next time comes, we can't be caught unprepared. Ajax is helping Odysseus. He knows something. Maybe even how Odysseus is reaching our walls unseen. If I can get him to reveal it, Andromache would—"

Cyrrian kneels in front of me so that his staggering eyes are level with mine. "I am not talking about Andromache. I am talking about you. Have you no care for your own life?"

"Of course I do!" My voice rises the way it always does when Cyrrian and I argue, which is whenever we speak. "It's one meeting. I'll let him say what he will, discover what he knows, and then I'll take my leave."

Cyrrian's nostrils flare. "You are far too clever to be this naïve."

His words are a double-edged blade. Praise on one side. Insult on the other. As always with Cyrrian of the Two Shadows, one side cuts just a little deeper.

I glare at him. "I've survived this long because of my ability to judge people well. Ajax means me no harm."

"Ajax, son of Telamon, is no ordinary Achaean. He is easily the deadliest warrior to set foot on our shores despite the odes the bards heap on his cousin. More importantly, he is a man." Cyrrian's knuckles turn white against the edge of the offering shelf. "I'm afraid you aren't so good at judging those."

"I am not a child."

"No, Rhea. You aren't." The air between us grows smothering.

My face blazes as I study the stone floor, wishing I could sink beneath it. This is another one of Cyrrian's games. A way to put me in my place by forcing me to speak the truth we both know full well: I am no Helen. No Chryseis or Briseis. Whatever Ajax's reason for meeting me, it is unlikely to involve impugning my honor.

"I'm not questioning your loyalty, Rhea." Cyrrian's tone gentles. "It's his intentions I don't trust."

Tears prick my eyes. This is the cruelest sort of mockery. I am not the sort of prize men fight wars over. I'm not even the sort of woman who merits a lingering glance. That he would manipulate my secret desire to believe it just to rob me of this one chance to use what gifts the Mother gave me hurts more than it should.

I take a deep breath and swallow any bitter words I might say. Cyrrian doesn't want to be here. He wants to be with Hector lying in wait for Odysseus's men near the east gate. Instead of fighting for Troy, he will spend this night sitting in a cold stone temple, waiting for me, someone he does not even particularly like. I don't begrudge him his anger. But I also don't deserve it.

"Would you say the same to Andromache?" I ask.

"I wouldn't presume to tell that woman anything. I place too high a value on my own life."

"And what of Salama? Where were your dire warnings for her?"

Exasperation flashes across his handsome face. "You aren't like either of them."

"How? How am I different?"

For once, he does not have a ready answer. But I do. It's the same as it's been all of my life. I am too small, too weak, too helpless. I am the one who needs protecting.

"You just are," he says at last.

I turn toward the waiting dark. "Help me or leave. Either way, you won't stop me."

"I won't take your choices from you. No matter how witless they are." Cyrrian seems to release all the vehemence of that statement in one audible breath.

"I'll be back before morning." I'm already moving toward the tunnel. Odysseus will have his hands full with Andromache's allies on the east side of the city. I am headed northwest. It shouldn't take long to pacify Ajax and learn his part in Odysseus's plans. The festival is set to begin after sunrise, and I wouldn't miss Andromache's moment of triumph for all the gold in Egypt.

Please, Mother. Be with her tonight.

Fingers wrap around my wrist. The intimacy of Cyrrian's touch sends my pulse racing. My breath releases in a gasp so sharp he cannot help but hear it.

"Rhea." The catch in Cyrrian's voice begs me to look at him, but I can't. I'm still too humiliated by the truths he made me admit. Even to myself.

"What?"

"I . . . Be careful. Please."

"I am always careful." I wait for him to release my wrist. When he doesn't, I finally meet his gaze. Mysteries swim in his eyes. For one hopeful moment, I think they might spill from his lips. But in the end, Cyrrian does what he does best. He clenches his jaw, and he keeps his secrets to himself.

"My path will keep me far from the plain where Odysseus and his men will be moving," I say, even though Cyrrian knows this path better than anyone. After all, he was the one who charted it for me. "I'll return before the sun," I promise, and then I crawl through the tunnel without looking back.

But Cyrrian's words haunt me all the way to the Achaean camp.

The circular walls of the ancient shrine glow faintly in the moonlight up ahead. Nerves tangle in my stomach as I watch it from the shadows.

Is Cyrrian right? Am I walking into a trap?

"I thought you'd changed your mind."

I spin to the right just as Ajax steps out of the shadows in front of the latrines.

I force thoughts of Cyrrian aside and lift my chin. "I was kept later than expected."

"By Odysseus?" Ajax stares out over the swamp, the cords in his neck bunching. The question feels weighted. Does he know I lied about belonging to the Ithacan king?

If so, coming here was a mistake.

"No, Odysseus is busy tonight." I offer the truth and wait for some reaction. Some sign of recognition from Ajax. There is none. "I was doing errands for the infirmary," I say to hide my confusion.

"More stitching?" A half smile plays on his lips. The first time I saw it, I thought the expression sly. The more I watch Ajax, the more I realize there is nothing sly about him. If anything, the smile is almost . . . shy.

"Not since my last attempt."

Ajax moves toward me as if he's afraid any sudden movement will send me running. It isn't far from the truth.

"What did you want with Odysseus last night?" I ask the question before I can lose my nerve.

Ajax frowns down at me, searching. "He asked me to build something for him. I had come to tell him that the work was finished."

"You built something for Odysseus?"

That smile again. "I have a reputation for being good with my hands." The smile evaporates when he realizes how that sounds coming from a man many call the Butcher of Attica. "I built him a cart," Ajax says hurriedly. "One that could be easily broken down into smaller pieces and just as easily put back together. He needs it to move farm equipment across the cut."

His sincerity is impossible to deny. It fills me with disappointment. Whatever part Ajax has played in Odysseus's schemes, he has done so unwittingly.

If there is any more to know, it will not come from Ajax.

"I'll lift you up over the wall," he offers.

His body dwarfs mine, but it is the warmth emanating from him that has me taking a quick step backward. "Is that . . . really necessary?" This meeting has been a waste. The faster we conclude it, the better it will be for everyone.

The corner of his mouth twitches again.

No, not sly. But then again, not completely shy either.

"Is it the curse that makes you nervous, Rhea? Or is it me?"

"You." My response is immediate.

He nods. The gesture is defeated somehow. "Is it because of what they say? About the things I've done?"

I find myself answering his question with the same earnestness with which it was asked. "No. It's because I don't know what you want from me."

Surprise flickers in his eyes. "I want to give you something. By the fire, where you can see it. That's all. On my honor."

There are few things I think of less highly than Achaean honor. Nevertheless, his face is utterly without artifice. From what I've seen of the Achaean kings, this straightforwardness may set Ajax apart even more so than his size.

"All right. Just for a few minutes." I will let him give me what he wants, and then he will have no reason to come searching for me again. It isn't what I came for, but it is better than nothing. "This time, I prefer to try the climb on my own."

"Very well." His eyes study the ground before returning to mine. "I won't let you fall."

My pulse sounds in my ears as I face the least intimidating part of the wall. Using the few available footholds, I work my way slowly to the top. Triumphant, I glance down only to find the giant shaking his head.

"What?"

"I was just thinking that you climb about as well as you sew."

I stare at him in bewilderment. Is this beast of a man . . . teasing me?

Yes, I realize. He is. It catches me off guard, just as he means it to.

"Not all of us have legs as long as oars," I tell him.

He grins up at me, and his smile could almost make me forget who and what he is.

Despite my head start, Ajax gets to the ground first. Once again, there is a fire burning at the heart of the shrine. It throws flickering light over the walls, creating a glow that radiates around Ajax's golden head as we face each other inside the confines of the four standing stones. The running shadows highlight the square planes of his jaw and his rugged cheekbones.

I take another step back.

At my retreat, a shadow passes over his features.

He knows that I am afraid of him.

He doesn't want me to be.

"It's only a small token of appreciation." He says the words as if they've been rehearsed many times.

"You didn't have to do that." In fact, I wish more than anything that he hadn't.

"And you didn't have to help me, but here we are."

He reaches into the small sack attached to his war belt, removes a lump of cloth, and places the bundle in my hand. It is solid. No bigger than a loom weight and much lighter.

I stare at the bundle as if it might erupt on my palm.

A low laugh escapes Ajax where he's watching me from his dizzying height.

"What's so amusing?" I ask.

The dimple flashes at the edge of his mouth. "You." He grips the back of his neck. "You look absolutely terrified."

A smile tugs at the corner of my lips before my sense returns. Along with all the reasons I shouldn't linger. "My mother told me to beware of strangers bearing gifts."

This time he laughs outright. The sound echoes off the stones and into my chest, where it loosens something I hadn't known was wound tight.

He rubs both hands over the stubble on his jaw as if he can't for the life of him decide what he's doing here.

He is not alone.

"Well, Rhea, Anatolian girl with the name of a Greek goddess, mine told me to always accept a gift freely given."

This time, my frown is instant. It prompts another round of laughter from the giant, silent this time, but no less real.

I unfold the cloth and raise the object to the light. My heart does a strange sideways dance.

It is a horse. A Phrygian mare in full stride. Carved from a single piece of wood. The figurine steals my breath. There's so much movement to it. So much life. I stare at it as if I half expect it to gallop off my palm.

A strange burning starts in my eyes as I raise them to Ajax, watching me intently from his post against the stones.

One look at my face, and shutters fall across his. "You don't like it." He nods, accepting the verdict with a proud stoicism that reminds me of Hector. Unlike Hector, the traces of Ajax's disappointment shine through.

"It is beautiful."

He searches my expression, and then that smile breaks free again, so bright I'm forced to drop my gaze to the figurine in my hand.

"You said your father raised horses. I thought . . . it might remind you of home."

It's as if someone captured my past and my present and all my dreams for the future and shaped them into a single figurine.

"Where did you find something like this?" I force the words past the thickness in my throat.

"I made it."

My eyes drop to his giant's hands. How?

The craftsmanship is unique. Like nothing I've ever seen. It's as if the spirit of the animal has been enshrined in the wood itself. I can't even imagine how many hours it must've taken him to create something like this.

Ajax shrugs. Color stains his high cheekbones. "Like I said, I've always liked to make things. Small things, especially." His gaze races back to mine.

"My father once told me true gifts are callings from the gods."

His light dims. "And mine said whittling wood was a pastime for cripples and eunuchs."

"That isn't true." My fierce defense surprises no one more than me.

Ajax's dimple returns, but only fleetingly. "When one of our servants found the figurines I'd carved in secret, my father smashed them in his megaron while his men looked on."

"How old were you?"

"Six." He wears his shame openly, and for a moment, I see the boy he must have been. One who might have possessed the body of a man, but who had not yet grown the armor to match.

This time, the swell of sympathy is impossible to suppress. "What did you do?"

"My father sent me to Chiron so that I might train to become a warrior. Chiron waited until my father had gone, and then he gave me back my knife. He told me that if I followed his teachings, no man on earth would ever again take what was mine. I suppose in the end, my father and I both got what we wanted." The lines of his face harden, and I glimpse the warrior Cyrrian described. Brutal. Utterly without mercy. But as quickly as he comes, he disappears. "I was born to sack cities and bring honor to my father's line."

I stare down at the beautiful figurine. "You Achaeans speak much of honor. I think perhaps it means something different to you than it does to me."

He doesn't answer, and I realize I've given away too much.

"I had better go." I turn toward the lowest part of the wall, eager to escape this place and the safety Ajax has tricked me into feeling. Cyrrian will be waiting for me, and I don't want to cross paths with Odysseus as he moves in the dark.

"I want to see you again."

I turn slowly.

"Please," Ajax adds with an odd formality that has me staring as if he has sprouted a Gorgon head.

"Why?"

He rakes his fingers through his brassy mane. "Because I like listening to you talk." His hand drops back to his side. "Because I like the way you listen when I talk."

"I'm not much for talking."

That dimple flashes again. "True. But the few words you say are wise."

The ground I am standing on feels unsteady. "And you like this about me?"

"I thought we might be friends."

"Friends," I repeat dumbly.

Ajax squares his massive shoulders. "You asked me what I want from you. That's the answer."

His words make no sense. He is a warrior. And he believes I'm the property of Odysseus, his peer. For any sort of contact to exist between us, I wouldn't be the only one accepting risk.

"I don't think that's a good idea."

What it is, is sheer madness.

"I can't argue with that." Ajax tosses a stick sideways into the fire. "If you refuse, I'll understand."

I need time to breathe . . . to think. There may be an opportunity here. One hidden below the more obvious danger. Ajax is a member of King Agamemnon's inner circle. He's in a position to know many things I might never otherwise learn. Not in months or seasons at the bathhouse or the infirmary. Meeting with him could be a way directly into Agamemnon's head. Whether or not Hector and Andromache ensnare Odysseus tonight, such insight beyond the Ithacan's domain would be priceless to Troy. And still, a small voice inside cries out a warning.

"Do you not have friends? Among the men?"

Ajax shrugs. "There are many men I would kill for. Some that I would die for. If that's what you mean."

I'm not sure that it is. "So why don't you seek them out?"

Another stick hits the fire, sending up a cloud of sparks. "I've grown tired of their company." Flames dance. "I've grown tired of who I am when I am with them."

"And who is that?"

"Ajax the Great." He makes two fists. "A man who was born to break things."

"And is that not who you are?"

"That is exactly who I am," Ajax replies in a quiet voice I've not yet heard him use.

"Then why do you do it?"

Ajax laughs again, but this time, the sound is dark. Wrong. "At birth I was twice the size of a normal babe. My father said it was a sign that I was destined for battle. What I want doesn't matter. Only what is expected of me. But sometimes . . ."

"Sometimes what?"

"Sometimes I wish that the gods had been a touch more sparing when they made me."

His words echo through the most secret parts of me. The ones I keep hidden even from myself.

"Do you believe our fates are truly fixed, or is it something we have the power to alter?" Ajax asks before I can compose myself.

"I don't know." I turn over the beautiful figurine, work of a giant's hands. "But perhaps the truth of who we are lies less in how we are made and more in the things we do when nobody else is watching."

My thoughts race back to Andromache, defending a city that will never know all she risked to save it. And then to Helen. Her fingers digging into the soil on the top of Kallikolone as lightning flashed and rain streaked down her bare face.

"And if someone is always watching?" Ajax asks quietly.

"Better than passing through the world a shadow." I place the figurine inside my basket and wrap my arms around it. "Do deeds even matter if there is no one to witness them?"

"They matter."

The light has touched Ajax's face again. The one that has nothing to do with the fire. He doesn't move toward me, but I can sense some strong emotion rising inside him. "Maybe that's what this shrine can be for us. A place to be who we would if the world gave us a choice. A place to live only the truth."

But even the closest of relationships are filled with truths unspoken.

Andromache's face flashes before my mind again. The warmth in her gaze as she pressed a prayer into my forehead. As she thanked the Mother night after night for my safe return even as I failed her. "And if the truth hurts? If it has the power to destroy everything you've grown to love?"

It is Ajax's turn to frown. "If the truth destroys, it is like fire. Returning everything to soil so that something new might grow. Nothing beautiful has ever grown from a lie."

All the breath leaves my lungs in a rush.

Ajax sits up straighter. "What is it? What did I say?"

"Nothing. Everything." A laugh escapes as I shake my head. The first thing I'll do when I return to Troy is tell Andromache about Helen. No matter the consequences. I owe it to them both. A strange lightness comes over me at having made the decision, and it does not escape me that I have the strangest person to thank for it. "I think perhaps you are the wise one."

He grins and clasps his hands behind his head. "I suppose there is a first time for everything."

I bite my cheek to hide my smile while I consider what he is offering. "Odysseus wouldn't like me coming here."

"He wouldn't," Ajax agrees, instantly sober. "Discovery wouldn't be good for either of us."

No. But not for the reasons he supposes.

"I'll see that no harm comes to you. You have my word."

My grip on my basket tightens. I told Cyrrian I wouldn't linger, but . . . what harm could it do to stay just a little longer? Odysseus will move his men when the moon is high. Waiting here until the third watch will give Andromache and Hector the time they need to capture Odysseus, making the path back to Troy safer than it has ever been.

"What would we have to talk about?" I ask.

Ajax grins and unwinds his tall frame to sit down by the fire. I mirror him at a safe distance. As if the meager space could somehow protect me from him. Ajax doesn't laugh, but his eyes dance all the same.

"You could start by telling me more about your family. And your horses."

So I do. Carefully, at first, and then not carefully at all. Words tumble from my mouth, and Ajax collects them eagerly. Listening quietly until it's his turn. And then he tells me about Salamis, his home, about his brothers and sisters, and Chiron, the old man who gave him back his knife and his pride.

Our voices blend together, rising and falling with the wind. They rise and fall for a long, long time.

39

ANDROMACHE

"YOU ARE ASKING me to do *what*?"

Hector stares at me across the fortress of flatbread Bodecca has engineered on the kitchen table in preparation for the festival.

The night has fallen black and thick over the courtyard outside, where Bodecca and our servants are covering enough roasted meat to feed the entire Lower City. It is already long past the hour the servants would normally retire to bed, but tonight, none of us will sleep.

"Have the guards above the east gate stand down." When Hector's stony face does not change, I add, "It's the only way the allies will be able to intercept Odysseus without alerting the Citadel. If Odysseus senses something isn't right, he will not step foot into the trap we have set for him. There can be no mistakes, Hector. This is about more than our cattle. Tonight we apprehend Odysseus once and for all, and we finally learn how he is getting so close to our walls."

Hector has to hear me. Not only so this plan can succeed, but so I can execute it knowing his trust in me has been restored.

He silently weighs my words. One day we may have the chance to be a normal wife and husband who argue and are then given the space to fully reconcile, but that is not a luxury afforded to Troy's commander and his Harsa. Too many people depend on us.

"If the east gate is left unguarded, then I insist on having Peirous and his mounted Thracians ready and waiting just inside," Hector says finally. "They will ride down Odysseus if Pandarus's and Glaucus's men aren't able to subdue them on their own. We cannot risk our cattle. Not even for a prize as hefty as Odysseus. Troy's people will not survive without them. Especially when we have already slaughtered so many for the festival."

I set down my cup of tea so hard it echoes. "But if we send out riders, Odysseus will know we are waiting for him." And we also cannot afford to raise his suspicions.

"He won't if Odysseus's head ends up at the tip of one of our men's spears." Hector's eyes glisten with a bloodlust I don't often see. But there is something else. The desire to protect a girl who has become like our own, all while doing his duty to the men under his command.

I gesture to the hearth behind us. "And I would love to hang that fine display on our wall. But using the horses *must* be a last resort."

Hector nods. "Agreed. We will not open the east gate unless it is to save our allies or usher in prisoners."

"There is one more thing." I begin with some hesitation. "You ought to let Polydorus join you at the gate. Even better, give him some simple task to keep him occupied. We don't want him moping around the Citadel raising suspicions."

Hector sighs. "He hasn't stopped pestering me about letting him fight. Perhaps I can have him escort the prisoners we capture back inside the walls."

Merely envisioning Odysseus being prodded by the eager boy's spear is enough to lighten my mood. "I hear the king of Ithaca has a son close to the same age. Perhaps Polydorus can remind him of what he's missing back home."

Hector doesn't give up a smile, but I see it treading water in his eyes. He may be on the verge of forgiving me for all I kept from him, but before things can ever be fully right between us, I must show him it was worth everything those secrets cost.

"You do understand what is at stake?" he asks.

Only the loss of our primary food source, resulting in the entire city's starvation. And on the eve of the festival where the succession of Hector to Troy's throne *must* be confirmed.

"I do."

As Hector puts on his helmet, the veins in his forearms throb. We are risking everything, but once he dons that horsehair plume, Troy's commander will not show fear. Hector pushes out the kitchen chair in one forceful motion, nearly undoing my own composure. Such a simple gesture that harbors all the emotions he must keep hidden. I only hope that after my own reveal tomorrow, we have a few moments to release those feelings in our long-cold bed.

Hector marches toward the kitchen door. When he reaches it, he turns, jaw clenched with all the words we have no time to speak. He strides back to me, planting a brisk kiss on top of my head.

"Stay inside the walls, Andromache. No matter how things fare beyond them."

Once Hector is gone, Bodecca and her kitchen maids enter to prepare for their own part in this plan. Pots of honey salve and strips of linen to dress wounds cover Bodecca's workspace, a preparation for what may await us if my mission fails. I pull a chair up to the fire, but all I can do is stare at the glowing embers. Minutes pass. Perhaps more.

I hate waiting. I hate it even more when I must do it in silence. The last time I spent time in this kitchen, Paris's trophy sat across from me with her pleading, perfect eyes. What has become of Helen? I wonder. I haven't seen her floating around the Citadel in some time. Perhaps Paris's shame following the duel has become her own.

A wife's shame I will surely share in if these risks I convinced Hector to take backfire.

"The water doesn't warm any faster the harder you stare at it." Bodecca drops several bundles of herbs down on the table. After untying the twine, she crushes the dried lavender petals into the pot, releasing a scent that does not sit well with me. But it is necessary. If any of Pandarus's or Glaucus's men are hurt, they have strict orders to be brought here and only here.

"I pray none of it will be needed." A growl erupts from my throat, causing Bodecca to startle. "I hate doing nothing."

"I'm glad you think so highly of my work," Bodecca snaps back. "If you need a task, you could always find more help. Flesh wounds don't dress themselves."

Other than a few of Bodecca's kitchen girls who can be trusted to keep quiet, who else would I ask?

Unprompted, Bodecca shoots me a leveling glance.

"No."

"She's a trained healer, that's all I'm saying."

"And an even more proficient liar," I reply. "It's too dangerous. Paris can't find out about tonight. Not when his concubine has grown too big for her tunic in more ways than one. He would do anything to ensure that the succession tomorrow goes his way."

Bodecca releases a long sigh. "Where will you go to watch?"

I narrow my eyes at this old woman who has gotten too good at reading my thoughts. "It must be high if I am to see as far as the grazing fields to the east of the Lower City. Even higher than the ramparts."

"There is only one place, then." Bodecca soaks a handful of linen strips in the boiling mixture, stirring it with a long spoon. My mouth goes dry. Cassandra's tower is the highest point in the city by far, but the thought of entering her lair stirs a dormant fear within me.

"Make sure you are armed," Bodecca orders. "It is a full moon. Who knows what face the princess will be wearing."

If there is a voice within Cassandra that isn't terrifying, I haven't met it yet.

"You are an oracle of good news, Bodecca."

The woman scoffs as I impulsively kiss her cheek. Then I depart to my rooms before the scent of lavender grows too strong.

Penthesilea's breastplate is laid out on the bed.

Tears scratch at the back of my throat. Hector knows better than anyone why a commander should dress the part, whether leading the charge from the front or standing at the rear as a figurehead.

Hector also knows me.

I put on the breastplate, but it is tighter than it once was and will no longer cinch around my middle. An indication that my Amazon armor would be useless if I actually entered the fray. Even though I won't be, I grab my bow and quiver, heeding Bodecca's warning.

The walk to the Dardanian gate is short, and the guards do not stop me. As I follow the maze of corridors and staircases leading to Cassandra's tower, it strikes me that I haven't taken this route through the Citadel in years.

A white-haired man rises from his chair beside the entrance to Cassandra's chambers. He is much too old to be in the King's Guard, yet the horses of Priam's house woven into his tunic say otherwise.

"I need to speak with the princess."

The old guard's eyes travel up the growing curves of my body. Not in a lecherous way, but as if to verify my identity. Satisfied, he opens the door and steps aside.

A small dagger sits in the leather belt beneath my cloak, but the pressure against my hip is a small comfort when I step into the shadowy chamber, lit only by a single torch and the dying embers in the hearth. Slowly, I scan the unadorned room. There is no sign of Cassandra, not in the chair by the fire, nor in the bed of rumpled blankets that sits in the far corner.

Turning back to the now-closed door, I take a deep breath. The air gathers in my chest as a bolt of panic rushes through me.

She steps out from her hiding place behind the door. Behind me.

Her face glows white in the light of the moon. Neck bent at an unnatural angle, she moves forward with jerky movements.

I feel a slight lurch in my womb.

The Wraith. It does not speak. It just stares through a curtain of oily tendrils, the dark eyes that supposedly belong to Cassandra now an abyss of misery.

"Do not fear. I am only here to watch something through your window." I slink toward it without turning my back on the Wraith.

No movement. No response. An upright corpse.

The lower part of the small window sits right at my eye level. From this height, I can see far beyond Troy's walls to the olive groves that sit to the east. Bodecca was right—with the bright moon, it is the ideal view, as well as the perfect night for sabotage.

My heart sinks slightly. The fields just south of the olive groves where the cattle graze are at the edge of the frame this window provides. Still, it will have to do.

A flash of light beyond the wall signals that Pandarus and Glaucus are on the move, their men dressed in the loose tunics of common cowherds. Since those herders always carry torches to light their way, doing otherwise would make Odysseus wonder. And we need the element of surprise on our side. Sporadic lights flicker below, but they do not move quickly or aggressively. Nothing seems to be happening. I strain my neck, but the glow of Pandarus's torches soon disappears beyond my line of sight.

A low wheeze fills the darkness behind me. Slowly, I turn.

Cassandra stands in the glowing square of moonlight that bathes the floor. Something gleams in her hand. A knife. Why anyone would let her have one is beyond me.

Her dead eyes glide across my belly. A rush of panic has me reaching for the dagger on my belt, but I stop. No matter how alien she appears at this moment, the Wraith is Hector's sister, whom he loves dearly.

My bare hands, then.

The two black orbs of her eyes seem to be searching. With a sudden lurch to the right, Cassandra darts toward the wall, jabbing the blade into the mortar with all the intent of a spearman piercing his target. She works ferociously, until a thick brick pops out of the wall. With practiced fingers, she guides it free and places it on the ground at her feet.

Flinging the knife aside, Cassandra crouches in front of the neat, square hole, beckoning me closer. As soon as I'm at her level, her ice-cold hand grabs my chin, thrusting my face forward.

Through the makeshift window, I can see everything. From the olive groves all the way south to the fields across from the east gate where Hector sits inside with Peirous and a handful of his Thracians.

Odysseus will surely approach those fields from even farther east, and when we capture him and his men, we will make them tell us of the hidden route that led them there. By whatever means necessary.

Suddenly, the lights scatter, darting in a dozen directions across the grazing field. Pandarus's and Glaucus's men must be routing the Achaeans as they approach to attack the herds. When the many lights converge, they stop and form a small ring.

A moment later, the east gate cracks open. Not for the Thracian riders, but for Hector's chariot to collect its prisoners—driven tonight by Polydorus rather than Cyrrian.

My pounding heart gives up a smile. They have done it. They have stopped the attack on our cattle and captured Odysseus's men.

And they have done it so . . . quickly.

All unsettledness dissipates when Polydorus releases a war cry whose whoop echoes across the field. The young prince will have his initiation into manhood as he escorts the prisoners back to the wall, and I can imagine how proud Hector will be to witness it.

I'm about to release a celebratory shout of my own when sudden movement to the northeast draws my gaze. The night sky must be playing tricks with my eyes. The shining silver leaves of an olive tree surely look similar to the glint of swords beneath a full moon. But then, even closer to the city— shadows slinking in the night. Right along our walls. Right in the wake of Hector's chariot.

The moon ducks behind the clouds, yet I see them before they are bathed in darkness. More Ithacans. A silent enemy closing in on my men from two directions, the olive grove and the wall.

And the allies have no idea. They are not looking. Why would they? They think they have already won.

All the blood in my body seems to rush to my head as I strain forward through the hole in the wall. A small noise at my back makes me whirl around. Cassandra is standing there, calmly holding one of the arrows from my quiver.

"If he is the horse, then you must be the fire," she says in a voice eerily like her own. "If you both become who you were always meant to be, you will set the world ablaze."

My chest burns with her prophecy like I've swallowed hot coals. I take the arrow she offers and glance around the room. On a stone ledge near Cassandra's bed sits a collection of odd trinkets. Dead plants rotting in their clay pots. Bird feathers and animal bones. And, startlingly out of place among the debris, the most finely woven scarf I have ever laid eyes on, its fabric dyed the rich color of Minoan saffron.

"Helen made that for me," Cassandra says with a disturbingly slow smile. "Did you know she sits with me sometimes? The Spartan knows many things. About many men."

No doubt, I think as I grab the golden scarf, plunge it into the oil of a nearby lamp, and wrap the fabric around my arrow. Queen Penthesilea's voice rings in my head as I nock the arrow and slip the end through the hole. I pull back my arm as far as it will go, but the angle isn't right. No arrow I fire from here will have the height to reach the distance I require.

And I cannot afford to miss.

Odysseus's second contingent is drawing closer to my men, but they are too busy boasting and taunting their prisoners. I could scream through the hole, but the wind would steal the warning from my lungs. If Hector and the allies even heard me, they wouldn't know the first place to look for the threat that has gathered silently all around them.

On trembling legs, I rise and scan the room again, but there are no easy solutions. There will be no more help from Cassandra either. The Wraith has returned. Her neck disjointed and her tongue silent, as if rotted right out of her head. Two gnarled fingers almost seem to be gesturing behind her. Pointing.

The north wind howls through the balcony doors.

I unclip my breastplate and follow it forward.

Grabbing a torch from a nearby sconce, I step out onto the balcony, though to even call the structure that is generous. The stone slab is barely wide enough for a single person to stand on, and there's no railing. It is a narrow ledge that follows the tower's perimeter, but not an ideal place to enjoy the view. One slip and the fall ends in the Underworld.

One might think that was exactly what the king and queen of Troy had in mind when they banished their unseemly daughter here.

I press my back against the tower's exterior wall and begin to inch east, the wind caressing the swell that prevents me from looking straight down. I must stop often to steady my shaking hands and my breathing. Not only for me, but for the one with the most direct view of the Citadel streets below. The child who has not consented to take this risk.

There will be nothing left for him unless you do.

A few more steps and I am far enough east to shoot the arrow as far as it needs to go. Now I just need the leverage. But in order to get it, I must step away from the wall.

I must lean into the wind and trust it will keep me standing.

With the torch, I light the oil-soaked scarf secured around the arrowhead. The wind whips through my hair and rustles my robes, but it does not betray me. Two sharp breaths as I home in on my target. One long exhale. I release the arrow with all my strength.

The flame sails like a star falling across the black sky. Time stops and the wind roars.

See it, Hector. Please.

The arrow lands on the open plain not far from the olive grove, but the flame only burns for a passing moment. Then, like all of us, it goes out.

Pulse racing, I fall back against the wall, praying to the Mother that Hector has seen my sign and understood it. For a few moments, all is silent except for my own labored breathing. Soon, I hear muffled shouts.

Followed by the low creak of the east gate parting.

At a hard gallop, the white-haired Peirous and four Thracian riders race across the fields to form a half moon around the other allies just before the lurking Ithacans reach them. Whatever happens next happens fast. The clash of bronze tells me there's fighting, but my men were not caught unawares. And we have the advantage of a cavalry.

Moments later, I see Hector's chariot racing back to Troy's walls. My hot lungs release a breath I've been holding for nearly as long.

"I must meet him at the gate," I tell a catatonic Cassandra, leaping back inside her room. I start to crouch down to refit my breastplate when a sharp pain has me doubling over.

No.

Something warm travels down the curve of my inner thigh. Desperately, I reach for the source, as if walling up this levee will somehow save the life behind it. Hand trembling, I slowly lift it to the glow cast by Arma's fickle moon.

My fingers are painted red.

A low moan escapes my throat. I am collapsing in on myself when I feel something cold against my abdomen. A flash of ice overtakes the heat of the fear spreading through me.

The knife. Where is the knife?

My eyes drop in anticipation of another kind of searing pain. But instead of a silver flash followed by a pool of blood, I glimpse a hand that has not recently seen the sun.

Cassandra rests her icy palm across my belly, the small smile on her lips a ghost of the lost girl trapped in the deep recesses of her mind.

The girl who knew Odysseus was coming, and from which direction. The girl who has already spared a city that has never showed her a single kindness.

"Your child will rise up against his enemies like the Scamander in spring."

Another burning breath flees my chest as I raise the hand marked by my guilt. "*Look.* How can you say something so cruel?"

"Because it is the truth, and a fool has nothing to gain by speaking it. But first you must eat *your* words, sister. They may go down bitter, but I promise you. The aftertaste will be sweet." Cassandra gives me another unsettling smile. "You need her, and she needs you even more."

Who is she talking about? Rhea?

Fear fans within me anew.

"But what of the child?" Fire meets ice as my other hand falls on hers and grips it tight. "You are certain he will take his first breath?"

She stares down at our linked hands for a moment. The sudden softness in Cassandra's eyes tells me this is what she misses most—*touch.* Her hand seems to warm on my belly as her smile spreads into something . . . human. For once, we understand each other perfectly.

40

HELEN

THE WIND BLOWS, blasting my face with frigid mist.

Rain. Dripping softly at first. Then harder and harder.

My swollen eye cracks open, yet not without a fight. I blink until the blur comes into focus. The world is tilted upside down.

No. It is me who is sideways, face pressed against the stone wall. Splattered with blood, not rain. *My* blood. The reason for it floods in with a surge of fresh suffering.

I remember everything.

How he'd found me on the balcony. How I'd nearly escaped.

Have only hours passed since then? Or has it been days?

Kairos is long gone, and Kronos will not speak.

With a moan, I try to straighten my right leg. My teeth grit against the agony as I force my hands to feel the tender bones beneath mottled skin.

It isn't broken, but it might as well be. Just like my every hope.

The halo at the edge of my vision closes in again. Footsteps echo down the hall.

Please. Let it be anyone else.

The door creaks. It takes every drop of strength I have left to lift my head.

There is no one there. Did he mean to leave it open?

Does it matter?

Another groan escapes as I pull myself onto all fours. The white-hot pain sends me back onto my stomach. Instead, I crawl.

Closing a narrow gap each time, just before another wave of black pain rises up, towing me back under. My mouth goes dry as the shattered pieces of memory come together. I recall the cloying taste of the wine he forced on me, turning its honey sweetness bitter, though my every muscle wanted it. Craved it like a vine reaching for the sun.

All those wasted years. The hours I sat indifferently in the fog, unwilling to act, not wanting to choose. Begging my god for some way out, for answers that never came.

Because they were around and within you already.

I shiver at the whisper, and another memory surfaces. Andromache at the Fair Winds, looking *to me.*

"What do you say, Theana?"

Yet even if the Unnamed One opened that path, I could not make her listen. There was no help when I asked for it, and there will be no help for me now.

There is only this expanse between me and the door.

I lurch forward. My leg throbs and the black cloud descends.

More minutes pass. Maybe hours.

When I wake, it is full night. The moon is bright but shadows lurk at the corners. All my pleading thoughts are like water slipping through my fingers.

I hold on to the only cry that matters.

Give me the strength.

A gust tinged with smoke blows in from the balcony, sending the spindle from my loom rolling across the floor. With a deep breath, I follow it. Broken. Stripped. As low as I've ever been.

And therein lies your power.

A sudden glow fills the room. I stare at the open door.

Radiant light dances along its edges, yet a yawning shadow fills most of the space. It is an unusual shape, but one I somehow know. Barrel-chested. Low to the ground like the animals he once bred. And that unruly mane— the gods have given him more hair than they typically offer three men.

Odysseus?

Here to take me back to the children others have raised in our stead?

The shadow looks down on my effort to escape and instantly transforms. Whereas Odysseus knows exactly who he is because his feet are planted on the earth, the shadow standing in my doorway has only one skill set—and that is playing a part. A performance requiring a dozen false masks, each one leaving him both more arrogant and more fearful. He pretends to be a god because he is fully aware that he will never come close to touching divinity.

"I thought we were past this, my love."

I raise my eyes to the voice, to the light. Higher and higher.

Not light. Darkness.

It is all-consuming as it spreads. I open my mouth to scream. For the first time since I've set foot on Trojan soil, I scream until my throat burns and I can scream no more.

⌒ ୨ ৎ ⌒

THE BRUISED FLESH of the golden apple becomes visible when I hold it up to the glow of the moon. I bite into the overripe fruit, letting its juice dribble down my chin. Leaning forward, I stare into the bronze basin of the shallow bowl, searching for similar blemishes, for any sign of the old age I would welcome.

Paris has done his part to hasten the process, I'll give him that.

Since he left a few hours ago, one eye still will not open. My lower lip is split down the middle, and my skin is mottled in many colors. There is no amount of henna in the east or kohl in the west to fix the damage Paris's fists have done.

And yet a smile lurks.

I hold up a small, curved blade. The tool is meant for peeling fruit, but it is plenty sharp. Sharp enough that Clymene should have been more discerning when she delivered the late-night meal I have barely touched.

Pregnancy certainly makes some forgetful, yet of the many expecting women I have cared for, I have never seen it make anyone as cruel and confident as it has made Clymene. Then again, there have not been many servants with reason to believe their child may one day be named Troy's king.

Again, I peer into the basin. He has used my face for his own purposes, and he has beaten it like the hide of a farm animal. He has run his fingers through my uncovered hair, and he has used those same strands to strangle and silence me. To keep me under his control.

He has taken everything from me, but he will not take this.

In this prison within a prison, he will not take the one thing I might still have a say over.

I raise the blade and begin to saw. Slowly. Carefully. Right at the root. The first thick tendril fights the hardest, but the task grows easier with each handful of curls.

Before long, I am staring at thousands upon thousands of radiant threads. Threads that once wove a tapestry that could not be falser. I peer into the shallow bowl for the last time. After this, there will be no need to stare.

Yes. This picture is more to my liking.

My swollen lips stretch as they bask in the glow of the truth.

These strands of silk tangled among my fingers are little more than dust. They are not true beauty. Beauty is what radiated from my daughter's eyes when she held my face in her chubby hands. A gaze of pure love that would have been there all the same, even if I were less rose and more dandelion.

My chin jerks toward the door. The sound of desperate pounding forces me to my feet with a wince. Why would Aethra or Clymene bother knocking?

I breathe in sharply, pausing to lean against the chair. The leg he mangled when he threw me against the wall still aches. It is a wound that may never heal completely. Yet it can be lived with.

Much, I am learning, can be lived with.

What should be tolerated is another matter entirely.

Two more shuffles and I'm nearly to the door. Whoever waits on the other side must finally realize the latch is secured from the outside. The door opens.

Andromache's face swims across mine. Her expression goes from resolute to stunned, though I feel nothing at the sight of it. Not hope, and not relief.

For this is not the same bold woman who pounded on Lower City hovels to rouse mothers and whores. She blinks rapidly, her eyes glistening with either sorrow or regret as they run over the pitiful thing I have become.

Hector's Harsa pulls her robes tightly around her body, as if hiding something. As if she doesn't know whether to enter my chambers or turn around and flee.

Andromache so uncertain is something I never thought I'd witness.

"*He* did this," she says finally. Andromache steps into the room in the manner I'd expect. She circles the halo of fallen hair like a hound working itself up on a fox's scent.

"You are surprised?"

She doesn't respond. Of course she doesn't. She was there when Paris struck me in her kitchen. She knows.

In the space of her silence, a wave of rage that could rival Poseidon rises up and overtakes me. For once, I let it. I let myself feel all the things I needed to feel when he ripped my child from my arms, when he brought me to this land against my will, and when nearly every woman who was here to greet me has heaped on me nothing but scorn.

All sentiments I numbed and then drowned. To survive.

Yet I am not that person anymore. I will say what needs to be said. I will scream and grieve all that needs to be screamed and grieved. Razed hair is only the beginning of my lament. My loss is total, and there is nothing Andromache can ever do to make it up to me.

"Helen, I—" she begins to say with no shortage of stumbling.

"Don't." I cut her off. "Don't offer words of comfort you do not mean."

I can't begin to guess how many moons have waxed and waned since Paris dragged me from her home, unleashing the full range of his retribution. All I know is that I, another woman, cried out to her in need, and she turned her back. I sacrificed everything to give her that which might open her womb, yet she could not open her mind. Not for one moment.

As a consequence, I have spent a thousand moments writhing on a filthy pallet in this darkened room. Alone. Replaying the instant when she turned away from me, a poem sung on the stage of my mind as more welts surfaced and each bruise reached its full ripeness. Even then, I still wished I had the strength to act as she does—in my own interest above all else.

"This was not what I expected to find when I came here," Andromache says slowly as she paces the room, her hands clenching as they would around a spear. It makes sense that she would view this confrontation as a battle. I suspect she can count the times she has admitted to being wrong on one hand.

"The truth was right in front of you," I snap, insides recoiling. "It just wasn't the truth you wanted. Not when it was easier to blame me for all that has befallen Troy."

Andromache's face hardens as her pace quickens. Her hands keep on clenching, but her mouth is dammed shut.

Another surge of rage hits me. Why is this so hard for her? Why does this woman who can surely brawl with the best of men find it so difficult to admit that she was wrong?

Would it even matter if she did?

"What made you doubt your own infallible judgment?" I ask, striking her in the place she takes the most pride in, the place where the wound will smart most fiercely.

"Cassandra." Andromache's shoulders slump. "It was something she said. About having to eat my words."

The visual almost brings a smile to my lips. Yet the triumph is fleeting. Andromache falls to the ground in front of me.

"You owe me nothing. I know that I have done you wrong, but please . . ." Andromache opens her robes with a desperation I do not recognize. "Help me. You're the only one who can."

All the breath in my chest departs. The bottom half of the tunic beneath Andromache's robes is covered in enough blood to smother my anger and flare my fear.

"I can't lose this child, Helen. I *can't.*"

Tears pour down Andromache's ash-streaked cheeks while she claws at her robes. Suddenly, *finally,* she is one of us. Not a woman seeking to break into a man's domain because she thinks herself so much better, but a woman begging to be let into the only sisterhood that can save her.

Her normally stern face is transformed. All the force that animates her equally strong features is gone. She embraces my knees like a prisoner begging his enemy for mercy.

Compassion wells up within me, but I push it back down.

"I am sorry Hector and I didn't intervene with Paris sooner. We will discuss the matter in time, but for now . . . *please.*"

I study her for more signs of sincerity, though it's impossible that her red eyes and blotchy skin are an act. Be that as it may, only the gods have the power to forgive all that Andromache has done. And all she has left undone.

I gesture to my bed all the same. "Take off your robes."

I am still a Paeana, after all. And no Paeana would turn away a woman who feared for the life of her child.

Andromache gets to her feet and does as I command. While I wash my hands in the basin beside my fallen hair, I ask her, "When did the bleeding start?"

"Not long ago. A little over an hour, perhaps. Odysseus's men led a raid on our cattle tonight. We stopped them, but I had to . . . take action. I fear I may have . . ." Her tears well up again as Andromache lies back on the bed, still sprinkled with my own blood.

Despite the way they tremble, Andromache's legs part decisively. And then she is laid out before me, every wall down. Every shield lowered.

"What do you see? Did I hurt the baby? Can you tell?"

I can't tell much, but she isn't bleeding now, which is a good sign. When I press gently on her abdomen, Andromache does not flinch or yelp. Thank Eileithyia.

"You are spotting, but the blood loss wasn't too great," I say on a long exhale. "It is not uncommon, but you will have to be cautious. *Much* more cautious. At some point, you may even need to stay in your bed."

Andromache shoots up from mine. "What? But I am needed! I cannot just—"

"I understand. Yet the fate of your child may depend on you making the one sacrifice you do not wish to make."

"And what is that?"

"Surrendering to rest."

Andromache bristles, but her shoulders sink as if her soul could use the reprieve even more than her body. In the end, I know Andromache will do what needs to be done. She is here, after all.

At the crossroads the Unnamed One has led us to.

Andromache pulls her robe back on and begins to pace once more, mind churning with some new stratagem. "Fortunately, what I need your help with at today's festival does not require much movement from either of us."

Making sure the child in her womb is alive and well is one thing, but it appears Andromache does not know when to stop. "What more could you want from me?"

"Your alliance. Our chance has finally come."

"*Our* chance?" I scoff, taking a moment to tongue the crack in my lip. It splits the scab again, and I taste blood. Only this time, there is a fruity ripeness to it that wasn't there before.

Andromache stares, seemingly caught off guard by this new spine I have grown, even while other parts of me have shattered. "Your chance, then. To free yourself from him. Paris has wronged us both, and it is time to show all of Troy what he really is."

I limp a few paces toward her, embittered by Kairos's failed promise. "And why would I bother with that now? What good will fighting do me? Whether the Achaeans win this war or the Trojans, my fate remains the same."

Andromache shakes her head. "No. You still have choices. We always have choices." She grasps my hand and thrusts it to her belly. This time, the soft warmth has my palm retreating like it has grazed an open flame.

"Take this as proof that your earlier efforts were not in vain."

The tea.

"How did you find out?"

"I didn't. Not until now." Andromache gestures toward a table covered in herbs laid out to dry what now feels like ages ago. "Then I remembered you in my kitchen, poking around my tea bag." She smiles slightly. "Boiling water, indeed."

I stare at her small but definite swell, waiting to feel some tinge of sympathy. For the life that has rounded her center to fill the emptiness in mine. "I am happy for you. For Hector."

"Thank you. For everything." Andromache watches me closely, the tense silence between us stretching into something . . . new. "It is strange," she says finally. "This child. I expected only the joy of triumph, but whenever I stop and think about what it will all mean, it feels more like I am about to undergo . . ." She glances around my chamber, as if the right words might be found in the shadowy corners. "A death."

I nod. "It may well seem like one. I was hardly more than a child when I gave birth to Hermione. I discovered who I was in the discovery of my love for her."

The brutal truth is the only blow I am fit to issue Andromache, and I trust she will not loathe me for it. "It will be much harder for you."

Andromache's inhale sounds like a stifled laugh. "Because I'm so much older. Is that it?"

"Hardly." My own lips have forgotten how to smile. "You've simply had more time to become acquainted with the woman you are about to lose."

She sighs. "That is most reassuring."

"It should be." I pause to breathe in a memory of honey hair and chubby fingers. "To give of yourself fully, you first need a self to give."

Andromache studies me for another long moment before turning toward the balcony and the golden glow of Kallikolone beyond. "You must join us, Helen."

"*Must* I?" My voice comes out shriller than I intend, but after all the words we've spoken, I will not return to shrinking from the authority she lords over me. "You come here seeking my aid on two fronts, and yet you turned away when I needed your help most. You left me here to rot."

Andromache's cheeks drain all over again. "I had no idea Paris would—"

My voice swells into a torrent. "Curse the gods, Andromache! How do you *think* I came to be in Troy? Do you think I wanted this? That I would leave my daughter all alone to be bartered over by brutes just like I was? That I would risk the fate of both our peoples for a man who could do *this* to the wife he supposedly thought was worth a war?"

For several breaths, her eyes study the pattern of the tile floor. Pacing and clenching, pacing and clenching. She finally lifts her head. "I was wrong, and I am sorry. For all of it."

"They are just words," I say, waving my hand as Paris has so often done to me. And yet they have more weight than I want them to. Enough to create the sensation that a massive stone is dragging me down. Only to what end?

"You don't understand," Andromache sputters suddenly. "You think I don't know that this . . . me . . . isn't easy for Hector? That the insults Paris flings burn because they contain some truth?"

I stand a little taller, unclear what any of this has to do with what she wants from me now. "I've never berated you for being who you are, Andromache. As the heir of Troy, Hector could have chosen any number of demure beauties from here to the Euphrates. But he didn't."

Her eyes flash before she releases a mirthless chuckle. "Perhaps he wishes he had."

"Then he would find himself at a significant disadvantage. There is little room for gentleness in Troy, believe me." The words have a thawing effect as soon as they leave my bruised lips. "Many would have crumbled years ago. Instead, you have been the other pillar that has held up his roof."

Andromache grunts. "A pillar . . ." She smooths her bloodied tunic over a small heart that thankfully beats beneath it. "Sometimes, I wonder if perhaps what Hector needs, what he truly deserves, is a soft place to land."

I shrug. "Then provide it."

Andromache looks like if I've asked the entire world of her. And maybe I have. She'd probably be less frightened if I'd said the only solution to her marital woes was to battle Achilles at daybreak.

"I did not come here to discuss my marriage," Andromache continues. "But if there was ever a time for you to save yourself from yours, *now* is that time."

A laugh of disbelief escapes me. "And why would that matter to you?"

"Because it matters to Troy."

"Troy." I shake my head. "How much more evil will be excused on her behalf?"

"Perhaps much more will not be required." She pauses, as if weighing whether to continue. She does. "During last night's raid, we took a prisoner. We had hoped to capture more, but in the end, one is enough. It is one of Odysseus's men."

"And what do you want from me?"

"To identify the man." Andromache's gaze narrows. "I know Menelaus hosted Ithacans often at his table, so you may recognize him, especially if he is to Odysseus what he appears to be. Once we know the man's name, we can use him as a negotiation tool."

Use. A word that does not sit well with me. Paeanas will use every gift of the earth, but it is a part of our vow never to use people. What would the women who taught me think if I agree to what Andromache is asking?

She must read my hesitation. "My mentor, Queen Penthesilea, often said that in the service of life, less savory tactics must sometimes be employed to achieve greater ends."

"The excuse given by every tyrant who has ever drawn breath."

Andromache frowns. Then, suddenly, her face softens and her hands fall. "Then don't do it for me. Or for Troy. Do it for them. The children who do not get to decide."

My response catches in my throat. Any words I might say are overshadowed by the ache that ripples through me like an endless labor pain.

For her sake.

Hermione's is the first face I see when I turn to take in the slowly expanding light. Then I see them. Hundreds of them, if not more. All floating before me as small, lifeless shades that Ares is eager to usher down to the Underworld.

A city of several thousand women means thousands more children, both within the womb and without. What would those mothers of war, what would any mother, do for the chance to spare them? To end the suffering that will be riding on the chariots of the rising sun now that the rains have stopped?

"If I agree to what you have in mind, and Paris finds out I helped you . . ."

"Hector and I will protect you. We'll make it so you never have to come back to these rooms. I give you my word." Andromache pulls her shoulders back, and then, almost self-consciously, reaches for a lock of her own long hair. "Why did you do it, Helen?"

It may be the first time I have heard my name on her lips without malice. I run a hand over my lamb-shorn head, over the patches of fuzz and the fresh scabs, then down the puffy flesh of my cheek. "He used to say it was his greatest weapon."

Andromache looks confused. "What was?"

"My face." I meet her gaze without flinching.

Understanding mixed with no small amount of admiration brings the color back to her cheeks like a strong wine. Andromache scoops up my fallen hair from the floor and grabs both of my hands, wrapping them in golden threads like she is making a vow.

"Trust me. Paris has no idea how right he was. But soon, he will."

41

~⁓~

RHEA

A SCREAM CUTS through the night. A hawk. Its shadow streaks across the stars, which have somehow shifted when I was not looking.

I scramble to my feet. "I have to go."

Ajax frowns as if he too is surprised by how quickly the night has passed. "If I don't appear at my settlement soon, Teucer will come looking."

"You go first, then," I offer quickly. "I'll wait until you walk out onto the ridge before I follow."

I will do no such thing. Instead, I am headed straight back to Troy, where Andromache and her allies will have started the celebrations early after routing Odysseus. Today, Andromache will have her victory with all of Troy as her witness, and I will be there in the crowd. It feels like a shift not just for the city but for me. A balancing of the scales as I take one small step toward repaying the great debts that I owe.

Ajax gently lifts me back over the wall. His touch is less tentative this time, and my pulse only accelerates briefly when his big hands wrap around my waist.

My body thrums with anticipation. I can already feel the excitement of the people as they learn of Hector and Andromache's joy; hear the reluctant prayers of Priam's priest echoing through the festival square as he anoints Hector as the heir.

"Meet me again. Two nights from now." Ajax must misread the look on my face, because he rushes to explain, "Tomorrow night Teucer and I have promised to feast with my cousin in his settlement."

"You mean Achilles?"

Ajax sighs. "Who else? Nestor has enlisted my aid as an intermediary. Teucer and I are meant to talk him back around, but it's a lost cause." Something passes over his face. "I worry for him."

"You worry? For Achilles?"

Ajax lifts a golden brow. "He may be a gifted killer, but that is not all he is. Even the greatest warriors have their weaknesses." His eyes dart away from mine before they return again with a new intensity. "Two nights from now."

He waits for me to nod before he grins. And then he disappears in the shadows that lead behind the Achaean latrines.

I watch him go. When I'm sure he won't be coming back, I run.

The moon glows behind a gossamer veil of clouds. While I was not looking, it crested in its arc and began a slow sink toward the horizon. I should not have stayed so long, but there's more than enough time to reach Troy before the festival starts. Especially if I take the plains directly east instead of my usual longer path north around the city by way of the bay. Odysseus would have moved to capture Troy's cattle when the moon was highest. By now his men will have been killed or captured, making the plains as safe tonight as they will ever be.

The black of the sky has bled to dark blue in the east when my small boat runs up on the eastern bank of the Scamander. From here, it is a long walk around the camp Hector's troops have made just west of Troy's walls. I am starting for the sandy beach that sits below the plateau when movement draws my gaze southeast.

At first, I assume the dark shapes are sheep some inattentive shepherd has let wander. It isn't until the clouds break over the lightening sky, revealing the sharp edge of bronze spears, that I realize what is creeping across the Trojan plain.

A chill wind blows over the Scamander, making the grasses tremble. There are at least fifty Achaeans, fully armed and moving carefully in the dark. Slight breaks appear in their line—gaps where some of them are dragging large objects behind them with ropes.

Chariots' wheels.

A wild thudding starts in my chest as my gaze moves down the serpentine line stretching out in the opposite direction of my own path. These men might circumvent Hector's soldiers on the plain, but they will never approach the walls unseen unless . . .

The figure at the head of the Achaean party is unmistakable with his rolling gait.

Odysseus.

But Andromache and her men . . . Words rise up in my mind. The ones Odysseus himself spoke.

"Silinus and I will take the rest of the men and finish what we started."

"It is what we have been waiting for. There is no one else I trust to do this, Polites."

"My men and I are farmers by trade. We are merely returning to our roots."

The weight of the entire sky seems to grind me into the earth as a dozen moments come together, flashes of bright images and the utterances of foreign words, all twisting and rearranging. I squeeze my eyes shut, but it does nothing to erase the sight of the army moving against Troy. A Troy full of eager, unsuspecting people who have no idea what is coming for them. They have no idea, because I did not warn them.

Two more of Odysseus's men join the line, dragging a felled tree stump. One that is just the right length to block a city gate from the outside. They are followed by even more men carrying an intricately constructed bed of wood. More pieces appear and its shape becomes clear. A cart. The sides are being used as pallets to transport rows of carefully secured arrows and large jars with glistening mouths. The wind carries the stench of cedar pitch.

I glance back toward the safety of the beach. I could run back to Troy and let Andromache know that the cattle were not Odysseus's only targets tonight. But if I'm right about what is moving across the plain, it is already too late to stop it. Not unless I follow Odysseus and find out exactly how he is bringing his men up to the walls.

"Be careful. Please."

Cyrrian's words wind through my head, where they are quickly drowned out by the ones Ajax said to me.

"Even the greatest warriors have their weaknesses."

They are not alone. I did not recognize the full extent of Odysseus's intentions until it was too late. Hector and Andromache risked everything on a plan built around the words I spoke. They loved and trusted me, and I cannot let that trust become their weakness.

I won't.

My eyes follow the men moving toward Troy, and it strikes me that maybe Odysseus too has a weakness. After months of owning these plains at night, he does not know he now shares them. With *me*.

If I can uncover his secret route, maybe I can bring that information back to Troy. Andromache will know what to do. She will find some way to turn Odysseus's own trap against him. But that won't happen if I run back to the Mother temple now. This is my chance. My one turn to do the saving.

My eyes trace the sky with new urgency. The dark is heavy enough. There is an hour, maybe two left before dawn. I can figure out the route the Ithacans are using to reach the walls and tell Andromache before the first flag of the festival is hung.

Above me, a shadow separates from the others and dives low over the plain. The hawk again. It circles the clump of juniper bushes where I am hidden before returning with its kill back to Troy.

So many shadows. So many games playing out in the dark. There is only one thing left to decide.

North or south?

Follow or run?

Hunter or prey?

I grit my teeth and move out into the open. Quietly, I follow Odysseus's men as they make their wide loop around the Lower City. The first traces of purple are visible behind the Hill of Kallikolone when we finally reach the fields on the east side of Troy. Cattle graze with only a few herdsmen to guard them. Not Andromache's allies. They have already come and gone. These are boys. Andromache must have succeeded there, at least, or she would never have left the cattle out here undefended. But with the city streets set to fill for the festival, she wouldn't have brought them back through the gates either. It would only add to the crowds.

A churning starts in my gut as I watch the men move around the grazing animals up the rocky terrain that leads to the olive grove sitting on a low hill east of the city. The grove is thick with trees and several large boulders that could easily be used for cover.

There. Whatever Odysseus is doing to reach the walls, everything inside me screams that it has something to do with the shelter of that olive grove.

The distant crown of Mount Ida turns a deep pink in the southeast.

Soon the light will sweep across the plain. If I don't go now, I won't make it in time. I am turning back the way I came when something moves at Troy's east gate. At the base of the wall. A clump of grass lifts and falls aside, and an Achaean in a boar-tusk helmet climbs out of the hole the missing swatch of earth reveals. Soundlessly, he slides into the murky trench that sits several dozen paces in front of the walls.

My gaze moves farther down Troy's east wall. Now that I know what to look for, I can make out more Achaeans emerging from separate tunnels that let out at the foot of Troy's walls. Painted in mud, they waste no time descending into the trenches that are Troy's first line of chariot defense. A defense that is now being carefully used against us.

But where do the tunnels start?

The last of Odysseus's men reach the olive grove. I track their movements until I have my answer. On the highest point of the grove, behind a dead tree surrounded by boulders, half a dozen men have gathered. It becomes quickly obvious that the boulders are not boulders at all. They are piles of dirt.

I know how Odysseus is approaching the walls unseen.

The tunnel starts in the olive grove, where the higher ground is still dry enough to dig. It must run below the eastern field, where it divides into five fingers like a hand reaching for the walls of Troy.

The festival.

Movement in my periphery causes me to freeze.

A spear emerges from the tall grasses not three paces from where I lie crouched. Only the tight grip of fear around my throat prevents me from screaming.

An armed warrior follows the spear out into the open. He is so focused on the guards watching from Troy's towers that he does not turn his head. If he did, he could not miss me.

The warrior passes me slowly. When his back is turned, I sink down to the earth. I'm sliding backward on my stomach when the next warrior comes out of the grass. His sandals crush the wet stalks less than a foot from where my cheek lies pressed to the earth.

I squeeze my eyes shut. Most of this second wave of Achaeans make their way across the field to the olive grove, where they take the tunnels and disappear into the muddy trenches under the unsuspecting ramparts of Troy.

But some . . . some stay camped in the grasses all around me, waiting. But for what?

The third night watch has come and gone. Overhead, light streaks across the sky. The weight of the dawn seems to press the air from my lungs. I can't think. I can't even breathe. It is the same as the night I lay in the hay of our stable and watched my world burn.

The sensation that I'm about to watch it all go up in flames again builds with every careful Achaean footstep closing in around me.

Only this time, there is no one to save me.

This time, there is nowhere to run.

42

HELEN

"YOU ARE MAD."

Andromache releases a gravelly chuckle. "That may well be true."

Yet her admission does not stop the old tingle from returning to my hands as they prepare to create. I dip my pale fingers in paint made from crushed cochineals, then reach out to trace Andromache's belly in an array of red swirls. When I'm done, the design reminds me of a lotus flower. Or a flame.

"It is either madness, or the Muses have paid a visit to your dreams."

"We shall soon find out." Andromache rises from her chair to fan her front while the paint dries. The wind offers its aid by flapping through the hide door of the tent she was given to dress for the festival games.

"Do Amazons truly ride into battle so . . ."

"Naked?" Andromache supplies. A flash of a smile. "No, but they always make an entrance." She stares down at her bare midsection. "Though I can't claim *this* as a widespread custom."

"You are convinced it will work?" I ask.

"If by 'work' you mean get the council's attention, then yes." She throws her quiver over her shoulder, tightening the thick strap between the twin moons of her crimson breasts. "Ah, your Achaean compatriot has arrived," she says when the tent door flaps again.

"Harsa?"

It is not an Achaean standing in the doorway, but rather a stable boy whose face turns as red as the paint on Andromache's bare chest. A small group of warriors pulling a bound and hooded man are right behind him.

"What is it, Larion?"

"Cyrrian of the Two Shadows. He has been looking for you since before dawn." The boy drops his gaze to his shuffling feet. "Also, I . . . I have your horse."

"Thank you. Cyrrian can wait. My horse cannot. But first, we must find a plow for Kasirga to pull." Andromache steps out into the bright sunlight. "Welcome, Glaucus. Pandarus. I see you come bearing gifts."

The two men freeze outside the tent, mouths parting as wide eyes run up the painted, half-nude Amazon before them. Glaucus clears his throat before kicking his shackled prisoner through the doorway. "If you count a foul-mouthed, stubborn bastard as a prize."

"In my experience, the foul-mouthed ones scream loudest when their feet are held to the fire." Andromache studies the men who have entered her tent, men who don't even seem to notice me sitting in the corner beneath her imposing shadow. It makes my stomach flutter with possibilities, this way I have become invisible. "But before we continue, I need your word that you will not tell anyone what you are about to hear." She looks down at her crimson belly again. "Nor what you have seen. I promise that you will not have to keep my secrets long."

Pandarus and Glaucus give her a firm nod.

"Helen." Andromache extends her arm to me without turning my way. These men who have seen years of battle look upon my face with horror. "She has come to see our new friend, who may well be an old friend of hers."

As I approach, the captains pull back their prisoner's hood, revealing a confused face that stares at mine without recognition. The Ithacan has deep-set eyes and a rapidly receding hairline. Yet that is common in men his age. What gives him away is the jutting prow of his nose. When seated next to the short Odysseus with his wild mane, the two men made an almost comical pair. Maybe that was why they used to talk with me like I was a real person. They lacked the vanity and arrogance of younger men.

And I am about to return that respect with betrayal.

"His name is Polites. He is Odysseus's closest companion," I say quietly, insides squirming. I gave Andromache my word, and I know the man is not innocent—who among us is by this point?—but still. This Ithacan sailed to Troy on my behalf, and my words may have sentenced him to a fate more agonizing than death.

That may be the game men at war play, but it is not the way of Paeanas.

Polites's glare screams *Traitor!* His bloodied lips twist into a sneer as he says low words meant only for me. "Not to worry, my queen. You will be reunited with your rightful master soon."

Andromache holds her enemy's gaze. "As you may be reunited with yours. So long as you give us what we need."

"He caught them by surprise, you know," Polites continues unfazed, his words reverberating through the tent like a gong. "Your brothers. They were out beyond Thebe's walls grazing their herds. If my memory serves, the youngest was playing a little pipe."

Polites's smile spreads as Andromache's fades, yet the blatant cruelty of it is all wrong. The Ithacan is as battle-hardened as the rest of them, but this spitefulness is beneath the man of honor I once knew. "And then comes Achilles, charging right out of the woods like a lion or a boar. It was all over before the rest of us even had the chance to play."

Andromache reaches for her blade. I swear I see Polites lean forward, offering his neck. Goading her on.

But why? Surely Odysseus would pay any ransom for his closest friend.

Unless Polites fears talking under torture and betraying that friend first.

Glaucus extends a hand, holding Andromache back. "Give us ten minutes with him, Harsa, and he will soon be singing the Achaeans' secrets."

Andromache pulls her shoulders back, regaining composure. "After the festival. There will be plenty of time to get what we need from him."

"And that is something I must speak to you about, Andromache." I frown at how high and lyrelike my voice sounds compared to the others. Yet this time, I will be heard. She owes me that much.

When the men depart the tent, Andromache turns toward me. The shadows of her revived grief still hang below her eyes, but her face is alight with imminent victory. She is Artemis incarnate, minus the rather obvious lack of virginity: her bronze armguards gleaming, her hide riding breeches hugging her muscular thighs. Down her back hangs a long Phrygian-style braid, thick like a whip. Only the loose copper tendril at her forehead will not be contained.

"What is it, Helen?"

"Polites. I knew the man well. Let me talk to him before you . . . use harsher means."

Andromache studies me closely. "Compassion may have been possible within the safety of the Citadel, but I assure you, there is little place for it here."

"Be that as it may, to share in another's suffering is often the best way to loosen their tongue. Not all battles are won at the tip of a spear, Andromache."

Her face softens like the words are a half-remembered truth. "You can have a few moments with him before the feast for the allied captains tonight. I'll have my men escort you to the winehouse where he'll be guarded. But first, I need Polites's assistance here, and I can't promise you it will be without pain."

I nod and hand Andromache a cloak. When her copper skin disappears into its heavy fabric, I cover my face with an almost equally opaque veil, though one still light enough not to aggravate the tender bruises.

Her eyes spark when they meet mine. Polites's fate may be hanging in the balance, but it is time for Paris to learn of his. "Remember," Andromache says as we head toward the door. "Do not show yourself. Wait until I join you. Not a moment sooner."

"I will wait for you." It's not as if I don't have nine years of practice.

The minute we exit the festival tent, we are pummeled by all the smells that animals make and every sound a human can produce. Andromache immediately climbs onto the gray gelding Larion left tied up outside.

Before she rides off, she shoots me a look that again screams *Wait*.

Because she wishes for me to share in her triumph, or because waiting is what will best serve her cause?

Either way, I made my choice. There is no turning back now.

Once the dust the horse kicks up settles and Andromache's swinging braid disappears, I slip back into the tent to retrieve an additional layer of security. If Paris learns I am here too soon, everything else will unravel.

The last piece of my festival costume is the Death Mask. Despite the day's growing heat, my somewhat labored breathing inside the mask has the comforting timbre of an old friend. Andromache can issue her demands, but I will not sit by and miss every step of Paris's downfall.

Beyond the cluster of royal tents, the grounds for the Festival of the Divine Twins has taken over most of the Lower City. I limp through streets decorated with colorful banners from all the lands of Troy's allies, bringing my performance as an old war widow to new heights. Given the laughter and lute music echoing out of each courtyard, the city's people are in as good spirits as I have ever seen them.

Even if I can't force myself to feel unbridled joy for everything Andromache has gained at my expense, I am satisfied knowing her triumph is one that will be shared by all of Troy.

Three little girls race down the street in front of me, holding hands and giggling, the petals from their flower crowns fluttering to the ground behind them. A glimmer of a smile pulls at my battered lips.

I do not mind the pain it brings. In the early summer, Hermione often woke me with a shower of wildflowers scattered across my pillow. The stray memory loosens the tangled knot of my resentment. Maybe Andromache is truly doing this for them. For her own stubborn pride, yes, but also for them. And who among us does not act from more than one motive?

More limping steps carry me to the central arena and platform where King Priam and his family sit. The place where many fates will be sealed by games that are anything but.

Hector rests at the edge of his chair, his hair pulled back in a knot as tight as his clean-shaven jawline. His white linen tunic is simple, but he dons the same horned tiara worn by all of Priam's children, along with his gold signet ring. Hector's dark eyes flit anxiously in search of Andromache, who should be seated in the chair beside him. I'm not sure what to make of Hector at this moment, if he even realizes what is at stake. He does not wear the tortured expression of a man who is on the verge of losing everything. Whatever the outcome of the succession, it is clear Hector intends to hold his head high.

Every stifled prayer inside me burns. For her sake. But even more for his.

At the sudden blast of a war horn, all eyes shift to the pounding of hooves. "Here come the Dioscuri," roars a voice in the crowd. "Here come the Divine Twins!"

The shout is followed by excited chattering as a chariot rimmed with gold rolls into the arena from the direction of the allied camp. It is indeed pulled by twins—two stallions whose clean coats are as white as Hector's tunic.

An enormous man—made even larger by the furs he wears despite the heat—steps off the chariot. Elaborate etchings no Trojan metalworker would bother with decorate his face shield. For a moment, the warrior's bronze face seems to lock onto mine, as if he senses a kind of masked kinship.

When I turn back to the platform, Hector has descended it and is crossing the square with open arms. I press up against the hastily constructed partition so I can hear what the two men say.

"Welcome, King Rhesus," Hector calls out as he reaches for the man's thick arm. "We did not expect you so soon."

"Your Fair Winds inn is aptly named and its beds are even finer," the fur-covered man replies. "The gods saw fit to give us safe passage through the Dardanelles, and a speedy one too."

King Rhesus of Thrace. Another frequent visitor at Menelaus's table. Though clearly the hospitality was not so grand that he wouldn't think to fight against him now.

A second horn blasts, causing Hector and the Thracian king to move closer to me at the edge of the arena. The ground rumbles as more chariots roll forward. Paris's black horses are in the lead. He dons the same gleaming armor he wore the day he disgraced himself at Menelaus's feet, though it has a few dents and scuffs this time around. At the sight of his haughtily plumed head, I fight for air. For room to breathe.

Paris disembarks his chariot and takes his seat on the royal platform beside his father, who will usher in the official start of the games any moment. Or maybe King Priam plans to announce the succession first.

Suddenly, rising over the hush in the crowd following two ostentatious entrances, comes the sound of a single horse's hooves. When the dappled gray enters the arena, the gasp the people expel is one. Not only is Andromache riding the horse like there is no place she feels more secure, she rides by the grip of her thighs alone, with no leads to grasp. No breastplate to shield her naked, vulnerable condition.

And yet, even with her brazen belly swinging before her, one hand clutches her bow, the other a flaming torch.

Behind Andromache's horse, Hector's youngest brother, Polydorus, drags Polites into the arena by a rope. The beaming boy prince struts, basking in this moment at such a slow pace that his Ithacan prisoner has no trouble keeping his footing though his legs are bound.

The entire city holds its breath.

If the Trojan people ever wondered what it would be like to encounter an

Amazon on the battlefield, they are getting a glimpse of it now. Andromache guides her horse around to the stands where the entire council sits below the stone-faced king, his horrified queen, and a scowling Paris. Satisfied, Andromache turns her back on the Old Blood. When she taps her horse with her heels and the gelding breaks into a trot, the silence shatters.

The people are taking in the full view of her now, a woman who does not wear armor forged by the hammer of the gods, but the sagging, nourishing flesh of a mother. They gape at her bare breasts and slowly swelling stomach, all three spheres painted the color of life. The color of death. All three swaying with the movements of the horse, who trots gently, as if he knows who else he carries and what the child is worth.

I look to where Hector stood beside the king of Thrace, but the prince is no longer there. My eyes seek out Paris again. He is focused on the bow resting in his lap, which shields his expression. Yet I can imagine it is thoroughly enraged.

Near the sacrificial altar at the center of the arena, Andromache swings her leg over the horse and slides—carefully, I'm glad to see—off the gelding's back. Polydorus proudly brings her prisoner around from behind the horse, hand ready on the hilt of his sword.

"People of Troy," Andromache begins, her sure voice ringing like a bell across the open square. "I present to you the enemy who brought the plague inside our walls. The enemy who in the dark of night attempted to steal our cattle and make this festival an occasion for grief, not joy."

Polites stumbles forward when Polydorus gives the chain a hard tug. His oiled Achaean beard is proof that shines in the Anatolian sun for all to see.

Again, the city falls silent in a way no city should. It is like the deep inhale before a scream. When that scream comes, it erupts as a chorus of cheers.

Only their eyes are not on Polites. They are on her. The people of Troy do not merely admire Andromache for these two hidden victories made visible. They *love* her for them. I can see it painted on their faces as they take in the work of art her body has become.

The Old Bloods, notably, shift in their seats. King Priam, Antenor, Laocoon—none of them seems certain of how to react, yet not one of these leaders stands in respect or does anything that might cause the other council members to follow, granting Andromache the approval or recognition she deserves.

But they know. That, I can also see. And then, nobody is looking at them anymore. Least of all Andromache.

One man breaks from the platform where the Old Bloods sit. The man all of this is for. He races across the arena, and the cheering in the stands grows even louder. When he reaches for his wife, I can almost feel the heat of his touch when he pulled me up from the floor in his hall—warm and restrained, gentle yet firm. All at once. Andromache glides into his arms as gracefully as she slid from the horse. A seamless fit. Their embrace is like the collision of two stars. The sight of their rejoicing melts whatever remains of my rancor. A knowing wind seems to blow across the arena, whispering to all of us through the scattered dust.

It is a rare thing, this. *So very, very rare.*

And I find I understand. Why she did everything she has done. Hector and Andromache are the only ones who can save this city.

Even if everything is what it has cost me.

Only how will Paris respond?

I search the platform once more, but Paris is no longer sitting comfortably. He is standing on the sidelines, like he often is, gripping his bow so hard I can see the whites of his knuckles from here. I can also see his face, and it is not defeated like I would expect. No, it is hungry. Starving to fulfill the plan that has been driving him since the very beginning. The scheme that brought me here.

An arrow that has always been aimed at Hector.

My hands go rigid. All of a sudden, it's as if I am the one standing nude in the middle of an arena with the city looking on. I follow the gust that has given me such a violent chill.

Turning slowly, my eyes come to rest on Polites. Despite the celebration that swirls around his humiliation, the Ithacan stares at me as if he can see right through my Death Mask.

His lips quirk. The small smile of one who has a terrible secret.

43

ANDROMACHE

"YOU HAVE BEEN keeping secrets." Hector gathers my half-naked body into his arms, beaming as if the city of onlookers has all but disappeared.

"I wanted to be sure."

With a boyish grin, Hector pulls back to scan the length of me. "I'd say there can be no doubt."

Delight shines in his eyes, but there is something else. Forgiveness? Trust? Not because I gave him what he needed, but because I did it the way only I could.

A sound between a laugh and a sob erupts from my chest. The jubilant throng is cheering so loudly, I'm forced to shout above the roar, "And now all of Troy knows it."

My neck tingles, pulling my gaze toward the royal platform. But the eyes staring at us so intently do not belong to Priam or Paris. They belong to the Ithacan prisoner, Polites. The captive's mouth is bleeding into his beard, but there is something odd about the expression he wears. Satisfaction. It makes me feel as if someone I can't see is poised to launch a spear at my head.

I glance over my other shoulder to the defeated chariot rolling away from the arena. Helmet down, Paris passes us with his gaze fixed straight ahead. He has no desire to witness what comes next. For once, he does not even feign happiness for his brother.

For once, Paris does not pretend to be anything other than what he is.

The thrumming in my chest quickens as I take in the stands of people who do not even notice Paris's departure. This is everything we have waited for, and the entire city is here to witness the triumph. Young women and old men I recognize from the Fair Winds. Children from the asylum camps who are still in faded rags but don the brightest smiles. Even Madam Morgestia stands in the front row, waving a veil that is the same Aegean blue of the sky, streaks of kohl running down her saggy cheeks.

Still, the face I long to see most is the one I do not.

Where are you, Rhea?

Unwilling to give in to fear, I grab Hector's hands and place both across my belly. The horse nickers, nuzzling each of our necks as our foreheads touch.

Hector is utterly still. Eyes closed, he breathes in deeply as he holds the small dome of our entire world.

He looks up, racked by wonder. In the next breath, the prince of Troy is sinking to his knees. He wraps his arms around my legs, taking slow and steady inhales against me.

And then he laughs. With his king, his allies, his people looking on as he kneels before his wife, Hector laughs, even as tears stream down his face. The purest of sounds echoes across the square.

I have never heard anything like it. Not in all the years I have loved him.

Rising to his feet, Hector cups my face in his hands, consummating his joy with a gentle kiss. When he pulls away, his chestnut eyes are still shining. More tears escape freely, the pride of any Trojan man capable of grief and gladness and everything in between. I press my mouth against his cheek. In the salt, I can almost taste the preservative that might just save this city.

Save *us*.

I give the council members below the king's platform the briefest glance, but the truth is, I no longer seek their recognition. I have the other half of my soul in my arms, his child beneath my heart, and the love of a people too long overlooked embracing all three of us.

My whisper reaches for my husband's ear. "They have no reason to stop us now."

"I couldn't care less about them or their succession." Hector kisses me again, more hungry than grateful this time. "Boy or girl, this child is *ours*."

The gentleness of his words feels like a promise of all that is to come. Hector the proud father. Hector rocking our baby in the cradle he made and one day teaching his child to ride, whether that child is a daughter or son. As the lines around his eyes deepen, I realize there has never been a version of him more enticing or beloved.

"What is it?" I ask, his catching laughter filling me up as well.

"Your smile. You are beaming, Andromache." Almost shyly, Hector pulls his eyes from my heavy breasts. "It is . . . strange."

"Then let us not waste this opportunity," I say, turning to the two men who approach us from the royal platform.

King Priam's gem-studded scepter mostly serves as a cane, but he is never without this reminder of the former power that has been gradually slipping with his mind. The priest Laocoon walks by his side in a blur of flowing robes. Hector and I meet the men at the stone altar in the center of the square.

Laocoon washes his hands in a bronze basin. He takes a large amphora of wine and adds it to a silver cup with two handles, partially filled already with the blood of a lamb. After scattering barley around the altar, the priest raises the cup and utters a prayer before pouring out the splash of a libation in the dirt. Laocoon then hands the silver vessel to Priam, who presses a thumb dipped into the blood-wine against Hector's forehead.

The old king's eyes radiate pride as he wordlessly confirms his chosen heir.

That glow dims somewhat when they pass to me. I have done my duty to him as a daughter, and he will at least acknowledge that, even if he chooses not to see everything else I have done on Troy's behalf. The king hands me the depas cup. I take a sip of the metallic mixture, then give the cup to Hector. Not to drink—he has been visibly marked, whereas I must bear the burden within me—but rather to share.

And he knows from the nod I give him who he must share it with.

Hector turns away from the royal platform and walks over to the standing rows of common people. The shocked silence becomes a deafening pulse as strong as the glares of the slighted Old Bloods at our back.

Hector stops before a family at the front of the crowd. A family made up of four brothers who have recently welcomed a baby sister, proving the folklore of Aetheopia about figs and dates trustworthy. The warmth blazing within me spreads as Hector hands the merchant Ekon the cup. He is bewildered, but when Hector nods, Ekon drinks. He then shares the sacred elixir with his radiant wife and the eldest son I've been watching for among the ranks, Zaidan, who passes the cup to his brothers and then beyond. Farther up and farther into the stands. I suspect more will taste this fruit of the gods than we can imagine. These people are used to getting by on little, but they will have *this* king's best, not his scraps.

I turn to Priam and Laocoon. "Hector and I hope you will join us at the feast tonight for Troy's allies. Your presence would do them great honor."

Neither man responds. They are too busy gaping at what Hector has done to upset the balance of . . . everything.

The succession ceremony completed, Hector and I move to the royal platform where Queen Hecuba waits on the stairs, her henna-dyed hair escaping her headscarf as her equally red smile grows.

"The heir of Troy will have a son!" Hecuba cries for the crowd. She raises her arms high, reigniting the celebration as if her beloved Hector has not just transgressed every norm.

As we take our seats, Hecuba hands me a cloak. "I admire your ability to make an announcement that will not soon be forgotten. But the time for trekking in the wilderness has come to an end. You are a warrior woman no longer." She stares at my bare stomach, some of her elation fading.

"Of course, Mother," I agree as amiably as I can, glancing down the row to make sure the queen I actually need to consult is here. And she is. Waiting behind Helenus in the shadows. "But before we move on to the festival games, there's something I would like to say."

Dropping Hecuba's cloak into my seat, I reach for a tightly veiled Helen and pull her into the daylight beside me, before moving both of us to the edge of the platform. No one looks more stunned at what I am doing than Hector. "Andromache, what is—"

"People of Troy!" I announce with a force that comes from the very core of me. "Today is a blessed day for Prince Hector. You have shared in our joy, and so you must also share in the truth, even when it is tinged in sorrow."

I glance at Helen, her pale arms trembling. There is hesitation in her eyes. Not fear exactly. Just the look of someone who is about to leap from a great height. "Remember your promise," Helen whispers.

I realize then that what she is uncertain of is *me*. Will I answer her cry for help the next time it comes, or will I turn my back on her again?

My voice rings out to reassure her. "You all deserve to know that there would not *be* an heir of Troy if it weren't for the hands of a most gifted healer."

I cast Helen a firm nod.

She lowers her veil. The unified gasp that follows is even louder than the cry that arose during my botched fertility rite all those years ago.

"I give you Helen of Troy."

And I give her with high cheekbones bruised and a broken nose. Every inch of porcelain perfection a picture of chaos. Even still, the poised woman stands with her chin lifted and her back arrow-straight. Silent tears stream down Helen's swollen face as something inside her cracks open.

There are few things more unbearable than suffering that is not seen.

But they see her now. They see everything.

And they know who is to blame.

Startled cries descend into grumbling as the collective eye of Troy searches the arena for Paris. But he is long gone. Still, one day he will be made to account for his actions, of that I have no doubt.

Helen trembles as she takes her seat. She has just delivered a fatal blow. Paris was shamed as a warrior at Menelaus's hand, but it was his own hand that mortified him as a man.

And he will never recover. I do not need to see his rage to know it.

Unwilling to dampen her favorite son's triumph any further, Queen Hecuba orders the lute and lyre players into the square. A few songs later and the people are chirping merrily again. Soon a pair of wrestlers take to the field to stretch their sinewy limbs.

"That took great courage," I say to Helen once the festivities have recommenced.

Her restless eyes sweep the crowd.

"He can't hurt you anymore."

"You underestimate him," she says. "Just as he has always underestimated you."

"I have offered you my protection, and I will hold to my word. Just give me a few more hours and Paris will hold sway over no one. Least of all you."

Helen swallows hard, casting me a weary look that says there is nothing she desires more than to go lie down. But we both know she cannot leave until the festival is finished and she can return home safely. With us.

As the music of lutes and lyres fades, I look to the muddy wrestling pit on our right. Hector leans over and whispers, "You're blushing, my *alev*. Should I be worried?"

"This is . . . unexpected. That's all."

Not only that Sarpedon of Lycia is restored enough from his voyage to be attending these games at all, but that he is striding across the ring in the nude.

It seems I am not the only one who lacks shame, though his brazenness is according to accepted custom.

The Lycian captain and the Trojan warrior he is about to wrestle are both as naked as the day they were born. Their muscular bodies are drenched in olive oil and coated with a layer of sand to defend them from the wind and the sun.

I reach down to grab the sprigs of jasmine laid at the edge of the platform by my feet, casting a smile to the three girls who placed them there. Sisters, by the look of them. They bow shyly, eyeing Helen like she is still the most stunning woman they have ever seen. It didn't take long for the people's gifts to pile up. Small tokens, mostly. Flowers. Homemade bread. A woven cap for the baby.

I prize them more than all the gold in Troy.

My hand grazes my front, grasping for this strange culmination that feels more like a beginning than an end. We have a child, and that child will find he still has a city with plenty of cattle to feed it—all thanks to three young girls whose bravery these cheering people will never know. Along with the willingness of our allies to drive Odysseus back to his dung heap.

We have won on every front.

Back in the ring, Glaucus and Sarpedon bend their heads close together. Glaucus traces something on his cousin's chest with what appears to be a bit of charcoal. An odd custom, though perhaps my red war paint inspired it. I can't see the design from here, but I do not care where it comes from so long as it brings good fortune.

"I was right," Hector says. "You've taken to this pirate." He leans back, resting his feet on the railing in front of us. "Or he has taken to you."

I gesture to the top half of me. "Or perhaps the rumors are true and Lycians just really love their mothers."

Hector chuckles and we refocus on the muddy arena. As Sarpedon stretches his limbs, he glances up often, as if searching the sky for the good omen of an eagle. But I can tell he's really scanning the platform, making sure that I see him.

I do.

The two warriors lean forward to clasp wrists as a sign of goodwill. When the match begins, the Trojan dives for Sarpedon's legs, but the Lycian takes a nimble leap to the left and his opponent falls face-first in the mud. Sarpedon, along with the rest of the crowd, roars with laughter.

"Which one are we rooting for again? My Trojan?" Hector teases.

"Captain Sarpedon deserves the win. This festival wouldn't have been possible without the use of his fast ship and skilled crew to deliver the supplies."

"Of course." Hector's lips twitch, but there isn't a hint of envy in his eyes. I'm struck by what a rarity it is—to be part of a union so solid, both husband and wife can appreciate another person's strength or beauty for what it is.

And Sarpedon has both. He isn't as large as Hector, but there's a gracefulness about his lean, athletic frame. His stocky opponent, on the other hand, scrounges about like a beetle in the dirt—all effort but no form. In a matter of minutes, both panting men wear mud from head to foot, a parting gift of the recent rains. Sarpedon stands tall, his arm raised high in the air by Glaucus. His face is a wall of mud except for the white flash of his haughty smile.

The Lycian saunters over to the raised platform, where I force my eyes to remain fixed on his face. He appears to be doing the same. With a deerlike leap that makes Hecuba clutch her godstone, Sarpedon throws his bare torso over the railing, extending a long arm to me.

"Your veil, please, Harsa," Sarpedon says with the wry grin I wouldn't know him without. "It will bring me good fortune in the next match."

Hector rolls his eyes. Like me, he recognizes this moment for what it is. He knows the allied captains must be mine, just as Troy's army is his. And now I must claim them. With the entire city looking on.

"It doesn't appear that you—any of you—require much luck, Captain." I glance around to where our other allies are competing in a variety of games. And winning them more often than not. "Our extra training in your absence is clearly paying off."

"That's not how I heard the men speak of it. Unless training is how the Amazons refer to such acts of torture?"

With a throaty laugh, I hand Sarpedon the unused veil hanging over the back of my chair. "Then be glad you missed it. Still, I'm willing to stake far more than fabric on your future victories." Removing the gold signet ring stamped with my flame, I thread the veil through the sign of authority. "Be sure to bring this back to me."

Sarpedon clutches the headscarf carefully. "And what if I decide to keep both for myself instead?"

"Careful, brother," Hector growls, though there is good humor in it.

"My apologies, Prince Hector." For a fraction of a heartbeat, Sarpedon's sardonic face turns serious. "I merely wish to pay respects to the Alev, and to remind the commander of Troy's armies of how graciously he has been blessed by the gods."

The Lycian slips off the platform railing and saunters back to the middle of the arena, where the people have adorned the ground with tossed flowers. As he walks off, Sarpedon slips my ring into the leather pouch at his belt. Glaucus hands him a strip of linen that he uses to clean himself off before tying my veil around his neck like a scarf. I catch a final flash of the marking on his chest, but it is smeared from the match and I still can't make it out.

"*The* Alev?"

I suppress a smile. "I have no idea."

With a grunt, Hector goes from sitting at attention to slumping in his chair. "That man grows too bold. They *all* grow too bold."

"Perhaps." I cast Hector a hooded glance. As the day goes on, it becomes clear Sarpedon isn't the only allied captain who stands out. Hippothous is dominating the stone throw. Akamas wins the horseback race. Nhorcys the Strong proves he is worthy of the name.

"I wish to take a walk," I tell Hector after a few hours of sitting. "Will you join me, Helen?"

She nods, her face drained even more after watching acts of lesser violence that still point to the more vicious ones to come when the war resumes.

But we have time. Rhea's girls are watching the enemy camps, and Odysseus will need to regroup. With our allied forces bolstered with fresh recruits, we will be ready for the king of Ithaca when he comes circling our gates again.

As soon as Helen and I leave the platform, a rush of excitement passes through me. Women in the stands sway their hips to the beat of Anatolian drums while their children chew on skewers of roasted meat. I can feel something building, something *growing* at every turn. Its verdant scent in every raw, rich aroma.

It is hope, and it is blowing through this festival on the wings of the wind.

But it is also change. A kind of freshness, like the first days of spring. In a thousand lifetimes, I never would have imagined walking with Helen's comforting silence at my side. Even more, I never imagined wishing I might absorb some of the openness she has always worn like a fine garment—a perceived weakness that may be the true source of the power behind her face, battered or not.

No wonder Paris kept it hidden. A face that hospitable and hopeful draws weary wanderers to it like the most welcoming hearth.

It is the face of the Mother herself.

A low roar pulls our attention back to the games. To our left, Memnon, captain of the Aethiopians, has just won a boxing match. When I stop to watch his victory celebration, I notice a smeared mark, just a shade darker than the tawny skin of his glistening chest, in the same spot where Glaucus marked Sarpedon.

In the ring across the way, Peirous is competing in the spearthrow. It is not the old Thracian's greatest gift, but apparently his shoulder is still stronger than the Trojan warriors who've spent these idle weeks arm-wrestling in winehouses. His weapon flies across the ring, landing in the sand right below the platform where the royal family sits.

My breath catches. He too has the mark.

An itch crawls between my shoulder blades from the platform above. King Priam and his brother Antenor. Observing my captains. Weighing, measuring, judging. Seeing for themselves the truth their ears would never hear when it was issued by my voice.

Still . . . why this strange, sudden weight?

"You feel it too?" Helen says as I glance around the games.

"Feel what?" I'm curious to know what she means and if it matches my own disquiet. The Anatolian sun beats heavy on our backs even as a cool gale blows.

"The inhale before the scream," she says softly.

Yes. That is it exactly.

"It's the prisoner Polites," Helen continues. "Something about his manner. He does not act like a man who cares for his life. I . . . I should talk with him sooner rather than later, Andromache."

The fearful look she gives me is a scream of its own. A scream we have heard before.

Three times.

We may laugh and dance and sing this day away, but we must also enjoy it fully. With the plague and the rains behind us, there can be no doubt that our time of victory will not last forever.

Every inch of my stretching skin can sense it on the wind.

THE HAWK

Blood on the wind.
The Hawk glides
through billows of black smoke.
Flood of water turned rain of arrows.
The Hawk dives in and out of shafts,
deadly tips winking in the sun.

The Hawk tastes fear.
Sing to me, cries the Hawk as men scream.
The time for singing is done.
Screams come faster.
Clashing bronze.
The Voice cries through the Hawk.
Shriek of hope and dread,
proclaiming the truth to those below.

One storm is over.
Another is about to begin.

~⌒~

44

ANDROMACHE

"YOU WILL NOT have long with him," I tell Helen.

The sky over our heads glows with the pink and purple swirls of the setting sun. As the evening settles in the southernmost corner of the Lower City, the cool air carries a hundred different spices, all mixed with the smoky tang of charred meat.

The first time I visited this place, misery was as dense as the haphazard asylum camp hastily erected in the shadow of the south wall. Tonight, laughter echoes off the ramparts. The shadows under the eyes of the serving-women Bodecca recruited for our feast seem lighter. Perhaps because tonight their children will go to sleep with sticky fingers and full bellies. It is a victory that required neither sword nor spear, and for that, I know Queen Penthesilea would be proud.

"If you can convince Polites to talk, that would spare us all a great deal of trouble. If not . . ."

"I understand," Helen says.

"He is in there." I point to the building directly north of the refugee camp and the south wall. A lair of sensual delights that will soon become a cavern of pain if Polites does not talk willingly.

Helen takes in the arched entrance of the brothel, hung with a dozen veils. "It is interesting company you keep these days, Andromache."

"These days, I take my friends where I can find them."

She studies me with a thoughtful expression. Then Helen walks over to the armed guards waiting to escort her under the arch without looking back.

My men wait in the winehouse next to Madam Morgestia's. A circle of torches glows around the perimeter of the large courtyard just visible at the end of a narrow alleyway between the two establishments. The same courtyard and winehouse where I first met a dueling Sarpedon and Akamas all those weeks ago.

It seemed a fitting place for a reunion.

"Are you ready?" Hector approaches from the alleyway and offers me his arm.

I take a deep, steadying breath. Despite our recent history here, the allies gathered in the courtyard are captains and kings in their own lands. Regardless of how well we drill and feed them, nothing can make up for the fact that they are dining in a common winehouse and not at King Priam's table where they belong.

"You are their liaison. They are waiting for you to start," Hector says.

"I have already given too many speeches," I confess. "I have no more inspiration to offer."

He lifts my chin. "You speak most truthfully when you speak from the heart. And it is the truth that makes men come alive." Hector threads my arm through his. "Besides, I will be standing right beside you. Your bumbling, inarticulate husband."

My laugh precedes us into the courtyard.

A fire blazes in the raised rectangular hearth that takes up the north side, where Larion is busy turning a rack of beef over the flames. The musicians playing in the corner put down their instruments as Hector and I approach the long table that has been prepared with a cloth of the deepest Phoenician purple. Nearly twenty captains, all dressed in the formal attire of their homelands, sit in hushed expectation. I am surprised, but pleased, to see Laocoon standing off to the side. It seems at least one member of the King's Council recognizes the son of Troy who will soon lead it.

"You start," I whisper.

Hector does not miss a beat. "Welcome, allies," he announces in the Luwian that binds us. "Our high priest has joined us to make an offering in honor of the Divine Twins."

The old priest moves in front of the fire, barefoot and without his usual pageantry. In the past, Laocoon's gaze carried nothing but disdain whenever he looked my way, but tonight his face is impenetrable. Lifting his muttering lips to the heavens, Laocoon throws the bloody organs and entrails of a goat onto the grill rack resting across the fire. A flagon of wine makes the embers steam.

A northern wind blows over the high southern wall, filling the courtyard with a low moaning. Like the anguished cry of the dead woman they say walks Troy's highest ramparts. I pull my shawl tighter around my shoulders, uttering my own silent prayer that Helen can use her unique power to un- cover the Ithacans' secret path to our walls. I will have the information from Polites one way or another, but I'd prefer that the only blood spilled tonight be that of the animals we have offered the gods.

The sacrifice concluded, Laocoon passes around a platter of the charred offering for each man seated at the table. I force down a bite of a blackened kidney.

Bodecca's servants then bring out platter after platter. Figs drizzled in honey. Wild boar and smoked venison. Along with countless foreign dishes I've never seen. Each time a captain glimpses a delicacy from his homeland, he reaches excitedly for the bowl or plate like he is a child again, at home in his mother's kitchen. To my right, Peirous shakes his head while Nhorcys the Strong flirts artlessly with a red-faced Faria as she refills wine. To my left, Akamas and Sarpedon hold Polydorus immobile between them while Hippothous balances a pomegranate on his head. King Rhesus laughs loudly when Pandarus takes aim with an imaginary bow.

"They are more united already," Hector murmurs into his wine cup.

I smile and take a bite of tuna doused in lemon juice, a dish from Percote on the Dardanelles. It's been so long since we feasted on fresh fish, the food of kings. I'd nearly forgotten that there are as many flavors in this world as there are races of men.

My gaze drifts to Laocoon, where he sits apart. The empty seats around him meant for Troy's own captains and council members are a glaring slight. My eyes land on the seat set in the position of highest honor, and the fish turns sour in my mouth.

Even still. Even after he has named Hector his heir, Priam refuses to humble himself before the people his son loves, and who would love him in return.

I take a sip of watered-down wine to wash the bad taste away and turn my attention to the masculine grunts and crude jokes flying across the courtyard. In the alleyway beyond, laughter echoes from the open ground where the allied soldiers and the common people are having feasts of their own. They are joyful sounds. Sounds of hope that will not be overshadowed by the loud absence of petty leaders who do not know the meaning of the titles they hold.

Hector gives me an urging look.

A speech is expected, and since the king of Troy is not here to give it, the duty falls to us.

But duty alone does not win wars.

I take in the sea of foreigners we are depending on, a courtyard full of captains who still have more cause to resent Troy than die for her. Men whose presence here has more to do with the treasure they will take home and the oaths they swore that urge them to uphold their honor.

"Andromache?" Hector says. "What's wrong?"

I pause a little longer, mind churning but heart knowing. "How can mere words ever move men who speak in so many tongues to sacrifice themselves for strangers?"

Silence is his only answer.

"Andromache!" This time, my name comes not from the man beside me but from a figure moving hurriedly through the courtyard entrance.

Something in Cyrrian's expression has me pushing my chair back and walking briskly to where he stands in the shadows of the alleyway.

"Rhea did not make it back to the walls last night," he says in a rush. "I've been looking for you since dawn. Not even Bodecca knew where to find you."

"I was with Helen." Ignoring the obvious question in his eyes, I focus on what matters. "Rhea is clever. With Odysseus on the move last night, she must have thought returning to the city was too great a risk."

She would have been right. And yet something in my reasoning rings hollow.

"No." Cyrrian shakes his head. "She knew you were expecting her. She wouldn't have missed the festival. Not by choice."

"Rhea is resourceful," I say the words again, for my comfort as much as his. "If she remained in the camps, there is a good reason for it."

"We shouldn't have let her go back."

I study him closely. There is more he isn't telling me, but with Cyrrian of the Two Shadows, there usually is.

"Wherever she is, she has a purpose. Trust her, Cyrrian. As I do. She has earned it."

"Something is wrong, Andromache. I can feel it." His voice is haunted. Ringing with the pain I only ever glimpse on those nights we sit together on the wall high above the stables, singing our sorrows to the wind.

That same wind finds us now in this cramped alleyway. Despite the air of celebration, I feel the nagging disquiet too. It has been hanging over me since the festival. Only my concerns have less to do with Rhea than they do with our prisoner and what he isn't saying.

"Feelings can lie." I give Cyrrian's arm an encouraging squeeze before abruptly dropping my hand.

Just like words.

On their own, they are not enough.

"Come with me." I do not give Cyrrian the chance to argue. I turn back to the central table, where the feasting shows no signs of slowing. I can feel Hector's eyes on me as I walk toward the gathered musicians and remove a lyre from a startled bard's grip.

"I promise I will return it in one piece," I assure him before thrusting the instrument into Cyrrian's hands. "Accompany me. You know the tune."

"It is getting dark. I should go back and wait for Rhea in the temple." Cyrrian's eyes burn with frustration to do something.

"Waiting will not make her reappear any faster. Trust her and trust me." I gesture to the men behind us. "Now is the time to make all the risks we have taken count for something."

I hum the first few notes and understanding dawns. Cyrrian's throat bobs once before he nods.

Cyrrian's fingers deftly work the strings. Each note ignites the verses in my mind.

It is an old song. One that sprang from the lush gardens and life waters of the east, where the very first city was built by human hands. "*A city in the sky,*" my mother used to say. I knew without asking that she was not speaking of Mount Olympus. For this city was home to men, not immortals who had never tasted death nor felt its sting. A city where a river flowed beside an ancient oak, its streets populated by people of every tongue and tribe. Only there was no need for walls or kings because every man, woman, and child was free to rule themselves. Free to *be.*

Cyrrian's clear tenor joins me at each chorus in the Hittite style, but my gaze remains fixed on the faint stars appearing in the wine-stained sky. I do not dare look at the captains until the last note of the lyre is plucked and our paired voices flee into the night. When I glance up, the faces staring at me are seeped with longing. The longing for a home that can never be invaded or sacked, and for the bonds of brotherhood that keep a city standing far longer than the thickest walls.

As I scan the rest of the courtyard, I find Helen watching me from the hearth with glistening eyes. I search her face for some sign of success with Polites, but she merely shakes her head. The stab of disappointment is brief. Unlike Helen, a part of me wants to give the enemy what he has coming to him. I am motioning her toward me when Sarpedon stands abruptly, wiping the tears from his eyes. My headscarf is still tied around his neck. He pulls it down to reveal the flame mark on his chest.

"The Lycians will stay and fight with Troy, but they will only take their fire from the Alev." He places a hand over his chest. "May it ever burn bright."

Pandarus rises to mimic the same gesture. "May it ever burn bright."

He is followed by Glaucus. Nhorcys the Strong. Peirous. Adrestus. Pyraechmes.

It feels as though the child in my womb is crawling into my throat as, one by one, the rest of the men stand to reveal their marks.

"I will remain your liaison," I tell them, unsure of what is happening. "If you decide to stay, that will not change."

"We do not need a liaison. We need a leader. One we all can agree upon. That is you, Alev." Sarpedon lifts something from under the table. His shield. The proud Lion of Lycia roars at the center. Directly above it, a new symbol shines in fresh black paint.

The only sound in the courtyard comes from the crackling fire.

"You wish for my wife to lead you? Under a separate banner than that of the kings of Troy?" Hector's voice is flat. Measured. Not even I can read it.

"No disrespect to Troy or her princes," Sarpedon says. "But Troy is not our city. If we are to shed blood over a woman, we choose to do it on behalf of a warrior queen."

As one, the captains look to me.

"You must know I could not ride out with you into battle. Not now." The only thing I find harder to believe than my words is that they no longer taste of regret.

"Forgive me, Harsa. Your archer's arm is impressive, but as you once told us yourself, that isn't your greatest asset." Sarpedon cracks a smile.

"Our request is not meant as an insult," Glaucus adds when Hector still does not speak. "If anything, it is a tribute to the kind of man you are off the battlefield as well as on, to have a wife other men would follow."

Sarpedon's gaze does not leave my face. "But make no mistake about what we want. For it is not what the Alev does. It is who she is."

Of all the allied captains, only Hippothous does not stand to reveal a mark of his own. I seek him out at the far end of the table, his hardened gaze locked on something over my shoulder.

A hunched figure draped in ceremonial robes steps through the court-yard gate.

"Father." A smile breaks across Hector's face. "You honor us. We had hoped you—"

"What is this?" King Priam scans the courtyard, studying our foreign allies united under a charcoal flame. He rests his arm against the wall as if he needs its help to stand.

Paris enters on the king's heels with two dozen royal guards and archers. He takes in the ring of captains with my mark emblazoned across their chests.

Allies of Troy who apparently require an armed entourage to receive a visit from the Citadel.

Helen flinches at my side, drawing Paris's notice. Something almost like regret twists his fine features, but his eyes meet mine with a simmering hatred.

"Would someone like to explain what is going on here?" Paris's gaze is calculating. Even with his hopes for the succession dashed, he is still search-ing for some way to claw his way back to the top of the Citadel.

"We are celebrating that our allies have agreed to stay," I tell him.

"But they would do so under your banner rather than the black stallion of Troy?" says King Priam, more lucid than I have ever seen him.

For once, the shock Paris wears is entirely real. "That is a slight to our ancient house and every man who bears her mark."

"It is no slight to give honor where honor is due," Sarpedon answers coolly. "Strength is not shown by dominating the weak but by kneeling when the situation requires."

Paris snorts. "What halfwit Lycian bard do we have to thank for such sagacity?"

Sarpedon's jaw goes rigid. "My mother."

"This is Troy, not Lycia." King Priam lifts his head like it weighs more than the rest of his body. "Kneeling is not our way."

"But it is our way." Akamas lends his voice to Sarpedon's. "And it is *our* choice. Years ago, we came here for you, but we have found Troy's hospitality wanting. We will stay only for the Alev."

Their request is not treason. But it surely feels that way to Priam. The men at this table may be our allies out of necessity of the common threats we face, but many have also been our enemies in the past. Blood once spilled is never truly wiped clean, and there has been much of it on all sides.

It wasn't so long ago that Priam watched his own father slaughtered at the hands of a Hittite ally, a man invited into the gates of Troy as a friend, but who took the throne for himself until Priam took it back.

Power is never easily shared. Not then, and not now. Not even with a daughter-in-law who may well carry the future king.

"Have you nothing to say, brother?" Paris asks Hector, whose silence is deafening.

"I say that our friends have chosen well. And so have I."

Our gazes tangle. Heat and pride. Understanding without words.

"You'd allow your pregnant wife to ride onto the plain to meet our enemies, bare-chested like some vulgar whore?" Paris asks, incredulous.

With great difficulty, I tear my eyes from my husband. "I don't need to set foot on the battlefield to lead these men. Who would know this better than you?"

Paris's cheeks go bloodless. "Come, Helen. We are leaving this place."

Helen's small cry breaks through the hard shell of my rage. When she shrinks back, I step forward.

"Helen stays."

"She is my wife. Some of us still know what that means."

A deep trench cuts across King Priam's brow as his glassy gaze passes between Paris and Helen. For a moment, I think he will intervene, but then, he turns away.

From the wounds on Helen's skin.

From the terror in her eyes that she cannot hide.

Hector goes rigid, his body trembling with the restraints of duty and blood that bind him.

But they do not bind me.

Paris bolts toward us, reaching for Helen. I grab the spear of the man next to me. My fingers close around the wooden shaft and thrust. The flat edge catches the collar of Paris's tunic.

"Take one more step and what you are due to receive at Menelaus's hands will feel like a warm embrace in comparison."

"You go too far, Andromache." Red climbs the withered vines of King Priam's neck. "It is a punishable crime to lay hands on a prince of Troy."

At the unspoken threat, the allied captains behind me reach for their weapons. Across the courtyard, the Trojan soldiers at Paris's back do the same. Violence dances through the air. A part of me craves it. Wants nothing more than to exact justice for all the wrongs that have been done. To all of us.

But whom would that serve?

"Our fight lies outside these walls. Not with each other." I lower the spear. "Still, I'll not sit by and watch you harm a defenseless woman."

Never again.

"*Bitch.* You care nothing for Helen. You only wish to use her for your own ends. As you have so skillfully used my brother."

"Paris!" Hector's voice booms through the courtyard.

Paris's face contorts. "What, Hector? Would you betray me *again*, all for the sake of this unnatural woman who—"

The crack of bone echoes through the courtyard.

Paris drops to his knees. When he straightens, his nose is a red ruin. There is no more pleasant veneer. There is only shock. Then hurt. And finally, blinding hatred. For us both.

"I looked up to you once, brother." Paris spits out a mouthful of blood. "You could do no wrong. But then you turned away, just like the rest of them." Cords pop at his throat. "I labor for Troy in the shadows while you bask openly in her sun, and yet they worship the ground you tread on. Everything you have has been given to you, and you deserve *none* of it."

A shrill cry pierces the courtyard.

I follow Helen's gaze over the winehouse walls. Suddenly, the night is alive with the light of a hundred stars burning across the sky. They fall through the darkness in a high arch over the walls as they head directly toward . . .

"Andromache!" Hector's voice is an echo from somewhere far away.

The air is knocked from my lungs as someone dives into me with the force of a charging bull. Strong arms twist me in the air, cushioning my middle from the fall. I glance down at the hard body below me, expecting to find Hector. Hippothous's face greets me instead.

He flips us over and covers us both with his shield.

Metal resounds like our roof in a hailstorm. Men shout. Servant girls scream. Then a moment of silence that magnifies the roar in my head. Hippothous hurls his shield and rolls off me. For a moment, we lie face-to-face, panting in the dirt.

Then Hector is there, pulling me to my feet. Flaming arrows stick in the ground all around us. His hands tremble as he strokes my cheek. One breath. It is all he allows himself before he transforms from my husband into the commander of Troy's army.

"Raise the tables!"

Pottery smashes as our allies upend the long tables and set them sideways to provide a rudimentary barrier. Through the haze of smoke, I see that at least two of our allied captains have been wounded, along with several of Paris's archers. The rest grab their weapons, prepared for whatever comes next.

And something is coming.

No, not coming. It is already here.

Three times.

Hector pulls me underneath the winehouse awning as more arrows light the night sky over our heads. They fall upon the Lower City in a deadly half ring of fire that stretches from east to west. I watch them arc high over the walls, dropping onto the thatched roofs of houses and businesses closest to our exterior defenses. The drastic upward tilt of their flight tells me everything I need to know. Unlike men, the path of an arrow does not lie.

The Lower City is surrounded.

Judging by the number of arrows, there are easily a hundred men outside our gates, possibly many more.

But how? The Achaeans should never have been able to come so close in such numbers without sounding an alarm.

"Your men in the camps outside the west wall?" I ask Hector.

"We cut the numbers in half for the festival." His voice is grim. "After our success with the raid last night I thought . . ."

His somber expression says it all. Whatever men he left in those camps, they were the first to fall. While we were feasting, the Achaeans were closing in. By covert means we never did uncover. We thought we'd won, and in the end, it will be that pride, not our walls, that will be our downfall.

My pride. My downfall.

"Rhea." Her name escapes as a moan.

She would never have let Odysseus move against the Lower City without returning to warn us. Or trying to.

Another barrage of arrows. They fall in rhythmic waves, speaking of a tight coordination that fans the flames of my desperation. Distant screams force me back to the horror of the present moment, a moment that is far from over.

I cannot see the rest of the city from this low elevation, but I do not need to in order to glimpse what is at stake. The Achaean bow is deadly, but it has a limited range. The damage that fire can do to the Lower City is vast, especially here where the buildings are overcrowded and fire is a danger even in the most peaceful of times. Our system of spring-fed wells and inner walls of stone are intended to mitigate such a threat. It is unlikely any fire destruction should reach the upper levels of Troy. Even if the Lower City is lost, the Citadel will be safe.

Which is exactly as it has been designed.

"Peirous! Secure our prisoner!"

Questions about Odysseus's movements and Rhea's whereabouts whirl through my head as Hector bellows for the white-haired warrior, who nods at him before ducking out of the courtyard and breaking hard for the entrance to Madam Morgestia's.

Desperate cries fill the night along with the acrid stench of smoke. All around us, the roofs of the buildings closest to the walls are already starting to burn. Depending on how quickly it moves, it could engulf entire sections of the Lower City in minutes, trapping the people inside.

Women. Children. The elderly and infirm.

Hector and my allies.

We cannot let that happen.

We also cannot stop it by any means that belong to mortals.

I lift my eyes to the clear night sky, pleading with Tarhunt to send a storm cloud.

Instead, more flaming arrows rain down.

45

ANDROMACHE

SHIELDS RISE IN a wall from my left to my right to block the fall of arrows. When the Achaeans stop to reload, Peirous appears at the courtyard entrance, dragging Polites behind him. Hector pulls me back, but I yank my arm free. I need answers, and Polites is the only one who can give them. He is Odysseus's right hand. The one man he trusted to steal our cattle.

Cattle that at this moment are grazing unguarded in the fields beyond our eastern wall.

Polites takes in the destruction all around him. He smiles.

Icy dread spreads through me. The Ithacan prisoner knew this was coming. He knew, and he let us revel in our victory because it would only leave us distracted.

But I see everything now. Every angle.

Troy's walls are her greatest defense. But they are also a potential weakness. One the king of Ithaca has exploited thoroughly.

"Hector!" I cry. "The gates."

He looks at me. I know the moment he understands. A flash of fear he cannot hide.

Mother, forgive me. I have been such a fool.

More screams echo through the Lower City. The latest shower of fire pierces the high trellis of the courtyard, now scattered with broken pottery and scraps of our forgotten meal.

To my left, Pandarus blocks an arrow before it reaches the table where Faria, Larion, and Polydorus are hiding. Another flaming tip lands in the dirt not three steps from where I crouch. A third strikes the calf of a servant with lavender sprigs in her hair. She cries out and falls to her knees.

Akamas sprints into the open. With one hand, he throws the girl over a shoulder and makes his way back under the awning.

Out of the corner of my eye, I see Helen move toward them. Paris starts for her but is driven back by another wave of arrows.

"Stay back!" I raise my voice above the din, but most of the men have already taken shelter where they can. Stray arrows break through in regular waves, but the soldiers have their shields to protect them.

The people of the Lower City have no such armor.

A river of images runs through my head. Shy girls with work-worn hands and downcast eyes laying flower chains at my feet. Old men in rags bowing to offer me respect. Mothers with deeply lined faces watching their children play between rows of huts made in haste but tended with care.

Huts made of wood, not stone.

A gust of wind clears the worst of the smoke, driving it toward the untouched Citadel, where the Old Blood remain safe behind Troy's innermost walls.

All around me, arrows stick out of thatched roofs, the straw and mud-brick beneath them already blackening. I have knocked on these doors, and I have seen the faces of the women and children who make their homes behind them.

The smoke is getting thicker now, riding north on the wind, carrying sparks to those rows of homes the arrows have not yet reached. It has not rained in days. Something that had felt like the answer to our prayers a mere hour ago. The ground is still wet in places, but the thatched roofs have dried out in the hot sun.

Dark clouds drift toward us from the brothel next door. Sobs choke the air as the barefaced girls pour out of the doors, thrown wide open. Hector takes in the horrors, seeing the same things I see.

A groan draws my gaze to the end of the alleyway, where an old woman is pressed against the south wall, holding a child by the hand. Ash coats the woman's face and dark red stains her robes around the protruding end of an arrow. Her crooked legs tremble with effort, but still, she presses the little boy to the stone behind her.

"I see them, Alev."

Peirous's cloud of white hair appears at my side. At his signal, two Thracians scramble into the alley. One grabs an overturned cart and lifts it high, as the others move to collect the woman and the boy. I do not see where they take them.

Hector helps me to my feet. His next words are halted by the arrival of reinforcements, bearing a familiar crest on their shield. A black horse. The horse of Troy.

My blood runs cold.

"Hector, where is . . ."

I look back to find Priam in the middle of the courtyard, beholding the clouds of smoke as they billow over the walls, threatening the city that was ruled by his father, and his father before him.

I hear the wails of the oncoming arrows before their flames streak the sky.

"Father!"

Hector and Paris both lunge forward.

A single arrow blazes a path through the night. It is almost upon Priam when a figure lurches out from behind an upturned table. I recognize the man's muscular frame before I do his face.

A grunt echoes through the courtyard as Nhorcys the Strong knocks the king aside, stepping into the path of the flaming arrow. It grazes the back of his head before it hits the winehouse wall. The Phrygian's oiled braids catch like a torch.

Nhorcys screams in surprise.

Akamas is on him before he hits the ground. The Thracian rips off his tunic and uses it to smother the flames. Behind them, Sarpedon steps into the open space in front of the king.

"Are you all right?" I call out to Nhorcys where he leans against the winehouse wall. Ash streaks his skin, and raw patches of scalp show through his singed braids. His normally tan face is deathly pale.

"How is the king?" comes his only reply.

"He'll live." Peirous helps the king in question to his feet.

Priam takes in the grizzled Thracian on his left and the stocky Phrygian on his right. Something moves behind the clouds of his eyes as they meet mine across the ruined courtyard.

Every word I have ever said.

Every warning I have uttered that fell on deaf ears seems to howl in the air between us.

For the first time, the king of Troy looks at me. Really *looks* at me.

As cries rise in the night all around us, I find that I no longer care.

Paris's men move at once, forming a line of Trojan shields before their king.

"Who is that lunatic?"

I follow Hippothous's finger down the street hugging the south wall. A street that is rapidly filling with flames as the asylum camp catches fire, sending up thick black smoke.

"A man who believes himself blessed by the gods." I grit my teeth and watch Aeneas sprint toward us.

"They have blocked all of the gates, pinning us inside!" Aeneas pants as he takes his place at Hector's side, confirming what I already guessed. "Their barriers are weakest at the Scaean gate, but it would still take the help of every last god to break through it." He takes stock of our surroundings. "This fire will soon rage out of control. We must get these people to the shelter below the Citadel. The stone there will protect us. It is their only chance."

A woman in garish silks stumbles past the courtyard opening. A few girls follow on her heels, each clutching baskets as they make their way to the well near the outer wall. Larion and Polydorus move to help.

"Leave it!" Aeneas calls the boys back. They pause. Beyond them, the woman attempts to drag her full basket to the burning brothel. Feet tangle in the hem of her robes and she lands on her knees a few paces away, the contents of her basket running through the mud.

Instead of kohl, dirt streaks Madam Morgestia's cheeks as she lifts her eyes to mine.

"These are their homes," I tell Aeneas. "Many here have already been driven from their lands once. Where are they supposed to go if the Lower City burns?"

Paris pushes his way through the line of shields to stand before King Priam. "Father, we must marshal the men and make for the Scaean gate. If there is any give in those doors, my warriors can push through them. Let us go out and meet the Achaeans like men."

"No!" I cry. "Every able-bodied man here has been conscripted into the army. We cannot leave their women and children to put out these fires alone. And we must put them out, or there will be no city left worth saving."

"Our men are warriors," Paris snaps. "If the Lower City burns, we can rebuild it."

"Can you also resurrect the dead?" I ask. "Because an army of corpses is what you'll have if you try to march through those gates one by one."

Think, Paris. For once, just stop and think.

"Troy's cattle are back in the fields," I continue. "Odysseus does not need to breach the walls if he can burn our food stores in the Lower City and starve us out instead. If he has left a pathway through the Scaean gate, it is because he is funneling you. Take that path and good Trojan men will die."

My gaze races to the sky. The arrows are coming slower now, but the realization brings me no comfort. The fire has already done its work. Smoke billows over us, making it difficult to see beyond the alleyway to the asylum camp. At least when the Achaeans were firing, I could pinpoint their position. The sudden quiet leaves me with the eerie sense that Odysseus's men are moving around us in the dark. Repositioning. Preparing to release more of Ares's wrath.

"At least it will be a glorious death," Paris says, drawing my attention back to him. "Fighting with spear and sword in hand. Not in some back alley surrounded by homeless men and wailing women."

"Hector!" If they won't listen to me, they will listen to him. They must.

"These are your people, Father." Hector flanks Priam. "If we don't fight for them, who will?"

"Listen to yourself," Paris sneers. "She is still jerking your lead, and you can't even see it. She doesn't care what happens to Troy. She despises us and everything we stand for."

Out of the corner of my eye, I glimpse Helen's blood-covered hands tearing a strip of cloth from her gown to bandage a servant's leg.

We do not have time for this.

"Troy is my city," I say through gritted teeth. "*All* of her."

"And yet with every flouting action you take, you seek to destroy her" Paris turns away from me in disgust. "*I am Troy. Please, Father. Give leave to defend her, and I swear to all the gods, I will not fail you.*" He g Priam's hands, and for one flickering moment, it is not a spoiled man k ing there, but a child begging to be seen.

Priam nods.

The desperate need for redemption stiffens Paris's spine. This is his chance to be the hero he has never been, and he will buy it at the cost of as many lives as it takes.

Orders ring off the walls as Paris's men take King Priam and head for Troy's inner gates, the ones that lead out of the Lower City. In disbelief, I follow them out into the street, past the south wall, where old men and women struggle to gather water to keep their homes from burning. Below their feet, the bright garlands from the festival lie trampled in the dirt.

The people stop and stare as their king and his men walk past, abandoning them to their fate. Children's wails mix with the groans of the wounded and dying.

Aeneas's voice cuts through the song of my failure. "Andromache is right. There will be a second slaughter at the gates, cousin."

Hector's calloused palm finds the back of my neck in a wordless apology.

"Go." Fire floods my veins. "See to your army, Hector. Leave me to mine."

"Andromache—"

"Do not ask me to hide."

His shoulders sag but there is pride in his eyes. And trust.

It fills me with a fire no mortal could put out.

"Go," I say again. "Your men need you."

"We will guard the Alev." Sarpedon appears at my side, his face ash-smeared, and for the first time, deadly serious. "On the name of the Mother, no harm will come to her."

"Do not make promises you cannot keep," Hector says quietly. "Not even the best commander can see how this battle will end."

Sarpedon nods. "But it is up to us to decide how those battles will be fought."

Something weighty passes between them.

"Take no unnecessary risks." Hector's hard hands cup the swell of my omach.

I cover his hands with my own. A silent promise. One neither of us ws if we will be able to keep.

'ith a searing kiss to my lips, Hector turns to make his way through rings to the Scaean gate. He is the only one who may be able to mitigate the bloodbath the king has given Paris the power to unleash. That is Hector's battle to fight. But *this*, this is mine

The grim set of Aeneas's mouth suggests we have all lost our minds. Still, he follows Hector without argument.

I spin on my heels and march back into the courtyard. "Nhorcys!"

"He cannot answer." Helen presses the fabric of her gown to burns on the side of the unconscious Phrygian's head. There is no time to indulge my fear for him now.

"Sarpedon," I say. "Take your men and help these women carry water from the south well."

"It will take more than water." Hippothous speaks up beside me.

My gaze flies across the smoldering rooflines. Quickly, I shuck my cloak and dunk it into a passing bucket before walking up to the men from Pityeia and Mount Tereia. "Birrus, if your men can climb the flat sides of stables, they should be able to manage those houses." I toss him the wet cloak, now a weapon.

Understanding lights his eyes. "Yes, Alev."

One by one his men strip their tunics and drench them in water. Muscles glide under bronzed skin as they scale the houses that lie closest to the south wall, up to the flat roofs where the arrows are doing the worst damage.

"Larion!" The boy appears at my side. "Go ask the girls next door for some of the blankets from their beds. They will hold more water and should work better than tunics to smother the flames."

"I'll go with him," Cyrrian offers before the two of them break for the brothel.

Another gust of smoke fills the courtyard, drawing a chorus of coughs from the surrounding men.

It won't be enough. Even if we manage to put out these fires, Odysseus will send more arrows to light them again. We won't save the Lower City. Not unless Hector finds a way to get past the blocked gates and drive the Achaeans out of firing range.

As if to underscore the point, an arrow strikes one of Birrus's m
through the neck while he tries to put out the flames on the brothel's r
It is a long fall to the ground. The man whose name I never learned
there, unmoving. Two of the allies quickly drag him toward the cour
but I already know there is nothing to be done for him.

We are fighting a losing battle. Without knowing what Odysseus is doing beyond our walls, where he is coming from and how he is bringing more men to our gates, we stand no chance of getting a single step ahead.

Stumbling back through the alleyway, I turn left toward the south well, where Glaucus and Sarpedon are tossing soaked blankets up to the bare-chested Adresteians poised on the nearby roofs. The ramshackle huts along the south wall are beyond saving. I watch Polydorus and Peirous attempt to direct the women and children who lived there toward the upper rings of Troy.

I find Cyrrian in a thick clump of Lycians at the well. "Is there an access point nearby that leads up the ramparts?" I ask.

He wipes the sweat from his eyes. "There is a ladder built for the archers directly across from the winehouse. Why?"

Not bothering with explanations, I start toward the spot on the south wall he described. I've reached the winehouse when the sound of distant twanging has me diving back into the alleyway.

Another volley of arrows comes over the south wall. These are not dipped in fire, which only means they are impossible to see against the night sky and block with a shield.

A dozen arrows pierce the earth between the winehouse and the wall. Just beyond the ruined remains of the asylum camp, I can make out the ladder that Cyrrian described.

"Sarpedon!"

The Lycian lifts his head from the well and starts toward me.

"What are you doing, Andromache?" Helen suddenly appears at my side. The remaining material of her gown not used for bandages now hangs off her in rags.

"I need to see how the Achaeans are positioned. Follow Polydorus and Larion. They will lead you out of the Lower City to safety."

"I will stay here with you and the people." She does not ask for my permission. She does not need it.

"My men have quenched the flames over the winehouse. Stay with Boca in the courtyard. I will have the allies bring any wounded there. But, n . . ." My mouth forms her name without the slightest bitterness. "The too widespread and our manpower is limited. Do not leave the court-r I cannot guarantee your safety." I wait for her to nod her agreement before turning back to Troy's outer wall. It looms across twenty paces of open ground. Another volley of arrows cuts through the night as Cyrrian and Sarpedon reach me.

"They are trying to keep us on the defensive so we don't send archers onto the walls," Sarpedon says grimly.

"There has to be a way for us to get Pandarus and some of his men up those ladders," Cyrrian adds. "It would buy us a little respite from their bows."

On the heels of his statement, those bows twang in the dark behind the walls.

Shields raise to meet the clang. Then lower.

"It will be impossible unless we can determine where Odysseus has stationed his men. We need some sense of their numbers and positions." Following Helen's example, I take a fistful of my skirt and tear. The material gives easily at the seams, freeing my legs.

"You're mad," Cyrrian growls, not the first time I have heard these words. But he lifts his shield above my head anyway. An instant later, his shield is joined by Sarpedon's.

"To the Alev!" Sarpedon roars to a group of warriors behind us.

Glaucus answers his cousin's call, followed by Akamas and Hippothous, until nearly all of our allied captains have created a bridge of shields for me to run beneath. Another wave of arrows rains down as I sprint for the ladder.

The rungs have been carved directly into the stone. They reach as high as the parapets, more than thirty feet above my head. Thick black smoke blocks out the moon and stars. Only the glow of fires at my back lights my way as I take the rungs one at a time.

The ground drops out beneath me. For a moment, I am alone in a world made of smoke and stone. A northern gust blows hard over the parapet. I grip the ladder to steady myself. Everything teeters, and for one breath, I am back on the roof of Cassandra's tower with nothing but wind to catch me on every side.

Hector's voice rises up, holding me steady.

"Not even the best commander can see how this battle will end."

No, but she can still get the best possible view.

I grip the ladder tightly and ascend the last rungs. The archers' spills out onto the battlements facing the southern field. From r perch, I can see the entire world split by the Trojan walls. Outside them, small bands of Achaeans stand before our three main gates, blocking them from the outside with felled logs. There are fewer Achaeans gathered at the south gate, where the fire has done most of the work for them.

A handful of archers stand in a widely spaced line beyond the Lower City walls. The source of the sporadic arrows. Having sufficiently set his fires to occupy us, Odysseus has pulled most of his men to the gates, where they are now holding us captive inside.

Hector's camp outside the west wall lies in ruin. The dozens of tents that have been a permanent feature of the plain since this war began are now a sea of flame. In the flickering light, I can make out the still forms of fallen bodies and a few dozen Achaeans confiscating the chariots and horses that survived the attack.

Low bleating draws my gaze to the east. In the grazing fields, five hundred of our cattle lumber away from the scent of smoke. Our herds are cutting a path southeast toward the foothills of Mount Ida. If we cannot find a way past those blockades on our gates, it will be a simple matter for Odysseus to round them up and drive them across the Scamander to the Achaean camps, leaving us with a burned-out city on the verge of starvation.

I turn my attention back to the city behind the walls. We have managed to control the fire here by the south wall, but the parts of the Lower City to the west where Rhea and I found the plague-ridden body still glow dangerously bright. Hundreds of people are crowding each of Troy's inner gates, seeking to climb to higher rings, searching for shelter from the smoke.

Farther north, just inside the Scaean gate, the bulk of Troy's army is gathered. Men are packed shoulder to shoulder, and still, many are relegated to the training grounds, where they wait for an opening that will never come. Even with the full strength of our forces concentrated on one door, we've barely managed to wedge the gates open a shoulder width. The log that is being used to block them does not look in any danger of breaking.

A figure in familiar armor stands at the front, directing men through the rrow slit two at a time. Paris's helmeted face is the last thing these men before they charge through.

Most are cut down before they even manage to lift their spears.

"ow does it look?" Peirous asks when I return to solid ground.

"ey hold us hostage with a force of a hundred. This isn't Agamemnon's army. It is Odysseus and his men." And though that does not change what is, our superiority in numbers does give us a chance. If only we can break through the chains holding us to exploit it. "They are four men deep across each of our gates, which they have blocked with felled timber. Any men we manage to push through are funneled directly into their waiting spears."

"A chariot could break their lines," Cyrrian says, hands fisting at his sides.

"Even if we could pry the gates wide enough to let a chariot through, it would never survive contact with the barriers they have erected across the gates to hold them shut." My teeth grind together. "Odysseus has seen to that."

"He knows how defensively you Trojans fight," Sarpedon says. "And he is using it against you."

My heart breaks into a jerky trot as my eyes scan the gathered men around me.

"Peirous, where are your horses?" I ask.

He wipes at the blood on his ebony brow. "Akamas ordered them pulled back to the Merchant Quarter, out of reach of the fire. He is there now with young Polydorus, helping the women and the children make their way through the inner gates." A pause. "We could follow."

We could. Retreating with the rest of these people to the upper rings of Troy would keep us safe. But for how long? The safety of those stone Citadel walls is nothing more than an illusion—one that will shatter as soon as Troy's meat and bread run out. We need our cattle. We need the Lower City ovens that bake our bread.

We need the people who make Troy what she is.

I meet the red gazes of the men around me, and I see the same knowledge painted with the sweat across their faces.

"They deserve better," Hippothous says simply.

The rest of the men do not speak. There is no need.

"If this is a battle we must fight, then we will do it the way *we* choose." I direct my next order to Peirous, whose hair has gone gray with ash. "Take your men and find Akamas and the horses. Limit yourselves to the lightest of armor." At the question in his gaze, I raise a brow. "Do you remember the first day in the training grounds? The fence?"

Realization dawns across the old warrior's face.

He remembers.

"Pandarus." I turn my attention to the archer. "Take some of your men up the archers' access. There is just enough cover at the top of the south wall to hide you. Do not reveal yourselves. Wait until our Thracian friends make their way out of the south gate, and then disable the Achaean archers before they can take aim at our riders."

Pandarus wastes no time carrying out my order. I wait for him and his company to ascend the ladder before I turn back to Peirous. "Paris is sending men out to the slaughter at the Scaean gate. You will never make it through on horseback. Exit through the south gate instead. The fire is still making its way through the asylum camps, but it is also the access least guarded by the Achaeans."

"How will you open it?" he asks.

"Just get your horses ready." I grip the older man's shoulder. "Once you are clear of the walls, ride hard for the Scaean gate. Disable the men who block it and give Hector a path. His men will do the rest. Tell Akamas. Just as we have trained."

Peirous nods once and is gone.

"Hippothous." I meet the Pelasgian's dark eyes where they are watching me steadily. He grips the long spear that never leaves his side. "The Thracians will need a gap to ride through."

The silence hangs heavy between us as he gathers my meaning. "The Pelasgians will see it done, Alev." A dip of his chin and he too is gone, leaving me alone with Cyrrian at the base of the south wall.

I glance back up the ladder. Pandarus's men have taken their positions above us on the southern battlements.

"Don't even think about it," Cyrrian growls. "Once was enough."

I reach for the first rung.

"No, Andromache. Hector would strangle me with my own reins."

"Hector is not here. I will move you if I must."

Cyrrian lets out a pained breath. "Fine." He ducks past me. "But this time, I am going first."

The scene that greets us on the ramparts is unchanged but for the number of Trojan dead. At least a dozen bodies lie on the red-stained earth outside the Scaean gate.

The line of Ithacan archers surrounding the city below lets out another volley. On the walls to my left and my right, Pandarus and his men stay crouched behind the battlements. Hidden. Hands twitch on their bows, but they hold steady for my command.

"We are too exposed here," Cyrrian says.

"Just one more moment."

One moment turns into two. Then ten. Still, there is no sign of the Thracian riders.

An arrow whizzes past my head. Cyrrian looks as if he is ready to toss me over his shoulder and carry me back down the ladder when screams ride through the Lower City on a peal of thunder. Not from the sky, but from the ground.

Rumble of a hundred hoofbeats.

The Thracians and their horses shoot like stones from a sling from within Troy's second inner gate. As one, they take a hard turn into the Lower City, charging through streets that quickly clear in front of them. Cyrrian presses my body back against the battlement when they fly past the wall below us. Dust swirls in their wake as they ride hard for the south gate that leads out to the plain.

Hippothous and his men are waiting for them. The Pelasgians have used their long spears to wedge open the gates. It isn't a wide opening, but it does not have to be.

A rider with a torch of red hair is the first through the narrow gap. Akamas hits the gate at a full gallop. His horse lifts its front hooves and sails over the log pinning the doors shut, coming down hard on the Achaean warrior standing on the other side. One by one, the Thracian riders follow. Their graceful animals leap over the high barrier that would have stopped even the finest chariot.

Screams ride the wind. Only this time, they are Achaean, not Trojan.

Pandarus and his men finally unleash their arrows from the ramparts. They fall on the Achaean archers before the enemy can so much as change the direction of their bows. And then Akamas and his men are right there. He cuts down an Achaean archer with a rock from his sling and gallops hard around our exterior walls for another gate that lies north.

Their lines broken, the Achaeans flee from our gates toward a cluster of chariots beyond the smoking remains of our camp. Others make for the olive groves to the east. With the gates open and Troy's might unleashed, we have the numbers on our side, and so they do not wait. They move with a purpose that suggests that failure was an eventuality they had planned for, dragging their wounded toward a large cart that waits in the olive grove.

Akamas pulls on his reins as he watches them go. His horse's hooves dance, as eager as his master to give chase. A moment passes before he yanks his mount's head away from the retreating Achaeans and breaks hard for the Scaean gate. Peirous reaches those gates first. He and several other Thracians dismount to dismantle the blockade from the outside and throw the doors wide. The Trojan army marches through them, weapons bared, only to find the enemy already fleeing across the Scamander plain.

Firelight dances off the recognizable crest of Hector's helmet. I search the growing crowd of soldiers outside the gates, but Paris is nowhere to be seen.

Cyrrian and I descend into a street now crowded with women and old men. They are running again, but this time, they are coming from Troy's inner gates. Moving toward the flames, not away from them. Carrying water. Working with those allies who are focused not on the Achaeans outside but instead on battling for them inside our walls.

I glimpse Sarpedon next to Glaucus on the far side of the alley near the south well. Weapons and shields lie discarded on the ground, freeing their hands for the heavy jugs passed down a long line toward the winehouse. The sky is full of smoke, but no more arrows. Sarpedon meets my gaze through the haze. At his silent question, I nod. His answering smile blazes white-hot against his soot-streaked face. I return it with one just as bright.

Time ceases to have meaning. We work through the night. Putting out the fires. Sending the injured to the courtyard where they are tended by women led by Bodecca and Helen. Glaucus and Cyrrian take turns enforcing rest upon me, but as the second watch creeps into the third, I stop recognizing faces. Everything is a blur of sweat and soot and exhaustion. Hector finds me in the darkest hour. He tucks my bronze streak behind my ear, and we share a single embrace that makes words unnecessary. Then he and Aeneas leave again with a group of men to work on the fires that still threaten the structures on the eastern side of the city, which unlike those to the west might be saved.

It is long past the end of the third watch when I finally look up again.

A wind drives hard across the plains as the day breaks over Troy, bathing the Citadel in a gauzy, muted gold. On the parapets, a studded crown of robed figures watch from the safety of Troy's highest walls. They cannot see me, but from that vantage point, every twist and turn of this battle will have been perfectly marked. These men might pick and choose whose words they believe, but there will be no denying the truth of their eyes. Tonight, the Lower City was spared because of the courage of those who have too long been forgotten. And from the lowest hut to the highest tower, all of Troy will know who stood their ground. And who ran to save themselves.

I am moving toward the well where Lycians are organizing the distribution of water when a scream cuts through the rising dawn.

Its familiar edge stops me cold.

Helen.

"Where are you going, Andromache?"

Cyrrian's voice rings at my back as I fight against the crowd leading into the courtyard, which bears Helen's mark in the neatly organized rows of injured.

Bodecca's body seems to wilt when she sees me. "Thank Hannahanna. I was afraid—"

"Where's Helen?"

"She followed a young girl with a babe on her hip. Said their mother was trapped and needed help." Bodecca frowns. "It was some time ago. She should be back by now."

I grip her arm. "Which way?"

"West, the girl said west. Near the outer wall."

My mouth goes dry. It is the only part of the city where the flames still rage unchecked.

"Andromache, wait!"

Smoke streaks my vision as I move down the street.

A hand closes around my wrist. "Andromache, *stop*," Cyrrian demands.

"Helen. I have to find her." I pull free of his grip and duck down the alley to my right, searching for some sign of Helen. Finding none, I push down more streets filled with more people dragging baskets of water, using sodden blankets and fistfuls of dirt or whatever they can find to put out the flames that dot the Lower City like a hundred open pyres.

The farther west we go, the thicker the smoke and the thinner the crowds become. Until it is like we are walking through a city of the dead.

The worst of the destruction is centered on the small corner of homes where the exterior west wall meets the inner walls separating the different rings of Troy. Just beyond that barrier lie the stables and the training grounds that Hector and I call home.

"This section is still in chaos," Cyrrian says, reading my mind. "She could be anywhere. The fire is isolated to this northwest corner. It will arrive at the stone wall dividers from both the south and the west and will burn itself out."

A weak wail draws me back down the street we just passed. An infant lies bundled in a trench outside a house I recognize easily despite the billows of black smoke pouring out of the door. It's the home of the widow Watti and her daughter, Lannaka.

I lift the squalling baby from the trench. A familiar scar twists her tiny upper lip. She is wrapped in something soft and gossamer.

Helen's veil.

I start toward the house but stop when a woman emerges from the smoking doorway.

My cracked lips part in a choked gasp. Coughing violently, the woman lifts her face.

"Give her to me." Lannaka rushes forward, tearing her daughter out of the veil in my arms.

"Lannaka!" When she starts to move past me, I hold her fast. "Lannaka, where is Helen?"

"I told her Mother was trapped inside." The young woman's voice sounds worlds away.

Dread coats my insides in ice.

Cyrrian pulls me away from the house. "Get back. This whole structure is about to collapse."

"I think Helen is inside."

Cyrrian's expression goes slack as he beholds the flames on the roof. Mouth setting in grim acceptance, he pulls his tunic over his head and wraps it around his lower face. He's taken a step forward when we are hit by a wave of blistering heat.

I cringe away, shielding the child inside me from the explosion of fire. Blackness floods my vision. Tears blind me as I look back at the building. Now a smoking ruin.

Beside me, Lannaka screams.

The sound cuts through me, filling me with a thousand regrets. A thousand griefs I do not have time to indulge.

Helen.

"We need to go east." My voice is a hoarse croak.

"So we can encounter the Achaeans once they pass through our gates?" Lannaka's lips are blistered, her eyes shot through with wild, crimson threads. There is something vacant about them. Something missing. It is as if dark spirits have worked their way inside to claim some part of her.

"Lannaka, listen to me. The Achaeans are gone." I grip her arms. "We have to go west, where it is safe."

She does not hear me. Wherever the girl's mind has fled in its grief, it is somewhere much too far to reach. Lannaka clutches the naked babe to her chest and spins out of my grip. She runs north toward the wall that connects to the inner circles of Troy.

My gaze runs down the rows of packed houses, where the fire closes in on that wall from every angle.

"Andromache, we have to go now!"

I take a small step toward Cyrrian before I turn back toward the burning street down which Lannaka fled. At the thought of the little girl in her arms, my hand moves to my stomach. To the child I would not even have if another woman had not risked everything to help me. Even when I refused to help her.

I clutch Helen's veil in my fist and run toward the inner wall.

"Lannaka!" Smoke fills my lungs, making it difficult to speak. I press the gauzy material to my nose and mouth. "Lannaka, where are you?"

Crying up ahead draws my gaze to a small animal shed pressed close to the wall. I can just hear the panicked sounds of the horses in the stables that lie beyond it.

Lannaka uses the lower roof of the shed to climb onto the awning of the building directly beside it. One that sits flush against the wall. The fronds beneath her feet are already smoking, but she moves forward with the child in her arms as if she cannot feel the heat.

My eyes follow the girl's crazed scramble until I see her goal. A small group of Trojan soldiers stand along the inner wall. They are looking down on the fire, unable to do anything to stop it from where they stand. One of them wears a helmet that is much too large. It nearly swallows his child's head.

Polydorus. And next to him, a barefaced Larion.

Hector's youngest brother yells something I cannot make out. But Lannaka sees him. Every line of her body points the way.

Polydorus calls for a rope, but the flames below move faster than the men above them. They lash at Lannaka's legs. A few more breaths and the edge of her tunic catches fire.

Her cries fill the air, but she reaches up, arms trembling as she raises the baby as high as she can.

Polydorus reaches back, but the chasm between them is too wide.

And then Polydorus is sliding over the wall headfirst. Larion grips one of his ankles while the soldier beside him grips the other. His arms come down to encircle the child.

The mother lets out one long, ragged scream as she hands her baby to safety. And then she lets go.

There is silence when she falls. So loud it seems to shatter everything around it. I don't have time to process the horror I've just witnessed. The bravery. I cannot even draw a breath, because suddenly Cyrrian's hand is around my arm, spinning me toward the danger stalking us from behind.

A large shape barrels toward us through the smoke. The wrath of the Furies on four legs.

Hector's fire horse.

Grit and ash streak his crimson coat.

The fire horse stops in the center of the street. He blocks our escape, this animal not even my husband could break, and for a moment that feels endless, the red beast and I stand face-to-face.

Bright embers dance through the air between us.

The stallion hooves the ground.

"Andromache." Cyrrian's urgent whisper comes from my left. "Do. Not. Move."

My father's blade burns against my thigh. Fingers twitch toward it.

That is all it takes.

The animal charges. Cyrrian wraps his arms around my waist from behind, thrusting me aside just as the beast gallops past us. I scream as the top of a nearby roof slides sideways. It crashes into the street directly where Cyrrian and I were standing just moments ago.

The fire horse rears up at the edge of the flames. He makes a tight circle and charges past us before stopping again. Waiting for acknowledgment. Recognition.

Someone approaches down the street behind him. A child with an animal pelt lifted over her head as a shield from the falling ash. The child moves past the dangerous animal as if he were not there.

No. Not a child.

"Rhea!"

I do not know which of us screams her name first, but Cyrrian and I move as one. Cyrrian gets to her before I do. His arms reach for her, dropping to his sides at the last moment. I have no such qualms. I throw my arms around Rhea and draw her as close as the wolf's pelt and my tender side will allow.

"I'm sorry," she says into my shoulder. "I'm so sorry, Andromache. I tried to   "

"None of us could have stopped this." I pull her back to look into her tear-streaked face. "But we survived it. That is enough."

The fire horse rears up again. Thunder peals through the streets behind him. At first, I assume it is Akamas and his Thracians coming back into the city, but they would never risk bringing their horses this close to the fire.

And yet horses gallop toward us.

They move through the smoke, a sea of muscle and sinew made up of every shape and color stolen from the palette of the gods. There are a hundred. Maybe more. A spot of stormy gray draws my eyes to Kasirga where he gallops in between Hector's beasts, Golden and Lightfoot.

A wave of chaos, they crash toward us. The thought crosses my mind that it is a fitting death for the wife of Hector. But then the fire horse turns and gallops, splitting the center of the herd. As one, the horses switch course around him to fall in line. They run back through the Lower City, between two rows of burning buildings. If they fear the fire, they have been trained too well to show it. Our Rhea has seen to that.

"Ishtar! Carris!" Rhea starts toward the herd. "I have to get them back to the stables."

"But how did they get out?" I ask.

"The fire would not have reached the training grounds," Cyrrian wheezes, clutching his ribs.

And yet, the size of the herd running away from us suggests every stable door in Troy has been thrown wide open.

"After I came in through the Mother's pass, I went home first to look for you," Rhea says. "Zikari was frantic. He said someone had let all the horses out."

"Who would do such a thing?"

No sooner have the words left my lips than a shadow slinks in the fire horse's wake.

"Helen?" Hope brings me to my knees.

The figure turns toward me.

Yawning pupils. Endless darkness.

If this is now a city of the dead, then the Fury is its queen.

"Cassandra." I step toward her. "What are you doing down here? It isn't safe . . ."

The words dry up on my tongue when the creature wearing Cassandra's face picks something off the ground. Her head snaps to the side as she considers it, sending a shudder through me.

Shoulders bow and spine collapses. A groan, followed by a giggle. Hunching and straightening and hunching again. I can't tear my eyes away from the horror as she stalks toward me.

Features ripple like water. Then all is still.

The face that finally emerges is one I've seen before. That night in her tower when she placed her hands on my belly and spoke of things she could not possibly know. But did.

Cassandra's fingers tremble as she presses a Death Mask in my hands. Helen's.

"Do not mourn," Cassandra says, as self-possessed as I have ever seen her. "Sometimes the fire must burn hot, returning everything to soil so that something new might grow."

Beside me, Rhea gasps.

Troy's forgotten princess looks between us. She smiles.

It lasts less than a breath before the Fury returns. Revenge and violence with nowhere to go. She screams. A song of suffering that can only come from Hades himself. The Fury follows Troy's horses down the streets leading west to the Lower City. A place, to my knowledge, she has never been allowed to walk unguarded.

My knees give out, and I slide to the stones.

Rhea crouches beside me, clutching Helen's Death Mask. The relief of the solid weight of her hand in mine is almost enough to drown out every other pain. Every other loss.

Cyrrian and Rhea help me to my feet. Together, we stumble east, away from where the fire is burning itself out against our stone walls. We stop next to the first home untouched by the destruction.

"Will you both be all right here?" Cyrrian wipes the grit from his eyes as he glances between us. "I should find Cassandra. This part of the city is still dangerous, and the Fury is unpredictable."

Leaning against the wall, I rest the side of my head against Rhea's shoulder, unable to banish Cassandra's strange smile from my mind.

A smile full of secrets.

I look down at the ash-streaked veil in my hand.

"The Crone. The Child. The Wraith. The Fury." Swallowing mouthfuls of air, I count off the faces of Cassandra's that I know. "I've heard there is a fifth."

Cyrrian's gaze is ringed with sadness as he stares down the street where the Fury just fled. He starts after her but turns at the last moment to look back at us. "It was the first," he says. "The one that revealed itself when she was just a child. Hector and I would find her walking barefoot on the balcony ledge, flapping her arms and threatening to fly away."

"Fly?" Rhea asks.

A fresh breeze from the coastline cuts through some of the smoke. I follow Cyrrian's gaze up to a sky thick with orange haze, hanging over a city that has been saved. For now, at least. A victory won at great cost, though I fear it is only the beginning of a reignited war that is far from over.

"Yes." Cyrrian's gaze passes from me to Rhea, who also hangs on his every word. "She believed she was a Hawk."

46

CASSANDRA

HE CAME TO me in the Light.

Dawn was painting the white walls of my bedroom when he appeared in my window. Black shadow blocking the bright burning sun. I could not make out his face, just his form—wide shoulders and a narrow waist. Enough to know that it was him. The god.

The one I had seen in my dreams.

My heart leapt. This was the moment. Dream I'd had for as long as I could remember. A god who had chosen me above all others. Not in spite of my strangeness, but because of it. Being cut out of sunlight. Only this . . . this was not a vision. The god was *here* to change my life forever.

And he did. Just not in the ways I thought he would.

The god in my window stepped out of my dreams and into the reality of my bedroom. Each one of his strides brought him out of the direct light, so that I could more clearly see his face.

The greeting died on my lips as one by one, his features were revealed. Sun-darkened skin with cracks around the eyes. Thin mouth that seemed anchored down on one side.

I knew those eyes; had felt them watching me across my father's table.

I knew that mouth; had seen it smile a secret smile just for me.

In an instant, other things became clear in a way they had not been before. The slope of shoulders. Curls that had appeared golden in my dreams, actually brittle straw set fire by the rising sun. The rush of blood, a roar as he approached my bed.

It was happening. Every moment transpiring exactly as I had foreseen it. Only now, everything looked different. For that is the way of visions. The things they show you speak less of truth than they do of your own desires.

Clarity, not certainty.

He approached. Not a god. A man—one I thought I knew.

He came, and he told me to be quiet if I wanted to live, and then he joined me on my bed. He settled under my blankets, and he found the small shape of my hand, which he guided. It was the first time I left my body behind, and I escaped the only way open to me. I went down

down

into the well. Beautiful darkness where the light could not reach. And in that darkness, there you were.

A Crone.

Sitting on a ledge at the edge of my mind, as if you had been waiting for me.

You sat and you rocked me back and forth like my mother had done before she recognized a strangeness in me she could not love. When it was over, you told me I could visit again, but I could not stay, and you led me back up to the world by my little hand. You said I must be brave. That I must speak the truth even if nobody could hear it, because the act of speaking itself was power. And the truth was not for them at all, but for *me*.

So I left you in the darkness, and I came back to my body, aching and broken. I crawled across the room to the corner, far away from the Light. There I hid until darkness fell.

I went to my mother. My father. I covered my eyes as I told them what the false god had done. When my story was over, I dropped my hands and found them looking at me. Not with the hesitant affection that had always been there before. Not with horror at what had been done to me. No, they looked at me the way the rest of the world did.

With suspicion. *Fear.*

I had told them a truth they were unwilling to hear, and so they invented lies instead. A story about a god and a bargain and a curse that no one but a fool should have believed. But they did. People believed, and it was not my truth but their lies that would echo through the ages.

I suppose the songs are right about one thing.

He came to me again and again, and why wouldn't he? There was nobody there to stop him.

It would have been unbearable if it had not been for you. Whenever the Light became too much, there you were, waiting for me in the dark. Ready to hold me until it was over, and I loved you for that. After a while, you showed me there were others hiding in the shadows with us.

A Child for me to play with.

A Wraith. Her eyes bloated orbs in sockets of exposed bone. She frightened me at first, but I grew to love her too. Crooked neck and sad silence. Rotted tongue that could not speak, so she would sit and hold my hand, lending me comfort with her nearness.

There was a Fury who drank the fear of men like wine.

And a Hawk that flew far and wide, taking me with him so that, for a while, I might forget.

It was a torment, but I survived it because of each of you. And when he would have killed me to ensure my silence, it was you again who saved me.

The last morning he climbed through my window was like the others, only this time, it was the Fury waiting for him. She lay still and quiet, a knife clutched in her hand. And when his weight hit the bed, it was her hands that knew what to do. The knife slashed down his chest. Blood on the blankets. For once, *his*, not mine, and it made the Fury's heart sing with joy inside my chest.

She did not kill him even though she could have, but she hurt him enough to let him know.

I wasn't alone. Not anymore.

He never came again. Twelve years, and I still sleep with that knife beside my bed.

I know the stories the ages will tell. I've heard the echoes of their songs—songs that will outlive us all. They will speak of great heroes. Of gods and prophecies and curses. Of favors granted and denied. They will drown the truth of my life in the lies told by men, and that is how it will be.

But this story is not theirs. It is mine. I will tell it now as I did twelve years ago because speaking is power, and the truth I offer is not for them at all, but for *me*.

The truth is that I was nine years old.

The truth is that it wasn't a god that came to me, but a man. And there was no bargain. No question, because he did not ask, he *took*, and when he did, visions of burning cities flew across my eyes as the blood dripped down my thighs.

The truth is that I did not cry because by then, I already knew.

What was the point of crying when there was no one to hear me?

Speaking is power, you said, and so it is. I have waited and I have watched and I have ached with the knowledge that it was not yet time. I have swallowed the truth. Bit down on my tongue until my mouth was full of blood, but now they are here, and the waiting at last is over. I have seen them.

The Hawk whose wings I ride.

The Mouse.

The Weaver.

The Spindle.

The Horse. Creature not of ash, but of fire.

The moment for truth has come, even if the world will never hear it.

Not for the ages. Not for those who would not listen when the way ahead was not yet drawn in blood.

For me. For *us*. For the prices we will pay.

The end is coming fast now. Spiders moving in the dark. It is too late to change it, and I would not even if I could. The time is now.

Hear me.

My name is Cassandra.

And I have work to do.

AUTHORS' NOTE

In writing *Horses of Fire*, we combined elements of mythology, archaeology, and the fascinating but largely opaque history of the Late Bronze Age. There have been many stories of the Trojan War, but most of these portrayals paint a Trojan world that is largely indistinguishable from the kingdoms of Mycenaean Greece. This includes the *Iliad*, composed by the Greek poet (or group of poets) known as Homer hundreds of years after the legendary war it depicts. And yet, if the city of Troy really existed (which many scholars believe is likely and have identified as the ancient site of Hisarlik in Turkey), then the people who lived there surely had their own unique culture and traditions. Although most of these cultural details remain a mystery that scholars continue to unravel, we wanted to infuse our Troy with the character and dazzling complexity that existed in ancient Anatolia. As a result, some of the names and pantheons we incorporated may be unfamiliar. These were drawn primarily from ancient Luwian, Hittite, Hurrian, and Hattian origins. Though the Troy depicted in *Horses of Fire* is represented as being Luwian in part, there is ongoing debate and research about who the Trojans actually were. Our aim, therefore, was to represent Troy as we imagined it *might* have been, given its strategic position at the crossroads of several major trading routes—a melting pot of the many cultures that existed in this region during the Late Bronze Age. A city of different peoples that stood at one of the most important gateways in the ancient world and on the fault line between two great empires.

Another aspect that captured our imaginations when writing this story is the historical enigma known as the Late Bronze Age Collapse. Many scholars have dated the Trojan War to approximately 1200 BCE, which also coincides with a period of cultural decline and previously unparalleled turbulence that rewrote the map of the ancient world. Major cities in the Mediterranean and Near East were destroyed, massive empires disappeared into thin air, writing systems vanished, and trade routes halted abruptly. The reasons for this unprecedented collapse remain one of the greatest unsolved mysteries of human history. Scholars have presented climate change, natural disasters, plagues, political instability, internal rebellions, and the mass migration of people as potential factors—all possibilities that feel eerily similar to the geopolitics of our present day and reflect many of the images we witnessed on nightly news programs while we were writing. The theory that there may have been Bronze Age seafaring raiders (often referred to as "the Sea Peoples") who razed coastal cities from Egypt to Crete was another fascinating possibility we incorporated into the backdrop of our Trojan War in order to explore this speculative history and give our story an even more sweeping scope. If some of the events in *Horses of Fire* seem unfamiliar to readers of Homer's *Iliad* and *Odyssey*, that is because the *Iliad* begins in the tenth year of the war, and in our version, we wanted to imagine some of the choices that might have come before those few days described by Homer. As a result, we altered or dragged out the timeline of events in the *Iliad* in order to make them more realistic and plausible.

One of the most incredible gifts we receive when engaging with myths is the opportunity to explore timeless questions. Myths are by nature multilayered, and so often they tell us as much about the period in which they were written as the distant past they are trying to memorialize. Myths have always been retold in different times and contexts, and we are thrilled to be taking part in this long tradition. For example, there are two Andromaches in Greek mythology: the wife of Hector of Troy, and an Amazon warrior. In our portrayal of Andromache, we thought combining these two elements would be compelling for modern readers. Although we adore and are indebted to the *Iliad* and *Odyssey*, any intentional departures from Homer's storyline were made with the reassurance that even these foundational texts are but one version of the ancient drama we now call the Trojan War. It is a truly epic story featuring larger-than-life personalities, a story big enough for many versions that encourage us to reflect on what it means to be human.

Some of the terms and names in the novel are derived from available sources (see our website for a complete list). Some have been altered for reader ease (the ancients were very fond of names that began with *P* and *A*). Other terms (i.e., *Harsa* and *Paeana*) are works of our own imagination created to give the story the epic atmosphere of the historical and fantasy novels that made us voracious readers. Among the scholarly research we are most indebted to are: J. V. Luce's *Celebrating Homer's Landscapes: Troy and Ithaca Revisited*; *The Modern Scholar: Archaeology and the* Iliad*: The Trojan War in Homer and History* lectures by Eric Cline; *The Trojan War: A New History* by Barry Strauss; and *In Search of the Trojan War* by Michael Wood. Also, Manfred Hutter's chapter on "Aspects of Luwian Religion" from *The Luwians*, edited by H. Craig Melchert. Terms like *Alev* and *Atesh* we drew from the modern Turkish language—our nod to the incredible land of such rich history where one can still visit what many believe are the remains of ancient Troy. Count us among the believers.

ACKNOWLEDGMENTS

We would like to thank our incredible agent, Shannon Hassan, who did not balk when we sent her a three-hundred-thousand-word epic of the Trojan War partially narrated by a bird. We are grateful for your willingness to not only read our many words many times, but also for your pivotal early advice to divide our giant epic into two slightly less giant books. What we are left with is the story we always wanted to tell.

Thank you to our brilliant editor at Dutton, Cassidy Sachs, who became the fourth member of our coven. From that first conversation, we knew we'd found the person who understood the story in our hearts and would help us share it with readers. We are incredibly grateful for your keen insights, your faith in this story, your tireless championing of it, and for all you have done to make our dream a reality.

Our deep gratitude to the amazing team at Dutton. We can start with the incredible art team, whose beautiful work wraps these pages, both inside and out. Your talent blew us away. We cannot thank you enough for all you did to make our words come alive. Thank you to our wonderful marketer, Caroline Payne, and publicist, Sarah Thegeby, for all your hard work and guidance. To the copyeditors and proofreaders who made us look smarter than we are. Thank you to the wider team at Penguin Random House, whose enthusiasm and support we have felt at every turn. We feel incredibly lucky to be a part of your book family.

We are forever grateful to our first readers: Julie Cremin, Elena Patel, Maureen Cremin, Mark Cremin, and Loretta Cremin. Your enthusiasm for this story and early feedback made this novel what it is today. Thank you to Lisa Maxwell, not only for your willingness to champion our work but also for helping us turn our "soggy middle" into an ending worthy of these characters. You are magical and so talented. Thank you to Olivia Hinebaugh for reading a million times and for lending your endless artistic gifts to the beautiful map at the beginning of this book. Your support, vital insight about the Andromache-Helen conflict, and enthusiasm for this project as a whole have meant the world to us. Thank you also to Lancia and Peter Smith for the love and support you show so many writers, even from afar.

We never would have been able to write this story without the support of our families and the military service that brought us together in Germany over two decades ago. The values you gave us and the world you opened up for us lie between every line that we write. Thank you to our parents, Steven and Lea Anne Chowen; and Mark and Loretta Cremin. From you we learned the bravery, strength, and selflessness of those who serve both with and without uniforms. Our siblings: Haylee and Mollee; and Kevin, David, and Thomas. Our brothers- and sisters-in-law: Nate, Gabe, Bryana, and Zach; and Krista, Charlotte, Laura, Lonnie, and Audra. We are also very grateful for the support and encouragement of our fathers- and mothers-in-law: David and Anita Cowles; and Frank and Brenda Stinson. And our dear friends John and Polly Miller. You all are the village who keeps us afloat and makes it possible for us to write with six kids between us.

To our grandmothers, Joy Adams and Arletta Chowen. And to Marianna Rizzo and Marie Cremin, who are no longer with us. Your courage and perseverance in times of struggle are the models we strive to live by. Thank you for sharing stories of the past with us when we were children. We hold them in our hearts. They shape everything that we do.

We are forever grateful to our husbands, Jordan and Josh, whose steadfast love and support make it possible for us to pursue this calling. Thank you for holding down the fort while we escape—either to each other or to the worlds inside our heads. We love you dearly.

To our beloved children: Isla and Jack; and Uriah, Isaac, Daniel, and Caleb. Our wish for you is that you might always look for Light and Beauty in this world, no matter how dark it seems. And that you will never forget that your greatest power lies in your potential to be that Light and Beauty for others.

ABOUT THE AUTHORS

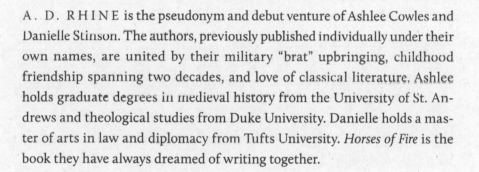

A. D. RHINE is the pseudonym and debut venture of Ashlee Cowles and Danielle Stinson. The authors, previously published individually under their own names, are united by their military "brat" upbringing, childhood friendship spanning two decades, and love of classical literature. Ashlee holds graduate degrees in medieval history from the University of St. Andrews and theological studies from Duke University. Danielle holds a master of arts in law and diplomacy from Tufts University. *Horses of Fire* is the book they have always dreamed of writing together.